THE COLLECTED WORKS

of
ERNST GRAF

in one sperm-sodden volume
1999-2019

ERNST GRAF

FOREWORD

"I say! You fellows! Yes, you fellows down there! You misshapen fellows, stunted, twisted, unfortunate faces—who look like you cannot count to 10, or recite your alphabets, and have to wear slip-on shoes all your life as you don't know how to tie your own shoelaces, you there! What IS it about me that upsets you so?"

This book is probably as close to an autobiography as the world will ever get from me. All of my writing is essentially a diary (or travel diary), and this book follows my progress through life year by year. There are gaps, years when nothing much happened, and the years 2008-13 when I was, in a sense, living instead of writing. I was having 'a relationship' instead of writing. This book will be the standard textbook for all those interested in the life & times of Ernst Graf, the mysterious Marquis de Vaccine, 1999-2019.

"A Bible of degeneracy," as my mother puts it.

What is this book? A record of one man's journey through life. Nothing more, nothing less.

—Ernst Graf, the Marquis de Vaccine, 24th December 2020, Charing Cross, London.

CONTENTS

✝

AUTISMUS

1999-2001

ERNST GRAF

CHAPTER 1
YOU ARE REALLY GETTING TO PEOPLE NOW

YOU ARE REALLY GETTING TO PEOPLE NOW. THIS IS HOW MY SITUATIONIST REVOLUTION IS PROGRESSING. I WILL BE GOING ON A SITUATIONIST GEO-PSYCHIC TOUR OF EUROPE. LADY TARA IS THE MUSE AND ONLY DESIRE OBJECT OF THE SITUATIONISTS. VIOLENT EROTICISM IS MY WEAPON. MY INSOLENT DISPLAY OF LUXURY. LADY TARA IS THE ONE THING OF WARMTH IN THIS MAD, RUTHLESSLY LOGICAL, SITUATIONIST REVOLUTION. IT IS ALL RIGHT TO BE UNHAPPY IN YOUR LIFE. IT IS ALL RIGHT TO KEEP BEARING EXCRUCIATING EMOTIONAL PAIN AND EXCRUCIATING PERMANENT, CONSTANT, RED-HOT HUMILIATION—BECAUSE YOU CAN BEAR IT. THIS IS THE CENTRAL MESSAGE OF THE REVOLUTION. OSCAR WILDE SUFFERED APPALLING BASENESS EVERY DAY OF HIS LIFE AFTER HIS TRIAL. VINCENT VAN GOGH SUFFERED APPALLING BASENESS EVERY DAY OF HIS LIFE AFTER HE BECAME A PAINTER. WE CAN READ THESE THINGS AND BECOME WISER. WE WILL NOT BE TORMENTED BY OUR PERVERSITY. WE SHALL EXULT IN IT. WE SHALL FLAUNT IT, AND WALLOW IN IT, AND LUXURIATE IN IT. AS WE ALSO WALLOW, AND LUXURIATE IN OUR LOVE FOR LADY TARA. BUT THIS WE DO WITH TOTAL HUMBLENESS, SPREADEAGLED WITH HELPLESS WONDER BEFORE THE STARRY COSMOS LIKE BEETHOVEN IN HIS ODE TO JOY. WE SHALL FORCE OTHER PEOPLE INTO BASENESS, BY OUR CONTINUED FLAUNTING OF OUR VIOLENT SEXUALITY. BUT THEN BEFORE LADY TARA WE INSTANTLY BECOME SO HUMBLE. THIS IS NOTHING IF IT IS NOT A MANIFESTO FOR FIGHTING. A MANIFESTO FOR GLEEFUL WAR. A MANIFESTO FOR REVOLUTION. THIS IS MY DARWIN'S ORIGIN OF SPECIES. THIS IS MY MARX'S COMMUNIST MANIFESTO OF 1848.

THIS IS MY FREUD'S INTERPRETATION OF DREAMS. THIS IS MY EINSTEIN'S THEORY OF RELATIVITY. IT IS NOT A SENSIBLE JOURNEY, IT WILL BE A SITUATIONIST JOURNEY. THE POPE IS GOING ON HIS MILLENNIUM PILGRIMAGE, GOING THROUGH ALL THE HOLY SITES, AND THAT IS WHAT I AM GOING TO DO, VISITING ALL MY HOLY SITES—NAPOLEON'S TOMB, AUSTERLITZ, GRANADA. I WANT TO GET FAR AWAY FROM LADY TARA, BECAUSE I LOVE HER, AND I WANT THE PAIN OF BEING SEPARATED FROM HER

JUST BECAUSE YOU HAVE TO BEAR CONSTANT DAILY EXCRUCIATING PAIN, THAT IS NO CAUSE TO THINK YOU ARE A BAD PERSON, THAT IS NO CAUSE TO BE UNHAPPY. REMAIN JOYOUS THAT YOU ARE MORE INTELLIGENT AND MORE BEAUTIFUL THAN THE PEOPLE WHO ATTACK YOU, THAT IS WHY THEY ATTACK YOU. THEY CANNOT BEAR ANYONE SO MUCH BETTER THAN THEM TO GO ON LIVING. SARAH KANE KILLED HERSELF. EVEN SOMEONE AS TALENTED AND SUCCESSFUL AS HER COULD TAKE NO MORE PAIN BY THE AGE OF 28. TAKE STRENGTH FROM THE BLESSED, BEAUTIFUL SARAH KANE, SHE DIED THAT YOU MIGHT STOP YOURSELF AT THE LAST MOMENT. THE PAIN CAN BE BORNE.

THE SITUATIONIST REVOLUTION, IF IT IS ANYTHING, MUST MIX AUTISM, STRATEGIC IMMORALITY, MATHEMATICS, LOGIC, PRECISION, BEAUTY, POETRY, ART, HISTORY, GEOGRAPHY, CINEMA, MEMORY, LADY TARA, HOLD ON TO LOVE, HOLD ON TO LOVE. BUT I CAN'T, BUT I CAN'T. IF YOU KNOW HOW HOLDING ON TO LOVE IS TO BE ACHIEVED, THEN PLEASE LET ME KNOW. I AM GLAD I HAVE CREATED THIS FAME FOR MYSELF, THIS NOTORIETY, THIS REVOLUTIONARY MODEL. I AM GLAD PEOPLE ARE ALL FASCINATED BY ME, AS I AM FASCINATED ONLY BY LADY TARA.

IN THE MAW OF ANY REVOLUTION COMES THE TERROR, THE RUTHLESS GUILLOTINE OF MY LOGIC. ONLY ONE PERSON WILL BE SAFE FROM IT: LADY TARA. IS THIS LOVE LETTER, MANIFESTO, OR SUICIDE NOTE? IT IS ALL THREE. I HOPE TO DIE DURING THIS MONTH IN EUROPE.

2

I LIVE FOR THE SIMPLE PLEASURES IN LIFE. LISTENING TO THE PROMS EVERY NIGHT ON RADIO 3. READING MY LORCA. FINISHING MY BOOK. I AM NOT A SOCIAL CREATURE. I AM AN AUTISTIC CREATURE. I AM A DENIZEN OF THE KINGDOM OF DEATH. I AM ONE OF PRINCESS MORT'S SERVANTS. I AM HER MOST LOYAL AND BELOVED SERVANT. I AM HER GOLDEN BOY, I AM HER FAVOURITE,

I AM HER DARLING, I AM HER PET. SHE WILL DO ANYTHING FOR ME. "MY LITTLE SEBASTIAN". NOW I REALISE WITH A SHOCK PRINCESS MORT IS LADY TARA! THEY ARE ONE AND THE SAME PERSON. I DON'T HAVE TO WORRY ABOUT GIVING MYSELF TO ONE OR THE OTHER. I DON'T HAVE TO WORRY ABOUT DEBAUCHING MYSELF IN THE KINGDOM OF DEATH THEN HAVING TO COME BACK TO FACE LADY TARA AFTERWARDS. SHE KNOWS, BECAUSE SHE RULES OVER THE KINGDOM OF DEATH ALREADY. SHE IS PRINCESS MORT ALL THE TIME. IT IS LIKE FINDING OUT DARTH VADER IS MY FATHER AND PRINCESS LEIA IS MY SISTER ROLLED INTO ONE. I DON'T BELONG IN SOCIAL RELATIONSHIPS. I DON'T BELONG IN SOCIAL PLACES. I AM THE DARK POET. I AM THE DARK ANGEL. I AM RESEARCHING THOSE DEADLY PLACES. KEEP PUSHING THE SOCIAL PEOPLE, KEEP PUSHING THEM. I just want to get away from Lady Tara forever. This book will be a record of my love for Lady Tara. THE REVOLUTION IS BEING WAGED. THEY ARE THINKING ABOUT ME BECAUSE MY LIFE IS MORE DEPRAVED THAN THEIRS. THE SOUNDS OF THE JUNGLE ARE SO BEAUTIFUL! I AM DON GIOVANNI. I AM JERZY K. "But despite his literary success, Crane was a profoundly tormented man. Poetry sustained him in a life that otherwise teetered on the brink of collapse. When he wasn't writing, he spent much of his time engaged in fleeting homosexual encounters and alcohol binges. In 1932, three years after meeting Lorca, Crane committed suicide by leaping from a ship into the Caribbean." The people's lives in the Citadel are a case of suspended agony. I AM DEVOTED TO ALWAYS DOING THE WRONG THING. IT IS A MATTER OF PRINCIPLE TO ME. TO SHOW IT CAN BE DONE. "YOU CAN HATE ME NOW, BUT I WON'T STOP NOW". I WOULD GO TO THE ARMY & NAVY AND BACK FOR PRINCESS MORT. IN THE UNDERWORLD I MAY BE JUST A LOWLY SERVANT BURIED AT THE BOTTOM OF SEVERAL LAYERS OF HIERARCHY, *BUT I AM HER MOST BELOVED SERVANT!* FOR THAT PRIVILEGE I WILL DO LITERALLY ANYTHING FOR PRINCESS MORT.

3

This is a desperate attempt to communicate my last messages from the testing ground of world destruction before the end of the world, before my transmitter is detected and I am closed down. My reports are rambling, confessional, despairing, exultant, but the cries of a hunted man, in the Last Days of Mankind, in a feverish 1914 Vienna.

If these are the Last Days of Mankind, and if I am going to die soon, I want to leave this record behind me. I seem to have built my own testing ground for world destruction to live in. I have built this experimental station for world destruction. They are all living in Vienna 1914, this experimental station for world destruction, in the Last Days of Mankind, without even realising it. They were so smug and cocky, and they didn't realise how diseased, and filthy, and poisoned they were. Their society was about to explode. I will do everything I can to put the black sparkling bomb under it myself. There is only one person in this hell I would save if I could. My job is to tempt people into stupidity, into betraying their baseness for all the world to see, to constantly tweak society's noses, to get under their skin, and make them obsessed by me; even though they were killing themselves laughing at me, thinking this their moment of greatest victory, they would start to melt and scream like the Nazi at the end of *Raiders of the Lost Ark*. Moral imagination. I will roam like W.G.Sebald from the Citadel to Berlin to Vienna to Budapest to Paris to Granada to Stockholm. I will roam between these Berlins and Viennas of the mind. I will visit them for real only to help me concentrate and focus on the journey I am making in my mind. Like Robinson's journey around London. Tara is my everything. I know I am such a good person and it puzzles me why I am the most reviled person I have ever met. It does not get me down because I have been used to it almost from the earliest time I can remember. I was never popular. I have always worn my lack of popularity as a badge of pride, because the people who attack me are so stupid and ugly. I am proud to be attacked by such people. The time to worry would be if they ever started to accept me. That truly would be a black day for me.

4

I am on a higher level to them. I have higher intelligence, higher culture, higher sensitivity. I am Oscar Wilde, I am Karl Kraus, I am the Marquis de Sade. I am Lord Byron. Transgression is not only possible, it is beautiful. I must live on that dangerous line: always courting my own destruction. It is my murderous intention to take on everybody, to stir everybody up more and more. I am not backing down. I am not becoming ashamed. I could be living a beautiful, peaceful life now. But you can't remove the storms from your history; they formed me. The storms kept me alive and do so still. I can only write my testament. They don't understand me; I am beyond them. They fear me. I am the dark blue poet. I have shown I can do anything. I have no respect for society's morality. I refuse to back down and be a member of their society; their fetid, putrid, pig-stupid society. Their malice tells you everything you need to know about them. They have a slight lack of intelligence. They feel small. They are bitter and jealous, of my beautiful freedom. I am writing my Die Fackel, to record the 1914 Vienna in the Last

Days of Mankind. I need to keep pushing them more and more. It is like squeezing a drop of blue ink into a beaker of putrid, fetid water and watching to see how it spreads; then squeezing a drop of green ink in and watching how that spreads; then red. Squeezing one drop after another and always watching the results, transfixed by the beautiful swirling colours. I am devoted to being an anti-hero. Into building as much of a black reverse image of what society wants me to be as I possibly can.

5

Berg's Violin Concerto suited my mood so well now. I couldn't listen to pop music anymore; there was too much boy-meets-girl emotion in it, like cinema; I just wanted the pain of the classical music. Sibelius, Bartok. This is sign I am moving further into NOTHINGNESS. I will move further and further away from Lady Tara and watch her from that great distance, instead of moving closer and closer to her and melding with her, isn't this insane? But I feel I cannot move closer, it is not that welcome, so unable to stay in between, as ever, if I cannot merge I must remove myself to a great distance in the cold. Stockholm. Helsinki. I look at Lady Tara with such desire, but she is another representative of my fatal ancestral tragedy. What do I want in my life? I want Nothingness. If I can't have Semele I want nothingness. I will work long hours at the citadel and earn my money, and return to my nothingness, my Bartok, and Berg and Sibelius. My cold, icy world, with my cold, icy hands. But somewhere in me is a heart that burns for Lady Tara. I use my life as a work of art. I use my diary as a work of art, like Tracey Emin. Eva Mudocci. The only woman Edvard Munch truly ever wanted to fuck. Nietzsche. Freud. Munch. Lady Tara left me to rot in that machine, as I steadily went mad. Perhaps I shouldn't see this Nothingness as a defeat now, as sign of my failure: maybe I should see it as the vital next stage I had clambered up to and achieved, at long last. Maybe after trekking through the jungles, scaling the escarpment, I had at last managed to complete my descent into the black hole, of the Lost World, where wonders await me. Perhaps this was the great leap forward I had been searching for since 1989. I expected a great leap forward after 1989 but it never happened, the engine stuttered and died and I was left black and rudderless for nine years. Now at last I am ready for the next stage to begin. I just live for work, and then coming home to my Berg and Bartok and Sibelius; nothing in between. Cultivating my nothingness now, making it grow. What's this? I'm just growing stronger? What's this? I'm just growing richer? SEEDS OF THE POPE. The record of a war. A study of narcissism. A romance. The roaring thunderous cadences of Sibelius speak to me of the triumph of the autistic will. "All of us are in the gutter, but some of us are

5

looking at the stars". I have to write SEEDS OF THE POPE because of my love for autistic people and my need for someone to forgive me, my need to make contact. When I write "I don't like real people", that is the heart of the tragedy. I am preparing my testament to leave behind me. So one day Semele will understand. I don't mind anything; I am autistic, and I like that about myself.

6

I want to make myself more extreme; bleak; and go to Stockholm. Stay alone in an expensive hotel like *The Silence*. If I want the nothing and silence of the Stockholm hotel room I should enjoy the nothing and silence of the Citadel. My one great extravagance is luxury hotels. Stockholm is my new Boston. My greatest heroine is Gunilla Gerland. But it is the town of Greta Garbo, too. I will now indulge my autism. Give myself up to my true nature. I am going mad. The Citadel was such a safe harbour; why did I let the madness get the better of me again? It has made it more interesting, hasn't it! I want an end to all passions now. Me leaving for Stockholm in particular means something. It means I am giving up on another tormented tortuous attempt to form a relationship and trying to sink myself in Asperger's Syndrome. I want to stay out of the way from now on. I have got into enough trouble. Whenever I forget I am not a real person and try to engage with people, it ends in disaster. It would be progressing quite well, but then my madness would come galloping behind, the volcano would rise, and pick it up and dash it to destruction. I crave darkness, and shadows, and night. I crave icy weather and a warm hotel room fire. I want to live in Ingmar Bergman's *The Silence*. I want to spend my life alone with my mind, never having to engage with real people at all. I want to go back to how things were in the first four years. I resent the world for having taken that four years away from me, and now I want to insist on it back again. Perhaps after this explosion I might find a new equilibrium. Beneath the renewed tormenting twitch in my right cheek, I sense there is a new sunrise about to dawn inside me. But it depends upon the reaction of the people I am set to leave behind.

7

I am beautiful, and intelligent: like Kaspar Hauser. The pain keeps building up and building up. You think it must break soon—but it never does break. This pain: I am mining a completely new seam. It is building up in their consciences. It is an examination of pain. Whither now, Kaspar? Do nothing. Be nothing. The only way to survive this pain; like Chauncey Gardiner. So you wanted to be alone; well, no one's ever been more alone and isolated than you are now. I am devoting my life to giving birth to a new writing, for the good of mankind. I am turning into something else like Leto turned into a giant sandworm in *God Emperor of Dune*. "Strauss's mother periodically suffered severe mental breakdowns. The terrifying exploration of neurosis in his operas *Salome* and *Electra* has less to do with either Freud or sensationalism than with the impact of a private tragedy...Nietzsche became another Straussian hero, yet though he professed to follow his philosophy, he more often than not drew back from it. Many of Strauss's characters—Don Juan, Till Eulenspiegel, Salome, Elektra—attempt to pass into a territory of pure amorality ('beyond good and evil', as Nietzsche put it)—but they are always destroyed in the process."

8

The secret perhaps lies in fever after all. I am Richard Gerstl. That is why I go to Vienna. I am sick, diseased in this sick, diseased fever town. I feel mortified again. Flushed and hot all the time, because I have destroyed things with Semele again. I will take more interest in the psychosis of Vienna before 1914. Richard Gerstl killed himself. Unable to bear the misery and despair and desires of that fever town any longer. The only sickness that I have got is lovesickness. The only fear that I have got is repressed desire. Normal companionship is not possible for me. It never has been and never will be. People are cruel the world over. This nervous weakness in my right cheek is sign of the neurotic fever town I live in, during the last days of mankind. Mourning my missed chances with my perfect woman: Semele. My stupid repression and failure to be relaxed with her. Whenever I am split from her will be the last straw, like the split between Gauguin and Van Gogh was the last straw for Van Gogh. His madness careered out of control after that. Semele has been my biggest strength but also my biggest weakness. That is why I am Richard Gerstl. I want her so much. She is the only person warm to me in this cruel and vicious world; my heart is bleeding for her. I tried to control my loneliness when I was with Semele, and not get crazy. Life without love is worth nothing. Semele is the one I love. What will life be worth without her? Just people's enmity and ridicule and no warmth from her to counterbalance it. I have something missing from my brain. I am Richard Gerstl. I am too hypersensitive to survive this neurosis. I am bleeding inside from my desire for Semele.

9

I am the Pope. But I feel weak with uselessness. I have no more conversation left in me. I am Kaspar Hauser. But I am the Pope. The crimson Borgia Pope. My chest is in such pain. I have never felt so dull and dead. I have sunk back into the worst disillusion and deadness of my life. It feels terminal. There are no more stimuli that can break through this fog. I am back on the seas again, enveloped in the thickest fog mankind has ever known. My steam yacht is drifting lifelessly, all power gone, all engines dead. The memory of my failed connection with Semele my only company. A connection that failed only because of my silence. A silence terrifying and remorseless and gripping and clammy. I want to scream to break the repressiveness of this fog, but it would carry nowhere, to no one. The sound would become muffled as it left my mouth. I would not hear it myself. What a fate this is, to be killed by fog, this fog that has descended around me, this fog that has descended in me. I want to cut myself just to check that there is still some red colour in this world, that there is still some feeling left in me. But I know I would feel nothing, and the blood would come out grey. This has happened when Semele has turned her greatest rays of warmth upon me, and I have felt myself so inadequate in my ability to respond, I have inadvertently formed this fog around myself. What a farce this life is. When will it ever emerge from this fog? I don't believe I ever shall now. I have found my foggy grave, and I shall lie in this grave for whatever time is left to me. I relied on Semele for the only life that was possible to me. I am the Pope. I am carving my own canali in life. I am finding my own path. I am formulating my own philosophy. All I have is the silence. The silence of a grand hotel.

10

I am Volpone. I trick the vicious out of their victory. I am a man for whom abuse has become a drug. DEBAUCHED BORGIA POPE HID HIS LIFE OF DESPAIR. "Munch was infatuated with Juell, a feminist before her time who advocated free love. He believed that the point of sexual ecstacy was the moment 'when life and death join hands' and painted Juell obsessively in Berlin between 1894 and 1895. Despite his hangdog devotion, she married someone else. A spokeswoman for Christie's, which is selling the painting for an unnamed European collector, said: 'The painting tells us a lot about the secret emotions of his life, his traumatic initiations to love, jealousy and rejection.'" It is Edvard Munch and Dagny Juell. It is Friedrich Nietzsche and Lou Andreas Salome.

11

Some days I will be more silent than others. I must accept that about myself and not stop loving myself because of it. I need me to keep loving me. One day I will tell her about Gunilla Gerland and *A Real Person*. The social component is missing from my brain. I live in a realm of deep sleep. I have never had a single friendship, not with another man, nor with a woman. This may seem remarkable to someone, for example, like Semele, she would perhaps be unable to comprehend the full extent of what I was saying, but it doesn't seem remarkable to me. A silent person cannot imagine the real life that real people lead, with real relationships and real friendships, real interactions with the world around them; as much as a real person cannot imagine the complete nothingness of a silent person's life. My black hollowed eyes seem to stare out from another world like a painting by Munch.

12

I am going to become more provocative, more vile, more mischievous, more annoying to them. I am playing with you! This is revolution. They don't realise that their minds are being changed by me, whether they like it or not. I am poisoning and diseasing them, I am smuggling myself under their skin and into their bloodstream, so that they take me home with them, and then I can infect their wives and their children, and their friends and workmates, and now they are sickening and dying. I am smuggling Soho pornography and prostitution into their living rooms. I am smuggling my white sperm into their living rooms. Now I am being meek and mild, and the good angel, but my red-blooded self is in there waiting to come out again when the moment is right and indulge all the pleasures that are open to me but barred to them! How they hate me for it. They abuse and try to shame me, and I just smile at them and do something even more illicit and debauched, right under their noses! My fountains of white sperm. My insolent display of luxury. I want all of Paris to worship my sovereign nudity. I am Nana on the stage of the Théâtre des Variétés, in just a single-piece of see-through gauzy fabric. The golden fly. "Socks. How do you plead?" "Horny as hell!" "Take him down!" My Soho life is just sleeping. I can always return to it, whereas they are not allowed. I will return to it with a vengeance, and provoke them more and more and more, because they see—I cannot be destroyed! I feel powerful because I can always indulge my Soho desires when I want to.

13

If people don't like me, then that is their problem, it is not my problem! I should wake up happy every day for the material I am going to collect. Smile mischievously because they cannot stop me being ME, Kaspar Hauser, supreme being, and writing my book about me. I like being me, leading my Soho life, getting everybody thinking about ME; this only would be enough for me if it wasn't for Semele, making me sad that I haven't got what she's got. I am an artist, I love the Soho life. I am Kaspar Hauser, I wander precisely where I want to, unconcerned of any social conventions or taboos or disapproval. I LOVE disapproval! I am devoted to living as disgustingly as possible, to show you can still breeze through it. Because I am Kaspar Hauser, first man of the new superbreed. They understand what my project is. My mission to stir society up as much as I possibly can, to foment them into viciousness and vileness, so they are exposed in their true colours, and they can demean themselves. I need to be pushed into a more extreme place, so I can write the things I need to write. My project to show you can do precisely what you want, no matter what society thinks about it, and be much happier that way, as a Kaspar Hauser free spirit. I believe in being as eccentric and debauched as possible. I am devoted to exploring the sinful side, testing one wire after another, to see what effect it has on people around me. Semele has got time on her hands, she puts it into her friends; I have got time on my hands, I put it into my books. I do it all with a mischievous laugh. I am devoted to stirring people up, so I cannot lose. My job is to reveal the stupid people, like going along a wooden wall to knock at the panels until I find the hollow sound and the secret door. Note that one down and carry on knocking looking for the next one. I live for different things, I don't live for friendships. The thought of having to be with anyone other than Semele is horrible to me.

14

If I left the Citadel now the nothingness would destroy me. The Citadel is the only thing holding me together. By going to Stockholm, I feel I am going away from the action: the action is in Berlin and Vienna. But that was the point of going to Stockholm: to nihilistically remove myself from the action completely. I love the myth that Semele has become to me. I wanted to remove myself from the action, to purify my body and mind. But Berlin and Vienna are important to me. Just go everywhere and do what I want to do and ignore the people. Because people are the one thing I don't like about this world.

15

I am Steerpike. I am Švejk. I am a born troublemaker and subversive. The abuse I stir up pushes me into the extreme place I need to be. I need the quality of loneliness I would find in Stockholm to push me even more into an extreme place. I love my free life; I am powerful enough to lead it. I'm in an interesting new phase now, the richest phase of my life. I just see my life as a fascinating journey. I am just on a train recording each new place it brings me to. I <u>want</u> to be the one Semele relies on. "The type of the turn of the century, the personality which destroys itself". In that destroying myself I bloom and blossom. My life is so rich and stimulating now!

16

I am an explorer, as intrepid as Shackleton. I have just started out on the moral icefields on my way south.

17

How can there be any end to this pain? When will this pain in the chest ever end? Stockholm will not cure it. NO SALVATION IN BERLIN FOR SCHRÖDER. Only she can cure it but that is the ridiculous hope that causes the pain. I am a closed person. A silent person. A recessive person. A non-existent person. That is what my books are about; non-existence. Sarah Kane will understand the pain I am feeling now in my chest. LULU. SEEDS OF THE POPE. SEMELE. I must try to bear this pain, while tasting the poison in my mouth, to write the books. I have no social life that she has, I have a book life. I have a fearsome book life: I am giving my whole existence over to it. It is a black hole swallowing me up until there is nothing more to be seen of me. Even the soles of my boots have disappeared from Semele's view now. I have given myself totally over to non-existence. The emptiness of my life previously was filled with the pornography and prostitution of Soho, feasting with panthers, but now that is no longer desirable by me, there is just the emptiness remaining. The sadness at my emptiness. The devastating sense of inadequacy with Semele beside her incredible fullness, her unbelievably busy and packed social life. The constant pain in my chest. Am I really as non-existent as I feel when I am beside her? I have got the books. I will make them everything. I have made them everything. There is just nothing else. I want to...what? Be with Semele? Be inside Semele? Merge myself out of existence with her, so that I don't have to feel this anymore? Always Semele or not Semele; but a principle: a light in the darkness. That is what she has been: a light in the dark, but not somebody warm and real that I could ever be a partner with, just a light, that relieved the darkness certainly, but not something that I could hold and possess.

18

I am going to the country of Karl Marx, Friedrich Nietzsche and Kaspar Hauser. "Marx, weary of Committees and Societies and Leagues, retreated into the British Museum reading room, ten minutes' walk from Dean Street, and applied himself to the ambitious task of political economy—the monumental project that was to become *Capital*...Marx needed to keep himself in a state of seething fury—whether at the endless domestic disasters that beset him, at his wretched ill-health or at the half-wits who dared to challenge his superior wisdom. While writing *Capital*, he vowed that the bourgeois would have good reason to remember the frequent carbuncles which caused him such pain and kept his temper foul. His living conditions might have been expressly designed to keep him from lapsing into contentment...In a graveside oration, Engels described him as a revolutionary genius who had become the most hated and calumniated man of his time, predicting that 'his name and work will endure through the ages'". My wildness is my strength; if they tame me they have won. I have places, and artistic heroes, who mean a lot to me. Semele has real friends who mean a lot to her. We are different creatures. I must relish my wildness. Rhinemaidens. In mini-dresses made of little Deutsche Marks, like Ginger Rogers at the start of *The Gold Diggers of 1933*. I am going to the town of Alban Berg, Anton Webern, Arnold Schoenberg, Egon Schiele, Karl Kraus, Richard Gerstl, Georg Trakl and Sigmund Freud.

19

I am changing. I am evolving. I have become disillusioned with Chelsea. Cinema. Soho. I have fallen back on just the book. Semele is stunned that she cannot find any sign of life in me. She hadn't expected it to be this bad. I need to push myself to a very extreme place. Then I would change and become the monster that I need to be. I will reach that extreme point I need to reach. The moment I met the most desirable Queen of my life was the moment I completed my journey to monsterhood. I had nothing to write about, so I wrote about the gutter, the only place that was accessible to me. I am disillusioned with it all. I need a woman to restore my faith in life. Semele alone fitted the bill, but such a thing has never been possible for me. I seek solitude. I don't care for people at all. Semele is the only person I can feel anything for. She tries to get to know me but finds there is nothing to get to know. That nothingness is the essential me. This makes me feel so useless that I could cry. How to accept what is me? I am as unhappy as Sarah Kane. These black words are all that keep me alive. These black words are all that exist of me in this world.

20

"You will be buried alive. You will have the flesh torn from your bones. You will be tortured in many horrible and primitive ways. But you will realise that genius which you sometimes have suspected you possess."—German explorer Voss.

21

On the train home, I practiced for being on the train across Germany by watching the passing scenery and letting my despair over Semele flood into my eyes. It produced a quality of despair hitherto unknown to me; a new shade had been added to my spectrum of misery. I will go to the Black Forest. I will go to Nuremberg. I will take the Romantic Road. This is my Creation of New Ideals, my Revaluation of all Values. Immorality is worthless, and love is impossible. I want to spend lots of time in Germany, probing my morbid romanticism, before going to Stockholm. I will take the Romantic Road, fuelled by my rejection by Semele.

22

I've cured the twitch in my cheek anyway! All I feel for Semele now is resentment. I imagine seeing her again when I return, and I'm sitting by the window as she's coming towards me at 9 o'clock, with bitterness. The rightful heir to the throne of Baden. Whit Monday, 1828. Nuremberg. "He is taken up by this eccentric English aristocrat, Lord Stanhope, and he seems to have conceived also some sort of passion for Kaspar in which the dynastic and the sexual seems to be uneasily mixed. He seems to have had ideas, as people have had since, that this child was some sort of potential messiah. His effect on Kaspar in the end was wholly detrimental. He seems to have taken him up, offered him adoption, corrupted him in that sense, given him ideas of a grand status, and then to have dropped him. And whilst it can't be said that he occasions the murder, he certainly does nothing to prevent it. He leaves him adrift." "And he is murdered in the end?" "He is, indeed, then murdered after only five and a half years or so, in the daylight." What I did was violent with Semele. I will be more violent on my own in Europe. I will write her violent postcards. Sarcastic, violent postcards. Because I like writing. I want things to become more violent, more revolutionary. Because there is no further I can move in the other direction: I cannot become more normal, more a respected, liked member of society, more warmed by a real relationship. So stop hovering around waiting for it. I need passion and drive to my life again. I need to be powered along the hanging track by my instincts. It will get me into trouble but at least it will get me somewhere. Trouble is better than nothing. Trouble is better than waiting at Semele's door to be patted on the head, for being a good boy.

CHAPTER 2
THE
GRAND
TOUR

"This is where I have been today, Neuschwanstein, home of Mad King Ludwig II of Bavaria, one of my greatest heroes. He was a compulsive masturbator and fantasist, who spent millions making his fantasies real. The castle took seventeen years to build, and then he lived in it for just six months, before the Bavarian government sent troops to arrest him in his bedroom because they said he was suffering from a mental illness (but really because he was spending all of Bavaria's money). They took him to another castle where the next morning he was found drowned in a lake. King Ludwig's favourite animal was a swan, and there are pictures of swans throughout the castle, even the door-handles to all the rooms are in the shape of swans' heads, and that is where the castle's name comes from. Wagner was Ludwig's greatest hero, and the walls of all his rooms are covered from floor to ceiling with paintings depicting scenes from Wagner operas. The walls of Ludwig's bedroom are covered with scenes from *Tristan und Isolde*. It was very moving for me to be standing in the room where King Ludwig used to sleep, walking the same gloomy corridors he walked, leaning out the windows looking into the wall of white mist that he would have done. This is the place I would most like to live in all the world.

Leaving the castle, I headed up the steep path through the forest which suddenly comes to the Marienbrücke, a little rickety wooden bridge suspended over a very narrow and very deep gorge. When you get to the middle of the bridge all you see over the railings on either side of you is a solid wall of white mist, and beneath you a tiny little waterfall and stream. It was very scary but very breathtaking. I thought I was going to pass out, or that someone was going to come up behind me and tip me over the icy railing. I live in permanent fear of assassination attempts from people trying to finish me off, like they did to poor King Ludwig, and like they did to poor Kaspar Hauser, who I'm going to Nuremberg to make pilgrimage to tomorrow."

24

We wouldn't be here if it wasn't for tension. If not for the tension of sexual congress between your mother and father resulting in the climactic explosion, we would not be here. Without the tension there would be no orgasmic explosion. It is the tension that produces the explosion. There would be no universe if not for the tension. The Big Bang would not have happened without the tension. I need the tension. Sturm und drang. Storm and stress. That is what Goethe is symbol of to me. That is what Weimar is symbol of. Lou Salomé seemed to help a lot of them increase that tension, Rilke, Nietzsche, but they had to release it in the explosion of their work. That is what Semele does for me. An extraordinary, intelligent, beautiful young woman, she inspires so much work I've produced, but the only explosion she will allow me is in my work. They are spiritual masturbators, but only spiritual. That is the only service they will provide. Weimar, the capital of storm and stress. Goethe, its figurehead. I am always looking for things that will put me into the trance I need that will enable me to shut people out successfully. They hate me because I have got my own personal style; when they have got no style at all, they are herd animals; they are sheep, concerned only with fitting in. Like Kaspar Hauser had his own style, like King Ludwig II had his own style. I am proud of having my own personal style, which so few people do. Now I am poisoning and polluting the people of München—that is good. Sehr gut. I just feel excited now; I just feel stimulated. I am flaunting my Kaspar Hauserness in their faces.

25

I know I am a good person, and I know Kaspar Hauser was, and I know Vincent Van Gogh was, and I know Jesus was, and I know F.G.Lorca was, and I know Oscar Wilde was—and yet all these people were viciously pursued and eventually destroyed by the members of society they lived in. What does this tell us about "normal" society? Discuss. If we added up the achievements of all the normal members of society who did so much to destroy these people, what would it come to, compared to the achievements of the people they destroyed? Discuss. If you want to, that is. If you don't feel comfortable with this subject matter, then that's fine, we'll just leave it for another time.

26

So I saw the plaque to Kaspar Hauser in Unschlittplatz. It felt kaleidoscopic to be there in that little odd-shaped square, as twilight started to fall, cobbled and sloping in all different directions, vertiginous and dizzying, things were spinning around me—this was the square where Kaspar Hauser arrived in the world as a fully-formed 15-year-old child, on May 26, 1828, as Frankenstein's monster arrived in the world a fully-formed man, in Ingolstadt, just down the romantic road. No one knew how to cope with Kaspar nor he with them. It brought out the best that human beings can be in him, and the worst that they can be in them. This Grand Tour is a series of deeply personal pilgrimages. I will want to come back to Kaspar Hauser's plaque every year, as I will want to return to Schloss Neuschwanstein and Marienbrücke every year. They killed him because he was a Holy Fool. His innocence, and his beauty, made them feel ashamed. They could not live with that shame every day, so they had to remove their source of it: Kaspar. Semele has enabled me to go to Neuschwanstein and Nuremberg; it would not have happened without her. I am magnificent in my specialness; I am no good being like them. I AM ON THEIR MINDS. I AM ON THEIR MINDS. Fu Manchu has poisoned London, München and Nürnberg, and now he is going to poison Wien. Sturm und drang. I need this storm and stress. That is why I will be going to Weimar, the capital of storm and stress. I still wonder whether I should be making some Marxian pilgrimage, by going to Trier, and Frankfurt, home of the 1848 parliament and the black-gold-red German flag, as well as birthplace of Goethe and *The Sorrows of Young Werther*. That can wait until next time perhaps. On my way back to Nürnberg and then the mountains. I am so happy and content in my own little world, and the fact that they try so hard to bother me must mean I am really getting to them. The people of Nürnberg have not improved since 171 years ago. No wonder there is no mention of Kaspar in their guide books or in their tourist information offices. That is not something they want to remember. It might offer them nothing but disturbing lessons, so better to erase it altogether from the collective memory. They don't like the fact that I have arrived asking about him, stirring things up again. Like the pinch-faced man in München tourist information office didn't like it when I was asking him about Hitler's Eagle's Nest in Berchtesgaden, it stirred things up that were best left forgotten. I know. That it seems is to be my role in life. I will come back on May 26th next year.

27

Normal people like being in groups laughing and joking with each other; I don't. I like being on my own thinking and writing. To be non-sociable is a crime in society. You will never stop being punished. I love heading towards the mountains. There are less people there and the air is colder. I love this strategy of tension. This storm and stress. Without storm and stress there would be nothing. I am Švejk. Smilingly tottering on his way, apparently oblivious of all the viciousness raining down on him from all sides. Švejk in the First World War. I am a 1914 figure. Semele has protected me because she needs me. I have helped her because I need her protection. Semele has been warm to me. I am born troublemaker and subversive. My muteness and my head down is my subversion.

28

What is life worth if you don't give in to temptation?

VIENNA

The more people attack me the more determined I become to go on to Berlin and Stockholm and Helsinki. To go to the capital of storm and stress itself: Weimar! Vienna for me stands for the 1914 feverhouse, the experimental station for world destruction, in the last days of mankind. The Vienna that Karl Kraus wrote about, of 2 million souls and him. And he was going to take them all on himself. The Vienna of the neurosis and hysteria that made the too sensitive like Richard Gerstl take their own lives, that made Egon Schiele paint the way he did, that made Arnold Schoenberg start composing music the way he did. By coming here, and just looking all around me with the shutters of my eyes fixed open like a camera so it will all just be recorded on my photographic plate, I am tapping into all that.

30

Berlin for me means the sado-masochistic love of defeat of the Weimar Republic, the 20s and 30s that Grosz and Dix painted. The strategic immorality that Louise Brooks wrote about. If something had broken down, they were going to keep pushing it while laughing hysterically until it was totally destroyed forever. They were going to go all the way now; and they certainly did.

Stockholm is for me Gunilla Gerland, her book about not being a real person.

Helsinki for me is this autism taken on a stage further, more extreme; it is Sibelius's Finlandia. The absolute despair at now standing on the very precipice of an experience, the verge of a lifetime of pain that is just increasing every day, standing on that edge with just the sheer black threshold of the night ahead of me—and feeling exultant. That exultation when you should be feeling the final total despair that Camus wrote about in *L'Étranger*.

31
Vienna for me is the Etna of hate that was inside Karl Kraus.

32
I am Švejk. Everything they do to hurt me just thrills me even more. Everything they do just fills me up with power and delights me further. How terribly annoying for them. You are, I take it, terribly annoyed? I have a talent for provoking the stupid and the ugly, the dissatisfied and the resentful, the conformists and homophobes of all stripes everywhere. I flaunt myself in their faces, like Nana on the stage of the Théâtre des Variétés in a little flimsy see-through piece of white fabric. I invite the whole of Paris back to my gigantic bedroom to worship my sovereign nudity, my insolent display of luxury. I am the Golden Butterfly on the shit heap of Turn of the Century 1990s society. I am Walt Whitman. I am all the ships on the ocean, all the stars in the sky, I am the baby suckling at its mother's breast! I contain multitudes!

33
I make people do things; they are like Pavlov's dogs. I provokingly ring their bell all day long. Standing on the balcony in the Museum de Stadt Wien looking out to the Karlskirche church to my left and all the glorious buildings before me, I was thinking wouldn't it be nice if the illusion of being the only person in Vienna at that moment were real. If the city had been emptied by plague and I had the whole place to myself forever, like the man in *War of the Worlds* walks a world devoid of all human beings, wiped out by Martians. Like Cole comes up to a world devoid of all human beings in his sealed suit in *Twelve Monkeys*. If that could be me! If I could be the one person left inhabiting Vienna, the only person left in the world. I have rejected their normal society because to me it is foul and repulsive, being based as it is on socialising, talking, conversation, friendship, all things that have no meaning for me. I exist in an alternative world, of blackness, night, silence, despair and the exultation that only comes at the very moment of total final despair. Stockholm for me is representative of all that. I just want nothing to do with people. They play no part in my scheme of things. They are completely just in the way.

34

I still had no idea if other places had been affected the same as Vienna had, or whether it was just confined to this one city. When I turned the radio on there was just the sound of static hissing and I could find no programmes whatsoever. I thought this must mean a fairly large local area must have been affected but then when I turned on the television all the TV channels were dead as well, which led me to think the whole world had been depopulated! I felt the urge to take my clothes off and to be naked in the Staatsoper. Removing every stitch of my clothing, I felt the intense frisson of excitement of being naked in a public place, the pleasure of breaking that taboo. But at the same time, I felt the rotting sensation of doing something sinful alone, and not with Semele. The flickerings of sexual desire that were trying to break through my blanket of dull longing and despair for Semele were being smothered by the feeling that I should only be naked when it was with her permission and when I was alone with her. I left the director's office, and walked onto the red carpet landing, padding down the vast white marble steps. I went through the door into the auditorium and stood at the back of the stalls. Naked and in a state of some semi-excitement I padded down the aisle and up onto the stage. I stood there on the stage naked, with the hundreds of seats staring at me in the stalls, and dress circle and balcony. I wanted Semele to be in every one of them. As much as I felt the frisson of excitement at being nude in such a public place where I shouldn't be nude, I felt despair that I was alone, and that I could not be doing this with her. I felt despair and self-contempt and self-loathing and mournful misery.

35

I step through Munich, Nuremberg, Vienna, Berlin, Stockholm, provoking abuse and hatred everywhere like Kaspar Hauser. I cut a swathe and leave people poisoned in my wake. I have got my own style. I am as wild as Salvador Dali; as wild as Oscar Wilde. As Aubrey Beardsley, Egon Schiele. I will be torn apart like Sebastian in *Suddenly Last Summer*. I will be pierced with arrows like Saint Sebastian. "Yet Kraus himself was a regular visitor to the coffee house, first of all the Greinsteidl and then the Café Central but saw himself in literary terms more as an outsider. He founded and ran his own journal, the Fackel, the mouthpiece for his own cultural criticism. As a protest against the madness of the war, he wrote *Die letzten Tage der Menschheit* (1918/19), an extensive collage of texts, it was his main dramatic text, one which, as he said, he had written for a 'theatre on Mars', he himself imagining it to be unperformable. At the same time this critic of language and the age wrote unerring essays, satires, aphorisms and poems." The real world is only possible if you have a relationship; I will never have a relationship, so the real world has never been possible for me; I will always necessarily live in the dream world. In the steamy, erotic ferns & fronds of some Central European porn cinema, surrounded by other men with their big fat cocks out of their trousers in the flickering half-light of the screen. Dreamy, like Noodles in his opium den. This is my paradise; and a paradise that I am sure will be over soon enough.

36

The heart of the Karl Kraus exhibition (literally) was the mortal agony of his relationship with Sidonie Nádherný; a countess from above his station, he could never be sure of her feelings for him, so lived in constant lovestruck torture. But that was what inspired his creative imagination. "To love, to be betrayed, to be jealous in that order is easy; it is much more uncomfortable to be jealous, to be betrayed, and to love."

BERLIN

Stockholm for me equals science. Science of the mind. More so than Vienna. I take the abuse as my due homage. It is very hard, but I must put myself through it. I have stirred people up magnificently: stage one has been completed. The great separation has been achieved. Now the room has been opened up enabling me to do something worthwhile. I am as excited and stimulated by the mind now as I was by sex. This is a fantastic development on my part. My science protects me against the world. I am looking forward to getting to Stockholm for the chance to sleep and wash as much as anything else!

38

I am famous in Europe: my fame has preceded me. I am happy about that. To Munich, to Nuremberg, to Vienna, to Berlin. Probably to Stockholm also. They try to distract me from my researches; they try to knock me out of the trance. They just provide me with richer material. Berlin has been hellish—and absolutely invaluable! I regard my setting eyes on Die Sünde by Franz von Stuck in Munich's New Pinakothek, my emotions as I walked the corridors and bedroom of King Ludwig in Neuschwanstein, the Karl Kraus exhibition in Vienna, and my hellish experience in Berlin, as the great spectacular leaps forward in the continuing formation of my science. These notes are being written in the Reisezentrum hall of Berlin's Zoo station. I include this note for future biographers and idolators who wish to make pilgrimage in a century's time. They should put up crosses in the various places where the ego landed, like the cross erected at Charing Cross and elsewhere. These people who attack me have no idea what excitement my scientific research fills me with, and how they are but moths banging their heads against the blazing lighthouse. All these loving couples are so close in Berlin Zoo's Reisezentrum and sightseeing in all the cities I've been in, and I think of Semele being that close to someone, with a pain. The Berlin abuse started with the first step I took out of Berlin Zoo station after having deposited my bag in the locker. As the abuse started with the first step I took outside my front door as I started my journey. These things still seem extraordinary even to me, yet they are commonplace now. The abuse of Munich, Nuremberg, Vienna and Berlin has been more fierce than that I face at home: for them it is their great chance to get their kick in which might never come again, so it has been like a feeding frenzy, like when the Sainsbury's money comes in to the P.O.C.L. I am going to Stockholm to stay in my hotel room and WRITE; that is no doubt why I am looking forward to it. Berlin has been hellish, and that is no doubt why I have written more in Berlin than in any of the previous places. I am writing in the Reisezentrum of Berlin Zoo. I'm only trying to kill four hours until my night train to Stockholm gets in. There are red lights all around me; it would have been so easy to have killed all this time in the good old days. I am not sure what my good behaviour is gaining me. I hope you appreciate it. I hate Berlin and that is why I love it: it has been the most invaluable visit of my entire grand tour. I love Berlin now because it brought my hatred to new sublime levels. I am engaged on an absolutely thrilling scientific research in the most ferocious, poisonous seas imaginable, a veritable Jason and the Argonauts voyage between sheer rock faces, and the horrors of Berlin have brought my research onto a new, even more sublime level. Berlin has been horrible, and I feel at my most excited.

39

I feel as if I have taken root in Berlin Zoo's Reisezentrum, and my beanstalk is shooting up big and strong with each minute that passes. I have written such a lot of stuff here; in the place that I hate so much, my beanstalk will always stand now as a memorial to one of these rare moments when my ink really flowed.

40

W— has given a poison to the world, it has spread around in Europe; and W— is famous now as being the centre of it, as Nuremberg became famous for just such a reason. W— has become a capital of Europe. All these people in Europe who know me now will ask where does this man come from? Where is the home base of this person, where does this cancer radiate out

21

from, where is the smoking gun that has been shooting out all these seeds, and the answer is W—, and all the people of Europe will be going to their atlases to look up W—. Never before in history will the people of Europe have been sent to their atlases to look up W—. This seems an extraordinary moment in world history. It must surely be W—'s finest moment. For this poison it has created, this manure it has spread, like Nuremberg is famous for the way it destroyed Kaspar Hauser and the Nazi war crimes trials. W— has made itself the new Nuremberg. It has put itself on the map of Europe. This is such an extraordinary thing. It has put itself on the map of Europe. It will mean as much to the people of Europe as does London. The two places will be marked for them in their minds by the same great big black spot and star, as if they were both such huge capital metropolises. No longer will London be a great black spot and W— a miniscule little black speck if mentioned at all; they will both be absolutely equal great black spots. This has been achieved by my enemies; no, let's be fair, by me and my enemies. Together we have brought about W—'s greatest moment in world history, perhaps opened up a whole new vein in history's blood supply, a whole new branch of history has begun, and W— will grow to have permanent standing the way Nuremberg has. It is the most amazing thing that has happened. I must now be the most abused man in Europe. Is there any man in the world today who will be abused the moment he sets foot on the station platform of Munich, Nuremberg, Vienna and Berlin? Bomber Harris himself wouldn't have had to put up with this sort of vilification.

41

So I end up leaving Berlin in a joyous frame of mind. It will always mean a lot to me because of this moment. I will have fond memories of the sublime degree of nothingness it pushed me into, the quality of the pain. Everything they do helps me; I have a determination to make everything they do help me. I am writing notes in my book on the platform as the trains go past like a train spotter. It has given me this moment of epiphany. The moon in the black milky seas above me. The white Mercedes-Benz sign revolving slightly bigger, and slightly more brilliant. The gold clock of the Kaiser Wilhelm splinter glowing beautifully. The giraffe on the side of the office block. The blue neon of the Grundig and other signs. The trees of the Zoo lit brightly green by the white lamps. The traffic slowly passing, hissing along wet roads. I have had a pleasant stay. Thank you so much, Berlin.

STOCKHOLM

I like the idea of seeing these cities at just a tangent, just passing through the edge of them in a straight slice at a time, seeing the great monuments of the city from the bridge on the train across the river as it is leaving the place. It is very appropriate for me to be in the city of Gunilla Gerland and to stay in my hotel room on my one night there. Stockholm is beautiful but once again there are far too many people here. This grand tour has finally finished me off as far as people are concerned. This is a good thing. Before I always felt mournful that I didn't have the fraternal, socialising life of Semele; but now all I want is to be left with my book in my room, and I am happy to admit it. This has been the eye of the needle I had to go through.

43

I've been away for too long and I'm really desperate to come home. But I feel sad I didn't get to Helsinki or Oslo, or Gothenburg, and I'd like to return to Malmo, and Vienna. But not now because I've had enough, and my T-shirts and underwear have run out.

44

The science is all that matters. My "autism book" is all that matters. I've been pretending to be like a normal person on this holiday. That has stopped now. I have got what I needed. I got what I came for. A change has been brought about. I'm happy when in my own little world. With my nose in a book I am in my element. Without someone to explode and be yourself with, you must always remain behind your mask. Bartok had some release, I have none. Only in my reading and my writing. I am Gunilla Gerland. I am Greta Garbo. There is great warmth in me, but I am so different from them, I want to be alone. I had to go away so I could come back and enjoy what I had before. I am a scientific researcher. That is all I care about.

45

I want to make an impact on everybody. That is my mission. There exists very little scientific psychology about autism, and what there is has been done by outsiders i.e. normal doctors, or else books written by autistic people subjectively. Gunilla Gerland is my model. Never talk unless you are with Semele. I forgot to get my Stockholm postcard; perhaps symptom of the fact that I was never really there. I must buy and read lots of autism books when I get back. Write to the N.A.S. again. The seeds of my proposed science had been germinating for some time, but I needed some light and warmth thrown on them to make them shoot. That is, you understand, the autistic light and warmth i.e. the blackness and coldness of being alone at night in strange cities. In the blackness I might become imbued with the presence of Kaspar Hauser, Egon Schiele, Richard Gerstl, Sigmund Freud, Karl Kraus, *The Night Porter*, *Bad Timing*, *Pandora's Box*, *Cabaret*, *The Serpent's Egg*, Otto Dix, George Grosz, Edvard Munch, and in that greenhouse canopy some necessary mutations would take place. Then when I returned home my scientific seeds would be green shoots. I love being exposed and white and skinless in the city streets: it is how I am hypersensitive. It is how an autistic person is. In Stockholm I think my moment of becoming a pure autistic person did happen. Not by seeing the sights but by shutting myself inside my room. I had bludgeoned myself into submission in the preceding fourteen days and now I was ready to become pure sadness. Pure mute. Pure silent. I am so much looking forward to Alan Green's voice on Radio 5 football commentaries again. I am so much looking forward to the night train back from work, back to my science, to my room. The sight of people is repulsive to me. I am changing into the giant sand worm like Leto. It is necessary to become the God Emperor. I need the hostility of the people around me to keep germinating the seeds: it is the permanent heat that needs to be beating down on them. Freud, Marx, are my great heroes and role models. Next time I must visit Trier, Frankfurt, and Weimar. I've done the big centres this time, next time it will be a tour of the small places. Göteborg, too.

46

Vienna is the one place I feel I could return to and settle back into, the Rathaus. The pornography on TV, the nice stairs, the quiet side street no doubt are all vital considerata. It feels an old city; it still feels the city of *The Third Man*. Next time I will visit Trier, Frankfurt, Weimar briefly, before staying 8 or 9 days in Vienna.

47

I am the Kaspar Hauser who survived to turn his scientific gaze upon himself, his own mind, and the society that hounds him, to become a leading expert in the subject of P.S.D. (Psycho-Social Dwarfism). Gunilla Gerland is my heroine. I would also like to read the books of Dorothy Asner and Philip O'Connor. My time in society, as well as in psychotherapy in particular, got to the point where I said, "I'm sorry, it is plain beyond cavil that my ideas are totally incompatible with those of people around me, and we must completely break." With that I became the Pope, and the war commenced. I could no longer go on being down on myself because I was not like them, to keep twisting myself into agonisingly embarrassing positions in trying to pretend to be like them. It had to stop, so I stopped it. I got off the merry-go-round. In more fin-de-millennium terms, I got off the

Big Wheel (the symbol that now connects Vienna with fin-de-millennium London, unfortunately). When I think back to that Pope week, *Erotica in the Shadow of Death*, the week the Great War against me was really unleashed, the pictures of Blackadder, Pope Pius XII, blonde woman killer in that tight white top through which her dark nipples shone, Olympia, how incredibly pleasurable and thrilling it is! Of course, this was just before I started work and met Semele. It will perhaps have to wait until my time with Semele ends before I can go back to the pleasures of the Pope period.

48

"I forgot to get a postcard before I left Stockholm, so I've had to get this one in Malmo, before getting the katamaran back to Kopenhagen. I have been away so long. I am missing you so much. Malmo, Stockholm, and Kopenhagen are all incredibly pretty, at least the bits by the water are, which is all I've seen. There was never anything I wanted to see in Stockholm, it was just to be there to make a pilgrimage to Gunilla Gerland (as well as being the home of the great Greta Garbo, of course, and *I Am Curious Blue*), so I stayed in my hotel room and just wrote, which was very pleasant. The best parts of my holiday have been when I have got back to my hotel room and been able to write, and the long train journeys. Writers need somewhere to hide out in and just write in peace, the hotels next to the railway station are my favourite so I can go across to the station to buy my rolls and ham and newspaper then return back to my hotel to eat. I have done too much sightseeing this time, it has worn me out, so I'll be glad to have the next couple of weeks at home. That will be nice."

49

It could be that I am making a little colony on the edge of my resistance, like a little volcanic colony on the edge of a black smoker. Because it is fertile here. But I am not probing into anything. Maybe I am probing the fact of my resistance rather than removing it and going beyond it. Maybe. In that case this will be a study of resistance. A whole lifetime's resistance, for people like me have no other choice. Beyond the resistance is a vast abyss, and all bridges were destroyed at birth, were in fact never built. We mutes must live forever on the isolated side of this abyss with the impossibility of building bridges clear to us, but disputed by psychotherapists, and viciously mocked by the rest. Maybe just a powerful black demon took over my mind and he convinced me over the years that there are no bridges, and none could be built, because it was in his interest to do so, and so maintain dominion over me.

50

My resistance is all I have, beyond it is nothing. I would not know how to stop resisting. I feel a permanent black tension within me. I do not turn a dynamo all day to create this. It is there permanently. I am being held on the edge of the resistance, like Maximilian Schell on the lip of the Black Hole, the waterfall into the abyss. My mind must keep furiously rowing to resist being thrown into the abyss, but it can never move further upstream to safety, it can only hold its position on the verge. Perhaps this is a study of resistance. Their world seems horrible to me. Semele's world. But some people are trapped in resistance by the non-growth of their brain at birth because of no stimulation, and no bridges were built, and a hairline fracture opens up between them and the rest of the people around them which with every year that passes spreads more and more until it becomes a vast terrifying cleavage like only the German Romantic painters knew (if a vast cleavage can ever be thought of as anything other than magnificent), and these people deserve study, in order for them to be helped to live their extremely painful life.

51

Semele has been fascinating and beautiful for me because it has allowed me to get close enough to someone to study what separates me from them. Needing each other has brought a certain closeness between us, which cannot hide the fact the gap between us being no more than the gap between one synapse and its partner, it is still a cleavage completely unbridgeable even if we had all the granite blocks and iron girders in the world. Never connect. That real emotional connection is not possible for me. I am too weird, too blocked, too resistant, or my brain just never grew the bridges at birth. I feel I have put down markers for future visits. I feel safe to go back to Vienna and write. I feel safe to go back to Malmo and write. I would go back to Berlin only to kill myself. Like Emil Nolde I perhaps prefer small towns. I would prefer to go to Göteborg rather than Stockholm, for some reason. It is the town where Gunilla Gerland found the right answer whereas in Stockholm she found only sweeping under the carpet, of which I am so familiar.

BRUSSELS

The abuse back at Brussels Eurostar is already intense; like the fire facing the Messerschmidts as they approached the British coast. My science is a great solace to me. I missed the 8.03 because I spotted that Gellar magazine, and now the 8.57 is delayed due to technical problems. Welcome back to Britain! It is so predictable I could cry. Now we are moving. Just one more train after this. If you survive this, you can survive anything. This is the vital test by fire I need, for in the fire the revelations will be discovered. Keep your nerve, because you are stirring them up, and getting a book out of it. I have taken a different path in life. It is giving me my book.

CHAPTER 3
AN AUTISTIC JOURNEY THROUGH NORWAY

I am always writing, writing, writing. The way Friedrich Nietzsche spent every minute of his life writing. The way Vincent Van Gogh spent every moment painting, painting. Trying obsessively to solve the problems in his art and his life. On the train from Berlin to Hamburg the bunch of young businessmen started saying "English?" "English" then whispering where they had been talking very loudly, before bursting out laughing. On the train from Hamburg to København the man and woman opposite me started saying "English?" "English" and then something like "always schreibing" and laughed. I am the wild child of modern day Europe. The autistic wild child of Europe who does not mix, does not socialise, does not talk, does not make eye contact with strangers. This has made me famous throughout Europe and the world. This trait of mine is so severe that I even did not speak to P when she wanted me to. Even if I had met with her I wonder if we would really have been able to speak to each other in any deep way. My difficulties in this area are severe. The fact that she was prepared to build the bridge and was prepared to more than come halfway to meet me might indicate she would have put up with my reticences, and we might have made a success of it. The best thing for my writing is to be on a train surrounded by people. I am forced to get my pen out in order to keep my head down. This is why all my writing from my last European journey was from Berlin Zoo-Stockholm-Malmo-København-Hamburg. They were all day trains, so I was surrounded by people. Now on the train from Hamburg to København I have written my first words of this journey. I ran to Europe to escape from the horror of P not being there anymore but in every city I have come to I have had to flee from the emptiness of her not being there with me. The man and woman opposite me are talking away to each other, and I don't think they met each other before, and I think how do they do it? When the Italian barmaid started talking to me in the Berlin pub I instinctively started looking for the door. I cannot talk to people. Even if I had met with P there is a strong possibility that I would not have been able to talk to her. Though before that I had very good feelings for her. She opened me up to all the love and kindness that there is undeniably somewhere deep inside me. She opened me up and then shut the door on me. All this love and kindness is now flowing out of me but with nowhere to go now, no one to receive it. I am bleeding into the ground.

54

I am happy as if a little child watching the scenery pass, thinking my thoughts, thinking about Bartok and Schoenberg, thinking about P. I am more in a world of my own this time than last because of the horror I feel about what happened with P. I seem cut off from all emotions. I could just wander around Europe forever now; it is only money that stops me. I have lost even any feeling for home. I only want to return because I fret about the money I am spending to no purpose as it will not bring P back. Home for me should have been me with P, and now I have lost that I will find none other. Society attacks me because I am always writing instead of talking, the way they attacked Vincent for always painting, the way they attacked Orpheus for only thinking about his lost Eurydice. I am boring because I do not talk but despite that they all seem very fascinated by me. Not only do I not talk, I do not even seem to cough, sneeze or sniffle. My soft footsteps make no sound. Even mute people do not cast such a deep silence on a room as I do. It is like I bring a black hole into every room I enter, and it sucks up all the frivolity and laughter into it. I cast my net like a giant black spider's web on the room and they have to struggle to get out of it. When I am amongst people, on these trains, I can examine myself in society and my effect on society most productively. I am sleeping beauty and P was the Prince who might have woken me with a kiss. SLEEPING BEAUTY, is that my title?

55

Sarah Kane killed herself at 28. That is the amazing thing. Things have not got that bad for me yet. Vincent killed himself at 32. I seem to have put myself at the extreme edge. I seem to want to make things as difficult for myself as they can possibly be. Despite everything one person decided to reach their hand out in friendship to me and I spurned even that. I am a scientific writer. I write about the terribilita of autism; the terribilita of being dead behind these eyes; the terribilita of just writing and never talking. TERRIBILITA. My PRINCIPIA TERRIBILITA. Society punishes me because I do not talk. Because I do not give love; when there is so much love locked up inside me. I think there are few people in this world with such deep love inside them as I have. That is the terrible irony. Yet with apparently no way of transmitting it or communicating it. I am still searching for my hotel by the sea. It is symbol I suppose of my aversion to people, which always grows with every day of holiday that passes, and my yearning to be alone with nature. Better to keep moving and get to Gothenburg and Oslo and Bergen as quickly as possible. Then from there start my rush back to Paris, helter skelter!

56

The brown splinter of the Kaiser Wilhelm church gives a glimpse of how charming Berlin would be today if not for the bombing of the war. It would be as lovable as Vienna or Brussels. It is so sad that it was wiped out like that. That is how I feel about myself. It is a tragedy that I ended up this way; I could have been so charming. The near total destruction I suffered at birth wiped that out and left me quite charmless and functional. Cold and dead. The sad thing is I am still terribly pretty. Some of the great beauties of the age have been drawn towards me only to be repelled by my lack of response. I am eccentric. I am pleasingly batty. I am crazier than a coconut. This inures me to the enmity I have to face. I am on a pilgrimage to the Munch Museum in Oslo and Bergen. Along the way I will pass through the personally significant town of Gothenburg as that is where Gunilla Gerland was finally diagnosed as autistic. The worst thing is to feel that you have let someone down. I was perfectly happy in my secluded life, not bothered by the world against me, until P came along. That is what brought about my downfall. I let her down. Despite everything, I actually hate letting people down. So few people are nice to me that it really slaughters me if I then let them down. She caught me on my Achilles heel. I am so strong against all the attacks I must face but totally defenceless against friendship. I sat trying to look on the positive side and raise a smile but there was nothing there. I let myself down and her down. That is a feeling which is difficult to get over. I am not into people. I don't travel with the aim of meeting people. There has been nothing on this holiday to match the visit to Schloss Neuschwanstein. The grey-trousered girl in the Brussels modern art museum maybe. Her trousers so tight they were like a second skin, and from the way her buttocks bounced she quite obviously was wearing no knickers beneath them. I am so irresponsible. *A man like me is dead in places other men feel liberated.* Finding the rings in Am Hof market then having the Ottakring beer in the bar next to it, then having the lovely meal in Wegenstein's.

57

The funny thing about this holiday is I have discovered the joys of eating in restaurants. The Dorint meal and the steak I had on the ferry between Hamburg and København were lovely, too, with a beer or two to wash it down. There is a lesson in this. The first afternoon I spent in Vienna exploring the Gurtel looking for Tallulah was nowhere near as enjoyable as the second afternoon I spent buying my rings, drinking and eating a meal. The third afternoon I spent traipsing around three museums felt like a sham, as moving as seeing Archduke Ferdinand's car was, which was only redeemed by the lovely meal I had in the Dorint just before leaving. The Berlin visit did not go well. I felt so ill by the time I arrived there. The hotel had no beer. I spent my one afternoon there looking for Tallulah rather than going to the Holocaust Museum and The Oscar Wilde pub as I had wanted to do. The roll I had opposite the Zoo station just before getting my train almost redeemed everything again! The meal I had on the ferry from Puttland to Rødby was very pleasurable.

OSLO

I sat in a crowded compartment for the train journey up to Oslo. The young woman conductress seemed to take an instant dislike to me. At one point, as she came in checking the tickets of people who had got on at the last stop, I saw her and an old lady passenger glancing in my direction, "Melancholisch!" I heard the old woman laughing & the conductress was sniggering too. As we arrived in Oslo the conductress stood in her doorway saying goodbye to everybody, as I passed she stepped back out of sight into her room, and then reappeared to say goodbye to the people behind me. It is incredible the effect I have on people the whole world over.

I felt so fragile today. My face felt so tense and anxious. The rest of my body feels so fine, it is only one's face that betrays one. So nervous. I came back from the Munch Museum, had something to eat, came back to hotel for my coat but could not face going out again to the National Gallery so stayed in, and am writing this instead. I really feel disintegrated today. My good, strong moments are so few and far between, like when I arrived last night, or when I was walking around Gothenburg's main square (circle) getting hotel prices. Even then I am bleeding inside all the time. I do whatever makes me feel comfortable. I did not feel comfortable with the idea of going out again, so I did not. Slowly I can start to relax again and regain some equilibrium. I think I was a bit shaken by the Munch Museum, especially the film. When I arrived, it was just saying how Edvard's terminally ill 31-year-old mother took her young son out into the woods for a last walk,

31

and he was thinking "Mama, why are you walking so slowly?" I always find things like that terribly moving, I don't know why exactly. I'm not sure if it reminds me of — or mother, or rather of a third non-existent woman who I regard as my real mother. The fact my real mother and the mother I really love are not one and the same person is difficult for me and leads me to blending the two to create my Madonna-like mother figure. Always unpossessable because she never existed. Then there was all that talk about Munch's enemies trying to poison him, shouting outside his window "There he is! Now shoot him!" This was after he had rejected Tulla Larsen, feeling he had to choose between work and love, and that was when the war against him really started. That was what drove him to his breakdown. Also moving was his grief and guilt at the death of his father, with whom he had had a difficult relationship, wishing he could have explained to him why he was often so irascible and anxious, dead and cold. His close relationship with his Aunt Karen and sister Inger was also moving. At the end he no longer even wanted to see his friends or go to any social gatherings; he just wanted to be left alone with his pictures. I think the film and the exhibition stirred up many emotions for me, and I was already disintegrated before I left. During the film I was of course thinking about P, and how whenever I feel desire I try to fight it, and how ridiculous that is. I had such strong feelings for P, but I fought against them, until I had killed her feelings for me. A long-haired girl came in to the film and sat in the back row with me. I felt very threatened. Red jumper, black miniskirt, black stockings, long thick matted yellow-blonde hair, red face, looking more than anything like Gunilla Gerland. She was gorgeous. In my disintegrated state it was too much for me.

59

I felt exposed today. I think it is better for me if I do not try to go beyond my limits. If I only feel comfortable going down to drink in the hotel bar, then that is what I should do. I will find that an enjoyable and pleasurable experience because I stayed safe. I think this cold stark weather makes it worse. I really should come in summer next time. The blazing hot sun and the heat on one's skin makes one feel protected, like a hot bath. I choose winter so the night trains will be emptier but there are enough people on them even in October. I think I almost feel more comfortable in the beating heat of summer, and more steamy and turned on, than in the cold dampness and stark street lighting of winter. There was a very interesting picture in the Munch Museum of top-hatted men ogling dancing girls on stage who are sitting with legs apart for them, like a typical Berlin cabaret/brothel of the 1890s to Weimar period, and it was called

Tingel-Tangel! This could be my new name for Tallulah. Tension makes a tangle. I will not go to Bergen now. It is a bridge too far. I have made my point. I want to start pulling myself in again now. I have stretched myself far enough by coming to Malmo then Gothenburg then Oslo. Bergen would take me past my breaking point. I want to start letting my rubber band relax back into place now by going back to Gothenburg tomorrow. Maybe staying a night in Hotel Opera or maybe not. Then being in Malmo Saturday so I can try to see the Kaspar Hauser musical at the Musiktheater. The name Gothenburg still has a charge for me as it was where Gunilla Gerland finally received her diagnosis of autism, but I am not sure whether I will find what I am looking for there. I want to make somewhere the centre for my writing. But money is draining away, and maybe I should regretfully pass straight through Gothenburg to Malmo, so I get there Friday night and just trust that I will find a hotel myself. Still, for its scientific importance I would like to try to spend a night in Gothenburg.

60

It was funny seeing that woman who looked so much like Gunilla Gerland in the Museum today. It is important to treasure and savour the moments when one feels nervous as much as anything else. They are as valuable an experience as any. With a drink or a cigarette it is nice to feel those nerves fading away, if they do. Sometimes they don't. Sometimes the feeling of disintegration persists. Whatever did P see in me? I always ask myself this whenever any woman shows an interest in me. Like Munch, I do not believe it is possible for anyone to love me. Whatever P thought she saw in me I wish I could be it. I see nothing in myself. I felt desire for P, but I fought against it. Why on Earth did I let myself do that? It would have been easier to have P as my partner now than to still be alone. To still be alone was the difficult option. I am all prickly and spiky, like a hedgehog or a porcupine. I do not know how anyone can love me or be warm to me. I can't imagine it. It is the failure of my imagination that is responsible for the loneliness of my life. Solitude is a peaceful word, a relaxing word. But what goes with it is being exposed, and to feel exposed is tiring, and stressful, and devastating. Company is a threatening, panic-making word but only company brings comfort and protection, I suppose. I have never had company, so it can only be a supposition. The presence of anyone beside me has always had me looking for the door. Maybe with P it would have been the same but now I will never know.

61

I think it will be seen that P was my last chance of life. And that my refusal to respond to her will stand as my last bewildering enigma. Everywhere's empty if you're on your own. Everything's pointless if you're on your own. I could be at home with P now in our own place together. The phrase "moral support" cropped up in that Munch film as well. On the train that we both got every night, I always sat in the same seat and one night on the window frame by my seat I saw the words 'I need your moral support' written in pencil in a feminine hand. I was sure it was her who had written it. I wanted to grab the chance with her so much. I wonder if deep down she suspects that is the case, and realises it was only my fear, and the ingrained years of solitude that made me not respond to her on that night. It is the saddest mistake of my life. Perhaps she knows deep down that I do feel love for her and do feel desire for her and do have strong feelings for her. For some reason, I fought against all of them until I killed her feelings for me. I am such a good and kind person, but I am mocked and abused and hounded everywhere I go. Edvard Munch knew this, Ernest Dowson knew this, Oscar Wilde knew this, Vincent Van Gogh knew this. We are too sensitive. I could not cope with beautiful P's assault on my masculinity. I cannot cope with femininity. Therefore, in most cases, I am rather revolted by it, and so they become revolted by me. It is very rare that there is prolonged mutual attraction like between P and me. I have turned her feelings to revulsion as well now. In the end we were just ships that passed in the night.

62

This is my PRINCIPIA TERRIBILITA. Filled with scientific measurements of the horror of my life. My life has moved onto a new more terrible level than before now. It always scarcely seems possible that my life can get any worse, but it has a habit of doing so. I travel around just to be held in suspension on the trains. I have had no normal relationships in my life. The fuel line to that part of my brain was ruptured at birth by my mother's madness. I have been dysfunctional ever since; to all intents and purposes autistic. Socially backward. A psychosocial dwarf. P.S.D. I am glad I managed to get to the Munch Museum today. That was moving. The onset of one of my debilitating nervous attacks unfortunately made it impossible for me to go on to the National Gallery, or to even contemplate the journey to Bergen. I feel so exposed when I walk down a street, like I have been stripped bare of all my skin; but Alfred Hitchcock felt like that, Tennessee Williams felt like that, many people do. You must not get down on yourself because of that. The easiest thing is to feel bad about feeling bad. To think that because you feel completely exposed and defenceless you must be a pathetic person. It just means that you are more sensitive than other people, and this is a great quality to possess. Hypersensitivity opens you up to enormous pain and distress, but also great insight and understanding. You must just weather the terrible nervous storms, even though like on Jupiter they are constant, and keep plugging away doing whatever it is you want to do, making your contribution to the world which will stand as your epitaph and monument long after you are gone. I just live to create that body of work that will stand for me after I am gone. It is the only thing that keeps me going. The chances to have something else to live for, like P, are behind me now. I will never forget the yellow-haired girl in red jumper and black miniskirt in the Munch Museum who looked so much like Gunilla Gerland. The precious memories will live with me. They are the jewels on the jungle path in *The Night of the Iguana*.

63

I am starting my homeward journey now. It is now Thursday night. I will be home by Tuesday night. In between I will spend nights in Gothenburg and Malmo, and travel through København and Hamburg to get to Paris. Touching moments of this doom-laden holiday? The grey-trousered girl in the Brussels Museum of Modern Art without knickers, which contained Alfred Stevens's Salome and Geef's Génie du Mal. I could wander around Europe forever. I feel no compunction to return home whatsoever. It is only my money which is bleeding into the ground that scares me. I would like to wander forever around Europe like a ghost, inevitably giving in to Tingle-Tangle in the end. If I was a millionaire that is what I would do. I do not say I would enjoy it, but it would be less horrible than returning home. All I feel is this loneliness, this emptiness, this pointlessness. The Am Hof market in Vienna where I bought my rings, followed by the Ottakring bar and Wegenstein's. The car of Archduke Ferdinand. The meal I had in the Hotel Dorint restaurant before catching the train to Berlin. In Berlin, the gorgeous belegte roll I had before catching the train to Hamburg, Copenhagen and Malmo. The gorgeous black & white pork & beef steak meal I had on the ferry. The yellow-blonde girl in red jumper and black miniskirt who looked like Gunilla Gerland in the Oslo Munch Museum, and the moving Edvard Munch film. I want just one memory from each city I visit, that is enough for me. Time to consult the timetables.

64

Suddenly I looked across and saw with horror the wild grey hair of the previously elegant middle-aged woman next to me, grown prematurely old from proximity to me. The hotel staff kept letting themselves into my room at night to relieve themselves in my lavatory. I was too shocked to do or say anything, so they all came in one after the other for hours on end, not even bothering to turn the bathroom light off, just shooting me a leering glance as I cowered under the covers as they went in and out, some even did poos. The automatic doors of the hotel entrance were no longer opening for me; my presence had become so weak and insubstantial. I was a dead man and a ghost. When I was forced to speak my voice sounded so far away even to my own ears; people retorted sharply "What's that? Speak up! I cannot hear you!" The two receptionist girls were openly laughing in my face as they checked me out, with absolutely open contempt, perhaps because of the porn films on my bill I wondered? But no, I don't think it was just because of that.

<h1 style="text-align:center">65</h1>

In me you see what happens when a baby does not receive love or affection when he is born. He does not know how to receive love from then on, throughout his entire life. Feeling threatened by it whenever it comes close, because it is something unknown, he inadvertently destroys it to keep himself safe. I am in depression. I never received any love from my mother. Because of that I do not know how to give love or how to receive love. Because of that I am viciously abused and attacked wherever I go, punished for something which is in itself already a punishment. But I am glad I am on the right side. I am glad it is them doing it, not me. I am glad I have stayed pure and beautiful. The Spanish Girl Making Cigarettes by William Donat was very affecting in the National Gallery. Yes, I got there in the end; forced myself to go there on my last morning in Oslo before rushing back to catch my train. In the street outside the museum I was passed by two teenage girls, who started laughing when they saw me and said—in English—loud enough for me to catch, "Oh no! He's still here!" The wall with Self-Portrait, Madonna, The Scream, Ashes and Puberty on it. Portrait of Sister Inger. Cabaret by Per Krohg. The Sohlenberg pictures. The Ruins with Statue of Marcus Aurelius in the Roman exhibition, and The Arch of Titus in the Forum Romana. That idea of a wilderness with classical ruins dotted amongst it is always moving to me. It always reminds me of my dream of a world returned to nature and forests, when I am the last man left. Like the Grand Tourists of the 18th century. The Romantic Imagination. Frankenstein. I do not know how to be with someone. I am beautiful, and kind, and intelligent, but I do not know how to be with someone. I would not have known how to be with P. I am not made for love.

COLLECTED WORKS

COLLECTED WORKS

LOTTA

2002

ERNST GRAF

COLLECTED WORKS

CHAPTER 1
THIS IS SHAPING UP TO BE A REAL AUTISTIC HOLIDAY ALREADY

THIS IS SHAPING UP TO BE A REAL AUTISTIC HOLIDAY ALREADY. Getting drunk in the bar of the Hotel Ibis. I have got the most beautiful room I have ever stayed in. 32 channels on the TV. Chauncey Gardiner and Thomas Newton would have been in their element. Pink's Morphine is No.1. I just watched it on Top of the Pops. It is such a shame to check out after just one night. But I must get on the Munich train Saturday night. I feel like Michael Palin in *Around the World in 80 Days*. The time pressure I am under is that I cannot afford many nights in these lovely hotels, and their bars. What is the point of this journey? I am not travelling with a broken heart for the first time ever. It is to see as many treasures as I can. It is to stir up as much pond life as I possibly can. I am starting to feel the Autistic glory and getting over my conventional nerves. "It is almost as if you're being held in suspended animation & someone is about to wave a magic wand & restore your vitality. But that person is you. Thanks to Mercury's reflective influence, you can awaken from a trance and see what's really missing in your life."

2

So I saw the girls by the Gare du Nord. I saw some good pictures in the Museum of Modern Art: Dali's The Temptation of St Anthony being the best of them. There was also a Bacon, which is always a fantastic visceral shock and pleasure, and it was a Pope at that, a gorgeous maroon and pink one. It is the one picture in the gallery you really can't tear yourself away from. There were so many other great pictures I do not remember from last time. One of the ones I do remember from last time, Alfred Stevens's Salome, had gone, replaced by an Ophelia, but the Trésors de Satan next to it was still there, as was Geef's mesmeric Génie du Mal just around the corner. The Delvaux pictures were very good. My hotel room in the Ibis is so beautiful, the best I've ever seen. I wish I could stay there forever. The window was set in a low archway. The whole room felt arched. After checking in I went out for a stroll but felt so uncomfortable. I came back to the hotel bar for two Stellas and went out again and felt much better. I got back to my room after 0030 and watched TV until about 2. Before going to bed I opened the curtains to see it was thick mist outside. Arriving at the hotel I put the TV on to see Top of the Pops, and Pink at No.1. When I woke up in the morning I was switching continually between MCM, MTV and VH1. So many great videos that we never get to see on mainstream TV in England. The Ketchup Song the best of them; Mirwais's Rolling Stones cover, Pink, Avril Lavigne. It is my habit to spend mornings in the hotels watching MTV until 12 midday, then going out to explore. Already this night train to Munich seems more busy than usual. I am travelling in September instead of October. The Oktoberfest is still going. I still wonder whether to go back to Sweden and Norway. I will perhaps head for Prague and Budapest and Venice this time instead. "Run, just as fast as I can, to the middle of nowhere."

3

I haven't wanted a relationship with anyone I've met on this holiday. I just want to get on my own. I am not natural. I am autistic. All I think about is my next beer and w—ing. I am constantly nervous, edgy, tense, strings stretched taut. That is why Chess Goddess eventually fled from me in horror. A woman wants a man who is confident. That is why the music of Schoenberg, Berg and Webern is so incredibly vital to me. It is the music of my brainwaves. The violin playing of Jascha Heifetz, Itzhak Perlman, Jelly D'Aranyi, Jennifer Pike. Where do I really want to go on this holiday? Vienna. Munich Pinakothek and Lenbachhaus. Venice. Berlin Oscar Wilde Pub and Holocaust Museum.

4

I have pronounced the Euro a great success. It has made my life easier anyway. The train is very busy. I will travel in late October again next year. I prefer the cold weather to people. I don't know what inspired me to leave earlier this time. Put on the classical music. Shut everything out. Open the door to my inner realms. I look at the map and think I could go to Köln, and I could go to Frankfurt, and I could go to Weimar, but then I think well what would I do when I got there? The fact that I am not already going to those places suggests there is not enough reason for me to go there. They are in the middle places, whereas Brussels and Vienna and Berlin are terminal places. What I really like to do is find a nice hotel in a big city and lose myself there and do my writing there. The Ibis in Brussels is fine, the Dorint in Vienna. I need to find such a place in Berlin. The other place I really want to go on this expedition is Venice. So go there—and don't feel guilty or inadequate because I'm not doing Köln or Frankfurt or Trier or Weimar! I obviously don't want to go to those places enough or I would have been there. I want to go there, yes, but they don't shine on my horizon like Venice does now. I don't want to stretch myself too thin, doing things that I feel I have to do; as if somehow I will feel ashamed if I don't go out of my hotel enough when I am in Berlin. What is important to me is to have a hotel room to come back to, with a shower, a lavatory, a bed and a television. I need to lead a certain hermetic, sealed existence even on holiday. So—let us concentrate on Ibis Brussels, Vienna, and this time Venice, maybe coming back to Vienna to get to Berlin, and then home via Paris. That, after all, is quite a lot! So, I am not doing all the small places in between. I would have no resources left, no money left, no psychic defences left. Travelling alone can be psychologically very tiring. You need to shut yourself away for spells at a time to recover your equilibrium, let your well fill up again. Too much sightseeing, traipsing around museums, town centres, is not good for me. I am autistic. Like Chauncey Gardiner and Thomas Newton, the most important thing to me is to have a TV in my hotel room with at least 50 channels—MTV especially. If I've got that, my own bed, my own shower and my own lavatory, I am happy. After my few hours stopover in Munich I will spend a few days in Vienna before making my way to Venice. "Ah, Venice." Then I will head up to Berlin, from where I can make my way back to Paris. The Ibis in Brussels was beautiful: I could have stayed there forever. I could have used Brussels as a base to go on daytrips to Antwerp & Bruges. The incredible iron girders of Köln Station. Now for sure I will be joined by company. I just need to find a restaurant in Brussels I like. I have found several bars: the Pullman in the Gare du Midi, the Ibis bar, the Casa Manuel in the Grand Place. I was sorry to leave my Ibis hotel room. I wish I was still there now. There are so many pictures in the Musée d'Art Moderne I would like to go back to see again & again. My rail pass lasts for a month: I could pop back to Brussels on my few days off from work. I think I would really like to put the time & effort into getting to know Brussels really well. And putting the effort into getting to know Vienna really well. Better to make an effort getting to know a couple of places really well than stretching myself too thin and rushing about from town to town, feeling uncomfortable and new everywhere I go. You can never enjoy a place until you get to know it and feel at home there. Rushing around from place to place I will never get to know anywhere.

5

Köln and Frankfurt both look such spectacularly impressive cities, but I would need time to do them justice. They are worth more than a one-night stand. And by doing them justice I mean staying for three or four days, getting to feel at home in them. My privacy ended at Frankfurt Airport, as it always does. I hope I can find a hotel room in Munich—at 630AM on Sunday morning. I would give my kingdom for a bed. And a TV with MTV Europe on it. It is important to stay places for a few days at a time. Constant travelling is psychologically exhausting, not to say destructive. Having to face up to one new city after another whittles away at one. To be able to sleep in the same bed three nights at a time. People probably wonder why I come away on holiday on my own. What is the point? I ask myself the same question, a thousand times a day. It is such hard work. Where is the reward? It is walking into my Ibis hotel room and being hit by such a beautiful sight. Is this someone who doesn't talk inevitably the same as someone nasty? This is the big moral question I am posing. I don't think it is a big moral question, but apparently other people do. I am blissfully happy, I will help anyone, yet I am very disliked because I do not talk.

6

So, what did I gain out of München? The train to Wien is so busy I cannot believe it. I saw Die Sünde and Salome again. I had a lovely meal in the Rechthaler Hof, which I will return to again & again. 155 Furs for a F. So many Oktoberfest people on the train. I will never travel during Oktoberfest again. I have found a bar in München as well.

WIEN

I've rediscovered the desire to explore Wien again. Having satisfied the erotic itch—the *Eyes Wide Shut/La Ronde* impulse—I am once more turned on by the culture. The good thing about Brussels was discovering a Brussels base for myself in the Ibis, with its incredibly beautiful room and very nice bar.

8

"I have been staying in some very nice hotels. My room in the Brussels Ibis was the most beautiful I have ever stayed in, and the bar is very nice too. I now look at the Night Managers in a new light in every hotel I stay in, to see if they come up to my and —'s high standards, and quite frankly they have been found wanting. And it goes without saying that they are not a patch on —. The barstaff, quite honestly, have not been fit to piss in —'s ice bucket. And the receptionists, well! They've been pretty good actually. I am missing — very much. I know — likes lists of beers. In Brussels I drink lots of Stella and Maes. In Munich Augustiner, and I found a nice little restaurant. In Wien, Zipfer and Gösser, and re-found my favourite restaurant from last time. I have already seen the Holy Roman Emperor's crown that Charlemagne used to wear, Beethoven's grave, and the car Archduke Ferdinand was shot in that started the First World War. Dead Famous People. I did *The Third Man* tour last time I came here but I want to go to the Ferris Wheel in the Prater, and also because it is where Ludwig Wittgenstein used to creep at night in search of boys".

CHAPTER 2
VENICE

Dirk Bogarde is one of my great film idols. It was Vienna where he made *The Night Porter*, with Charlotte Rampling, which is the reason I wanted to work in hotels, and Venice is where he made *Death in Venice*. Every corner I turn I think I'm going to see the little red mac gargoyle with the meat cleaver from *Don't Look Now*. Every time I come out of the hotel I say to myself "Ah, Venice", like Indiana Jones in the *Last Crusade*. I watch too many films. I should get out more. Oh, but the best thing about having a holiday is I get to watch MTV Europe all the time. Last year I became hooked on Alcazar's Crying at the Discotheque, and now it is Las Ketchup with the Ketchup Song. I can't afford a gondola ride. They are more expensive than C— Cars.

10

St Mark's. When I look at Lotta I can't think straight. Sophia was just like a friend, so I could talk to her easier.

11

I do not want to try to get involved with anyone in the hotel, because it just tears me apart, and rips me up. What is life worth without people, though? There is no point carrying a camera with me on holiday and taking photos; all photos are worthless without people in them. The pictures of Lotta & Sophia together at Schönbrunn and in their room are proof of that. The sounds of a group of people sitting around a restaurant table below my Venice hotel window, talking & roaring with laughter, reminds me of being with Lotta & Sophia & Edi in the Chinese restaurant, and how lovely that was, and how much I have missed out on in life by not doing this before, by not <u>being able</u> to do this. They were lovely to me to put up with me and make me feel at ease, but I always feel I have to apologise for my presence anywhere. Drinking alone in the Brussels Ibis bar, sitting alone in my beautiful Brussels Ibis room, sitting alone in the München restaurant, eating alone in the Wien Wegenstein's: what a cold air blows through me, and how ridiculous and worthless it is all made to feel by my brief bit of contact and illusion of conviviality with Lotta & Sophia. I want to be with

46

them all the time now, but it would just be to suck up some of their life, to sponge off their warm blood & happiness & easy conviviality: I could bring nothing of my own to the table. They would get nothing out of it, as they scarcely did that night. I am just a sad, desperately cursed vampire, like Klaus Kinski in the Venice vampire film. Like the trapped self-loathing of Brad Pitt in *Interview With A Vampire*. "I haven't been human for 200 years". How that line haunts me, and rings so true to me. I can honestly say the same thing and mean it with full sincerity. I want to be with them all the time, and I want to have my own set of all those photographs they showed me, for the life in them, to suck it up for myself: not because I am cruel & evil but because I desperately need an injection of their warm blood to keep me alive; I am Autistic; white, & parched & dessicated. Phèdre, longing to seduce long after seduction has lost all its pleasure. I am withering away for lack of just this bit of life. Being with them & then being forced to come away from them has cruelly brought that home to me more than ever. That is why I do not even try to get close to another person; it is so devastating when it does not go well—as it cannot, because of the way I am, because of what I am: A Vampire; Autistic—and then when I have to come away on my own again. What is the point of seeing Lotta again? We would both sit there not talking again. And yet I love her, I adore her. All I can do is gaze on her with silent adoration, and that makes a girl very cross & disgusted. All I can do is travel alone & be alone. So, the cold air continues. I do not try to get close to someone. Isn't that better than the repeated embarrassing humiliation of trying & failing? To be brought face to face with the screaming realisation that I am incapable? I am killing myself with self-loathing again. Like after Chess Goddess. Now Lotta & Sophia.

12

When I stepped off the boat to San Marco and set foot on land, coming from one of the stalls the first sound I heard was the Ketchup Song. That has been the sound of this holiday. I said that to Lotta & Sophia and Sophia said that it was the same for them. This emptiness at the heart of me, which people don't at first suspect but then soon discover, to their alarm. I told them last year it had been the Swedish band Alcazar with Crying at the Discotheque, and they were horrified, Alcazar made them ashamed to be Swedish. I have decided I like to keep myself to myself and go to the cold icy air of the mountains like Nietzsche: because the humiliation of trying & failing to connect with girls like Lotta & Sophia is so painful. So, stop trying. I went to the top of the Campanile bell tower of St Mark's—one of the two things I came to Venice to do. The view to the north was good, the view to the west gave me my first sight of La Fenice (the other thing I came to

Venice to do), grey stone and grey plastic sheeting, but the view to the south gave me one of those rare moments of epiphany that are what I travel for. Looking out over the bay (as I think of it; the canal in actual fact), sliced this way & that by boats of every size and description, St Giorgio, the island of La Giudecca, further to the left the landing stages where I had set foot, and beneath me the Place de San Marco itself, the pigeons, the Loggia, the people, the two columns. The sky & sea just seemed to merge into each other. There was no discernible horizon. The morning had started grey but had turned to a haze that the sun was trying to burn through. By the time I left the tower (about 45 minutes later!) it had done so. It was here, gazing over the bay to the island of St.Giorgio, that I was able for the first time to think about the previous night I had spent with Lotta & Sophia, and the agony of not being able to be with Lotta the way I wanted to be, and how I wished I could get talking to Sophia when I went back & tell her how I felt about Lotta, how whenever I look at Lotta I cannot think straight, how I can never think of what to say to her and consequently why I talk to Sophia more than to Lotta, because Sophia is just like a friend to me. I thought about the photos they had showed me and how I wished I could take a set home with me. I kept thinking the same thing over & over as I gazed out towards St.Giorgio. It was an incredibly powerful, painful, overwhelming moment of epiphany, the like of which I haven't had since the Sydney Opera House and Sydney Harbour Bridge in the pouring rain from the grass bank below the old Government House two years before. I felt so much love flooding my heart for Sophia & Lotta (particularly, of course, Lotta) at that moment I couldn't tear myself away from that spot. I took root by that window, transfixed by the view and the emotions now coursing through me, as I kept trying to absorb the moment, the sights, soak it all up like a sponge, to keep reconjuring the moment of orgasmic epiphany. This is a place I will return to. I am such a disappointment to people. I was such a disappointment to Chess Goddess, and I was such a disappointment to Lotta, and the pain of that was at this moment overwhelming. I am never on the same wavelength as the people I love and that is upsetting. The one moment I did feel on the same wavelength was when me & Sophia were sharing our mutual love for Ralph Fiennes & *The English Patient* with each other. I heard Lotta turn to Edi and say "what shall we talk about?" as me & Sophia were eulogising together, but I did not want to lose the moment of connection so stayed locked together with Sophia for those one or two precious minutes. Every time I looked at Lotta was painful because I knew I could not experience such a bonding moment with her. A couple of times I had to briefly relinquish my position at the south window, and move to the east window, to experience almost as great a moment of epiphany to find myself looking down at the five magnificent domes of the Basilica San Marco. I am ashamed to say it just instantly and powerfully reminded me of the magnificent domes of the Swedish girls, perhaps the four most beautiful breasts I have ever seen in my life. When Lotta and I were walking around the Butterfly House together several times we bumped into each other and I felt her breasts really prominently poking into me. Sophia's are the equal of them. These profane things I confess I thought as I gazed again and again at the magnificent domes of the Basilica St Marco, this sacred place. I returned repeatedly to my former position, until 12 o'clock when the bell just behind me, & barely four inches above my head height, started tolling. An incredible moment. If I had walked under it at that moment & stood on tiptoe I would have been hit and killed by the great clapper, putting a suitably ludicrous end to my ludicrous holiday & ludicrous life. Eventually I forced myself to go back down to the Square, and went inside the Basilica, to see the domes from the inside. The side-chapel on the left was reserved for real worshippers/mourners/supplicants/prayers/whatever, and it was incredibly moving to see people kneeling there, weeping or with faces full of distress & worry or heads bowed & hands together in prayer. Going from one tourist spot to another it was quite a jolt to be brought face to face with people with real reason to be there. I set out to find my way to the Fenice then & stopped off in the Hotel Cavaletto for the two most expensive bottles of lager I have ever had in my life, but I got to sit on the balcony watching the gondoliers in the Bacino Orseolo and stayed there for almost an hour, in the blazing sunshine. Eventually I tore myself away from this as well & staggered from the shock of the bill once more in the hopeful direction of the Fenice. I found it eventually and leaned on the parapet looking at the boats of the contractors as they loaded the stuff into the building. It was moving to finally be so close to La Fenice, & to see it being rebuilt with my own eyes. It must be very hollow inside because a tractor kept pulling up to the boat to pick up another load of concrete or earth or something then speeding back in reverse into the interior again. My two reasons for coming to Venice now satisfied I made my complicated way back to the boat (via the Bridge of Sighs). I sat at the front of the boat out in the open for the trip back in the sunshine, evoking memories of the Sydney Harbour boat trip and, more powerfully in the circumstances, of my hydrofoil ride from Malmo harbour.

13

On the way back from the Chinese restaurant to Westbahnhof the previous night I had been walking with Sophia while Edi was ahead of us with her arm around Lotta's waist, & Sophia said to me "I'm guessing about 26" and nonplussed at first, I then realised she was talking about my age. She guessed again, 29, and finally got it right, 32. "Oh, so you're decomposing then!" she joked. "You're rotting away!" But she was of course more right than she knew. In Westbahnhof I kissed Lotta goodbye on her cheek and made to kiss her other cheek as well, but she put her arm around my neck and hugged me instead. I kissed Edi on both cheeks and the same with Sophia. She told me to have a good time in Venice and I said I would try. I then with great difficulty got my bag from the out of order lockers and realised my train was leaving in 18 minutes from Sudbahnhof not West. The taxi just about got me there in time. I shared the compartment with two Pakistani dentists, in Wien for their annual world conference and just going on a daytrip to Venice, and a 24-year-old Czech girl who worked for a Formula 3000 racing team, and thanks to the two Pakistanis the conversation flowed very easily and the four of us stayed up until about 230 in the morning, drinking beer & talking. In the morning, though, it's a bit like after a one-night stand, you just mumble "morning" to each other and then disappear out the door without saying goodbye. I was a bit sad Katya never said goodbye to me, but the Pakistanis I kept bumping into repeatedly over the next one & a half hours! At the Tourist Information queue, an hour later at the boat queue, then on the boat landing platform itself. They were like a Pakistani Laurel & Hardy, comically miserable faces because no one spoke English. The fatter one kept asking me every time we re-met each other if I knew if there were any day tours of Venice & I had to keep explaining I had never been to Venice before & didn't know, which didn't stop him asking me each subsequent time he saw me. The boat came & I & everyone else jumped on & I thought they had, too, but as it pulled away, I just saw the two solitary Pakistanis standing alone on the platform as we sailed off. Standing at the top of the belltower looking down I was convinced I would see them again below me or tapping me on the shoulder behind me asking me if I knew if there were any day tours of Venice, but sadly I never did. Maybe when I get back to Vienna. Unfortunately, they made me say hello to their video camera while on the train. Someone also took my picture in the belltower and then a man took my picture while I was on the balcony of the Hotel Cavaletto with my beer. People are so fascinated by me and fascinated in particular by how very boring I apparently am, which is quite a contradiction in terms.

14

I could say so much about Lotta & Sophia, which really puts the rest of my holiday into its proper perspective of sad pointlessness. My loneliness in Brussels, Munich, & Vienna the first two days, my loneliness here in Venice.

He shoots. He misses. Some players are just frightened to score. How much longer is it worth continuing this expensive amble around Europe? I'll be back in Vienna 930PM Friday night, go to the Am Hof & the Prater on Saturday, stay in my room all Sunday. Leave—leave Lotta & Sophia—Monday. Where for? Budapest. Vörösmarty Square? Berlin. Holocaust Memorial & Oscar Wilde Pub? Weimar. Goethe's house & Nietzsche? It will not be any less depressing staying at home than staying away, so I might as well plunge on a while longer. Nice. Montpellier. Paris. This has been my *Death in Venice*. The lonely, sad repressed man coming by himself to Venice, obsessed with desire for the young Swedish girl Lotta he met in his hotel. Tortured & tormented self-loathing in this diseased, fever town. My enjoyment on this holiday only started when I met Lotta on Monday afternoon. I think of Vienna as being home now, as that is where she is.

15

I am sunk in misery because of the lacerations of travel, although I keep bobbing back up to the surface. My face feels tense & nervous. In the snack bar my hand was shaking so much when I lifted the coke to my lips I nearly spilt it. I had something like the nervous attack I had in the Munch Museum in Oslo. I was attacked as I was leaving the hotel, in the station café queue, as I was re-entering the station after I had been sitting outside on the steps for half an hour, on the platform before boarding the Carlo Goldoni. In conjunction with the attacks the previous night which started to multiply and come thick & fast after I had left St.Mark's & Fenice & turned to make the journey back. The journey back is always hardest, as Napoleon found out. All my holidays are rather like Napoleon's trip to Moscow. I travel with such hope & optimism & then get there & sit there & think "what was the point?"; then I have to turn and make a sprint for home with my enemies now falling upon me from all sides. But that is OK—I am different. That is the way my life is lived. It after all does not kill me, and my hope & my optimism before long soon returns again. It leaves not a mark on me, so there is nothing to complain about, and I am happy & cheerful & with love in my heart for everybody once more. That is the thing: there is such love in my heart for everybody—the same as Kaspar Hauser, & Oscar Wilde, & F.G.Lorca, & Van Gogh, & Jesus Christ, & all the other Holy Fools—yet I am reviled & attacked everywhere I go. This of course says more about them than it does about me. Autistic people are not understood, and not liked. Like the two most famous cinematic autistic characters, Chauncey Gardiner in *Being There* and Thomas Newton in *The Man Who Fell to Earth*, I could happily sit in my hotel room watching my 50-channel TV all day & night

51

long, never having to go outside & meet people. I give out no warmth, so that makes people shiver & dislike me.

16

A black-haired Italian woman, around about 30, followed me into the snack bar, and while I was sitting eating I looked up after about ten minutes to find she was looking at me. I looked away out of politeness, as one does, in case it was just an accidental meeting of eyes, then looked back again to check if there was anything more in it, to find she was still watching me. I did not look back again. I had enough to cope with just holding my cup steady. I finished and went to the station. I first went to find the lockers, and then thought it was no longer worth it, I would carry my bag onto the boat for my final farewell trip to San Marco & back. I went back outside and queued for the boat ticket, before deciding I did not have time for that either and went back inside the station. I joined the queue in the buffet bar to pay for a beer and turned to see the same Italian woman walking towards me meeting my gaze directly and joining the queue directly behind me. I paid for my beer, collected it, drank it, went & sat outside on the steps for half an hour, came back in & got on my train. I did not see her again.

17

Beautiful black-wavy-haired train conductress just came in to punch my ticket. We said "Grazie" to each other and she left, closing the door behind her.

18

I get so nervous around people, not just girls although that is what saddens me most, of course, that getting close to them could never be possible for me. Has never been possible and will never be possible. It would involve someone making an incredible sacrifice & not wanting a lot of things that an affair is supposed to provide as a matter of course. I see the couples passing me on the steps of Santa Lucia station hand in hand and I think that could never be me. I cannot imagine how their minds work, are wired, what their minds look like, as they cannot imagine mine. We are a different species. Lotta found that out on Wednesday night. She is just the latest.

19

Forty-five minutes into my seven-hour forty-five-minute journey back to Wien. I should perhaps have used Venice as my springboard to go on to Pisa & Roma. Instead I will spend Saturday doing a couple more things in Vienna, and then go on a daytrip to Budapest's Vörösmarty Square on

Sunday. I can go out with a girl, a Chess Goddess, a Lotta, as they make it quite clear they are attracted to me and would rather like me to ask, but I do not ever get any closer to her. I do not know how getting close is done. I am hardly with her even when I am going to the same places at the same time as her. There is an abyss between us, a black yawning chasm, which bewilders & disappoints & annoys them. There is this great rift valley running through the story of my life like the gorge in *Under the Volcano* & I will end up being thrown into it or throwing myself into it. I live on the edge of the abyss. People like Lotta cannot imagine the place where I live. It is the entrance to hell.

20

Venice was warm, the sun was just starting to burn through the haze again; with every mile back to Wien I go, however, it gets colder & greyer. I should maybe go to Weimar, but I can't face returning to Germany. Already I wish I was staying in Italy. I want to turn around and go back to Rome & Pisa. Perhaps I will, on Monday. I will leave Wien once more to return to Italy! Crazy the way I live my life, like a lost person. The lost boy. I am one of the Lost Boys like Peter Pan, seeking eternally for a Young Mother. Lotta is just my latest ideal young mother figure I have put on my pedestal. It sounds pathetic & sentimental to talk about Peter Pan, & Wendy, & the Lost Boys, Never-Never-Land, the boy who never grew up because he lost his mother, but it is such a cuttingly accurate depiction of Autism. What it is like for us. Again, I must stop & qualify my use of the word Autism, when some would say Autism is something different. Whatever you call it—autism, psychosocial dwarfism, maternal deprivation, emotional deprivation, Kaspar Hauser Syndrome—I believe it is a form of Autism, and Autism is the best catch-all word to describe those of us separated from their mother at birth, who are never taught how to give or receive love, how to talk, converse, & so grow up unable to form close relationships for the rest of their lives. When I use the word Autism that is what I mean by it, anyway (Orphanism?). I have been invited to step down through the window and join the warm bosom of family life so many times, but I am always...scared? Incompetent? Incapable? It never happens anyway. I did step through Chess Goddess's window down into her bedroom, almost, and then when she found out for herself how incapable I was of living that kind of life, a Lost Boy is all I can be, she sent me packing out the window again. Defenestration. But after spending some time trying to be a real boy I lose my power to fly for a while and after being thrown out the window I just hit the ground, before gradually the power to hover in the air returns to me.

21

Udine. It is getting so cold as we head back north. I have to pull my jumper out of my bag. I may need to put the coat on as well. *Peter Pan* is childish & therefore hard to actually read, but it is such a sacred text of Autism. Alongside *Under the Volcano* by Malcolm Lowry, *Being There* by Jerzy Kosiński, *Once Upon a Time in America* by Sergio Leone, *The Man Who Fell to Earth* by Nicolas Roeg, & others. The moment David Bowie is in the bathroom peeling off his skin & removing his lenses to reveal his alien eyes and Candy Clark walks in and catches him and runs screaming from the room is a particularly primal, seminal one in the sacred Autistic literature. It is the scene I lived through with Lotta on Wednesday. The scene I lived through with Chess Goddess back in the summer. All Autistic people know this moment, when the person they love and have let get close to them discover what they are really like. "You're really lovely, underneath it all." The No Doubt song & video which is one of the Proustian paving stones of this holiday. I may be really lovely underneath it all, but I am also really an alien, a man who fell to Earth, underneath it all. That is the hard moment anyone who wants to get close to us has to go through. That is why we avoid letting anyone get close to us because we dread this inevitable scene arriving again. It is too painful. We so much want to let our guard down, our mask slip, peel our skin off & let the person we love so much, & want so much to be our perfect Young Mother, see us as we really are; but when it happens they just run screaming from the room, and you think I am never bothering to try again; I am never even trying to get close to someone & let them get close to me again; because I do not want to live through this scene again. So, you go back to having nothing to do with other people whatsoever. You give up work, become a hermit again. Then I can never afford to travel, which I tell myself is the best thing, even though, as I say, all my holidays turn into Napoleon.

22

I have just come out of a series of tunnels after Udine to find a huge mountain on either side of me just growing up out of the flat fields. What a fantastic sight. And the streams running down from them are so blue amid the stony scree I feel I could drink from them. Ha-ha. Lotta & Sophia were so funny Wednesday night laughing about how Viennese have mineral water with everything: tea, beer, coke, everything has to have mineral water mixed with it. This landscape reminds me of the Sweden to Norway journey, and even more of the mountains around Oberammergau when I was going to Neuschwanstein & Linderhof. They are, after all I suppose, the same mountains, just the other side. This is the cold Nietzschean icy air of the mountains I talked so much about. I do not want to return to the built-up areas & flatlands of northern Germany anymore now.

23

After Chess Goddess left I never wanted to return to South Kensington. After Lotta & Sophia leave I will not really want to return to Vienna. It will always seem so empty without them; there will always be such a hole there (I, after all, feel the hole everywhere, I carry it around with me, but there it would be biggest & most black & massive). But it would be an Epiphanic moment to return to the Schmetterling House, I suppose. It was about the only time I made Lotta laugh, when I said that was why they called it the Butterfly House, because there was only one butterfly, & that if there had been more it would have been called the Butterflies House. I can only travel alone, I can only walk around a city alone. I do not know how to <u>be</u> with another person. I just want to be holding her, kissing her, telling her how much I love her: I cannot do polite small talk or friendly conversation. I have little to say apart from what is in my heart & that is not something that is ever easy to find the right moment for, as one cannot just plunge into that sort of talk right from the start, even though it is all I am feeling right from the start.

24

Everything is only exciting when you see it the first time. It was probably a mistake to go back to see Stuck's Die Sünde and Salome in Munich. I should have preserved them as a perfect memory. The same with the Génie du Mal & Death of Marat & Trésors de Satan in Brussels, though there were the new delights of the Francis Bacon Pope & La Tentation d'Antoine by Dali. The Belvedere was a disappointment because Richard Gerstl's Laughing Self-Portrait was not on show as half of one floor was shut off. There are not many views or sights that never pall. I think the Campanile of St Mark's will be one that remains special, though, because it is where my love & despair for Lotta & Sophia hit me with full force & really flooded my system, as I gazed out over the bay & the square in the haze just as the sun was burning through, & the boats were criss-crossing the shimmering glistening water to & fro so it seemed impossible that there were not collisions. When I go back there I will be reminded so powerfully of Lotta & Sophia. For me Place San Marco is now the Place of Lotta & Sophia, & it is the Basilica of Lotta & Sophia that I look down on. Getting so close to the Fenice was also a powerful moment for me. Perhaps I should not repeat these experiences either, though! So they remain perfect unspoiled memories.

25

We are now two & a half hours into my seven & three-quarter hour journey back to Wien. We have crossed the Italian-Austrian border at Tarvisio Boscoverde. We have left the green uniforms of the Italian railway employees behind. The Oberammergau scenery continues. When I go out socialising with people I just cannot keep up with them. I do not know how to kill myself laughing the way they do. I do not know how to have fun.

26

Art excites in us emotions it cannot itself satisfy. For me it is the same with Lotta. I can only gaze at Lotta & yearn for her, without ever being able to satisfy the yearning. Now I have left Italy to return to Wien, there is nowhere I can think of going next more than Rome & Pisa.

27

You have to keep going to new places, seeing new sights. The Austrian woman in my compartment keeps getting calls on her mobile & talking to her different friends. Unimaginable to me. A different world. Rome. Pisa. Nice. Montpellier. Paris Musée d'Orsay. Napoleon's Tomb. Sacre Coeur. Oscar Wilde's grave. Now someone is in my compartment I can no longer think clearly to write. Going home means going to classical music concerts. That is my entire life at home. Just let me stay in suspension. So I don't have to face the reality that the relationship with Lotta is over. Just keep travelling, blindly, pointlessly.

28

Some people go through life as part of a group; some go through life alone. Is one any better than the other? If someone lives socially as part of a group always does that make them a good person; and if someone goes through life alone does that make him a bad person? If you prick us do we not bleed? My real uselessness with people. My real uselessness with relationships.

CHAPTER 3
THE RETREAT FROM MOSCOW ANALOGY HOLDS TRUE FOR RELATIONSHIPS TOO

The retreat from Moscow analogy holds true for relationships, too. I am now forced to pull back from Lotta, & I just want to turn & run for home, but the attacks have started on me & they are devastating. I now feel Sophia & Lotta's hostility & contempt for me lacerating me like shards of glass. I feel like they wouldn't pick me up if they found me lying in the street. On Wednesday night we kissed & hugged goodbye. I now realise that meant she hoped she'd never have to see me again. Today has been absolutely devastating. One of those appalling days where I just wander aimlessly around, half-heartedly intending to do one thing but then when I get there finding I have no real desire for it at all. I stumbled around Wien like a dead man today, trying to convince myself I was doing something meaningful & worthwhile, but all I was really thinking of was Lotta. Now Sophia & Lotta have turned against me: the lacerating attacks have begun to come thick & fast, as my heart turns from the site of its once beautiful hope & optimism & starts to race for home. And how I dread it when I do get home & click that front door shut behind me! That is the one & only time since Moscow that Napoleon would have let himself fall back against the door & sink down to the ground & sob his heart out as he now finally admits to himself the devastating, annihilating, humiliating defeat he has suffered. The defeat of Lotta & Sophia will only hammer its nails into my coffin the moment that front door clicks shut behind me back at home. I have got to get out of Wien so I don't have to see the contempt in the two Swedish girls' faces, & see that what could & should have been so wonderful, & gone so right, has turned into a vicious hatred, but I do not want to get home because that is when I will break down & cry. Napoleon never cried all the time he was battling back from Moscow. Only when the door of his Paris apartment shut behind him did he let the tears come, as one can imagine that they would have done for hours, far into the night.

30

I have £375 credit left on my Visa. After the Dorint take this £300 I will be down to £75 left. In effect, when I leave Wien Monday lunchtime I can afford just one more night in a hotel. This is the stark reality of my situation. Where did it all go? There is only £130 left in my Woolwich as well.

31

—, what have you done to me? Kaspar Hauser never recovered from what was done to him & neither have I. The two Swedish girls are just the latest devastating proof of that. Wearily, I let myself get my hopes up that it might be different this time, but the shattering of the delusion is always crushing. We will always have the Butterfly House. I am being soul-murdered every day like Kaspar Hauser, like Sarah Kane. There will never come a day when I cannot take it anymore, as happened to Kane, & Van Gogh, & Plath; I don't think so. I will keep plodding on, absorbing all the pain until I am flooded with it, writing about it until I die of sheer exhaustion & despair. That is how Ernest Dowson ended. He died of drink & despair. The same for Oscar Wilde. Despair brought about his premature death. Like an abandoned, emotionally deprived child physically withers for lack of love, so too do grown men & women when their life takes a wrong turn or reaches its inevitable wrong end. Despair, and lack of love, physically & rapidly deteriorates them. I am a vessel of pain. Filled to the brim with it. Has there ever been any account of pain as minutely detailed and honest as this? The funny thing is, after a day walking around rejecting all possible things to do as empty, I now really want to go back to see the Egon Schiele paintings, I really need to see that Richard Gerstl Laughing Self-Portrait, I would really like to go back to the Schoenberg Foundation to watch that film about his struggle to create his new music. Will I ever be understood? Will I ever be cared for, & loved, even though I am the way I am? Will Lotta ever one day understand & feel some sense of affection for me, despite everything? I want to make Lotta one day understand, & love me, & love my memory. She abhors me now, but I will not rest (my pen will not rest) until I have turned that abhorrence around into, after all, a fond memory of me. A strange boy who tried to love her. Very badly, but he tried. That is something to give my life purpose.

32

I started this holiday able to get enjoyment out of little things. I could stand in front of a painting & get a real intellectual pleasure out of it, & did not feel empty, & was able to draw nourishment out of it. I said how this was the first holiday I've taken where I haven't had a broken heart & what a relief that was & how much easier it would be to enjoy it because of that. Then I met the two Swedish girls & suddenly everything else felt empty. Paintings meant nothing to me. I walked around blindly in a daze, like the Lovis Corinth blind man with bandages over his eyes. How empty that picture would have seemed to me as well. I have wandered around Vienna today in a stupor, like a ghost. My spirit all gone, so, rather, not a ghost as a ghost is all spirit, but a shell, a husk, a zombie. Without love & care & affection & kissing & holding, we live as zombies. Monsters. Frankenstein's monsters abandoned by our mother. Lost Boys in a Never-Never-Land of dreams & idolisations of women on pedestals who we hope could consent to become our mother. After tonight's events, however, if I saw Lovis Corinth's blind man now it would be a minor epiphanic moment. If only Richard Gerstl's Laughing Self-Portrait was still on display in the Belvedere! I really need to see that now. I will go to the internet shop & log in to my website, so I can see it there. I really want to go see that Schoenberg film again. On the train back to Wien from Venezia I played my Webern, Berg & Schoenberg tape the whole time, & I remember thinking that there is so little sign of them when you get to Vienna! Everything is Mozart & Strauss & musicians dressed up in ridiculous wigs & frock coats. There is a Mozart & Strauss concert EVERY NIGHT in Vienna. Why is there not a Schoenberg, Berg, Webern concert EVERY NIGHT? There is no trace of them here. The same way when I went to Nuremberg I found no <u>trace</u> of Kaspar Hauser. Eventually I went back & found the plaque but the girl in the Tourist Office could find nothing to give me about him! It is extraordinary to come to Vienna & find no trace of Schoenberg, Berg, Webern. My humiliating failure with Lotta has really distressed me. After Schoenberg's wife Mathilde left Richard Gerstl & returned to her husband, Richard Gerstl shaved off all his hair, painted the Laughing Self-Portrait of himself, put his brush down & hanged himself, while simultaneously stabbing himself in the heart. The fever town had claimed another victim. <u>Now</u> I want to go to the Jewish Museum. "We had such dignity it made my heart overflow with respect". I wear a yellow star. That is how everyone recognises me. I will not compromise one bit. I will not flinch. I will keep writing.

33

What about a tactical retreat? Return home now. Wait for the new funds to arrive in my bank account—another £600?—then return to do Paris, Antwerp, Montpellier, Nice.

34

Society is trying to ruin me. They are deliberately trying to psychologically destroy a man every single day in every single way. They did this to Kaspar Hauser, Oscar Wilde, Vincent Van Gogh, F.G.Lorca, Jesus Christ, so I am in good company. Needless to add, the names I have just mentioned are now generally recognised to be among the most beautiful, sensitive, kind human beings who have ever lived. It was ever thus. This is precisely the type society hates most & tries hardest to destroy. For a moment I thought there was a break in the clouds with the two Swedish girls—no, I never thought it, not for a moment, I never believed in it, that was the problem, I wearily submitted to going out with Lotta with a sense of complete resignation of what would happen next. If I went with optimism & positivity it might have turned out better. But one cannot manufacture false optimism & false positivity if it is not naturally occurring. My pessimism & certainty about what would happen ruined my date with Lotta & therefore made it happen. A Self-Fulfilled Prophecy, No.927. Well done.

35

As always, I tend at these times to think: —, this is your fault. I cannot avoid that accusation.

36

But there is nothing I want to see in Budapest—the attraction of the Eastern Europe places passed a long time ago! However, I certainly don't want to be walking around Vienna on Sunday so considering it will mean no extra cost I might as well go for a ride to Budapest as do anything else. I could, of course, leave Vienna altogether. But now I do want to see that Schoenberg film again. Is that justification enough for staying & prolonging the agony that Swedish Girl Vienna has become for me any longer? Where did Berg live & compose? Where was *The Night Porter* filmed? Why don't I know these things? Falling in love with Lotta has totally made me lose the plot & the ability to derive joy from these things. To be able to see *The Night Porter* hotel, where Berg & Webern lived, these are the treasures that I thought I could enjoy on this holiday being unburdened for once by a broken heart! In Brussels I was able to enjoy the Temptation of St Anthony by Dali, and the Bacon Pope. For a couple of days I got my hopes up that I might be able to return to London glowing with my happiness with the two Swedish girls. Now these hopes have come crashing down in humiliating red-faced shame & embarrassment I return to the emotional austerity, not letting myself ever get my hopes up, that enables me to find such deep joy in things, for example, like the Schoenberg film. To be in the city of Schoenberg, for God's sake!—this is where he wrote Pierrot Lunaire! Why isn't Pierrot Lunaire performed every week here? Why isn't Transfigured Night? For God's sake, I am in the city of Verklärte Nacht! I have forgotten all that. I am in the city of *The Night Porter*. All forgotten by stupid emotional hopes & softness brought on by a fleeting glimpse of happiness with two Swedish girls. I became giddy as a schoolboy. I fell in love with Lotta. I became crazy. Now I get a grip of myself again. I am in the city of Transfigured Night! I am in the city of Pierrot Lunaire! I am in the city of Berg's *Lulu*! I am in the city of Webern! But of course one cannot satisfy these feelings. Nothing satisfies one when one has thought oneself close to a naked Swedish girl's soft pussy. Transfer that despair into music. The only way I will hear Schoenberg, Berg, Webern in Vienna is to carry my walkman everywhere with me.

37
I think I will go straight home now; if not tomorrow then Monday. But there will be no more thoughts of Rome & Pisa, or Berlin & Weimar, or Paris & Nice. Vienna has become a ruin. A flowering, burning inferno. I will not return here until after Christmas, when the Swedish girls have returned to Sweden, & I can then just be free to return to walk through the black ashes that is all that is left of Vienna. Only one building will be standing, like the A-Bomb Dome in Hiroshima or the Kaiser Wilhelm Church in Berlin as they were at the epicentre of the firestorm & so miraculously survived, and that of course will be the Butterfly House. There will be nothing left standing in Vienna except that.

38
I imagine a Vienna with permanent black skies, a spectral eerie landscape of ruins & black ashes, amidst which one finds one building miraculously still standing untouched, glowing emerald green like some Hound of the Baskervilles, the Butterfly House. It will be like the romantic road Grand Tourists going to the ruins of Rome & Naples & Pompeii, except my ruins are in Vienna under permanent black skies with the low murmur of music of Schoenberg, Berg, Webern bursting out of pockets of ash on occasion.

This is my Revaluation of Values. This is my blackened Creation of New Ideals.

39

How can standing in front of a picture in an art museum satisfy anything in me now when I could have been in bed with a Swedish girl right this minute? Of course everything seems pointless. Life is pointless. I never want to see Weimar. I must find a new memorial to what has happened with Lotta & Sophia. Maybe I should go to Schönbrunn & the Ferris Wheel, so they will be my last memory of Vienna. Of course despair comes from sexual frustration. Ernest Dowson yearned to be with Adelaide as I yearn to be with Lotta, so that was how he fell into drink & drug addiction & pneumonia that killed him. "Last night, ah yesternight, betwixt her lips and mine, there fell thy shadow Cynara". Lotta will be my Cynara. For the rest of time, she has officially become the Cynara of my life. "Even now the fragrance of your hair has brushed my cheek, & once, in passing by, your hand upon my hand lay tranquilly". How many times, in passing by, did her prominent breasts poke and press into me as we turned in the Butterfly House and Leopold Museum & bumped into each other. Christ, those amazing breasts! Did Sophia just murder me tonight? Was that her? Doing Lotta's dirty work for her? What a foul & infamous black Saturday night this has been.

40

Still I am no nearer to deciding what to do next. I have no more money left so that decides it: I must—those dread words—go home. So then I can shut my door behind me & my defeat will really hit me & I will finally break down & sob, sob tears that will last all night, like Napoleon after he returned to his Paris apartments after his sprint from Moscow. Can anyone imagine the tears Napoleon cried that night when he was alone in his room as the door just clicked behind him? I can tonight.

41

It is unclear whether it is really my financial devastation or in fact my emotional devastation that is making me say, after all, I have to return home now. I blame the lack of money in my bank account to excuse me from admitting I am heartbroken and emotionally shattered. Like the shock as of a sudden blow to the solar plexus that Lorca felt when he discovered Salvador Dali had gone to Paris to make *Un Chien Andalou* & Emilio Aladren had abandoned him for a woman. Emotional refusals & cruel denials of intimacy. Wasn't it I who shut out the two Swedish girls? I was so scared. I wanted it so much & that is what made me so scared. I couldn't eat or drink today. In Wegenstein's I had to leave both the meal unfinished & the beer. The staff were slaughtering me as well—absolutely open mockery. Laughing in my face. As I say, on the retreat from Moscow everyone suddenly springs out of the ground & falls upon you with savage vengeance. I travel around Europe like Gulliver around Lilliput. Great men will always try to be pulled down by the small men. By the time I got back to Westbahnhof on my way back to the hotel they were coming thick & fast. Like bats flying at me all at once. A shot, a couple of shots, then just an endless round of machine gun fire. Thinking I had seen Lotta standing outside the hotel & turning her back on me so I did not see her while she waited for another man I returned to my room crazed with jealousy. I went out again trying to pass her again, but she had gone, whoever it was, but on my next time coming back to the hotel there was Sophia whistling as loud as she liked as soon as she spotted me while looking past me. It now seems the first one wasn't Lotta, but the second one was definitely, I think, Sophia. I went out again to pass her again, but she had gone, too. I went & sat in the bar, because I had watched her from my 6th floor window after she had whistled as I passed her coming in, & she was looking into the bar waiting for someone to come out. Leaving the bar, I returned to my room & eventually decided to ring their room, to see if they were there. Both of them were. So had it been Sophia outside? If so, we passed in the lifts! A woman deprived of the company of men, pines. A man deprived of the company of women becomes stupid. Chekhov's words ring very true tonight. What a night.

42

I have been rejected by the world, like Frankenstein's Monster. For a while the two Swedish girls accepted me. Now they have turned, too. After the debacle of the two Swedish girls it is clear that there is no point going on with this holiday any further. If I hadn't met them I would have gone from art museum to art museum, sight to sight, very nicely, enjoying things at a very shallow & safe level. But then Lotta started talking to me and made me fall in love with her. Now that has cut a deep gash. That has brought the holiday to an end.

43

I was now in the emotional state of Dirk Bogarde in *Despair*. I had lost it. Sarah Kane took her own life because she could no more stand the catastrophes of love. It is good to get crazy over a girl once in a while and make a fool of yourself. It reminds you that you are alive. It is clear I have been in the grip of a sexual obsession like *Bad Timing*. My attempts to find love are like Lily Bart's in *The House of Mirth*. I am running just as fast as I can, from Lotta's love. I did not give her a chance to love me. I stabbed her before she got close. I am in real despair and distress over the ending of the relationship with Lotta. I really cared about her.

44

Only if I turn my despair and distress into a science do I feel I can survive it. Sarah Kane killed herself after the repeated catastrophes of love. Vincent Van Gogh was the same.

CHAPTER 4
I'VE GOT TO START SEEING THINGS IN THE RIGHT LIGHT AGAIN

I've got to start seeing things in the right light again. I am in the land of Bartok. That mysterious night music with the jazzy syncopations. I would maybe like to stay in Wien longer now, more like the eight days I stayed in München the first time & use it to go on lots of daytrips. I really want to take my time in Wien again now. Take time to go to the Schoenberg Foundation, the Prater, & Schönbrunn. Rediscover the real intellectual delights again. How much Schoenberg, Berg & Webern mean to me—and I am in their city! Where are they buried? Where is *The Night Porter* hotel? The Swedish girls waylaid me & totally stopped me thinking straight. It was a nice dream for a couple of days, in the City of Dreams. I am in the city of *The Third Man*. Lotta totally blew away my perceptual filters so all I could think about was her. It was raining as I left the hotel at speed early this morning & raining now on the train to Budapest. I am feeling sad but hard. Salvador Dali & Emilio Aladren have left me. Dali has gone to Buñuel in Paris to make *Un Chien Andalou*, and I implicitly am the dog. I thought he was my friend. Feeling emotionally betrayed, but, after all, not surprised. I am feeling sad about many things. "Cos I'm a creep. I'm a weirdo. What the hell am I doing here? I don't belong here". In the loving bosom of two Swedish girls. I must rediscover a cold, hard, thrilling intellectualism. Enough of desire, and love. Enough of starting to really care about someone. How laughable that I started thinking about these things again. I am not made for them, after all. Return to the cold hard cynicism of Harry Lime stealing penicillin from the children's hospital to sell on the black market. That is what life is really like, old man. No Alida Valli, though. I do not want to leave Vienna. I want to stay here forever because the two Swedish girls are here, but I never want to have to talk to them again. Just to know I am under the same roof as them. To leave will be to face reality & accept facts, always hard for me. I can afford maybe one more night in Wien, then I must rush back to Paris. The Musée d'Orsay, Eiffel Tower, Napoleon's Tomb, *Last Tango* house, Oscar Wilde's grave. Those names all fall heavily in my heart like stones. Vienna is the only place I want to be.

46

Wow! This is probably as far east as I have ever been. I feel a slight masochistic desire to explore Eastern Europe after all, the site of my lost empire, my lost socialist utopia. To go to Bucharest, the city of *Fortunes of War*. To sail across the Black Sea down to Istanbul. Then to Cairo. To do a real Michael Palinesque voyage. I should do that. Just to give some purpose to the empty experience of travelling alone, make a point of travelling in a chain of cities so I come back to my starting point in a circle. It's a cold hard wintery world. You must make your own romance. Bartok. Kodály's 'Háry János'. Vörösmarty Square. Goulash communism. Imre Nagy. Personal meanings. But from a long time ago. A dusty antique distant past 1986-89. Before I knew love & betrayal. Ha! In the era of Michael Moorcock, before I knew Karl Marx & Friedrich Nietzsche. The era of Jean-Luc Godard & Anna Karina. The era of Throwing Muses & REM & 10,000 Maniacs & the Lemonheads. The era of Mudhoney, 'Sweet Young Thing Ain't Sweet No More'. The memory of this holiday: Lotta's breasts poking into my arm whenever we turned & bumped into each other. I love living in the memory of a failed love affair. It gives everything such deep personal meaning. One experiences so many epiphanic moments. My misery is laid like a patina over every street & every building. I can gorge on it like a mother eating her own placenta. I should go on lots of these cross-border daytrips. Travelling in suspension is the best thing. It is when I have to come to a stop & settle & be with people that I scream.

47

I am morbidly gloomy and that is as beautiful & pure as anything else. I exult in my difference. Other people see only our deadness. We only feel our hypersensitivity. I feel stronger & happier, more in my element, with every mile we get closer to the Austrian border. When I returned from Venezia to Wien I was dreading how to continue the relationship with Lotta. Now I return from Budapest clear in the knowledge that it is already over so nothing more is required of me. When I rang her room to ask her to come up for a drink I was almost relieved when she said no. That is why I am still a bachelor.

48

It seems to me I might have come out into a new clean air, on the other side of falling in love & starting to care for someone. I can now enjoy the fruits of my beautiful difference again. This is the second time this has happened on this holiday. I started off with intellectual hopes, but quickly became waylaid by Eros. I overindulged & quickly became sated with Eros & with relief was past it, to the other side—but almost immediately Lotta started speaking to me, & I was waylaid, shanghai'd, KO'd by love. Now I am through that little storm, that petit blizzard, & once more into clean, beautiful intellectual air on the other side. Yea, right. Sophia complained Lotta says "fitta" all the time, pussy, and I can't deny that I am still haunted by thought of Lotta's fitta. The last morning in Venezia I had a nervous attack. Last night in the hotel I had an attack of lovesickness. I have lost "my way" twice on this holiday. Once at the start, because of overpowering Eros, then when that was thoroughly sated, & exhausted, it was taken over by love. I have regained my way & am back on my journey. Congratulations. A normal person would have combined the Eros & the love, in the shape of Lotta, & would be living happily with her now.

49

People get annoyed at me because I don't keep them entertained. But what am I—their entertainment officer? The one time I have ever lived with other people I felt like my housemate was my girlfriend! If I wasn't attentive enough he got really pissy. Has he no interior life of his own? No inner resources of his own? I live my life differently. The Swedish girls now learn I am a different creature. They choose to punish me for it. Why not respect that I am a different creature, and be nice to me just the same? I fascinate people. That someone is as absent as I am. A miniature black hole has entered the room. It absolutely dominates everybody's thinking who is in that room with it. What they can't stand is that I have got some life which they are shut out from:- my inner life. They punish me for shutting them out of that.

50

How much nastiness there is in the world. Nastiness created by them and directed at me. I have created nothing but pure beauty and serenity for all people. They have brewed so much poison and pumped it into all the seas and wells and drinking supplies. They have created an ugliness of an unimaginable magnitude in this world.

CHAPTER 5
THIS HOLIDAY WAS GOING TO BE ABOUT SO MANY THINGS

This holiday was going to be about so many things, & last for so long, & involve going to so many different places; but as soon as I met Lotta in Wien it all just became about her & the holiday effectively ended with her. Still it was a very poignant & emotional episode for me, so it is worth its weight in gold for that alone, I suppose. After Lotta there was nowhere else I wanted to travel to, because it would just be taking me away from her, and yet she did not want to see me again, so the holiday just died a painful death. Now I will be lucky to get two hours in Paris before catching the Eurostar home. Home, when the door closes behind me for another year, & the reality of losing Lotta forever & never seeing her again hits me for real, & I sink down to the floor & cry. We will always have the Butterfly House.

52

I was going to travel with the joy this time of not having a broken heart, but I acquired one after the first four days.

53

I've been told this is the last night I can stay away, as the hotel is fully booked the next night. I was going to go to Berlin on the sleeper, come back on the sleeper, passing a couple of nights cheaply without needing a hotel, then check back into Wien again. But what for? I've done the cemetery (at last), the Schoenberg Foundation, the Belvedere, the Leopold, the Butterfly House (!), the Holy Roman Emperor's Crown, the Bibliothek. All that is left is the Prater Ferris Wheel, walking back through some of *The Third Man* sights, & maybe the Vienna Opera House tour. At the end of *The Third Man* Anna walks straight past Holly at the cemetery without even looking at him. If I did come back to Wien again in a couple of days there would be absolutely nothing left to do. And I would just be coming back to be close to

Lotta at the same time as not going anywhere near her & avoiding the restaurant & bar whenever I know she is there! I have got to stop moping around just for the sake of being under the same roof as her. As it turns out, my work has refused me extra leave & moreover told me I am expected back Thursday instead of next Monday as I had thought! So that has ended the return to Wien/Lotta idea for good anyway. Tomorrow morning I will maybe see Lotta for the last time, if she is even working tomorrow, & after that we will never see each other again. And another part of me will die with it. The Schoenberg Foundation was wonderful, by the way, but I can't write of it now. I am too tired, physically & emotionally exhausted, & I must to bed. There is nothing left in my tank. I feel battered & defeated. Defeated by Lotta.

54

A slight rapprochement with Lotta, which in its way seems a minor miracle. After going first to the station to check my E-mails & book my train ticket, a short journey which nevertheless saw me slaughtered by all & sundry, I re-entered the Klimt bar for the first time during the day since Saturday when I spoke to Sophia & she told me Lotta was off. I was so nervous, but it turned out Michi was there. I had a siderl & sat down at the table, realising that typical of my luck, Lotta was not working today & so I had lost my last chance to ever see her, & that my Wednesday night hug & kiss before Venezia was my last sight of her. For the hell of it I had a second beer thinking I needed it to face all the attacks I would suffer making my way to the Prater. I drank while staring out the window through the Klimt curtains, thinking about how I had mucked everything up with Lotta, & what this room meant to me, & would always mean to me for the next 40 or 50 years, the place where I had met Lotta. A few minutes into my second beer, while I was gazing left blindly through the curtain, I became aware of a white-shirted figure to my right, & I looked up to see it was Lotta, smiling down at me. The Second Coming of Jesus Christ, or the apparition of the Virgin Mary, could not affect anyone more than this sight affected me. She was so friendly, & warm, albeit with that nervousness & discomfort there is always between us. I could say a million words about the couple of dozen that passed between us in that moment, before she returned to pretending to be busy behind the bar. We spoke a little bit more, she served me my last siderl, before we shook hands, foolishly I also kissed it, & said goodbye. I do not know why I did not stay talking to her until the end of her shift. Because I thought it would make her uncomfortable, & I am always too considerate of the other person's feelings, so that I reject myself so they don't have to.

55

I didn't even see Lotta coming (in every sense of the word). I had the beer glass grasped in my hand but held unmovingly at my lips, as I gazed blindly like Lovis Corinth's blind man out the Klimt window. All of a sudden there she was standing at the arm of my chair. It was as though I had conjured her up by my own powers of concentration. I had summoned her because I wanted to see her so badly. I was thinking so hard about her I never saw or heard her approach until she was standing there, smiling down at me. A miracle.

56

Being so polite I then all but ran away from her, even though she said to me "are you going to keep me company?" I didn't want to make her feel awkward so after getting her E-mail address and asking her if she would send me a photo of herself I said goodbye to her and left for the Prater. How stupid. Why didn't I spend every last minute of my last meeting with her? She asked me what time my Paris train was, and what time was it now (it was 12.15). Maybe she would have gone somewhere with me again if I had asked. But I was a coward and did not ask. That is why I am still a bachelor at 32. After asking her if she would send me a photograph I returned to my seat and started to write my address for her, and to my surprise she came up to me with a scrap of paper with her E-mail address on it, before I even had to ask.

57

It was so nice that we were able to part on these good terms, with warmth on both sides, though still the same discomfort on both sides. While in the restaurant 730PM that night I actually saw her again. Two girls came out of the staff door from the kitchen & were going into the lobby. I vaguely recognised them, Lotta in long black quilted coat buttoned up all the way to the ankles, & Sophia in a beige jumper with long hair. It was Sophia who recognised me & stopped & waved & told Lotta who popped her head around the door, too. I asked where they were going & they came to tell me they had just eaten & were now going back up to their room. Lotta said goodbye & turned to go smiling back over her shoulder, and after a couple of steps turned & smiled back over her shoulder one last time. Then she was gone.

58

My last words to Lotta in the bar after kissing her hand, were "You're the best thing in Vienna". I'm glad I managed to get that compliment in.

59

I had no desire at all to see Paris. Lotta was not in Paris so that meant there was nothing I wanted to see in Paris. I transferred straight from the 14-hour train from Vienna to Paris Est, to the Eurostar from Paris Nord to get me back to London before the rush hour began.

60

If I can take my mind off of Lotta for a moment (really the most incredibly beautiful bust I have ever seen, constrained in that tight white blouse and in that push up bra?) what are my best memories of this holiday? The floodlit Jesus Christ statue in the Budapest Basilica, really the most beautiful basilica I have been to. The St Mark's belltower which gave me an Epiphany thinking about the two Swedish girls I had left behind gazing out over the bay in the blazing sunshine with emotions suddenly flooding my system. Looking down at the domes of the St Mark's Basilica and being so overwhelmingly reminded of the Swedish girls' bosoms. The moment at 12 midday when the massive bell started gonging right behind my head, which was the cue for all the other bells in Venezia to start ringing. An incredible moment. If I had walked right under the bell & stood on tiptoe the clapper would have hit me & killed me. I didn't go to as many places as I wanted, mainly because something kept me in Wien much longer than expected & made me for some reason unable to tear myself away, & the fact I was called back to work four days earlier than expected, & a lot sooner than I had been hoping. In Brussels, The Temptation of St Anthony by Salvador Dali and a gorgeous Francis Bacon screaming Pope. Wherever I am in the world, whenever I see a Bacon picture I am transported right back home. It was also nice to see again the Génie du Mal, the most lifelike statue I have ever seen, & the Death of Marat. In Venezia, getting as close as I could to the Fenice opera house, even as the builders were busy working away at it, loading the materials inside it from the boats pulled alongside on the canal around the back. In Wien, the exhibition in the Arnold Schoenberg Foundation. I put the headphones on and turned the music up as loud as it would go. Finally making the effort to see Beethoven's, Mozart's, and particularly Arnold Schoenberg's graves in the Zentralfriedhof. Finally making the effort to go on the Prater Ferris Wheel and revisiting some of the sites from *The Third Man*, particularly the Rupert Stairs. In the Ferris Wheel car I was the only one standing in the corner looking in to the car, while everyone else was admiring the view outside, as for me the thrill was picturing Harry Lime & Holly Martins standing there with Orson Welles giving his Swiss cuckoo clock speech: the high moment in British cinema history, of course. We are in the tunnel now under the Channel. The dream is over for another year.

Don't say that! Don't say it!

The Ketchup Song, of course. Beautiful blue skies over England. Puddle of Mud's She Fucking Hates Me. No Doubt's Underneath It All. Pink's Morphine. Avril Lavigne's Complicated. I came out of Venezia's Santa Lucia station, straight onto the boat for St Mark's, stepped up onto the quay and from the nearest souvenir stall the first sound I heard was the Ketchup Song coming from the radio. 2Raumwohnung's Ich und Elaine. TokTok vs Soffy O I Don't Claim Any Riches. I bought another ring in the Am Hof Saturday flea market so that is now my Lotta ring (the Am Hof being one of the very most important sites from *The Third Man*, of course).

And the Butterfly House, of course. As Humphrey Bogart says to Ingrid Bergman in *Casablanca*, we will always have the Butterfly House.

61

Lotta was the reason I didn't go to as many places as I was planning. I stayed so long in Vienna just to be close to her: and yet...avoided making any real effort to get close to her. I feel so much like Gustav von Aschenbach in *Death in Venice*, falling in love with the beautiful Polish boy, & being tormented & tortured by his own repression. I was so repressed around Lotta. I know her name is not spelt like that, but I just love the sound of her name so much I have to write it like that.

62

I think there was some mutual attraction between Lotta and me but as usual it soon vanished when she went out with me and realised what I was like. *The Man Who Fell to Earth* bathroom moment. I'm glad I'm not with Chess Goddess because I would not have met Lotta. I'm glad I'm not with P— because I would never have met Chess Goddess. And so on. I am autistic. I will always be alone.

63

The incredible sadness of the failed relationship with Lotta, as I return home and get off at cold wintry dark London. I travel to test myself against the extreme. Forge myself in fire. And I was certainly put through a trial by fire this time.

EPILOGUE
MORE THAN EVER
NOW I LIVE IN THE
MYTH OF WIEN

More than ever now I live in the myth of Wien: Gustav Klimt & Egon Schiele & Karl Kraus & Arnold Kubin & Sigmund Freud & Schoenberg & Berg & Webern & Beethoven & Mozart & Richard Gerstl & *The Third Man* & *Bad Timing* & *The Night Porter*. Lotta has fixed my heart and soul there forever. My centres are the Klimt Hotel, the Schoenberg Foundation and the Butterfly House. I cast my mind back now to that first night sitting in the Brussels Ibis bar, contemplating the loneliness and pointlessness stretching in front of me. It is like jumping off of a skyscraper: I just close my eyes and throw myself into the emptiness. I envisaged a dispiriting battle between Art & Eros. I did not consider Love. That was not on my horizon. The day before you came. The three days just before Lotta came are as legendary to me as the ones that came after. In Brussels and all the way to Munich and from Munich I was obsessively panickingly questioning myself, racking my brain, as to the point of what I was doing. Then Monday afternoon I met Lotta in the Klimt bar.

I was not nervous at work this week because I was lost in contemplation of the holiday, and what happened with Lotta & Sophia. Events at the hotel became irrelevant to me. I was so churned up remembering the feelings I experienced in Brussels & Munich & Wien & Venezia. Now I am into the anniversary of my first trip to Europe in 1999 and being flooded by all the emotions and Proustian memories from that holiday as well! Lotta is on my mind so much at the moment it is stopping me worrying about anything else. I am thinking a lot about Brussels as well, the night I spent there, to try to remember how I felt before just before I met Lotta, compared to how my heart blossomed and I went crazy after I met her. Brussels always seems a very black place, somehow. A place to celebrate a black mass, with satanic rituals. All those rain-soaked cobbles, and all those rumours of vast paedophile networks among the police and judiciary and politicians, & James Ensor, & Ysaÿe, & Geef's Génie du Mal & Georges Simenon. There is something very dark and evil about Brussels to me. Maybe it is because I always arrive at night! Whereas I tend to get night trains everywhere else & arrive in the mornings! I always get the impression of something slithering through the darkness in Brussels that I don't feel anywhere else. Brussels always haunts me after I return from holiday. Like the Abba song 'The Day Before You Came' it is really strange trying to remember those last two or three days before Lotta came along. "And at the time I never even noticed I was blue." Well, I did notice it all right. "Without really knowing anything I hid a part of me away." I knew that all too well. As I sat in the Ibis bar watching the trams and people passing I was thinking about little else except how I hid all of myself away. Before going down to the bar I dropped my stuff in my beautiful room, turned on Top of the Pops just in time to see the Pink 'Morphine' video at No.1. It is such a black Gothic video, seemingly set in a madhouse, that that too now always reminds me of Brussels. Last year it was Natalie Imbruglia's 'That Day'. Now it is Pink's 'Just Like A Pill'. I am obsessively picking over those first few hours in Brussels to try to explain to myself what happened next when I got to Wien and met Lotta. I so cannot wait to get back to Brussels.

I loved getting back from Venezia, the exquisite agony of returning to the hotel where Lotta was, knowing she would not want to go out with me again, but that we were under the same roof, that I was just three floors above her. I dumped my bags in my room and went straight down to the bar and stayed there getting drunk until the bar closed at 1.15AM. It had been years since I had drunk so much, and I returned to my room, to fight against being sick. It has been more than ten years since I came that close. I then endured one of the most horrible, wretched Saturdays in my life, at the end of which I realised my retreat from Moscow would have to begin. I avoided Lotta for two whole days, until my final Tuesday morning, when I went in to say goodbye. She was not there, and I sank into my seat clutching my beer in despair. I had gone into the bar with my heart racing, so nervous was I of this last meeting with the 18-year-old Swedish girl I had fallen in love with, and she was not there. Staring through the window clutching my second beer, a white-shirted figure appeared at the arm of my chair, and I looked up, and it was her, smiling down at me, like the Virgin Mary. There were explosions inside me. It was one of the more incredible moments of my life. If only my life had ended then.

I returned to the Grand Hotel to find a second girl in the hotel declaring her love for me. I let this boat sail without me as well and felt deeply ashamed of myself because of it.

Lotta will always remain my angel. My 18-year-old Swedish angel. I felt so black and loathsome and treacly, like molasses, and unworthy of her. It came two months after my beautiful heart was broken by the beautiful Asturian violinist in my German class, where I had gone in order to get over Mina from three months before that. Three extraordinarily beautiful young women who showed some interest in me, before realising their terrible, terrible mistake.

Wien is the centre of my life. It is where Schoenberg, Berg & Webern come from, it is where Egon Schiele, Gustav Klimt and Richard Gerstl came from, it is where Beethoven, Mozart and Brahms are buried, it is the city of *The Third Man, The Night Porter*, and *Bad Timing*, it is the city of Sigmund Freud, Karl Kraus and Robert Musil, and more than anything it is where I met Lotta & Sophia, and collapsed instantly, like Dirk Bogarde in *Death in Venice*. I will return to Venezia, but it will be a mistake, like Donald Sutherland and Julie Christie in *Don't Look Now*. I will return to St Mark's belltower and La Fenice and wish I hadn't. I will return to Budapest Basilica and go to the Budapest Opera House, where Lotta went with her mother. I will go on to Bucharest and Istanbul. I will then return to Wien, and go to the Butterfly House, before dining well in the Café Klimt, and returning home via Paris. This time I will go to the Musée d'Orsay, and Oscar Wilde's grave, and Napoleon's tomb.

I was intoxicated by the two Swedish girls. The intoxication is still not yet out of my system. I am still drunk with them.

COLLECTED WORKS

THE COLD ICY AIR OF THE MOUNTAINS

2003-2004

ERNST GRAF

CHAPTER 1
I REALLY LOVE
THIS
HOTEL

I REALLY LOVE THIS HOTEL. WISH I COULD STAY HERE FOREVER. THE WEATHER IS LOVELY. CLEAR BLUE SKIES EVERY DAY. HAVING A VERY PEACEFUL TIME. I GOT LOST IN THE MUSEUM OF MODERN ART AND COULDN'T FIND MY WAY OUT. ANYONE'S IDEA OF HELL, YOU MIGHT THINK. I SAW THE STATUE OF THE LITTLE BOY PLEASURING HIMSELF. THE CHAMBERMAIDS ARE MUCH BETTER THAN OURS. I AM WRITING TO YOU FROM THE HOTEL BAR, WHERE I HAVE SPENT MOST OF MY TIME ACTUALLY. I HAD A FEW TOO MANY DOUBLE VODKAS LAST NIGHT, WHICH IS —'S FAULT, WATCHING THE ARSENAL GET BEAT (SO IT SERVES HIM RIGHT), SO AM FEELING A BIT FRAGILE TODAY. I GET THE TRAIN TONIGHT TO BERLIN. BON SOIR. I VAGUELY REMEMBER LYING NAKED ON THE COLD BATHROOM TILES WITH MY HEAD AGAINST THE COLD LAVATORY BOWL SAYING "I WANT TO DIE", UNTIL THE RECEPTIONIST CAME IN TO TELL ME I WOULD HAVE TO PUT MY CLOTHES ON AND GO UP TO MY ROOM NOW.

2

The Bourse McDonald's, white-blue shirt, blue skirt, brown hair in a bun; and the girl with the really happy smiling face before that, almost an American accent. I got an erection in the Museum of Modern Art, which I always enjoy. I always get erections in art galleries. It is the slow pace of walking, and you tend to follow the same single young woman around from gallery to gallery. Lots of 18-year-old student types in there in groups and twos. It was fantastic to see The Temptation of St Anthony again, and the Paul Delvaux pictures. The Paul Delvaux pictures gave me another erection. I had to move away because I could hear the student group coming up the stairs and the sight of the bulge in my trousers would most likely have caused a massive commotion. Nocturne, Pygmalion, Le Musée Spitzner, Le Voix Publique. I feel ready for Berlin. I wonder if I will do anything there or not. Almost tempted to go back to Munich for the cinema, and that incredibly voluptuous stripper, and Vienna for the TV at night and the videokabins and live sex show. Maybe Berlin will have something to offer me.

3

I have not really enjoyed today, despite the erections in the Museum. It felt like the Saturday in Vienna, when I wandered around wretchedly, because of getting too drunk the night before. I missed the *Angela* film because of that as well. I feel a bit like death, the way I did last time I arrived in Berlin. Hope I feel better when I get there tomorrow! At least I have got a hotel to go straight to—hopefully—though I might be too early to be allowed to check in. I hope I sleep on the train tonight anyway. Best things about Brussels: the brunette woman in white jumper on the first night; the chambermaid on the first morning; Alizée on MCM, the erections in the Museum of Modern Art, the orange-haired girl & her friend who turned twice and looked over their shoulders at me by the Pullman bar. The Swedish blonde who made eye contact with me this morning in the same place. At least I haven't fallen in love this time. Thank God. That really spoiled my last holiday. The holiday before that I was in mourning for P—, and before that for R—. This has really been the calmest and strongest I have ever felt. I vividly recall sitting at this same seat in the Café Belge last year, feeling so appallingly lonely and isolated, thinking what have I done, why have I come away for? Not this time. I just feel strong, looking forward to maybe misbehaving appallingly in Berlin.

BERLIN

I am emptiness. I am a cipher. Here I am in Berlin, the city that was wiped out, the man who was wiped out. Berlin a beautiful, modern, elegant city. Now I know why Wittgenstein took himself away to small towns, Berlin, Vienna, London being, as Spender says, "haunts of anonymous promiscuity". Wittgenstein took himself away from temptation. Berlin and Vienna are all temptation. It eats my brain away. I don't know what I am doing. My life is a sham. My trips to Europe are as pointless as Shackleton's trips back to Antarctica. "After the Great War Shackleton went back South one last time, with many of the Endurance crew, but died of a heart attack at South Georgia where he was buried. The really amazing thing about it was that 'the expedition had no clear aim. All that mattered was that they were heading south again.' What kind of emptiness propels a man like Shackleton back to the ice, or Lawrence back to the desert, or the rest of us to the bottle?" What kind of emptiness keeps propelling me back to Europe on Eurostar, to Brussels, Berlin, Vienna? When I get here I find there is nothing here for me, like Napoleon in Moscow, and eventually have to turn around and run for home again. With the Kaiser Wilhelm Church just to my left, the Marmorhaus and Wertheim's dead opposite me. I love the Kaiser Wilhelm Church, I love Berlin Zoo station.

5

My brain is riddled with holes, like Swiss cheese. Tonight, in Berlin, looking out to the Full Moon (nearly) over Wertheim's Department Store & the Marmorhaus I feel I have reached a turning point. A Rilkean turning point, when you feel so low, things have reached such a low point, that they bounce and turn back. You start to see the value in small things. Classical music, Schoenberg, Berg, Webern, tropical ferns. I can start to really enjoy the intellectual things again. What do I do it for? Because I love to be on my own in a strange city. That is why I keep coming back to Brussels, Berlin, Vienna. That is why Shackleton kept going back to the ice. I am only unhappy because I have spent so much money and have hardly any left. It is a luxury to be sitting here in a Berlin Ku'Damm hotel sobbing how unhappy I am. If I had the money I would delightedly stay here forever. What I want in my life is to be alone. I am alone tonight, so I am happy. I love being alone, & I love studying myself in that aloneness, and learning better & better ways of enjoying that aloneness. Refining the joys of that aloneness, and distilling it, almost so I can bottle it as a tonic or a perfume. I am a singularity. I am a mote. I am an island. I am a lighthouse. That is why I keep coming back to the ice.

6

I like Hotels, because they enable me to hide from the world. I find somewhere to eat & drink & bury my head in my newspaper, as close to the hotel as possible, if not in the Hotel, and I only stay in hotels right next to the main railway station, so my entry into the city can be as quick & easy as possible.

7

Whenever I let love in again, like with Chess Goddess & like with Lotta, it reduces me to rubble, & wipes me out, & I have to rebuild myself all over again. It kills me if I let it in, & it kills me if I shut it out and send it away. It is like wave after wave of bombers that I pray will return again. It is the Zeppelin heading over the Bismarck mansion on the first of the night's bombing raids, while Una Persson comes in and shoots Prinz Lobkowitz and his lover Eva Knecht. It is the destruction I pray for when in peacetime.

8

I have stepped back from the brink here in Berlin, because I just didn't feel comfortable enough, and now I really can't afford to spend the money. The temptation is always here, though. It is already starting to eat me away again. That is why I think I should leave a day early and return to Brussels as soon as possible. I'm always crying, and bent double and racked with desire, and racked with shame like Dirk Bogarde in *Death in Venice*. You so much want to indulge it, & yet the thought disgusts you as much as it excites you. Now I know why Stephen Spender says Wittgenstein stayed away from big towns. The temptation to creep back into the Prater at night is always overwhelming. If I had money, however, I mean millions of pounds, then I do not think I should care at all, which as usual makes me think about exactly <u>why</u> I did not give in to temptation. It is nothing to do with shame, just worry about how I am going to afford it.

9

If Coleridge, Oscar Wilde, Bill Clinton, suffered from "a derangement in their intellectual and moral constitution", I think it is a derangement that a lot of us can relate to. Happy families is not enough for us. There is a demon in us that propels us to do worse, to destroy what we have got and waste what we have been given. There is something glorious in that, I think. To burn like fireflies, then expire before our time. Each man kills the things he loves.

10

I'll pop out later, and pay my respects, to the people of Berlin.

11

I sometimes think these old civilisations were more advanced than us. When you see the Ishtar Gate and Pergamon Altar and see reconstructions of the city in which they came from, and how they would have looked in full colour, you think there is nothing in our world today which can match the effect these buildings would have had on people three, four thousand years ago. There is nothing in our world today that can take your breath away like the Ishtar Gate would have done, or the Pergamon Altar, or the Parthenon, or Tower of Babel, or Hanging Gardens of Babylon. We seem to build so small. All right, we've got Sydney Opera House, Sydney Harbour Bridge, Statue of Liberty, Eiffel Tower—these are the "wonders" of our world—but they're nothing on the scale of the Great Pyramids, the Sphinx, the giant Colossus of Rhodes. For so long the Ishtar Gate had meant something very significant to me, and I can no longer remember why; perhaps since Chess Goddess used to tell me she was learning German so she could move to Berlin and start teaching music there, and somehow I saw the Ishtar Gate as the symbolic entry point to Berlin, and therefore symbol of my loss of Chess Goddess; she was going through the Ishtar Gate without me; so to stand in front of it, and then to walk through it, was an incredible moment of epiphany. One of the most powerful moments of my life. I came out of the museum floating on an extraordinary high. I had passed through the Ishtar Gate.

12

I now know Berlin is the most beautiful city I have seen. Or maybe the Ku'Damm is just the most beautiful street I have seen. As I came out of the Story of Berlin exhibition and rushed along the Ku'Damm to get my bags from the hotel and catch my train, the sun was blazing down, it was boiling hot, blazing blue skies, beautiful Berlin girls, I had quite an epiphany. I so much regretted having to leave the Story of Berlin exhibition halfway through and I so much regretted having to rush away from Berlin. I think for me the Story of Berlin exhibition will become here what the Schoenberg Foundation exhibition is in Wien, a place I can always go back to and spend an entire afternoon immersed in the sound and picture world. The cinema, in particular, showing clips from great Berlin films of the past, like *Blue Angel, M, Caligari*, will be a particular warm bath I will always sink back into. I never even saw Nefertiti. There is so much to come back to Berlin for. I will return to The Oscar Wilde pub, the Ishtar Gate, the Story of Berlin, and there are so many more places I haven't been to at all. The Altes Museum, the National Gallery, the Deutsche Oper, the Komische Oper, the Philharmonie. I thought there was not much I wanted to do in Berlin, but now I realised I have barely even scratched the surface. Rome I will surely find more beautiful than Berlin, but I have not been there yet! I have fallen in love with Berlin! It has finally happened. I was sure it would. I hated my first brief visit, I hated my second brief visit, but I vowed to keep going back, to bludgeon myself into finally falling in love with it, if it was the last thing I did, and now it has happened. It is like getting the girl you have always wanted (not that I would know about that). Berlin has been important to me for so long, for its history, for what it stood for, for its personal symbology to me as a metaphor for my own destruction and self-destruction, so I so much wanted to like it and become at home in it. Now ideal and reality have become as one. We have come together, in all senses of the words.

BRUSSELS

Every single day I was away there were clear blue skies, I did not see a single cloud the whole time, then as I came out of the hotel this morning to get the Eurostar home, it is grey and misty and drizzling with rain, gorgeous rain. A depression had settled over Brussels that morning. As always, I am convinced that I affect the weather. I avoided falling in love for the whole time I spent in Brussels, then Berlin, then on my final night back in Brussels I look at Stephanie and cannot take my eyes off of her. She seemed so beautiful. I liked her the first time but tonight she was gorgeous, radiant, glowing. Every so often her laughter rings out over the reception and bar area and makes the whole hotel feel alive. Once she is gone it feels empty. She makes such a difference. I should have asked her to have a drink with me. I wish I had asked, then I would have known, & could have left happily. As it is now, I am tormented by another missed opportunity. That is why after eight days of clear blue skies Brussels was sunk in gloom and rain this morning. I was so happy for the whole holiday, completely unencumbered by feelings of unrequited love for anybody, and then I go and fall for Stephanie on my last night, and, moreover, throw away my golden chance when it is presented to me. I cannot wait to return to Brussels now. As soon as I get the money I will be back on Eurostar & back to see Stephanie. But it is already too late. You must take your chances when they come. It is amazing how beautiful she looked. It is amazing the way her laughter fills that place and brings it to life. The other star of the holiday was the Irish barmaid in The Oscar Wilde. I never asked her name and I wanted to.

CHAPTER 2
WELL NOW I WILL BE CARRYING A TORCH FOR STEPHANIE

Well, now I will be carrying a torch for Stephanie, for however many months until I can get back to Brussels. I return literally under a cloud and a depression, when last night I checked in feeling so happy. It was probably because I was feeling so happy that Stephanie looked so beautiful to me. When nervous I keep my head down and do not make eye contact so do not really get a good look at people. Last night, I was happy and relieved because I'd managed to get some money out of the machine over the road without which I would have had to have slept in the station, so I went into the lobby of the hotel feeling so good, and that is why I felt quite confident with Stephanie and chatted away to her quite easily and looked at her more fully than I had done before. She was absolutely beautiful, gorgeous, radiant, glowing. A little bit red in the face which is always attractive. And then I had my chance to ask her for a drink and I blew it, because I was too drunk to think straight. No good would have come of it anyway, of course.

15

I know the tears Napoleon cried as he woke up every morning. Napoleon had a terrible time in Moscow, and he had a terrible time getting back from Moscow, but it wasn't until he was back in the luxury of his Paris apartments that his emptiness and grief would have hit him. Every day when he woke up in his Paris room and suddenly remembered all over again what had just happened, and he shook with tears of rage and grief all over again. He had it all, in the palm of his hand, and somehow conspired with himself to throw it all away. I loved Stephanie so much and did so little about it. It never occurred to me to do something about it. I thought "I'll think about it later, I'll do something later." It was the same with P—. I kept putting off and putting off, knowing that if I did let her in, it would turn into a disaster like with Chess Goddess and Lotta. I am damned if I don't let them in, damned if I do. Damned if I do make an effort, and damned if I don't. I left my heart in Brussels.

16

"You could get yourself involved in a rather messy emotional entanglement soon—but it's one that you wouldn't miss for the world. It appears your feelings are aroused over some matter. Moreover, you will be inclined to take a stand or make a bold statement of some sort. By all means, enjoy the pleasure of the moment, but bear in mind that it could be no more than that—a moment."

17

"It is unlike you to become a slave to love—but that is a strong possibility now that someone or something has got properly under your skin. You are aching to get out there and experience some hidden promise and what's more, you're willing to pay the price. That means that somewhere, a lucky recipient is going to have your undivided and devoted attention."

18

I know I should just let go. It will be a mistake to go back to see Stephanie again so soon. But it will be an adventure, won't it? At least after that I will be able to eat properly again. I am not a sensible person. I am Quixotic. If I am in love I will drop everything and follow them to the other side of the world at a moment's notice with no thought of consequences or what might happen when I get there. "You are aching to get out there and experience some hidden promise and what's more, you're willing to pay the price." I am aching to get back to Brussels, despite knowing it will be a mistake and that the moment has passed. Stephanie is my Libussa. There was something between us that night, if only fleetingly. It is that fleeting moment I am going back in search of. I cannot just give up on it, without trying, just once. This visit to Brussels and Berlin has left a very deep mark on me, more than any journey before. I have fallen deeply in love with both places. I have passed through the Ishtar Gate.

CHAPTER 3
LOOKING
FOR
LOVE

Looking for love. "If I was you, I wouldn't start from here." I am learning about love. I am teaching myself about love. When you receive none when you are born, you receive no loving mother's touch, you can go through life without ever knowing what it is. Now I am really trying to work it out. It has become my mission. If it is the last thing I do, I will find love. And then when I find it I will beat it to within an inch of its life.

20

I am crippled with regret for what I didn't do with American girl. I wonder if I will have a chance to rescue this holiday before it is over. This time the missed opportunity came on the train to Brussels. A beautiful young voluptuous American girl. Sitting in a packed Eurostar carriage, I picked up my bag and walked through the train until I found an empty carriage and room to spread out in. Amazingly, after a couple of minutes, this voluptuous American girl does the same thing and in an otherwise completely empty carriage chooses to sit in the seats directly across the aisle from me! How incredible! A cold sweat broke out upon my forehead. I so much wanted to talk to her but just sat there for the next THREE HOURS desperately thinking "What can I say? What can I say?" So, of course, got off the train having said nothing. We got off the train together, I was held up in the queue for EU passports, while she disappeared through the non-EU channel and I never saw her again, though I searched the station for her. I get the chances, I just never take them. Today was blazing hot, blazing blue skies. I had an almost permanent erection in the Museum of Modern Art over two women at the same time. How I wish I could have American girl back now. By my second night in Brussels I am already lost in pain & regret. I had a nice chat with Stephanie as I was checking in again. I want her so much. It was nice, too, to see the Bourse McDonald's girl in white blouse. Brussels opera house feels like a tiny shoebox after the Coliseum. I realise now my book is about love. Love comes unthinkingly and naturally to most people because they are born into it.

21

I feel like The Talented Mr Ripley. I am a fake. I am a sham. I am empty and a cipher. I look at myself in the mirror and don't know who I am. There is not enough of a person there to have an identity. I flick backwards and forwards through my 52 TV channels like Chauncey Gardiner in *Being There*, and Thomas Newton in *The Man Who Fell to Earth*. They, like the Talented Mr Ripley, and me, are empty, ciphers. I keep coming back to Brussels because I like to live in suspension. Complete peace and quiet, and nothingness. With the possibilities of relationships all around me, with Stephanie, with Nephania (a 16-year-old college girl I met on my previous trip to Brussels two weeks earlier), with American Girl, but spurned. Every time I come away I kill love stone dead. Something should have happened between me and American Girl, but I let it die stillborn. I am calm about it, but only because I am already a dead person. I am Mike in *My Own Private Idaho*. Spending my life in the daze of sleep and drunkenness searching for someone I will never find.

22

Girls are always so brave, and I always let them down. They are always so brave and forward in letting you know they like you, and then waiting for you to take your cue. I always miss my cue, unless they actually hit me over the head with it, like Nephania. At least Nephania & I shared a couple of drinks together. Thank goodness I behaved like a perfect gentleman; in the words of Michael Caine, "She was only six-*teen* years old".

23

Today I got drunk in the Pullman, as usual, then after the Bourse Grand Egg went and lay on the grass by the Parliament fountain, staring up at the blazing blue skies through the green leaves of the tree. Every time the wind blew the spray from the fountain came all over me as I lay there. It was lovely, and peaceful. I will come back here.

24

Elena Prokina was the best thing I have ever seen on an opera stage. Her first aria was the loveliest sound I have ever heard. In pale eggshell blue dress, like a 1920s flapper, she looked like the new hotel night porter's uniforms. The Brussels opera house is unprepossessing from the outside, inside it looked like a shoebox, but once that curtain opened—the most beautiful staging I have ever seen. The stage a tilted glass map of Venice. The costumes 1920s. Elena Prokina the greatest thing I have ever seen on an opera stage. I stayed on the edge of my seat until the end, not something I can often say about opera. Being such a small theatre, the sound seemed very loud. I could feel the vibrations of the singers' voices on my face. All this contributed to making this better than almost anything I have seen in Moloch. I will come here again.

25

So, what has this trip to Brussels produced? It all went wrong before I got off the train, when I missed my chance with American Girl. What an idiot. So what I have been back to the Modern Art Museum, paid my first visit to the opera, and lain on the grass by the Parliament fountain? I haven't seen Stephanie since the night I checked in. Where has she been? I can only get over the American Girl if I make some breakthrough with Stephanie. Fat chance. American Girl was quite something. Stephanie was quite something. I don't want to go back to London with nothing, as I always do. Sunday morning looms very large in front of me. How nightmarish that journey will be. I cannot escape it. I know how hard it will be. I feel like I live in Brussels. But what is the only interest I have received? The American Girl on the Eurostar to Brussels. What is the most beautiful girl I have seen? The American Girl on the train to Brussels. This trip was ruined before I got here. First it was Stephanie I fell for but ruined. Then Nephania—although she was too young. Then American Girl. Always something happens. It is extraordinary. But I cannot get over American Girl. I always like to have some tragedy to mourn. Missed opportunities feel worse the more time goes by since they happened. Every day American Girl has cut through me more, as I have become lonelier and lonelier. Loneliness does not bother me as such, as I can always drink, or sleep. Still, I think about her.

26

I have just seen the biggest cock I have ever seen in my life. A black African man in the toilets—his friend told him to show it to me—it <u>was</u> fantastic. It has turned me on. Does this mean I am gay, or just desperate for a woman? It <u>was</u> one of the most fantastic things I have ever seen in my life. One must not be squeamish about these things. One must celebrate beauty when one sees it. It has reignited my appetite for Tallulah, Esmeralda, everything.

27

I cannot believe I missed my chance with American Girl. Gilt-edged chances like that do not come along so often. Once again, I hesitated & hesitated & held back & held back, until she was gone and out of sight. I feel bitter & sombre again. Humiliated by myself. These girls shock me out of my complacency, and leave me appalled at how empty I am. I get sucked into the vortex of the wash they leave behind, pulled down into the maelstrom of shame & regret. I am Chauncey Gardiner, I am Thomas Newton, I am Mike in *My Own Private Idaho*, I am Samantha Morton in *Minority Report*, Samantha Morton in *Morvern Callar*. I am The Talented Mr Ripley. Evanescence, 'Bring Me to Life'. The pain of a missed opportunity just gets worse with every day more that passes, as the loneliness cuts in & really starts to bite. I stand on my balcony during the day and look out over a Granada totally empty for me. Under blazing blue skies, the green trees gently whisper in an occasional breeze. Because I sent her away. Because I closed the door on myself. I did not let something good happen. Terrified of the volcano I started to feel rising up in myself, because love & care were being stirred up, I stuck the knife in her and ran. People like Jack cannot love. He wanted to believe in what Lulu was offering him but couldn't.

28

I always come to Brussels quite childishly full of hope, but always return home to Moloch in despair like Orphée from the Underworld having found Eurydice miraculously only to then lose her for good. He puts in such a massive effort to get down into the Underworld, past all the obstacles and guardians, across the River Lethe, and with his great skill and beauty wins Eurydice back for himself, only to throw it all away in one split-second of madness. "What madness has befallen us!" Then he has to trudge back to everyday life without her. I go through the mirror every time I come to Brussels and descend down into some classical Greek ruined landscape glowing phosphorescent white under permanent black skies. But I am half in love with death. I am quite torn between Princess Mort and my beloved Eurydice. I love Eurydice with all my heart, and long for her, but am bewitched by Princess Mort. I loved American Girl so very much. I only met her once on a train.

29

I am all I. Self-obsessed and solipsistic, in a stupor.

30

I cannot stop thinking about that African cock. It was really massive. Fat & fleshy & pulsing. I wanted to hold it in my hands, I wanted to see it grow stiff & erect, I wanted to put it in my mouth. I hope those gentlemen are still in the hotel, so I might see it again. I cannot bear to look at my own anymore, it seems as puny as a pencil. It has, after all, been another adventure this trip. There was American Girl on the train, Elena Prokina in pale eggshell blue at the opera, lying on the grass by the Belgian Parliament fountain looking up at the blazing blue skies through the green trees as the spray occasionally cooled my face, that massive chocolate black African cock. I am lost in solipsism and contemplation—that is why I could not act with American Girl when I had the chance. I really loved her.

31

I will travel back to Moloch on Sunday morning, what a dread prospect, mourning American Girl, as I travelled back mourning Nephania last time—although she was too young, and mourning Stephanie the time before that. Stephanie happened right at the end of my holiday, Nephania right in the middle, and American Girl right at the start. I am so funny. Such a comedian. I am Pierrot Lunaire. I am Wozzeck. I am Elektra. I am the shattered, sharp-edged, taut strings of Schoenberg, Berg & Webern. I am all splinters and shards in the moonlight. The cold white, milky, sperm-like moonlight. The moon winks on & off behind the stormclouds as I walk back along the Boulevard du Jardin Botanique to the Gardens themselves. I splash through the puddles the storm has left behind, the skies are still black and menacing, but silent now. The Zeppelins have dropped their incendiaries for the night and returned to base over the Bismarck mansion where Una Persson has shot Prinz Lobkowitz and his jealous lover Eva Knecht through the heart, before loading an insensate, crying Jerry Cornelius onto her truck, still in his box. "Not much we can do for him, I'm afraid, poor old chap."

32

Bartok's wonderful night music starts up from somewhere around me in the night, in the rustling bushes, in the whispering black trees, as I pass by the iron railings of the Botanic Gardens. I dream of lying with white T-shirt American Girl on the grass by the Belgian Parliament fountain, of drinking with her on O'Reilly's balcony across from the Bourse, of eating with her in Le Grand Egg over the road. Of sitting with her on the bench in the Place de Mont Monnaie during the interval of *Foscari*. Of sucking with her on that massive black African cock. All this I could have done, all this could have been a reality. All this should have come to pass. It was easier for this to have happened. I snatched a miraculous defeat from the jaws of an almost certain victory once again. I really loved American Girl.

33

I have adventures, but they are autistic adventures. My path never actually intersects with that of another. Other people's paths cross & merge & mingle all the time, but mine remains determinedly singular, & unique. It is quite an achievement for my path not to intersect with that of another. It would seem almost impossible for it not to do so. Like atoms smashed in a particle accelerator, the traces of particles are captured flying off all over the place, but one of them never actually touches the trajectory of any of its fellows. That is me. I am a strange particle. I am a particle that attracts others to me, yet when they come close I have an internal force that repels me from them. This attraction-repulsion is the boom-bust seesaw oscillation of my life. And it is played out in the leafy green, blazing blue-skied crucible of Brussels every time. American Girl has become my latest Libussa. Stephanie is also my Libussa, too.

34

Next time I will go to Berlin instead, and degrade myself, like Weimar Berlin still exists. That massive African cock has given me a taste for degradation. It is my Josephine Baker shaking her breasts wearing nothing but a girdle of bananas moment as the Berlin gentlemen bayed & howled with lust, frigging themselves to death with their fat cocks poking out of their trousers. They rage there at the cage like animals in a menagerie. It is quarter past 7 A.M. on a Saturday morning in Brussels. There are some clouds in the sky this morning, but it is still predominantly blue. Satellite dishes are everywhere on the backs of the old houses around me. Coming away gives me the chance to confront myself, without any distraction or interruption. It is indeed an atom-smasher, so I can study the results. Still I avoid all relationships. Getting involved is a mystery that passes all my understanding. These, technically, are not autistic holidays, but schizoid personality disorder ones, as the gorgeous voluptuous Susi at the Maudsley diagnosed it. Stretched on the cross, I go out again. I cannot breathe. Stifled, smothered because I want American Girl, or Stephanie, so much. I am gasping for breath. I am asphyxiating. Once more, all of a sudden, I am lost in a Great Smog. I cannot see my own feet. A steaming, dripping, hissing fog has descended on the city of Brussels around me. I go out onto the balcony and stand there naked in the heat, and already cannot see the room behind me. I yearn to turn and just feel that African cock in my hand now. I am dying of loneliness here in Brussels, and secretly loving it? Really quite enjoying it? No. I am dying of loneliness here in Brussels and am sombre and in despair.

35

American Girl was just like that red cardigan American woman in the Story of Berlin exhibition. Big, voluptuous, quiet, intelligent, totally beautiful and gorgeous. Fleshy, Rubenesque American females. I wanted her so much in the Story of Berlin but was in too much of a tearing hurry to get around and get out and get back and catch my train to even think about it. Then there was the gorgeous brown bob schoolgirl also in red who sat in front of me in the cinema. The two white tunic & trousers clinic girls I passed in the Ku'Damm doorway in the blazing sunshine. The bouncy blonde Teutonic princess in brown skirt and beige sweater. If I go back to Berlin I will misbehave. I will bring sin back into the Hotel Eden; or, at least, I will wrestle with Eros for a day and a night like Jakob Wrestling with the Angel, or Gandalf wrestling the Balrog. It is time to give Brussels a rest.

36

Foscari was one of the best nights at the opera I have ever had. I took a chance and was handsomely rewarded. I should have taken a chance with American Girl on the train. I should have taken a chance with American woman in the Story of Berlin. So why not take a chance with Stephanie? I cannot.

37

The hotel is so quiet this morning. I think I must be the only one left. During the night everyone else packed up and quietly went away. I have been left in a Marie Celeste of a hotel. Like my dream of coming out into Vienna to find I was the last human being left and going to the Opera House and standing there naked among the red plush seats. The desolation and emptiness I feel inside seem to have become manifest in the hotel around me. This smog muffles all noises. I am living like money is no object. I am living like I am a rich man with limitless resources. I am living like John Paul Getty. My sombreness and despair have driven everyone away from me. My journey back to Moloch tomorrow does not bear thinking about, still less my journey back to work tomorrow night. It is hard to see how I can come back from this. I must admit, I am struggling to see it. Tuesday evening I was touched by grace & beauty. There were angels around my head. There were beautiful women everywhere. Since I went to bed that night there has been nothing, but a big black African cock.

38

I am passive & observational. I am not a participant. I am a spectator. I do not participate in affairs or relationships. I feel assailed by complete emptiness because I attempted nothing with Stephanie. Just waiting for another chance to come along again. I wanted something to happen between me and Stephanie but did absolutely nothing to make it happen. I can only live in dreams and fantasies. I am incapable of conversation, and conversation is the lubricating oil of relationships. There is this kind of invisible barrier, or imaginary barrier, perhaps, preventing me from having relationships. It is a mental block. Because I had no relationship with my mother, but was totally ignored, I can have no relationship with anybody now. I want to be desired and lusted after, the same as everybody else, but then I just bask in it, and do nothing about it, so it swiftly ends.

39

I feel low, and depressed. In reality, this has been the least successful of all my trips. After the American Girl and Stephanie on the first evening there has been nothing. Because of my failure to respond, more than anything. If you go looking for it, or expecting it, you will never find it. It only comes when you least expect it, and are thinking about something completely different, and are completely unprepared for it. I keep coming away in order to keep exploring. Shackleton kept going back to the ice time & time again, and the last time there was no clear aim to it whatsoever, it was "enough just to be heading South again". That is the spirit that propels me back to Brussels. It never has any clear aim, just some muddled hope that I will "meet" someone, I suppose, but more than anything it is enough that I am travelling again. What attracts me to hotel living is having everything done for me (chambermaids who will not leave your doorway until you have let them do at least something for you) and complete peace & quiet. The muddled hope that I might "meet" someone. Well, I met American Girl, didn't I. I met Stephanie. And I did nothing about it, either time. I met Nephania—although she was too young. So I keep coming back, time after time after time. Like Kenneth Williams in Tangier, no one visit was ever really entirely successful, but it was important because it kept the pendulum swinging. None of these trips has ever been what I can say is successful. But the absurd optimism and hope I always travel with, and the gloom and despair I travel home with, speak much for how much they mean to me all the same. They must be doing something good for me otherwise I would not keep doing them. If I had not come I would never have met Stephanie, would never have met American Girl, would never have met Nephania—although she was too young. So not much good ever came of any of them, but I am still very glad I met all of them. I never "meet" anyone in Moloch, do I? Only at classical music concerts it seems!

40

How gorgeous was American Girl? The most gorgeous girl I have seen on the entire trip, and she was seen on the Eurostar coming here. She was the high point of the holiday. It all was an anti-climax after that. There is nothing sexier than thinking someone likes you. What a complete failure this trip has been—because of my complete failure with American Girl. Everything since then has been pointless, wandering around aimlessly, killing time. Still, better than staying at home. That's why Shackleton kept going back to the ice: it was, after all, better than staying at home. I am crying inside. I am bleeding inside. The train back out of the Underworld is on its way, before carrying me beneath the Lethe, and back to everyday life. The trip out is always filled with romance and excitement, the trip back always filled with sadness and despair. That is why Shackleton kept going back to the ice. I am someone who goes through life alone.

41

I have felt invisible since my first night in Brussels. If I had responded to Stephanie or American Girl, then much might have happened for me. I hesitated, and let the moment go, and was invisible from that moment on. No one paid me the slightest attention. I passed amongst people like a wraith because I had let American Girl go.

42

It will be a long time before I go back to Brussels. It has been ruined for me now by memory of the two shameful failures in love, as Vienna has been ruined for me by Lotta & Sophia. It is like a dirty bomb has been detonated in those places, and the radioactivity will prevent me returning there for many years. I feel lonely and fed up. I must try to recapture the joys of being alone, or at least kid myself again that there are some. I always come back from my holidays in such depression.

CHAPTER 4
I DON'T THINK I CAN EVER GO BACK TO BRUSSELS

I don't think I can ever go back to Brussels. It has been drowned in so much sadness and despair and regrets at missed opportunities. I re-enact the same thing over and over. I have firebombed Brussels to the ground now, the way I did Vienna. I have drunk Brussels and Vienna into the ground. I drank a lot in Brussels because I was ashamed of my desire for Stephanie. The whole time spent bent double like Dirk Bogarde in *Death in Venice*, because he so much wanted the boy Tadzio but was so ashamed of wanting him, terrified of giving in to the impulse he so much wanted to give in to. Whenever I am not in love I pray to be in love again, only to be burned and tortured in the fires again. The destruction I pray for in peacetime.

44

Those three devastating return trips from Brussels. They have become part of the legend of my life. Three times I opened up a chance for myself in Brussels, first with Stephanie, then Nephania—although she was too young, then American Girl, only to flunk my opportunity every time. Boy, do you want love in your life? Boy, you will fall into the river. I am terrified of returning to Brussels now. It is in ruins, it has been firebombed to the ground, and every night more Zeppelins come over to drop more incendiaries, the same as what has happened to Vienna. I long to return to the Westbahnhof Café, and St Stephen's, and the Butterfly House, but they have been firebombed into the ground by my devastating broken heart called Lotta. Those awful nights trying to walk along the Boulevard du Jardin Botanique in the driving lashing rain and howling wind, one side of my face frozen like cold ice, to get back to the Van Gogh Youth Hostel! Incredible, extraordinary lunacy! Surreal, fantastical farce! Even though I was overage (significantly) they took pity on me and let me in; I headed up to my room and in the corridor all the doors were open and a bunch of teenage girls were shouting and laughing with each other until they saw this man coming out of the lift towards them, sobbing, snot hanging from his nose, absolutely soaking wet like a drowned rat, face white like Ahab's ivory stump in *Moby Dick,* and they all ran screaming back into their respective rooms slamming the doors shut. I could still hear their screaming as I locked myself in my own room. I can still hear their screams to this day. My arrival at the Van Gogh Youth Hostel is a thing of legend and people in Brussels still talk about it. Elena Prokina. That massive African cock. All parts of the legend now. The sadness of Stephanie and American Girl still pains me. I am still bleeding from it.

45

My last trip to Brussels was like a wake. The pain I felt watching Elena Prokina in pale eggshell blue at the opera. Getting back to my big empty hotel room. I cannot wait to get back to Europe again, though, to be at Waterloo Eurostar Terminal or Heathrow waiting to embark. Travel is the greatest thing. Just to go and blow several hundred pounds in the space of a few days. Why do it? Like Shackleton going back to the ice. Kenneth Williams going back to Tangier, none of the visits were ever really completely successful but they were important in that they "kept the pendulum swinging". They are sad experiences, but there I can wallow in the sadness, like Aschenbach in Venice, whereas at home, at work, one has to keep putting on a mask of cheerfulness, forcing jollity into one's voice. So I travel then so I can be sad? Yes!

46

My trips to Brussels were a symphony of repression in three movements. I wanted Stephanie so much, but each time left without doing anything about it.

47

Forget Greece, Turkey. Egypt, Malta. Everything is geared to getting me back to Munich, Vienna and Berlin now. The cradle of civilisation. I want to sleep with a Munich whore, a Vienna whore, and a Berlin whore. I am going to do it this time. I open the French windows and step out into the 545AM gardens, cool, blissfully cool. I look into the clear blue skies of the hot day to come and the red glow of the sunrise, and I ask myself "what are the good things in life?", and the answer is only: Whores. They are the secret oar & petals of love. I don't want a relationship with Sandra, the Head Chambermaid, though I love her very much, because I would have to be

97

with her and talk with her all the time. I just want to go to whores on my time off. Some people are born latently homosexual and remain homosexual in their habits all their life. I was born with a latent tendency towards whores and I shall remain that way all my life. I will spend a night in Brussels in order to revisit the Museum of Modern Art—the Génie du Mal, the Pope with Owl, Death of Marat, Les Trésors de Satan, and Dali's La Tentation de Saint Antoine—then get the train to Munich. For Franz von Stuck, Salome and Die Sünde, and then the "dolly bars" of Goethestraße and Schillerstraße. Then on to Vienna, for the Schoenberg Foundation, the Belvedere, the Butterfly House, and then the brothels of the Gurtel and Felberstraße, with maybe a daytrip to Budapest and Venice. Then on to Berlin, to Nefertiti, the Ishtar Gate, the Story of Berlin exhibition, and the whores of Stuttgarter Platz. Then I shall fly back home from Tempelhof. How much money will I need for all this? Eurostar, one night in the Ibis Brussels, two nights in Munich, two nights in the Dorint Vienna, one night in Venice, then three nights in Berlin. That is a minimum of ten nights! That is a thousand pounds easily! Where am I now? I want to check the parlous state of my finances, so I can really enjoy being at work! I have got just six weeks to get myself ready for October now.

48

Brussels has become an erotic site for me now—thanks to all my romantic repressions and agonised self-tortures! My erections in the Museum of Modern Art, looking at the Temptation of St Anthony and the Trésors de Satan, looking ahead to the sinful deeds I will be committing once I get to Munich and Vienna and Berlin! Though last time I went to Berlin I did nothing. This time I hope I shall be drunk enough and brave enough.

49

I want to go back to Europe before all my favourite places disappear, like the Carnival Strip Club and Astral Cinema have disappeared in Soho.

50

I am infected. I am more sick than I have ever been before. I am living like Second Empire Paris, Weimar Berlin, Habsburg Vienna, living lubriciously with nothing in my mind but pleasure, seemingly unaware that there will be any consequences, and that there will be any price to pay but money. There have been some awful, depressing, miserable encounters, but then there have been the great nights that have made my flesh and spirit sing. That is why I keep going back. I will be destroyed because of it. It is better to go down in a blaze of glory, however, if one has to go down at all, and after all, society will always be set on bringing me down anyway, so I might as well enjoy it and go down on my own terms. In for a penny, in for a pound. If they are going to damn me anyway, let me have a really wild time while they do it. It is the cynicism of Weimar Berlin. Nothing is worth anything anyway, so you might as well live for sexual pleasure while you still can. Living my life of tormented and ecstatic decay. Diving deeper into darkness.

51

I have got the first feel of the cold icy air of the mountains. This as ever comes in the melting heat of August, so hot last night I felt ill—my mind starts to yearn for the cool of winter, and my October train journey back to Europe. This is going to be the dirtiest holiday of my life. I will set myself a task—To fuck a whore in every city I visit. Brussels, München, Wien, Berlin. I know where to go in Brussels now, Munich is easy, Wien is easy, Berlin is easy. Atmosphere is everything, the same as with anything else. Forward momentum is everything. Cutting a swathe. You have to attack the traffic. Everything is about confidence.

52

I am now totally depraved. Totally corrupt. Totally beyond redemption. I no longer even think about the possibility of a relationship. Another night in the Flying Scotsman and Soho Cinema. The Scotsman was poor, nothing until Thais turned up at 7 dancing, of course, to The Kinks' 'Lola', Paloma dancing to Eminem's 'Superman'. I left then because some Irish man kept talking to me and wouldn't leave me alone. The chips were too hot. Nothing was quite right tonight, as I knew it wouldn't be. The Soho films were very average, *The Devil Deep Inside* with the fantastic Michelle Wild, and *Sexxx #2*. The films went off at 11 and we were chucked out. I was the last to leave, because my erection wouldn't go down, pushing my way through the iron gates, as two Boulevard girls came down the stairs behind me. I felt happy and euthymic, however, as I headed back to Charing Cross. Incredible black Amazonian girl in black miniskirt by Oscar Wilde's coffin. I love the fact that my erection wouldn't go down, and never does when I leave the rooms. Throughout the films I was thinking so much about Munich and Wien, the girls giving men blowjobs in the Munich sex cinema with everyone else crowding around to watch, the Wien brothels. I cannot wait to get there. It will be interesting to see how far I go. I love it when I feel really cut up. That is when I start to think things and feel things clearly. It is in those moods that I can write. When I am in those extreme places, right on the edge of existence. That is where I like to be. That is why I travel. I am Jokanaan. People hate my goodness, my quietness, and my stillness. I am a Holy Fool, and holy fools send everyone around them into a frenzy. I look at the books by Kierkegaard and Nietzsche and think that is what I want, I have never read the book I want to read so must write it myself. TALLULAH. Is that the title? Whores, sex films, strippers. This is my world.

53

The question people need to ask themselves is just why are they so desperate to bring me down? I have infected people with an inability NOT to react to me. But that is what small people do: they react. Great people just carry on doing what they want.

54

I am like a cross between Kaspar Hauser and Lord Byron. People are fascinated by me wherever I go. Both for the desires I give myself up to, and the appalling asocial inertness. It is a strange mixture. It is the deadness of a *Young Adam*, or a Meursault. I can feel nothing. I have become consumed by complete nihilism, like the sensation of suddenly finding oneself whisked up into the clouds, flying like a bird, leaving everyone behind.

55

I felt the most extraordinary deadness smother me this morning. The fog descended around me. It was my travel autism. The most total feeling of anomie. It was horrifying, terrifying, yet thrilling. I gave myself up to it. It felt naughty, illicit. I give myself up to this smothering deadness when alone in private, but here I was indulging it in front of everyone. I wanted more and more deadness. It was like a lust for it. I have become this bloated depleted creature. I am out of control like Klaus Kinski in Venice. I have had out of control spells before that lasted for a month or two at a time, but now it is permanent, it has become every day. I cannot stop myself or rein myself back. I have lived my life by a boom & bust cycle of agonised tormented repression and ashamed flooding indulgence, but now it is all indulgence. The only love I can ever envisage is fast love. I crave it.

56

I am a scopophiliac. Then you think if it is your nature why cure yourself of it? The thought of a naked voluptuous woman in my hands is mildly titillating but how much more thrilling is the cinematic image of a naked woman in front of me. "This is sick, and you need help to get over it!" Why cure oneself of one's nature? I need to be in an extreme place. To write I need to feel at my most alienated. Alienated by my extremes of sinful shameful indulgence or smothering fog-like deadness. Cut me and no blood would come out, and if it did it would be slow and grey. Then to break the fog, the slow dreamy white paraphrases. I am in the super-trance of travel. I have gone into it a week early, while still surrounded by people. People look at me in shock, concern and amused embarrassment. They don't know where to put their eyes. I am changing from Jekyll to Hyde in front of them. These are Munich cold blue skies and green & yellow trees. I feel like I am in southern Germany and Wien already. I have had extraordinary wet dreams two or three nights in a row. Appalling, fantastic, filthily erotic dreams, almost like opium visions. So I move further and further away from the people around me in the hotel. We stare at each other in horror like from separate continents, separate universes, standing face to face. I am Jekyll. I am Kinski. The transformation has begun before I even start my journey. My trips to Europe are like Kenneth Williams's to Tangier. No one trip could ever be said to have been completely successful, but they are essential, because they *keep the pendulum swinging*. I am becoming closer to Joe Orton's "do what you want with your genitals" now, and really meaning it, rather than just trying to think like that, like Kenneth Williams tried to. I am becoming a laughing, gleeful monster. Like Oscar Wilde my ashamed indulgences are becoming rampant, out of control, careless, reckless orgies in front of the whole world. I have lost all restraint. I am glad of it, and horrified, fascinated by looking at my new appalling self. I watch myself making love to Lydia like Herman in *Despair*. I have gone now. The madness is taking me over. I am giving myself up to it. I have lost touch with all reality. It is totally exhilarating. I can do anything. I can commit worse and worse (better and better) crimes and feel no shame. Just exaltation and joy. This is why people hate and fear and envy me. I am off the scale. I cannot be held back. I have broken their rules, and finding myself not destroyed, realise I am beyond their rules, and can break them more and more. This is a terrifying, infuriating moment for the society around me. It is the moment Logan goes on the run with Jenny Agutter. How dare I think I can be free when they cannot!

57

I am now giving myself up to my true nature, like Oscar Wilde did, and started "feasting with panthers". Like Lord Byron did, Kaspar Hauser. It seems it is when I feel most dead that I come alive. Then I enter that other universe, the universe of fog and smothered beautiful greyness, where I can indulge the most exhilarating nihilism, and the most insane acts of public licentiousness. I found myself horrified, appalled, and yet—ecstatic!

CHAPTER 5
I FEAR MY OWN ARROGANCE

I fear my own arrogance. Last time I travelled, the most perfect chance presented itself, in the voluptuous shape of American Girl. How I bled around Brussels after missing my chance with her. Two maybe three attacks so far. One by a woman who desired me, but I ignored. The first manifestation of the Salome Complex so far. I have but two plans in Brussels: the Wiertz Museum and the Museum of Modern Art. My first two erotic stations of the cross. I love — so much. I show it so little.

59

Love, Art & Eros. The eternal battle has recommenced. I have been reduced to ruins so many times, and have rebuilt myself stronger, risen like a phoenix from the flames, stronger every time. Annihilation in love is the story of my life, yet I seek it again & again. I want to get back on the stage and flaunt myself like Nana every time. Inviting the whole of Paris to worship my sovereign nudity. I am the Golden Fly on the shit-heap of Europe. My pace is increasing faster & faster. I am doing worse and worse. When, pray, are you going to destroy me? I've been waiting so long. I've been getting away with it so long. I revel in my own sinfulness. Sin has been all there is. It has been my reason for being. Everything else exists only to serve it. Welcome to France. Sin has saved my life from boredom. Whoredom, indeed, has replaced boredom. Diving deeper into darkness. The sublime & ridiculous world of me.

60

As ever my visits to Brussels start in the Wiertz Museum. L'Orgueil. A Scene in Hell. The trompe l'oeil. La Philosophie qu'on ne pense. Le Suicide. Things can never hold the thrill they did the first time you saw them, but they acquire another power. If you keep coming back to see them, they become stations of the cross. Vital staging posts along the way of the pilgrimage. And so it is I left the Wiertz with my customarily throbbing arousal and returned to the Museum of Modern Art.

61

There is one spot I can stand in, and see Salome, Trésors de Satan, Génie du Mal and Figure Tombale all at the same time. This spot might be my favourite place in all the world.

62

There are some places that are so powerful, I cannot tear myself away from them. The top of the St Mark's belltower was one of them, and now the spot in the Brussels Museum of Modern Art where you can see Salome, Trésors, Figure Tombale and Génie du Mal is another. I lingered and lingered and could not bring myself to leave. An extraordinary moment of epiphany.

63

I slept when I got back to the hotel (no more sign of Stephanie), until 10PM. Then went for a few drinks until 1130ish, before heading up to Gare du Nord. As luck would have it, while looking for the lavatories, I came out of an exit and found myself in Rue d'Aerschot! Girls sitting in windows right in front of me! I was so happy. This was my territory. I do not belong with real people, in polite society. I have no fellow feeling with them. I can only live in the illicit world, where you can just give in to your urges and desires, and do not have to worry about saying the right thing, thinking of something to say, being good company. I didn't finally leave until about 315AM. On the way back saw some promising places by the Place Brouckère and went down the stairs of the Guest Bar behind the Opera, a table-dancing place that looked okay. It's amazing how you never notice these places are there during daytime but lit up by red neon in the black night they are so obvious and so tempting, and so welcoming. There was also a place right at the top of the Boulevard Adolphe Max just across from the Hotel le Dôme. It wasn't a fantastic experience, but I was pleased that I had done it. I got it out of the way. On the way back to the hotel, I was thinking what is the point of going to München now? But I'm sure my well will have filled up by the time I get there. 243 euros in my hotel. Maybe another 90 in Rue d'Aerschot. Another 10 in the Pullman bar. 6 in McDonald's. 5 in the Metro. 10 for the train to Köln. I realise again I could never be in a relationship with someone. I am too much of a strange and recessive personality. Brussels felt very fulfilling. I did everything I wanted to do. I got to know it a lot better than ever before. And had the city to myself at 3:30 in the morning, which is always beautiful.

64

Thank God, we are in the Holy Land at last. Aachen is behind us and we move deeper into Germany.

65

If I don't have a drink I really start to feel drunk. My nerves build up & the tension gathers itself around my eyes, until I feel such stress and such bags appear under my eyes and my eyeballs become bloodshot, and people say have you been drinking? I feel like I have, my head hurts, I feel really smashed. This is the sign of an alcoholic. Withdrawal symptoms. I really look forward to the end of my train journey, arriving at my hotel, whatever, so I can get straight to the bar to calm myself again. For someone who lives his life alone, walks down every crowded street alone, enters every crowded room alone, relaxation is important and valuable and treasured.

66

I helped two pretty German girls with their cases in Köln station. They gave me nice smiles. When you come into the entrance hall at Köln station and see the fantastic Köln Cathedral towering above you outside, it is always a tremendous moment. I pray my hotel has a bar.

MUNICH

I really felt I got to know München a bit better today. What is the difference between now and how I was the last two times I was in München? I feel much more confident now. It is a marked difference in me. I checked out the Inter City Hotel bar. Then went to see Ludwig's tomb in St Michael's church, then up to Neue Pinakothek (closed) and the Moderne. I'd forgotten that I'd been here before, which says a lot. There was only one picture worth seeing, typically a Bacon. Kreuzigung. It is always a joy and a relief to see a Bacon when far from home. He is the most striking painter. Then back to Lenbachhaus to see Salome, again the only picture worth seeing in the place. It is actually quite strange that it is there, because it is so different from all the others and quite out of place. Russian blonde in red T-shirt. I had a vodka in the Polish café which was packed, and another in the restaurant, and a beer in the Hotel Wolff (135 euros for a room!). The Europäisch is cheap but has no bar.

68

Every time I come on holiday, something happens to knock me out of my smooth equilibrium and destroy my confidence. My *Chute* moment, when I should have done something but hesitated and hesitated and didn't do it. I should have made an effort with Susi. I was so happy and carefree and confident for my two days in Brussels, my two days in München, then last night I threw it all away. The usual battle between Love, Art & Eros has blown up in my face and struck me a mortal blow, as it always does, and now I am bleeding on the train to Ansbach.

69

I threw myself into the Love/Art/Eros battle, gung-ho and reckless and full of courage and confidence, and for a few days it goes well, people fall back before my onslaught, but then soon enough a woman gets the chance to slip a little tiny dagger between my ribcage and delicately pierce my heart. A small tiny little asp creeps through my defences and punctures my breast. Now I feel grim and sombre, bitter and drawn. The same thing happened with Lotta, with Stephanie, with Nephania, with American Girl. Now Susi. Now I'm stuck in the moment and I can't get out of it.

70

As usual, as I came out of the hotel this morning, there was a girl coming along the street towards me, who I only realised afterwards happened to be the splitting image of Susi. Tall, slim, long curly brown hair, long brown coat and jeans, a blue folder clutched to her chest. It could have been Susi, but thinking so much about Susi, I completely forgot to look. This always happens. You see lookalikes everywhere and are then tormented by was that her? Against All Odds. Eternal Flame.

71

I felt it was a bad omen when I could not get to see Die Sünde in Neue Pinakothek as it was closed in preparation for its 150th birthday and had to content myself with Salome in the Lenbachhaus. I have met my own real-life Salome in München now. She has sliced my head off, because I kept pure and resisted her temptation, though I desired her and so much wanted to give in, and now she has it on a plate. Salome haunts me. Unable to cope with women, they will always be Salomes to me. The Army has got on the train at Anyling. I imagine they are Herod's soldiers in German uniforms.

72

It is good I feel this sadness now, it enables me to enjoy things like this trip to Ansbach, the Schoenberg Foundation, etc. I have turned to Art for consolation again, after losing my senses in Eros and being murdered by Love, as ever. It always happens like this. Salome danced her Dance of the

Seven Veils for me all right. I was Jokanaan to a T. Until she gave up in disgust. We caught each other's eyes right from the start. We saw each other from across the White Coffin bar, and there was some spark that passed between us. Later, I stroked her arms, and ran my hands over her lovely arse, and kissed her on the cheek, but I would not go into the room alone with her. She said first have a drink with me in private and I said no even to that. Why? Why did I say no? Now I am a wreck, and a ruin. Wasted and empty. That fire-bombed Munich mansion.

73

Now I do not want to leave Munich. It has been reduced to ruins. When Eros turns to Love there is always a huge cataclysmic explosion, which annihilates everything. This happened in Vienna, too. Under permanently black skies, only the phosphorescent green butterfly house was left standing. It happened in Brussels, too. Maudlin and morose, I just want to wander in the hot burning ruins and never leave. Salome has closed the door on me, but I cannot bear to close the door on her by leaving. Having saved my money, foolishly, stupidly, on Susi, I was at least glad I did not waste it on anybody else. Susi's friend Amelia was going back to Bratislava today, so I expect Susi to have gone with her. There will be no point returning to the White Coffin except to drown myself in the music and the darkness and the beer. Love is the wages of sin. It is my punishment for sinning too much. Love always strikes me like a thunderbolt in the midst of my Eros wastefulness.

74

The sickly sticky eroticism of Von Stuck's Munich has claimed me at last. I have met my Salome. I have wallowed in appalling degradation but fatefully, fatally, did not go through with it. If I had gone through with it and given in to my temptation to follow Susi into the séparée I would be happy now and flying. The lesson again is that repression hurts more than indulgence. At the last moment I repressed myself; in the midst of all the appalling degradation I was already swimming in, I pulled back from actually experiencing real pleasure, real joy, with Susi. Because she seemed to be the only one with the spectre of almost a real relationship, of some sort. That was why in the end I could not follow her. I thought I might enjoy it too much and actually get carried away and for the first time in my life actually lose my guardedness and for the first time in my life really let someone beneath my guard. Susi so nearly got under my guard, and the fact I slammed it down on her at the last moment is why I am bleeding and decapitated now. Grim, dark, cold, rain-heavy skies. Tormented by what I didn't do with Susi. What I did not give in to. I didn't give in, so I lost.

75

I stayed locked in my private world. Sickly and closed. A swamp, full of diseases. No clean water ever replaces the old. Mosquitos & fireflies thicken the air. I remain in the midst of it, as cold as ice. Seeming to wallow in silence & loneliness as if it were a matter of pride. While on my quest for a serene initiation to Love. A cold air blows around me, from within me, and chills whosoever is foolish enough to come near. I keep writing, like Nietzsche. There is nothing else.

76

It is good. I want to not get involved. She was just trying to prize a fool from his money. The only thing is—I was attracted to her, and I think she was maybe even a bit to me, above & beyond the usual commerce of it all. It was like Jack being reluctantly dragged up the stairs by Lulu, "Come on. I like you." Yes, I was attracted by her, and that was why I distrusted her so. It just made it easier for her to get money out of me, so I had to close the shutters down on her more than I would someone I had no feelings for. My logic is perfect, just is completely in reverse. There are always good reasons, and well thought out ones, why I've done all the things I've done, and led my life into ruins as I have done. Every time I come on holiday I am hoping for some romantic spark, just so I can kill it dead and extinguish it and leave myself in ruins again. There is always one person who touches my heart, and I cannot forgive them for that.

77

Oh! But I really liked her!

78

Travelling to small towns is always exhausting and I wonder why I bothered. In Ansbach I saw Kaspar Hauser's statues and his memorial in the Hofgarten park at the place he was stabbed and (I think) the house he died in. Ansbach is such a pretty little town (everywhere I've seen in Germany is), with so many strange and beautiful statues. The statue of Kaspar stooping, almost bent double, his face hidden by his hair, holding out his letter, is particularly affecting. You can really imagine the total blanked out fear this boy must have been feeling when he was dumped in Nuremberg, 175 years ago, with no idea how to cope with all these people he suddenly found around him. I saw the plaque to Kaspar Hauser in

Unschlittplatz, Nuremberg, four years ago, and now have walked in the park and seen the spot where he was killed, while trying to meet someone who promised to tell him about his mother. It is like *My Own Private Idaho*.

79

I feel quite down now. Thursday night's mistake with Susi and then Friday's tiring long trip to Ansbach has left me low. I stayed in Friday night and will do so today as well, unless I can find somewhere showing Turkey v England! Tomorrow I hope to move on to Vienna—though what for? What for am I in München? More than anything it was to go to the White Coffin and when there I thought "was this really what I came all this way to Munich for?!", until I walked back into the bar from one of the four or five porn kinos surrounding it and out of the corner of my eyes saw a brown-haired girl sitting on the other side, and before looking again I knew I would love her.

80

So now I've let Susi go, maybe I will find someone to love in Wien. I can go to the Schoenberg Foundation, the Belvedere, and most important of all I need to go back to the Butterfly House. Then, after that, the Gurtel. I would still like to go on to Venice, to stand in the top of the St Mark's belltower and see La Fenice and this time do the Accademia as well. It will be good to explore the hotel bars in Wien the way I have done here in Munich, too. And when I return to Brussels as well. That is a good new game.

81

Being in a small town scares me. The closer I got back to Munich the more my equilibrium returned. Gorgeous long brown-haired girl in brown jacket and grey trousers looking at me on — platform. Blonde in black coat and red scarf all the way back to Munich.

82

It is always amazing how many English & Irish people there are in a place far from home. Ned Kelly's and Killian's were absolutely jam-packed with them. I watched the first half of Turkey v England in Ned Kelly's and went down into Killian's for the second half. I asked the beautiful brown polo-necked jumper, brown-trousered Regent Hotel girl for directions to an English pub. She is so gorgeous and has very large bosoms. I meant to ask her name. Talking to her put me in a good mood and turned me on for the rest of the day. It was the concierge in the Hotel Eden Wolff who suggested the place I eventually went to. The two pubs are in the same building just behind the Frauenkirche. The trees around the church all have light-bulbs in them at night. After the football I headed back to the White Coffin, and tonight it really felt like the best place in the world. Being a Saturday night, it was packed so there was a great atmosphere. All the girls seem to be Brazilian or Russian—just like London! The stunning Norwegian blonde who looks like Anne Marie Foss turned out to be Russian—Irina. She stepped to me. She was incredibly gorgeous. She let me stroke her arse while pressing her tits into my chest. A bit later as she went by she just ran her hand down my back and looked back over her shoulder smiling. I was ready to go into the séparée with her, but she then spent the rest of the evening sitting around the bar with five Russian guys and did not seem interested in private dancing anymore. I left feeling disappointed. I drank an enormous amount, in the afternoon before the football, during the football, and then at the club until about 1 or 2AM. After that I looked into a few of the dolly bars, but no one was interested in selling anymore it seemed, so I returned to the hotel about 4AM, frustrated but feeling glad I had done the right thing, to save my money for Wien.

83

I went into the Inter City to have a word with Nancy again, and just double-check if they had rooms that night and they did, plenty, so the blonde guy must have point blank lied to me Friday night when he told me they were going to be absolutely full up. It made me determined to stay one more night in München on my way back from Wien, just so I can stay in the Inter City, to spite him. It will also give me an excuse to go back to White Coffin one more time, to maybe get that dance from Irina. The little brown ponytail girl with the perfect sexy arse in little lace knickers was fantastic, too. So poised and sexy. She sat on the TV side in front of me in lacy trousers, legs wide apart. I could look at her all night. She went into the séparée for ages with a young guy and it made me so jealous. The dancing was fantastic. Elena dancing to an incredible French track with an accordion, 'Tu m'as promis' or something, then Irina dancing to two Russian songs. The White Coffin is really fantastic. All the girls are knock out beautiful. I now know I will come back to Munich many times. Like in April I finally fell in love with Berlin, now I have finally fallen in love with München.

84

What am I going to Wien for, then? So I can come back to München and be relieved to be back. I will stay in the Dorint tonight but must find somewhere else for Monday. It seems now I am completely depraved. I think about nothing but sex. So what? What's wrong with that? It is no worse than thinking about nothing but work, or one's children, one's family. I would like to go on to Venice just to provide some pinnacle to my holiday. I do now see the day I passed through the Ishtar Gate as the turning point in my life. I have become much freer since then.

85

I am not a new kind of creature, I think. Before me there have been Edvard Munch, Friedrich Nietzsche, Egon Schiele, Vincent Van Gogh (as I pass a field of sunflowers), Ludwig Wittgenstein, etc. The difference being that they were all talented. I can do nothing except write journals, recording my path through life. Recording my life from the very edge, poised on the precipice of the universe, a blink away from annihilation. There is, however, some value in this recording, I think. There have been lives like mine, both famous artistic geniuses and unknown 'ordinary' people, but none have recorded their passage through life as it is happening the way I do. It has been a life worth living. It may have had a propensity towards infantile eroticism, that lately has blossomed into a full-blown addiction, but it has been worth living all the same. There have been times, it is true, when the pain of being me has been almost overwhelming—a sobering reminder of those days coming in Ansbach, which after all is where Kaspar was killed—but I have come through it richer and stronger and better for it. I feel my power increasing with every year that passes. The pain of being me, moreover, has actually been eased and I could even say cured by my Eroticism. It is my joy & pleasure.

VIENNA

I returned to the Butterfly House. There were so many butterflies there this time! And so many exotic little birds walking along the pathways, you have to be careful not to tread on them. I focused on three butterflies which were following each other around in fornication. Quite worried they were going to poop on my head, but I don't know if butterflies do that. You wonder what they do all day, they don't have work to go to. They probably just fuck all day long. That's why there are so many of them.

87

There are only two things keeping me in Vienna, and they both belong to Fraulein W—.

88

I am no longer in any hurry to leave Vienna, yet I have got to get to Venice and back again. I want to hang around just to see Fraulein W— again. The Dorint always has the most gorgeous nubile girls. Arriving in Wien Sunday night, coming out of the Westbahnhof station and crossing the dark night-time car park towards the glowing Dorint, was an extraordinary magical feeling. To be back in Wien, after what it came to mean to me because of Lotta & Sophia a year before, was overwhelming. I felt honoured and privileged to be back. Yet still I didn't really know what I was going to do here. Seeing the two Dorint bar girls the next morning gave me all the answers I needed. I would kill time in Vienna—the city of *The Third Man, Bad Timing, The Night Porter*—just to be around them. Buoyant, intoxicated, aroused, I headed to St Stephen's Cathedral, always my starting place when I come to Wien. This time I even went inside, such was my good mood. Then I went to see the Lobkowitz Palace before returning to the Butterfly House. There were so many more butterflies than last time, the air was filled with them. And beautiful exotic little birds would keep walking out onto the muddy pathways, so you had to be careful not to tread on them. I sat on the little bench me and Lotta sat on last time, and it was a very intense epiphanic moment, for which I was grateful. Then on to the Schoenberg Centre, to spend an hour listening to the audio commentary in the exhibition. Another very intense and moving experience. By the time I came out, however, the drinks I had consumed in various establishments beforehand—Dorint, Continental, Sofitel—were wearing off and my equilibrium and feeling of power began to disintegrate until I became a nervous wreck. Sitting down for my evening meal back in the Dorint, a beer and several vodkas helped repair my state of mind, and I headed out to the ML Revue where I spent nearly two hours, but wishing I was back in the White Coffin all the while. Walked back past Tête-à-Tête for my usual titillating peek through the window—a young lady turned her quite glorious back—then to bed for the night. Now, after this debauchery, I felt the need to go on to Venice for my purification. It is where I go to atone for all my vices, and mourn all my lost loves, and to be blessed.

89
Mariahilferstraße is as dry as Oxford Street. Dryer, in fact.

90
I feel the Second World War inside me, it is in my DNA. The First War too. I look over to Westbahnhof and think of the TV pictures I saw of it in 1945, bombed and in rubble, and it is very powerful to look at it, and the surrounding buildings now. Every place has its memories locked up inside

them, and there are some places where I can really feel them, and this is one. I went to the Belvedere, of course. There is really not much there that makes me feel really excited. The one real treasure is the gold-framed Laughing Self Portrait by Richard Gerstl. That is the sole reason why I always come back here.

91

I trace my way across Europe by a network of important staging posts. The Ibis in Brussels, the Regent in Munich, the Dorint in Wien. Last night I ate in the Dorint, even though I had bought the chicken in the Westbahnhof. It was nice to see Natalia again. We are like old friends now. We exchanged E-mail addresses and I kissed her politely on both cheeks. As I arrived Fraulein W— was just leaving, shock of blonde hair falling around her face, long beige fur-trimmed coat like Maria Schneider, over grey sweater, blue jeans, she looked gorgeous. Christ, her young knockers are sensational! My relations with women can only be these fleeting attractions, however. I am not capable of anything more. Having only really stayed in Wien because of her, this is the only other glimpse I have had of her.

92

I have missed the Bela Bartok for the second time but have caught the Stefan Zweig instead. The blonde ponytail in see-through white jumper over a black halter-neck bra and big spreading tits in the Leopold. I became enamoured three times in the Leopold, once with her, then in the exhibition of Klimt & Schiele pencil drawings of nude girls, and then with the big voluptuous black-haired scarf woman in the Gerstl room. The Toulouse-Lautrec exhibition had little effect on me. The Schiele rooms were the best, Revelation and (Self-Portrait with Foreskin Pulled Right Back, did I imagine that?) Self-Portrait with Chinese Lantern Plant were good, but Mourning Woman was the absolute treasure. If I always return to the Belvedere to see Laughing Self-Portrait, and to Neue Pinakothek to see Die Sünde, Lenbachhaus to see Salome, then I will always return to the Leopold to see Mourning Woman. She doesn't look like Mourning at all, she has a quite dirty look in her eye (and who doesn't in a Schiele picture?), like her and her lover have just bumped her husband off, so they might indulge their carnal appetite unfettered. Revelation looks like the boy is giving the man a hand job. If Munich is thick with the sickly eroticism of Von Stuck, then Wien is the same with that of Schiele & Klimt. I stood in front of the big window that gives a panoramic view over Vienna, where a year earlier I had said to Lotta "This is the best picture in the whole museum" and she had laughed that she was just thinking exactly the same thing. Before the

Leopold I went to see the just opened Francis Bacon exhibition in the Kunsthistorisches Museum. My first impressions were that it was quite overwhelming. To walk into the first room and be surrounded by 11 Popes, 7 of them Bacons, moved me to the brink of tears. If the later 1970s works wore me out a little bit, that does not change the fact this was one of the great exhibitions of my life, all the more so because it was so far from home. Apart from the Popes the other great joy was to see the Study for a Nude 1952/3, which I have loved for so long. The Diving Deeper into Darkness picture.

93

If I keep coming back to the same place it is to test how much I have grown since last time. I felt so much more confident in Wien this time than I have ever done before. So, what was the point of coming here? Some good points did emerge. I got on really well with Natalia; Fraulein W—'s incredible breasts; the Butterfly House with its fantastic profusion of butterflies and exotic birds; the great surprise of the Francis Bacon exhibition; four really treasurable memories. Four epiphanies in their way. And added to that is Egon Schiele's Mourning Woman and Richard Gerstl's Laughing Self-Portrait. The great pleasures from Munich were watching the Turkey v England match in Ned Kelly/Killian's; Susi & Irina in the White Coffin; the brown jumper girl in the Regent. And Stuck's Salome. From Brussels, the incredible thrill of seeing Alfred Stevens's Salome again, in juxtaposition with Trésors de Satan, Figure Tombale and Génie du Mal. The closest I came to any love this time was the real desire I felt for Fraulein W— in the Dorint. And Susi in the White Coffin. They were the only real fleeting flickers of electricity. I would have liked to have taken things further with Fraulein W—, and Susi, and the brown jumper girl in the Regent, but if this holiday belongs to anyone then it belongs to Natalia.

MUNICH

I have fallen in love with München this time, the way I fell in love with Berlin back in April. The moment when I made eye contact with Susi was the single greatest moment of the holiday. I regret I did not make it to Venice, but it was the right decision. Next time I will spend less time in Brussels, München and Wien, and more time in Venice; maybe even finally crossing the Rubicon (literally) and going on to Rome. That must be my goal for next time.

95

I want to write a small monograph of my travels, like a Fabergé egg of a book, a Horta Lamp of a book, like Goethe's *Italian Journey*. After the psychological hell of my Norway trip, and the Lotta & Sophia-inspired disaster of my last Vienna holiday, how my travels have improved now. This has been the best holiday of my life.

96

My return to Munich has been difficult so far, fraught with little problems and misunderstandings. You should never return. I got several nice smiles from Eva in the Inter City breakfast this morning, yet nothing when I tipped her or asked her name. The smiles were really cute though. I do not want to leave München.

97

I realise now I am someone scared of relationships, who actively tries to stay out of the clutches of women. This trip to Wien and München has shown me this. I play hard to get, like a woman. Complete erotic devastation. Last night, to see Irina leave with another man just after 11, having laughed she would be spending the night with me, sleeping with me, coming back to my hotel. Because of that I could not bring myself to leave München this morning and ended up returning to the Regent for one more night. Having stayed, I now cannot face returning to the White Coffin tonight! I yearn to get on the 23:58 night train direct to Brussels and get out of here as quickly as possible! The bomb that caused chaos. I am in a mess now. Plus ça change. My holidays all end up like this. Because I cannot overcome my repression. I return home sombre and bitter, like Napoleon from Moscow. My features drawn and brooding. A Russian Salome this time. She lopped my head off 11 o'clock last night. It would restore much of my pride if I stayed in München tonight and did not go to the White Coffin. I do want yet another night of drunken debauchery. [I suspect I meant to say "I do NOT want another night of drunken debauchery" but accidentally missed out the "not"; a typically revealing Freudian slip]. I am tired of it. I have overdone it and left myself low and depleted and horribly sick of myself. Just for once, I want to be strong and not go back tonight.

98

I am bleeding to death. My bank account has suffered a massive haemorrhage. I do not know how I will recover. I have been on a journey of the soul on this holiday as always when one travels. I always return home emotionally cut up, bruised & battered, by emotional failures in love, and as

J.G.Ballard says all failures are ultimately failures in love. It ends, then, with a whimper not a bang.

99

My emeralds, bracelets & armbands, show a man fatally, tragically in love with himself, and frightened of getting involved with anybody else. That is why Susi & Irina & B— could not break through. Why I am now in a mess.

100

As time goes by I will increasingly come to think it is a good thing that I stayed pure and did not let myself get involved with Susi and Irina—but before I even finish the sentence I am overwhelmed by sadness if I do come to see it as a good thing. It would be desperately sad if I ever stopped feeling sad about what happened or didn't happen. Jokanaan should surely have f—ked Salome, all over the palace, at all times of day & night, and brought pleasure into his life and hers. Self-denying abnegation is a cause only for regret and shame.

101

At least once a week there comes a moment when I feel I am too autistic to keep on doing my job at the hotel and think I cannot go on and will have to relinquish my position. Every day of my life is hard when I have to try to get on with people. Sometimes it overwhelms me, and I want to break down and cry, really I do. *The Man Who Wasn't There*. Bela Bartok. "As a personality he almost didn't exist; but his impersonality was <u>tremendous</u>." Kaspar Hauser. King Ludwig II. Vincent Van Gogh. Edvard Munch. Friedrich Nietzsche. Søren Kierkegaard. Isaac Newton. I take shelter and solace in this community of fellow sufferers. Call it autism, call it schizoid personality disorder, call it Kaspar Hauser Syndrome, whatever it is it is a deep inability to relate to <u>people,</u> and in this world that does not forgive that it can be a crushing handicap. So one seeks silence and loneliness, to find relief from the crushing social pressure, like John Proctor having stones piled on his back in *The Crucible* until he confesses to something he didn't do. I have nothing to apologise for. Not much, anyway. Questing always, like Paul Delvaux—who was also frightened of women—for a serene initiation into love but ending up instead always in the firebombed Munich mansion. Any time I try to touch love the Zeppelins come over on their bombing raid and firebomb me to smithereens. Courting unpopularity. I got to see Prinz Lobkowitz's Palace, at last, in Vienna, which also saw the first performance of Beethoven's 3rd Symphony, another man who suffered terribly from his inability with women. Moonlight Sonata. Yet if I truly became a hermit I would miss out on the fleeting moments of conversation like all those I enjoyed with Natalia, for example, the kindest and warmest encounter of these two weeks in Europe. Yet I would have feared asking her out and feared even more if she had said yes. I am tired now, and just want to be home. With —. I read today that the superb Newsnight reporter Michael Crick lives with his mother, reminding me of Peter Sellers and Kenneth Williams who were inseparable from their mothers. There is something terribly touching about a man who lives with his mother, revealing a singular helplessness in their character which is lovable.

102

I'm like the Staten Island ferryman who apparently motionlessly, emotionlessly, let his ship crash into the pier, only then springing into action and sprinting from the scene without even bothering to pick up his keys, running 3 miles to his home, breaking in and barricading himself in his room, whereupon he tried to slit his wrists and shoot himself in the head and chest with an air gun. I know how he feels. What makes me freeze, as we sleepwalk into certain known disaster, urgently alive when it has happened, and it is too late to ever get the moment back again? It is, as ever, the Judge, in *La Chute*, the most terrifying, heartrending book ever written. "Now you're stuck in the moment and can't get out of it." It is Camus's Meursault, who cannot cry at his mother's funeral, and cannot feel anything, until he is finally on the scaffold on the edge of the starry night sky and surrounded by all the people yelling hatred at him—then he experienced his orgasm of pleasure, and joy, and exultation. Camus, who wrote in *The First Man* of his mother just staring out the window, singing to herself, and never cuddling him.

103

It is Lulu, whose lifetime dream was to be killed by a sex maniac and who finally got her wish when she met Jack. "Come on, I like you." My failure to let in Susi and Irina, my frozen inability to respond to the certain destruction, until they just got up and walked away, is the central defining mystery of this holiday, as it has been of my life. It is the mystery of love. Some part of me sees a certain charm, or glory, in having remained an inscrutable enigma to them, which will always make them freeze into sadness when they think about me, but, as I say, I think it is terribly sad that I think like that, even fleetingly. After all, my logic says, if I had slept with them, I would have been instantly forgettable to them, so this way I am guaranteed to stay in their memories for ever, the strange man who liked them but said no to them, and just walked away. Ha! Now you will always remember me. No one would remember Jokanaan and Salome if he had said yes to her. They would have done it and gone their separate ways (it probably would have been a disappointment). Instead he said no, and it has become one of the great stories of the world. The story of me and Susi & Irina has become the great, tragic pain-filled story of this holiday. The irony is that if they had said to me 50 Euros for sex I would have instantly said yes and done it with them, got it over with there & then. If they had let me pay them I would have instantly felt comfortable. Left in the minefield of emotion, however, and I could not take a step. I feared if I had said yes it would have turned into a disaster like Lotta and Chess Goddess, so instead, agonised, tortured, wanting so much but fearing so much, preferred to turn it into a disaster like P— and Stephanie and American Girl, et al. I fear more than anything not coming up to scratch, as I know I won't, and being let go. This of course stems from the moment I was born, when I did not come up to scratch and was let go. That has shaped my whole life. It is incredibly hard to get over it, and as I write, — years down the line, therefore impossible. To feel wanted, like when Susi's eyes met mine across the bar, and when Irina said she wanted to spend the night with me, is of course incredibly thrilling; but I always let the moment go, and never act on it; like I say, because I know I will not come up to scratch and will be let go, so better not to put myself in that position where they can let me go. This is my self-destructiveness. I let them go so they can't let me go.

104
Oh! But I really liked them!

105
Some people seem to warm to me, and accept me just fine the way I am, like Natalia, whereas others feel very uncomfortable to be around me. It requires a pretty amazing person who can accept me the way I am, I think. I will always remain as a question mark to Susi, and Irina. An unsolvable mystery. And part of me likes that, which makes me feel very sad. Something noble in saying no? No.

106
The nightmare will not end. Now I cannot get out of München. There were no seats left on the midnight train to Brussels, so I have come back to the hotel. I should have been home by now if I had left this morning as planned. I just want classical music and ferns again.

107

117

Beautiful clear blue skies over glowing green red yellow autumnal trees—the classic München weather. I am on my way home at last. Slate grey unmoving cloudy skies are Vienna's weather. I feared if I had said yes to Susi it would have opened up the floodgates, and I couldn't have that now, could I; like Sherlock Holmes with Irene Adler.

108

It is a cliché to say German railways are very efficient and well-run, but they really are fantastic. A German person perhaps could not comprehend the level of shock an English person experiences on a daily basis while using the German railway system. Oh, and the double-decker trains! The greatest culture shock of my first Grand Tour to Europe was the sight of double-decker trains! Absolutely startling! It is with a permanent sense of magical wonderment that English people encounter the Deutsche Bahn.

109

It is true that this has been the best holiday of my life—everything is relative—yet I still return home with deep melancholy: because of Susi & Irina. Acute sadness. As usual, by the end of my holiday, I have nothing left to give. I am running on empty. At an emotional and spiritual zero, because of my failure to take the opportunities for relationships that were offered to me. Susi. Irina. Natalia. S.I.N. A neat trick that fate has played on me. I stayed self-enclosed, pure and autistic and didn't let anyone get close to me, under my guard, yet they got under my skin all the same. It's always what you don't do that haunts you more than what you do. My missed opportunities are like a severed limb, and it takes several days for the bleeding to stop, the weeping to stop, and for the wound to start to close. We are now in the Channel Tunnel. The holiday is over. Orpheus has left the underworld.

110

Put everything behind you, and just hold onto the thought of seeing Susi again. My whole life revolves around that now. I must try to stop drinking before work. That would save me £40 a week to start with. £160 a month. Two nights in a hotel. By January I will have earned myself the train fare and four nights hotel money, just on savings alone. I cannot wait to get back to Brussels, and Munich and Wien. I still haven't got back to Berlin yet, and next time I must finally get to Rome. And cross the Rubicon to do it. We are now in England I think though it is night so hard to tell. Only by the change in sound do I tell we are out of the tunnel, but everything is pitch black, whereas we entered the tunnel under blue skies, with just a reddy hue to the clouds. So welcome back to the doom and Stygian gloom of England. A very apt transition. The young German couple suddenly get up and rush for the bar. I know how they feel.

111

I want to go back to München just to confirm that the spark with Susi is over, then I can go on with relief. I love being in love with some unobtainable woman. It in fact constitutes my ideal relationship.

CHAPTER 6
ON A SCALE
OF 1-10

On a scale of 1-10, my Enthusiasm Quotient when I left the house was no more than a 2. How to find the enthusiasm I need for this adventure? It seems as misguided as my return trip to see Stephanie in Brussels, and what a disaster that was when I arrived! Though I then met Nephania while watching Rooney make his debut for England v Turkey, which was a pretty amazing episode in my life. I require all of my old enthusiasm. The Oslo Spirit. Now, for the first time in my life, I am in a Lufthansa aeroplane. It is the haves vs the have nots. I did feel increasingly excited as the tube neared Heathrow. For the first time in my life, I am on a Lufthansa aeroplane.

113
We are flying into the night.

114
I was woken up by the bump of the plane landing on the runway. It was night already. Munich airport was shrouded in mist. Dreadfully beautiful. Then I noticed everywhere was white. The airport was covered in snow. Only the runways were clear of it. They say Munich is one of the best places in the world for Christmas, and I wish I had come here two weeks ago to spend Christmas here. Next Christmas I will do that. We taxied speeding past rows of parked Lufthansa planes. The Lufthansa bird a yellow phoenix from the flames. Munich airport was virtually empty, white, shiny, sparklingly clean, like a hospital (not an English hospital). Like Una Persson in *The Entropy Tango*. I found my way easily enough down onto the S-Bahn, changed at F—, onto a U-Bahn for the ride into Hauptbahnhof and the hotel. The same pretty receptionist from last time. It was 7PM and the bar/restaurant was empty. Just a group of people around one table. This hotel seems just as empty as the one I had just left in Moloch. The whoring scene in Munich seems more complicated than in London. There is a whole courtship ritual to go through here! You have to go to the bar, buy an

expensive drink, sit with the girl talking to her, buying her an even more expensive drink, then go to a room, have a bottle of champagne, very expensive massage before sex(?). In London it is so quick and easy and animal. There is too much talking required here. Socialising. I am not comfortable in the Munich clubs. They make me too self-conscious. Vienna is the same. I fear they would be disasters. Anyway, the sexiest contacts are in the opera house, the concert halls, the art museums and cathedrals. I make my home in Munich between the Inter City, the Regent Hotel bar and restaurant, the Wolff, the Opera. Trapattoni is going to Spurs. *Lost in Translation* has just come out. A man alone in a strange city.

115
The more you do, the more you get back. The more wild & brave & delirious you are, the more reward you get.

116
How I upset the lowlifes.

117
I got the No.19 tram to the opera to buy my *Fledermaus* ticket, then walked to St Peter's church and the incredible Asamkirche—a must see for anyone coming to Munich. I bought some Puccini boots and then had the most beautiful meal of my life in Lamm's in Sendlinger Tor Platz. Got the No.27 then up to Neue Pinakothek. It was incredibly powerful to see Die Sünde. I couldn't find it at first and was walking around and around in circles thinking it had been removed, until I asked an attendant and she led me to it. After that, all of the pictures seemed so much better.

118
No Doubt It's My Life. Maurice Denis The Crown 1901. Lovis Corinth Thomas & Wilhelmina 1916. The Red Child 1922. Egon Schiele Agony 1912. Cathedral Towering Over a Town 1813. Karl Friedrich Schinkel. Building of the Devil's Bridge. Blechen 1830/32. Picasso's Head of Jester 1905. The Ecstatic Virgin Anna Katharina Emmerich. Gabriel von Max 1885. The Anatomist 1865. Khnopff I locked my door upon myself 1891. Redon The Cathedral 1914. Degas Woman Ironing 1869. Anna Netrebko. Evanescence Immortal. Junior Senior. Frank Popp Ensemble Hip Teens (Don't Wear Blue Jeans). J-Lo Let's Get Loud. Jay Z Threat. Like A Virgin. Shut Up. Limp Bizkit. Luisa Blabusch. So the era of Susi & Irina is over. It is funny, after I got back from Munich last time, I thought Heidi Klum really reminded me of Susi. Now outside my hotel room is a 30ft billboard poster

of Heidi Klum lying on her back in black bra and knickers. I look down on the three pink top telephones and the entrance to the station. The back of the Coca-Cola sign. I wish I had a camera with me. Patricia was the only one still there from last time. No one else special. Nothing like last time. No Susi. No Irina. No Romanian in the tight trousers. The music was good though. A really great song at the beginning which I infuriatingly cannot remember. I have got to go to the opera tonight, so I won't get back there until late.

119

The Neue Pinakothek now rivals the Museum of Modern Art in Brussels as a site of pilgrimage. Massive-breasted American black woman in brown jumper in the Inter City lobby, waiting with cases. Katerina in the bar serving me my three vodka & cokes. The Asamkirche. The Puccini boots. The Alt Wiener Rostbraten in Lamm's. Die Sünde in the N.P. My hotel room 305 looking down on the Hauptbahnhof entrance, the back of the Coca-Cola sign, the three pink top telephones, and opposite the Heidi Klum poster. Patricia in the White Coffin. She is so funny on stage, and such a fantastic dancer. She is so full of life and livens up the deadest proceedings with her sheer good nature. The incredibly beautiful black girl in the Limp Bizkit video. "And my dreams they are just empty." Sugababes Lost in You.

120

A lot of the shops and restaurants have still got some Christmas trees outside their doorways. I am definitely going to spend Christmas in Munich this year, God willing. "Du hast mein herz". This must be the first trip I've been on where I haven't fallen in love with someone! Last year it was Stephanie, and Nephania and American girl, then Susi & Irina. Before that Lotta & Sophia. I have had no erotic encounters at all. Not one returned gaze. I have, after all, only been here one day. Thursday was spent just getting here. I am so relieved Susi & Irina weren't there. I walked in, dreading the moment when they set eyes on me. Motel corridor walls with glowing hieroglyphic writing covering the walls. Today I just want to try to buy a disposable camera to take a picture of Heidi Klum, have lunch at Lamm's again, then go to the opera and back to the White Coffin.

121

As usual, the morning after the night before, I feel sad and down. Empty. I overslept and so missed the chance to go to the opera, going straight to the club instead, feeling so sleepy. B— came and sat straightaway on my lap, kissed me open wet kisses which I could not respond to. She gave me her

Brazil flag and pulled me in to watch her dance. Afterwards she came back to me, kissing me wet kisses and tongues. Again, I could not respond, and we had nothing more to do with each other after that. I felt bad and ashamed. Patricia came and draped one leg over mine, asking me if I wanted a dance. When I said no she pointed at B— and screamed accusingly as if it were her fault "Pah!" She is incredibly sexy, though, and as the night wore on I wanted her more and more. At ten to one I went out and got more money, came back in. There were just four people left. She came off stage, went to man to my left, then to me, and this time I said yes. She was very hot. I got my cock out and she put some kitchen roll over her breasts to catch my issue. I, of course, was too tight to finish. That's the thing I feel most sad and empty about this morning. If I could have come over her, it would have been fantastic. "No fucking! No fucking!" I want her again. It was the sexiest, hottest, dirtiest encounter of my life. Afterwards, she wouldn't even look at me. Both of us just politely kept out of each other's way. Earlier, she had been pulling her top back on in the cubicle behind me, having just finished a lap dance for someone. That was the first close up look I got at her incredible breasts, beautiful nipples. That was when I started to want her. As she came past me she squeezed the back of my neck. Later, just before I went with her, she squeezed my nipple as she went past, saying "what's up darling?" I want to come back to Munich to see her again.

122

Scooter Weekend. Benny Benassi Satisfaction (Dirty). "When you get into a serious drug dependency, the tendency is to push it as far as you can". The Boogie Pimps Somebody to Love. Lovestern Galaktika Project Superstar. Junior Senior. Steve Murano Passion. Paul van Dyk Nobody but You. Joy Kitikonti Porno Joy. There is no doubt the 1970s are the golden age of porn. "I want to kiss you, but I want it too much".

123

I hate leaving. I went to my window one last time to say goodbye to Heidi Klum. I realise she is looking right at me. Lying on her back, looking right in at me. I should have got a few of those Moleskine notebooks, they are just perfect. No doubt I will be back in München in a few weeks' time. It is no hardship to go back to the N.P. I am living on the never-never. Always spending money that I haven't got. I was so nervous in the hotel this morning. Like I say, I hate leaving. If I could only learn German and get a job in a Munich hotel.

124

I feel sort of ashamed, or humiliated, or embarrassed by my behaviour in the club, especially with Patricia. At the same time, it is my most thrilling memory of this trip to Munich, and it excites me to think of it even now. I really regret that I was too tight to really get my pleasure from it. I have never done something so deliciously rude, and shocking, and debauched, and depraved. In a séparée by no means closed off to others' gazes I made love to Patricia who let me come all over her breasts (if I had been able). While feverishly mauling her I at one point looked up and saw the back of two people's heads on the other side of the gangway, just four feet away—and we still kept on doing it. For European males this is perhaps quite common and normal, but for someone coming from tightly ruled and constricted London where such behaviour would be strictly verboten and quite possibly an arrestable offence it was quite quite thrilling and intoxicating. Séparées! Ah, séparées! The glory of Europe—of Berlin and Munich and Vienna—is the séparée. The greatest thing Central Europe has given to civilisation; and as Freud teaches us civilisation is based on the suppression of the erotic. Here in the séparée it may be gloriously channelled and released. I want it again. I want Patricia again. Illicit sex in London is up back alleyways, up back stairways. Here in Germany and Austria it is in stripclubs and girlie bars, gloriously celebrated and exultantly carried out.

125

My train has got to split in two, like a worm, and the two halves are going to different places. I hope I am on the right half of the worm. Out here by the airport the snow is still very much on the ground, albeit patchy. A lovely big Airbus coming, a puny little Lufthansa pig going back home. Me going to Munich and Vienna and Berlin is in the tradition of people like Joe Orton and Kenneth Williams and innumerable others going to Tangier in the 50s and 60s. I will get eaten as inevitably as Sebastian in *Suddenly Last Summer*. F.G.Lorca in Cuba. "Yes, it was a very powerful election."

126

My sex life causes me unhappiness and shame. All fake love, fake passion, which nevertheless occasionally approaches moments of real tenderness. Just because a financial transaction has taken place it does not preclude real attraction, closeness, desire, tenderness. But it is always short-lived and can never last. I think I did cross some barrier this time. Crossed some Rubicon. Last year I would not go into the sépareé with Susi & Irina, and so lost the chance to get closer to them. Can you imagine what an opportunity I lost! Particularly with Irina. Can you imagine that towering 6ft white blonde

Russian Amazonian goddess right on top of me? I certainly leave Munich in better spirits than last time, though still sad, down, troubled, under a cloud...about what? That I entered into only bad relationships. By that meaning I did not manage to form any good or happy relationships. My attempts to form relationships on this trip were not successful. From somewhere close to me on the plane I can suddenly smell Patricia's perfume.

127

I was quite incredibly unattacked in this three-night stay in Munich. I was attacked before I got to — Station. Then I cannot remember the next attack until getting off the train at the airport. I was still nervous about going out most of the time, which required me getting drunk before leaving my room or the hotel, which resulted in me oversleeping and missing the opera I wanted to go to see. So what fleeting relationships did I flirt with entering into? The receptionist who checked me in. We exchanged some nice encouraging smiles. Met Katerina in the bar and again exchanged some nice smiles. Maria from before. Frosty stony glare from woman at the opera. Station café lady with tight purple trousers was nice. Did OK in Lamm's. Got quite close with B— on my first night in the club, but withdrew from her totally on the second night, which must have bewildered and hurt her a bit, as it did myself.

128

I only had two full days in Munich, the Friday and Saturday. On the Friday I did well, went to the opera to buy my ticket, went to St Peter's, Asamkirche, bought my sexy Italian boots, had the most gorgeous meal of my life in Lamm's, went back out to the club in the evening and had my first ever séparée experience, with B—, which bought some real closeness between us. She must have told Patricia that I wanted to fuck, as everyone turned around to look at me. Patricia stepped up to me with B— by her side. I cannot remember what she said at first but after I told her I had no money it was "No money, no fucking". It did tickle me. I left about 11:30 to get to Sexyland, looking forward to the same great films as last time, but that was a disaster. I got back to my hotel feeling somewhat frustrated, feeling I had in some way repressed myself and held back from going all the way with something. Probably because I did not pursue the closeness with B—; she wanted me to buy her a glass of red wine—at normal prices not the exorbitant mark ups when buying drinks for the girls—she looked hurt when I said no, but grinned when I said how much is it, and fetched me a beer from the bar. We were getting on well and I ruined it the next night by doing nothing at all, withdrawing from her completely. Anyway, I should have gone on to do something with Patricia as well that first night. The fact is I got back to my hotel feeling frustrated because I had not fucked.

129

Saturday, I hardly did anything at all, apart from my vodkas in the bar (5) before stepping outside the hotel. I enjoyed another gorgeous meal in Lamm's but nearly fell asleep at my table trying to finish my beer. Popped into Hertie on the way back to buy a disposable camera, having told everybody I wanted to take a picture of Heidi Klum in her underwear outside my window. "Pussy!" said Maria to the other barmaid, quite surprisingly actually. Got the fluffy giant dog, which was a mistake, and went back to the hotel. Then fell into a deep alcoholic sleep and missed the opera. Woke up 8PM and went straight to the club, my head full of cotton wool and cobwebs, deep sleepiness, which affected my ability to walk and left me feeling dead and lifeless and killed the relationship with B—, who greeted me so warmly and enthusiastically. Sitting on my lap, giving me her Brazil flag, pulling me by the hand inside to watch her dance, telling everybody "He's my man". How that echoes Lela who kept singing "I'm Your Man" over and over the night before my birthday. B— kept giving me deep open mouth kisses which I had no vitality to respond to. She obviously felt this and became increasingly hurt until we had no further contact whatsoever.

130

So Saturday was a bit of a drunken waste. I didn't feel like drinking for hours, so drank a lot more than I wanted to try to force myself into wanting to drink. I am really angered at myself for missing the opera. It would have been the highlight and centrepiece of the trip, like *I Due Foscari* in Brussels was. But at least it ended on a suitably dangerous note when I all but fucked Patricia in the séparée. Patricia was actually going to let me come on her breasts and I would have done so had I not been too tight to come. I think what hurt me though was that she made no effort to continue the relationship outside the séparée. In fact, very pointedly ignored me when I came out, a few minutes after her. That hurt me, perhaps on purpose, as they perhaps felt I had hurt her friend B—. I finally left the club about 2 when it was just closing. B— and Patricia were there with their jeans and coats on. Why did I get back to the hotel with such a nagging gnawing sense of things having gone wrong, the feeling which now clouds my homeward journey with worry? What could I have done differently? Drunk less so I had come over Patricia. What a chance missed! Got on better with her afterwards, but that was not really my fault. It would have been nice if we could have at least parted warmly. Then I head sobbing back to London. Hard to take waking up Sunday to pack and get the train to the airport.

131

A relationship based on love. Ha! That would be a first. My relationships are all based on lust and money having changed hands. What could have gone better? I could have come with Patricia and gone to the opera. I could have continued the frisky relationship with B— instead of cutting her, though it was beyond my control. I was powerless to inject any life into my interaction with her on the second night. Again, echoes of my relationship with Lela. I burst through barriers to bring myself to something real with them, then throw it away again the very next time I see them. Hurting them and confusing them and making them angry and bitter towards me.

132

It was incredible how little attacked I was in Munich. Ha! We'll see how that changes when I set foot in Moloch. Like Messerschmidts approaching the English coast, as my Lufthansa pig does now, the wall of flak will hit me. Since they announced we had commenced our final approach to London we have seen absolutely nothing. Thick dirty grey fog outside the window. When we finally emerge out of it we will probably see that London is not there anymore. You always worry when you come back that London is not going to be there, don't you? Like when the Millennium Falcon comes out of hyperspace to find Alderaan is not there. "I've got a very bad feeling about this." With the butterflies on my wrist I perhaps proclaim a slight effeminacy. Good old London! Wind and lashing rain as we finally emerge from the cloud just seconds before hitting the runway. It is so reassuring to come back to good old English weather. Now we taxi past one British Airways plane after another, as we taxied past one Lufthansa plane after another at Munich.

CHAPTER 7
THE
WHITE
COFFIN

The White Coffin is a fantastic club. Every time I come back from there I feel I have been through some intense emotional experience. The man getting a blowjob from a girl in the corner, with everyone crowding around. Then Susi & Irina. Now B— and Patricia. The music is great, loud and thumping. The dancers are fantastic, Brazilian mainly (!). My bad behaviour is now accelerating rather than coming to an end. Like the jet plane suddenly putting its foot down and surging along the runway I want to get back on those planes and back to Munich and Berlin and Brussels.

134

It would be good if I could go back to Munich every month. I want Patricia again. Yet I will become as tired of it as I have become of the Scotsman if I am not careful. I want to try Berlin as well. Yet Berlin frightens me. In Munich it is so easy and relaxed. In Berlin I want to see Nefertiti and the Story of Berlin exhibition. I have left so much blood on the tracks in Munich, though. I feel no desire to go anywhere else. I feel exposed in Berlin in a way I don't in Munich or Vienna. I need to pay a series of visits back to Munich, one after the other, the way I did with Brussels last year. It is the only way to get it out of my system. Yes, I will become tired of it, and I will spoil it, and do it to death, but if I tried to go anywhere else I would just be wishing I was in Munich. The only way to avoid temptation is to give in to it. Each man kills the thing he loves. I loved Brussels until I killed it, with my increasingly sickly morbidity. I will kill Munich, too. I have to kill it before I can be free of it & move on. I have to completely use it up and suck it dry, until I throw away the used husk, and I move on bloated and replete, sated and sick, to find somewhere else to feed my lust. It is Munich that has stimulated my lust now. I must see it through to the end, the way I saw

Brussels through to the end. I am hooked into a fatal morbid obsession with it now. I have just noticed we have an Orlowsky staying in the hotel at the moment. Having just missed *Die Fledermaus* on Saturday this seems a little shocking. The performance I missed was the fourth of eight. I have another chance on 20, 22 and 24 of February. Once something catches my attention I become obsessive about it, until I do it to death. My visits to Munich can revolve around the opera! I discover what I had once known but long forgotten, that Peter Jonah is the head of the Munich opera! Like my debauchery in London always revolved around my nights at the opera it will now become that way with Munich. Oh, but how can I find the money?! My whole life now revolves around getting back to Munich as often as I can, to go to the opera.

135

I haven't been with it at all since I got back from Munich. Stressed and tense, feeling ill at ease. I think I am slowly getting my excitement back now, though. The growing feeling that, yes, I will definitely be going back to Munich within the next two weeks is exciting me and lifting my spirits. I go to Munich to "court the wicked woman". For the delicious "moral decline". As represented by von Stuck's Die Sünde in the Neue Pinakothek. Now the delicious idea of permanently linking the opera and the brothel, as once I used to do in Moloch, has regenerated me.

136

München is the town of Von Stuck. I feel small, and squeezed tight, shrivelled like a prune. The Intercity was built in the 1870s in fine jugendstil style but was blown to bits in World War II. The same for the Europäischer Hof. Oh God. Mein Gott, I can't wait to get back there now. To lose myself in the jugendstil memories of the Intercity. In Von Stuck's Salome and Die Sünde. In Henriette Hardenberg. There are just tiny minimalist modernist touches that are traces of the Intercity's 1870 jugendstil past. The curling silver lampstands. The globe lamps. I hate it when things go wrong. When everything feels soured. The only thing that can make me feel better, then, is the misfortune of others. I feel better for opening my heart to people, to show them how upset I was feeling. I draw positivity from that. It is good to show one's vulnerability. You're allowed one mistake; but of course I do not feel that. I am going back to lose myself in the jungle of Munich. "Dusk, shed by a lamp, brightens the tears." I lie still and fearless when you enter. I am feeling small, and defeated, at this moment; but it will pass. Damn. Damn my moment of taking my eye off the ball. I will learn from it and be stronger from it.

137

There is no one I want in London. Only people I want in Munich. Who would have thought Munich would have become my most important place? I always used to stop off in Munich on the way from Brussels to Wien, but I always used to think: what for? That all changed when I came through the doorway and set eyes on Susi. The city of Franz von Stuck. Of Salome and Die Sünde.

CHAPTER 8
THIS
IS
MADNESS

This is madness. Every time I go back to Munich I am just digging at an old wound—the wound of having missed my chance with Susi—so it is not at all a healthy thing for me to do. It is, however, in keeping with the mood of sickly morbid eroticism that is my life, that is the eternal flame at the heart of me. If my enthusiasm quotient was 2 last time, this time it is even less. Sonia Ganassi was good. I very much enjoyed it. And it was pleasant before that in the Calcutta. I finally relented and put some money in the jukebox. It was fantastic to bring that place back to life again. I even got a smile from Aureline. The selection is not very large but there was at least Sugababes Hole in the Head, Jamelia, Benny Benassi, Avril Lavigne. What am I going back to Munich for? To go back to the White Coffin, the opera, get a Philharmonie listing, visit Stuck's grave.

139

My journey to Munich seemed so much easier than last time. I had some extraordinary eye contact with three different girls at Heathrow. The pretty Indian girl explaining cameras in Dixons. I got a lovely smile from her as I left. The brown ponytail girl in red leather jacket, grey trousers in the departure lounge and in red striped top on the plane. I got from the airport to the hotel easily. Same receptionist and manager from last time, they just took my signature and the girl had a little smile on her face (which I attributed to me leaving the giant white fluffy dog in my room when I left last time, with a note stuck on him in pidgin German, asking someone to find a loving home for him. 'The only person I know here is Maria, in the bar'). After a beer and two vodkas in the bar I went straight out to the White Coffin. As I expected it was much busier and prettier than before. The place was very crowded. B— was there but very low profile and almost invisible tonight, when normally she is so dominant. Later I got a little kiss and a hug from her, but she still looked sad and hurt. By contrast, Patricia was all over me. Kissing me on the lips, turning my head around with her hands to look at what the barber had done to me. She was happy and smiling. Then it was her turn to dance and as she moved away I pulled her back by her knickers, so she screamed and came back and hit me with her wrap. Later, she two or three times came by me and pressed the wrap over my eyes. She was lovely. Also there was Vanessa and Daniella, two new Romanians, Christina and the absolutely sensational Michelle. Long black-haired, beautiful sexy face, incredible breasts. I told her "Saturday" and she smiled "I don't believe you". I had two beers, three vodka & cokes, and two more beers. 38 Euros. Then I crossed another personal Rubicon by going into two of the girlie bars. As I got into the first one I spoke to a blonde girl who explained the rules and was laughing because I was "sweet". It would be 45 Euros and you would maybe get a blowjob only. I'd had so much to drink I could not contemplate giving in to temptation. It was just a reconnaissance mission. Like Roy Scheider's "You're going to need a bigger boat" I suddenly realised "You're going to need more money!" Now I know I can go into those places completely relaxedly, just buy a beer, someone will come to me and I can go for a 45 Euros. I will not go to the White Coffin but will maybe try one of the other bars.

140

I was sick in the lavatory when I got back to my hotel, the first time that has happened for 13 years! Being sick was by no means as bad as I remembered it. I met Andy the young German in the hotel bar. We were passed by ten American women, some of them with very enormous breasts. Just now, looking at the little pig in the toy shop, I turned to go and saw the incredible shoe shop girl in tight red jumper. I went back into Asamkirche as I was passing to Lamm's. I have got to go back to the opera, get a new programme, then probably back to the hotel. I don't know what the matter with me is. I feel so listless. I didn't really want to go down for breakfast, didn't really want to go to the opera, the club, private dance, anything. Beautiful black-haired girl waiting for tram outside Lamm's. She looked up as I got off, then another one getting the tram back from the opera. She walked to & fro past me a couple of times. I was feeling a bit frazzled by the time I got back to Hauptbahnhof. No tickets left for *Rhinegold* tonight or even *Robert Devereux* last night. I will try the Philharmonie tonight. And N.P. I feel so flat and becalmed. Lost in a fog.

141

Augustiner is a nice beer. Brewed in Munich since 1328! I think I just lost my nerve a bit in Munich this time. On the first night, just off the plane, I was on a high, excited to be back in Munich. Lovely to see Patricia again, Michelle seemed so sexy. Friday night was a big mistake. Michelle had no effect on me whatsoever. I didn't get turned on once. "So sau, so sau" Patricia said to me twice, near the end, grabbing my crotch. It was nice, it was the first time she had acknowledged me after three hours. I left soon after that. Another 20 in Lamm's. The prevailing trait of my life "I give up on myself". I am scared to go with Patricia again, even more scared of the intelligent, saucy Michelle.

142

It is crazy what Germany did to itself. All right, they were British and American bombs, but Germany brought this on itself. The pictures of Munich in 1945 are incredible. The Trummelbahns. I have got to get out of Munich. It was an adventure. Strange things. Things that once seemed incredible now become usual. I can't even remember her name. Emily, was it? She was from Romania anyway. The news from Patricia blew my mind and sent me wildly off the rails for the rest of the night. It knocked me for six. "Why not? Why not?" I kept asking her, as this time she would not let me remove my cock from my trousers. "B—, B—," she kept muttering, before finally coming out with it in faltering English. "Because B—, I love you. You understand? B—, I love you." "B— loves me?" "Yes." And because Patricia is B—'s friend from Brazil she could no longer do anything with me or touch me. "But I love YOU," I said. "You must love B—," she said. Her smile was so lovely, like the Virgin Mary to the Baby Jesus. There was now no longer any reason not to drink so I went straight for the double vodkas. From there my path of destruction commenced. I came out into the thick and new and continuing never-ending snowstorm. I went into the first club from before. So moved on to the second and there met Emily and could not control myself. I could not control myself to the tune of 275. "I'm not a houri!" she said giggling. "In English?" A whore, I said. "Yes! I am not a whore!", killing herself laughing. That covers a three-night stay in the hotel. So, I just will not travel again when I was going to, to make up for it. There may be further repercussions, however, but hey, it was an adventure. It was an incredible adventure. After that I walked around in the snow, putting off returning to my hotel time and again in heavy snowfall. I didn't even feel drunk and I didn't even feel cold. A quite extraordinary straightness and nihilistic serenity had settled over me as deeply as the snow. I walked to Karlsplatz—an incredibly beautiful sight in the snow—then back along Bayerstraβe to Hauptbahnhof. I had a nice exchange with the night manager. "Isn't it beautiful?" I said. He looked baffled. "The snow!" I said. "Is it snowing?" he said, in shock. Then went to the window "My God!" It had been snowing for 8 hours non-stop, there was deep snow covering Munich everywhere, and he remained completely oblivious to it until I told him. I left him gazing out the front door to look at it.

143

I watched the snow falling and the trams passing in it for another half-hour or so from my window. It started snowing again just as I came into the hotel to get the tram back to the Flughafen. It was Munich like the Busby Babes knew it, the icy morgue as their plane tried to take off from the snowbound airport. I told Patricia I was going back to London tomorrow. "When will you be back?" she said. "One month," I said. But it will be at least six months before I travel again. Things got too intense this time. I went too far. Coming out of the clubs I thought to myself "To think I wasn't going to come out tonight!" It is quite incredible what I would have missed. What has to be the most incredible night of my life. Patricia was smiling fondly to me as she told me how B— talked about me, "That's my baby. That's my baby". When I saw B— Thursday night she seemed so quiet and subdued. She wasn't the same person from before. A change had come over her. Michelle is lovely, and so is Masha. They both remind me a lot of Susi. How far ago that incident now seems. How far I have left that behind and dived ever deeper into darkness. Every time you travel something happens, but this time too much happened, and I have scared myself. No, it was an adventure, and I am pleased with all of it. I went too far, and it is only then that things become enjoyable. I am sure I have not heard the last of my night at Club F.

144

I have to get out of Munich. Its morbid sickly eroticism totally consumed me on Saturday night. The big black snake around Die Sünde's neck coiled itself around me and crushed me to death. I courted the wicked woman. I gave in to sin. Now more than ever like *The VIPs* my flight to London has been cancelled due to the snow and the fact the plane is not where it should be. I must now go 55 minutes later and changing at Frankfurt. I feel stressed, thrilled, worried about repercussions. It is an amazing thing, however, to have someone tell you that somebody else loves you. I was doing brilliantly with my spending, until the very last moment. I went out with a bang.

145

This trip to Munich was more farcical, more comical, more tragic, more beautiful, more scandalous, than anything before. Yet still I am sure I have barely even scratched the surface of what sin can offer. I have barely even dipped my toe in the waters. The further I go the further I realise there is for me to go. Every time you enter a new room you see a whole vista of doorways & halls & staircases leading to other places in front of you. My Eros was opening up like a rosebud blooming & blossoming & unfolding all its petals. Something quite wonderful was happening to me.

146

The grey gun-metal hangars at Frankfurt Airport look so familiar then I remember they are Zeppelinesque. They look like Zeppelin sheds. The dark grey of USAF KC-135s and Starlifters I always used to see at Mildenhall and Lakenheath.

CHAPTER 9
INCREDIBLE
NEW
POSSIBILITIES

Incredible new possibilities have opened up for me. I now know I can walk into the bars in Vienna totally relaxed. And in Berlin. Whole new vistas have opened up for me.

148

Did it all really happen? As always, I am still in another world when I return to work from holiday. I have been living in such an unreal world for four days it is hard to come back to reality. As usual, I crucify myself for every little cretinous mistake I make. And torture myself with self-loathing and self-consciousness. Patricia, B—, Michaela. Emily. "The dreams in which I'm dying are the best I've ever had". I always suffer a post-holiday crisis of confidence. Instead of days on end fuelled by drink and fantasy and sex, I spend days on end sober. My identity disintegrates. I feel very aware of my own loathsomeness and uselessness at this moment. You're made to feel so desirable living in that Wedekindian world of brothels. The hour of the flesh goes on and on and you don't want it to ever end. The world seems so grey afterwards. It is a drug. It is an addiction. When can I get back to Munich again? But it will be so much better if I leave it a long while. If I wait until March or April. Annoy people more and more, that is always an inspiration. Do worse and worse. I have got a good job, and I should value it. It is a safe place for me. A safe harbour from the storms. Somewhere I can always come back to. I only want to live in that world. Munich has got into my bloodstream, in the way no other place has. I am infected with it. "The tendency is to push it as far as you can".

149

Once again I am crippled by mortification. I am so easily mortified. What Patricia told me was a good thing. At first things are easy. Then the longer you go on the more you become aware you are walking in a minefield. You become increasingly fearful of taking a single step lest you put a foot wrong and feel amazed that you were never blown up before. So many people come in all happy and confident, and become increasingly troubled and hesitant as time goes by. Nietzsche and Kraus are my gods.

150

I never knew there was a naked woman in *The Third Man* before. In a very strange scene, Holly Martins, after being shown the evidence of and finally believing his friend's guilt, goes to a go-go bar to get drunk, and while he watches the topless girl dancing on stage, six girls sitting at the bar watch him. After what Patricia told me I did the same thing. When Ernest Dowson was drunk it is said he became quite literally insane, and it has much the same effect on me. On my return from Munich the matinée films on Channel 4 on consecutive days were *The Third Man* and *The Man Between*.

151

A life of whoring and drinking. What I do between times in the hotel is irrelevant to me. I couldn't care less about anything there. The real life is increasingly unreal to me. Only the phantom world feels real now. What Vienna was to me, Brussels became to me, then what Brussels had become to me, Munich became to me.

152

All I want to do is travel and write. I am diving deeper into darkness and it is absolutely fantastic. Every time I travel I cross another Rubicon and go further than ever before. I am losing it. I should be grateful just to hang onto the job I've got. I've made two bad mistakes in the last two weeks, brought about by my difficulty in coping with the return to reality after the fantasies of my Munich trips. I am living in Never-Never Land. It is frightening how far I am now going and how aware I am that I have barely even started. Exploring sin. My mind has not been right since Christmas.

153

I went to the *Wagner and his World* exhibition in the Munich Stadtmuseum. It produced several epiphanies in me, several orgasms of the soul. That to me is spirituality. I was moved and transported and carried away, like the people in the marvellous Beardsley pictures that the exhibition also included. How fantastic to be brought face to face with

Beardsley so far from home! As it is an epiphany to turn a corner to see a Bacon, especially a Pope. What an epiphanic moment it was in Vienna in October to enter the room and find myself surrounded by a dozen or more Popes on every side of me, on all four walls. After the Wagner, moved, not wanting to go, I went into the city history part of the museum and was moved by all the pictures of Munich in rubble after the war. It is mind-numbing what the Germans did to themselves, what they brought on themselves. The pain they had to live through for so many dark, cold years before they pulled themselves up by their bootstraps and got back on their feet again. That is why I love Germany so much. They have destroyed themselves so many times, then picked themselves up and became powerful again. Moved, I did not want to go home after what Patricia told me either, and walked around in the thick snow, as the snow kept falling, and found my way eventually to Emily. That, too, was an epiphany. After that I just walked in the deepening snow and increasing snowfall, to Sonnenstraße, to Stacchus and the Justiz Palast, then back to Hauptbahnhof, and through the Hauptbahnhof from the other side, back to my hotel by the longest route possible. Then I spoke to the night manager, turning at last to take the concluding steps up to bed, and even then, knelt at my window for an hour watching the snow fall, and the night trams pass. It was the night to end all nights.

154

What did I do in Munich? Crazy things. Many crazy things. It is amazing what I am capable of. It is quite glorious. I have these great lost treasures: the statuette. The pack of 1970s playing cards. The *Nana* programme. If I had these cards I wouldn't need to go and do a lot of things that I go and do. I may never even have started. I can't stop now. I want my room to look like a Berlin study. "I think they've tapped into the zeitgeist." "Isn't that dangerous?"

155

I have left so much blood on the tracks in Munich all right. Munich is awash with my blood. I am choking on it. On my last night I came out of my hotel at 9PM to find it had started snowing. My fate was sealed. From the doorway of the White Coffin I watched the snow continuing to fall all night. I stood mesmerised by it. I cannot remember the last time I've seen snow falling. Snow is normally only ever something I open the bedroom curtains in the morning to find covering the gardens. I have never I think been out & about in an actual snowstorm. Thrilled, enervated, dangerously sensitised, I renewed my tryst with Patricia only to learn that her friend was in love with

138

me. Devastated, shocked, blown away, I started drinking, having at that point only been holding a cup of coke in my hands. I left soon afterwards, out into the still falling snow, now thick and deep and beautiful underfoot. I went in another club, then The Three Cats, where I met Emily, and lost myself. When I emerged it was after 3, the snow was ever deeper, and falling ever more heavily. I walked in as big a circle as I could find to get back to my hotel. The night manager knew nothing of the snow, even though it had been falling without stop for 8 hours and was shocked when I pointed it out to him and I left him rushing to the front door to look at it. The walk back to the hotel through the snow will always rank as one of the most beautiful epiphanic moments of my life. This is what I travel for. Still shaking from what Patricia had told me, and what I had just shared with the Romanian, the snow lifted my feelings onto a whole different plane where they have never been before.

156
Now I am going to the city of George Grosz and Otto Dix. Of Hildegard Knef and Head Status: Chopped Off.

157
It is amazing to think I have been to Berlin three times now and I have still not even dipped my toes into sin there. I hope to put that right this time.

CHAPTER 10
THE MOST
AMAZING
SERENDIPITY

The most amazing serendipity blessed my last trip to Munich. I travelled under lucky stars. From the moment I left home to the moment I returned to my room in the early hours I felt I was living a charmed life. There is none of that feeling now, as I prepare to go to Berlin. I am tense, and a bundle of nerves, suppression, repressions from the past. I have never in my life felt as turned on as I do at the start of this journey to Berlin. As I left the house the most incredible feeling of elation and anticipation rose up in me. It helps that today—February 11th—feels like the first day of spring. As I left the hotel this morning and headed the short distance up Oxford Street towards Marble Arch everywhere was grey, heavy, steamy, and oppressive. A coat was quite unnecessary. Coming down the station approach birds were twittering in the trees like it was an idyllic cherry blossom summer day. I expected to see daffodils, and bluebells. I am dangerously excited. I also feel a lot of fear, too. Berlin is the most important city in the world to me, and for that reason I come home filled with trepidation and foreboding. I am scared of feeling so excited. I have never done anything in Berlin before, and I am scared of my nerve failing me again. Incredible to be going past the Grosvenor Park Hotel on the No.73 bus this morning, and the Dorchester, when in a few hours I can be going past the Eden, and the Adlon. How fantastic that Berlin's main railway station is Berlin Zoo. After the long journey across Europe, across the German border, alongside the Rhine, past Köln, one finally ends one's journey by pulling to a halt in Berlin Zoo, conjuring up images of Rousseau, and lush tranquillity, macaws & parrots & howler monkeys.

159

You are entering the jungle now. The rails of iron are entering the jungle. There is soot on the leaves. We are Edwardnauts. Voyaging into another age, another epoch, another universe.

160
I have lost my Berlin virginity.

161
A good way to make up for all the repression of previous visits.

162
Now I want THE OSCAR WILDE, ALTE NATIONAL GALLERY, PERGAMON, STAATSOPER, KONZERTHAUS.

163
The receptionist at the Kant Hotel this morning, brown sweater, small but beautiful breasts, beautiful sexy face, brown ponytail. She booked the *Tannhauser* ticket for me. The most beautiful girl I have seen for a long time.

164
The smoky taste on the lips of the prostitutes. Yulia here in Berlin, Emily in Munich. It is so cheap here. For 50 euros, everything. When was the last time I came with a girl? Mai probably, in November. They are all obsessed with horoscopes, "what star sign are you?" I came out of the videokabins of the Berlin Erotic Centre in Lewishamstraße (!) with a massive erection that would not go down—pausing in a snowy side-street to piss up against a tree despite my erection. Back to the nightbars of Stuttgarter Platz, was it Stutti Frutti or Mon Cheri I went in? Either way, I sat in the glorious, dark Alphonse Mucha lounge and was joined by black-haired voluptuous Polish girl Yulia. After a quick drink together, we went upstairs to a black as sin fantastically grandiose, opulent Wilhelmine bedroom, lit by a single red-shaded bedside lamp, windows completely covered from floor to ceiling by massive black drapes like black-out curtains, with a massive black four-poster canopied bed with mirror above you. I took my pleasure with Yulia in every position in the Stygian gloom. It was a mind-blowingly dirty experience. On a different scale to anything I had enjoyed in Soho all these years, and on a different scale to my brief experiences in Brussels. This was sex the way it should be, this was sinning red in tooth & claw. The greatest high of my life. The bar keeps getting raised with each month that passes. I am in a daze at how unbelievably wonderful my life is becoming.

165

Tilla Durieux Depicting Circe 1913. A Die Sünde 1912. Ludwig von Hofmann Traumerei 1898 (Dreaming). De Chirico's Serenade 1910. Covinth's Blinded Samson that I saw in the Tate five years ago. I always look at it and think it is a portrait of me. Max Klinger. All Souls Day 1896. Franz Skarbina. The smell in the Adolph Menzel room was extraordinary. Kirche Ennere (Barock Alter) 1852-55. Alter in ein Barockkirche 1880-90. Rodin Thinker 1881-83. Rodin's green The Bronze Age 1875/76. Aristide Maillot's Torso. Hans Makart The Summer (Sketch) 1880. Nollendorfplatz by Night 1925—Lesser Ury. Salome with Jokanaan's Head 1870—Victor Müller. Frau Ehre Grunewald 1877. The blonde. The tall girl in stockings. The black goth. The black-haired Czech girl.

166

Verona Feldbusch. Alida Nadine-Kurras. They've rebuilt their city so prettily. Who is responsible for the look of Germany post-1945? Berliner Kindl. Berliner Flair. The girl in the hotel really hates me. Ha! She smiled yesterday, but not today, as if she knew what I had got up to during the night. Yesterday, The Oscar Wilde pub, nice fish & chips. Walked back to the Alte National Galerie. Fantastic. A new Die Sünde and Die Circe. I am getting to know Berlin a lot better. The Beersaloon in Ku'Damm is awesome. Hiccups. This morning, the Filmmuseum. Fantastic to see a section devoted to Hildegard Knef. Clips from *The Murderers Are Among Us, Die Sünderin*, and *The Snows of Kilimanjaro*. Also great the Marlene Dietrich section. Potsdamer Platz: the big tent structure over the top is quite awesome. It always fascinates me how much more confident I feel when I come back to these places. Compare how I feel walking along Ku'Damm to the Beer Saloon today to October. What is left to do in Berlin? The Nefertiti Museum and Schloss Charlottenburg. Story of Berlin. To be honest, there has been no romantic interest here in Berlin at all! I have two more nights here. The Berliner Dom is awesome. The Ishtar Gate as awesome as before. *Jenufa* tonight at the Komische Opera.

167

I think I will go back to Sybelstraße videokabins again before I go home. But tonight I want to go to *Jenufa*, then get fucked. Try Bon Bon and the Erotic Centre. Tomorrow Story of Berlin and Nefertiti and *Der Ferne Klang* at night. All I can really think about is getting fucked tonight, after *Jenufa*. I felt so turned on in *Tannhauser* last night. I had to come out at the interval to go to the Berlin Erotic Centre. The videokabins were fine but the cinema was a great disappointment. No girls? I will leave *Jenufa* later and come straight back to...Bon Bon and the Erotic Centre, then the Kaiser-Friedrich-Straße places. Just to drink and drink and drink. Until someone special turns up.

168

I have done the Berlin thing, and now I am thoroughly disgusted with myself. You have to go to the end of any experience.

169

BERLIN ZOO, NEWSPAPER & TERRASSE, STORY OF BERLIN, NEFERTITI. STAATSOPER. I am thoroughly repentant and penitent and ashamed. Not by what I have done, but at how much money I have spent. This has cured me of the travel bug for a long time, though. I feel just ready for Oslo & Gothenburg the next trip I take. This has been a big discovery expedition to Berlin. I have crossed many more Rubicons. It seems I am crossing another Rubicon every day. Passing through Ishtar Gates. It is amazing how much more at ease I am travelling around the city compared to last time. Was it really March I came here last? It seems a lifetime away. I like opposition. I need opposition to derive pleasure out of anything. Like Christina Aguilera, and David Beckham, they made me a fighter. They gave me a fighting spirit which has enabled me to gain a lot more enjoyment from life in general. I saw two beautiful girls with two boys coming out of a restaurant—Voltaire—and thought would I like to have been sitting at that restaurant table with them? And the answer, as always, is no! No, I really wouldn't! I would die to have to be sat at that table with them, as gorgeous and beautiful as they are. I cannot exist in that situation. So, we are going to have to think of something else. There isn't just one way of being. There is no one in my heart at the moment at all. No Susi, no Irina. No Lotta, no Sophia. I do not think I can feel love anymore. U2's With or Without You. "And you give yourself away."

170

There is a young couple below me at the opera, and unfortunately I cannot help but overhear their irritating lovey-dovey conversation. I could not do that; I could not play any part in it. Could not exist in such a situation. It is hideous. Repulsive. Just endless, endless conversation, small talk, giggling. Do I protest too much? It is Valentine's Night, Saturday 14th February, in the Unter den Linden. We are in the interval of Franz Schreker's *Der Ferne Klang* at the Staatsoper. How impossibly glamorous. It is a cool, fresh night. I stepped outside to get some air. The place is half-empty again, the same as the Komische Oper last night for *Jenufa,* and the Deutsche Oper the night before that for *Tannhauser.* I do not know how Berlin functions. They have got three opera houses, all playing to half-empty. The public transport system operates on an "honour system"—they trust that you have paid! Coming from London these things seem extraordinary. My hotel—the Kanthotel in Kantstraße—has 70 rooms and only 35 of them are occupied tonight. I cannot think why anyone would choose the Kanthotel for its location. It is not near anything worth being near to except the brothels. The young lovers' continual inane pointless conversation is driving me crazy. What on Earth is the use of it? Conversation!

171

Today I finally made my way back to the Story of Berlin exhibition and completed the full circuit this time. The bits about the Berlin airlift almost made me cry. So immersed was I in this world it was very difficult coming out afterwards. I had a nervous attack, complete identity disintegration again. I forced myself to make my way up to the Egyptian Museum to see Nefertiti. She is incredibly beautiful. The bust does have an incredible aura about it. I like a nice bust. Back to the hotel for a brief respite. From somewhere on the plane With or Without You starts up.

172

I like the Kanthotel, I think. Its location is good in that it is right in front of a bus stop and next to Wilmersdorf U-Bahn and McDonald's. Having said I have been cured of the travel bug for a long time I am already ready to come back. There were no special highlights in particular on this trip, no romantic sparks at all, but the whole trip was just deeply pleasurable. And finally, I lost my Berlin virginity—with one of *the* great fucks of my young life. Three nights at the opera in a row—*Tannhauser, Jenufa,* and *Der Ferne Klang*—the Alte National Gallery, Pergamon Museum, Ishtar Gate, Berliner Dom, Film Museum, Nefertiti, The Story of Berlin, The Oscar Wilde pub, the Beersaloon. Next time I must finally go to the Reichstag. *Ariadne auf Naxos* at the Staatsoper. Sybelstraße. Maybe just go for two nights to save money. The Berlin girls are not all that beautiful compared to the Munich girls, but they are cheaper and will do plenty for the money. The real precious moments of this trip were seeing the two Von Stuck pictures in the Alte National Gallery, Circe and Die Sünde; getting to sit in the front row at the beautiful Komische Oper, the look I exchanged with black-haired Czech girl in the Berliner Dom; but, above all, Anne Schwanewilms in *Der Ferne Klang.* The occasional glances exchanged with the brunette in the front row. We have come out of the clouds right above the Viagra Tower. London seems so small, and pathetic and insignificant. Nothing to compare with Berlin. Perhaps it is just my over-familiarity talking. If I was a Berliner, London would seem as exciting to me as Berlin does.

CHAPTER 11
I AM DOING
TOO
MANY
DRUGS

I am doing too many drugs; and in my case as always drugs means sex and whoring, cabarets and brothels. I stood entranced before Nefertiti's beauty, mesmerised, thinking "Where have I seen such beauty?"; then I realised: in myself! I had spotted a family resemblance, between Nefertiti and I. That profile, those eyes, that mouth. It was like looking at myself.

174

I am an extreme Englishman. I crave silence, solitude, isolation. That is my nature. Nature meaning I grew naturally that way, in a world of silence and lack of love, so such a world is all that seems natural now, so such a world is the only one I can live in. The central texts of this world are *The Silence* by Ingmar Bergman, *The Man Who Fell to Earth* by Nicolas Roeg, *Being There* with Peter Sellers.

175

I feel I have finally cracked the Berlin nut. With this four days in Berlin I hoped to crack it, having made good initial preparatory moves toward it the previous March, and now I feel I have. For sure, there were bad mistakes, wrong moves, I spent way too much money unwisely, I chose often poorly; but as I always say one cannot make an omelette without breaking some eggs. All my wrong steps, mistakes, were necessary exploratory movements, to test the ground, feel my way. In doing so I was finally cracking the nut. The moment of consummation came in the Staatsoper with Anne Schwanewilms in *Der Ferne Klang*, and at the interval outside, and after it ended, in the Unter den Linden. Has Moloch anything to compare with the

Unter den Linden, with Kurfürstendamm, with Berlin Zoo station, with Potsdamer Platz? Maybe I am jaded, and bored with overfamiliarity, but I can no longer feel any excitement in Moloch like I do in Berlin, or even Munich or Vienna. It is only by going too far that you know you have gone too far, it is only by getting lost that you know you are going in the wrong direction, so you learn to treasure the going too far, and the getting lost, as much as getting things exactly right, or finding one's way absolutely effortlessly.

176

And in cracking the Berlin nut I have done something far more profound: I cracked myself. I broke through some kind of barrier, crossed some great Rubicon, passed beneath some great Ishtar Gate of the soul, split the black spider web veils that had been smothering me, to emerge from the chrysalis like some great butterfly. In feeling at home in Berlin I have learned to feel at home in myself. Berlin for me has always been the greatest city in the world, Potsdamer Platz in fact the exact centre of that world, and so in feeling at ease in Berlin I have at last found some understanding of myself. I overturned all that was most holy, all right, in excessive displays of exhibitionism. I cried like Nana on the stage of the Théâtre des Variétés in nothing but a flimsy piece of gauzy fabric, for the whole of Paris to worship my sovereign nudity, riding along Kurfürstendamm like Maria Schneider in *Last Tango in Paris*, proclaiming my chariot is my cunt. Such "understanding" of oneself, such letting oneself go, usually precedes inevitable destruction like Oscar Wilde feasting with panthers. So be it: destruction is my destiny. Like Lulu always dreamed of being killed by a sex murderer until her deepest desire came true. She had been craving it, and inviting it, all her life, luring it in and luring it in, like luring the moth in to the still imploring flame, luring the bombers into the skies above Berlin: Come, bomb me! Destroy me again! Bring it on! Like Francis Bacon with his shirt off, in India, without a passport, screaming: "Come and get me you cunts!" That is all the world wants, says Hirst, that defiance, that out there on the edge of the universe, on the edge of the precipice, come and get me you cunts spirit. Do your fucking worst! Because I can take everything you can possibly throw at me, take every bomb you can possibly drop on me, take every prick you can possibly ram into me, and still pick myself up from the ground, pull myself up by the bootstraps, and come back for more. It is Robert De Niro in *Raging Bull*: "You never got me down, Ray. You never got me down." It is Juliette Binoche in *Damage*: "Damaged people are dangerous. Because they cannot be hurt."

177

Berlin has had everything done to it now, and it still came back for more. How can you look at that city today—at the Philharmonie, at Potsdamer Platz, at the Bahn Tower, at the Sony Centre "tent", at the Kurfürstendamm, at Wertheims, at the Kaiser Wilhelm Memorial Church, at Unter den Linden, at the Staatsoper—and not bow down in shock and awe before it.

178

This brief high point in my life, this momentary & largely illusory Golden Age, can only be a precursor to my total doom and destruction. Well, bring it on.

179

By going to Berlin, I feel I am setting out to conquer the Nile. Some personal Nile of the soul, which no man has ever journeyed for its entire length. Looking back to when I started these journals, with AUTISMUS at the end of 1999, I feel I have been on a great journey. The speed of my travelling is now accelerating, and we are getting to great new places almost every week that passes. On my trips to Munich and Berlin so far this year I have crossed some personal Rubicon on almost every single day. I am a mountaineer like Messner, scaling ever greater peaks on every expedition. I am a buffoon, like Austria's last emperor, 30 years old, looking like a 20-year-old, behaving like a 10-year-old. I still rely on my mother to feed me and clothe me and give me shelter from the world. Like Peter Sellers or Kenneth Williams, I will be close to her always. I rely on the cabaret and the brothel for my entire emotional sustenance. In those places very little socialising or conversation is required so I feel completely comfortable. The hour of the flesh has become my entire life. Drinking and whoring, interspersed with nights at the opera, and concerts by pretty young pianists and violinists. Sex and violins. This year already Sonia Ganassi, Ruth Palmer, Mihaela Ursuleasa, the Russian Chamber Orchestra of London, Ekaterina Apekisheva. While at *Tannhauser* and *Jenufa* I sat in my seat feeling an overwhelming sexual longing rising up in me and had to rush away at the interval to satisfy it. Opera has always been the greatest aphrodisiac to me. When a "real" girl lets me know she likes me I run away, as I cannot exist in that world.

180

Do I ever meet someone I even could love? Yes, sometimes. Sometimes when I'm sitting in the fourth row at the opera and there's a woman sitting in the front row, and we exchange glances two or three times, like the woman at *Der Ferne Klang*, and I think I could love her. Of course, I never do anything about it. I wish we lived in a world where the women do the asking. Coming to think of it, it was Valentine's Night, she should have done.

181

How fantastic I might find the Strand if I was a Berliner coming to London for the first time! The Strand of Mack the Knife. The Kurfürstendamm of London. How fantastic to go to the world-famous Fleet Street, Scotland Yard, 221B Baker Street of Sherlock Holmes. How fantastic when I went on the bus tour of London, and suddenly turned a corner and there was St Paul's Cathedral looming above us! As impressive as Berliner Dom is, it is no more impressive than this! I ignore my own city. I always look forward to coming to work every night, though. To come out of Charing Cross Station and see the Strand in front of me. To stand at the bus stop looking up at St Martin in the Fields, imagine the black skies behind it turning boiling blood red, and imagine Jack looking up at the Christchurch next to the Ten Bells as he stands here in his black cloak and top hat, as this will be the night for another attack. The blood is boiling in his veins, boiling in his brain, he has got himself up to such a high, maybe with opium or laudanum, or gin or beer, and as he looks up at the spire of the Christchurch the skies behind it turn a broiling blood red as well, and he thinks yes, it is a right thing that he is doing, and tonight is to be the night. When the bus comes I am also thrilled as it crosses Trafalgar Square then sweeps round the suddenly white phosphorescent brightness of Piccadilly Circus, and look up at black Eros, past Liberty, and Selfridges until we get to Marble Arch. How fantastic all the theatres of London must seem to a Berliner, the Coliseum and the Royal Opera House. How fantastic to find warm inviting pubs on virtually every street corner. London is a big messy fantastic city. I take it for granted. How excited a Berliner must feel coming on the underground from Heathrow, and pulling into Piccadilly Circus tube station, as I am when the U-Bahn pulls into Potsdamer Platz.

182

The dangerous excitement in my blood that I carried around with me in Berlin and Munich has followed me back to Moloch, I now realise. I feel powered by a latency. Some kind of gathering madness is engulfing me, and I wonder how it is all going to end. I am a bewildered spectator of what my life is becoming. These repeated trips back to Munich and Berlin, Brussels and Vienna, for opera and whoring. I am falling in love with Carla. She is the sex goddess non plus ultra of the city of Moloch. She floats my boat. Every time I see the Queen Mary II I think of the desire I feel for Carla.

183
I went into psychotherapy feeling so incredibly guilty. For 26 years I had people criticising me and trying to make me feel ashamed for the way I was. I came to Sara to find forgiveness and understanding, and—although, puzzled, she did murmur the words "I forgive you"—I found she just piled more stones on my back, like they did to John Proctor in *The Crucible*. I felt all my life people were viciously trying to get me to confess to something I had not done, just to make themselves feel better about themselves. Psychotherapy, which I went to while in ruins, like Germany after the war, marked the moment where I almost, almost, gave in. Thank God I stopped myself in time, and instead rose out of the ruins like a phoenix from the flames, like the Lufthansa bird.

184
I had the whole of society against me, but they were never quite able to mount enough resistance against me, to stop me coming into my kingdom, into my power, to stop the butterfly emerging from the chrysalis and flying free. They had me on the ropes once, but they let me escape, and now they can never get me back again.

185
I am becoming completely sex obsessed. But I do not feel like it is a problem. I have a steady job, earning steady money, and so that means I can spend it on sex, and that feels fine. What else is it worth spending money on? I am addicted to the drug, but I enjoy it, so what is the problem?

186
They hate me. And the more I keep on getting away with it, the more they hate me. I drive them insane. I drive them crazy with frustration and jealousy. I shouldn't still be alive. By rights, I should have been beaten down by the whole of society against me long ago. Instead I rose up out of the shit-heap they made of their world like a butterfly, like a phoenix from the flames. Now I flutter over them in my iridescent beauty, out of their reach, I infuriate them even more.

187
They sought to wear me down; instead they inspired me.

188

The more they attack me the more I enjoy doing the things I do. Jesus is representative of one man standing up to the whole of society and taking them on. Just because society are in the majority doesn't necessarily mean they are wrong, but usually it does. People hurl insults at me, or gently tip them my way, which bothers me not at all as it is the sincerest form of flattery, and I think how can they live with that insult on their conscience? I feel sad for them. The idea of deliberating insulting another person is mind-boggling to me. Why on Earth would you ever deliberately want to hurt another human being? It passes all my understanding. This is what the term Holy Fool means to me. People who are incapable of understanding the impulse to hurt another person. Society is unnerved by such people, and if there is one thing society cannot stand it is to be unnerved, and so tries to make them look ridiculous in everybody's eyes, tries to bring shame and ignominy on them, so they are destroyed. The Holy Fool's goodness throws an uncomfortable light, is an unflattering mirror, on society's pettiness, and society is unnerved, exposed, until this light, this mirror, can be removed. Society is ruled by the Great Lie, and it will try to destroy anyone who uncovers this great lie, points out the Emperor's new clothes, the way Jesus did.

189

I really crossed some Rubicon in Berlin. I really went through some Ishtar Gate. I came back from Berlin and on my first night out in London I re-met Carla and she asked for my number. Then I met Melani. Then I got that extraordinary little look from Vicky. I would like real love. When I think of real love I think of the glances I exchanged with the woman in the front row at *Der Ferne Klang* in Berlin. I feel real love for her. Nothing like it for people I actually know at the moment. I am not capable of it. When people get to know me, they realise I am empty, a hollow shell. So I avoid letting anyone get to know me, and keep my wall up at all times. Sometimes I put the wall up against someone I really wanted to let in, and it causes me great pain and grief for a long time afterwards, like with Susi, and American Girl. I am capable of great love and tenderness yet spend all my time with dancers and whores. Paying for company.

190

The fact is, in a burst of three quick ascents in January and February, I have raised my life onto a new level. After my first visit to Munich I had got myself up to one plateau, after my second I got myself up to a newer higher plateau, and with the Berlin trip I got myself up to the highest plateau of all.

Back in Moloch I have been continuing to climb. When I feel hungry I get an overwhelming urge to go back to Lamm's in Munich. Or the roll shop opposite Berlin Zoo station for a belegte. After those three lung-bursting rapid leaps upward in Germany I needed a period of rest and recuperation in London, making just small incremental climbs at a time, so as not to lose momentum entirely. I am now at an all-time high, an oxygen-thin rarefied level with the whole world below me. I feel like Zarathustra. I feel like Messner.

191

The people of Moloch are obsessed and twisted by their jealousy of me. I am more beautiful than them, I am more intelligent than them, it must be intensely annoying for them. And I am having more sexual partners than them. It must be hard for them to get me off their minds. President Clinton got under people's skins in this way. Oscar Wilde did. Beauty and intelligence is always what puts other people's backs up and brews resentment to start with, but then when they discover how much dirty, dirty sex you are enjoying as well, it drives them over the edge, they become insane in their hatred of you. How dare you be allowed to get away with it! But here we are, like Joe Orton, still getting away with it.

192

I WANT TO HEAR SOME CLASSICAL MUSIC. I HAVE A NEED FOR PURITY. FOR FERNS.

THIS TIME LAST YEAR I WAS LEAVING MY BAGS WITH THE FRONT DESK AT THE BEST WESTERN AM BOULEVARD KURFÜRSTENDAMM BECAUSE IT WAS TOO EARLY TO CHECK IN, AND RIDING UP & DOWN KANTSTRAβE ON THE BUS, BEFORE WRESTLING WITH EROS ALL NIGHT, IN MISERY. THE BIG FULL MOON OVER WERTHEIMS OPPOSITE ME. A SALOME MOON. WATCHING ME. IMPASSIVE. MOCKING ME WITH ITS IMPASSIVENESS, AS I FOUGHT AN EPIC BATTLE WITH EROS, LIKE JAKOB WRESTLING WITH THE ANGEL.

HOW MUCH STRONGER I AM A YEAR ON.

I FOUND OUT LELA HAS GONE, "MONTHS AGO". SHE JUST PACKED IT IN, DIDN'T WANT TO DO IT ANYMORE, I CAN'T HELP FEELING IT IS BECAUSE OF ME. THE FIRST THREE OR FOUR TIMES I WENT TO HER SHE WAS ALWAYS SO HAPPY, SO BEAUTIFUL, SO SEXY, GLOWING, VOLUPTUOUS, WITH THE MOST BEAUTIFUL RUBY LIPS,

SO SMILING, SO RELAXED, SO UP, SO CONFIDENT, SO STRONG. THAT LAST TIME—THE NIGHT BEFORE MY –TH BIRTHDAY AND ENGLAND WINNING THE RUGBY WORLD CUP IN AUSTRALIA—SHE LOOKED BROKEN-HEARTED, AND EMPTY, NOTHING LEFT TO GIVE.

I DRIFT THROUGH MY LIFE IN A DREAM AND ALWAYS FIND IT AMAZING TO DISCOVER THAT I HAVE HAD AN EFFECT ON SOMEONE.

CHAPTER 12
SALOME

Salome at the Staatsoper. I was sitting down the front after the interval, in row 4, so I could be close to the action. The production, as ever, was fantastic. The dresses so beautiful. Opera in Berlin is the best. There is real pain in my heart. And I can still feel blood trickling in my nose, almost ready to drip again. I am so tense. On arriving the previous night I was tempted to stay in watching *Lola Montez* on my hotel TV, but instead I went straight out and met Riccarda in Mon Cheri. A young Berlin blonde with a peroxide blonde bob. The most beautiful girl I have ever slept with. I felt like I was f—king Marilyn Monroe.

194

I had a belegte in Thobens at Berlin Zoo watching all the Hansa Berlin fans arriving, then bought a paper and went in Café am Zoo for a beer. It is nice there and I shall be back. Huge-breasted Turkish woman behind the bar in red top. I went to the Irish Pub to watch the Arsenal-Manchester United FA Cup Semi-Final. I had another vodka in the Football Café, only because I needed to use their lavatory, then back to the hotel for half an hour, then back out to the Komische Oper for *Fledermaus*. While sitting at the Kanthotel bar before leaving for the opera it started to rain, and you could feel breaths of that lovely summery smell. I just missed three buses, while trying to finish my drink, then two more went by because they were too full. The No.100 bus from Zoo then took 35 minutes just to get as far as the Reichstag. Crawling ten metres then stopping again, all the way. The driver made some announcement at Zoo which of course I did not understand. Probably something sexual. I could tell by his voice, and I caught a quick glimpse of his face as I was getting on the bus, and it was a face of complete depravity and bestial instincts; or maybe I just caught my reflection in the glass, I'm not sure. By Reichstag I felt like killing myself and got off and walked the rest of the way, through the Brandenburg Gate and along Unter den Linden to Glinkastraße and the Komische Oper, ten minutes late. One of the ushers already had a fag in her mouth! Only in Berlin. She got me my ticket from the pocket of her colleague and directed me to the second ring, wishing me a nice evening. I was just in three little seats right at the back next to the lighting equipment, with two pillars in front of me on either side and drapes, so I felt like I was in the Royal Box. There seemed to be many topical jokes inserted into the speaking parts of the opera as the audience laughed a lot and clapped to show their agreement at some points. The only topical reference I got was when he held up a bottle of that darkest blue vodka and said "Gorbachev!" Dagmar Hallender was gorgeous in black & red with a definite cleavage, a bit like a Hanna Schygulla. I felt lustful thoughts. The coat room lady was in absolute frenzy returning people's coats at the end, like she was having some kind of orgy of coat returning. From there I went to Sarah Young which was not as good as last night, of course, though I felt it was necessary. It is always better to go too much than feel you should have gone once more. Instead of coming out aroused I came out depressed therefore, feeling really ill in my stomach because of all the vodka I'd had during the day.

195

Another glimpse of Conchita before leaving for the opera last night. In black pants and pink low-cut sweater this time, naturally her sweater was small and tight. I do not now want to know her real name because she is so like Conchita in *That Obscure Object of Desire*.

196

The real jewel of the Alte National Gallerie is not in fact Tilla Durieux As Circe, or the poorer twin sister of the Munich Die Sünde, but Viktor Müller's Salome with Jokanaan's Head. The lips look so soft and rubious one feels one could kiss them, and it is an effort to restrain oneself from doing so, lest one be thought a pervert. Also great is Hans Makart's The Summer, and the two baroque altar pictures of Adolph Menzel. It is as if there was something about this altar that actively prevented him from depicting it, no matter how hard he tried. Some kind of block that at the last moment prevented him from filling in the details. They are two very mysterious paintings. I queued for half an hour to get into the New York MOMA exhibition at the Neue National Gallerie. All of Berlin seemed to be there. I can't say there was anything in the exhibition which really stuck in my mind at all. A Magritte, De Chirico's End of a Day, but that was about all that really affected me. As ever I was looking for a Francis Bacon but there was not one. The greatest work of art was all the pretty attendants in pink MOMA T-shirts. In the evening *Salome* at the Staatsoper. This was simply my greatest night at the opera I have ever had. To be seeing *Salome* at the Staatsoper has overwhelming meaning for me anyway, as it recreates the scene from *The Man Between* with the great Ljuba Welitsch screeching in the background.

This time it was the great Evelyn Herlitzius and I am happy to call her great. It is thrilling when the jungle music starts up signalling the start of the Dance of the Seven Veils. One does feel tense in anticipation of this, like one does at the start of *Last Tango in Paris* when Maria Schneider passes Marlon Brando under the bridge and we know they are very soon to be fucking each other up in the apartment. It is fantastic when Salome first hears Jokanaan, and edges slowly from around a corner as if not daring to see if he is really as beautiful as she thinks. Then after he has refused her she lays flat out face down with arms spread wide, then suddenly leans up, like a sphinx, as the idea occurs to her of what she should do.

197

On the way to the opera me and the big voluptuous blonde woman with red fingernails next to me kept checking our watches every couple of minutes, so that it became increasingly obvious that we were going to the same place. She asked me if this bus went to Staatsoper and after I asked her to translate into English we exchanged some small talk. I left her in the foyer of the opera as we went our separate ways and I wondered if I might have met her on the bus back afterward but did not. She was very gorgeous, big, beautiful, in her 30s. I wanted to ask her if she was meeting someone there but did not. When I got into the auditorium itself, the whole place reeked of sweat. Quite overpowering.

198

I went back out at night to Sarah Young, expecting little, having found her so disappointing on the Wednesday night. Tonight she was magnificent! I stayed there two hours before forcing myself to leave and go back to Mon Cheri. Stutti Frutti was closed and would not reopen for a couple of months because of no girls. Mon Cheri was busy (well, three men, keeping the three girls occupied). Riccarda was on stage dancing as I arrived. I forgot what a fantastic body she had, quite voluptuous in fact, like watching Marilyn Monroe striptease dancing. When she had stripped completely naked she put her dress back on and rejoined the guy at the table with another girl. One guy was sitting on a couch alone as there were no girls for him, just watching Riccarda and the other girl at their table. I sat at the bar. After a while Riccarda looked around the corner to see if I was still there and grinned at me and winked. I was by now getting drunk again, and then when two more men came in, I got up and left. I want to save Riccarda for next time to give myself something to look forward to.

199

Coming back from Sarah Young last night, feeling ill and down, I was thinking what was the most erotic moment of my whole trip, and it was in fact the blonde girl with the baby on the platform at — station right at the start. Then there was Conchita, two glimpses of her in her beige jumper and then the pink one. And then Riccarda. Every time I come on holiday I cross another Rubicon and go a little further than I have ever done before. There was Patricia in Munich, then next time there was Emily, then Yulia in Berlin, and now Riccarda. Only someone who ever actually f—ked Marilyn Monroe will know how I felt with Riccarda.

200

So was this trip worth it? What special epiphanies will I be taking home with me? Riccarda. *Salome* at the Staatsoper. The Komische Oper itself. Viktor Müller's Salome. The two baroque altars, disturbing by their omissions, by what he does NOT paint. The blonde on the bus. Sybelstraße. Conchita. I look forward to coming back in two weeks.

CHAPTER 13
THE
BERLIN PLAZA

The Berlin Plaza is the kind of hotel where you seem to see so many familiar faces amongst the staff, even though it is my first time there. The woman in the bar instantly seemed such a familiar face. The beautiful-looking blonde receptionist seemed such a familiar face. I'm sure I've seen them both before, yet I cannot have done. It is that kind of hotel. You feel so at home and happy straightaway. *Carmina Burana* was absolutely fantastic. Once again, my best ever night at the opera. The barrier keeps being broken. The bar keeps getting raised. Those legendary Munich nights. And now these extraordinary, unbelievable Berlin experiences.

202
Travelling with someone I don't think you can really notice things as much as when you travel alone. For example, standing in the pouring rain on my last night in Sydney, looking back at the Opera House and Harbour Bridge lit up against the night sky. That was a moment one had to enjoy on one's own, and they are the moments I travel for. Aloneness, isolation, quite often desolation, sharpens one's emotions, and gives a keen edge to one's responses.

203
I am completely in love with this idea of the lonely traveller, this idea of Nietzsche writing with blue hands in unheated rooms in cold icy mountains, Schubert's Winterreise. This is the noble ideal I aspire to. The idea of being happily married with 2.4 children, a house, a mortgage, a car on the drive, holidaying two weeks a year in Spain, is surreal to a man like me—"I want love but on my own terms", the superb Elton John video with Robert Downey Jr—and completely out of my reach, whether I wanted it or not, and I am quite prepared to accept that if it were within one's reach one inevitably would want it, as it would be lovely to live one's life so safely, so free from dangers and alarms and loneliness and the hostility one always

has to suffer when one is alone. To be alone is something one obviously has to be punished for. I accept my punishment without complaint. I cannot help seeing it as no more than the revenge of the Lilliputians against Gulliver and so am comforted by it. I prefer to see every attack as proof that I am indeed still on the right track. If the stupid people are attacking me, then I must be doing something right. It is when one finds oneself accepted by the stupid people, i.e. society, that one has cause for dismay. People are always amazed when they ask me who I am travelling with, and I say no one, and then they say, "why, have you got friends out there then?", and I say no, and there is an awkward silence, when their mouths just open and close like a fish and they can't quite comprehend the magnitude of what you are saying. And yet to me it is completely normal, and it is the idea of travelling with someone that is completely bizarre and unthinkable. I cannot really imagine their lives any more than they can imagine mine.

204

I am a Kaspar Hauser, a Steerpike, a Peter Pan, a Noodles in *Once Upon a Time in America*, a Geoffrey Firmin in *Under the Volcano*, a Thomas Newton in *The Man Who Fell to Earth*, a Chauncey Gardiner in *Being There*, a Will Penny, a Friedrich Nietzsche, an Edvard Munch, a Strindberg, a Kierkegaard. For people who can't understand me this should help them and make it all clear (if they knew who any of these people were in the first place). I am a Greta Garbo, a Marilyn Monroe, a Louise Brooks. I am a Sherlock Holmes. Throwing myself into complex intellectual puzzles in order to keep loneliness at bay. Taking myself to violin recitals by beautiful young nubile violinists or piano recitals by beautiful young nubile pianists, in order to keep loneliness at bay. Never letting myself even think about opening my heart to a woman, say for example a Chess Goddess or a Lotta, because I know from experience that it will, like it did Holmes with Irene Adler in *A Scandal in Bohemia*, completely capsize me. There is one moment in cinema that always makes me cry: when Robin Williams's shrink is pinning Will Hunting to the wall and telling him over and over "It's not your fault. It's not your fault. It's not your fault" until Will himself breaks down and cries his heart out. It gets me every time.

205

The world is full of Salomes, and Charlotte Cordays. So many women become vicious when you do not respond to their direct looks and their hair twirling. I live in a different world to them. Anything that requires emotions I am afraid I am not equipped for and cannot help them with. I cannot enter into any such arrangement. So I surround myself with whores, the only women I have ever been able to talk to, and feel a closeness to. I feel comfortable because I am paying for it, and we both know where we stand. I feel love for the ones who show real warmth and generosity. I feel love for them for putting up with me, as I would not wish me on anyone. I am like Vincent Van Gogh in this. I am like Henri de Toulouse-Lautrec, an incredibly kind and gentle and caring soul who in many ways has so much to offer, yet I spend all my time with whores, looking for love in all the wrong places, so when I don't find it I can say "See! This proves I was right! I am incapable of love!" One always likes to be proved right. Women are often, it seems, attracted to me. Indeed, I could say some of the great beauties of the age have made attempts on my fortress. Yet any that I let in are almost immediately disappointed with what they find. That I have nothing to offer. I am incapable of company. I am bewildered by the concept of talking. I sit in silence desperately racking my brains for something to say. Words, indeed, don't come easy to me. And yet—and this is one of the funniest things in my life—when I am with the whores they ALL criticise me because I will not stop talking for the entire duration of our congress! Ha-ha! "Are you a reporter or something? A policeman?" They are so suspicious of me because I want to make conversation with them! "No," I say, "I work in a hotel." "Bollocks!" they explode. They never believe I work in a hotel. "Why don't you believe I work in a hotel?" I ask, amused, bewildered. "Fine. You work in a hotel. Whatever you say." But still they do not believe me. When I am making love to her I want to know everything about her, what is her name, where does she come from, how long has she been here, what does she like about here, how long has she been doing this job? I cannot make love without talking. Ha-ha! And yet outside of a brothel no one can get a word out of me. This I always think is one of the most hilarious paradoxes of my strange personality.

206

It is important for us to talk about scopophilia—for if I suffer from anything it is that. Autism, yes, in many ways, Schizoid Personality Disorder, yes, Kaspar Hauser Syndrome, yes. Orphanism, perhaps. More than anything, however, I am a scopophiliac. Patricia in Munich kept coming up to me and pressing her silk scarf over my eyes, to stop me looking, to stop me seeing, to stop me gazing, maybe to guard herself from my pretty eyes which is always the only thing that attracts women to me. The subject of the Gaze fascinates me. I have over-developed visual organs, I believe. They have grown strong and dominant to the detriment of everything else, which is why I love to look and look but do not ever actually want to do anything. I love going to whores, so I can see them, naked.

207
Actually, despite everything, I have still not quite lost my Munich virginity.
All but, but not quite.

208
I would say last year was the first good year of my life; the first time when I
could actually start to bear living in my own skin.

209
I have hardly written about my Norway journey before. It was a Munchian
pilgrimage. It is funny. In the Munch Museum I watched the film about
him, which included the incident where he pulled out of his engagement to
Tulla Larsen and that was the moment the whole of society turned against
him and tried to destroy him. Kierkegaard, similarly, pulled out of his
engagement to Regine Olsen and that was the moment society turned
against him and tried to destroy him. I travelled to Norway mortified and
horrified at my own refusal to respond to P—'s beguilements. I was close to
mental meltdown at having let my chance with her go. People seemed to
pick up on this and fell upon me with gleeful hatred. They tried their best to
tear me to shreds with absolute glee and delight. It was like Christmas for
them to have me in their sights and in their clutches. I experienced such
savagery while in Norway, but I always think you carry the weather with
you. If you are mentally disintegrating because you are ashamed or
guilt-ridden about something, people will pick up on it and bring you the
punishment you seem to be asking for. They can see it in your face, you are
begging to have your face shoved in the shit. Like a dog only bites those who
are frightened of it, it can sense those who don't like it, society only attacks
those who are uncomfortable. If I am feeling uncomfortable, feeling like I
have no skin on, I know I will be attacked mercilessly. If I am feeling
confident, flying high on drink or drugs or a smile from a pretty girl, I am
hardly ever attacked. It is like I am protected by a force field, a visible aura,
like the Ready Brek boy on his way to school on a snowy morning. I was
close to insanity when I went to Norway, in short, and was absolutely ripped
to shreds. Savaged. That is why that is the one place in the world I want to
go back to more than any other. I have left so much blood on the tracks in
Oslo. It will be so delicious to go back and eat it.

210
This was the first time I have stayed in Berlin and had MTV in my room. It
makes such a difference to me. It is funny that three separate songs being

played on MTV during my three nights in Berlin featured the f-word—Eamonn's Fuck It, Amiel's Lovesong, and Pink's Last to Know. Also, two songs were on the same theme of men who thought the girl would sleep with him when they got back to the room and didn't want to know when she wouldn't: Pink's Last to Know and Avril Lavigne's Don't Tell Me. How I love having music channels in my hotel room.

211

I seem to be permanently on the verge of a nosebleed when in Berlin. My blood pressure must be very high when I am there. It is the temptation of the whores. Hoping I will be in the right frame of mind when I get there. Hoping I will get a good one and not get stuck with one I went with before and would feel honour-bound to go with again just so as not to hurt their feelings. It is like the lottery, waiting for your balls to drop. You never know what one you are going to get. It is also the fact that I am drinking so much when I am in Berlin. Morning, noon and night. Permanently inebriated.

212

I cannot cope with reciprocated love, reciprocated passion. I can only adore my goddesses from a distance, with them above me on a pedestal. Once they come down and offer themselves to me, body and soul, I leave. I am horrified, chilled, deadened. All life leaves me. I become a wooden Pinocchio.

213

I went back to Iga the second night and couldn't be bothered to do anything. She had to pull me through the whole thing, do all the work. It was horrible. I had gone completely cold. I was desperate for a pin to stick into myself, to wake myself up. WAKE UP! But I had gone into sleep mode. Shut down. Even though I wanted to kiss her on the lips the first night, when she started to kiss me deep in the mouth when I went back the next night, I could not respond. I do not want it when they give it to me. I do not like kissing actually. When they let me, I discover I hate it. I do not like sex all that much. When they let me, I suddenly lose all feeling for it. I now love Iga so much, but it has been mixed in with my own shame that I could not respond to her kisses, and any further contact will be so awkward. It was like this with Lela.

214

I have been waiting all my life for society to turn on me and rip me to shreds like a pack of dogs. I always knew it was going to happen, even as a child, and I think I had spent my whole life breathlessly expecting it at any moment, and that tension in anticipation of imminent savagery was a permanent feature of my existence. I instinctively knew the barbarity of dunces was waiting for me, as Lulu instinctively knew she would one day be killed by a sex murderer. She in fact yearned for it—like Francis Bacon wanted to be tied up and beaten, like that German man apparently wanted to be eaten—and it was in fact her deepest wish, as it had become my deepest wish to be torn to pieces by society as if by a pack of dogs and yearned for it—for only then could I finally show my contempt for them and laugh in their faces even as they were ripping me limb from limb, realising that in that ultimate moment I had stolen their victory from them; for it was not until their seething jealousy and resentment of me came out into the open with an orgiastic riot of barbaric savagery, that my seething contempt and scorn for them and invincibility to them could also come out into the open.

215
They need to ask themselves why they feel the need to pick on me, single me out. What is it about me? What was it about Oscar Wilde? What was it about Van Gogh? What was it about Lorca? Could it perhaps be our beauty and our intelligence and our goodness, and "the fact that they could not do without us, nor discompose us, to the slightest degree, but had to bear our sometimes insolent witticisms behind gritted teeth" while all the time raging with jealous hatred of us on the inside? We must beware about letting "arrogance seep into our behaviour patterns", but oh, it is so hard not to, when people around you make themselves look so stupid, reveal themselves as being such dunces, every single day. When you deliberately try to hurt another person, I think you have revealed yourself for all to see as one of the dunces. I hold to Cocteau's one true law: "Never hurt others. Never diminish others. Never answer insults". I have always had so many people trying to hurt me, trying to diminish me—desperately, obsessively, blindly—that I could never do it to another. I hurt people in different ways and am hurt in different ways. I am hurt when a person, like a Lela, or an Iga, tries to love me, and I cannot respond. And I hurt others when they try to love me, and I close the door on them.

MUNICH

I feel I have lost my job. I feel physically sick. I live dangerously. I research the outer reaches. I am autistic. I am eccentric. I do everything differently. I am stunned when people take offence. I have a warped view of reality, a strange sense of humour.

217

Susi at the White Coffin. And Amelia. Amazing things. Patricia appeared out of nowhere. B— in Brazil for a month. Smiles from Susi at first, she was on stage in a sparkling silver & diamond dress when I walked in. Amazing fantastical wonders. Susi was on stage when I walked in, but then when I didn't respond, her looks became cold and angry. She looked unhappy for the rest of the night. I tried talking but she just answered my questions and did not push the conversation. I think she was expecting me to try harder. She danced to 'I Would Die for You' and Sting's 'I Still Want You' and looked at me expressionlessly. She affects me more than anybody else in my life. My person of the year for last year. How amazing to meet her again. She disappeared when I thought her surrounded, then dropped in my midst, splashing me with her waves, when I had forgotten all about her.

218

I ask myself why do I go back to the same art galleries every time I come to a city? Today in the N.P. there must have been about twenty pictures I have never seen before or just never noticed before. Even the pictures I knew from before affected me greater today. My worries about the hotel have now lent me a higher sensibility to everything.

219

Trying to see what you do in a positive light. To have no regrets. To love one's mistakes. If you don't write your thoughts down, you just have your thoughts and that's it. You just keep saying those words to yourself over and over in your head and that's it. By writing it down, you get it out of the way, and clear the way for the next thoughts, which usually follow right behind it to fill the gap. I am very unhappy with myself at the moment. I dislike everything about myself. I have been under a cloud here in Munich, and it makes me feel incredibly small and humble. I feel like Rodin's Age of Bronze, broken and decapitated, and all hollow inside. Completely empty. I have to keep pushing people; just to provoke a reaction. I can't just get on with people nicely.

220

It finally happened—my nose poured with blood. The tensions I had been feeling and the pressure I had been under during this three days in Munich finally burst; like after a long hot torrid summer's day, black clouds slowly gather and then it starts raining, hard, persistent rain. Like the rain as I left the White Coffin and Viktoriya last night, like last time when I left The Three Cats and Emily and found it was still snowing and had been for hours. This time, after Viktoriya, I didn't want to go back to my hotel but just walked around and around in the rain, working my way with no enthusiasm in as big a circle as I could find to get back to the Inter City. The rain was constant but not heavy. It was pleasant. Once again, I was disintegrating, crying inside, a mixture of some dark euphoria and abject despair. I walked past the magnificent Justizpalast, stopped in the rain and looked up at it, went up its steps and stood in its doorway, like Harry Lime in *The Third Man*, before standing looking up at it some more then pressing on. Hertie, Eisenhof, Intercity. "Abend, Mr Night Manager." Go and kill myself in my room.

221

I am autistic. I am the autistic wildboy. The Kaspar Hauser wildechild. *Lulu* at the Staatsoper was poor. De Arellano was fantastic, but the 1980s kitsch American production was awful, each scene more relentlessly banal than the last. A great disappointment. Unbelievably for *Lulu* it wasn't even sexy. It was like they took all the sex out of the story. Reading the interview with the director at breakfast this morning he talks about how she is passive, almost autistic. As I always say, for me Kaspar Hauser and Lulu could be brother and sister. I have really fallen in love with Viktoriya.

222

A devastating trip to Munich.

223

I have left more blood on the tracks in Munich than ever, literally. My nose-bleed on the final morning the worst I have ever had. It was a devastating trip because of the extraordinary emotions that it had stirred up. To meet Susi and Irina again was quite simply extraordinary. How can one not think that the gods are playing tricks on one? Stepping into the White Coffin I saw Susi and her friend Amelia's pictures on the wall. Buying my drink at the bar, Patricia, a fire from my recent White Coffin past, appeared at my side from out of nowhere, smiling and kissing me and leading me inside. There on the stage, as gracefully beautiful as I remember her, was Susi. Our eyes met twice, and she smiled radiantly, happily, both times, but I just looked back expressionlessly, stunned into silence, and she did not smile at me, or scarcely anyone else, for the rest of the night. Still hanging on my arm Patricia led me to the séparée, and there inside, straddling a man's lap, was a tall, incredibly beautiful, stunningly blonde blonde. After she came out I realised it was Irina. The joke was complete. I felt the trap shutting around me. Well, that's a good one. It was Lulu that brought me back to Munich on this particular week.

224

All my trips are devastating. Full of bitter emptiness and abject despair. That's what I travel for, I suppose. The possibility of just going and lying on a beach for a few days and having a "great" time is not open to me, it seems. I am cut out for other things. Emotionally devastating lacerating days in some German far away capital, leaving behind massive amounts of sticky blood on the tracks.

225

I am an incredible creature. I just seem to live for whoring, though get no real pleasure out of it as I am always drunk, because I wouldn't have the courage to do it if I wasn't. I spend all my money on whores, travelling to places to have those whores, drinking to get the nerve to have those whores. And yet what better thing is there to spend one's money on? One can go out to a concert, or an art gallery, or a film, but one will always come home feeling incomplete. Only after whoring does one feel one has done something worthwhile with one's night.

226

My whole life revolves around getting back to Munich now, to see Susi again. And Viktoriya and Irina. I will save all my money, and tighten my belt, and not do anything in Moloch, just to enable me to go on that train journey back to Brussels, and Munich, and Vienna, and Berlin, and Malmo, Gothenburg and Oslo. This is going to be Grand Tour revisited. On the fifth anniversary of my original life-changing journey. I am going back to Berlin to see Riccarda and Iga and Maya and Vanessa and Karolina again. Back to Vienna to see Fraulein W— again. But more than anything to see Susi, and Viktoriya, and Irina.

CHAPTER 14
I DON'T CARE
ABOUT
ANYONE

I don't care about anyone. Except mother. And Viktoriya. Susi and Irina. Iga. So I don't care about what anyone thinks of me or what I do. You can attack me all you want but I am now meeting the most incredible Tallulahs and Esmeraldas and having the most unbelievably high nights of my life. Dangerously high. I am losing my head over these florid & lurid butterflies of the sépareé and the Tingel-Tangel.

228

I always want them to fall in love with me afterwards. I go away feeling so choked and rejected because they didn't. Louise Brooks's description of Berlin has become true for me. Things got off to a good start by watching Sharapova winning Wimbledon on the screen in Heathrow Terminal 1. Then Stefania Bonfadelli in *La Traviata* at the Deutsche Oper straight on the bus from the airport still with my big bag. Only after that checking in to my beautiful Berlin Plaza. Two beers and a knesepfanne then off to Sybelstraβe and Club. Maya and Carolina from Poland. In Monte Carlo sex kino I sat on the hard black bench looking up at the porn on the TV screen above. Bulgarian Maya came to me. We retreated into the small cubicle behind a curtain to the side of the screen, and I stripped completely stark naked while she took my money to the bar and came back with the condoms. To be standing there alone stark naked in a Berlin sex kino; how weird and exhilarating it felt! As she bent over the armchair, I took her from behind; dressed, pulled curtain aside and sat back down on the black bench to carry on watching the film and drinking my bottle of Berliner Kindl. Every time I try to go further than before. I have become completely cynical (in the football sense of the word). I just want gratification and am cynically ruthless about it.

229

Berlin blondes. It is not that there are more blonde women in Berlin than elsewhere, though there maybe, it is just that as soon as you see one you can't help thinking "Ah, a Berlin blonde". They are a separate species. A fantastic race. As unique and distinctive as Vienna redheads. Red Vienna is a very true soubriquet but it's because of women's hair. All the clubs in Berlin have their own unique flair and atmosphere. The Monte Carlo is all Bulgarians. The Sissi black. The Starlight is Thais. The Blue Bananas seems less full on sexual than the others, less dirty and sleazy. No screen playing porn is probably the reason. There is a certain type of species called a Berlin blonde. They are quite unique. Of course, you see a million blondes when you are in London, in Paris or New York or anywhere. But nowhere is a blonde so perfectly blonde as she is in Berlin. Riccarda intrigues me. I have met her four times now, and every time she seems quite different. Like a different person. That is fascinating to me. She is like a Maria Sharapova of the séparée. Berlin blondes look different from blondes anywhere else in the world, I swear they do.

230

Well, this is as empty as I have ever felt. I will be killed on the streets of Berlin one night, like Chopin.

231

I return in anguish. A sad and tawdry end. I really like Riccarda. But she is like an angel of death. White hair, black eyes. Bony shoulder blades. She has deteriorated so much since I first met her in February. I wish I spoke German, so I could talk to her. Now, I don't want to sleep, I don't want to stay awake. I don't want to be with her now, but I miss her. What is wrong with me? As soon as I start to like someone, like Lela, or Riccarda, then I find I cannot be with them. All passion goes. I am so tragically sick of myself, of the way I disappeared from Riccarda even when I was with her, when she was giving me so much affection. She is a girl who gives so much and gets so little back. She needs a lot of love. It was like fucking Maria Sharapova. She is a girl like a giraffe who has got lost in her life. She is diving deeper into darkness. If I saw her again in two months I think she would be even worse. She is a beautiful girl, but she is doing something terrible to herself.

232

I never went back to Iga. I don't like things when they become emotional, because I can't follow them there. I looked at Riccarda, and thought you are death. You are death. After I finished she took my condom off, threw it away, and waited for me to put myself in again. Then she really would be death, I think. She wanted to take me with her.

233

I feel completely sad and lost and empty, about how I behaved with Riccarda. I am very fond of her, she is in my heart, but try as I might I could not respond erotically to her. She is my Ester. I am not capable of a relationship with anyone. I flirt with rescue when I have no intention of being saved, like the man in *Smiles of a Summer Night*. Riccarda was so impossibly sweet, but there is something about her of death. A white-haired black-eyed Death. She is wasting away like Violetta in *La Traviata* which I saw on my first night (but this is how Violetta would really look, not like the beautiful, voluptuous Stefania Bonfadelli). When I held her, her shoulder-blades felt like razor blades. When we were going up the stairs to the room she was gasping for breath long before we got to the top. She is dying. That girl is dying. That girl is killing herself, and my heart was bleeding for her. When you look at her beautiful face, you think she should be the most beautiful woman in the world. When I first met her five months ago I felt like I was fucking Marilyn Monroe. Now I felt like I was fucking a blonde-haired skeletal Death. It was like she was reaching out to me to save her, and I, horrified, let her go. I could not have saved her, she would just have dragged me down with her. So I let her go. I love her, and I let her go. She is the most haunting figure of my life. I want to cry because of shame that I could not respond in kind to all the affection and passion she was trying to give me.

234

I feel so ashamed and depraved now; but I would do the same things all over again. Sarah Young was great; the Monte Carlo was the best. I have managed to dismiss Sissi and Blue Bananas and Golden Gate and probably Mon Cheri. What else did I do? Went back to the Alte National Galerie, saw four operas but left at the interval of every one, so desperate was I to fuck.

235

I haven't had my nosebleed yet.

236

I'm crying for Riccarda.

COLLECTED WORKS

CHAPTER 15
THE
FOUR
OPERAS

The four operas I went to were extravagant and wasteful. The *Traviata* I went to on the first night, with the stunning Stefania Bonfadelli, was the only one I can justify, as it is such a topical subject with personal meaning. Over the next two nights it was to acquire even greater meaning to me, in retrospect, after my two encounters with Riccarda, the fatal Riccarda. You never get the real sense of Violetta as consumptive because she is always played by a voluptuous, well-fed, trollop of an opera singer—only after I slept with Riccarda on my last night did I know how Violetta would really have looked in those final minutes with Alfredo. Going up the couple of short flights of stairs to the bedroom she was gasping for breath long before we got to the top. It was deeply disturbing and saddening and frightening, and heart-breaking. This beautiful girl who was one of the most beautiful girls in the world and should still have been and who I felt love for, seemed to be dying. It was so hard to go through with the sex. Her shoulder blades were like razor blades. Afterwards, I could say nothing to her. We dressed in silence and she started off down the stairs like a skeleton in her long white boots. Downstairs in the bar I could still say nothing to her, not a word. I was shocked. She got up and went back to the bar, coming back once for a final try to get me to want her. I was feeling choked. She must have been so hurt, so cut. She looks like someone who is dying and knows it. She is my real-life Violetta.

238 .
I am terrified to see her again yet cannot not. It will be two months before I can travel again and maybe longer before I return to Berlin, but I know I must go back to see her. I am drawn to her like a moth to the fatal white flame. She fascinates me. She completely fascinates me. I have seen her five

times now and every time she is quite different. The first time she was beautiful, white blonde-bobbed, sexy, modern, voluptuous, I felt like I was fucking Marilyn Monroe. I went back two nights later and there was a voluptuous blonde stripping on stage and I didn't recognise her. Only after she came off stage and was drinking and smiling at me did I realise it was her. Two months went by and I saw her again. This time she was sniffing like she had just sniffed some coke. She sat down beside me but almost immediately became hurt and angry at me and got up and left me. After chatting briefly with two of the other girls I got up and left without a backwards glance. And now, this time, a skeletal tall blonde comes towards me smiling like she likes me, like she knows me. When I ask her name, I am shocked, really shocked, to hear her say "Riccarda". For the first time her hair is pulled back in a tight ponytail making her look even slimmer. I did not sleep with her the first night, as I was too drunk, but some fatal obsession, some morbid determination made me go back and straightaway go to the room with her the next night. Almost immediately I knew it was a mistake. Terrifyingly, when I had finished, she pulled off my condom, screwed it up and very deliberately threw it away, lying back again and smiling into my eyes, wanting me to put myself in her again. I stared at her horrified. It was like she was dying and now she wanted to kill me too. Afterwards, and downstairs, I could not say anything to her, and I think she must have been so hurt by that. When I finally left, I said "Ciao" to the bar in general and when she didn't even glance up, I said "Ciao Riccarda" to her in particular, and she glanced at me and blew me the saddest of kisses. With that I was gone. A desperately painful encounter to me and maybe even for her. It seemed like she had wanted something from me, some affection which I felt but could not show. As always after I have hurt someone, I feel overwhelming love for them and remorse. My shame and remorse is translated into love. I now love Riccarda desperately, but I think she is dying. Looking at her is too painful, I cannot say a word.

239

How can she have changed from the sexy voluptuous sassy blonde-bobbed Marilyn Monroe Sharon Stone in *Sliver*-like girl of February, to this frail stick insect pathetically needing of my affection in July? It is the saddest thing in my life.

240

She just very quietly got up and left me because I could not think of anything to say to her, and I just let her go and sat on my own and sometime later just said goodbye to her and shut the door behind me, and that must have hurt her inside so much. I walked home in the horrible bright blue Berlin 4:20 dawn with the birds singing and I don't know how I put one foot in front of the other. I felt choked by shame, that I had done this to her, choked with love for her, choked with horror at what had happened to her, choked that she was dying and she knew it, choked that she had seemed so pathetically needy of my affection for her, and I could not give her any, choked that she had after a short while got up and quietly walked away, and choked that I had let her, choked that I had later just got up and walked away with no more than a "Ciao Riccarda" and a glance in her direction.

241
I went back to Berlin and never even bothered to say hello to Iga.

242
I have got the funny, eccentric, charming habit of sending postcards to my favourite whores after I have got back home. Feeling that I have hurt them by not giving them as much love and affection as they gave to me. I don't want them to think it meant nothing to me, that I just used them as a hole. I want them to know that I care for them and miss them and love them.

243
Once again, I did go further and deeper than ever before. I always say I have done this, and it seems hard to think how I could continue going on going further and deeper than before, but I do. I had a numbing bad relationship with most of the hotel staff, but also some good ones—Anna, Patricia and Yvette at the Café am Zoo for example. In Thobens, mixed. I will go looking for George Grosz (and Otto Dix) next time I go to Berlin. It amazes me that he is not everywhere, like it amazes me when I go to Wien that there aren't concerts every night of Schoenberg, Berg and Webern but instead all Mozart. Berlin this time was in the grip of *Spiderman*, and still of the New York MOMA exhibition.

244
Maybe I am quite wrong about Riccarda, and when I go back I will find her strong and brave again. I sincerely hope so. But by now I am sure I have turned her against me forever, like happened with Lela. Even other people instantly seem to pick up on it. When Edvard Munch rejected Tulla Larsen people gathered beneath his window, on one occasion catching sight of him, "There he is! Now kill him!"—all this because he rejected his fiancée! When Kierkegaard rejected his fiancée, he became attacked and abused by all and

173

sundry in Copenhagen. Home after leaving Riccarda I got myself up and forced myself to go out. I found myself being attacked everywhere I went. It was like this after I refused to respond to P—. I took myself off in a state of psychological meltdown to Berlin and Malmo and Gothenburg and Oslo and felt myself relentlessly mocked and pilloried everywhere I went. Oslo was the worst and most vicious I have ever experienced. It always seems a reflection of how I feel inside. When I am happy and powerful I am never attacked. When I am feeling shamed and remorseful about some wrong I have inflicted on someone, by not giving out my love, I become relentlessly hounded by all and sundry. And don't tell me it is just my paranoid imagination.

245

I'm the Sphinx, and people have been taking pot shots at me for centuries. But I will live on, long after they are forgotten.

246

Riccarda is becoming a recurrent figure in my life, like Susi in Munich. Riccarda took me by surprise. I was surprised to see her again, I was surprised to see how thin and sickly she looked, I was surprised to find I had fallen in love with her. But at the end of March, start of April, she had been the most spectacularly stunning woman I had ever seen. Sleeping with her was like sleeping with Marilyn Monroe. The beautiful ones never do it for long. I was shocked to see someone as stunning as her doing it at all, even more shocked she was still there at the end of April, even more at the start of July.

247

I do often get sentimental about Tallulahs and Esmeraldas. It is inevitable. They are the only women I mix with, so it is inevitable from time to time I will get sentimental about one of them. Cities that live on fault lines or next to volcanoes will from time to time get totally destroyed or severely damaged, so if I mix only with Tallulahs and Esmeraldas it is inevitable that I will sometimes get destroyed or severely damaged by one of them. I have this sentimental habit of sending postcards to Esmeraldas I have fallen in love with, after I have got back home to Moloch.

248

I want to go back to see if Riccarda's decline has continued, or whether it was just a blip, or just my imagination, and she has staged a recovery to full voluptuous bloom again.

249

I can cry about all the money I'm spending, bleeding into the ground, but you have to live your life all the way, don't waste it. This is the time I am burning brightest. I want to push people more, I want to push the travelling more, I want to push the envelope. I always say, in wonder, that every time I travel I go further than ever before—experience-wise. This last time in Berlin I felt quite bored about the prospect of going and didn't think I could push things any further, but sure enough I did. I opened up new doorways.

250

If you live in ice and high mountains, then the only love you will find will be with Tallulahs and Esmeraldas. In the world of Tingel-Tangels. From the moment I set foot in Norway people were so vicious to me. In fact, from the moment I set foot in Sweden. I really must have upset Scandinavians somehow; so, I am going back to upset them some more. I have followed the life and career of Edvard Munch very closely; I have followed the life and career of Kierkegaard very closely; so it is a thrill to go back to Copenhagen, Malmo, Gothenburg, and Oslo. I cannot wait to get to Oslo now. I am a hermit. I wait alone until my mutation comes.

251

When I read back through my notebooks, and look back through my newspaper cuttings, my life seems like a terrible drug-addled nightmare. A series of opium dreams, like Berlioz's *Symphonie Fantastique* written while in love with the actress Harriet Smithson. Can it really be as horrible, and farcical, as I depict it? And yes, it is in fact even more horrible and farcical than my embarrassment will allow me to say. These are my *Confessions of an English Opium Eater*. My opium has been drink and Tallulah, which I have relied on as a crutch to support me against my crippling shyness and self-consciousness. "Dracula started out as Victorian gent Bram Stoker's dirty dream about three young lady vampires in see-through nighties. In another age, such thoughts might have inspired him to set up his own West End nightclub, Stoker's. Instead, repressed and well-read as he was, he mapped out one of the best-known horror tales in the English language, a tale of sexual dependency and moral depravity among the idle rich." Sexual dependency and moral depravity: the twin pillars of my life. Dracula obsessed by Mina, as Berlioz was by Harriet Smithson, Rossetti by Lizzie Siddal. Women are the flames that draw our moths to their destruction and therefore give purpose to our life. As one should try to have a good war, one should always seek a good destruction, destruction just being another word for life. Whether you have a 70-year destruction or a 30-year destruction, it is all the same. People who are not actively engaged in pursuing their destruction are not really living.

252

I am a broken-down person, with so many problems that had been there since birth & had never been addressed. I spent all my life just papering over my cracks trying to hold all my millions of splinters together, like the Austro-Hungarian Empire, and eventually I could do it no more. Everything came undone. It was only when everyone turned against me that I was able to fuse myself together into a coherent whole, and find myself, who I wanted to be, what I wanted to do.

253

Crowds queued up to see the space where the Mona Lisa used to be after it was stolen in 1911. I suppose when I get to Oslo next month I will go to see the space where The Scream and Madonna used to be in the Munch Museum. You have to suffer in order to make great discoveries. Like the Belgians in the Antarctic. People queue up to see the space where my personality used to be. Where my presence used to be. They are as fascinated by it as they were by the space left by the stolen Mona Lisa in 1911 or the stolen Scream now. They are captivated by my enigmatic emptiness, as they were by Garbo's or Bartok's. I go among people the way Bartok went around Hungary collecting folk tunes. At first people always thought he was a tax inspector or some other government official and were suspicious why he was asking them all these questions. People are suspicious of me. What am I up to? Why is he content to work alone at nights, in a silent hotel, like a church mouse? Like Dirk Bogarde's Night Porter, if I live like a church mouse I have my reasons. I haven't finished with hotels yet. My *Night Porter* existence in thrall to Dirk Bogarde and Charlotte Rampling and the revolving door is still not over yet.

254

I resisted the impulse to Tallulah & Tingel-Tangel & Esmeralda and I feel much better for it. Fellini's *Casanova* did turn me on, especially the opening scene with the nun in red underwear & beautiful fuckable arse, and I felt like going to Stephanie and Sunset, but luckily I was so tired from having drunk six pints in the Calcutta that it was not possible. My long vigil at the Calcutta was quite enjoyable. I hooked another two: the pink T-shirt brunette and the orange top Turkish girl. Several other beautiful big-breasted girls in tight white blouses in the hot weather. The pink halter neck top girl getting on at E— and running to get on my door so I could see her big breasts bouncing. The black top girl running for the train at Charing Cross, so I could see her big breasts bouncing over the top. Three brunette students on tube back to Charing Cross, the nearest one, short skirt, black jumper, enormous bulging big breasts. In Calcutta, coming in, spectacles, long blonde hair, big voluptuous Swedish girl in beige cardigan open over big chest in white boob tube. She sat alongside from me reading. Suddenly I felt like I was in Sweden or Norway, in the bar of the Ibis Copenhagen or the Scandic Byporten Oslo, drinking alone in the bar and spotted by some woman drinking alone. It made me so excited to get to Copenhagen and Oslo! Sweden is a dead loss—prostitution is illegal and the man will get arrested!—so no point going to Stockholm, and certainly I do not want to linger in Malmo; we shall see if I can find any excitement in Gothenburg. The bar of the Brussels Ibis will be fantastic to get back to, and the Pullman. It is a shame I will not be able to go to the Wiertz Museum, but I will go back to the Museum of Modern Art, the Cathedral, and maybe even the European Parliament this time. At nights I have got the Gare du Nord and I will also try the American Bar and try to find some others. I will end my journey in Berlin, at *Die Entführung aus dem Serail* and Sybelstraße and Monte Carlo. I am so much like Fellini's Casanova, a throbbing, gasping, white loathsome thing, gasping for its drug of sex with whoever my eyes set upon, Casanova as Dracula, as Nosferatu, as Kinski in Venezia. "The surreal nightmare world of Casanova's lost wanderings of the obscure cities of 15th century Europe comes alive and his willing enslavement to his own lust given free reign, in sex scenes which are only disturbing, could leave you wondering if you would be any different given the same freedoms." "I think you are a Casanova," Viktoriya said to me, right at the end, and now I think she is right, in the sense of being a pathetic individual whose life is governed only by the lust for sex.

255

I am just 16 days away from getting on Eurostar at Waterloo! It scarcely seems possible. It is here at last. I have got the Interrail pass and my Eurostar ticket.

256

I was thinking I do like to spend all my £3,300 all the time. As long as I have got the hotel I can keep paying it off and keep spending it again. It is OK to earn enough to pay off your debts and keep your head above water. What I have gained by trips to Munich this year—Heidi Klum and the night with Patricia (1), the night with the Romanian & the snow (2), the nights with Susi, and Irina, and Viktoriya (3); what I have gained by my trips to Berlin—Yulia and *Der Ferne Klang* (1), Riccarda and *Salome* at the Staatsoper (2), Iga and *Salome* at the Deutsche Oper (3), *Traviata* and Monte Carlo (4). What more I might gain by my trip to Brussels and Scandinavia in 16 days' time. Spend the £3,300. It is invaluable experience. Always keep spending the £3,300 and keep working at the hotel to pay it off. Then I will take an English degree and travel around Eastern Europe giving English lessons like Michael York in *Cabaret* to pay my way. I will be a perpetual traveller.

257

I am not paranoid, but I swear someone once shouted 'Kaspar Hauser' at me from a doorway as I passed, and a parrot in an Australian zoo once shouted the word 'wanker' at me. I count Oscar Wilde, Byron, Vincent Van Gogh, Edvard Munch among my friends. I live for drinking and whoring, and travelling, to be permanently held in suspension, never having to face the reality of social relationships, and partnership, and real life. Never coming down to the ground. The brothel was a regular part of life for Ernest Dowson, Edvard Munch, Van Gogh, Oscar Wilde. It is the milieu of the artist. For Freud a sexually abstinent artist was inconceivable. It is completely natural. Von Aschenbach's visits to Esmeralda in *Death in Venice* as she plays Für Elise. I have liberated myself now. The hour of the flesh is a perfectly normal part of life. Tallulah. Tingel-Tangel.

258

I have been abstinent for 22 days. No Tallulah, Tingel-Tangel, Esmeralda—nothing.

259

The purpose of my travels is now purely impure! Tallulah solely. My journeys used to be an epic three-way battle between Love, Art and Eros. I would bat between one then the other, like a ricocheting pinball. No longer. I have achieved a unity between the three, as everything serves my lust for Tallulah. I feel I have lost a lot by the exclusivity of my focus, but it is better to be free of the repression that used to make my stays abroad such epically miserable affairs. I only pursue intellectual interests that will fuel my lust, so I can later indulge that lust, where I will also inevitably fall in love with the object of that lust. "I think you are a Casanova," Viktoriya archly observed, in almost the last thing she ever said to me. At the time I thought she might mean in the sense of charming women into my embrace which was patently absurd, but now I see she meant in the sense of being a loathsome white gasping creature that feeds on the blood of women in a completely cynical way, until he falls to the side bloated, and replete, until the next day at least. Having just seen Fellini's *Casanova* I have come into this self-knowledge, and only now does Viktoriya's typically perceptive remark gain added resonance. Of all the women I have ever met in my life Viktoriya is the one I would most like to spend my life with. As we sat down with our drinks her first urgent words to me—"I am not proud of what I do"—touched me more than I can say.

CHAPTER 16
WHY DID I COMMIT MYSELF TO UNDERTAKE THIS GREAT LONG TRAIN JOURNEY ACROSS EUROPE?

Why did I commit myself to undertake this great long train journey across Europe? It is baffling. Once again, I set off like Orpheus into the Underworld, in search of Euridice. A great rift valley has opened up in my soul. A great abyss has been rent through my life, and I have fallen into it, like the Consul in *Under the Volcano*. I am dangerously lost and lonely and out of control.

261

The Modern Art Museum had almost no effect on me. Remember last time, how almost every picture had such a profound impact on me? The Paul Delvaux room, especially Nocturnes, used to turn me on so much, I would physically have to try to hide my massive erection from the other people; this time nothing. Lola de Valence, La Goulue, Les Profundeurs de Plaisir. The Temptation of St Antony was gone (!), on loan to another museum. The timing of this holiday seems more than ever like a mistake. I cannot go to Munich like I want to because of Oktoberfest, Wiertz Museum is closed, Munch Museum will be closed when I get to Oslo, and The Temptation of St Antony is gone. In the museum I was thinking it was because I really want to be in Munich and I really want to see Viktoriya again. Being in Brussels does not excite me at all—for the first time ever. Sitting in the bar of the Café Belge watching the trams & buses did not excite me as it used to (even my favourite corner tables were gone). Drinking in the Pullman does not interest me. What is it I'm waiting for? Is it just because I want Viktoriya?

262

All my senses are dulled. I am not ready for this holiday. Not thinking sharply. I forgot to take my umbrella this time and got soaked. I went to the Cathedral, but it did not move me either. I feel blanketed from the world, nothing registers or excites me. I am not even taking a reverse autistic pleasure in things. A real deadness. What the hell will I do in Oslo for three days? I wonder if something will happen to snap me out of this.

263

Brussels is where Karl Marx wrote the Communist Manifesto, 1848.

264

This is becoming a holiday about what I can't see. I can't see the Munch Museum, the Wiertz Museum, The Temptation of St Anthony. The spiralling nightmare this holiday is becoming. I needn't think it is a waste of money if I just come to Brussels and stay in my hotel every day, drinking and sleeping. I like to hide out in hotels. This is my deepest pleasure in life. This holiday is going to be so ruinously expensive that I will not be able to get back to Munich this year so better to go there this time, even for one night, while I have got the rail pass. That will sate my urge to go there, and make this holiday seem worthwhile and fulfilled. I won't need to travel again this year if I go to Munich now, however expensive it will prove during Oktoberfest. I think it will work out cheaper in the long run, to go to Munich now however much it costs. Then that will be it, the end of my travelling this year.

265

I am so relieved that I discovered my credit card stolen 8AM this morning. At the last moment it stopped me getting that 828 train to Kopenhagen and Oslo. Everything that happens is for the best. I was freed from a trip I didn't really want to make. I feel incredible relief. Now I can just take it lazy in Brussels, pop to Munich, then take it lazy in Berlin for three days. There is the gorgeous voluptuous blonde by No.42 Rue d'Aerschot that I want to see again and return to Sexy World. I am pleased that I got to the Palais de Justice today, by Louise Metro Station. I am fascinated in justice in the sense of the justice of the universe, natural fair play, versus its opposite, corruption. Corruption to me means the corruption of those who attack me and my own corruption inside. Justice also has a double meaning, then, not just fair play, but being "good", in the procedural sense of society insisting you be good and then damning you and persecuting you heavily if you are not. Justice and corruption fascinate me, which is why Palais de Justices in every city I visit are so incredibly moving to me. This one especially so, as there is a small shrine of flowers and photographs under its main portal, dedicated to the disappeared Belgian children lost to paedophiles. I got the metro to Louise, walked all around the Palais de Justice, touched its doors, looked at the skies, came back again.

266

In the Café Belge this morning I suddenly realised Maria Sharapova was on TV, playing in the Chinese Open. It was a heart-stopping moment to see her again and be reminded how much like Viktoriya she is (though Viktoriya is rather shorter and curvier). In Brussels I live on tuna & tomato melts, and ham baguettes. I sat there in the Café Belge, so pleased to still be in Brussels. That was what inspired me to make the effort to go to the Palais de Justice, to say my thanks. Really, I am so pleased my card was stolen. It stopped me from an awful journey.

267

I am still frustrated. Last night was typically thwarted, the story of this holiday. Preparing for that gorgeous whore at No.42, I came in my pants in the Sexy World kabins and wasted the opportunity. Then I went in Guest Bar, and it was disappointing, nothing to compare with Munich or Berlin, though there was one adorable heart-shaped face, my favourite girl who I would have loved to have talked to. There is no point going back there, though, as nothing is going on there. I am looking forward to tonight. More drinks in the Café Belge, tuna & tomato melt, then up to Gare du Nord for tingel-tangel, before the whores.

268

The Palais de Justice was good because it was somewhere new. It seems to sit on the edge of a cliff, on a very precipice.

269

The two Swedish blonde women in the Café Belge Saturday night, the bigger more voluptuous one. Saw her again coming out of the lift this morning. I don't know what it is I want. As soon as I get close to a woman I want to run away. Like Jack with Lulu. The incredible brunette whore in green swimsuit, black hat, massive breasts. I wanted her so much but had come again in the kabins. I went in Gascogne Cabaret opposite the Dome Hotel. Girls dance and ask you to come and put money in their knickers but I didn't. Then the Guest again. I bought a drink for the Belgian girl, who looks like something out of a Paul Delvaux picture. Then blonde and Tilly. Laura the boss was sexy. It started to get boring at about 4. I found my way back to the hotel so easily. All these years I've been going the wrong way!

270

I am so glad I had my card stolen. That spared me those awful long train ordeals to Köln, then to Hamburg, then to København, on the next morning to Gothenburg and Oslo, and then all over again, coming back. Having said that I saw a leaflet for Ibis København just now and I really felt I would like to stay there. Tomorrow is about organising my trip to Munich and Berlin. I will find out if there is an Ibis in Munich, then try the Intercity and the Senefelder. I will probably stay in Munich Tuesday and Wednesday night, before making my way to Berlin Thursday and Friday which is already paid for. If there is still no tuna I will go to Bourse and eat in McDonald's. I want my work to send me more money.

271

"Sir William Erskine—an inept, unstable Peninsular War general blamed for allowing a besieged French force to escape by forgetting to send an order after writing it out—whose last words, after jumping from a window, were 'Why did I do that?'" I feel very close to Sir William Erskine. Here in Brussels, for my fifth night, I cannot escape the notion that this holiday has been dreadfully pointless. I have pretty much taken it easy, and been very lazy, which after all is what holidays are meant to be for. I only went out on Friday and Saturday nights, saw a mindbogglingly sexy whore but resisted the temptation, or at least putting it off until next Saturday when I am due back in Brussels. Now I head to Munich. Full of trepidation. Both scared of meeting Viktoriya again and longing to meet Viktoriya again. I look forward to eating a proper meal again in Lamm's and returning to the Neue Pinakothek, and finally seeing inside the Frauenkirche. Then, as always, the White Coffin.

272

TALLULAH. I am nothing but my addiction to drink and whores.

273

183

Something has gone wrong with my hearing. I cannot hear properly. My ear seems blocked up somehow. All senses are dulled. Being cocooned in a hotel room pretty much continuously for five days has had this effect on me, and too much drink. I feel more than ever like the two sisters in *The Silence*. I am Thomas Newton, I am Chauncey Gardiner, I am Kaspar Hauser. All I want to do is write. What is wrong with that? So I will never have any money. Just earning enough living like a church mouse in a hotel night manager's job to enable me to travel a few times a year, repeatedly, to the same places, Brussels, Munich, Berlin, Vienna. Like Kenneth Williams & Joe Orton kept going back to Tangier. No one visit was ever truly successful, but the pendulum was kept swinging—that's the important thing. It is a release valve.

274

Five past seven in the morning, and still as black as sin, as we head towards the Holy Land. I am squeezed up tight in the corner of the train. Not so much through tiredness as fear, scared about Munich, feeling unprotected because I am not drunk, scared by the amount of money I am spending. A few drinks would make everything feel better but that is another seven hours away. Amazingly, last night someone tried to pick my pocket AGAIN; and using the same tactic: "Excusez-moi, do you have a light? Ah, English! David Beckham!" then shaking my hand and hooking one leg around mine in a playful mock football tackle, while obviously slipping his other hand into my pocket. Forewarned by the previous night's heist I shooed him away. "Be gone, my good man. There'll be no more of your thievery tonight. And I would advise you not to besmirch an England footballer's good name like that!" The really wonderful thing about the theft of my credit cards the previous night from my right-hand trouser pocket was that in my untouched left-hand trouser pocket was a rolled-up bundle of 400 euros in banknotes. I got away with that one.

275

After all, I think my short three or four-day trips by plane are better than these long trans-European train journeys. Ten or twelve days is too long when you are drinking every day. One tires of drinking every day and whoring every single night. Mars disarmed by Venus and her Nymphs, that fantastic epic picture in the entrance hall of Brussels Museum of Modern Art, opposite The Fountain of Inspiration, suddenly feels very appropriate. There was Trésors de Satan, Alfred Stevens's Salome, the Génie du Mal and Figure Tombale, but no Temptation of Anthony. I have scarcely even felt tempted on this holiday, my lust lost beneath an all-pervading blanket of sadness and ennui. My ever-present awareness of my parlous financial situation, spending money which isn't really mine to an extreme degree, coupled with the theft of my card is partly responsible for this, I think. That is why the notion of currency is so powerful to me and why I visit the Bourse in every city I visit along with the Palais de Justice, the Cathedral and the Opera House. Monetary currency is irrevocably linked with bodily currency, the exchange value of things. As my experience of love has always been as a result of money having changed hands, currency is therefore symbolic of bodily juices being exchanged. Every coin and every banknote becomes an erotic object therefore, charged with incredible lustful power. The Bourse therefore is every city's temple to the power of money to buy Eros.

276

Tallulah, Pandora, Lulu, Eve, Venus—my life is governed by these great erotic female archetypes. I live for these sexual goddesses. When a woman relents and indicates she would like to actually talk and get to know me better, then I run for the door, terrified, I stick the knife into her like Jack into Lulu, though he wanted what she was offering him—tenderness, affection, love—more than anything in the world, the volcano suddenly erupted inside him (all his lifelong repressed desperate longings for these things) and destroyed it. Each man kills the thing he loves. I like paying for Esmeraldas because there are no emotions involved, so it is safe. I like to push the encounters towards emotionalism, by trying to make her fall in love with me, just to flirt with that terrifying danger, that inferno, knowing I can jump back to safety at the very last moment. Like someone standing on a railway line in front of an approaching train. I flirt with the volcano, and get burnt by its fiery heat, knowing the elastic rope I am on can always pull me back to safety in an instant, like a whiplash. I lower myself on this elastic into the depths of the volcano, getting as close to the molten magma as I can get, stirring it up to its eruption, and escaping with my life just at the last moment. This was the model for my encounter with Susi in Munich, Irina in Munich, Viktoriya in Munich, Riccarda in Berlin, Iga in Berlin, Lela in Moloch, Ana Maria in Moloch, and of course innumerable others. I am frightened of love. As Claudia Cardinale gleefully tells Marcello in Fellini's 8½, "You are incapable of love! You are incapable of love! You are incapable of love!" I am a Casanova, a filthy bloated loathsome creature whose life is governed only by Eros, lustfully taking what he needs from every woman until replete and sated. But the overwhelming need comes back again so quickly. As soon as the need is emptied it starts to fill up again. I like paying for Eros, because you both know what you are getting: she gets what she wants, and you get what you want, and you are both happy. And you can always flirt with the volcano and get out again when it erupts, though not without getting burnt a bit. The moth always burns its wings. "I am not ready for repentance, nor to match regrets. For the moth bends no more than the still-imploring flame." Those fantastic words of Hart Crane, another drunk who lost himself in fleeting erotic encounters with innumerable strangers. "The sexuality of woman is the primal spring at which the intellectuality of man finds renewal." Kraus. How exciting it is to come out of Brussels Gare du Nord station into the Rue d'Aerschot and see all the women in their windows! How it fires the blood and makes a man's spirit soar. "True spirituality lies in regeneration of the flesh." The one in the black hat and the two strips of green material that almost made a swimsuit who will haunt me forever if I do not get the chance to go back and have her.

277

Eros rules my life and in every city I visit I go to pay homage to the temples of that Eros—the Palais de Justice, the Bourse, the Opera House and the Cathedral. Before beginning my night-time searches of the brothels and clubs, searching for the whore who will be the one for that night. Nights of Tingel-Tangel and Tallulah, searching for my Esmeralda, as she calls me in by playing Für Elise on her piano, half naked. I will go and become infected and die, achieving my heart's lifelong desire, as Lulu does when she is killed by a sex-murderer on Christmas Eve. Anarchic promiscuity. My favourite words in the English language are Promiscuous, Voluptuous, and Slut, which put together accurately sum up my ideal woman. The Yulias in Berlin, the Emilys in Munich.

278

Life is dramatic. Life is tense. All I feel is tension and nerves, heading towards the one I love. I cannot cope with emotions. I feel bitter and sombre. I am mining a seam in my life, by coming here to Europe for ten days. In Moloch I have a couple of whores I am fond of, Lydia and Ana Maria. There is nothing else. I want to be alone, but it is very lonely. I love the Rue d'Aerschot, and Schillerstraße, and Stuttgarter Platz, and the Gurtel. What kind of artist would I be if I didn't feel ashamed? I am Francis Bacon in India, shirt off, without a passport, standing there on a cliff, shouting, "Come and get me you cunts!" I am Kenneth Williams in Tangier, keeping the pendulum swinging. Lust is all right, it is love that is the devil. My happiest, freest, most relaxed, soul-soaring high moments in life have been down to lust. Emily in Munich on the night of the snow, Yulia, the red top girl in the Sunset Cinema. Andrea the young Greek girl in Soho with most enormous knockers in white nightie, the Egyptian, Ana Maria. I have no happy memories of love, only painful, humiliating ones. "From love I have had only trouble," Viktoriya texted me. "I am not afraid of love, but I hate it."

279

Passport Control Guards who come onto the trains always regard me as suspicious. In a full carriage, they only ask two people to show passports, me and another single man. In Malmo, once, I was escorted from the train and actually strip-searched and bag-searched in their office, while the married couple who had been sitting alongside me were never even asked to show their passports. No one arouses so much suspicion as a single man.

280

Imagine being so sexually desirable that men will PAY to have sex with you!

281

I feel there is worse to come, another blow to fall. I feel I am teetering on the edge of a precipice on this holiday. My financial exposure had already created the abyss I would have been peering over; the theft of my card nearly pushed me over it, and now I am just hanging. It could go either way. Every time I go to my cash machine now I just close my eyes and cross my fingers and am amazed when it lets me have money.

282

How Germany really is the Holy Land. We passed an Intercity Express train called Ingolstadt. Town of Frankenstein. Now we pull into Nuremberg, where Kaspar Hauser appeared in the world. Perhaps it is only when one comes to Bavaria that it becomes the Holy Land, when one hits the Romantic Road. German Romanticism is what makes it Holy. Nuremberg, Ingolstadt, Wurzburg, Augsburg, Regensburg, are its Antiochs and Tyres, but Jerusalem will always be Berlin. As I write these words the sun breaks out from behind a cloud and I feel its hot rays for the first time since I left home six days ago.

283

I think on balance the short 3 or 4-day plane journeys are better than these long European rail journeys. On the train you get to each new place with less energy and enthusiasm than the last. Not to mention less money. The excitement is not there, coming to Munich from five days in Brussels, as it would be if I came straight on a plane from Moloch. I prefer guerrilla raids.

I get more out of them in a shorter space of time. The only thing that can be said for the longer train holidays is that I write a lot more, which, after all, counts for a lot. More clearly than before I have crystallised my feelings about the Palais de Justice and the Bourse, to set alongside the Opera House and the Basilica. I passed by an Esmeralda in Brussels I would very much like to return to. Coming to Munich now is a mistake, but there are some mistakes you have to make, before you can move on.

284
Whenever I see a woman I instantly feel weak and inadequate. I am terrified that if I met Viktoriya I might actually have to go out with her on a 'date', and actually have to think of things to say, in a conversation. Safer to remain in the club, in the artificial world, governed by the exchange of money for her favours. This is what led to the break with Lela and her crying when I saw her again. The same thing happened with Ana Maria. She was reproachful and scornful of me, would not let me kiss her or touch her, because I had not been back for so many weeks? It is so strange, and mind-blowing, when a whore gets attached and you have to apologise to them for your ill-attention the way you would to a wife. That always throws me completely and makes me giddy, like the night Patricia told me B— loved me. I lost my head completely and went along Schillerstraße, eventually meeting the extraordinary Emily on the night of the snow. Then there is Susi. My belief is that my relationship with women cannot exist outside the sealed atmosphere of the brothel. Outside of that is just a black vacuum, with whirling galaxies, and no air to breathe, so the relationship dies an almost instantaneous death, when it had been so good inside. I got on fine with Chess Goddess in the Goethe Institute, the flirting between us in the classroom so incredibly thrilling, the lunchbreak she took me back to her Royal College of Music locker with her so incredibly thrilling, but once we got outside it died an instant death. Never let it go further has become my guiding principle ever since.

285
I have been called a cripple, a leper, the alien in the corner, and other more vulgar terms and this is not at school where a mild four-eyes and glasses might be all I could really expect, but in the last few years, in my thirties! People retreat to childishness when they deal with me. They make themselves look stupid. They humiliate themselves. Hatred always does more harm to the hater than the victim. The victim must just play them like a piano, like a king in his counting house, counting out his money. My calmness infuriates. My Kaspar Hauser-like almost Švejk-like implacability

enrages. I am an anarchist revolutionary. My wilful, violent, rebellious ways are my defence against my own crippling shyness and self-consciousness which makes it hard sometimes to walk down a street. Tennessee Williams knew this, Alfred Hitchcock knew this. When one learns this one does not feel so bad about one's own weaknesses and guesses that it is in fact quite common. After all, I would rather be too sensitive than not sensitive at all.

286
I am Thomas Newton, I am Kaspar Hauser, I am Chauncey Gardiner.

287
So I did nothing with Susi, and just forced myself to walk away. I did nothing with Irina, and just forced myself to walk away. I tried to put that right in my visits back to Munich this year. I threw myself at Patricia with wild abandon, I threw myself at Emily with wild abandon, I threw myself at Viktoriya with wild abandon, haunted by memory of how I had hurt myself with Susi and Irina.

288
I am going to the town of the Oktoberfest!

MUNICH

What to say, about my first day back in Munich? It is not the Munich I know! I came out of the station and did not recognise the city in front of me. I do not like it. Oxana in White Coffin told me Viktoriya is in Nuremberg. I was so excited I forgot to test her knowledge, to prove if she was telling the truth or just stringing me a line. The Caribic? Did she make up Nuremberg on the spot? And the Caribic? She says Viktoriya and Irina are there together, but I do not believe her. They are probably upstairs. Emily, the Romanian from the Night of the Snow, is not around either. She works one or two days a week, usually Friday or Saturday. Munich is a madhouse. Like a living hell. I will go to Nuremberg tomorrow to look for Viktoriya and Irina, under cover of a pilgrimage to Kaspar Hauser. It will be good to be out of Munich. One of the more incredible days of my life.

290
Just one more day of this madness to get through, before I can escape to the honest whores of Berlin.

291

Why Korn's Word Up video is so sexy whereas the White Coffin was not? My head is not right. The blonde bob was gorgeous. The brunette with balcony bra. Under normal circumstances I might have enjoyed it there. It is my inexorable destiny to go to Nuremberg to look for Viktoriya. Munich has lost its innocence for me now. Could I ever go back to just visits to the New Pinakothek, Lenbachhaus, St Michael's Church, Asamkirche, and then enjoying some innocent pleasures in the White Coffin at night? Maybe once Oktoberfest is over, it will go back to being my Munich. I feel I have really lost it now. Coming here to Munich was an emotional impulse, and now I am sliding downhill on a sheer slope of ice. It will be a relief to get back to Berlin, and out of it. This terrible fondness. Thank God, this is my last night. Then tomorrow I can go to Berlin. Straight to Sybelstraße and Monte Carlo. Then back to Rue d'Aerschot Saturday night.

NUREMBERG

A goodbye would have been lovely. It still meant everything to see you again. I still want to marry you in the Asamkirche. I don't think we will ever meet again. Lucky you. If we do I will marry you. I met Viktoriya in Nuremberg, but the meeting did not go well. I was so nervous as my train approached Nuremberg Hauptbahnhof in the dark I was almost hyperventilating. I had several beers in the station bar to give me Dutch Courage, and when I finally got into the Caribic and found her she was contemptuous of me, because I was so drunk. Irina was there, too, on the distant far side of the vast circular stage, lying on a chaise-longue, gazing at me. She never moved from that chaise-longue the whole time I was there. As I was leaving, stumbling to the exit, I realised I had left my umbrella behind, and had to go back into the club, asking the girls if they had seen it. Viktoriya came out of the sépareé with it and handed it to me without a word, walking away without a backward glance. At least I didn't lose my brolly.

293
You mess my head up. You pull me apart. I got back to my hotel 645AM! Opened the paper & was reading about a couple who split up, so she started walking along the Great Wall of China from one end, and he from the other, and after having both walked 1,500 miles they met in the middle, and said goodbye, and never saw each other again. Isn't that lovely? Nuremberg felt like that. I came out of Nuremberg station and did not know which way to turn, and there in front of me was a huge office block with 'Victoria' written all around it in blue neon in the darkness. This seemed a good omen.

294

Last night was when I finally exploded. All the emotional tension that had been building up to such a climax was released like a thunderstorm. I dived deep into darkness. I'm tired and just want to go home. To what? I feel so empty. As empty as I did walking home in the bright Berlin 4AM morning after leaving Riccarda. As empty as I did standing in the Justizpalast doorway in Munich after leaving Viktoriya the first time. Sombre and bitter. Munich has been firebombed into the ground. Lost all its magic and its innocence. Nuremberg is site of the most awful pain, now not only because of Kaspar Hauser. Walking towards Nuremberg city centre, how must Kaspar have felt? Much as I felt as I approached Nuremberg on the train last night, not knowing what I would face, what my reception would be. Helpless, completely reliant on others' kindness.

BERLIN

I arrived in Berlin and have never felt so much I just didn't want to be here. All I can feel is my despair and shame over Viktoriya. My sombreness & bitterness. But it was a gateway I had to go through, a Rubicon I had to cross. A mistake I had to make. A disaster that had to happen, before I could move on. Just another broken heart. It was incredible to see her again. One of the most incredible things to have happened to me. It was painful, actively humiliating, but it had to happen. I had to do it. I had to see her again. Meeting Diana in the Pils Bar was also a lovely thing to come from going to Nuremberg. I would like to see her again, but Martina, even more so. While I sat at the bar with Diana, Martina lounged on the chaise-longue behind us, with the most ginormous bosoms I have ever seen in my life, naked bosoms, covered by nothing but innumerable necklaces; why I spent my time and money on Diana and not Martina I will never know, as lovely as Diana was. I think I was just too much of an English gentleman to send Diana away and say I preferred Martina, but it was Martina I was lusting after. The Caribic was once again completely unsexy, as White Coffin was, as Sexyland was. The Pils Bar had a red velvety, curtained atmosphere about it, the way the Monte Carlo does.

296

Ten days of absolute insanity. Five days in Brussels, two days in Munich & Nuremberg, two days in Berlin. Humiliated everywhere. Lost it with Viktoriya and with Iga. Viktoriya was everything. Now Iga is everything.

297

It has been an adventure, hasn't it? An autistic adventure. More than ever I am the lost boy, Peter Pan pining after one Wendy after another—Susi, Irina, Emily, Ana Maria, Viktoriya, Iga. So, in time-honoured tradition, what were the highlights of this holiday? There are almost nothing but painful memories. Munich has been destroyed for me. Nuremberg was good for meeting Diana and the incredible Martina. Repairing my relationship with Iga and Riccarda. Being shocked by how beautiful Iga was. When Riccarda squeezed onto the end of the Mon Cheri couch with me & Hannah, while talking to Hannah I was reaching behind her and stroking Riccarda's back while she was reaching past Hannah to stroke my hair. The real exclamation of shock when Iga met me outside the Golden Gate. Her attempts to explain herself to me when she came back in. Her kisses. While I sat at the bar after we finished, her coming back and tapping me on the back to ask, "What is happening now?" Then, later, her soft "liebling". "Darling. Will you give me one kiss?" What beguiling words to hear! There were just these fleeting moments of tenderness, despite everything, amidst the commerce. From behind me, almost like a voice from a dream, or another world. Teasing me with its hint of tenderness.

298

"To love, to be betrayed, to be jealous, in that order, is easy. It is much more uncomfortable to be jealous, to be betrayed, and to love"—Karl Kraus—isn't that lovely? I must admit it hurt me to see you with another man. I was shocked by how jealous I felt. Of course I want you all for myself. I am an egoist, like you said. Seeing you again was so nice. I fell in love with you all over again, just like the first time I met you. That black dress & white hair. I had forgotten the effect you had on me. Why didn't I go to the room with you? I really wanted to. Why didn't I? You say I don't understand. I understand perfectly. I place you above all women. You are No.1 for me. Why did you give me your telephone number? (I'm not sure it even left Berlin with me, I was so loathsomely drunk on the night of your birthday, I certainly have never seen it since). This time cut me deeper than last time. I will be **bleeding** until I can see you again.

299

The nightmare received a new twist and reached even greater proportions, as I approached the door of the Golden Gate only to find Iga coming out of the Golden Gate, then followed by a guy in grey suit. What horror! Her shock and horror was the same as mine, as she let out a shocked "Oh!" The whole 10 days was an awful nightmare, but meeting Iga and Riccarda just made it worthwhile. This is where the revisionism begins. I am trying to see good in the darkest blackness. Meeting Diana was lovely, and the incredible Martina. All of a sudden we are in Belgium. The city of Horta. Adorable creature. All in black & white. I can't tell you how much it hurt. That you fancied him and not me. I was just thinking Iga is my Esmeralda, the whore playing Für Elise on the piano in *Death in Venice*, when the tune starts playing on the woman's mobile phone in front of me. Another one of those strange little coincidences that have been following me over the past few months. You could not make it up.

300

These maybe the 10 days that change the course of my life. Though I will still go back to Lydia, and to Iga and Riccarda in Berlin. I will cut out so much else. Everything that happens is for the best. I have been cured of Viktoriya, which is what I needed. There was no painless way to cut her out, so it was always going to hurt and be bloody and be expensive and be mythical. It was an exciting adventure. I made new contacts with Diana and Martina, renewed old contacts with Riccarda and Iga. Iga's sexiness was the best thing about the holiday.

BRUSSELS

I only ever fall in love with unobtainable women. Girls who like me I run away from. Maybe that is why I spend so much time in places like the Golden Gate. I feel safer paying for a girl's company. There is no pressure then. You made a much bigger impact on me this time than you did in April. I know you feel the same. I am writing this in bed in the Brussels hotel, having had a horrific journey back from Berlin thinking about you all the way. I am a Romantic. I need to be in love with someone unobtainable. I feel safer that way. Why didn't I go to the room with you? I really wanted to. I go to these places because I don't want emotions. I just want sex without emotion. Then I meet someone like you who I feel emotions for and it screws my head up. There is nothing that can be done for it. You don't like me as much as I like you. You are dangerous for me. I am addicted. Like any drug, I will need stronger and stronger doses of it to give me the same effect and will spend more and more money on it. I am an addictive personality. I am lost in my life, to be honest. I am missing you already. It was quite a shock to see you again. You make me wish I lived in Berlin. You looked so gorgeous in that black dress with that white hair. I had forgotten how beautiful you were. I thought about you all the way home. How much I want you. That makes you dangerous. It makes me crazy. I wish I had gone to the room with you. It did really hurt to see you with that man. I was shocked to feel so jealous. How come you never took me to a room? Never even asked if I wanted to. I wanted to test myself against the emptiness. I failed the test. I lost myself. I exploded first with Viktoriya, then with Iga.

302

I praise you above all women. You are No.1.

303

I had a pretty horrible 10 days away from home, and seeing you with that man on the way to the hotel was the final twist of the knife. Of course, it just makes me love you more. The gods are playing games with me again.

304

We are out of the tunnel and, alas, back in England. Pouring with rain. I remember the last time I went to the New Pinakothek, how thrilling it was. How much it meant to me. I was so alive to it. The last time I went to the Modern Art in Brussels. How thrilling it was. I was so alive to it. This time, nothing. I was lost in a fog of longing for Viktoriya which destroyed everything else. When I finally found her, in Nuremberg, on her last night there, I realised how stupid I'd been. I came back to Berlin, wanting a familiar face, and met Iga—who shocked me by how beautiful she was. I had forgotten. I fell in love with her. This was a deeper cut than the first time. On something of a high, I went to see Riccarda as well, and this time got on better with her, which meant a lot to me. I felt I repaired the damage of last time. She looks much healthier than I remember. She had put on some weight again and had her hair long in a bob again and looked more like her old self. I was relieved and pleased. Happily, I went back to Iga the next night, and just as I was approaching the Golden Gate, out she came in blonde hair and black dress and black handbag and followed by a man, on their way to the hotel next door. It was a shock to us both. Nuremberg was a madness, but it was a madness that had to happen. It happened with inexorable destiny. From that, falling in love again with Iga was a surprise.

CHAPTER 17
I THINK THESE 10 DAYS

I think these 10 days, these 10 nightmarish, hellish days, will change the course of my life. It was when the way I have been living my life finally blew up in my face. I have been so sick, and now I need to pull back, and clean up. I will still indulge in Tallulah occasionally, but more selectively. Only seeing the people I like, Lydia in London, Iga & Riccarda in Berlin. Maybe an Emily in Munich. But <u>can</u> Tallulah be controlled this time? I doubt it. But I know I must try to repair my bank. I have nearly bankrupted myself during these 10 days in Europe. God knows how many months it will be before I can pay it all back. I doubt whether I will be able to travel again until the New Year. Ten days is too long a time to be away when I am drinking every day without it having an accumulative degenerative effect, which resulted in the explosion of self-destructiveness with Viktoriya and Diana in Nuremberg, and then Iga in Berlin. I will set myself the target of trying to spend Christmas in Berlin. It will mean not going outside the door between now and then which will be a good thing. I will spend all my time on my writing, as I should have done for the past few years.

306

I will always want to come back to see you. You are in my blood now. I am Leontes to your Hermione. Sexual jealousy has deepened the feelings I already had for you. Seeing you rushing to the hotel next door with that man was perhaps the single most dramatic moment of my life. Even you cried out in shock when you saw me: "Oh!" That wait for you to come back in having finished with your trick will always rate as one of the most exquisitely masochistic moments of my life. It was the Epiphanic moment of this holiday. I knew I would never be free of you now. You had claimed me forever. Sexual jealousy had chained me to you forever. I am helplessly fascinated by everything about you.

307

Whenever anyone comes back from holiday and you ask them if they had a nice time, they always without fail say "FAN-tastic!" or "Won-derful!" or some equally emphatic variation. My holidays are always emotionally devastating. I always come back feeling ruined—financially, emotionally, sexually, mentally, every kind of ruin. I always feel I have been through so many doorways—so many Ishtar Gates—of the soul, crossed so many Rubicons, changed so much as a person during the course of the 4 days or 10 days or whatever it was. I have been on eight trips now this year, and every one of them I feel has taken me up to another level, like a mountaineer breaking out from one base camp and days later establishing a new one higher up—or maybe I go down a long way each time, descending the abyss, diving deeper into darkness—but the point is I always come back feeling I have really gone on some *journey*, meaning some journey of the soul and spirit which has taken me to a new place in my life. My holidays are real experiences, often nightmarish, hellish, farcical, but experiences nonetheless. These people who go and lie on a beach for a week, what do they really get out of that? I would not be able to do that, just lie on the beach or a sun-bed around a pool, doing nothing.

308

I want to go back to Berlin this Christmas—to see the *treasures*. During this 10 days in Europe I completely neglected the treasures, so obsessed was I by thoughts of Viktoriya. After Viktoriya, in despair, needing badly to see a friendly face, I found Iga again. I have never felt love like this, but I have probably said that before. So the daisy chain continues. So La Ronde continues.

309

I always say I always go further than ever before when I go on holiday and wonder if it is possible to keep going further than ever before. This time was looking like a very uneventful trip, but in Nuremberg and then Berlin I did indeed once again take things further than I had ever done before. I dived deeper into darkness. With Viktoriya, Diana and Martina in Nuremberg, then Iga in Berlin. Once again, I explored further into new territory. I no longer mind the five days I spent in Brussels doing nothing, as that was very restful, and prepared me for the torments of Germany to come!

310

If I hadn't had my card stolen Friday night I wouldn't have gone to Munich, wouldn't have gone to Nuremberg, wouldn't have met Viktoriya, probably would not have gone to see Iga when I got back to Berlin. But wouldn't I have liked those three days in Norway, drinking in the bars of the Radisson SAS in Oslo?

311

I would like to go back to Munich, the city of Franz von Stuck, and not rush this time. Take time to see the Asamkirche, and spend a long time drinking in Lamm's before eating. Spend a night in a Nuremberg hotel to go to Unschlittplatz and Kaspar Hauser Platz, before ending in the Pils Bar. A nice time with Lydia in London has released me from the worst of my sadness about Iga and enabled me to regain my equilibrium. Feel happy that I had such a nice time with Iga and do not feel sad. I want to go back to Berlin for the Alte National Gallery and The Oscar Wilde, and the opera and the Belegtes. Lydia is a sumptuous Russian blonde from Siberia. The world I live in. Of courtesans and dance halls. "I might have lived my life in a dream, but I swear, this is real". It is amazing, but my favourite people are all whores: Iga, Riccarda, Lydia.

312

Sometimes I have wanted to make myself alive to every insult, be on alert for each one, record each one in detail; at other times, like now, I prefer to sink down into the middle of a raincloud, where nothing can reach me, blanketed from all the world & its doings. All I want to think about is Iga, and getting back to see her at Christmas, and my writing. At the same time I am alive to every insult, I am likewise alive to every sign of admiration, and cannot not look at every woman who passes. So it goes that when I retreat into my cloud I don't want to even see other women. There is just Iga, and my writing. There is such great purity in this way of being, such peace & transcendence. It is like being held in the suspension of a train journey—one does not have to live again until one arrives at one's destination—in my case, Christmas in Berlin, when I arrive like Louise Brooks arriving at Berlin Zoo to be met by Pabst & crowds & bunches of roses. Christmas in Berlin will be the most fascinating journey of my life. Something unexpected always happens, so even though my plan is all about Iga, I am sure it will not turn out to be anything like that. The gods have more tricks in store for me.

COLLECTED WORKS

CASANOVA

OR LOST WANDERINGS

2006
ERNST GRAF

COLLECTED WORKS

CHAPTER 1
I AM
A
BAD BOY

I AM A BAD BOY. I AM ERNEST DOWSON, I AM AUBREY BEARDSLEY, I AM FRANK WEDEKIND. I LIVE IN A WORLD OF PALM FRONDS FLOATING ON AN INDOOR LAKE, WITH CLAUDIA BARAINSKY ON A GRAMOPHONE SOMEWHERE SINGING *HERODIADE FRAGMENTS*. THEN A *SALOME*. I LIVE IN THE CLAUSTROPHOBIC STUFFY GRANDEUR OF AN OLD BERLIN BEDROOM WITH A FOUR-POSTER BED WITH A MIRROR ON THE CEILING. I CELEBRATE MY VICES. I CENTRE MYSELF AROUND THE FLYING SCOTSMAN, AND SUNSET STRIP—THESE ARE MY CAFÉ CENTRAL AND GRIENSTEIDL, THESE ARE MY ROMANISCHES CAFÉ—AND KARL KRAUS. AROUND MY CITADEL, WITH ITS TROPICAL FERNS, ITS WORKS OF ART ON THE WALLS, ITS BIRGIT NILSSON, ITS ELENA PROKINA. I DO NOT NEED TO GET A NEW BETTER-PAID JOB, BECAUSE I DO NOT WANT TO TRAVEL ANYMORE.

YET THOSE INCREDIBLE FELICIEN ROPS PICTURES I WAS LOOKING AT THIS MORNING SO MUCH MAKE ME WANT TO GO BACK TO BRUSSELS AGAIN. IT HAS BECOME AN INCREDIBLY EROTIC PLACE AGAIN—THE TOWN OF ROPS, OF WIERTZ, OF CLARISSE. JUST TWO MORE NIGHTS TO GET THROUGH THEN I CAN GET BACK TO THE CALCUTTA & THE FLYING SCOTSMAN—I AM ADDICTED. I AM AN OPIUM ADDICT. HERE IN LONDON, IN KING'S CROSS AND CHARING CROSS; UNDER THE CHANNEL ON EUROSTAR TO BRUSSELS; IN BERLIN, AND IN VIENNA.

MY THEME: "THE VISCERAL PLEASURE IN DETACHMENT OF AN AUTISTIC PERSON".

THOSE INCREDIBLE FELICIEN ROPS AND WIERTZ PICTURES MAKE ME WANT TO GO BACK TO BRUSSELS (AND NAMUR, AND THE

201

EMPIRE AND THE GARE DU NORD). THOSE INCREDIBLE GEORGE GROSZ & OTTO DIX PICTURES, AND TILLA DURIEUX AS CIRCE AND VIKTOR MÜLLER'S SALOME HOLDING JOKANAAN'S HEAD MAKE ME WANT TO GO BACK TO BERLIN (AND MON CHERI & GOLDEN GATE & MONTE CARLO & CIRO). THOSE INCREDIBLE HANS MAKART PICTURES MAKE ME WANT TO GO BACK TO VIENNA (AND THE GURTEL).

MY OPIUM ADDICTION HAS ALREADY CAUSED ME TO RUN UP A £5,060 DEBT ON MY CREDIT CARDS. "GET TO GRIPS WITH THE IDEA THAT IT IS EATING AWAY AT YOUR MONEY, YOUR LOVE AND YOUR LIFE." NOW I WANT TO PLUNGE BACK TO BERLIN, & VIENNA, & BRUSSELS. DIVING DEEPER INTO DARKNESS! I AM COMPLETELY UNRESPONSIVE TO A WOMAN'S PROMPTINGS. I AM NARCISSUS, I AM DORIAN GRAY. I SEEM TO HAVE FORGOTTEN THE PASSION AND LOST THE DESIRE. *THE PRIVATE LIFE OF SHERLOCK HOLMES* IS "REALLY A CHARACTER STUDY OF A MAN FOR WHOM LOVE SEEMS AN IMPOSSIBILITY, AND SO HAS THROWN HIMSELF INTO HIS WORK IN AN EFFORT TO ESCAPE HIS SAD PREDICAMENT."

I never connect with anyone. I never want to become friends with anyone. I want to stay the stranger, alone & unknown. All the years I have been going to the Scotsman now, I do not know anyone there. I do not talk to anyone. Only one person has broken through my defences, and that was —, and when she gave me my chance, I just let her leave without saying a word. She is nice to me still, but will never give me another chance. I should have been a week & a half, or even two & half weeks into my relationship with — now. Instead here I am still shut outside the window, longing to be inside, but knowing it is too late. I am Stéphane in *Un Coeur en Hiver*. I am Noodles. I am Will Penny. I am Edvard Munch. At this moment, I do not like anyone. I do not care about anyone or anything. I am bitter and nihilistic.

YOU CAN BE STRANGE AS YOU WANT AT THE SCOTSMAN! BE STRANGE & ECCENTRIC, NOT DOWN & DEPRESSED! IF YOU ARE POSITIVE, & RADIATE HAPPINESS, PEOPLE WILL BE DRAWN TO YOU. I WILL LOSE MYSELF IN NIHILISM & SELF-DESTRUCTION TO PUNISH MYSELF FOR LOSING —, LIKE BERLIN IN THE 1920S. I WANT TO THROW A STONE INTO THE POND. I WANT TO THROW A BOMB & BE HELD RESPONSIBLE FOR IT. THAT IS WHY I MUST PUBLISH THE BOOK, *AUTISMUS*, & BE DAMNED FOR IT IF NECESSARY.

REMEMBER THE SWEETNESS OF KRISTINA LAUGHING & TELLING ME IT WAS HER FIRST DAY. REMEMBER THE SWEETNESS OF THE MCDONALD'S GIRLS. REMEMBER THAT — WANTED ME ALL THOSE MONTHS. I AM ERNEST DOWSON. I AM VINCENT VAN GOGH. I AM PATRICK CAULFIELD, SITTING ALONE IN LONDON PUBS JUST WATCHING THE WORLD PASS BY, AND LEAVING WHEN IT STARTED TO GET BUSY. GOING TO THE BAR AT THE THEATRE INTERVAL & NOT GOING BACK IN FOR THE SECOND ACT BUT STAYING DRINKING ALONE IN THE EMPTY BAR AS THE BAR STAFF CHATTED AMONGST THEMSELVES & BUSIED THEMSELVES CLEARING THE EMPTY GLASSES. I AM A STRANGE CREATURE. A STRANGE, ECCENTRIC, & DEPRESSIVE CREATURE. — KNOWS NOW THAT ALL IS NOT WELL WITH ME. I HOPE I SEE HER AGAIN. — KNOWS NOW I CAN NOT BE THE BOY FOR HER BUT SHE WILL ALWAYS HAVE FONDNESS FOR ME, I HOPE. THE WAY SHE STOOD IN FRONT OF ME & LET ME PULL HER HAIR TWICE, AND JUST TURNED AROUND & GRINNED EACH TIME, AND THEN NEXT TIME PUT HER HOOD UP & WAITED FOR ME TO TURN AROUND & NOTICE HER, BEFORE WALKING OFF GRINNING, SUGGESTS THAT. THE WAY I LOOKED AT HER FROM THE SIDE AND SHE JUST LOOKED BACK TELLS HER I CARE ABOUT ONLY HER & SHE KNOWS THAT.

I DRANK SO MUCH I BECAME STUPID ON SATURDAY NIGHT. THAT IS OK. I LIKE GETTING STUPID. I CAN LAUGH IT OFF. LIKE I SPILT THE DRINK OVER MYSELF WITH BECKY, BUT SHE HAS BEEN SO FRIENDLY & NICE SINCE THEN (WHY HAVEN'T I SEEN HER FOR SO LONG?). I AM ERNEST DOWSON. I BECOME A LITTLE BIT INSANE WHEN I DRINK. OF COURSE I MUST KEEP GOING TO THE SCOTSMAN. IT IS MY *TWENTY THOUSAND STREETS UNDER THE SKY* WORLD. I tell myself I earn the night-time drinking by doing my writing all day long. That is what I tell people. I need to make it true now. I feel justified going to the Scotsman and Sunset Strip every night, if I have been working on my book all day. THEN WHEN PEOPLE ASK ME WHY ARE YOU HERE ALL THE TIME, I CAN TELL THEM MY ROUTINE: "I WORK ALL DAY ON MY BOOKS, THEN AT NIGHT I REWARD MYSELF BY COMING OUT & DRINKING". I AM A WRITER. I STAND QUIETLY IN THE CORNER & OBSERVE & RECORD. I NEVER GET INVOLVED, EXCEPT WHEN I GET LURED OUT OF THE CASBAH LIKE PÉPÉ LE MOKO BY SOMEONE LIKE —. I NEEDED TO END IT WITH —. I HAD TO BRING THINGS TO THEIR CRISIS POINT SO IT COULD FINALLY BE OVER. I PUSHED IT ALL THE WAY THIS TIME, JUST SO I KNOW IT IS

DEFINITIVELY OVER. NOW I AM HAPPY & I CAN MOVE ON. I HAVE NEARLY GOT INVOLVED WITH ESMERALDAS BEFORE. I CAME SO CLOSE TO A RELATIONSHIP WITH LELA, WITH ANA MARIA, WITH LYDIA. MAYBE I WILL GO ALL THE WAY WITH PAMELA. NOW I CAN REALLY FLIRT WITH JANET. I WRITE SMALL MONOGRAPHS ABOUT PEOPLE WHO CANNOT LOVE, NO MORE THAN 45-46 PAGES EACH—*AUTISMUS, LOTTA, THE COLD ICY AIR OF THE MOUNTAINS* and *CASANOVA (OR LOST WANDERINGS)*.

PEOPLE DO NOT KNOW WHAT IT IS LIKE—TO NOT BE ABLE TO LOVE; TO NEVER HAVE BEEN IN A LOVING RELATIONSHIP WITH ANOTHER HUMAN BEING. ALREADY — IS AS CLOSE AS I HAVE EVER BEEN.
     WHAT HAPPENED BETWEEN ME AND — WAS THAT FATAL MOMENT OF HESITATION THAT TOOK PLACE BETWEEN BRANDO'S PAUL AND MARIA SCHNEIDER'S JEANNE WHEN SHE HAPPILY TELLS HIM SHE LOVES HIM. IT SHOCKED HIM INTO SILENCE. HEARTBROKEN, SHE THOUGHT SHE HAD BEEN REFUSED, AND KILLED HIM IN HER HEART, ONLY FOR HIM TO TURN UP TO TELL HER HE ACCEPTED, AND THAT HE LOVED HER, TOO—BUT IT WAS ALREADY TOO LATE. HE WHO HESITATES IN LOVE IS ALWAYS LOST. IF I HAD GONE WITH — THURSDAY NIGHT LOVE WOULD HAVE HAPPENED. IN THAT MOMENT I LET HER GO WITHOUT FOLLOWING, OUR LOVE DIED. "You see, an artist has to be very careful when he wants to marry someone, because an artist never realises his capacity for making his companion miserable. He's obsessed by his creative work and by the problems it poses. He lives a bit like a daydreamer and it's no joke for the woman he lives with. One always has to think of that when one wants to get married" (Ravel to Manuel Rosenthal). Artists are not made for conventional relationships, and I think that is why I let — go that night. THE AMAZING THING IS — NEVER SHOUTED BACK AT ME, HAS NEVER GOT ANNOYED AT ME. SHE STILL JUST WEATHERS MY CRAZY PERIODS, AND THEN TENTATIVELY SMILES AT ME THE NEXT TIME SHE SEES ME, TO SEE IF I AM OK AGAIN. WHAT AN AMAZINGLY LOVELY PERSON SHE IS. SHE WAS FORLORN & LONELY THOSE NIGHTS ON DECEMBER 28TH AND THE WEDNESDAY, AND PROBABLY RECOGNISES THAT I AM FORLORN & LONELY, TOO, AND DOES NOT WANT TO HURT ME.

CHAPTER 2
WELL WHERE DO I
GO
FROM HERE?

Well, where do I go from here? It has been a very stressful few months. I feel such tiredness & dread of me at work. THE ONLY WAY TO BEHAVE WHEN ATTACKED IS WITH MORE DEFIANCE! LIVE MORE WILDLY! DO WORSE! PROVOKE & PROVOKE THEM EVEN MORE! FLAUNT YOURSELF IN THEIR FACES! I AM FRANCIS BACON! I AM WEDEKIND! I AM KASPAR HAUSER! I AM *AUTISMUS*. I AM *LOTTA*. I AM *THE COLD ICY AIR OF THE MOUNTAINS*. I AM WALKING THROUGH THE ISHTAR GATE. I AM SEEING ELENA PROKINA IN *EUGENE ONEGIN*. I AM SEEING VIKTOR MÜLLER'S SALOME. I AM SEEING ADOLPH MENZEL'S BAROQUE ALTARS. Everyone is so contemptuous and scornful of me at the moment. So what? I am autistic. I am strange & eccentric. I am silent & withdrawn. "Solitary and private, in spite of the crowd around them, Roosters enjoy their dreams."

It was 14 years ago that I became addicted to opium, the opium that I call Tallulah. "My name is Tallulah, I live till I die. I take what you give me, and I don't ask why". I have been lost in Tallulah ever since. And, consequently, have fallen ever deeper and deeper into debt, which, further consequently, makes me ever more reliant on my mother. Baudelaire died in his mother's arms on August 31, 1867, in a Paris clinic. "We're obviously destined to love one another, to end our lives as honestly and gently as possible," Baudelaire had written in a letter to her. "And yet, in the awful circumstances in which I find myself, I'm convinced that one of us will kill the other." "I've made a lot of friends in exotic places. I don't remember names, but I remember faces". Ravel lived with his mother practically all his life up until her death. Three years after her death, when Ravel was thirty-nine, he wrote to a friend, "My despair increases daily. I'm thinking about it even more, since I have resumed work, that I no longer have this dear silent presence enveloping me with her infinite tenderness, which was, I see it now more than ever, my only reason for living." "Lonely? You don't have to be lonely. Just come and see Tallulah. We can chase your troubles away." Peter Sellers and Kenneth Williams, too, were completely inseparable from their mothers right up until the end. Little lost boys right until the end.

Whenever I feel depressed, my old sexual demon returns, and that banishes my despair in mad displays of wild exhibitionism. It is the Weimar Berlin spirit. It is Josephine Baker on the stage in nothing but a girdle of bananas. It is Anita Berber the sex dancer losing herself in opium and gin. It is George Grosz and Otto Dix. I progressed from The Flying Scotsman to harder stuff and then back to The Flying Scotsman again. I am pushing the boundaries of what The Flying Scotsman can offer however. How much I would like to fuck J—. How much I would like to fuck K—. How much I would like to fuck L—. I like to be on the edge. I like my CALCULATED madness with —, just pushing things as far as I wanted them to go—and then pulling back. So I had an effect on people & stirred things up. I like pushing things CALCULATEDLY with —. I would like to see Clarisse in Brussels again. Tuesday is the anniversary of *Lulu* at the E.N.O. and VIENNESE EROTICISM. Immerse myself in Berg, Webern and Schoenberg, the most sensually decadent music ever written. And, immersed in it, soaked in it like whiskey, go back to The Flying Scotsman! All I care about is my magazine, my Fackel. I have nothing else. I am a broken down man living in the ruins. — thought she wanted to get involved then changed her mind. What is important is to give style to one's character, and to turn one's mistakes into something that had to happen for the overall good, and one must not be without. The world's so quiet & silent at night.

I felt good & confident, & happy to be out in just my jumper with sleeves rolled up. I went into Charing Cross station feeling so happy, exchanged a nice smile with the Calcutta barman who already had my pint pouring before I got to the bar. They had the Hits Chart on the TV, with Charlotte Church first, & then during my second pint the most gorgeous voluptuous dark blonde girl came in. I sat watching her in profile as she was at the bar & she knew I was looking. Her hair was long & thick & combed so it hung down long on the right side of her face. She had a little black jacket on over red party dress, so low cut over massive massive voluptuous tits. She came & stood to the left of me so she could now see me, & before long was joined by a man in a suit. She had to get her own stool, so I could take another good look at her as she came back with it. They left after one drink. I had an erection as I was sitting there. Summer is here. I went in Sunset Cinema! The films were awful, but I really felt like it. It felt good to be moving from cinema to cinema with my big swollen cock out of my pants but just rolling inside my trousers. I went to Pamela. Then I looked for Renata but there was no answer at her door, so I went upstairs because I thought I heard her voice, but it was some Russian or Lithuanian. I stayed anyway which was stupid. A very expensive night.

All I want now is to lose myself in classical music. Just accept this will take a long while to get over. You are heading for ruin. Concentrate on the positives. Concentrate on writing with blue hands in cold stoveless rooms like Nietzsche, heading to the cold icy air of the mountains, where the air is thinner & there are less people. I always want to get to where there are less people. I seem to have lost interest in art museums, in classical music concerts. I am just lost in an emptiness. All there is is drinking. This coming week I will devote to writing, staying up all night, into the early hours of the morning. Funny how sweet & lovely to me the new brown top barmaid was; she was gorgeous to me. Jane was lovely to me. Even though my life is getting better year on year, there is always a period each year when I go into real psychological darkness & desperate straits.

Ernest Dowson and Hart Crane would both get drunk every night, and usually become violent & almost insane. I am driving myself almost to insanity every night at the Flying Scotsman. So where are my poems? Try to get into the habit of going to the Scotsman just once a week, and never again on a Saturday. If I go just once a week, then I can also go into Soho afterwards, for Sunset Strip, Sunset Cinema and maybe Pamela as well. The other two days off I will concentrate on staying in and writing through the night. I always love seeing Pamela. How good it felt to be in Sunset Cinema going up & down stairs between the two cinemas with my big swollen sore cock rolling inside my trousers. The sexual charge in those places is fantastic, and now summer is coming there may be more chance of finding some girls in there, too. All artists have to throw themselves into the gutter. Face it, the greatest memories of my life have come in the Astral Cinema, the Soho Cinema, and the Sunset Cinema. All the incredible hot erotic memories from those places! I drink to derange my senses & go into the dream world. From there I can go back to Soho and the Sunset Cinema. Just imagine if the Flying Scotsman did private dances as well! Thank God they do not! There is something glorious in my drunken stupidities at the Scotsman. But please—once a week! Then I will allow myself Sunset Cinema as well. Like Hart Crane cruising the violent & dangerous Brooklyn,

Manhattan & Hoboken shorefronts I cannot help but keep going back into Soho cinemas, despite the shame & ignominy & ruin it brings on myself—because the highs are so great & so exciting!

I like getting wilder & wilder. Audit Day today. The — is going to be audited. I am going to get caned. Infernal's From Paris to Berlin is No.4 in the charts! Reminding me so much of my travels. Also the Out of Touch, Out of Time video in the Calcutta. I love the excitement of travel. IN THE LAST TWO WEEKS I HAVE SPENT £422! I COULD HAVE GONE TO BERLIN INSTEAD & USED IT TO PAY FOR THE £165 BA FLIGHT & £225 BERLIN PLAZA FOR FOUR NIGHTS, STILL WITH BEER & KNESEPFANNE MONEY LEFT OVER! I COULD HAVE SEEN THE HEATHROW PON DE REPLAY WOMAN. THEY'VE SHOCKED US AND HELPED OUR UNDERSTANDING OF THE WORLD. TWELVE BOOKS THAT CHANGED THE WORLD. I WILL WRITE 12 BOOKS THAT WILL CHANGE THE WORLD. THE H.M.S. BEAGLE LANDED ON THE GALAPAGOS 1835. I AM A GENTLEMAN SCIENTIST. A SYNOPSIS OF HIS LIFE'S WORK. PUBLISHING IT WAS LIKE CONFESSING TO A MURDER. I shrank from all contact with the other children in nursery. I shrank from all contact with other pupils at school. I shrink from all contact with people now. One of the great things about me is my blissful uncaredness: I couldn't care what — or — think of me. I am in my private world, going there for my private reasons.

Oh, I get home feeling so down & depressed. I don't know what to do. I either go repeatedly to Flying Scotsman and Sunset Strip & derange my senses & watch strippers all night, or I stay put in the house and let another night go by inside the four walls. What a choice. Sometimes I will force myself to *Phaedra* or *As You Desire Me* or *The Gothic Imagination*, but I derive no real enjoyment from it—it seems so much less real than the sex dancers & the drink. I HAVE to do the writing to earn the drunkenness. I am cut off from everybody, & that's how I like to be, & that's how I want to be. S— told you she liked you. H— told you she liked you. — told you she liked you. I AM WRITING A BOOK ABOUT SEX DANCERS. ABOUT ANITA BERBER & JOSEPHINE BAKER. I USE THEM AS MY DRUGS. Poor bus stop girl. She doesn't realise what a resolutely silent person I am. Polish D—, G—, M—, were all so warm to me until they realised I am not going to talk to them, and then they become surly, & stony-faced, & contemptuous. I AM DEPRAVED. LIKE SALVADOR DALI. LIKE OSCAR WILDE FEASTING WITH PANTHERS. LIKE WITTGENSTEIN CREEPING INTO THE PRATER AT NIGHT IN SEARCH OF ROUGH TRADE. LIKE HART CRANE CRUISING THE DANGEROUS & VIOLENT MANHATTAN,

BROOKLYN & HOBOKEN WATERFRONTS AT NIGHT. What do I keep going to the place for to gaze at the girls dancing? I like to lose myself in it, enter another world.

I feel so sad & down now. I am so glad I managed to get some picture on BBC1 so I could watch *Dr Who* with Sophia Myles as Madame de Pompadour. While he is reading her mind, she instead reads his. "Lonely. So, so lonely." "Don't worry, it will pass," he tells her. "No," she says. "You. My lonely angel." And he is shocked into total silence. How shocking when someone understands us. I cannot even talk to my own mother. What is the matter with me? I love her more than anything in all the world and cannot say a word to her. How fickle I am. A few weeks ago — was all I wanted. Now I cannot stop thinking about Melani. I dream she is the one who will understand me, and see through the masks and veils I cover my loneliness with. The Doctor has always been so lonely and always will be. Sherlock Holmes has always been so lonely and always will be. Will Penny. Stéphane in *Un Coeur en Hiver*. Noodles. How lovely of Melani to instantly turn to me the moment the man went to the bar, to say hello to me and ask if I was OK. How naturally I went up to her and cradled her face and hair in my hands and kissed her. It felt like we belonged together. I have not even spoken to her for almost two months, I have passed so many times without even acknowledging her, how strange that it felt so natural & instinctive to kiss her and stroke her face & hair this time? Maybe she is thinking of that, too. There is something between us, and there always has been. But I thought that about —, too. I AM ERNEST DOWSON. I AM VINCENT VAN GOGH. I AM THE DOCTOR. LONELY. SO, SO LONELY. WHERE IS MY SOPHIA MYLES? IS IT MELANI? I got a message to say Lydia called 19:46, just as *Doctor Who* was ending. Maybe she was watching it, and thinks of me as her lonely angel, who steps through her fireplace or her mirror every now & again & then disappears again! I wish she was my Sophia Myles, but she cannot be. I thought she might be once, but I have lost those illusions. It has been raining, slowly, splattering rain, slowly hissing traffic, all evening since I got back to the house. The dark green trees below my balcony rustling & whispering in the breeze. It is a lovely sound. I love summer rain. I wish Melani could be my Sophia Myles. How could anyone ever love me? In — years it has never happened, not once, not one single time. It was so lovely of Melani to reach out to me on Wednesday. When I said "Well, I'll leave you with your boyfriend" she laughed so much & so loud. This *Dr Who* series has been one of the finest things on TV in recent memory, alongside *Casanova* and *Twenty Thousand Streets Under the Sky*.

You cannot complain. Look how you shut out —, look how you shut out —. Look how you shut out S— and H—. Do you not think all those girls felt humiliated? I REALLY HATE THOSE MORNINGS WAKING UP HUNG OVER, MY BRAIN FULL OF HOLES, JUST TOSSING & TURNING NOT WANTING TO GET UP UNTIL AFTERNOON. I DESPISE THEM. I WANT TO END THAT WAY OF LIFE. I HATE THOSE NIGHTS STAGGERING HOME DRUNK, JUST THROWING MY CLOTHES ON THE FLOOR & PASSING OUT IN BED. LET ME CHANGE THAT NOW. ONE NIGHT A WEEK ONLY I CAN DRINK. I LOVE SO MUCH BEING CLEAR-HEADED. I am interested in the men who depended so much on their mothers right until the end of their or their mother's lives, such as Peter Sellers, Kenneth Williams, Ravel. How DID I get such a good picture on BBC1 tonight? It was a wonderful piece of good fortune, and I am grateful for it.

*

A night of madness & insanity, worthy of Ernest Dowson. Coming to the bar of the Calcutta was a beautiful little brown-haired girl, hair held in bun, but one bit hanging down the side of her face, black trousers, tight light blue top over most massive breasts. I could not stop looking at those breasts. She couldn't get served so gave up in the end. Why do barstaff always serve women last? I would serve them first. After two & a half up to Sunset Strip. Melani was sitting at bar as I arrived & said hello & let me kiss her on the cheek, then she was saying something to Juliana in Brazilian, and Juliana was quite sweet to me after that. I had no further contact with Melani, apart from the fact when she came on stage she winked to me at the back. Elektra was sexy as ever but no eye contact this time. I watched most of the Middlesboro-Sevilla final until the end, but Melani was talking to an old man who looked like Sigmund Freud all night. She is bewitching. You could tell he was absolutely bewitched by her. I left before 10 & went to the cinema. I looked at the films & almost did not go in but saw the name Brandy Talore on one of them & stayed for that. As soon as I went upstairs, I found a mob of men gathered around & thought this is what I come to Sunset Cinema for! Some girl was leaning over the chairs at the back being vigorously fucked from behind while everyone else crowded around. I managed to squeeze in & was feeling her tits like stones & her arse, and even got a finger in her pussy. Then she said "tea break" & I saw she was about 50 years old. An hour later I went back up there & the same thing again. This time one man finished, another man took his place, she put the condom on, sucked him a bit, then bent over & he started pumping her. When he finished, a gap opened up & I took his place! She put the condom on me,

210

sucked me a bit but I was already so hard, bent over & let me pump away. I of course could feel nothing, so gave up & after that she took a break again. Back downstairs was brunette in white & grey slip dress with man, and she was sucking him off while he fingered her pussy. I sat down in the seat next to her with my big cock out. He told me not to touch her, but after about ten minutes I could not resist & stroked her thigh. She told him & he got angry at me & they left. I moved down the front to enjoy the rest of the Brandy Talore/Jessica Sweet film. It WAS really good. What a hot night in the Sunset! I rather think it is like this every night. You just have to be there every night & hang around for a couple of hours & something will always happen. Despite the excitement of the two girls I still was not ready to come, so I let some man get my cock out & wank me & then I started to feel on the verge. I stayed until the film ended & the lights came up & left still with my huge cock bulging in my trousers! I love walking the streets like that. Renata's place seemed to be shut up. I went in the first doorway around the corner. Upstairs was busy, and downstairs three Indian guys were knocking at door, and as it opened I saw it was black-haired Sicilian Demi from before, so I slipped in in front of them. My God, I forgot how sexy Demi was. Flat-chested yes but that face is so hot. She took my 20 and made me wait in room & did not even take a tip for maid. In room she put condom on me, sat on bed & sucked me to get me hard & I never even paid for French! In the waiting room she originally said 30 until I protested then straightaway she said "OK 20". With free suck thrown in! God, she was sexy. I wanted another ten minutes, but she had someone waiting. In kitchen she was on her phone, still sitting with no knickers because I could see her pussy. She refused to look up or acknowledge me, so I walked in & stroked her cheek. The maid said goodbye to me kindly, & that Demi was off two weeks after this week. Maybe I will go back Friday! I went to Pamela after that & my God I'm sure her breasts get bigger every time I see her. She turned around & let me fuck her doggy style but would not lie flat so I said don't bother. Fucking her was so nice but I still could not come. I paid £43 in total for twenty minutes. I told her again I wanted to see her & I wanted to take her home with me. She asked where do you live actually? On your own? "Alone, alone, alone. Isn't it lonely living on your own?" "You tell me," I said. "I've got a dog," she said. "A dog?" "Yes," she smiled. She smiled a lot & we got on well enough. Maybe she will finally relent, like Ana Maria did (nearly), and Lela (was just about to). I would love to bring her back here with me. She is really gorgeous. Ana Maria always kissed me so passionately, but she was Spanish; Lela let me sometimes kiss her chastely on the mouth, but she was Romanian; Swedish give you nothing!

After my haircut & after dinner I went back to Charing Cross. Had three in the Calcutta on a Friday night, one or two sexy girls but mostly older women! Then straight to Sunset Cinema but it was already nearly 22:30. After a while black jacket, black skirt, black-stockinged woman came in upstairs screen with man, medium brown hair, and they sat not doing much. I came back and sat just behind them & saw her skirt was pulled up high & she had suspenders showing. Man to my left started reaching around & grabbing her breasts, and with that it was like a whistle was blown, because everyone jumped from their seats & fell upon her. It was Kay, the same black dress woman I had seen before. I pulled down her dress from behind and was fondling her breasts, while one man stood in front of her wanking. I was rubbing my erect penis against her head, wrapping it in her hair, rubbing it against her cheek, all I could reach from the row behind. She kept saying "don't spunk on my black clothes." And "Don't come in my hair!" "Oral sex is all she will do" the man kept saying. I so much wanted to be around the front. Then she said something I didn't catch and the man next to me said kindly to me, "You didn't mean to, mate, did you. It was an accident, wasn't it." It got so hot she said it was like a sauna & eventually they gave up & went downstairs and were gone. I got a look at her in the bar to see her face for the first time & she is really pretty. Popped into Boulevard but the girls were so anonymous—another year until I go back! My cock is so hard now as I write this.

The Makropulos Case was good. One of the best things I have seen at the E.N.O. in 14 years. Each act was very short with two intervals which meant I could go down to the Lemon Tree three times! The first time I went in and in corner of my eye I saw the white top barmaid from before bending over, this time not in an open shirt but a tight white T-shirt over straining bra. My eyes popped out of my head, my heart burst out of my chest, my cock burst out of my trousers. I admired her very much every time she went collecting glasses. The second time I went for a half the two girls were talking & when I caught their attention white top did a pose, as if to say, "Oh sir, how can I help you?" She was so red hot. Her hair was up in a ponytail this time, but I am sure it is the same one. The sexiest barmaid in London. The Lemon Tree does it every time. I will definitely go back to see *The Makropulos Case* again, just so I can go back to the Lemon Tree. I have spent £462 in two weeks. There can be no more Pamela or cinema. I don't know. I feel crazy about all the money I am spending now. I must get my life in order.************I could not talk to Melani. I could not talk to Lemon Tree barmaid, as much as I love her breasts. I could not talk to bus stop girl, as much as I want to fuck her from behind. Pamela is easier. They are the four women vaguely in my life at the moment. Oh, and Demi. Cut off from all emotion. Cut off from all communication. Cut off from all conversation. Yet there was something so gentle & sensitive about me. Drinking myself to death, diligently, determinedly, patiently, quietly & without wanting to cause any fuss to anybody. It was very moving watching Emilia Marty. She had lived for 300 years & did not want to live anymore. She didn't care about anything anymore. There had been so many men in love with her, so many men killed themselves over her, so many men threatened to kill her. I already felt very old when I was a child, so tired of everything even as a child. I feel like I have lived 300 years already. I was reminded also of Phèdre, continuing to seduce long after seduction had ceased to be a pleasure. I still doggedly go back to Tallulah and Esmeralda, long after I ceased to get any real enjoyment out of them. I feel so incredibly unhappy now. I must become pure and small and humble and return to the writing.

I have got to pull myself together. But when have I ever been any different? I go from one addictive behaviour to another. If I don't go to the Flying Scotsman, I go to Sunset Strip and Sunset Cinema and Pamela; if I don't do that, I go to the E.N.O. and ogle the Lemon Tree barmaids in the intervals. All my life has been lost to the grip of addictive & obsessive behaviour. Because I am lost. I need a secure, loving relationship with a partner. Who are the current contenders? Melani or Pamela. I love it when I am at my lowest, because then I can write most bleakly & most starkly. Then I can write in blood, in cold, stoveless rooms with blue hands. There is so much pain inside me. That sounds melodramatic but I do not know what else to say. I am a vessel brimming over with pain. I long to be able to talk to my mother. I long for Melani or Pamela. If I died tomorrow my mother would not know the first thing about me. I record the pain of my life. I record the loneliness of my life*******Oh, but I have such soft feelings for Melani.***********Who are the women in my life now? Melani, the Lemon Tree barmaid, the bus stop girl, Pamela, Demi.***********Like it or not, my relationships with whores are the most important of my life: Lydia, Iga, Riccarda, Diana, Ana Maria, Lela, Pamela—all had a massive impact on my life. Not to mention the dancers, —, Anya, Sylvia. It's only when you go too far, you suddenly find yourself on a cliff, teetering over a precipice, like the Justice Palace in Brussels. Wasn't the time I spent with Pamela worth every minute? As was all the time I spent with Ana Maria, and Lela, and Iga & Riccarda & Diana & Viktoriya & Irina. That debt figure of £5,000 has a whole lot of pleasure & joy in it.***********All this money I have spent in the past two weeks was absolutely vital. It could not have been otherwise. I had to see Melani both times, I had to go to twenty minutes with Pamela, and then to thirty minutes. I had to go to *La Belle Helene* and *The Makropulos Case.* So what am I to reproach myself for? I had to go with Demi. I had to go to The Lemon Tree. It was obsessive, but I enjoyed all of it. All of it was intense. The debt I am running and pushing is absolutely essential money well spent. As I always say, I could be struck by lightning tomorrow, and what use to me if I tightened my belt and lived like a monk for a year just to owe zero pounds on my credit cards? I could don my hairshirt for two years and never go out, reducing my credit card to zero, then released to enjoy myself again, step outside the house & be struck by a lightning bolt. What then the use of those two years saving money & being a good boy? Better to always run a debt & keep having amazing experiences.

Do I feel good about myself now? No. Average films in the cinema, not completely mediocre. No girls there except the old one upstairs who lets everyone fuck her one after the other. I got nice and hard though and knew I was ready for Demi. She looked fantastic in black widow's weeds. Amazingly she turned over without complaint and from feeling nothing, I immediately started to come. I must insist Pamela turns over for me too. Nothing or no one else exciting. I missed the real substance of a night at the opera. Something to engage my brain and spirit. A low-key night all round. I miss Lemon Tree barmaid—I cannot get her off of my mind. Demi is like a black-haired Irina, with a bit of Famke Janssen thrown in. As she lay on her front, she kept her hand underneath her, and I almost got the feeling she was getting some pleasure out of it (remember that is the room Kimi said she was going to come, "Don't stop! Don't stop!"). She was certainly happy enough to turn over for me. I only slept for about two hours or so. I feel not hung over, not sleepy, just longing for someone to be with me. Someone to hold and cuddle and stroke. I suppose I will go back to Sunset a lot once the World Cup starts. There is no better place to watch football. ARIODANTE tonight I suppose.********I remember Demi the first time complimenting me on my toenails & then touching my cock. "And that's VERY good—if you didn't drink!" Now she turned over so readily and put her hand underneath herself as I fucked her from behind.

CHAPTER 3
IT IS QUITE FITTING THAT I SHOULD HAVE TROUBLE WITH MY EYES

It is quite fitting that I should have trouble with my eyes, given I devote so much of my life to "the gaze", to ogling at women on a stage, and elsewhere, to spending so much time looking at myself in mirrors, to writing & reading such small print on my computer. I feel like Nietzsche, who suffered such appalling, crippling health complaints, headaches & eye pain and such like, which so reduced his ability to work. I feel like Ernest Dowson, drinking too much, an appalling tragic wreck; like Hart Crane always looking "for bolts that linger". Oscar Wilde was ruined by a man, as I have been ruined by a woman, once before, and would surely be again if I went with Lydia to Russia. Phèdre hates herself because she is so full of sin. She is half animal, so she cannot help herself, but she hates herself for being what she is, and not being able to control her lusts. Phèdre is another Lulu, another Salome, another Traviata; women have to be killed if they cannot control their lusts. Well, what do people do to me? What did people do to Oscar Wilde, to Bill Clinton? Byron?

A time of illness, a time when we feel low, and hit rock bottom, is always good, because we can strip everything away, and just see what is really important to us. What we want to do, what we want to be, cut away all the superfluous things that have been allowed to encrust themselves to us, and concentrate on the simple essentials: classical music, ferns, the books. Then we can start to bounce back, and climb back out of the blackness, feeling

215

stronger, calmer. Who is my Helen of Troy now, imprisoned in London? Is it Pamela? Or Melani? Maybe yet Jolanda? And now the tooth ache returns. So that is two urgent appointments I must now make for next week. Now I am frightened to eat anything as well as wanting to close my eyes all the time.

To help deal with the pain I will try to get recordings of *Phèdre* by both Rameau and Britten...and something of Rosa Ponselle. I escape from the misery of my life into opera. From the misery of my eye problems, and my teeth problems. From the misery of the "catastrophes of love". It is transcendence. It is entering the Kingdom of Death, in love with Princess Mort. It is stepping through the mirror that turns into water, and escaping from the world. I am happiest in the Kingdom of Death, where the skies are always black & there is no sun. The white ruins are lit by a spectral light only. There I can meet the Kaiserin on her marble throne. I can meet Rosa Ponselle and Maria Callas. How can I explain that to people who keep asking if I am "all right", because I seem "very quiet"? Just all go away and leave me alone, please. It is floating on my back on a lake in a steaming palmhouse, amid the palm fronds and giant lilypads, listening to *Herodiade Fragments* on the ancient gramophone. Somewhere in the steam my odalisques wander, and stroll, and lounge, and fuck. Suffering makes us soulful, suffering makes us spiritual. We grow lovely out of our longing, wrote Henriette Hardenberg. Longing for freedom makes us beautiful. "I lie still and fearless as you enter."

I didn't get to the Calcutta until 645PM. Got to the Midnight Bell to discover that after missing Kelly & Zoe last time, I had now missed Arleni & Anya. Zoe was just finishing, then Amanda, Jasmine who kissed me on both cheeks then was banging her bottom against mine as she collected behind me until I put my hand on her arse & she smacked me before banging her bottom against mine a bit more, then Camilla, cousin of Tequila on her first day. I left after giving a pound to Nozumi & went back to the cinema for two decent films, *Hot Paradise* and *Cream Dream*. After just three pints I was ready to come very quickly, & I was just about ready to explode as I headed to Pamela. I got there ten past ten and was her first customer. This felt like a Lela moment, an Ana Maria moment. She let me kiss her nipples lightly, when she usually says "No, they're too sensitive", and this seemed significant. She was starting to open up & let me in. After I came, she just lay beside me looking at me smiling & made no move to go. We talked a little bit & she said how nice the hot weather is because you can go to the seaside, go swimming, & maybe she was hinting she would like me to take her to the seaside. I just lightly stroked her breast as we lay together. As I sat putting my socks on ("Red socks? Why?") she just sat on the bed facing me, something she had never done before. When I looked up, she was looking away shyly. After going to a knock at the door, she came back in & closed the door again even though I was obviously ready to leave, maybe giving me the chance to ask her something if I wanted to. I was now, however, assailed by doubt. When someone starts being nice to me & opening up, I go cold, so I left with just a polite kiss, and she, amazingly, slammed the door hard behind me. Feeling so low & quiet & down, I had a KFC I scarcely wanted & bought a tuna mayo before the bus home. I have been thinking about Pamela all night & all morning. As usual I woke at just 230AM and never really slept again after that. What to do with Pamela? I will have to ask her again, maybe next week, and she will say no again and that will be fine. She is going home to Sweden in August, and to Italy in July with friends. How I wish I could go to Italy! "Will you be here next week?" "Of course!" I wake up feeling defeated—by my shutting out Pamela. Defeated by myself.

I cannot stop the overheating of my world. A rise of 3°C is the least extreme scenario. That is if I totally control myself from here on in, and do not make anything worse, which is not likely. My greenhouse effect started to run out of control about four years ago, with my repeated trips to Brussels, then to Munich, then Berlin, and Vienna. Once I moved into my citadel, I knew I would never be able to repair the damage. Like a gambler returning to the roulette table with a handful of chips I can never resist the buzz. I woo a voluptuous young Swedish girl with love and tenderness, and no hope or thought of success, and am comforted by her constant polite refusals; until she starts to let me in & lets me know my suit is now welcome, and I become instantly cold and devoid of all feeling for her. I can only love from a distance. I set sail on the seas heading South many years ago, though like Shackleton none of my expeditions ever had any clear aim. It was enough to be heading South again. Like the man in Bergman's *Smiles of a Summer Night* I feel I owe Pamela an apology. "I am sorry. I flirted with rescue when I had no intention of being saved."

I am Phèdre, continuing to seduce long after seduction has ceased to be a pleasure. I am half animal. I cannot help myself, my passions, my lusts control me even though they no longer bring me any great pleasure or excitement. I smile out of bitter self-loathing for my bestial nature. If you do not pluck love when it is ripe on the bough, instead hesitating and hesitating, and leaving it hanging and hanging, longing for it and itching to reach for it but always at the last second just being too scared, eventually it will turn rotten and poisonous. — has become a pernicious poisonous influence in my life and I have become the same in hers, when once we were so sweetly fond of each other. All my relationships go like this. They go from promising beginning to poisonous end without anything ever actually happening in between. My habit of doing nothing and doing nothing, but just watching with my eyes, and wanting, and letting them know I want them but doing nothing about it even if they say "OK then", just go on watching instead with my scopophiliac eyes, bewilders them and annoys them and then my attention goes from being something sweet to something poisonous and pernicious. But I love this holding of their gaze, I love this looking and looking into their eyes, for as long as I can, pulling the strings of the violin as taut as I can like Schoenberg, Berg or Webern, doing nothing, just drawing the emotion out to its maximum tautness, this to me is sensuality, until it breaks, and they can take no more, and they hate me, and scorn me, and punish me. Yes, I am perverse, and people wonder about me and wonder with their limited imaginations if I am gay. No, I am not that.

*

How to gather together all the fragments of thoughts and impressions from this night? I went straight to Calcutta for two while watching the start of the Czech-Ghana match, then up to Sunset via Oxford Circus and Central Line. Elektra was there but it is three new girls who made the most impression on me. Luna, like another Giselle, Adriana and Helen. All beautifully voluptuous and sexy, but it was Luna especially who actually made me swell. For her second arrival she went to the pole nearest me, turned around and bent over to point her ass straight at me, as if to say this dance is for you. At 6 I went up and watched a bit of football. Foxy was there & she kept glancing round as if towards the street, and when she went in to dance, she looked anxiously back over her shoulder and I followed her with my eyes and we locked eyes with each other very intently. That was a thrilling moment. Elektra was dancing to a song "and the TV's on" "just a little baby" something like that. The music there is so loud, and bass-deep, and thumping. I was in one of those moods where every girl was sexy, even Nikita on her back as I came in, in a double act with blonde Emma. I left for the Royal Opera House via Holborn and Piccadilly Line to Covent Garden, had a pack of crisps in the pub opposite while watching the end of the Ghana game—how fantastic when a World Cup is on! To go from pub to pub watching bits of games! Once again I remembered why I thought I would

218

become a regular at the Royal Opera. From that balcony position C64 the view is fantastic. You feel so close to the action. It feels so exciting. Christine Rice was great in *Duke Bluebeard's Castle* in red dress. I really enjoyed it. I ached painfully when I thought I could have been in this position to see Alexandra von der Weth in *Boulevard Solitude* five years ago if I could have been bothered, and now will probably never see her. One of the great missed opportunities of my life, along with Violeta Urmana at the Wigmore. I was feeling very tired during *Bluebeard*, but forced myself back to pub just for a coke with ice while watching the Italy-USA game. I saw the Italy goal, the USA goal, and the Italy sending off, before I had to go back for *Erwartung*, which was also fantastic. It is so Vienna! It reminded me so much of the nights searching the Gurtel for Tallulah or Esmeraldas. That really is the music of the Viennese broken world. How you look for love and sensuality but it is always broken and twisted, and you can never believe in it. I found it very very moving, this lonely solitary questing after love and sex.

Back to Covent Garden, Holborn, Central Line to get back to Soho. So many breasts on display in this hot weather, the black dress girl with cleavage hanging out getting on tube as I got off. There were screens in the street around Frith Street and Bateman and crowds were gathered watching the end of the Italy game, a huge roar went up before I got there, but it was a miss. I decided to go back to Sunset as it cost me no more, to see some more action. I watched the last four minutes of the game, then went downstairs to find it packed! With four of five girls as well. I will come on Saturday nights more often. Ariana, a tall blonde was looking at me a lot at the back, Estee was in her element with a big crowd, Foxy too was great. I went back upstairs to sit a while and saw so many sexy girls there, the one in little red bra & knickers & devil's horns, Emilia?, a really beautiful girl smoking looking a bit like Samantha/Maria Moore. Sandra? Anna was the blonde girl from Boulevard. It closes at 1 with last admission at 1230, and I thought I might go back but didn't. The films did not look good at Sunset Cinema but I stayed anyway. Upstairs I walked in and saw man sitting there with massive big fat cock, the fattest I have ever seen. The Hot Rod Blue adverts near the end were the best thing (*Wicked Weapon, Rich Man's Bitch*), and I was really close to exploding, even after a total of six beers. The start of *The Power of Love* was good with Taylor St Claire and I knew I had to leave. I tried Demi, upstairs from Demi (with a Kay lookalike who said goodbye really nicely who I might go back for), Pamela's room with a Cristina M Bell lookalike, then Lydia. My sumptuous Siberian Cleopatra. I am saying nothing more except that she looked beautiful, especially at the end as she sat on bed waiting for me to dress with her hair down, black mascara running around her eyes. "Why did you come back?"

Quite a grey cool 7AM start to the day, as it so often is in summer. I just want to be going back to Sunset Strip and Sunset Cinema. I am a rebel and a revolutionary and I just do not care. I flaunt and provoke and scandalise. Just three nights to get through! Then Jolanda for sure early Wednesday. When the Bell? When my life is so empty and I am so bored, what else could I do but turn to pornography, strippers and whores? Is Lydia another one I have broken the heart of? Like Lela, and Ana Maria? Maybe Pamela, too? Viktoriya? Susi? If I didn't spend money like this is in Moloch, I would just save it so I could do the same things in Berlin and Vienna. Van Gogh, Dowson, Ravel spent their whole life with whores, it is what artists, writers, composers do. It is the bohemian way of life. And it leads to the madhouse, or the morgue. I love my little Gothic pile don't I?! To listen to Wagner *Tristan Prelude* and Schoenberg's *Erwartung* on my gramophone player, and then watching the Francesco man on the TV talking about Italy.

An incredible night on Streamway. I gravitated almost straight to OpenLegs4U; she was the only one I wanted to log into under my own name anyway. As usual, she was like stone, not an answer to anyone. Yet her face was so expressive, she was so happy and laughing, and smiling. Amazingly I broke through. "You are like the Sphinx. Beautiful, enigmatic, and mysterious." And then it came, in red: "Ty." It took all of our breaths away, I think. It was the only reply she'd given to anyone for hours. Thrilled, shaking, I pressed on. "You set men riddles that no man can solve." I then asked her to look me in the eyes for two seconds, which she did not do, which started off a raging argument between Stooge and Popi: "If you aren't gonna do that for sarge, why not live up to your namesake and open your legs?" "Don't be so rude." Then, amazingly, while the battle was raging, she DID seem to look into the camera, twice, for a couple of seconds each. It felt an amazing moment of connection. "You are the most fascinating woman on this site." Amazingly, another immediate, red, "Ty." "If you really think that," said Stooge, "you must have led a very sheltered life." "No not really," I replied. "All the others just seem the same. If you don't agree she is the most fascinating person on here, why Stooge are you still here?" "Waiting for some miracle, to show she has a brain or a personality." Someone then took her private & I wandered off to look at Melanic. When I came back, no one else seemed to be there for a while, until two or three new people emerged. By then I had found her email address in her photos & tracked her down on Google to her Yahoo site and more stunningly beautiful pictures.

"Littlewolf" I said to her only, and she kept her face impassive, though her heart & mind must have been racing inside. Then "Would you please look me in the eye once more before I go?", to which she without hesitation glanced sideways at me out of the corner of her eye.

I allow myself my guilty little pleasures. A couple of visits a week to Sunset Strip and the Midnight Bell, maybe one Sunset Cinema and one model a week. I was on OpenLegs4U from about 10PM to 330AM. I watched her for a long while as a guest laughing & joking with someone unseen in the house with her, but ignoring the webchat, occasionally looking at the camera, then I plunged in to see if there would be any facial reaction from her. Amazingly at the moment I logged in she started punching her arms in the air like she had just scored a goal, and rubbing her hands together in glee & delight. Only as the minutes passed & I made no comment did she become increasingly sad & began to look like she was going to cry. From the laughing & joking & happiness, people started to say "what's up, you look tired?" I finally made some comments about her being like a lighthouse, "you let the moths bash their brains out against your light. You let the waves crash over you. Implacable to the nth degree." I said I had been looking at her pictures in the other place, when incredibly there came a response that shocked all of us: "what other place?" Popi kept butting in now, "she asked you where sgt", and "wtf are you talking about?", until I had to reproach him that I was talking to her! I told her she looked like a model, or an actress, she should be in films, like Louise Brooks or Garbo, but that it would have to be silent films. Jim laughed at that, and Wilhelm said, "that's a good one sarge." I said how fantastic to have her face on a cinema screen in front of me 30ft high. I asked her if she had got my email, and amazingly she responded again "what mail?" I explained I sent it to her Yahoo email, and her screen then froze, like she had gone somewhere to check out her Yahoo mail maybe, and when she returned she was killing herself laughing with someone unseen again, as if she had forgotten all about her Yahoo site? She went private a couple of times and the crowd all disappeared. When she came back, I ventured "so you didn't get my mail then?" to which she did not respond, so I followed it up with "I'm a scopophiliac", to which she immediately burst out laughing. I asked if she knew what it meant, and it was Popi who replied, "a love of looking." I kept going back after her private intervals, and sometimes she looked irritated, and the last time smiled. Before I first logged in, she kept looking into the camera every now & again as if wondering if I was there, then, like I say, with my log in she cheered and laughed and was punching the air like a goalscoring footballer. Over the next few hours, she often looked into the camera and I felt it was to me. I am proud I am the only one who got a response from her apart from "hi", "29", "check the pics", and "in pvt." I felt bereft when she disappeared into private at 330AM and did not come back.

I feel now like what am I going to do with myself until Lilith comes back? She has become the most important thing in my life. The best thing was when she burst out laughing when I said I'm a scopophiliac. Is that sad? No. Not sad. It is nice when you meet someone new who fascinates you. How often do you meet someone fascinating? How often do you see a face you cannot take your eyes off of? It will pass but right now for this brief moment in time she seems like the centre of the web universe. Her star has risen into the ascendant.

God, I do not want to go to the —. I want to stay in the safety of the —. It is safe and familiar. It is my *Night Porter* hotel. Meeting Lilith was like the moment Dirk Bogarde looks up and sees Charlotte Rampling come through the revolving doors. You lure me in like a spider to your web. I have become hooked on you. You are my newest addiction. All points of the web compass radiate out from you, N, S, E, W. You glow in the dark like a night-time cigarette. Your light seems to offer shelter from the storm on the night-time seas. Then I just bash my head against your light like a moth against a lighthouse. Cruel Lilith. Give me a look. I am lost in the dark and there you are. You lure us in like a siren to be dashed against your implacable rocks. You are Circe. I don't know what to do with myself when Lilith is not there.

CHAPTER 4
ECSTATIC
OUTPOURINGS

Ecstatic outpourings.

It is easy to say I am wasting my life and my money on all these whores and strippers, in London and Berlin and Vienna and Brussels. Rather, aren't they the best thing about life? Aren't they the alpha and omega of life? Aren't they the brief moments that persuade us to put off suicide a little longer? Do they not provide the very greatest, and most precious and treasured memories of my life? Aren't my greatest regrets, indeed, that I did NOT do anything with Clarisse in Brussels, I did NOT do anything with the Ukrainian sisters Alla & Olga in Berlin, I did NOT do anything with Martina in Nuremberg? So what I owe £5,800 on my credit card? That seems like nothing. Isn't travelling around Europe and London in search of the biggest-breasted whores and strippers the greatest point of life, and the most worthwhile quest!?

So that is it, June is over. The first half of the year is over. Most of it lost in suffering over —, then recovering via Melani and Pamela and Demi.

I find it impossible to give anything with people at work, because I am just desperately counting down the nights and hours till I can get back to Sunset or the Scotsman or the cinema or a whore. That is all I think about.

I feel very depressed now. By all the above. There is nothing in my life except that, and the writing. I can only be alone. I cannot bear to be with another person. Nobody could bear to be with me. I WANT TO WRITE LIKE E.E.CUMMINGS. I WANT TO WRITE LIKE HART CRANE. I WANT TO WRITE LIKE PHILIP O'CONNOR. I WANT MY WORDS TO APPEAR IN OLD PAPERBACK BOOKS LIKE I FIND IN THE CHARING CROSS ROAD SECOND HAND BOOKSHOPS. I want to write about solipsism, and what it is like to never connect. To always live alone. To always retreat from people when they try to get close. Only when I feel most bleak and lonely can I write.

This is Fu Manchu weather. Black, steamy, hot and humid, but raining all the time. A permanent mist of rain in the hot, steamy conditions. It is like being in Phnom Penh. This is Cambodia weather. Two in the Calcutta with white shirt Katerina with no eye contact. Sylvie was first on in Sunset followed by Jolanda. Nina was next. She is so much like Melani, but Melani is Nina x100. Nina does not turn me on though she is so beautiful. Also there Angelina, and doing the middle shift, Sandra. A quiet small brunette but she was so sexy! She made eye contact with me a lot & really turned me on. I left about 5 because it is so empty on early shift I feel uncomfortable.

At the Scotsman was —. After dancing she marched straight to back & sat down with me again. I bought her another Red Bull. She was so sexy in little red tartan bra & knickers only. Drinking so much so quickly on empty stomach I was feeling randier than normal, and when she left to collect, & asked me to keep her drink safe for her, I stroked her bum and had a good feel of it. She looked at me in mock shock but she was so sexy on stage. While she was dancing however, a huge voluptuous red haired girl came in with two men to talk to Tina. They exchanged numbers & then she came & sat where — had been sitting, so I could get a good side on look at her. Those tits are the most massive I have ever seen in my life. Her arse was practically hanging out of her jeans & that was massive as well. She glanced at me a few times. If she ever danced there I would die with pleasure. It would be the greatest striptease I have ever seen in my life. Knocking even fat-bottomed silver-dressed girl at Carnival into the shade. They were like zeppelins. Looking past her, — suddenly seemed so ridiculously small. — came back for her drink & found the girl there & was then in animated conversation with her & they exchanged numbers as well.

I went back to look for Francesca but she was busy, so I went back to Sunset for Lana & Nikita, the end of Elektra, and one more from Sandra before she left at 9. I watched most of the France v Portugal second half then went to Sunset Cinema. The films were great. *Magma Swing Party, Nympho Nurses Naughty,* and *Tittenalarm 17*—all German films!—plus *Fresh Meat 18*. I thought I was turned on enough so I went back to Francesca. She lived up to her description. Her breasts are sensational. She is pretty enough as well. For an extra £5 I got her to turn over but still could not come. She offered a hand job AND TOOK THE CONDOM OFF TO GIVE IT! It is true, she lets you come over her tits just like that. Still I could not come, so I apologised & kissed her goodbye. She works Tuesday to Saturday but only to 10PM. I will for sure go back many times.

I went back to the cinema again for more of the great films. Upstairs was bald man with pretty brunette girl from last week but they do not seem to do much. This time I was ready to explode, & though I wanted to carry on watching the films, I made my way to Demi, but another girl was there, Savannah. She was pretty but £30. I was tempted but she walked off angrily, so her attitude turned me off though her body was great. I went back to Pamela. It was so nice sucking her tits and the edge of her nipples at least. I could not stop sucking and love biting her. For £25 she turned over & I came very nicely again. I made her lay with me for just a couple of minutes, but could not stop laughing for some reason. She did not stay with me as I got dressed this time. I was too drunk to ask her anything. I came home after that. There was a sexy brown ponytail girl stood behind me at bus stop then she came & sat in the corner seat just beneath me, in little pink vest & I could not help keep looking down at her cleavage & her face, and she knew I was looking & I think liked it. She got off Wandsworth Road just before me. Sitting in back seat opposite me our knees touching was most beautiful blonde in long skirt, jacket over little green top, with nice big tits & cleavage on show. I grabbed a few ogles & she was so beautiful. On the next corner seat was the purple blouse girl from before! In brown leather jacket, low cut shirt with tops of breasts visible, and tight brown skirt. Red lips. She was so sexy. Sitting side on ready to get off she knew I was looking at her so much. All in all, a very sexy night. A night of a thousand breasts, and a dozen super-voluptuous vixens. Jolanda, redhead at the Scotsman, Francesca, Pamela, girls at bus stop & on bus. Sandra.

Finally went private with Lilith. She was wearing black again, with really black eyes. Really red lips, like she was making an effort. Amazing she let me in at all. Not a smile from her, though. Spent $37 just talking to her. "Maybe the riddle is not supposed to be solved". When I was talking to her in free, telling her she looked like Kate Moss, someone else kept whisking her into private. I am sure that must have been —, so jealous when anyone else gets on with her. It happened twice. I told her I would send her another email and she replied "no ty". "You hate me that much?" "I don't hate you. I just don't see the point." I am more hooked then ever. I don't want to be hooked.

Sin, degradation, and despair. But enough of the good things in life. I have become so used to you, I no longer like it when the other girls reply to me. I now only become erotically aroused when ignored. When I first talked with Lilith in free, she had no lipstick on, just those black eye shadow & black mascara eyes. After she was whisked away from me into private (maybe she keeps taking herself private to lure me in?), she came back wearing that blood red lipstick again, and looking so beautiful. This time I had to take her private myself. ************No sign of Lilith tonight. I have a quandary. I'd have to be as rich as Croesus to pay $20 a time just for four minutes of conversation with you. Yet you do not talk for free. So what is left? I actually look forward to Sunday night back at work so I can look for her again. Like *Orphée into the Underworld*.

Another call from Lydia as I lay cutting up my newspapers. I let it ring out, but immediately felt guilty, & texted her back "Oh Lydia". This time I answered. "What you doing Wednesday & Thursday? You come swimming with me?" "Maybe." "Maybe, or yes?!" "I don't like swimming, but I like you." "All right, we will just go outside somewhere." Thursday. I feel excited. She always turns me on. I always want to lay with her and f–k her. I have loved her since the first time I met her. It has been almost two years now. Then there is —, who I am still addicted to. Then there is Lilith. "When you put your face close to the camera, it is like the greatest thing in the world. It is like the opening bars of Beethoven's 5th Symphony. Something great has just occurred. Like Norman Mailer wrote about *Last Tango in Paris*. When Marlon Brando first meets Maria Schneider in the apartment & without warning reaches down & rips her knickers off in one movement, the sound of that tear is as great a moment in Western civilisation as the opening Da-da-da-daas of Beethoven's 5th Symphony. It is lunacy but beautiful lunacy. When you put your face next to the screen, it is as great. You say you do this for connections. Yet you don't see the point. Maybe just not with me. You are on a different level to all the other girls. You are iconic. I am scopophile. Erotomane. If you don't talk, you become a fetish object. We gaze & gaze at you. No one else would be worth gazing at. Your face is addictive. There is more going on in your face & eyes than all the other 'models' put together. Men look, and women are looked at. I cannot believe there is anyone on the entire web as worth gazing at as you. You glow in the dark. Like the tip of your night-time cigarette. And the men gather to you, like moths around the flame. And if their wings burn, you know you're not to blame. Marlene Dietrich. Years ago, I used to go to old cinemas and gaze up at her face like I do to yours now. They say her glory was all down to the lighting. It is clever the way you light yourself as well. You just show us your face & shoulders, and lit by a spotlight. None of the other girls do that. I can scroll down the list of online girls so quickly knowing your face will leap out as soon as I get to it." Every meeting with Lydia is so charged and erotic. Every meeting with — is so charged and erotic. Every meeting with Lilith is so charged and erotic.

My afternoon with Lydia just brought home to me how white I am, but also how unhappy I am. From the moment I met her outside — tube she started saying "you are unhappy." I suppose I am. I live in a constant fog of unhappiness that I have got so used to, I no longer notice it. Only when I am forced to be with people I realise how shocking other people find me. And how white I am. I live in darkness, both literally and metaphorically. Who would I want to be with now? No one. Not Lydia. Not —. Not Pamela. I only want to be alone. Left alone with my writing the way Munch wanted to be left alone with his pictures. This is a wonderful world for an autistic person. As long as we can indulge it. After getting back to Charing Cross I had a small tuna & mayo from the grinning "how are you?" Alia, and "see you later!", before dragging myself back into the Calcutta. Only as I got on the 815 train I saw the huge voluptuous-titted blonde bouncing past the window, with that almost black lipstick pout she puts on in disgust when she knows men are looking at her tits, yet she always wears those ludicrously low-cut vests, this time green, that show off so much of the tops of her tits. How I would like to touch & taste & fuck those tits.

Can you imagine going to work in an office with your MASSIVE knockers almost on full display like that? Can you imagine being a man working in an office with a girl like that with her knockers on display all day? How on Earth would you get ANY work done? I would be masturbating all day long.

You could say I have got worse, and I am like someone who has given up and will try no more; or you could say I have got better. I am more myself now. I am purer. I have gone deeper into myself, and deeper into nothingness. And that is where I long to be and where I love to be. Even Thursday I felt so bored in the cinema, despite *Tittenalarm 18*, UNTIL the blonde came in with the man, and was kissing him, and had her knees drawn up so he could finger her and all the men in the seats in front were turning & looking up her. That suddenly was SO hot and sexy. I had to leave in a hurry because I wanted to explode straightaway with Demi, but still she is gone for another two weeks, so I went with Francesca, just in the one position and came easily. I will not go back. Demi will be the next one I go to. The Sunset rota is up but I just feel totally sated by it now. I have to stop my spending now.

I am pretty far gone, aren't I? Look at my face, the bags under my eyes. The way I cannot talk to people. I am like a drug addict. I have disappeared so far inside myself. It is almost impossible for me to be in a room with other people. I am like a wild child. No wonder people often think I am on drugs. I am a revolutionary at work. I am carrying out a revolution. A subversive one. A Situationist revolution. I am carrying out a Situationist revolution against the whole of society around me. It is fantastic to be in a porn cinema when a girl comes in. The high that gives you is just so absolutely incredible. Of course I will keep going to Sunset Cinema after the Scotsman, prior to Demi. Sex, sordid, sleazy sex, illicit thrills, Godzilla sex, vampire sex, is what I live for. Companionship is not possible, for I am a dead man, a ghost. My books are my revolutionary texts—AUTISMUS, LOTTA, THE COLD ICY AIR OF THE MOUNTAINS, and CASANOVA (LOST WANDERINGS). You create a revolution by doing nothing. You cause so much anger and nastiness to fly around your head just by being silent and doing nothing. Nature abhors a vacuum and society abhors it even more and will not forgive it. You are not allowed to not join their club. They cannot understand anyone who does not want to join their club. Society is warped by an abnormal person in its midst. Look how it couldn't cope with Oscar Wilde, Vincent Van Gogh, Jesus Christ, Kaspar Hauser. "You are like a ghost", Lydia was laughing, "like a dead man!", because my skin was so white and my hands and arms and face so icy cold. Small talk murders me. I can only live in the realm of thought. Everything I do at the hotel is part of my Situationist revolution. Every move I make is a deliberate part of my Situationist revolution. Everything I do on my days off is part of my Situationist revolution. I am Guy Debord. The point of life is seeking the perfect point of inebriation. Going to Moscow with my White Russian Princess and coming back with her as my wife is part of my Situationist revolution; part of the complicated joke I am playing at society's expense. And I am playing the long game.

How many times I have snatched defeat from the jaws of victory. How many more times have I just looked away when victory was sitting there waiting for me, like with Carol at Sunset. — & — at the Scotsman. —. They all presented themselves to me on a plate. Bus stop girl. "Oh you're so sweet, do you know that!" pigtail barmaid at the Calcutta. They all just offered themselves to me, while I was minding my own business. Ursula at the Calcutta. When opportunity arises, I go cold, like with Melani, and Lilith, and Pamela. I send them all away.

I am sure Lilith knows I am there from the moment I connect to her room. A look always comes over her face, and is it my imagination but does she always start readjusting her camera, just to give an excuse to look directly into the lens? The moment I logged in under — I am sure I saw her face freeze, as if suddenly desperate not to betray any emotion, but I am sure her heart started beating faster, because she started breathing deeper and faster.

CHAPTER 5
I
AM UNIQUE

I am unique. It is important to remember that. I am writer and eccentric, like Philip O'Connor, Friedrich Nietzsche in cold stoveless rooms, Ernest Dowson. I exist to write those extreme, bizarre, small little books, like *Autismus, Lotta, The Cold Icy Air of the Mountains*, and *Casanova*. 45 page long monographs about emptiness and nothingness. Smile from Calcutta blonde: "No ice today!" I need to focus on *Miami Vice, Rebels & Martyrs* exhibition, classical music concerts. The sexiest encounters of my life were at the Barbican and Wigmore Hall. I travel uniquely, to Berlin, Vienna and Brussels. I live a bizarre and nocturnal life. I will continue to use Sunset Cinema and Demi and Pamela. There is nothing like that excitement when a gentleman comes in with a woman and everyone crowds around with their cocks out. I am Ernest Dowson. Philip O'Connor. The Shining Roads will be exclusively in Soho. How thrilling it is to come out of the cinema with my huge cock rolling in my trousers, just around the corner to Demi or Pamela. My life revolves around drinking & pornography. I want to take a long train journey again, thinking and writing.

My greatest periods of unrestrained sexuality come at my times of greatest blackness & despair. I need to be low and black and destroyed. I feel like Munch in Christiana now. Too much drink and drugs and endless nights with scantily-clad women have overwhelmed my senses and driven me into a spiral of despair.

I want to write books the like of which have never been seen before. Journals of a man subsumed in a life of emptiness and nothingness, but who revels in and gorges himself on this emptiness and nothingness, like a mother eating her own placenta. Journals about the visceral pleasure in detachment of an autistic person. About transcendency, about finding lenses that enable one to focus all the rays of this emptiness and nothingness like a magnifying glass used to focus the rays of the sun to start a fire, like the mirror that Orphée steps through to enter the Underworld, and then the transcendency flares into life like a white phosphorescent explosion, and one orgies in the transcendency, in the sublime orgasmic detachment from everything and everyone around you, in the supreme quality of emptiness and nothingness stretched to the nth degree like a taut violin string that is at any moment about to break but never quite does; what exquisite pleasure is then to be found. If Guy Debord's view of life was to seek the perfect point of inebriation, mine is to locate the perfect point of transcendental orgasmic detachment. The nights I would go to the Coliseum and have to creep in the darkness to the gentlemen's toilets and furiously masturbate so aroused was I. The nights at the opera in Berlin, when I had to leave at the interval in search of Kant and cunt, so highly-strung and aroused had I become. It is possible to take an aesthetic appreciation in fine pornography, fine aids to arousal and ejaculation; indeed it is impossible not to. The night in Munich I had to leave Strauss's *Arabella* in desperate race back to Schiller and Goethe. It was Karl Kraus who said a woman can sometimes be an acceptable substitute for masturbation, but that it requires an awful lot of imagination. When I think of all the brief connections I have made this year with women, – , Melani, Amanda, Pamela, Lydia, I can say that not one of them gave me an iota of the pleasure that I felt when the woman in the cinema let the men crowd around her with their cocks out, and let me wrap her hair around my cock to masturbate with in the dark. Transgression is not only possible, but beautiful. I would go further. Transgression is not only beautiful, it is essential. The double life is absolutely essential in order to save one's life.

When the Esmeraldas and Tallulahs I have met in my life have been so extraordinary and stimulating and life enhancing, how can I give them up? The closest I have come to a real relationship has been with the Esmeraldas I have met in Moloch, namely Lela from Romania, Ana Maria from Spain, Lydia from Russia, and latterly Pamela from Sweden. I can only fall in love with Esmeraldas. I do not think I am capable of loving a normal girl, a respectable girl. There is so much of me that I have to hide from them, so much of the double life that I must keep secret from them, which is never necessary with Esmeraldas, because we know everything about each other from the beginning. What a relief to be able to talk so openly and honestly with an Esmeralda, when by necessity only one word out of every hundred I would like to say to a normal girl can be said out loud. Ninety-nine per cent of what is the most essential me must remain concealed from a normal girl, like a portrait in my attic, whereas with Esmeraldas I can be 100% open. That is why I love Esmeraldas so much. As much as for the sex, it is to just be able to be myself and speak freely. I have felt closer to true friendship with Esmeraldas than I ever have with a normal girl.

I am on such an exciting new project now. I am as thrilled by the prospect of tightening my belt, and living like a monk, and saving money now, as I used to be by living wildly and spraying my money around and living hedonistically. It will be such a slow process before I notice any difference though. Like a supertanker, your personal finances are very slow to turn around. Your Love Is Like Poison, the song that — put on & I felt it was aimed at me. Yes my love is like poison and my love of strippers had become like poison. Like alcohol poisoning your blood by too much drink, I had stripper poisoned by blood. My love was like poison to —, to Jolanda and to Melani. All of them started off liking me then wanted to avoid me. Finally now I have the chance to remove the poison from the blood and be clean again. *Confessions of an English Opium Eater* I carried around with me Friday, and really strippers has been my opium over the years, ever since I first fell into it on that dark, stormy September afternoon on the shining road of Dean Street 14 years ago. I have been in its thrall ever since. And yes in the early days it provided me with magical moments, supremely high moments, but increasingly over the years those high moments became fewer and further between as my addiction worsened, and became nothing but habit, with no joy or excitement left in it.

Those red wig days, Czech Boulevard girl days, gold dress days, Carnival days, are very far in my past now. Now there are only the desperate depraved addict's memories of my appalling behaviour. How thrilled I will be now by watching my Woolwich building society account filling up and rising from minus to plus, from plus 100 to 200 to 300. That will be my high now. That will be my addiction now—hoarding money. I will get as much thrill from hoarding money as I used to from spending it. Oh if only I could have had this revelation earlier, if only I could have had this road to Damascus conversion sooner! But it has to come when the moment is right. I had to wait until I suddenly became physically revolted. I had to wait till the poison became so bad that it reached the tipping point and where it suddenly physically made me sick.

It was only when I got the — job that I had the money to start travelling and travelling led to so many amazing breakthrough moments in my life and caused so many explosions in my mind and opened up so many new rooms in my mind that I never knew existed. I went through so many Ishtar Gates and crossed so many Rubicons, really starting from that first trip to Brussels on the hotel money where I saw Alizee's J'en ai marre & nothing has ever been the same again. So of course I must save my money and hoard it so fiercely and protect every penny I earn so lovingly, to enable me to keep travelling. I have stopped going through Ishtar Gates and so have fallen stagnant and become a fever infested swamp of lethargy and stripper addiction which brought no real joy or happiness.

The richer you are the more you can gamble, and the more you gamble the more you are going to enjoy spectacular wins. If you are poor you can only gamble very rarely and very small sums and so even if you do sometimes win it is only for very small rewards. How can I say Munich is boring? How can I say Vienna is boring? You carry the weather with you. If I travelled with £2,000 in my pocket I would have the time of my life there. If I went in with a million pounds I could fuck the Irina lookalike, fuck Maria, fuck Angelique, and have the time of my life. Even in Munich I could go from club to club having a drink with every girl I liked until I found the one with looser morals who would let me come on her breasts at least. But as it is now I cannot afford to look in so many clubs, I cannot afford to buy so many girls a drink in order to find the one I want, and I come away feeling frustrated & that Munich is over, when really it is only that I do not have the starting collateral to enable me to gamble freely. You have to speculate to accumulate. At the moment I cannot speculate. To do is to dare. At the moment, I can no longer dare. This is a very important thing I have realised. Munich can come back to life for me! Brussels can come back to life for me! Vienna can come back to life for me! All these places can bloom and blossom and shoot up above me letting me shelter under their glorious smutty fronds—if I repair my finances and hoard my gold coins in London so I can gamble wildly and speculate crazily and dare everything when I go back. In February and March I spent £617 on strippers and £547 on drink, another £1,164 in February and March alone. So together February-March-April-May-June-July I could have had an extra £2,700 in my Woolwich account, or £1,100 in my Woolwich account and my Barclaycard at zero! Then for sure Munich would be full of life for me and bloom and blossom. Then for sure Vienna would be full of life for me, and bloom and blossom. You should only go into those Munich clubs, Vienna clubs, Berlin bars, if you have a lot of cash to spend; there is absolutely no point if you are on a tight budget. Then no wonder you come home feeling frustrated and dispirited. My holidays have got increasingly worse as my debt has increased. Let me go back to those years of repression 1996, 1997, 1998, when I could only yearn for those occasional visits to the porn cinema and a whore. That repression was so sexy, I was like a tautly strung hair trigger, it was delicious. Since then, in contrast, I have been like a gambling addict, Merson or Rooney, going deeper and deeper into debt. That is over now. The girls always say in those places I look miserable. If I went in rich I would be happy & fuck them all.

Go into Brussels like pulling into a great palmhouse, gigantic tropical ferns and trees and butterflies all around me. A steaming primordial paradise. With soot on the leaves. Let it become an overheated, closed, hothouse. Go into Munich the same way. Go into Vienna the same way. The more poor I became the more I travelled miserably, to Empire, Atlantic City, Pour Platin, Golden Gate. When you are happy people are attracted to you like to a magnet & you have great times. As I get poorer, I become more miserable & only have bad times. How happy I will feel when I reduce my Barclaycard to zero! The long project starts here.

*

Why do I wake up at 2AM feeling so unhappy? I feel like I want to cry. I had such an unhappy dream. I was trapped on a long distance train going across Europe and I knew no longer wanted to be on it, but I was trapped. I had no choice. In reflection in the window I saw an old man with black holes where eyes should be. It is almost a premonition of myself in 20 or 30 years time. I felt like I was trapped on this train, and trapped in this travelling, without aim and without enjoyment. Maybe it is just the after effects of the drink. Drink causes depression and low moods. Such a reversal of how I felt on the train home last night. Instead of having my epiphany in the Calcutta, I had it on the train home. As the train neared home in the darkness from station to station closer to —, I imagined I was on my train in Europe, getting nearer and nearer to pulling in at my final destination of Munich, or Vienna, or Berlin, and I felt again that intense excitement of about to arrive. How exciting it is to arrive at a place by train, not by plane. It made me really want to be on that train to Munich, or Vienna, or Berlin. The great thing about arriving by train is I know my hotel is right next to the station in Munich, and in Vienna, and very close even in Berlin, and in Brussels. To arrive in Munich at night is so exciting, when everywhere is so dark, and all lit up, and the night is about to begin. Very soon I can be heading over the road to Atlantic City and the night can really begin. Now, however, this morning I feel like I do not want to travel to those places and do those tawdry things again. I am sick of those places, and throwing all my money away. As always in the mornings I am most conservative and frightened, and at night I am most wild and hedonistic.

The pleasure of travelling around Europe by train is so great, even if I'm lonely, because when I am lonely I write the most. It is Nietzsche in cold stoveless rooms writing with blue hands, while weeping, writing in blood. That is what I like best. So what I owe £6,000? You cannot take it with you. I might as well live intensely for the next few years while the rausch is on me. I am inclined to go to Berlin in January for *La Traviata* and *Carmina Burana*.

I have got £13,500 credit and I owe £5,900. With a Vienna holiday at Christmas that will increase temporarily, but so what? It is just like taking out a loan. I have taken out a £5,900 loan which I will pay back when I come back from Vienna. And with this loan I am doing amazing, extraordinary things. Burning bright like a firefly. You have to push yourself to the edge. It is only there that you can observe things & record your observations. I am excited about going to work from now, because my journey to Vienna has already started. Remember how I always used to enjoy going to work because it was just getting me through the two or three weeks till I could get back to Munich again, or get back to Berlin again, or get back to Vienna again? Am I really spending hundreds of pounds going all the way to Vienna just to have sex? The sex with the Vienna and Berlin whores is more expensive but it is better. They will do anything. Remember how Yulia, Riccarda, Maria, Diana, did absolutely everything? You do not get that in Soho. Once you have paid your 100 euros you do get an absolutely mind blowing experience. Now watching the Alizee J'en ai Marre video I know why I travel. If I had never travelled I would never have seen that video. If I had not gone to Berlin and bought the Observer that Sunday in the Café am Zoo I would never have discovered the Libertines. If I had not gone back to Brussels I would never have discovered Elena Prokina. Travel enriches you so much. Just as the flat costs me a lot of money but it would be a false economy to give it up, so travelling costs me a lot of money but it too would be a false economy to give it up. That night coming away from *Katarina & her Wild Stallions* with such a huge erection in my trousers it still had not gone down by the time I crossed the leaf-carpeted Ku'damm. Meeting Clarisse in Brussels. On a wild goose chase to Nuremberg to look for Viktoriya I met the incredible Martina with the most enormous breasts I have ever seen in my life.

"Boundless aestheticism and ambivalent premonitions of an imminent and inevitable decline brought about a unique atmosphere in turn-of-the-century imperial Vienna, and led to Early Austrian Expressionism." I am aware of the decline and decadence, the sensual

235

decadence, the diving deeper into darkness, the romantic nihilism in myself, so that is why I am attracted to Vienna around 1900, to Weimar Berlin. If I am to dive deeper into darkness, then let me do it when it is dark, in December! I think a new mature phase of my life is about to begin, it is struggling through its metamorphosis and is just about to emerge from its chrysalis! A new mature diving deeper into darkness! A new mature sensual decadence!

Why do I say I love travelling when the trips are filled with such sadness and despair? Because in the sadness and despair I still find jewels, and have incredible experiences, like Clarisse, Martina, Erika, etc, etc. And after all the sadness and despair is no different from what I feel at home. That is just who I am. I take it everywhere with me. Europe offers greater sensual pleasures that is all. The greatest moments have always involved the porn cinema or videokabins. It is almost a year ago I first met black dress Kay, what a sexy moment that was, as she stroked my cock with her hand, as the black guy put his huge cock in her mouth and other guy put condom on & fucked her before coming over her breasts!

For all that talk of big breasts I never really made the most of my opportunities: Clarisse I never even had a 5 euro dance in my seat & refused to talk to her; with Martina, I went with Diana instead; with Andrea I just had the £20 option instead of half an hour. I can worry about the sadness and despair of my last trips to Berlin, Munich, Brussels, but I always feel this sadness and despair so it is normal & I should enjoy it! There is a kernel inside my brain that only wants to be stimulated by pornographic films and prostitutes, and will never be able to feel anything in real relationships, so I should just understand that and enjoy it. Isn't it great that I now feel so happy in myself and so self-confident? I am writing, I have my own place, I am enjoying the porn films and the prostitutes the same as ever, and no one can touch me. How beaten down I used to be. Not anymore. I am taunting them with what I enjoy that they cannot. I am flaunting it in their angry faces, more and more. I am provoking them more and more. I am Beethoven. I am genius.

I lead a strange existence. I read and write for a couple of hours, then sleep for a couple of hours. Listen to some classical music for an hour, then read & write some more, then sleep some more.

What a great life this is. Sleep for a few hours, get up to read and write for a few hours, listen to classical music for a while, sleep some more, for three or four days a week. Even my bad trips still produced interesting experiences. I need complete isolation. Complete peace. Complete solitude. I can only exist in solipsism, and its military wing, Priapism. I enjoyed living in the broken world of strippers and whores. But I fell in love with one of the strippers and started embarrassing myself. I want to write a magazine like *Simplicissimus* and *Die Fackel*. My life revolves around strippers and whores and yet I cannot talk about that. 95% of my life would have to remain hidden under the surface leaving only the tip of the iceberg which is not worth talking about.

I wake up alone and how do I feel about that? Fine. There is no one I want to be with. I am so happy to be alone and free. I feel pain gripping my chest, though. I feel stressed because I have got to go back to the flat early in order to force myself to get to the *Rebels & Martyrs* exhibition at the National Gallery, and I have become so used to not going out, not doing anything. I have retreated so deep into my own little world, almost a hibernation, and liking it. Those drunken addictive years to strippers & whores seem so far away. It is so nice to be curled up small & protected. But always I fear everything being torn down, invaded, ripped away from me. As always I expect the great flood any moment & having to gather all my things together on a raft and starting all over again.

How lovely it was lying on the floor of my flat when I got home, just doing my newspapers, and I put the anglepoise lamp on for the first time in months. My little nest looked so lovely, with all those books starting to pile up against the wall. I slept on the floor again! I think I actually prefer it on the floor, I seem to sleep a lot longer, and have so many vivid dreams. I did not get up till 645pm again. Before sleeping I was listening to that tape & it was full of the Vienna 2002 songs! Avril Lavigne Complicated, Los Asejere The Tomato Song, Puddle of Mudd, No Doubt Underneath it All. It was amazing to hear them again. At the same time I have been thinking a lot about those great films, the German tramp in the forest with the girl in the fur coat, and at first he exposes himself, then she just touches him a bit, before they are full on fucking in the middle of the forest path where anyone can see them. And the *Last Bus to Boobsville*. And the women's hen night party. Incredible memories. This is why I travel. Watching it on your computer is not the same. It needs oxygen to become combustible and erotic and catch into flames. But do I really have to wait so long till December!?

CHAPTER 6
YES I QUESTION IF I WANT TO GO TO VIENNA

Yes I question if I want to go to Vienna wasting all that money after working so hard to save it, but that is to forget the excitement, the nervousness so intense I cannot breathe as my train pulls into Vienna.

I am a great believer that you carry the weather with you. If you travel with a spark, a dancing flame inside you, you will have a great time. If you travel unhappy, and in a black place, weighed down by worries and debts, you will have a sad time. I cannot say the well in Munich has run dry; probably it is my well that has run dry. When my well fills up again, by making myself happier, ridding myself of obsessions, financial worries, anxieties, paranoid depressions, I will find Munich's well is full to overbrimming again, "stars filling the throat to the crop", as it was absolutely full to overbrimming when I met Susi and Irina on the night of Turkey v England, Patricia, Emily on the Night of the Snow, Viktoriya in those four magical life-changing visits in the space of six months.

The fact that I have paid £600 off my Barclaycard in the space of a month shows what is possible. I don't think I am going to go to Vienna in December. I think I would rather keep waiting and keep saving. So when I do travel I will have a real war chest to travel with. I was thinking in the Calcutta on Thursday that there is nothing worth spending money on except sex. If it is a choice between seeing *Volver* or *A Scanner Darkly*, or going to see a girl take her knickers off to music, then there can only be one winner. You see people who go on beach holidays, or Amalfi, and I think how bored I would be. The only holiday that means anything is in red light districts. To meet new strippers and new Esmeraldas. What is wrong with running a high debt?

Nothing in the city matters except sex, the buying and selling of it, young women stripping for you, young women lying back on the bed and opening their legs for you, men all with their cocks out in a dark porn cinema. This is the reality of my life. Vienna is still a mystery to me. With three consecutive visits to Brussels, then three to Munich, then three to Berlin, I felt I cracked the nut of all those places. I still have not achieved that with Vienna. Viennese Eroticism is very important to me. *Primitive London.* I am very intellectual yet I live very primitively, my animal instincts always winning out over my cerebral ones. So much drink has sozzled my brain that I doubt I have any cerebral instincts left at all. What an animal I was with Anya at the stag party; how impressed Sylvia seemed to be after that & so much more warm and friendly to me than she had ever been before. When people write about my life 50 years from now, they will have to write about the Calcutta, the Flying Scotsman, Sunset Strip and Carnival. About Astral Cinema, Soho Cinema, and Sunset Cinema. About Atlantic City. About Stutti Frutti, Mon Cheri, Golden Gate, Monte Carlo and Ciro.

If I do not travel to Vienna and Berlin in December and the New Year I will have no chance to meet a new Irina or Susi, Patricia or Viktoriya. Things happen when you travel. In Brussels I met Clarisse. In Frankfurt Katerina. In Berlin Erika. It is important to keep exploring. I live in a kind of Francis Bacon London. I live in the gutter like him. My writing is visceral and from the guts, full of pinks and reds and purples, like his paintings. I too am fascinated by a Pope. I am visceral and fascinated and turned on by my naked self like Egon Schiele. Do not apologise for this. Exult in it. I am priapic and I will just do it more than ever. I am saving money by not doing it so much just so I can do it more. I am going to Vienna at Christmas to fuck a couple of Viennese whores. In strip clubs every night is like Sylvester's Eve; or Walpurgisnacht. The more bawdy and raucous the better; that is why I like the Bell on Saturday nights. In London all the strip pubs are packed with men; again I ask the question, where do all the men go in Berlin? In Vienna? In Brussels?

"Berlioz's unstinting lionisation of Beethoven in the pages of *La Revue et Gazette Musicale de Paris*, the most important and influential music journal in 19th-century France, also played a major role in establishing him at the centre of the repertory for the concert hall." In my journal, what would I write about, who would I lionise? I would lionise the Midnight Bell, perhaps, and its dancers, extolling the virtues of Sylvia and — and Janet above all others. Extolling them in messianic, apocalyptic, grandiose, diva-esque terms, like they are Sarah Bernhardts. Invoking Hungarian history. Giving reviews of their performances just the way one would with reviews of violinists or pianists. They are all on a stage, why not? Instead of one paragraph reviews of Anita Berber's Bethanien or Marlene Dietrich's grave, extend them into full page articles, enabling me to digress into talking about *The Blue Angel*, Lola, etc. Berber at the Romanisches Cafe, Tucholsky. It would be a journal devoted to the strip clubs of London, the pubs, to Berlin, and Vienna, and Brussels, and Munich. Talk about them the way you would about great opera singers of the 1880s, from the stage side box. Write a magazine where on one page there is a review of Barbara Fritoli at the Wigmore Hall on Wednesday night, and on the facing page, a review of the Flying Scotsman on Thursday night, each with equal analysis. My reviews are scurrilous and scandalous, like James Ellroy, Charles Bukowski. Winter is coming. Remember those cold icy days when I first moved in here? Remember the excitement of those Astral nights? The unable to breathe shaking with excitement as I headed down the steps not knowing what I was about to see? Remember that unbelievably huge breasted beautiful Czech girl at the Boulevard? It is almost like a dream. I cannot believe I witnessed something so spectacularly sexy as her and made so little of it. If only I knew where she was now.

I would like to write my own magazine like the *Fackel*, full of my hard-hitting sometimes scurrilous articles and reviews of London life. Write about Barbara Frittoli and the tyranny of not being able to write about the singer's beauty, and sexual allure, as if this must not be mentioned, like some guilty secret. Write about *La Traviata* at the ENO, a weepy opera about "some consumptive whore, when in real life whores are treated like the lowest of the low, yet here she is celebrated as something glorious".

I feel an almost physical revulsion at the thought of going back to Sunset and Demi and Pamela. But what else is there, so I will eventually. When I know the pleasures I have felt in those places felt so intense. I feel a physical revulsion for going back to those nighttime Vienna places and the nighttime Berlin places. I feel a physical revulsion for spending any money when I am in this saving mode. That is good. I have become allergic to spending money when before I seemed addicted to it. I feel an almost physical revulsion for women. I am a strange man. How can — or anyone have a relationship with a strange man like me? I am like Ralph Fiennes' Spider. I only learnt how to be alone when I was a baby, and I always will be. I love places where I can be alone surrounded by loud pounding music and naked girls, that is why I love the dream world of the Scotsman and Sunset Strip so much. It is the ultimate detachment. The ultimate transcendency. The ultimate lens. The ultimate gateway to the state of bliss that is the Kingdom of Death. Ultimate nothingness. That nervousness so intense I cannot breathe as the train nears Nuremberg & as I got off and walk along the corridor to the entrance hall, and the nervousness I felt so intense I could not breathe as I went down the steps at the Astral, I now feel when I walk to the Scotsman from the north from the 91 stop. I feel it too when I enter Sunset Cinema, hoping to find a woman being monickered, and also when I go up the models' stairs. That is the high. That is the drug.

"We drank hard and talked about what Debord, who drank persistently and prodigiously, had written about alcohol. 'I admire Debord as a perfect and dedicated drinker.' We talked about how, in the early years of his career as a drinker, Debord was always in pursuit of or just arriving at a perfect point of intoxication which, unlike paid labour or any other servile activity, would reveal 'the true taste of the passage of time'. Drinking was a beautiful poetic game, with its rules and protocols. Debord devoted pages to describing this notion."

Irina suddenly leaned over to me and said to me "I'm sorry, you're a nice guy, but you drink too much" before giving me the ultimate private dance. I said to Viktoriya "You don't like me, do you", and she exploded back with real hatred "Yes. Because you're always drunk".

I insist on the primacy of my own experience. My own vision. I can only be alone. I can only be in cold icy mountains.

Don't be unhappy, be happy! Think what immense power you have got! You have made the great separation & now live for pure Priapism. You have got money. Winter is coming. I can go to the Bell, the Sunset Strip, Sunset Cinema, Demi and Pamela. In January I can go to Berlin. This is going to be a season of the flesh. I have got a nice little job I enjoy. I have got money coming in. I have got my own little nest. I have got a week off in December and another week off in January to go to Berlin, for *La Traviata* and *Carmina Burana*.

"Where do you live actually?" said Pamela to me. The discipline of saving money is actually a really exciting one. It has made the Bell more exciting for me. It will no doubt make Sunset Strip more exciting for me eventually. I love the things I have got away with in the past, the things I get away with now, the things I will get away with in the future.

I have got my book-lined London home, filled with ferns, and classical music. I live like a church mouse in a little hotel earning the money to write my books, while enjoying the girls taking their knickers off to loud music, and travelling a couple of times a year to Berlin. I am still sad about

241

—. Do what you want with your genitals, otherwise you will regret it when you're dead.

There is nothing better than travelling around Europe to see my favourite opera singers. While there enjoying the brothels and strip clubs and pubs as well. Travel seems the only point to life. To travel is to be held in suspension. As soon as you come to rest, everything stops and falls. You are just left waiting until you can travel again. Between travels I will just drink and drink to make the time go faster.

I will go home today so I can get drunk while listening to music. That is all I do every day on my days off, get drunk. Just waiting for the time I can travel again. Thursday should be thundery, and Friday showers. The paper says we are heading for a period of high winds, torrential rain and abnormally high temperatures! Phnom Penh weather. It remains to be seen whether I can resist the lure of the illicit thrill during these atmospheric conditions. I do not want to go back to the Bell and Sunset Strip and Sunset Cinema and Demi and Pamela until I am also ready to travel. Even when I get September out of the way, there is still all of October, all of November, and all of December to get through! Can I really resist travelling in December? Maybe I will just pop to Brussels?

I live for gambling, I live for saving my money in periods of abstinence just so I can blow it again on wicked women in London and Brussels and Vienna and Munich and Berlin. This boom and bust is what I live for.

What a merry chase I lead people! I exult in it now. How I torment them and torture them with what I get away with and STILL get away with. I used to feel chased and hunted and hounded. Now I delight in leading them on a chase after me. See if you can keep up!

Everybody was waiting for me when I first went to Europe. They already knew me and they already knew I was on my way, and they already knew the date and time of my arrival. I feel like Bourne. They know who I am and I don't. What was it I did? Who was I? Why was everyone trying to kill me? When I went to the top of the St Mark's Belltower in Venice, the American kids knew me. They raised their camera and took my picture and then laughed sarcastically in my face: "Ha ha!"

Yes I am amused to feel like Bourne. But I also feel like Joe Orton—still getting away with it! Like Frank Wedekind, flaunting it in their faces! Pour épater le bourgeoisie. To do whatever it is I shouldn't do. I LIVE FOR THE WILD NIETZSCHEAN DIONYSIAN PLEASURE. I LIVE FOR STIRRING PEOPLE UP. I LIVE FOR DOING THINGS I SHOULDN'T. I

LIVE FOR DOING DANGEROUS THINGS WHICH WILL PUT ME ON THE VERGE OF SELF-DESTRUCTION. I LIVE FOR THE SLEAZY THRILL.

Royksopp What Else Is There? Yes I owe a massive £6000. Yes my monthly interest is a massive £80. But think of those nights in Munich Atlantic City watching Susi, Irina, Patricia, Bella Rosa, Viktoriya, or in Femina with Emily. Going to Nuremberg and meeting Martina in the Pils Bar. Those nights in Berlin with Yulia, Riccarda, Iga, Diana or Erika. Would I take any of it back? No!

I AM DEBAUCHED. Debauchery is the road to Taoist contentment. The pleasures are great. The rewards are great.

The rewards for that £6,000 have been great.

Oh God I love to get drunk and lose it! And I always will. Whether in London or Berlin or Munich or Vienna or Brussels. I will always want to get drunk and lose it. That is the point of life. Live for the moment. Live every moment like it's the last.

Why do I keep going back to the same places? For me, it is an attempt at time travel. I am trying to go back to the past & this time put right what I did wrong. I have left so much blood on the tracks, and I want to put it all right this time, with Susi, with Irina, with Viktoriya, and do the right thing this time. Please let me have that chance. So of course all my visits become increasingly forlorn.

What a lovely 30? 45? minutes I had with Harrietta in Angelique in Vienna.

I am quietly obsessed with recording my own life.

Für Elise is nostalgia for all the beautiful Esmeraldas you have fallen in love with & who you have had to leave behind.

What the hell happened to Pink? What a loss. What a brief golden age. How can I not love all the Tallulahs and Esmeraldas I have met? What magical, never to be forgotten high, special moments they have given me.

Yes I miss those nights at Atlantic City and Sexyland and Golden Gate & Mon Cheri & Monte Carlo & Ciro & Pour Platin and Empire and the Bell and Sunset Strip & Sunset Cinema, but you cannot keep doing it all the time. You cannot do it every week, 52 weeks a year. Yes I am missing out on all those experiences and all those heady nights and all those new people like Janet or Martini that might be arriving—but it is great to have some months when you do nothing, and then have some months when you go back to it. You have to deny yourself some things for a while, in order to enjoy them again. The longer I leave it the more I will appreciate it when I go back to my Pope life, my Francis Bacon life, my George Grosz life. The Broken

World. The Shining Road. Once again I pore over the weather forecasts. For signs, auguries, of when the right time will be to resume my former sinful profligate life. I divine things from the weather. My sexuality is linked to the weather as much as it is linked to finance and to justice and to cathedrals. I will indulge my sexuality when the weather indicators are right, and the financial indicators are right, and the scales of justice feel right, and when in the cathedral it feels right.

I love the wicked women. I have met some women I could trust in that broken world, Lela, for example, Ana Maria, Pamela. Diana in Berlin or Riccarda. Probably not Iga, as much as I love her! You can genuinely touch someone in that world and be touched by them, I think. I always go into that world looking for love, as I think they are the only women I could ever love. The clink of gold in the glass. The Tallulahs are probably no more cynical than the Esmeraldas. They are only nice to you as long as you are filling their glass with gold. Still, I think you can meet some exceptions, when something genuine passes between you, with Susi, with Janet, with —. And if I am wrong, then it does not matter. Fleetingly, it felt nice to real there was something real between us, if only in the blink of an eye. It is those moments that you keep go out looking for. That is what you keep gambling for, throwing so much money down on the roulette table for the very occasional moment when you get back more than you put in. That is what you keep trawling the broken world for, those fleeting moments when eye meets eye and some spark of electricity passes between you, and that current brings you back to life, for a couple of hours, or for one night, at least. That is what the poems of Hart Crane speak to me of: "The flesh assaults outright for bolts that linger". How you put on your beer goggles, so everything looks magical, everyone looks beautiful and desirable, and everyone seems to find you beautiful and desirable in return. If it is all commerce, simply, then no matter. There are just those brief moments when it seems so real, comes so close to being real, that it is as good as real.

In every city there is Helen of Troy locked up somewhere in a room. She lives on like Orlando, like Emilia Makropolus. You go out every night searching for her, as David Tennant's Casanova always searches for Laura Fraser. "The sight of a whore is profoundly thrilling to a man". As a scopophiliac, sight is everything to me, and I lose myself in that world. For two months I have had to abstain completely and withdraw from it, only so that I might return refreshed and enjoy it anew. "There is only one woman in the world for me, you know that". "Who is she? Tell me!""No. She is cruel to me." "Maybe you were cruel to her." "Ah, that's what a bleeding heart does to a man. It drips and leaks into his soul, and before long floods his soul, and saturates him, and all his thoughts and all his words and all his deeds become bloody." "What could a woman do to help such a man?" "Well, if you would just give me your hand for a moment..." "No! You're an animal!" "If you would just step into this dark corner with me for a moment..." "No! Never again! No more dark corners with you!"

How I walked away from Irina without seizing my moment. How I walked away from — without seizing my moment. How I walked away from Susi without seizing my moment. Maybe Riccarda, too. Pamela?

I live in the Ernest Dowson world. Don't stick your head above the parapet unless you want to get shot at. When I hear Maneater I want to see — dancing to it. I am obsessed with her.

CHAPTER 7
THE CALCUTTA

The Calcutta was very packed even for a Friday. I had 3½ pints before going to the Wigmore. To be honest, Frittoli was more voluptuous than I was expecting, in a three-layered black dress covered with silver diamante patterns, and I had to revise my plan to leave at the interval. She was gorgeous and fantastic. A special honour to see her and yet in my mind I conflated her and — together so it felt I was looking and worshipping both of them at the same time, while I muttered away still talking to —. I was reminded very much of the Prokina night when she turned and looked at me at the end as she sang the words "I still love him".

As I was leaving the flat last night, the little blonde Polish bob had just come in & was checking her postbox. She did not turn around but I said hello anyway and she turned around with such a big lovely smile & said hello back & she looked so gorgeous & I was glad I did something friendly. I was rewarded by meeting English teacher and Greek girl on the bus & having a good night in general. The more you give out the more you get back. It is difficult when you are in the depths and coils of a depression, but I hope to meet my Rilkean turning point, and bounce back. Given her flowers, Frittoli bowed low & all the rainwater from the flowers spilled onto the stage. Everyone laughed & she pretended to shower the front row with it. When she came out for her encore she very exaggeratedly stepped round the water & pretended to slip over. A true star, reminding me of Jochen Kowalski catching the bouquet with one hand at the Komische Oper.

As I entered the hall the ticket girl smiled at me "we are sold out so no one can cheat" and we grinned at each other. You will not get out of your depression by being moody and cold, you will only do it by being warm and friendly, and trying to smile and be nice to people, and then get warmth back. — on November 18th at the Horse & Groom looms hugely on my horizon. In the meantime if I do not see her at the Bell I know I can always go back and have a good night at the Sunset.

Of course I cannot travel to Berlin in the New Year. Especially when the one I love is behind me in London. Alone, alone, alone. Always alone. I have always been alone, and I always shall be. And yet travelling can mark the end of one period of your life, and when you come back you can find everything feels different, and you feel very liberated from it. Maybe after going to Berlin I will feel I can start again and turn over a new page, which I will not do just by staying the whole time in London, trapped in the same routine, silently morosely standing in the back corner of the Scotsman, longing for — and never even going over to talk to her. This year has been ALL about —. That would be a good title! ALL ABOUT —.

I am a dreamy boy, who lives in a world of his own. I am Ernest Dowson, seemingly always submerged in a dream. He spent all his money on drink and whores. He suffered the torture of the damned because his beloved Adelaide did not love him back. I need to go to see Demi and Pamela, to try to console me over my broken heart with —. "I have been faithful to thee, Cynara, in my fashion". But all the time I am fucking Demi or Pamela it will be really — I am imagining is beneath me.

I write books about a chronic inability to relate to people or to talk to them or to form relationships of any meaningful kind. About life lived with no companionship whatsoever even though much may be offered. AUTISMUS. LOTTA. THE COLD ICY AIR OF THE MOUNTAINS. CASANOVA. I go through life with no companionship, even though — offered me companionship and I threw the chance away. The chance to get to know another human being, and to be known by another human being, and I threw it away. "The harder we search for someone else, the more likely we are to find ourselves." "But it is not Turgenev's writing that interests Dessaix most, it is his life. Specifically, the 40 years Turgenev spent in supposedly chaste devotion to mezzo-soprano Pauline Viardot, trotting around Europe after her—and her husband—like a fuddy-duddy lapdog". "The greatest of the 19th-century novels always centred on the journey towards that moment when one person is known by another, and is transfigured—or believes she is transfigured, or wants to be transfigured—by intimacy. From Jane Austen to Charlotte Brontë to Tolstoy, novelists created and strengthened our faith in the absolute power of the love relationship to transform a life for good or ill".

You wait so long for something special to happen in your life, that when it does, you just watch it in amazement & do not realise you have to make a move to catch it before it is gone and lost. A man on a desert island for 36 years finally sees a ship sailing by and is so shocked it is gone before he realises he should do something to make it stop. It is clear I have got to go back and f–k either Demi or Pamela to cope with the pain of —. I haven't had sex since...Francesca on the 13th July, and both Francesca & Pamela the week before that. A lonely man, who never talks, just stands quietly on his own in the corner. When the girl he loves and pines for is just a few feet away on the other side of the pub, ready for him to talk to all night long if he wished, but still he stays on his own in the corner, talking to no one.

I am Ernest Dowson, wandering around Europe after his rejection by Adelaide, suffering the torture of the damned. That is how I like to be. Pining for —. Longing for —. Bleeding for —. I had a chance to get into her life and I let it go.

"But despite his literary success, Crane was a profoundly tormented man. Poetry sustained him in a life that otherwise teetered on the brink of collapse. When he wasn't writing, he spent much of his time engaged in fleeting homosexual encounters and alcohol binges. In 1932, three years after meeting Lorca, Crane committed suicide by leaping from a ship into the Caribbean".

I am a broken man. — can see that now.

OK I did great to "save" £900 in ten weeks, but that is over now. I am going to go wild again now. I cannot waste these gorgeous dark witching months. Forget Berlin. There is so much to taste here in London. That break has renewed my taste for it. "There's really no way to reach me." What I want to achieve in my books is simplicity. Strippers remind me of Anita Berber, Josephine Baker, Mata Hari. They are Salome dancing for dirty old man Herod so she can get to kiss the lips of John the Baptist.

*

"How are you?" the stunning tall blonde Amazonian (Moldovan) girl smiled to me. "Thou hast what's left of me:" I said. "For I am now sunk so low from what I was, thou findst me at my lowest watermark. The rivers that ran in and raised my fortunes are all dried up or take another course: What I have left is from my native spring; I've still a heart that swells in scorn of fate, and lifts me to my banks." "OK" she said, a little hesitant now. I ploughed on. "Already, Death, I feel thee in my veins. I go with such a will to find my lord that we shall quickly meet. A heavy numbness creeps through every limb, and now tis at my head; my eyelids fall, and my dear love is vanished in a mist. Where shall I find her, where? Oh turn me to her, and lay me on her breast!–Caesar, thy worst. Now part us if thou canst." She was visibly moved by my oration and had to rush to the other side of the room so as not to let me see her cry. I purchased another pint.

Like there can be sudden changes in the Earth's magnetic field, in February this year my soul suddenly became completely pointed towards —, and despite the catastrophe, despite my Actium, despite my Black Night of Downfall, my soul remains immovably pointed in her direction all of eight months later. Other women–Pamela, Melani–have come along and with their magnetic attraction have been able to flicker my pointer a fraction towards them for a short while, but it has never been strong enough to keep me from my overwhelming attraction to –. Even if Sylvia came back that would not change anything.

I want that Libertines world, that Hogarth world, that Dowson world. "The sight of a whore is profoundly thrilling to a man." It has been three days since I last saw – and already it feels like an eternity. My life is just going through the boring motions, work, work, work. The only thing that gives it a spark is my writing, and time spent with a loved one if such a thing were ever possible for me.

"They rage there as at meat in a menagerie." The introduction to *Pandora's Box*. It was going to see *Lulu* at King's Cross that I discovered and fell into the world of strip pubs like falling down a rabbit hole into wonderland. They've even, coincidentally, got an Alice. It was a treasure to stand there watching all those posh theatre-goers coming in, in their suits and mink coats and pearls, and their mouths dropping open when they saw the half-naked girls walking around (and totally stark naked one up on stage showing them everything she'd got), and then quickly turning around and leaving. To the uninitiated, they must have thought they had walked into a brothel. One of the great theatrical events in recent London history for that reason, and why I also supported the idea of the E.N.O. relocating to a King's Cross base.

You can stick your Stringfellows & your Sophisticats—the sexiest strippers in London are the Scotsman girls. Of course, it goes without saying London's and the British Empire's great gift to the world is the strip pub, and out of all them—White Horse, Nag's Head, Old Axe, Browns, Griffin, Queen Anne—the Flying Scot is far & away the best. The "Menu of the Day" list of girls is disturbingly reminiscent of Jack the Ripper's victims' board at the Ten Bells. In the space of twenty yards King's Cross used to boast Housman's bookshop, The Flying Scotsman, and the gloriously sleazy Scala Cinema. The Scala Cinema alas is no more, but thankfully these other two great treasures of the British Empire remain. Tenseness, eroticism and repulsive pathology. Fine for a Jimmy Riddle but those needing a Tom Tit should look elsewhere.

"As Nietzsche put it, while recovering from his intoxication with Wagner: 'What can be done well today, what can be masterly, is only what is small.'" Talk about the girls being great actresses. Like Sarah Bernhardt,

Mrs Patrick Campbell. When I see them on stage I am seeing Anita Berber, Mata Hari, Josephine Baker. Every dance is a mini-drama. Tense, erotic, pathological. I want to write a magazine reviewing their performances like an opera magazine would Maria Callas at Covent Garden. Yet it seems more personal, and to talk about them by name seems impertinent, and to betray a secret. One skirts around one's feelings. One beats around the bush. One does not name one's fears or one's loves.

THE SERPENT'S EGG
A Journal about The Flying Scotsman pub, and Other Things
How often I used to go to King's Cross for Housman's bookshop, for their science fiction and their Karl Marx and their Situationist and Anarchist literature, and passed by that old ramshackle pub over the road that looked like it had closed a long time ago without barely giving it a second look. How many hours of my misspent life I spent in the darkness of the Scala Cinema, watching Godard triple bills, Russ Meyer triple bills, Bertolucci triple bills, without realising what delights were in the pub just next door. Can I even imagine a time when I didn't drink? After loving the Otto Dix picture of Anita Berber for so long I went to see the Berber film *Anita: Dances of Vice* there, and though there were only about ten people in the vast 2,000 seat auditorium, some man who looked like Arthur Miller (but wasn't) came and sat right down next to me in the back row and proceeded to slowly slowly creepy creepy spider creep his hand towards my arm, trying to touch me. At the moment his finger touched the back of my hand I asked him to leave me alone; of course I did. You doubt me? He soon went down the front of the cinema & no doubt tried his luck with some other pretty young boy, before, bizarrely, about 40 minutes later coming & sitting back by me.

I am decadent and rotten. I can lust after the great sex dancers of the Flying Scotsman as much as I lust after the great pianists, Irina Botan, Mihaela Ursuleasa, Valentina Igoshina, Nadia Giliova; the great violinists Tatiana Burman, Janine Jansen, the great opera singers Elena Prokina, Barbara Frittoli, Anna Caterina Antonacci, Stefania Bonfadelli. Is this bad of me? Is this wrong of me? "Saw the same two men on the Cally Road". This will be my *Die Fackel*. This will be my *Simplicissimus*. Devoted to the Flying Scotsman pub, the Wigmore Hall, English National Opera, the Black Hole of Calcutta pub, the Lemon Tree. After my great depression of these last few weeks, I see now that depression was the chrysalis, in which some metamorphosis was taking place, to give birth to this beautiful butterfly. *Nana.* It seems sad, but as sad experiences go it is one of the best. Men lusting after women is the engine of the world.

Decorated all over by pictures of the Anna Friel *Lulu*. I live in a lush, overgrown, tropical paradise. I push through the great ferns and fronds, brushing the black train soot off the leaves, till I find the door of the Scotsman, and surreptitiously disappear inside, into the wonderland within that scarcely anyone passing by can imagine. How many times I myself passed by this door without it occurring to me what went on within. All those wasted years of my life!

Some days I think I am going to go in that door and find just a normal pub, like a Wetherspoons or an All Bar One, and I will realise I dreamed the whole thing. It will be like the wardrobe that the children went through to enter their snowy Narnia, but then one day just becomes—a wardrobe. "Frank Wedekind (1864-1918) German playwright, who began his career working in business and in a circus. He became an actor and singer, and a playwright. The plays, *Erdgeist (Earth Spirit)*, 1893, and *Die Busche der Pandora (Pandora's Box)*, 1904, depict a society riven by the demands of lust and greed reinforcing his main thesis that the repression of sexuality results in perversion and tragedy. The two plays were later staged together as the *Lulu* plays." "All Wedekind's plays, with their sex-ridden men, women and children, their gentlemen crooks, and their grotesque yet vivid cranks, typify the feverish spirit of the years before 1914. Perhaps less shocking now to our society they remain valid statements of repressed and thwarted sexuality." Repressed, and thwarted sexuality! My constant and dearest companions and bedfellows! You mean sexuality comes in any other kinds? Thus due to my bizarre and troubling psychopathology, my mummy never loved me, I was dropped on my head as a baby, or something, I am a Lost Boy, repressed and thwarted, my Eros bends instead, during interludes, to the butterflies and the nightingales of the Scotsman, my Midnight Bell. But increasingly I find the interludes are becoming longer and more enjoyable, and I do not want the real Acts to begin again. The interludes between the real thing are becoming more real to me than the real thing, and the real thing seems not worth a light. My life becomes one long dark pleasurable interlude between womb and tomb. It used to be my cure for a broken heart. Now it has become where my heart most wants to be. I cannot imagine loving any girl who was not a Salome dancing for Herod, or a Mata Hari. I want my Flying Scotsman magazine to be suffused with Anna Friel's *Lulu*, and with *Salome*, and with *Nana*, and with heady steamy sensuousness. Cloying, overpowering, romantic nihilistic sweetness. Tension, Eroticism, Repulsive Pathology. "The most over-perfumed drama in the language." "'Where is she who gave herself unto the Captains of Assyria, who have baldricks on their loins, and tiaras of divers colours on their heads?"

You've got to hide your love away; though it is the most natural thing in the world to want to sing it from the rooftops. Each man kills the thing he loves. They are all Salomes, dancing for King Herod.

If only I could have back all the thousands of pounds I have wasted on strippers and drink over the years, I would go out and spend it all on strippers and drink. Our sad tawdry addictions are the best of us. If I did not have things to be sadly addicted to, I would kill myself. Our vices are the best of us. They are when we glow brightest and most brilliant. Oscar Wilde would not be celebrated today, would not have the West End full of his plays, would not have his own statue in Adelaide Street and his own stained (of course) window in Westminster Abbey if not for his vice. To watch young women take their knickers off on a stage. What a sad, empty experience, but as sad, empty experiences go, one of the absolute best. And at the Scotsman it has been refined to its most pure and simple state. The Nag's Head and the Old Axe could be this good but are not. Dodgy doormen demanding an apparently arbitrary amount of pound coins in their hand before they will let you in, body searches for concealed...what? An endless stream of 20 or 30 girls constantly asking for private dances. The fact that the Flying Scotsman does not offer private dances seems to me one of the most beautiful things about it. Anyway, if any of my Scotsman girls gave me a private dance, I think I would die. It would be too much, after all this time longing for them.

People criticise the Flying Scotsman because nothing is spent on it to modernise it, but that seems to me the nub of its absolute charm. It is like stepping back into Victorian London. With the Thatcherite revolution, the Millenium, the old Soho basement strip clubs were replaced by the mirrors and champagne and poles of the Stringfellows, and Sophisticats, and For Your Eyes Onlys, and we were told it is all right to go to strip clubs now, because they had gone upmarket, and respectable. Since when should sex be respectable? Sex should be down and dirty and sleazy or what is the point of it at all? The Flying Scotsman shines out like a beacon in the Stygian gloom, a glowing candle in the peasouper fog, by having resisted the tide. It is as close as you can get to the old Soho experience. It is like a fly trapped in amber. It is a Lost World at the bottom of a hole on a high South American plateau, where Tyrannosaurus Rex still roams, and Pterodactyl still fly in the sky. It is the Pterodactyl brought back to London and escaping and circling above the Royal Geographical Society against a Full Moon.

KARL KRAUS. "Why do I always act so dumb, seem to fuck things up for fun. Just can't help behaving, as if my head needs rearranging". It is always something exotic, and steamy. Exotic, steamy, King's Cross.

For me, for a girl to be a dancer is the greatest thing in the world. And to not be crude but to use my favourite description, a sex dancer. I revere opera singers, violinists, pianists, and actresses, but I worship no one like I do sex dancers. Wine, women and song.

CHAPTER 8
THE REASON I AM
GOING CRAZY OVER
PAMELA

The reason I am going crazy over Pamela is my madness over —. The two are connected inextricably, I will never get anything from either.

Another five in the Calcutta. The Belle of the Calcutta came in at 530 with boyfriend, black boots, short black dress, white white legs, black lipstick, brown fur-trimmed coat, what a sex bomb. Later I sat at the round table so I could get a direct look at her apocalyptically beautiful breasts in that black silk dress. I have never wanted to fuck someone so much in all my life. From there I do not remember but I must have walked up to Leicester Square up the side-turning directly towards the Crooked Surgeon and straight into Pamela's door, "Emma" now. She was grinning as she opened the door, £50 for twenty minutes talking! Let me suck her breasts and did not stop me even when her nipples got hard, and let me lick her pussy as well.

Fantastic watching the Hogarth *Harlot's Progress* programme when I got back with Zoe Tapper again as the prostitute Mary Collins. How poignant to see Hogarth falling so infatuatedly in love with his whore.

<u>A Harlot's Progress</u>
"In 1731 the artist William Hogarth produced a graphic series of paintings which lifted the lid on 18th-century vice and established his enduring reputation as a remarkable social satirist and the greatest British artist of his day. With an all-star cast, *A Harlot's Progress* depicts Hogarth's exploration of sex trafficking and debauchery in Georgian London."

Yes I have spent £268 this week—but it was vital money to get me over — and start something new with Pamela. Pamela did repeat on Thursday that she doesn't go out with customers, but then she said "I cannot go out this week, and I cannot go out next week because I am busy every day". What about the week after? "I don't know what my plans are the week after". So she is not ruling it out then! Or am I clutching at straws?

254

I am under a lot of financial pressure now. I have steered myself towards some very tight straits, and the rock walls are closing in on me from both sides. Will my ship be able to squeeze through?

Not sure why I was quite so depressed after last night. Felt rejected by — covering her ears when I asked about private parties, and then by Pamela keep saying no to me, she is busy every day, then when I asked her if she had a boyfriend she announced she had a not-quite a boyfriend, a Frenchman, who she knew from when she first came to England. Did not wake up till 130PM, just in time to head back to Calcutta for four, then the Queen Anne. Clara, Lucy is Giselle from Sunset! Then R— A— appeared. I realised she is the huge-Zeppelined girl I had seen talking to — at the Scotsman. My God. She is everything she is cracked up to be and more. Changed into black businesswoman's jacket and skirt with nothing underneath. I had a private dance with her and she rubbed very hard against me. She is awesome. It will be so long till I see her again. Got to work just before 10. Fairly awful night as can be expected with six pints inside me.

Arleni, Maira, the unbelievably pretty Sol, Sam, Lena, Michelle, at the Flying Scotsman. And — who I avoided. Stupidly I went into Sunset Cinema, paid £12, just looked upstairs and downstairs then left straightaway. I was too drunk. *Big Naughty Titties* is the only title I can remember. Pamela was busy so I sat with maid waiting, She smiled hello when she saw me, in red bra & knickers, & hair pulled back tight. As I said I felt like she would always reject me and it will never happen. "Don't look sad" she said as I dressed, "I hate it when you look sad" At least I only spent £22 this time. All those gorgeous Berlin whores I could be fucking in Mon Cheri, Golden Gate and Monte Carlo. All those gorgeous Vienna whores. Clarisse in Brussels.

I love Pamela but cannot have her. Another unrequited love in my life, after —. At least with Pamela there is no madness, no great missed opportunity to torment me. There is just a sadness, when being with her is so lovely, she is so voluptuous and beautiful, it is so hard to come away. I will not see her again for a long time, I think. It is pointless, crazy, like it became with Lydia. And I am getting missed calls from her again, on the 9th, 10th, and 12th.

I was running late so did not get to the Calcutta until 540, I took the box seat and found the Calcutta Belle & her man already sitting there. She was sitting facing me & it was hard to resist looking at her & her humongous exposed boobs in the mirror. I left just after 6, after just one pint, as she was putting her coat on to leave as well. I got to the Scotsman just as — was coming back to collect from some men she had missed first time but did not approach me, yet when she got on stage she was looking at me with little smiles. She is fine. Very fine. Sam, Crystal, Lucky. Alison, Cindy, Kelly, Cristina finishing at 7 same as Arleni. Holland v England was on which saved me some money.

— served me first with a little smile. It did seem very busy in there; I wonder if people had been reading my recommendations! It was great to see Lucky & Alison again, but nothing else, and I left after three. Felt so steaming mad, and bad-tempered on the bus, just from the despair and unhappiness of my life. I would have loved a Dionysus but resisted. Looked in Sunset Cinema but could not be bothered, just wanted to see Pamela. £47. Finally understood now it will always be no. Sadness. She is so good to hold, and talk to. Her dog is a terrier, called —. "He loves me."

CHAPTER 9
I AM AN OPIUM
ADDICT &
A GAMBLER

I am an opium addict and a gambler.

I have gotten in over my head. Every so often I manage to rein myself in and cut back, but even when I cut back and come down a bit, I look down the cold icy mountainside and discover I am already so far above the place where I similarly cut back a year ago. I make my debts worse by 2 or 3,000 then every so often with great effort I manage to control myself and actually save 8 or 900 and I am so pleased with myself for saving that 900 and paying back that 900, before going mad again and spending another 2 or 3,000. I keep on climbing higher and higher up this cold icy mountain and I never seem to see the top of it, it seems to go on upwards forever, and I doomed to keep on climbing upwards forever. Leaving people further and further behind me. Further and further from warmth and affection. The air gets thinner and thinner and harder to breathe. My hallucinations get worse. Every so often I find the shoes or clothes or picks of those who have gone this way before me and fallen. Not made it back down again and found their icy grave on this mountain. Sometimes I pass by their frozen bodies. And still I keep climbing? Why? Because it is there. What else is there to do? I tell myself you are only young once. You cannot climb when you are old, so you must climb as high as you can while you are still young. No point spending a year or two going back down the mountain to the flat ground, only then to feel free to start climbing again. While I am as high as I am, I might as well keep going: until I reach the—what? I've come too far to turn back now. And the turning back is probably more difficult and dangerous and fraught with peril than the climbing upwards. No, so safer to keep going up. Keep going up and keep diving deeper into darkness.

Wickedness has only ever left me feeling high with fantastically rich memories. It is only love that brings catastrophes that destroy me. I wish I could learn how to love without being destroyed by it. It is like walking into a volcano. So I am an opium addict instead. I prefer the phantasmagoric dreams and I prefer to live permanently in these dreams rather than in reality. Sometimes I meet someone in this dream state who wants to love me, take me out of the trance into reality, and to replace the opium with love, and I either give in to them and let myself be lured out and am destroyed, or else I resist them, which also destroys me. Love then is the great danger, but it is also what I always look for, glimmers of it in the phantasy. I look for it, cultivate it, then run from it and shut it out. I want to be desired without ever having to actually do anything in return.

My love is like poison. My love was like poison to Lilith, and it is like poison to —. Because I am scopophiliac. I can just gaze and gaze at them with love and longing, and when they are flattered, and say OK then, I am letting you in, you just go on gazing and gazing, because that is all you are capable of. Then they feel ashamed and embarrassed at ever having opened up to you, and slam the door in your face, after having let someone else through it first. I can only stay outside the window like Peter Pan, when all the other Lost Boys accepted the invitation to become part of the Darling family, so he lost Wendy forever. You keep on smiling, a frozen smile on your face, like Noodles at the end of *Once Upon a Time in America*. Telling yourself everything is fine, you didn't want her anyway, you wanted to stay outside, you wanted to come to the opium den instead. You prefer to stay in the opium den, you don't want to get involved with no woman. And inside you die a little more. Self-negation. You negate yourself out of existence. All because you could not open up to love, all because you were so terrified of opening up to love and letting love in. Why is love so terrifying? The Consul prayed every day for Yvonne to come back to him, and when by some miracle she did, he got drunk and ran away into the jungle again. That is what the volcano inside does to a man. So I can never ever love anyone ever again.

I have to get drunk, because I cannot bear myself as I am. Now the devastating coldness of being shut out. I did not enter when I was invited so now I am forever shut out. I wander lost, shivering, weeping in the snow like Von Stuck's Devil. The catastrophes of love will get to me in the end. Every one takes so much out of you. I get drunk because I cannot cope with the pain sober.

It is Paris 1899. — is my drug. She is my opium. She has got into my blood and I cannot get rid of her. When you meet someone you really want to f—k I don't think you ever really get over that, until you have consummated it. I am never going to stop trying. The graph of my mental health depends on —. If I go to the Fly and find her not there my graph collapses. If she is there, and we get on OK, my graph holds steady and even improves a bit. We should have got together ten months ago, but at the last moment I hesitated, and destroyed everything.

COLLECTED WORKS

THE STRIPPER

Grand Guignol in a G-String

2007

ERNST GRAF

THIS IS MY *DESPAIR*.

NOW IS THE WINTER OF MY DESPAIR.

SNOW FALLING ON WINTRY BERLIN TREES. KU'DAMM MANSIONS. BLONDE ENGLISH ROSE WHORE. ENGLISH ANITA BERBER. ADELAIDE, MY SOHO SCHOOLGIRL FROM 8 YEARS AGO. NOW STRIPPING IN A BERLIN STRIP PUB, THE BLACK PIG, THE FINEST LITTLE STRIP PUB IN THE WORLD.

BERLIN. OPIUM. ADOLPH MENZEL.

When I discovered the Black Pig I felt I had found my home. Since then I had seen so many young men come into the Pig obviously for the first time and very quickly saw that they, like me, were now lost—or found. "It started with toothache. Thomas De Quincey bought a tincture of opium at a druggist's shop in 1804 and discovered that 'happiness might now be bought for a penny and carried in the waistcoat pocket.' It was the start of his 'opium career', as recounted in his *Confessions of an English Opium Eater* (1821), which influenced Baudelaire and Poe among others and did so much to romanticise the drug." Almost every one of the regulars of the Pig had first strolled in there completely unaware of what they would find, the initial shock and delight turning to a habit, to addiction, to way of life. To think that the happiness of seeing a beautiful voluptuous young woman stripping completely naked could be bought for just a 'pound' in a pot! If the 'strip pub' was not the greatest thing ever invented by man, I did not know what was, and the Black Pig was the best of them.

In Berlin everything revolved around the nexus of Berlin Zoo Station, the Alt Berlin restaurant just outside, the English newspaper shop, and the Black Pig itself. Filled with tropical ferns, newspapers, men from every strata of life mingling together; in the corner were the musicians, classically trained, some of whom had played with the Berlin Symphony Orchestra, and everywhere the florid & lurid floozies, some of whom had also played with the Berlin Symphony Orchestra but in a different way, in their lingerie and their evening gowns at all hours of the day. Sex and violins, the perfect combination. I loved the Black Pig and felt at home nowhere else. On this cold Christmas Day, after the coldest winter since records began in 1910, I got off my bus in the snow outside Berlin Zoo station just to see it and to pass it and pay my daily tribute to it, before descending the Black Pig's coiling black wrought iron staircase (or "overwrought" as Adelaide always insisted, "like our customers;"), pushed through the ferns and was hit by the warmth, the darkness, the bubble of conversation and conviviality, the violin music, to the back room and there on the stage was a girl in red furry Santa outfit dancing to first The Kinks' Lola then Goldfrapp's We Are Glitter. My pint of Berliner Kindl in my hand, my blonde beermat on my table, a busty blonde on the stage, my Christmas Day began.

Above us we could see the feet passing to and fro along the snowy pavement, hear the rumble and hiss and rattle of trains and buses, down here in the warm Christmas Day basement one girl after another slowly gyrated on the stage in front of us. "How beautiful they are!" cried Sir Richard Lovell sitting down at my table, quoting Robert Walser, "Women who fight their wounded feelings down. The brilliance of her eyes quite turns me on. White as alabaster her complexion now. I am inspired to be dauntless! I can't help it, her act has fortified my faith in myself. The beauty of an artiste, what is it for, if not to strengthen and enrich the soul?" "What indeed brave Sir Richard. Ill met by gaslight. Happy Christmas my friend!" We embraced heartily, clinking our beer glasses together.

"Flaubert said authors required a permanent erection, but he needs to be in between sleep and lucidity, and a good stripper audience is the same. This is the power of the stripper. She represents the side of dancing that is amoral, hedonistic, self-serving and red in tooth and claw, offering in place of noble aspirations a guiltier, more primal thrill: the licence not to give a damn. It makes the man with respectable profession, wife and family at home, not want to give a damn as well. They corrupt us, these Jezebels, and Christ knows we are well up for it."

"Strippers are supposed to be the ones contorting themselves into vulnerable positions, exploiting their body to make the rent. But more often than not, it's not the clothes-shedder who bares their soul, it's the audience member watching them."

"Strippers are popular because they generate anxiety but, at the same time, they reassure. They brush up against us, but touch others. It's like leaning over the edge of a precipice to step back at the last moment. You feel giddiness. Anxiety. But also relief. It's a subtle pleasure."

An English Salome

Suddenly thunder. Deafening crashing rolling thunder, the pub went black. There was a cry or two from the girls and one sensitive young man passed out hitting his head on the bar as he dropped, splattering it with his blood;

264

it was not thunder, it was jungle drums. Then oboes, screeching clarinets, it was the Dance of the Seven Veils from *Salome*, in the pitch black of the Black Pig. The curtain parted and there was Adelaide, my 16-year-old Soho schoolgirl from eight years ago, in brown fox fur around her neck and grey mink fur coat which she immediately shed to reveal her Salome costume, grinning at me, as she began dancing. She turned around & bent over & pointed her bottom at me, as if to say "This dance is for you!" "The secret of love is greater than the secret of death," whispered Sir Richard terrified, visibly shaking. *Salome* gave way to Flashdance and Adelaide began to dance ecstatically around the small Pig stage. "What a feeling indeed!" cheered Sir Richard excitedly. She clambered around the wooden shelves & arches surrounding the stage and hung there like a bat in the belfry. As I stood in the archway next to the stage, she hooked one of her legs right over my shoulder so there was nothing in front of me except her pussy. I could not speak. I could not breathe. As the girl I had dreamed of seeing naked for so long now stood there naked in front of me. Then Carly Simon Nobody Does It Better; but how did she know? She padded around the stage on the balls of her bare feet as Salome surely had done for King Herod. All sex dancers were Salome dancing for Herod. All sex dancers should dance in bare feet. They never look naked if they keep their high heels on after taking everything else off. Only when a stripper takes her shoes off as well does she truly become naked, do you only then see her as she would look in your bedroom. Unusually for a stripper Adelaide took off everything, bra, knickers, shoes AND stockings, so she finished completely and utterly naked.

Afterwards Adelaide came and sat with me and Sir Richard at our table and we drank champagne together. She held a sprig of mistletoe over her head and let both of us chastely peck her on the lips. She was glowing, beautiful, a hot Mata Hari, an English Lolita, face caked in make-up and glitter. "How's Soho these days?" "Empty without you!" "Ha! You should have tried harder to stop me leaving, then." "You look fantastic!" I smiled, running my fingers around her Salome costume, managing to accidentally on purpose stroke some of her side boob as I did so and she did not stop me. "You can take the girl out of Soho," she said, "but you can't take Soho out of the girl. Or the man!"

Lily was her stage name. She looked older—of course she did—she was older. It had been eight years earlier I had first met her in Soho when she was still a schoolgirl and she had told me that she was in love with me, and maybe we could make each other happy, and if I wanted her I should come

265

find her, and it was only her young age that deterred me, frightened I would get into trouble, and I lost her. The child had become a woman. Now she had a used look; sluttish; wonderfully sluttish; the kind of sluttish look that is pleasing to every man; glitter, heavy make-up, her thick black eye mascara smudged. Her body fuller, to say the least. "I only became a stripper because then you'd want me. Because they're the only type of girl you love, isn't it? I became dirty, and let myself become used, so I would turn you on. Because I know you are sick. You cannot deny it! Here you are! I was right! If I stayed a normal girl you would never have wanted me. You would never have felt safe with me. Never have trusted me. I love you but you always leave."

"Can I wait for you to finish?"

"No." But after a few weeks of asking, watching her, drinking champagne with her, I went to see her at the Wild Horses, some rough tiny edge of Berlin strip pub, and finally it became:

"Yes."

*

Adelaide lived in Kurfürstendamm, the 'Champs-Élysées of Berlin', in one large room in an old Berlin mansion that had once been a brothel, one of these wonderful pre-war buildings that still remained, pock-marked by bullet-holes and soot-blackened by bombs and half-covered with ivy. The black room was lit only by a single red lamp on the bedside cabinet, black-out-style curtains on the floor to ceiling windows, like we were expecting a bombing raid at any moment, and it was here, in this black-draped four-poster canopied bed with a mirror in the roof, that I made love for the first time with Adelaide. I started to get a condom out of my pocket but she just grinned and shook her head, and pulled me down to her. "It's all right. I'm on the pill. Just fuck me. FILL ME with your sperm!" I obliged. How uncanny to watch yourself fucking in the mirror above you. But—as Adelaide was to say to me many times—"When in Berlin, do as the Berliners do!" If Nana's bed was the glowing forge at the heart of Zola's Second Empire Paris, then Adelaide's vast black bed lit by a single red lamp became the glowing forge at the heart of 2007 Berlin. Waking, Adelaide rolled into my arms, opened her eyes, and grinned at me. "After all this time—we've found each other!" "But I've been here all night, my love—what do you mean?" "Oh shut up!"

On her balcony she could look down into the white ice of the Ku'damm itself. She stood out there now, 4AM, naked. It was freezing cold but she did not care. She called me to join her and as I rose from the massive black bed I started to pull my long johns on; "No!" she shouted. "Naked!" We stood out there on the cold balcony naked together, me with my tool pointing vertically up to the black sky, with snow gently falling around us. I had never loved anybody so much in all my life as I loved Adelaide in this moment now. "You know, you should have just fucked me when I was 16. It is not illegal. It would have got it over with. Lanced the boil. Cured our curiosity. Maybe it would have been a disaster. Maybe then we would have been happy to go our separate ways. Instead I've been unhappy for eight years thinking about you and you've been unhappy for eight years thinking about me. Perhaps it would have been amazing and we would still be living in Soho now, happy ever after. And I wouldn't be living this shitty life I do here now in Berlin. But you like this life, don't you. Watching girls take their knickers off on a stage?"

There was lingerie hanging all over the place, see-through lingerie, silk nighties, expensive glittering evening dresses, black stockings, vases of flowers. The whole place was like a strip club dressing room, or Mata Hari's bedroom. Her kitchen, lavatory, bathroom, handbasin, were all in the one room. 'Life is a Cabaret' playing on her gramophone. More than once while we were in bed, there would be men coming up the stairs and knocking at her apartment door. "Lily! Fraulein Lily!" "Ssshhh!" she whispered to me, "they will go away if they think I'm not here!" She said it was probably the landlord demanding the rent she owed him, but on a couple of occasions I looked through the spyhole and saw men with bunches of flowers in their hands, heading disappointedly back down the stairs. The landlord brought her flowers? Ha! She made me laugh. All the women I had ever loved most in my life were all whores or strippers, that was certainly not going to stop me loving Adelaide. On the contrary, it probably just made her all the more desirable to me. "It's a hand to mouth existence," she told me very sternly, then giggling and jumping on top of me naked. "Or cock to mouth! To be honest!"

I only had two in the Alt Berlin before it closed, but really wish I had got through the day without any. I have a real desire to not drink now & stay sober, for Adelaide. If I am loved by her I do not need to drink. I can write all day in my little nest as I always planned.***Adelaide just called 12:45 & said she is still in bed. "Can I join you?" "Yesss." "At your place?" "Nooo. Your place. Later." She will leave 6 or 7. She has got my germs & wants me to take them back. She had told me she did not want me drinking anymore and I was not allowed to cut my hair either. Not only Salome but now

Samson & Delilah, our affair was assuming Biblical proportions, but rather like Samson & Delilah in reverse, she REFUSED to let me cut my hair. "But short hair makes me feel strong, long hair makes me feel weak." "If you cut your hair off, I'll cut your cock off. If you drink, I'll cut your cock off. Your hair belongs to me now. Your cock belongs to me now. You must make sacrifices to be with beautiful young woman!" my Berlin Delilah explained kindly. "Or else you will sacrifice beautiful young woman!" "But my love, not cutting my hair makes me unhappy." "Shut up! Being with me is all the happiness you could ever possibly need!" "Schindler's Lifts!" she giggled, pointing at the brass company nameplate as we got in the lift on the ground floor of my building. "Always makes me laugh!"

Now I feel so melancholy & sad, because Adelaide has left. At 615AM. I always hate it when she leaves. As she sat up on the edge of my bed putting her pink stockings on, I said "I love you" and she hesitated, then said something back in German, what was that? "I love you". The previous night after ――, she lay with her head on the pillow, staring at me accusingly, angrily, & said "I am in love with you" then when I asked her to repeat it turned her face away "No. Bastard!" then "How can I talk to you if you are drunk?" Later I asked her how long, and she said two weeks, since the letter. Especially the bit where I said she is in my blood. Having got dressed she stood in front of the bathroom mirror looking at her cold sores absolutely covering the lower half of her face & said "How could you kiss me?" so I kissed her again & we kissed more than we ever did last night. She wore blue skirt, little tiny lime green top, long blue coat, black jackboots. I hate it when she leaves. Every time she leaves I feel it is over. "If you do not stop drinking, you are going to lose me" she said to me quietly in the night. Talking about what music we liked, she said Bryan Adams is playing in May, "you like?" "No." "OK, then, maybe Christina would like to go with me?" she says in a funny singsong mock hurt voice. Asking me again if I would like to go with her back to London in August, I said "yes of course, but, we might be enemies by then". She just quietly kissed me on the cheek.********235PM & still no word from Adelaide. I feel like it is already all over with her. I said to her "will you come back here again?" "When can I come?" "Tonight." "Is it all right if I just come for a short time?" "Yes." Feel it is already all over with Adelaide. I will not be going to London with her in August. Four months from now we will have no contact. I said "I don't go to strip clubs looking for a girlfriend, I go to avoid feeling anything for anyone, to just get drunk & lose myself in the music & the girls." "But that is not life."

It was amazing that she actually stayed with me. It got late & for the umpteenth time I said "stay" and this time she said "Are you sure? Are you sure?" She then got up, got out her toothpaste & toothbrush & went to brush her teeth. She did not stop holding me, & kissing me all night. Kissing my mouth, my cheek, my hand, all night. I love her so much. When I just went out at 5 for food, it was like a beautiful warm spring day. This was the first time I had been out since Adelaide stayed the night with me, & everything felt different about the world. I still feel so stupidly nervous, unsure of our relationship. Any moment it could end. I have no faith in relationships. 2050 Adelaide texts me: Hi baby England win ● I'll go to sleep now, see u tomorrow! Don't forget DONT DRINK ALCOOL xxX

"I'm in love with you," Adelaide said to me again today. "I told L— I'm in love with you. I prayed to God to send me someone nice, someone I could trust, someone I could love. I've found you." I'm stupid. "You are not stupid. You are brave....Once every week you asked to see me. It is brave if there is something that you want, you fight for it. You are brave." She gave me one of her little fluffy dogs, Fifi, to remind me of her when she is not there. She rang me before 8 from the Black Pig to say "I am missing you. I don't know what is wrong with me, I want to see you every day. My head is burning. What have you done to me? I think you have done some magic on me. I keep looking into your corner thinking you are there. I couldn't think before because I was running for the underground, and thought I was going to be late, then I was getting changed, then I had my first dance, and it was only then that I had time to think. You've done some magic on me." It's my germs. "No, it's not your germs!" I'm in your blood. Can I see you tonight? "No, not tonight. If I see you tonight I will want to come home with you & I can't tonight." There was someone knocking at her dressing room door, interrupting her,"Hi!", talking in German, saying something about —, & Adelaide talked to her for a while before coming back to me. "Bye sweetie." She will text me later & I can meet her when she finishes at 7 tomorrow. From the Black Pig she asked me, "Are you watching the football? England are playing. If you watch it in a pub, don't drink!"

Adelaide was very drunk on the top deck of the bus home from the Black Pig, which upset me greatly, as I had gone all day without drinking to please her, and had waited for her outside the Black Pig instead of going in. "I HAVE to drink—for work; you understand? Men like strippers who are drunk—they give us more money! It's not that I WANT to drink. You DO verstehen?" "Oh yes, my love. I DO verstehen." She looked stunning, in a neck-to-ankle red satin dress like Otto Dix's Anita Berber painting, a black bob wig that made her look like Diane Lane in *The Cotton Club*, still caked in lurid make-up & multi-coloured glitter, and kept putting her hand down my pants around the shaft of my cock, despite the disapproving looks of people all around us on the bus, and jealous looks of the men. Despite my sordid life, I was very puritanical at heart, especially when sober, when in public at least—when in public one should proceed with decorum—so this annoyed me as well. I wasn't allowed to get drunk & enjoy getting crazy so why should she? "Christina was saying an engagement ring costs £3,000, is that right? When are you going to buy me one?" "In ten years." I was in a proper bad mood now. She pouted her lips & pulled away from me & sat with arms crossed glaring at me. "Ten years?" She says "When do you want to have Phoebe?" "Next year." "Before we have Phoebe, I want us to be living together, as a family." What incredible words to be hearing from my Adelaide, my Lily! Saying these things to me! So I said "Have you found somewhere for us to live then?" In a sing-song voice "How can I? When I have been with you every day? Eh?"

Adelaide says Phoebe will have to be born in England, as it is too confusing for her here, where cars drive on the wrong side of the road. She says she missed me. She says on the day I get married I can drink as much as I want, but I must wait till then! She says you know where you are living now? I was confused, "Berlin?", then she pointed at the centre of her chest. "I told you! Stupid! Here! In my heart." It was so lovely waking with Adelaide this Friday morning, & knowing for the first time neither of us had to rush up & go anywhere, we could lay there as long as we liked. I was just about to text her last night to say I was coming to the salon, the more risqué private club where she only worked once a month or so (which always ended with 'THE BIG STICKY' when one of the girls would let all the men ejaculate on her), when she rang anyway, & said I could meet her 10 or 11 there. "Are you my boyfriend? Why no texts?" Later in bed I asked "What difference do texts make?" "Then I know you are thinking about me." I told her I am always thinking about her, for a whole eight years not a minute passed without me thinking about her, she grinned and leaned over and kissed & hugged me.

One night she said to me "you are so sweet, you never once complained about the mess I live in." And—blushing a little—"and the things I do." "You can do what you like with other men when you are working, as long as you come home to me." "Some men I've loved and liked and wanted to be with are disgusted by what I do, and so are disgusted by me." "We all have to make the most of our competitive advantage, don't we. You're more beautiful than the other girls so you should make the most of it." She grinned and threw herself on top of me and kissed me big wet kisses on the mouth, and face, and neck. "Thank you! Thank you! Thank you! I knew you'd be lovely! All the men at the Pig are unhappy now," she laughed, "as I won't go out with them anymore." When she said 'go out', I wondered what she really meant. "I hated going out with those old men. But I had to—you understand?" "Yes, I do. It is hard for all of us to put a roof over our heads. We all have to do whatever it takes to survive. I am just ashamed I earn such little money I can scarcely afford to help you at all. It is all I can do to pay my own rent." "You'll find something. Most men who start going out with a stripper straightaway want them to stop stripping," she laughed. "That's not going to be a problem with you, I don't think! Most people look down on me because I'm a stripper. You look UP to me because I'm a stripper! You ADORE me because I'm a stripper!" "I adore you because you're the most beautiful girl I have ever seen in my life." "Liar!" she cackled, punching me in the stomach, but pressing her wet mouth to mine. "But thank you anyway, mein Liebling!"

"How did you get started at the Pig?" "I just got off the train at Berlin Zoo, with my suitcase, not a word of German, I was walking around looking for a cheap place to stay and then I saw the Pig. I went down the stairs, saw the naked girls, asked if they had a job, and they asked me to audition. I put my suitcase down, had a beer, took my clothes off, and voila! Ecce femina! Behold the woman!—the rest is history! Everybody wanted to FUCK me! I became 'the star' of the Black Pig! The star of BERLIN, dahhhling!" Giggling, she fell into my arms, covering her face. "Why did you leave England?" "Because I was broken-hearted," she smiled sweetly. "I fell in love with some guy but he wasn't interested! Some fucking bullshit that I was 'too young'." Touché! She leaned close to me, cupped her hand over my ear and whispered conspiratorially, "I think he was A COWARD!" then giggling and laying her head back on her white pillow, looking up at her naked self in the mirror above us. "My mother had just died. She wasn't my real mother, she was my adopted mum, and after she went I had no family at all. My father was an alcoholic and had moved to Germany years before and I did not even remember what he looked like. I had some crazy idea I'd come to Germany to look for him, and, and I don't know what. I was lost, and I was sick. I didn't know why, but later I found out I had a problem with my kidneys. It comes & goes. I'm frightened I'm going to die young. All on my own. I suppose it makes me not really care much, about anything. I'd like to meet a nice man, a nice RICH man, who can look after me, with a nice big house, and we can have a baby, or two." She smiled at me, but a little sadly. "Could you be that man, I wonder? Do you even want to be?"

"You know I loved you since I first set eyes on you." "That's not what I asked you. Pity the girl who falls in love with a man who hates love."

"Have you been anywhere else in Europe?" "I stopped off in Paris for two nights on the way here. I hated it! It was horrible! The French men wouldn't leave me alone. They used to follow me along the streets. If I sat down at a café table they'd sit down with me and wouldn't leave. The hotel manager tried to rape me in my room. I had to stick a knife in him to get him to stop. Why are Frenchmen like that? I mean, here in Berlin all the men want to fuck me, of course they do, look at me, but they're respectful about it, you know what I mean? Paris is a beautiful city though. I'd like to go back one day, with someone—maybe you?" "Yes, we shall," I said. "For our honeymoon." "Ha! So romantic! I don't know if you can ever give up the life you live now. But I think you *have* changed, haven't you? Already. A little bit?" "Yes. I'm afraid so."

I wake tortured & tormented & filled with self loathing & self disgust & inadequacy again. These feelings of worthlessness never go away. My identity feels like it is melting like ice. For some men love is not a solution, more a kind of poison. Before I used to be the cold, hard, monolithic Antarctica. Cold, frozen, but hard, solid, together, I could walk around on solid ground. Now the ice is all melting to slush & as I try to walk it is cracking & melting under my feet & I feel I am falling through slush into the freezing water. Ha! I am with most beautiful girl. I should be arrogant & cocky & full of power. I feel more useless than ever. I feel unworthy of her. She is out of my league and I do not deserve her and I will not be able to hold her back for long. She can have any man she wants; why would she waste her time with me? She needed a rich man who could pay for her and look after her, and that I knew could never be me. I'd always been poor, and I didn't see any way I could change it. I did not have the knack of getting well-paid jobs. I don't know how other people did it. There is always an egg in my mouth. A Serpent's Egg. I can never talk to people or look them in the eye, still. At least, not when sober. I want to have a drink. I want to get my hair cut. Discover my Byronic power. Please! Before I lose her.**************Today is Foscari Day. Yesterday was Lulu Viennese Eroticism Day. As Nietzsche says, we must make our own Feast Days. Christmas Day, birthdays, New Year's Eve, meant nothing to me; days society brainwashes us into celebrating "because everybody does". This was not a good enough reason for me. My personal feast days were what I celebrated. I couldn't resist going to the Alt Berlin, therefore, for two pints from stony-faced Anna (she had always fancied me & was now contemptuous as she had obviously seen me there with Adelaide), then messaged Adelaide on the bus to the little hotel where I worked as Night Manager, walking around the creaky corridors at night naked, masturbating into the giant ferns at the end of each floor. In the morning guests checking out would say "What was that terrible noise in the night? Like a banshee wail, followed by the sound of someone in floods of tears?" "That was me," I would tell them. "Masturbating into the pot plant outside your door", and they would hurry off without another word, with me chasing after them along the street, shouting "Remember your Oscar Wilde, madame! Every impulse that we strive to strangle broods in the mind and poisons us!" Adelaide messaged back but I never saw it until about 845PM, torturing me further. Be WILD with Adelaide. Byronic. Gorgeous voluptuous cat face Russian whore at the hotel in the night, I had to rescue her from the basement after she had left some guest's room & we joked in the lift as I took her back up & showed her to the exit. I was sorely tempted to show her to an empty room. As I held the hotel front door open for her, she grinned and kissed me on the lips before disappearing into the night. She made my chest flutter & my groin stir. I could have stayed with her all night.

Be dark, brooding, & Byronic! Explore the sordid with Adelaide. "You sound weary," says my mother on the phone. Indeed I do. I barely have the heart or willpower or confidence to form any words at all. All I want to do is drink. Then I can be Byronic & sordid. Take drink & the Black Pig away from me and there is nothing left? I long for the dark sordid cinema, the wandering hands, the women coming in to be used by all & sundry, like I wanted to use that Russian whore in the hotel last night; I long for Evalina, & Iga, & Diana, & the Monte Carlo girls, & Olga & Alla, & the Ciro girls. "The sight of a whore is profoundly thrilling to a man." My life is ruinous. I feel always that it is over with Adelaide & me, because how can an English rose as lovely as her love me? Today marks four weeks together. My first girlfriend. I cannot believe it has lasted so long. I feel gutted and choked that it is over; I always feel like this. This is how Kafka had his relationships, and Munch, & Proust. They brought scarcely any joy or happiness, just pain, & jealousy, & the paranoia that it was already over. When Adelaide ends things, I will lose myself so totally in the sordid. Back to the cinema and back to London & Vienna with a vengeance. I will completely fucking destroy myself in the sordid. The whores of the Gare du Nord Brussels, the whores of Schillerstraße Munich, the whores of Stuttgarter Platz & Mazurka & Ciro Berlin, the whores of the Gurtel Vienna. And yet, just 730PM last night, Adelaide wrote to me "———" and how my heart leapt into my mouth. The ecstatic butterflies in my stomach. After insisting I fuck her one more time before she rushed for work, Adelaide called me giggling from the Black Pig to say when she stepped off stage after her first dance, one of the other girls told her "Lily, you have got something on your stockings", and it was my cum running down her leg.

Other MEN were watching MY sperm running down the leg of LILY, the sexiest stripper in Berlin! Talk about marking your territory!

YOU NEVER KNOW WHEN YOU ARE LUCKY!

One day Adelaide called me and suggested we meet at Dressler's close to where she lived in the Kurfürstendamm and asked me to bring her camera she'd left at my house; so I knew she was planning to tell me it was over. "I think you love Lily, not Adelaide. When it's just me you lose interest. I need someone to help support me. I'm dying on my arse here in Berlin. There are so many rich men here who'd set me up for life if I let them. I don't love them. Not at all. I love you. But I just think you only love 'Lily' on the stage, and you are bored with me. I need time to think. I think it better if we take a break until I've made up my mind. I will let you know when I am ready." "What about Phoebe?" "When I'm ready to make Phoebe I'll call you!" "What about Fifi?" "You can keep Fifi so she can keep an eye on you while I'm away. But don't do anything dirty with her, or she'll tell me!" She laughed & hugged me, kissing me on the lips, wet open mouth kisses, letting me massage her beautiful bra-less tits in her tight pink sweater as she unzipped my fly and stroked my erect tool faster & faster until I came in her hand. "This is how we break up in Berlin!" "We should break up more often!" Leaving Dressler's with me to go down onto the U-Bahn to get to her next job, some private party at some rich old man's house, she smiled back over her shoulder, "I have to run! Both of us!"

*

A PERIOD OF SILENCE FROM ME IS ESSENTIAL NOW. TO REGAIN MY MYSTERY, & MY POWER. OF COURSE I WILL RETURN TO THE STRIP CLUBS, NOT THE BLACK PIG, BUT PUSSY WILLOW, & THE SALON, TO SEE ADELAIDE. I WILL BE SILENT & BROODING, MYSTERIOUS & POWERFUL. STANDING AMIDST THE GIANT FERNS WITH A BEER IN ONE HAND AND MY ENGORGED TOOL IN THE OTHER, STROKING IT LANGUIDLY WHILE WATCHING SOME GIRL ON THE STAGE. I AM WRITER. I AM KARL KRAUS. FRANK WEDEKIND. NOT THIS CRYING ERNEST DOWSON CREATURE ANYMORE. I AM HENRY MILLER. I AM BYRON, SHELLEY, KEATS. "Let's face it I gave nothing in the relationship, it wasn't just the supporting you thing. I was passive like Stephane in *Un Coeur en Hiver*. Just let you go. How could I want you so much for all those years, then when I get you give nothing? Love makes me go cold. Watching someone on a stage turns me on. Because I only watched my mother from a distance, I have always thought, I am a scopophiliac." BE NAUGHTY. BE A DEVIL WITH ADELAIDE NOW. BE A RED REVOLUTIONARY, AN ANARCHIST SITUATIONIST REVOLUTIONARY. BUT AT THE SAME TIME GET A BETTER JOB, SO I CAN BUY HER BIG PRESENTS.

I CAN ONLY BE ALONE. DRINKING EVERY DAY ON MY DAYS OFF. GOING HOME ALONE, PASSING OUT ASLEEP, WAKING UP IN THE EARLY HOURS OF MORNING WITH SORE HEAD ALL ALONE, WITH NOTHING TO LOOK FORWARD TO. IS THIS WHAT I DID NOT GIVE EVERYTHING WITH ADELAIDE FOR? "I have always lived like an animal. Dr Jekyll by day writing in my room, quiet as a mouse, but at night I turn into Mr Hyde, a disgusting animal capable of the most appalling debauchery. And I was addicted to this transformation into Mr Hyde every night. And when I started with you, I didn't know how to live without being Mr Hyde. Mr Hyde has been the real me for so long, I do not know who I am without him. Maybe a drunk is all I can be. There is something very romantic about that, because all my greatest heroes were all drunks, & pissed their lives away while writing their great books, so I have always been attracted to that way of living." Maybe it would be better if it was over. It was Lily that I loved? Rather than Adelaide? Wouldn't it be a relief if it was over? Just live in a state of nothingness & denial for the rest of my sorry life. Living in memories of Adelaide & Lily. But after Adelaide/Lily all those prostitution places in Vienna & Berlin seem foul, and repulsive. After something so real & so good, how can I go back to the fake? Every time I was with Adelaide in her room I felt smothered and suffocated, claustrophobic, I could not breathe (she always had the heating turned up full blast, even in summer) so I would make an excuse and say I had to go back to my place, but before I'd even gone 20 yards away I felt so desperately lonely and missing her so much. Crying. What was wrong with me?

The tragedy is I love Adelaide with all my heart, but I can only be alone. No one can bear living with someone like me. "You only saw me at the Black Pig when I was on the way to transforming from Dr Jekyll to Mr Hyde, becoming an animal. I was always in some stage of that transformation to Mr Hyde style animal. For two months I have been trapped inside my Dr Jekyll repressed persona."

I NEED TO FEEL A DISGUST FOR ADELAIDE NOW, I NEED TO BE HUMILIATINGLY BRUTALLY REJECTED BY HER SO I CAN FEEL A DISGUST FOR HER. SOON THE HOT STICKY JUNE WEATHER WILL BE HERE & I WILL WANT STUTTGARTER PLATZ AGAIN. SWOLLEN COCK PERMANENTLY THROBBING PLEASURABLY ROLLING IN MY TROUSERS AS I GO FROM PUSSY WILLOW TO SEX KINO TO MON CHERI. IT WAS SO MUCH FU MANCHU WEATHER LAST NIGHT ON THE WAY TO WORK. BLACK ABOUT TO RAIN STEAMING HOT. OH GOD PILLARS OF HERCULES, MICHAEL CAINE IN MALTA WEATHER! DO SOMETHING! GET MOVING DON'T MOPE and DON'T DRINK! SLEEPING WHOLE DAYS IN HANGOVER! WRITE MY BOOKS. SEND *AUTISMUS* TO PUBLISHER. GET SOMETHING MOVING JUST ME & MY BOOKS, AND MY BEAUTIFUL MEMORIES OF ADELAIDE. SHE WAS JUST BORED OF YOU IT WAS AS SIMPLE AS THAT! THIS IS STILL A GAME! DON'T LOSE YOUR NERVE YET. THERE IS BUS STOP GIRL TO F–K. THAT VOLUPTUOUS BRAZILIAN. MAYBE I SHOULD GO TO CLASSICAL MUSIC CONCERTS JUST TO MEET GIRLS? LIKE THAT IRISH LUSH AT THE WIGMORE! ANYWAY SUMMER IS HERE NOW! TOO LATE!

Be MAD and WILD. FIGHT FOR HER*********Thank God I am out of that claustrophobic relationship. Thank God I can save some money now. BECOME SO COLD. TURN TO ICE. GO TO THE ICY MOUNTAINS TO WRITE WITH BLUE HANDS IN COLD STOVELESS ROOMS. "In the face of renewed fits of illness, in near isolation after a falling-out with his mother and sister regarding Salomé, and plagued by suicidal thoughts, Nietzsche fled to Rapallo, where he wrote the first part of *Thus Spoke Zarathustra* in only ten days." TURN TO ICE. BECOME SO COLD. GO EVERYWHERE TO SEE ADELAIDE DANCE. I AM AN OPIUM ADDICT. MY OPIUM IS WATCHING ADELAIDE DANCE. BERLIN. OPIUM. ADOLPH MENZEL. I AM NOT GOING TO STOP. I BADLY NEED SOMETHING TO GO RIGHT FOR ME, JOBWISE. THAT EXTRA MONEY WOULD GIVE ME SO MUCH CONFIDENCE, WITH ADELAIDE, WITH EVERYTHING. FACE IT! SHE WILL NEVER COME BACK TO YOU! YOU KNOW IT VERY WELL. I am crying, disintegrating, burning up. This obsession with Adelaide is not going away. I can only be a drinker in a pub watching strippers. But I cannot watch anyone but Adelaide now. I tried at Pussy Willow and the Black Pig and it is just not possible for me to watch anyone else. I can only go where Adelaide is. Good, I wanted to be ignored. OH 1751 ADELAIDE HAS JUST SIGNED IN! WHAT JOY! TO STILL SEE SHE IS STILL NOT BLOCKING ME! I WANT TO BECOME COLD, HARD, RUTHLESS, LET ADELAIDE

HATE ME I DO NOT CARE I JUST HAVE TO SEE HER DANCE. SHE IS MY ADDICTION.

"Works of art are indeed always products of having been in danger, of having gone to the very end in an experience, to where man can go no further." 1:27AM Light hissing of rain falling. So I get up and open my big balcony windows & leave the curtains open. Beautiful. I wish this moment could last forever, just me, the Full Moon, the rain falling at night. A Berlin balcony.

YOU SHOULD FEEL POWERFUL. YOU WERE THE ONE WHO GOT ADELAIDE, 'LILY', THE NUBILE YOUNG ENGLISH ROSE WHORE ALL OF BERLIN WANTED TO F—K. YOU WERE THE ONE WHO WAS LET INTO HER LIFE. YOU WERE THE ONE WHO WAS F—KING HER, AT HER HOUSE IN THAT BIG BLACK BED LIKE AN IMPERIAL THRONE LIT ONLY BY A SINGLE RED LAMP, AT MY HOUSE, AT THE SALON UPSTAIRS. YOU WERE THE ONE WHOSE SPERM WAS RUNNING DOWN HER LEG ON STAGE IN FRONT OF ALL THOSE BERLIN MEN. BE COCKY & POWERFUL. SO WHAT? NOW I CAN F—K SOMEONE ELSE! I NEED TO F—K SOMEONE ELSE. STOP CRYING! "I miss you. There's no way back for me to my old life. That door has closed on me. But now your door has closed on me too. So now I need to try to make a fresh start", OUTSIDE OF HOTELS PLEASE GOD. ACCEPT THAT, HOPEFULLY, THAT THERE IS STILL A LOT OF LOVE THERE BETWEEN US, & AFFECTION, & ALWAYS WILL BE. BE WARMED & COMFORTED & STRENGTHENED BY THAT. I CAN BE STRONG & HAPPY NOW. NOT ONLY DID I GET TO F—K ADELAIDE, BUT ALSO I HAVE GOT AWAY WITH IT, WITH STILL BEING SINGLE & POWERFUL & SAVING ALL MY MONEY & I HAVE BEEN RELEASED FROM THE IMPRISONMENT OF THE STRIP CLUBS. IT IS ALL WIN WIN WIN. LET'S FACE IT I CANNOT BE ANYTHING BUT ON MY OWN, IN MY OWN GROOVES. WITH MY CLASSICAL MUSIC, MY FERNS, MY BOOKS. WATCHING ADELAIDE STRIP AT PUBS, WITH LOVE & TENDERNESS ALWAYS THERE BETWEEN US. ARE YOU TOGETHER? WE WERE FOR A WHILE. SO WHAT? FOR A WHILE IS GOOD. IS WORTH A LOT. IT WOULD BE MUCH EASIER TO GET BACK TOGETHER IN THE FUTURE THAN IT WAS TO GET STARTED IN THE FIRST PLACE. I WAS SO WEDDED TO MY SINGLE MAN'S LIFE. I TRIED & FAILED. SHE STILL HAS FONDNESS FOR ME BUT SHE HAS TO MOVE ON NOW. NO ONE CAN EVER TAKE AWAY WHAT WE HAD TOGETHER & WHAT WE DID TOGETHER.

THE CRYING AGONY & TORMENT IS: DO I REALLY WANT HER BACK? ON STAGE, YES, WITHOUT A DOUBT I WANT TO SEE HER SHEDDING THAT GREY FUR COAT AND DANCING BAREFOOT & NAKED ON A STAGE AGAIN IN THAT STYGIAN RED GLOOM, BUT DO I WANT HER BACK? THAT CLAUSTROPHOBIA AND PRESSURE AND PERMANENT TENSION. IT WOULD NOT BE ANY DIFFERENT? IF WE HAD A PLACE OF OUR OWN I COULD AT LEAST GO OUT A LOT. I FEEL TENSION WITH PEOPLE AROUND ME ALL THE TIME. BUT I COULD WATCH HER GET READY FOR BED, THEN CLIMB IN & HUG ME. I COULD — HER ALL THE TIME. BE HAPPY! BE HAPPY GOING TO WORK THESE THREE NIGHTS BECAUSE I AM EARNING MONEY TO GIVE TO ADELAIDE. BE WILD. GET A GOOD JOB. THEN I WILL FEEL SO SEXY AND POWERFUL. I CAN EVEN GO TRAVELLING AGAIN.

I AM BECOMING SCANDALOUS AGAIN! DOING WHAT I SHOULDN'T DO. FLAUNTING MYSELF IN PEOPLES' FACES. SHOCKING THEM. DISAPPEARING FROM THEM, THEN DROPPING IN THE MIDDLE OF THEM WHEN THEY LEAST EXPECT IT AND SPLASHING THEM WITH MY WAVES. "Are you happy now?" I asked her at the salon. "I suppose so," she shrugged. "Are YOU happy? You must be happy, now you are on your own?" DRINK HEAVILY THIS WEEK. GET THE — LICENCE. START WRITING FOR JOBS STRAIGHTAWAY. IF IT DOES NOT BRING ADELAIDE BACK, SO WHAT, I CAN GO TRAVELLING AGAIN, THAT IS ALL I CARE ABOUT NOW. TO BRUSSELS FOR EMPIRE AND GARE DU NORD. MUNICH FOR ATLANTIC CITY & CARIBIC. VIENNA FOR THE GURTEL. WRITE MY JEWELS BOOKS. YOU'RE ALWAYS SO WORRIED WHAT PEOPLE WILL THINK! JUST GO BACK TO THE BLACK PIG AND DONE WITH IT! I AM STILL GOING TO BE SOMETHING MARVELLOUS. WITH THE BOOKS. AND MY NEW JOB. WE HAD A FLING! A PASSIONATE TWO-MONTH AFFAIR!

Adelaide said to me at the salon she couldn't understand why I had this tunnel vision, just sticking in a job that only pays £–, "What will you do when you are an old man, who will look after you?" I said all I cared about was paying my rent, and having enough money left over for drink, "and strippers" she said, completing the sentence for me. She said she was trying to earn the money to go back to England for the operation on her kidneys. The pain was worsening and she could not avoid it any longer.

"No, I am not stupid, but I am naughty, I am dirty, I am rebel. I am rake, libertine, scandal, wild card, untouchable one unpredictable one, I am Byron. I am the devil. This is the addict's revolt. I am *The Man With The*

Golden Arm. I go back to the Black Pig & Pussy Willow because I have contempt for myself. If you don't want me, then I am no good. I will destroy myself quite happily. Drinking is nice because for a while I feel powerful, and in control, and like a beautiful angel. When you think me surrounded, I will disappear from you. When you have forgotten all about me, I will land in your midst, splashing you with my waves."

*

I AM MAD. I AM CRAZY. I AM AN ALCOHOLIC. LIKE ERNEST DOWSON, WHEN DRUNK I BECOME VIRTUALLY INSANE, PRONE TO RANDOM ACTS OF THE MOST APPALLING VIOLENCE WITH PEOPLE I HAVE NO CHANCE TO DEFEND MYSELF AGAINST. OUR RELATIONSHIP IS FANTASTIC NOW. FIERY! VOLCANIC! BETTER THAN THAT FLAT CRYING CLAUSTROPHOBIA WALKING DOWN TO GET COFFEE FOR HER THINKING HOW CAN I GET OUT OF THIS? I WANT A FIERY RELATIONSHIP. IT IS LIKE RICHARD BURTON AND ELIZABETH TAYLOR EXCEPT HE USED TO BUY HER HUGE DIAMOND RINGS & NECKLACES AND I SOMETIMES BOUGHT YOU A JAR OF COFFEE FROM THE CORNER SHOP.

I returned to the Black Pig. Adelaide was on stage when I walked in. She looked disgusted, furious, contemptuous. She avoided all eye contact with me and cut her song short and grabbed her fur coat & lingerie and stormed behind the curtain and soon after I saw her leaving the pub. I have resumed going there every day. Seeing her at the salon once a month or so was acceptable to her; returning to the Pig was not. The relationship between us has become poisonous. All the girls have taken her side against me and become as cold to me as she was. The bar staff, however, take my side and become even kinder to me. The whole pub has become involved and taken sides in the battle between Ernst and Adelaide. It dominates the whole atmosphere of the Black Pig. Her songs have become pointed and obviously aimed at me: Jesse James by Cher, "You strolled into town like you're slinging a gun. Just a small town dude with a big city attitude"; Cabaret Sally Bowles 'Bye Bye Mein Lieber Herr'; Bruce Springsteen "Like a river that don't know where it's going, I took a wrong turn and I just kept going" "We took what we had & we ripped it apart"; Black Eyed Peas "If I took you home would you still be in love baby?"; Eddy Grant "I don't want to dance, dance for you no more baby"; Evanescence 'Call Me When You're Sober' "You only want it cos it's over".

The more vicious and spiteful she becomes to me to get me to leave, the less ashamed I feel about being there and more relaxed. The more she tries to force me to leave, the more I make sure I am always there. I have been going to the Black Pig long before she had! How dare she try to force *me* out!

Our relationship is like Dirk Bogarde and Charlotte Rampling in *The Night Porter*, where they are playing and laughing and chasing each other around their room, then she locks herself in the bathroom. He demands she opens the door IMMEDIATELY, but before she does she smashes one of her perfume bottles on the floor, so when he bursts through the door in bare feet he walks on the broken glass, and she just grins at him nervously, like a naughty girl. We seem to like to do little things to hurt each other; or at least we just can't seem to stop ourselves. It is becoming very sado-masochistic. I live on scraps. I scavenge in the ruins, around the marble throne where the Kaiserin once sat.

Throughout it all I felt she did still love me; I knew she did; so I knew I had a chance. If I ever talked and laughed and flirted with one of the other girls I saw how upset and heartbroken she looked, and I felt her doing things to try to catch my attention again. The thing that makes a girl want you is if she sees some other girl wants you as well. It is at the Black Pig I discovered this cardinal fact about women. The thing a girl finds sexiest about a man is if she sees *other women* find him sexy. She then cannot *stand* the thought of some other woman fucking him..

One night I cornered her at the Black Pig and offered to pay for her flight back to England for her operation, and some money to live on while she was there. She chewed her lip and pretended to look pensive. "What would you want in return?" "Nothing." "Haha!" she laughed, punching me in the stomach. "Pervert!"

The next day we met to buy her ticket and she then came home with me and made love with me more passionately than ever before. I stopped going to the Black Pig again in the last few days before she left. On her last night at the Black Pig before flying back to England I went to see her dance for one last time and she came to my corner and hugged and kissed me, and thanked me again, and apologised for not coming to see me at my flat before work as she had promised, as she had been too busy buying presents in KaDaWe to take back to her friends and family. "But you wanted to meet me here anyway, didn't you, you pig!" she laughed. It is always money that repairs a relationship between a man and a woman. Another lesson I learned in the Black Pig. After the Pig closed at 11PM I waited for her at her bus stop and she came running up in a little blue short dress. We kissed passionately, me running my hands up her bare legs to her bare bottom. "Careful!" she whispered. "I'm not wearing any knickers!" This of course made me want to touch her bottom even more. "Come on," she said, taking my hand and leading me hurriedly away from the bus stop. We walked and found a church graveyard and fucked standing up against a huge white tomb or mausoleum or something. I was too tight to finish, however, being so drunk. I slumped down to the grass, my cock still out and pulsing, she dropped down to her knees and sucked on me until I finally did cum in her mouth. "This is how we say goodbye in Berlin!" she grinned, my white sperm running down her chin and dripping onto her breasts. "We should say goodbye more often." "We will, my love. We will."

*

"I am a gambler risking all on one throw of the dice, and if he loses, he doesn't even care, as he knows this was a gamble worth taking. Afterwards he can say at least I tried. I have always gambled a lot on you, from the 'I lose myself' day onwards, money but more gambled on showing my emotions in front of everyone & risking humiliation, and I have always got a lot back! Most of the time I went home having lost, in suicidal shame and despair at what I had lost, at what it had cost me in money, and emotions, but when I won, the wins were SO big, that it made up for all the losses. Now the stakes are getting higher! I am gambling bigger than ever before! Laying down more money & risking more than ever before. But I am playing for something that is the only thing that makes life worth living. If I don't gamble big, I will lose it. To do is to dare. To dare is to do. You have to speculate to accumulate. What am I going to say, count my money, and add it up, add up the chances, and say no, it is too much of a risk, I'll just let Adelaide go!? I will always gamble everything on you, always risk everything on you, all my money, all my emotions. In front of everyone at the Pig I let my emotions show. At the Pig I am as naked as you are."

"Now I feel quite calm and happy again. I am frightened of the storm, and the fever, and the drunken depressions. I don't want them to come back again. I just want us to be calm, and happy." "People would often talk about him to me; they said he was unstable, moody, even neurotic; I liked being the only one who understood him." (Simone de Beauvour, talking about her friend Nelson Algren). "I like the fact that you are the only one who understands me. Algren wrote *The Man With The Golden Arm*. 'The addict's addiction is a kind of revolt.' I was addicted to drink & strippers & the addiction was never going to go away overnight, even though I had you to hold onto at nights. Slowly, though, I think the addictions are leaving me."

"I have always IDOLISED sex dancers (so much better word than 'strippers'). Like Mata Hari, the sex dancer during the first world war, who lured all the German and French and British officers to her flame and got them to tell her all their secrets, until the French shot her! Josephine Baker the black American girl who danced in 1920s Berlin wearing nothing but a girdle of bananas and drove all the men into a frenzy (they had probably never seen a black woman before, let alone a naked one, SEX-dancing)! And my all time heroine, Anita Berber. For me, when I used to come to see you on Saturday nights, I idolised you, the same way I idolise Mata Hari, Josephine Baker, Anita Berber. Up there in the spotlight, you were my GODDESS."

"It is like I have been on a ship in a terrible storm. ALSO in the grip of fever as well! At last the storm seems to be calming down. Hope I can get my head together while you are away. I am still in limbo about the — and therefore the new job. Hope by time you return something will be resolved one way or the other. Now you notice the rains have finally stopped & the sun has returned. I told you I affect the weather."

"I liked to be silent, unknown. Anonymous. Didn't want to get involved with any of the girls, or any of the other regulars. I just wanted to observe the madhouse, I didn't care which girls were there, it made no difference, I went to observe the grotesque and eccentric and beautiful cast of characters. Now, however, I suppose I have become one of the cast. Always was, the boy in the corner who never speaks. Then he became the boy who is crazy about Lily and shouts at her when he gets drunk haha. Someone SHOULD write a book about the Black Pig, it is unique, it is special, just no one would believe what you wrote! They would not believe the grotesque and eccentric picture could possibly be true. They would think you were exaggerating! There are so many tales to tell from that place—wouldn't it be a great book! Of course I only know a few tales, I only have witnessed a few hundred Pig events, but you have seen millions. What tales you could tell! Let us write the book together! You can write the dancers' version. It was always special, now it has become the place where I met you, the great love of my life. The Grand Passion of my life. The girl I am going to marry. But that's not real life you told me. That is why I liked it, that is why I went. I went to escape real life."

"All my adult life I have lived naughtily, dirtily, like a slut, like a lush, then I fell in love with you and those feelings didn't go away, they just became all focussed on you only. All that naughtiness, dirtiness, sluttishness, lushness, has become fixated on you. Only you can satisfy these feelings in me. I live like a slut, any hole will do, but when I fall in love, I become completely faithful."

"I felt like a ship in a storm for eight years. I have been UNHAPPY since the night I fell in love with you, 'I lose myself', 'You might find yourself.' Even the two months we were together I cannot say I ever really felt happy. Only since we booked the plane tickets have I felt calm. Suddenly it was like the storm was over & I was in calm waters. Tonight feels horrible though. Anyway, I think time in Berlin alone will give me time to get my head together a bit (I hope). I can stop drinking so much, I will probably spend ALL my time off at my mother's haha to save money and keep me out of trouble ("Yes, you should" she replied). Now we are apart, I want to talk to you about a million things. I loved living decadently, naughtily, sleazily, I went to those decadent naughty sleazy places to avoid love and stay safe from it, but then I fell in love with someone in one of those decadent naughty sleazy places, and now I have to change my behaviour in a number of important ways. Now you are the all consuming passion of my life. All my lushness, sluttishness, has lasered in on you. You are the great love of my life. You are the Grand Passion of my life. You are my Immortal Beloved. Yes, the Black Pig (especially Saturdays) was my drug, but then inside the Black Pig I found an even greater drug. I have always run away from women, then when they go I run after them crying 'Come back! I didn't mean it! Come back!' I tried to avoid falling in love with you for so long."

Depressed by the emptiness of these three days, Wednesday, Thursday, Friday. But thank God I am free of the Black Pig! I have saved some money. "Sooner or later we all succumb to our weaknesses, some drink, others smoke opium, others again act like brutes—some kind of folly comes over us all."—Stefan Zweig. "I want to be with you forever, but all I can see is me back in that corner at the Black Pig looking for you, if/when you have shut me out again." I feel vile and repulsive again. Emotions always make me feel like this. Feelings of worthlessness, and complete pointlessness. I must make myself a hero. I won her love after eight years of wanting her, then I lost it after just two months, then I won her love again. It is inevitable that I will lose it once more.

I am a slut and a lush and sometimes it feels good to go mad and indulge those lush tendencies again. It is boring being a good boy. Living like a monk in a monastery. I want to study financial issues again, accountancy issues, as they are now more central than ever to my life. When I was living my life on strippers and whores I needed to spend a lot of money I didn't have to sustain this bubble. Now I have replaced that sluttish and lush life with a real relationship, I find I am spending even more money that I do not have than I ever did before! Money, and liquidity, I now see is ever more central to the happiness of my life. I can be something of a revolution in her life, and offer her a way out of the place she is trapped in. For sure, she is a revolution in my life, offering me a way out of the place I was trapped in as well.

Drink-induced anger last night; I felt like I wanted to fight anyone who came near. Now 5AM awake, cannot sleep. Depressed. Gloom and despair about our relationship. She can never tell me enough that things are all right. She urged the telephone number on me, urged me to call her whenever I wanted to. "There always seems to have been so many ups & downs in our relationship. It has been exhausting. I feel like there has been a storm in my head ever since the day I fell in love with you (or REALISED I had fallen in love with you). I don't want to split up with you again. I need you, to save my life. I have lived like a slut and a lush all my life. If you leave me, I will go back to being a slut and a lush again, and stay that way for the rest of my life. It is hideous the amount of money I have spent on drink & strippers over the last ten years or so. I would much rather give that money to you." I like my intellectual solitude too much, don't I? I like my little nest too much. With its ferns, dark winter nights outside, classical music, lamps on floor. "The world of Casanova, peopled with Fellini's favoured cast of degenerates, freaks and idiot crowds is a stylised transposition of this decadent contemporary landscape. Fellini's approach is to unravel the myth of the great libertine and rewrite him as not merely depraved—this much is known—but as a romantic failure and a bankrupt cultural icon." Living like a slut and a lush in Brussels, Berlin, Munich, Vienna. If Adelaide leaves me now, I will go back to Brussels and fuck Clarisse, and go back to Nuremberg to fuck Martina, and go back to Vienna to fuck all of them. And I will go to the Black Pig every Saturday. "Casanova is not only the story of a man, it is also about a whole era—an era of grand opulence and grand waste. Casanova is depicted as a sexually-ravenous, and deeply cynical man. He is constantly searching for some kind of image of the perfect woman—an ideal which eventually leads to his own destruction."

I MUST MAKE MY LIFE MORE PERVERSE, BERLIN KINKY. SODOM ON THE SPREE. STOP BEING SUCH A GOOD BOY. SUCH AN ENGLISH GENTLEMAN. SO DISGUSTINGLY UNBEARABLY TAMED. I looked across Berlin from my balcony in the direction of Berlin Zoo and the Black

Pig, yearning to be there now. Drinking the nights away, until Adelaide was back. But if I went to the Black Pig, she would not come back to me. Of course for me to be watching the other girls at the Black Pig behind her back, in that steamy, crazy, extremely sexual, lubricious, drunken, wonderful wonderful fucking wonderful environment, she would see as a betrayal. But I was so bored without it. How as soon as I get involved with a girl I allow myself to be tamed. Even as rampant & sordid & scandalous a figure as I. Is it weakness, or a sign I am becoming healthy? Music playing from the gramophone player in the room behind me: Solomon? "Solomon had a thousand wives, and being mighty good he wanted all of them, to lead contented lives. So he bought each mama a platinum piana..." Is there any middle ground between being sordid, Dionysian, rampant, and being tamed, obedient, self-castrated? Willi, my kakapo night parrot, hops around me, pecking at my naked erect penis, but says nothing. Nubian statues, oriental rugs, lamps everywhere. Horta lamps, Tiffany lamps, huge portrait of Marilyn Monroe from *Some Like It Hot* on my wall. I loved my Berlin apartment but without Adelaide it felt like a tomb. There was no middle ground. You can only do one thing or the other. Lose Adelaide and be yourself. Or be with Adelaide and lose yourself. But I could not bear to be without her. Adelaide was the woman of my life and I knew I would love no other. She was my Cleopatra, my She, my Helen of Troy.

"Only when we drink poison are we well—we want, this fire so burns our brain tissue, to drown in the abyss—heaven or hell, who cares? Through the unknown, we'll find the new." "Pour us your poison to revive our soul! It cheers the burning quest that we pursue, Careless if Hell or Heaven be our goal, Beyond the known world to seek out the New!" "The atmosphere of carefree pleasure over a chasm". "Remember me, I'm the one who helped you baby". Yes, I will always remember how she has helped me. Without going to strip clubs, it is actually very hard for me to spend money! The odd cinema visit aside, I have no expenses in life. The jungle drums start again, at 2AM in the morning. Louder even than last night. Pounding, insistent now. Berlin was a jungle and Adelaide was my Jane. I want to provoke myself into self-perpetuating realms of brilliance like Nietzsche, or Oscar Wilde. This is an exciting new adventure I am starting, at G–. Perhaps with the Justice Palace. I have found a good new job at G– a long way away from the Black Pig, but I yearn to work at the Justice Palace, both because I love Justice Palaces but also because the Justice Palace was just up the road from the Black Pig. Sex dominates all my life decisions. Naked girls dominate all my life decisions. My river cuts its course to where the naked girls are.

I am slipping further and further from real life. I am becoming a ghost. It is so long since I have seen my love, 26 days, and now a week since we last spoke on the phone. I have not been outside my mother's house since I arrived Wednesday night. I am becoming a wraith. I do not shave, or wash (as much as I should). I smell almost poisonous. I will bath now, but I think it is too little too late—my body really needs to be BURNT. It cannot be cleansed! When I don't see her for so long I almost lose my nerve and become so shy, our affair seems increasingly like a dream, harder and harder to believe that we have ever really been together.

"When I drink I feel strong, and powerful, and in control. I feel like a beautiful angel. An illusion of course, but a powerful and comforting one. It gives me the confidence that I so often lack. 99% of the greatest (most shameful? most thrilling!) experiences of my life have been under the influence of the demon drink, and would not have happened otherwise. It propels me into situations and leads me to pushing situations to their crisis points so at last something HAPPENS, things get RESOLVED one way or the other, at least there is MOVEMENT. Without the fire of drink in my blood, I am fatally indolent and indecisive, and would do nothing for being unable to decide what to do." FAKE FAKE FALSE FALSE FALSE! I cannot stand prevarication, and have been meaning to say so for some time. People who make sweeping generalisations are idiots. Big windows open to black afternoon skies, soon to rain, when I shall open the windows wider still, I 'listen again' to Strauss's *Also Sprach Zarathustra*.

At the Black Pig tonight, Adelaide is making her triumphant return from England and all those men get to see her and I don't.

*

At last the cold icy air of the mountains. All those people who I feel dislike from and discomfort from, would Adelaide want to be with any of them? No. I have got the most special thing in the world. She came to see me the night after her return to the Black Pig, with lots of presents from England, and she said she had ordered a ring for me and one for her. Commitment rings. She looked impossibly adorable, like a 1920s flapper, like an exotic bird flown in from the rainforest, and my heart filled with love and lust for her again. The move to the Justice Palace had turned out to be a terrible mistake. It was Hell. It turned out I was earning less money than I got at G— and even less than I had been getting at my hotel. And I hated every single second of it. And I no longer even had the Black Pig to escape to.

286

I woke up with cold feet, literally, and it reminded me of the cold feet I always felt in bed in Brussels Ibis and Vienna Dorint, and I started to miss those journeys, Koln Presse girls, that Europe-wide search for big breasts. But Adelaide, Lily, is my girl! I miss my cold lonely life, all those long train journeys across Europe. Maybe I could still do them sometimes. That is something she has to allow me from time to time. I will give her money every week, and we I hope live together, but I must be allowed to travel sometimes. Lying together just before we left she said "Do you really want to live with me? Do you really want to live with me?" She told L— about me, that she made love with me, that she wants to have a relationship with me. She is now at last talking about us living together. What a hold I have over people, because of the sinful pleasurable things I have done. What power that gives me over them. And now I am with the sexiest stripper in Berlin, Lily of the Black Pig, that sluttish little English Lolita. How that shot them up the arse. "If we live together, will you bring your piles of newspapers with you?"

I cannot be cut off from Adelaide. But I must keep some independence. Those long train journeys across Europe. I want to shut myself away like a monk. I'm going to the Justice Palace to write my Die Fackel about autism and solipsism, and how I DON'T get on with anybody around me. Be the grumpy curmudgeon. As Antarctica's ice melts it causes more problems. The ice was deadly but the melting will be worse. Enjoy my curmudgeonliness. I can only live in ice and high mountains. A job often sounds good as an idea but then the reality of actually getting on with my colleagues always overwhelms me with horror and social inadequacy. Sometimes I am overwhelmed by horror and revulsion of my fellow man and crippled by feelings of wanting to escape from my affair. I've always been the odd one out. I've always been hard to get on with. I've always craved everybody just leaving me alone. There was one person I don't want to leave me alone. Now I wonder even if I want her to leave me alone. That would be a kind of death. How good it felt to come home from my day in Hell to find her hairdryer still on my window sill and note on pillow. To find she had left her hair conditioner in the bathroom as well as her spare knickers. To find her glitter on my bathroom floor. To find she had cleaned my kitchen and bathroom sinks. But I need aloneness. I need to disappoint people and sink inside myself in melancholy and despair.

"I'll be honest with you. I am totally in love with you, I like you. But I don't understand you." Adelaide called from the bus home from the Black Pig at 23:12 down, sad, upset, sounding like she'd been crying. "I think you don't love me." "I don't think you are ready, to be part of a family." "You put me in a box. Why you don't want your mum to know about me? She doesn't have to meet me." "Are you joking with me?" About what? "About everything. About loving me." "I am so confused. You are so strange."

Surreptitiously, subconsciously, I think I AM trying to make sure I only get a job at Zoo—so I can be close to the Black Pig. The opium addict or the alcoholic or the gambling addict even lies to themselves, and dissembles to themselves, and manages to hide their true motives from themselves. I am trying to work at Zoo so I can be close to the biggest and richest supply of my drug—Tallulah. I gave up the good G— job which I was very lucky to get after the hotel, in order to go to the Justice Palace knowing it was just up the road from the Black Pig. Hating that job, though, I am already hoping to get another Zoo job, even closer to the centre of my addiction. You can never change a man's true nature. The thought of going with another woman fills me with repugnance. I don't want to touch anyone but Adelaide. I had my hair cut. Wow. I look beautiful. How can I go to the Pig wasting money when she is there trying to earn it? Many nights I went to the Black Pig and spent more money than she had earned. What on Earth is the point of a woman being with a man who is doing that? Yet we loved each other. So....? Yet I loved the Black Pig. So....?

Only when I am living naughtily do I feel free. Only when I am being a slut and lush and doing things I shouldn't do, things I am ashamed of, do I feel strong and powerful and defended against everyone. It is my way of fucking the world. Then I feel free, I feel I am flying, I feel happy, I can open out. Perhaps we should try to split up for a while. See what she wants to do. This pressure is crushing me. Making life seem grey and flat and dead. Strip pubs are colour and life and sound and drama! I could work OVERTIME if I could always go do something naughty afterwards. It would be a relief. I will not make any money and cannot give her any, but I would be happier, until UNTIL I can find something else. I will not stop looking. I can only be an artist, and poor. I wasn't happy at G—. I had to leave. It is great to be at the Justice Palace, if I can just learn to fly there, but I need to be a slut and a lush to do that, but still give Adelaide money. I need to be alone in cold air and icy mountains. I am Nietzsche. What happened to me as a baby has left me incapable of relationships.

How lovely it is going somewhere to meet Adelaide. The old life is over. Just before she left, I asked her "Where is my ring?" and she didn't evade the question at all, she said it should be here soon, but it is taking so long to get here from London. She says she is stressed out, about the world.

Everything. Now she is confused. She took her knickers with her this time, did not leave any in my bathroom. This seems very significant. She said nothing about when she might see me again. Anyway, more than ever I want to be alone to write my red Die Fackels. Save my money to put towards the house with Adelaide. I said to her about her TWO friends, A— and A—, and she grinned, and started saying yes, she can always rely on them to do anything for her. "You cannot rely on me?" She smiled sadly, "I don't know. You are STRANGE." I need to stop thinking about her so much and think more of Kraus, Nietzsche, my red Die Fackels. My books are the perfect forum for the expression of my personality. Paperback books with my name on them are my goal in life. I went to Joanna's, a new spectacular voluptuous whore I had heard about in Charlottenburg, and waited with another guy just to see her, and she was not that big, nothing special, I ran away. "My old life is over. From now on, I am totally dedicated to YOU. And my writing. And classical music concerts. And tropical ferns. My lamps & my newspapers & my Oriental rugs. I feel happy now. Soon hopefully I will be out of Justice Palace Hell and in a job I can enjoy. I have been through a dark month & a half and I hope soon I can be free of it. I feel like someone climbing up out of a dark hole."

Lying in bed with her Saturday morning, Adelaide kept just stroking my face, like she always used to back in the early days at the Black Pig, almost in sadness. Just before she left, she smiled at me quietly and said "how can someone with such an angel face be so dirty?" She took her knickers with her & made no mention of when I might see her again. Yet she talked about how the ring should be here soon, it was in the post from England.

*

"How icy cold your bottom was Friday night, my love. Yet by the time I got in bed beside you how red hot your bottom was! It is little moments like this that I want to live with you for. For the loveliness of that day in the Tiergarten. My life hangs in the balance between ruin and success. Between moving in and getting engaged with you, or splitting up with you. The closer you get to everything you ever wanted the more fragile everything becomes. The royal road, the Via Imperii, becomes a perilous tightrope. This is our test of faith. Now you are the one who is confused. The Gothic Justice Palace has turned into a Gothic Horror. It nearly and perhaps still will cost me my relationship with you. 'I'll be honest with you, I am TOTALLY in love with you' you told me, confused and bewildered by my coldness, calling me on your bus home from the Black Pig. I could feel your pain and hurt but was powerless to say the loving words that would make things better. I was

289

too frozen, shrivelled up, by the horror of my predicament, the Gothic Horror of my Justice Palace Hell. Almost to yourself, 'You are so strange.' Then, decisively, not wanting to waste your love on someone not worth it again, you withdrew from me. If I could pin you down to make a date with you, you did not keep it. When I did track you down and confront you with your no longer loving me, you were unnaturally happy, laughing hysterically at everything I said, evading every question I put to you, giving me nothing, keeping me at arm's length until you could get away. Until at last you turned up, when I least expected it, with your icy bottom. Instead of leaving you at 330AM as I should have done to return to Hell, I stayed, waiting sleeplessly for you to wake at 7, when we at last had two hours when we could talk. It remains to be seen whether it salvaged anything, but I could not help noticing that you took your dirty knickers with you this time, instead of washing them and leaving them in my bathroom for next time, as if you did not think there will be a next time."

In desperation, as a last hope, I asked the Justice Palace if I could be moved on to night shifts and they said "Yes!" straightaway. "Why didn't you ask before?" And I loved it. They let me work six or seven nights a week so I was able to make some good money again. Loving Ernest Dowson's Cynara poem so much, I had bought a book of poetry by Horace, writer of the original Cynara poem, and took it with me to work every night. During my lunch break at 2 or 3am in the morning I would walk all the way to Black Pig and back, just so I could walk past it, even though it was all dark and shuttered up, having closed hours earlier. Just to see it and be close to it and imagine the girls who had been earlier. Imagine Adelaide who had been there earlier. And then I was offered a day job at – just around the corner from the Black Pig, so I knew I'd be able to go in every lunchtime to see the girls on my lunch break, and also at the same time I had a chance to go to work at the British Embassy, for even better money, on the other side of the city. What to do?

My mind is disintegrating under the pressures. To stay at the Justice Palace working every night of my life in a place I now like, or take the — job. But overwhelmingly this temptation to go back to the Black Pig to see the girls dancing, the drink, the lights, the colour, the sound, the action, the fun. I want to stay at Zoo for the wrong reasons, emotional reasons, onanistic reasons, weak erotic addiction reasons, for reasons of erotic drunkenness. I feel erotically drunk, dizzy, being so close to the Black Pig and Adelaide. How unbearable it was that every night every OTHER man could see Adelaide dancing at the Black Pig, and I could not. The man who was supposed to be her boyfriend was the only one not allowed to see her naked! Madness! Adelaide would be hard-headed and professional. — has talked me around again and I want to take the British Embassy job, get out of dangerous sultry sensuous sordid Zoo, preserve my mind. I am dying to get back to the Black Pig, that is the disgusting truth. I will always find jobs that enable me to stay close to the Black Pig.

*

Finally, I wrote to her: "Adelaide, please, I beg of you—before Christmas let me know what is going on with us. I don't want to be left on my own all over Christmas not knowing what is going on?"

"I don't think you're the man for me."

Then I saw the pictures of Adelaide back with her German "husband" from before, the one she lived with when she first came to Berlin but left when he cheated on her. I rang her, hysterical, on the brink of madness, and this time she answered. She told me she was at his house now; I could hear her saying something to him. "I told him I am going to speak to you to explain things, OK? I didn't want this to happen. I loved you and longed for you for so long; but you are so cold. I cannot do it anymore. I was the only one giving anything to the relationship. You only love me because I am a stripper. When I stop being a stripper, I think you'll stop loving me. I want someone to love me for me. You love the Black Pig more than you love me. Go! There are so many girls there you love, aren't there! I want someone who loves Adelaide. Not Lily."

Crying, I went to bed, opening my balcony windows wide to the icy cold and falling snow outside, as I desperately grabbed my Horace and read by the lamplight, urgently, sobbing, like only these words about Cynara could get me through this & keep me alive, until I could see Adelaide again.

"A desperate lover. So it's war again, Venus, after all this time. Spare me, for goddess's sake. I am not what I used to be in dear Cynara's days, or nights. Merciless mother of immoderate cravings, 50 years have made me callous of your soft commands. Try elsewhere, try to answer some young man's eager prayers, drive your silver swans to Paulus Maximus's house for instance. That's the right address for some fun. He's handsome, and high-minded. Always happy to speak on behalf of the helpless. He's the man with the talents to carry your banner of triumph wherever triumph carries him. And once he's duly vanquished some squandering rival he'll be likely

291

to erect under a cedar arbor, near Lake Alba, a marble statue to you. And there, inhaling sweet clouds of incense, and listening to music of flutes and lyres, and bare Cynthian horns, you will be pleased to be praised twice daily by boys and tender girls, dancing in your honour. Myself I have no use for tender girls or boys either, have abandoned all hope of love's return. Wine leaves me cold, and garlands only make me sneeze. Then why, Ligurinas, why do my eyes sometimes fill even spill over, why sometimes when I am talking do I suddenly have nothing to say? Why do I hold you in my arms in certain dreams, certain nights, and in others chase you endlessly across the Field of Mars into the swirling Tiber."

COLLECTED WORKS

TWELFTH NIGHT

2014

ERNST GRAF

SO TWELFTH NIGHT A RUMBLE OF THUNDER NOW IT IS RAINING.

"I need to put myself into a mood of sickly morbid eroticism again! Of despair! Desperate sexual hunger that comes with black psychological despair and morbid sickly eroticism. The ferns and fronds, violin music, as dancers slowly take their clothes off on stage. Fucking like rutting cats, in despair, to fuck the pain away. Roll away and get up and leave each other without a word or a glance. I need to lose myself in degrading, sleazy illicit thrills again. Go back to the gilded gutter life of Francis Bacon, the sublime and ridiculous world, diving deeper into darkness. Go back to an infantile sexuality, pure Priapism, the life of the cock."

"Yes, sir, I understand; but can you do your trousers up now & put your seatbelt on? We are about to take off."

The pilot is saying something in German; probably something of a sexual nature. I caught a look at his face as I got on and it was a face of absolutely bestial sexuality; or maybe I just caught my reflection in the glass. An old joke, but it always makes me laugh. The plane took off into quite Wagnerian skies; black night still, thick cloud, wind, rain, and what looked like lightning, but may have been the wingtip lights reflecting back from the clouds. I always seem to be cold, lifeless, frigid when I come to Vienna, unable to feel anything sexual, even though the very words 'Viennese Eroticism' have always thrilled me so much. I have got to unlock the sexuality here, like releasing the fly from the amber, bringing the woolly mammoth back to life from the ice. To finally 'crack the Vienna nut'. I need to imbue myself with the spirit of Hans Makart, the way I do with Franz von Stuck in Munich. Lose myself in sickly morbid eroticism. Ferns and fronds, violins, around a stage on which a girl dances while slowly removing all her clothes, before retreating into a séparée to be mauled feverishly in joyless, pointless intercourse. Joyless, pointless intercourse—is there anything better? Just sheer fucking animal lust, sheer fucking animal need, sheer fucking animal fucking. To make myself ready for this debauchery I have to drink so much that I can then no longer feel anything when I do it.

Before you even know it we are already more than halfway to Vienna. We only seemed to get up in the air five minutes ago, and soon enough we will be starting our descent. Always a shock to realise the speed of plane travel after several train journeys to Europe. I want to be like a bitch in heat. 43 minutes until Vienna. The plane smells like a lion's den, too many trousers, too many men sleeping in an enclosed space. A suffocating, fuggish atmosphere. Constant erection. I think of *Sherlock Holmes and the 7% Solution*—a great film when it was 45 minutes of character study, before the risible boring plot took over; same as the great

Mel Brooks films, like *High Anxiety, Young Frankenstein*; you want to just go on enjoying these rich marvellous characters and tell them please don't bother switching over to a plot that they always feel they have to. Like every Bond film has to end in hundreds of explosions and burning buildings; so predictable; so boring.

Christ already we are going down; ridiculously fast.

I think I will never find the strip club I really yearn for; I will have to win the lottery and open it myself. I will never find the adult cinema I really yearn for; I will have to open it myself. I will never see the pornographic film I really want to see; I will have to film it myself.

Adolf Loos's 'windows without eyelids' that caused such apoplexy to the Emperor Franz-Josef are now absolutely ubiquitous in Vienna. Just about every building has these eyelidless windows. It is such a signature of this city. Amazing to think I have been coming to the Dorint Hotel—4 Felberstraße—all these years, without even realising that Adolf Hitler lived at No.22 Felberstraße (for 9 months) in 1908/9. It does give one an incredible frisson. Not only did Adolf Hitler set foot on the streets I walk, but he actually for a time lived here. Well, no Lotta & Sophia here in the Dorint, that's for sure. What a miracle that was. But these are the miracles we keep travelling searching for.

I saw so many clubs on the way to the kino yesterday, probably just the shells of places that were shut down in 2010, Vienna Night Club, Night Dreams, Show Café Bar. I am so hungry to fall in love with an —, a Natalie Sawyer, a —. I am not going to find someone like that in Fortuna Kino or Weltspiegel or Love Kino. I drank one small and three large Zipfers in the bar then just missed a No.6 tram to Fortuna Kino so went down and got the U6 to Wahringer Straße. I walked around & around and could not find the cinema for ages. With my head in my map I managed to tread in/more sort of kick a pile of dog shit. I thought 'so this is how this trip to Vienna is going to be is it?' An absolute sense of panic gripped me. The first time I emerge from my hotel to begin my holiday in Vienna and I cannot even find the first place I am looking for, I was walking around & around the Wahringer Straße station and I cannot work out which side is left or right, or north or south, and I am panicking more & more, a sense of hysteria taking me over, and now I have got dog shit all over my left shoe. Finally I found it and got in and it was totally different from what I remembered! Four rooms all off of one corridor, so weird. One stark naked young man lying back on a sofa just wanking the whole time. I left and got back on the U and coming back down in bewilderment, distressed that my holiday had gone so wrong so quickly, I saw the cinema I was looking for at Josefstadter Straße! Idiot. I went to the wrong one. All last year I was saying I must go back to Wahringer Kino and it turns out I was thinking of Josefstadter Kino, the Weltspiegel, and had in fact never been to Wahringer Kino before in my life. So I went in this one, Weltspiegel (WSK), and sure enough there were the three black-haired handmaidens I remember from before. I got properly turned on watching the film, one of them came and sat down next to me and I fondled her breasts as she explained the prices. I came out and walked down the road with an erection as it started to get a bit dark. I went in Erotic Peep Show. No kabins open! Big girl on stage in peep show, I masturbated while watching her for 4 euros. Carried on walking down the road with an erection. I passed so many places that looked like nightbars, I wonder how many of them are actually trading still? Got the No.6 tram then to Fortuna Kino. The film was new but not great, the huge-breast blonde old woman came in, Nina (?), and we went to the sofa at the back, and I f—ked her from behind in the dark for 40 euros. Amazingly I actually got turned on enough to finish! That says something. Different from last time anyway. Obviously feeling totally down and empty now with my usual post-coital ennui and slightly shaky legs, I dragged myself back to the hotel just wanting to be indoors. I had one small beer in the Dorint bar with the same barmaid as last time but now bigger and blonder, then went back out and tried a zwiebelrostbraten in the corner restaurant. Pretty awful. The service was so surly and cold. After being molly-coddled and treated like God by all the staff in these fancy hotels it is a shock to come back to a real "local", an Austrian "pub", and realise you aren't really special at all, and your inability to speak the language is met only with derision and contempt, and no attempt to help you out, and you get the overwhelming impression that they would be quite happy if you turned around and fucked right off. The steak was the most pale thin anaemic thing I had ever seen. It was tasty enough and filled me up, but I will not go back there again! Maybe I will find somewhere in Burggasse. So ended my first day back in Vienna.

There is a table of four sitting close to me here in the Dorint bar, two couples I presume. They are sitting there talking and joking and laughing, and I still cannot imagine myself being able to exist in that situation. That never changes. I so overwhelmingly still can only bear to be alone, or with —.

My second day of four here in Vienna. I hope to find somewhere or someone that will make me want to come back. Some real heart-stopping beauty that electrifies me. Or some great restaurant that I feel so at home in. Or some great strip club (pretty much there are none in Vienna I think). But Vienna's speciality is kinos. This is an absolute paradise for those who like adult cinemas. She could have black hair, she could have real white-blonde Swedish type hair. I want to find a place in Vienna with some life in it—not these night bars on the Gurtel where you walk in and you are the only man there and all the girls come up to you one after the other. A club full of men so I can just sit anonymously in the corner and enjoy the atmosphere. I don't know if that exists in Vienna (or Berlin for that matter). In Munich yes. In London yes. Even in Brussels (Yellow Lily), yes. The eternal mystery, where do all the men go in Berlin and Vienna, continues to elude me. Presumably there are just as many horny men (locals & tourists) in Vienna & Berlin as there are in other places, so where the hell do they all go?

Looking back at your life there are so many perfect moments—meeting Lotta & Sophia in Vienna, f—king (all but) Patricia in the Atlantic City séparée in Munich, f—king (all but) Emily in the Femina séparée in Munich, Martina with the huge breasts in Nuremberg—and you wonder will I ever have moments like this again? As I get older my life seems to be increasingly about memories rather than new experiences, and I absolutely fight against this, and try so hard to find new experiences. With some success—Yellow Lily in Brussels is a new discovery, Alhambra Cinema, ABC Cinema (already gone), 77 in Berlin. In Vienna I wonder if I can find anything new, and electrifying. Well, I just f—ked some woman in Fortuna Cinema yesterday, didn't I? That wasn't a bad start!

I think I stopped reading fiction when I was 21. Since then it has been all biography, philosophy, psychology and diary. And that is all I am interested in writing. I want to record my life in minute detail, every hour of my life. I want to form an unparalleled record of one man's journey through life, day by day. It is funny, when I come to these hotels in Vienna, Berlin, Munich or Brussels, I am the only person who sits drinking on their own in the hotel bar. Am I really so unique? So strange? I find it so pleasurable, yet it seems so unusual. One day, when I become something fantastic and renowned, there will be young men who will want to follow in my footsteps and will want to come to Brussels, Munich, Vienna and Berlin and stay in all the hotels that I used to stay in. I believe this. Like I always believed that me and — would be together, despite her always being so patently, ridiculously out of my league; but it happened. The miracle that I wanted to happen happened. This gives me belief that the second miracle can really happen as well, if I want it enough and don't give up on it. That I will be world famous through my writing—like a Shakespeare, a Nietzsche, a Freud, a Marx, a Darwin, a Musil. Perhaps a Dr Kinsey? A Wilhelm Reich? I always remember Paula Yates once saying 'it is not getting what you want that is the hard thing in life, it is deciding what you want.' I think there is great truth in that. I am just at the foothills now of the great mountains of renown; I am still in the chrysalis, still undergoing a metamorphosis. This serves to make every day exciting and full of progress. Keep working towards that second miracle.

Not only does my life seem more about memories than new experiences, I actually increasingly mythologise my own life. I want BBC4 to make an *Arena* documentary (a *Bookmark* at least) about my travels and my life and my loves and my partners. I want young idolators to follow in my footsteps in years to come. I want a library to be set up to house all my writing, published and unpublished scribbles in book margins, diaries and notebooks, and of course on the internet. Does everyone feel this need for self-mythologising? Is it sign of some egomania or is it normal? I want to be recorded and revered and worshipped like a Shakespeare, a Goethe, a Schiller, a Kant, a Nietzsche. I want streets named after me in Germany and Austria. And I really have a quiet belief that I am able to bring this about. It is the fire at the centre of me. I never lose sight of or doubt my sense of uniqueness. There I am alone in the Dorint bar, as I am in the Berlin Plaza bar, or the Munich Rechthaler Hof, or Brussels Café du Dôme.

I fetishise my own life, even as I am living it: I fetishise the Dorint Hotel in Vienna, the Berlin Plaza in Berlin, the Intercity and Regent Hotels in Munich.

It is just one small sign of how shit London is that strip clubs are not allowed to have two girls dancing on stage at the same time anymore, it has to be only one. What on Earth is the danger they are frightened of if two girls (or more) are dancing at the same time? Some faux-lesbian action? And what exactly would happen if that occurred? It is so so so asinine. What is it exactly that the councils are so frightened of? So you come to Vienna and there are girls in every adult cinema ready to blow you and f—k you, and do you know what, Austrian civilisation does not collapse. Life goes on, happily, calmly, with graciousness and civility. So what exactly is the reason for banning TWO girls dancing on stage at the same time? Oh, London, what a shithole you have become. Quite similarly, men (consenting f—king adults) in the privacy of an adult cinema are not allowed to masturbate themselves or masturbate the man next to them. Oh, why? Exactly? To bring a little bit of pleasure into their own life, and into the life of the person next to them? Why is this banned? You want us to live our lives completely without pleasure, is that it? Any pleasure that we plebs may enjoy is such a disgrace and threat and anathema to you. Honestly, what will happen if TWO girls dance together? They might touch each other. And? What will go wrong if they touch each other? It is so completely brainless and disgusting and yet we meekly and politely acquiesce in this puritanical takeover of our rich, vibrant lives. They steal that naughtiness, that vibrancy from us, and turn us into banal, mundane frigidity. And we let them do it. As De Sade says, if there is to be a revolution it must first be a sexual revolution. The irony is Germany and Austria are two of the sexually freest countries left in Europe, and yet incredibly they are two of the safest and politest and most stable societies in Europe too. So sexual Babylon doesn't bring down their civilisations? So what is London so afraid of?

Do you think there are other gentlemen just like me? Maybe there are other gentlemen connoisseurs of bosom and buttock, gentlemen who *really know the difference* between a bosom & a buttock, going to Vienna, Berlin, Munich and Brussels, and drinking on their own in hotels and going to kinos and strip clubs and whores at night? Or am I quite strange and unique? Maybe there are other gentlemen not only doing it but writing about it too?

What a vibrant place the Dorint restaurant used to be back in 2002, and 2003 (the Café Klimt as was); what a vibrant place the hotel used to be when Lotta & Sophia were here. Rather than the Berlin tradition of a big night on my first night (Yulia, Riccarda, Iga all happened just a couple of hours after my arrival) I hope for the Munich tradition of a big last night (Susi, Emily, Viktoriya all happened on my last night). My breakfast consists of peanuts and beer.

So after 4½ Zipfers in the hotel bar I headed to Cinema Erotic in Sechshauser Straße. One main room (quite small) and I think three tiny rooms off of that. Left quite quickly, tried to find my way to the Love Kino in Michael-Bernhard-Gasse but walked for ages and did not seem to be getting close so gave up and walked back to ML Revue instead. A great Nadine Jansen video and Tiffany Treasures which kept me occupied, and the peep show girls (including a male-female couple having sex) were probably the best I have seen, but 'Cobi' (?) a brown ringlet-haired Brazilian was the absolute pick. If only you could do more than just watch them here. Back to McDonald's in the station and incredibly both Hamburger Royale TS and with Käse were off the menu! This left Big Macs (which I don't like) and chicken burgers. Shocking! I was forced to come back to the hotel and try a Zwiebelrostbraten and fortunately found it was a lot better than I remembered from last time. Nothing to compare with Rechthaler Hof or Brussels Grill steaks but it did the job. Some salad with it would be amazing but that seems to not be on offer. By now it was 830PM and I just was ready for bed so that was my second night in Vienna! I now only have one night left if I want to search the night bars of the Gurtel.

As always, I am still disappointed to find no more Lotta & Sophia here in the Dorint. I probably will need to change hotel to meet two girls like that again, but the Dorint is still too perfect in terms of location (plus music channel and ice cold mini bar!).

We let the authorities make the rules, we let the authorities take all this pleasure away from us; but how would you stop them? There has been nothing in the national press about the closure of the models' rooms, and the Pleasure Lounge strip club, and the Boulevard Striptease, and the Soho Cinema. Nobody cares (or at least no one will protest as that will advertise the fact that they use these places), so the authorities can get away with it. Not a single smile from the barman; the contrast with Lotta & Sophia ever more stark.

Vienna still feels an incredibly white city. On my third day I don't think I have seen a single black face yet. I feel the Turkish influence always; by its absence. It was at the Gates of Vienna that the Ottoman Turks were repelled (thus saving Western Europe, Christendom), yet from the coffee beans they left behind Vienna opened their first coffeehouses; from the Turkish cannons left behind St Stephen's Cathedral forged its great bell. Conflict enriches us (if we can survive it). Zipfer is a relatively new beer, 1858; it can't compare with Augustiner's 1328 in Munich. Still no relationship here in Vienna; nothing electrifying. No real electric spark. I got that from — in – before Christmas. One more night to try.

Finally found the nerve to go to St Stephen's and up the top to the Pummerin bell, and then to the Belvedere (I was going to the Butterfly House but headed off in the wrong direction and got lost; I mean when I checked the map later I discover I came out of St Stephen's and headed confidently absolutely due north when I should have gone due south; an internal compass I do not have). Amazing to see Hans Makart's Five Senses again, and Gerstl's Laughing Self-Portrait, for me greater treasures than Klimt's The Kiss, now given pride of place against a black wall. I came back to the hotel after that with some chicken & chips from the station (poor, as every meal I have in Vienna seems to be) and then slept through to 8PM. Then watching some music videos on Go TV and some pornography (*Band of Bastards 4*, then all Nadine Jansen) on my computer I worked my way through my four bottles of Gösser to prepare me for my last night in Vienna. I tell myself tonight is just a reconnaissance mission—to see if there is anything or anyone worth coming back for.

The Gurtel clubs are all so empty, probably because they're all so far outside of the Ringstraße and the centre of Vienna where all the rich people stay; the rich gentlemen will never venture out to the rough, rather scarily desolate-looking Gurtel, yet this is where so many of the clubs still are (well, the last few that are left). The prices surely are another factor: 100 euros for 20 minutes of sex, 130 for 30 minutes and 200 for an hour. Those are rich men's prices in a place where rich men do not venture. At the laufhaus you can get sex for 50. In the kinos you can get sex for 50.

I am ashamed to say (and astonished) that I got lost on my last night in Vienna. It was all so simple—U6 up to Josefstadter Straße and I saw some clubs open and lit up on the right-hand side, Dream Bar, Haus 6, Okay Bar, Angelique, but I thought I will stay on for just one more stop and walk back, in case there are any more a little further up. This was my 'fatal' mistake. The problem is the train is on an elevated line above the Gurtel and coming down from the train you take the steps which switch back & forward in a real zig-zag before depositing you at ground level, and you are now totally unsure which is left or right of the train you just got off, and which is north or south. The fact the train track completely cuts off one side of the Gurtel from the other, so you cannot see the other side makes things worse. I set off and walked a long way in one direction thinking I would imminently be back at the previous stop Josefstadter Straße. After a long walk not seeing any sign of it I panicked and thought I must be going in the wrong direction so crossed over to the other side of the track and walked back in the other direction. After another very long walk I still recognised nothing and then when I came to U-Bahn Michelbeuern-AKH (the station after Alser Straße, that is TWO stations after Josefstadter) I thought I don't believe it I have been walking in the wrong direction, and my first direction of walking was the right one, so I turned again and set off on a long long walk back the other way. My pace of walking was increasing all the time as I tried to make up for each mistake and all my ever-growing lost time. In panic I thought of all those florid and lurid houris sitting there in their bras & knickers & suspenders waiting for me to burst through their door and I could not even find them. A rising sense of hysteria once more had me in its grip. I was sweating like a pig (I know, pigs cannot sweat, which is why hot weather is so dangerous for them). I thought any minute now the sun is going to come up and it is going to be daylight, and the night will be over, and like Nosferatu I will realise it is too late. It is all over. After a long long time I still recognised nothing, and still had not reached Josefstadter Station, and by now was beginning to even doubt its very existence and my own sanity, how was it possible after all this walking so far in BOTH directions I had not stumbled back upon Josefstadter?, and then my nightmare came true when I arrived at U-Bahn Nußdorfer Straße, which is two stations AFTER Michelbeuern-AKH, and THREE after Alser Straße, and FOUR after Josefstadter!! I just stopped in my tracks and stared at it like Charlton

Heston at the Statue of Liberty sticking out of the sand at the end of *Planet of the Apes*. "Those fools. What have they done?" Unbelievable stupidity! Extraordinary farce! Whichever direction I walked, I got FURTHER from Josefstadter Straße; how on Earth was this possible? Now I was in a state of full-blown hysteria, on the point of breakdown. I just came out to have a grope and perhaps a fondle, even just an ogle, and now this, this extraordinary obscene odyssey without end without sense. But the Gurtel is so featureless, it is so hard to get your bearings. Stupidly I had left my map at the hotel thinking I did not need it, as I was after all just going three stops up the road to Josefstadter Straße which I knew so well and then walking straight back down from there, a very gentle walk. What lunacy. Realising I was now at Nußdorfer I started to turn and walk back, but then thought no, no way, not again, I cannot do this anymore, I will be in Czechoslovakia if I walk any further, and just got in a taxi to take me back to Josefstadter. Extraordinary farcical madness. I was by now exhausted, sweating, and the chafing on the inside of my right leg felt almost like it was bleeding it was so sore.

The taxi deposited me outside the Velvet Palace as it happened (after a high-speed ride down the Gurtel which must have taken at least ten minutes, which just goes to show how far I walked in the wrong direction). I paid 10 euros to get in, but it was as empty as these places always are. One old man was with a girl sitting next to the stage, and the girls were dancing one after the other for just the two of us, which of course made me feel so awkward. I turned them away and finished my drink as fast as I could and left. One girl tried to call me back, even though I was kind enough to leave her the two 'dollars' I had been given on entry, saying to me "You will never get married with an attitude like that!" A great line, but she did have the good grace to grin when I showed her my ring and said "I am already married!" The owner seemed like a decent nice man but looked strained, no doubt, how to survive when you have no customers every night, but at least he did not seem about to threaten me with physical violence for leaving without spending any money, as they often do e.g. at the Ciro in Berlin—the Ciro manager standing in front of the door when I went to leave, and after finally stepping aside, bidding me goodnight with a quite aggressive 'hasta la vista', so I half-expected to get coshed on the back of the head.

Leaving the Velvet Palace, I crossed to the other side, ignoring the Dream Bar, going in what I thought was Angelique but being called to go in the next door instead by two quite insistent girls. It turned out the first door is Grosse Angelique and the next is Kleine Angelique. Anyway, I had the beer, the girls came to me one after the other, I turned them away, but all the time I had my eye on the grosse busen girl standing behind the bar.

Finally she came to me, I had a piccolo with her (27 euros). An uber-busty very beautiful Hungarian girl called Lily. I was too drunk to contemplate doing anything, and I didn't want to drop my trousers as I feared my chafed leg was too unsightly, so left when I finished my beer. I knew I would find no one more beautiful than her this night so walked past Haus 6 and Okay and Manhattan and Tête-à-Tête and returned to my hotel to sleep. This was my last night in Vienna.

These places are really stupid charging such high prices—100 euros for twenty minutes, 200 for an hour?—no wonder they are always absolutely empty. A far cry from the incredibly-packed, vibrant Yellow Lily in Brussels—the greatest brothel bar I have ever been to. When you can choose a much more beautiful girl in a laufhaus for 50 or a low-end girl in a kino for 50 it is no wonder the Gurtel bars are always empty. Having said that, Lily is one of the greatest girls I have ever met in these places who I think might almost be worth it.

I never did get to the Love Kino in Michael-Bernard-Gasse, or the Peep Show in Burggasse, or the Laufhaus in Triestestraße (either of them), and I really would love to try the Café Westend opposite Westbahnhof, but I would feel so uncomfortable in a Viennese coffeehouse—I do not drink coffee, and I don't suppose they serve beer? It looks amazing though. 145PM Thursday. My flight is at 805PM. I will try to get up to Weltspiegel in the next hour or so for a last scopophiliac's debauch. Not really in the mood for it.

Incredible to look out the Dorint window and think I would have seen Hitler walking past the window every day during the 9 months he lived along the road at 22 Felberstraße in 1908/9. In London I am always in awe around Whitechapel & Aldgate knowing for a fact I am walking in the exact footsteps of Jack the Ripper—it is the same feeling here in Felberstraße, knowing for a fact I am walking in the exact footsteps of Hitler. Munich I think it must be even stronger, as he gave speeches in so many of those great beerhouses that still exist. Walking around the Niederhofstraße/Wilhemstraße district of Berlin is the greatest disturbing feeling of all, though, knowing this was the absolute epicentre of the evil of Nazism of the 1930s and 40s. Really quite overpowering.

So no, no great 'electrifying' adventures or encounters here in Vienna, nothing to make me come back for in particular, but nothing to make me not want to come back either. A lazy, sensual, three days out of time, drinking and sleeping more than anything, with some brief silent bouts of scopophilia and onanism in between the blackouts and the getting losts. I have to say the Dorint serves their peanuts in a small black dish with a small silver spoon. Does anybody eat peanuts with a spoon? Vienna is famous for serving coffee and everything with an accompanying glass of mineral water, like you are supposed to mix everything with mineral water, but to eat peanuts with a spoon is another strange concept. I need to drink faster to get me in the mood for Weltspiegel. But it just won't go down.

*

So can I say I have really finally cracked the Vienna nut? Yes. I have finally scaled the Vienna peak. How thrilling it was with old Nina in Fortuna and Amanda in WSK. Two of the greatest dirty experiences of my life, easily ranking alongside the Mon Cheris, and Feminas, and Atlantic Citys. After finally tearing myself away from the Dorint bar, I waddled up to WSK for my last hour in Vienna—quite possibly my last hour in Vienna ever, I thought. Seeing voluptuous Polish blonde Amanda in long red evening dress coming up the dark WSK cinema aisle towards where I sat on the sofa at the back blew my mind. I had never wanted someone so much in all my life. With the desperation of knowing this my last chance of doing something in Vienna, this time I said yes and we both undressed completely naked there on the sofa at the back of the cinema and made love in every position like wild animals as the film played on, and the few other customers carried on watching the film discreetly leaving us undisturbed to our bestial congress, despite my cries of "Don't do it! Don't do it! No, my love! No!" One of the greatest moments of my life. One of the most beautiful women I had ever 'slept with'. One of the greatest f—ks of my young life. I literally had to run back to my hotel, to just catch the Airport Bus just in time to catch my plane home. I had saved Vienna! I had saved Christendom! And now rather than going home thinking "I will never come to Vienna again", I knew I would be coming back at the very first chance I got.

How f—king good the sight of red dress Amanda was, before I even got my cock out and — her. One of the greatest moments of my life. So exciting. I cracked the Vienna nut in that very moment.

Vienna, Berlin, Munich, they shine so brightly on my horizon. When I die, you can bury me in all those places. My body in one place, my head in another, and my engorged shrivelled penis in the other. My writing and diaries and marginalia I wish to be left in a new library in my name for future researchers and idolators to study.

Why delay? Why on Earth delay? What is the point of delaying? Force myself to wait till the end of February, for what? Life is short, if I want to go, go now, What would I gain by forcing myself to delay? It is stupid, pointless.

Never delay. Go now and get sated with it quickly, then I can stay in London as long as I like. But better to get sated quickly.

INCREDIBLE! 10 DAYS TILL I AM BACK IN VIENNA. Why wait? Life is to be lived. Nothing to do in London, might as well keep going back to Vienna and Munich repeatedly. When I get tired of it, then I can stay in London happily. BETTER TO HAVE A DEBT AND ENJOY PLEASURE. If I waited till February 25th that would just be another 37 days of my life wasted in grey waiting. Better to go back at first opportunity! Live fast, like that fireball in Tintin & the Seven Crystal Balls!

A new golden age of travelling, I will spend all my money on going to Vienna, Munich, Berlin in these dark winter months, leave myself destitute, but I am addicted to these places. I've got to try that Augustiner beerhall opposite St Michael's Church as well in Munich. Amanda the Polish girl in Vienna has brought everything back to life for me.

"He accused the Republic of tolerating all types of perversions so as to draw attention away from itself. He also accused it of fermenting a 'hothouse of sexual imagery and stimulation' which threatened traditional values. 'It is no accident,' Hitler charged, 'that more and more kinds of diversion are constantly being invented.'"

I feel a sudden keen hunger to see Lilly again in Angelique. Her opulent body. Her body in glorious full bloom.

Going to Vienna, the many porn cinemas, the many night bars with their opulent full bodied whores, I feel like I am going back to how Soho was in the 1990s.

"According to Maurice, he and Hitler would sometimes drift from one night spot to another looking for women. Besides liking his women beautiful, young, sweet and dumb, Hitler also liked them full figured, especially big busted."

Christ the history of Vienna is so amazing, even after all these visits I have not even begun to scratch the surface. "Glitter and doom". The abysses of society!

Some people while away their hours in the Vienna coffeehouses. I while away my hours in the Vienna porn cinemas. Lazy, indolent, sensual, always a girl on hand when you want one. Of course this would not be allowed in London, which is why London is such a boring shithole, and a place only to work, to earn the money to get out of London at every opportunity. Once the cinemas all close at 10, you can stroll down to one of the night bars and have a piccolo with one of the Esmeraldas (perhaps 27 euros each glass), and if you are rich enough take her into a room for 100 euros for 20 minutes, or

200 for an hour! Obviously you would have to find someone pretty tempting to cough up these kind of prices.

Walking around the centre of Vienna every building looks like a palace, it is quite extraordinary. Even the McDonald's is in what seems like a palace. Hitler liked girls with big bosoms too. I am starting to form a real nucleus of places I like in Vienna that are very close together now. I have long had this nucleus in Munich, Berlin, and Brussels, but have lacked it in Vienna. With a bit of effort this time I have discovered it, and brought it to life. It is like the lights have finally been switched on in Vienna for me. I don't want to have to keep travelling far for my pleasures, I want everything close together, close to my hotel. So when I finish I just have a short stroll back to my hotel at night or the early hours. Mistakenly I always say I want to get back "home" now, forgetting I should say "my hotel". My hotels become my homes. I have never wanted a mortgage, and to own my own home, I always wanted to save all my money for staying in hotels. Ah, Sarasate-Zigeunerweisen has just come on the radio, at 430 in the morning, What a pleasure.

When I first started travelling to Europe I used to go every day to the normal tourist sites, the museums, cathedrals, etc, but did not have the nerve to go to the naughty places. Now I go to all the naughty places and I don't have the nerve to go to the normal places. I feel so at home in the kinos, strip clubs, night bars, it takes a real brave effort to force myself to go to the museums and cathedrals, though of course I always feel enriched and proud of myself when I do.

"Later they [Kraus and Wittels] would go on to the Cafe Frohner, situated in the luxurious Hotel Imperial. Kraus was a heavy smoker, but never took a drop of alcohol. He was a gifted conversationalist and on good days, Wittels recalls, he enchanted everyone. All kinds of people—senior government officials as well as artists, actors, and attractive girls—would come to his table; and Kraus made them feel they were the 'centre of the universe'. Later, feeling the need to escape from the stifling atmosphere of bourgeois coffee houses, Kraus and his circle would move on to lower-class cafes patronised by prostitutes and bookies." (Edward Timms, 'The 'Child-Woman': Kraus, Freud, Wittles, and Irma Karczewska', in Vienna 1900: from Altenberg to Wittgenstein, ed. E. Timms and R. Robertson). That is what I like, the lower class cafes patronised by prostitutes; much like the porn kinos in fact; you can get tea, coffee and beer there as well. Stay all day for 10 euros.

The Marquis in Europe: Munich, Berlin, Vienna and Brussels. A look at the places Ernst Graf used to frequent.

Vienna is a place where sexuality and eroticism is celebrated and enjoyed and indulged, as they know that sexuality is a vital part of life and people must have somewhere to go to enjoy it. This is one of the greatest most basic pleasures of life so it should be allowed, because it is a pleasure. How different from London, where sex is something disgusting, to be ashamed of, and stamped out. How disgusting that even in a London porn cinema a man is not allowed to masturbate, and if an inspector goes in and sees it the cinema can be closed down. Private parties where middle aged men can enjoy stripers are raided by police, for what? What harm is it doing to anyone?? No one knows it is there! If consenting men and women want to hold these parties for their mutual pleasure and benefit, then what harm is it doing to anyone?? London is disgusting. Eventually you know all of Europe will go the same way, even Belgium and Holland and Germany and Austria. For now we must enjoy and treasure them while we can. No sex please we're British, how fucking true that is. Puritanical pricks who get a real hard on from closing down strip clubs and porn cinemas, they are so full of themselves after every triumph in denying people a little bit of sexual pleasure in their lives.

The Pound is shooting up!

Incredible. It is an omen, I SHOULD be travelling now. My decision to travel again now is what is pushing the Pound vs the Euro up. Vienna coming back to life for me is lifting it like a balloon. Of course I have the power to affect the weather, and I have the power to affect currencies; this is now so commonplace I usually no longer even remark on it. The remarkable has become expected.

Westbahnhof is the centre of my Vienna, around which I centre myself. It helps that it is in the centre of the red light district, or what is left of it. As Munich Hauptbahnhof is the centre of my Munich, and of the Munich red light district.

*

Beautiful piano music here in the Café Westend. Amanda in WSK was indeed much less stunning than I remember her—as I feared. Still the best girl there. I can't even remember, we did something, not sure if we had sex, maybe, a little bit; but she was contemptuous of me, said "you are an alcoholic", and "you have a problem". I stayed long enough that the night bars would now be open. I went in the Alm, no one for me, though the black Cuban girl was sexy and simpatico. Ignoring Big Angelique, straight into

Little Angelique, and Lily again. Two piccolos again, but no sex this time either. She was as beautiful as I remembered her, long black hair, and massively voluptuous body, like a voluptuous Natalie Sawyer. As always, I feel so uncomfortable in the cafés. I sit down, and no one seems to notice me, I sit there all alone. I have to go to the till to ask someone to serve me, and even after that it is so hard to catch anyone's eyes to get another drink. There must be a skill to it that I need to learn. I dangled my empty Gösser bottle in front of her as she was taking the order from the man at the table next to me but apparently she did not see it and just walked off after taking his order.

I suffered such terrible indigestion in the night again, that is becoming a feature of my Vienna visits. I woke feeling depressed, thinking why did I come to Vienna for these two days? But once I start drinking I feel happy to be here again, and do not want to go home. It is encouraging that already I want to come back and for longer next time.

Ah, I caught my severe waitress's attention. I ask for another bottle of Gösser beer and get a bottle of Wieselburger, which is new to me. It seems okay. The faces in this place I think of as real Viennese faces. Real Viennese clothes, hats, manners. Rather severe, aristocratic, even at this, the fag end of Mariahilferstraße on the edge of the Fünfhaus (15th District) badlands. I told Lily my real name, and she told me hers. She is someone I could happily live with.

I always think that one day I will become a big scandal, convicted or charged with some big offence for which I am innocent, but which nevertheless brings me into the international public spotlight, and at that point people will discover my writings, my websites, and then I will be on the road to fame (or infamy). Then everybody in the world will want to buy my books. Someone told me many years ago that every time they look at me they think one day they will open their newspaper and find I have committed the crime that no one thought was possible, or I have broken the bank at Monte Carlo, or something spectacular like that. It was a strange comment, and yet I feel it about myself. I am still latent, still in the chrysalis, still waiting for some spectacular arrival in the world, some great fame/infamy.

On this truncated two-day trip I have no time to do anything cultural, so the KHM and the Butterfly House must wait for next time. At least I have done one new thing by coming here to the Café Westend. I must try to tie a knot in my bladder. There is a woman at the gates of the lavatories who demands tips for entering. I paid 2 Euros as I am new. She must make a fortune. The important thing is I feel comfortable here in the Westend. I will try the Rostbraten.

311

The WSK has become such a warm bath I can sink back into, in these icy very cold Vienna days. I can't ever imagine going again to a porn cinema where there are <u>not</u> hostesses available. It makes the films so much more pleasurable knowing there are young hostesses on hand whenever you want them. It is funny when you come to these places in Vienna, like the Café Westend, where you <u>don't</u> see any CCTV cameras above you. In London they are absolutely everywhere, so it is strange to come to a city where you do not see them. Finally, a fantastic meal in Vienna, here in the Café Westend. A gorgeous Wiener Zwiebelrostbraten, the way it should be. You actually get two steaks, not just one. Fantastic. The Westend has just won my Gold Seal. Now I just want to go back to my hotel and sleep; I don't care about any sinful pleasures. This meal has sated me so much.

I actually liked Amanda much better yesterday; and fancied her as much as I did when I first saw her three weeks ago. She was sweeter to me as well, because I was not so drunk. Again I stayed until after 9. I walked right past Dream Bar, Alm, Angelique 1 & 2, had a quick beer in Bar Haus 6, Okay Bar, and Manhattan (with a piccolo for Vivian), and two in Tête-à-Tête. A McDonald's then bed. Early Saturday morning and I feel depressed now, as always after drinking. When the fog of depression lifts though I think I will be keen to come back to Vienna for a third visit but stay longer next time, of course.

*

Waiting at the Vienna airport bus stop the sexiest, most beautiful little thing—blood red hair, black sleeveless vest, see through around shoulders, pale blue jeans over most gorgeous curvy bottom. So sexy. The kind of girl who instantly enters your list of 'most beautiful girls you have ever seen in your life'. I got on coach behind her and had an erection for most of the journey thinking about her. Lost sight of her as we got off at Westbahnhof. Checked into the Leonardo by the same receptionist as last time, with the black fingernails. She is sexy too. Then passing the Dorint as I crossed road blonde in black leather jacket and blue jeans over the most gorgeous voluptuous bottom. A fine start, anyway. About 1PM now.

Already it is worth coming to Vienna just to have seen that red-haired girl at the Airport bus stop. That is what I travel for—beauty. Sexiness. I work just to pay for these constant travels. Mortgage is not for me; saving for my old age is not for me. We could die at any moment. The world feels such a dangerous, vicious place these days. I think it is a constant miracle that any of us are still here at all. So many in the world today seem to live to kill, as many people as they can; to take all their pleasure in killing people as often as they can. So why care? My plane could crash tomorrow. Sadly, it also means I can never have a partner, and must always be alone. For a partner you want to save money so you can look after them as they get older, but that would mean I could never travel.

I have got to write a *Ulysses*. I feel I have it in me. I have just got to reach the right point in my life; the right point of fruition; of ripeness. It may take years to gestate, and write, and ultimately never be completed, like Musil's *A Man Without Qualities*. Investigate Musil, Zweig, Webern, Berg, Benjamin, further. Big breast models, and great writers and composers, I place them all on the same transcendental level of greatness. A great pornographic video is as great as a Beethoven symphony. There is no difference. I do not discriminate between high art and low art. Whatever moves me. My indulgence of my pleasures is my defiance against the world, and my victory over them.

Four 'pints' of Zipfer and I am still not feeling any high, just getting slowly sozzled. Is it me or is it the beer? I will choose a different bar tomorrow, and a different beer. OK now my vision is starting to blur. Now is the time to go to the Esmeraldas, now they start to seem attractive, and like Helen of Troy.

I drew three blanks on my first day back in Vienna. Fortuna Kino was rubbish. Some awful film, I waited for it to finish and next one start hoping for something better, but then they just restarted the same film. To ML Revue which was also rubbish. The girls were mediocre, and the stunning Brazilian from last time was not there. The Nadine Jansen film which seemed so exciting last time now seemed rubbish. To WSK which was empty, no doubt because of the gangbang at the Love Kino that night. Amanda was there, though, and it is always a pleasure to see her, even if she does not feel the same. All I wanted then was a nice zwiebelrostbraten in Café Westend, and they duly delivered (when I was able to attract their attention). I reconsider my thought of rebooking my flight to stay another day. Maybe three days is enough after all.

As soon as I get back in the Café Westend, I know I want to stay in Vienna forever.

Love Kino was a disappointment—no hostesses, and a strange collection of little rooms off of a central passageway that seems to be a feature of these Vienna kinos—Fortuna and WSK excepted; the only two that have hostesses. Left after about one minute to come back to WSK. I was saddened by the absence of Amanda, the best reason for coming here, until

313

the owner invited me to spend 30 euros on a gangbang with Amanda, and there she was. Not at all what I expected from a 'gangbang' which I thought would last for hours and involve lots of people. Here, there was perhaps 4 or 5 of us, she laid back on a trestle table with her legs akimbo, and it lasted about ten minutes. I felt happier alone with her later. I did not even bother with the night bars, just got the U6 straight back to my hotel. So that was my second day in Vienna.

Now I have enjoyed my third rostbraten in the Café Westend, and several Wieselburger beers, and feel like doing nothing except going back to bed. There were so many things I planned to do on this trip to Vienna: KHM, Justiz Palast, Butterfly House; but in the end I just did what I felt I wanted to do at any given moment. That meant spending all my time drinking and eating in the Café Westend, and then spending the rest of the evening at the WSK. A river cuts its own course. The rest of the time I enjoyed sleeping in my lovely big double bed.

Here in Vienna on my last night, in bed by 8PM already, listening to Ravel on Radio 3. Nowhere else I want to be except in bed listening to classical music, my big window wide open to the sounds of the traffic passing along the Gurtel outside. Feeling sad and down. The thought of returning to London so depressing. But let me shut myself away from the world and cocoon myself. Three days in the Café Westend, and three nights in the Weltspiegel Kino. This was my trip to Vienna. I don't even have the energy or motivation to go back to the airport in the morning. I feel no fever in this fever town. Three days of drinking and ejaculating have unsurprisingly left me low in energy. That is what I came to do, and my well will fill up soon enough. It will be a long time until I come back to Vienna again. What do I want that is any different then? Nothing. I don't want anything, and I don't want anyone. I just want to watch the traffic passing below me in the Gurtel while the classical music plays in the room behind me. Just to be held in suspension like this. Just watching the world pass by. The only real blessing that I am alone, and free to be as lifeless as I want. I am alone, and I am glad about that. What luxury to be feeling sad in a 7th floor Vienna hotel room, overlooking the Gurtel. This is my natural state. Oh, how I love my big white bed! How I love my big white pillows!

*

People can say I have had a sinful and sleazy life, going from strip club to brothel to porn cinema to night bar to Tingel Tangel, but at the end of the day what it has all been about is: a love of women. An absolute obsession

314

with women's beauty. And that is not such a bad thing I think. I groped after it in the dark like Gatsby chasing the green light at the end of Daisy's pier, or a Polish pilot looking for a runway in thick fog. It was a hole in me, and I chased feminine beauty to fill that hole, without ever of course succeeding, as once that hole exists it will always be there. Drink, drugs and women are just painkillers, they can never heal the wound. Morphine is a painkiller not a cure, and like so many I became addicted to the morphine and the morphine did more damage to me than the original injury.

Maybe that last trip to Vienna wasn't really all that exciting, but it was important as Kenneth Williams always said of his Tangier trips, in that it KEPT THE PENDULUM SWINGING. It kept my mechanism in motion, from stopping altogether, and I have come back and felt so much more relaxed. This is why these trips are so important, it is the after-effect more than anything that keeps me going for a while in London. When that momentum starts to run out, it is time to jump on a plane again, to set the pendulum swinging again. This sense of liberation is tremendously healthy to my mechanism, my system, my soul I believe. To be able to go where I want, when I want, with who I want (myself).

The first time I have seen *Bad Timing* at the cinema. Two things which immediately stand out is how brave Garfunkel was taking on this role, such an unpleasant unsympathetic character, but he does give such a true picture of obsession, what an illness it is, how it poisons and shrivels your own life. The other thing is how unsurprising it is that Nicolas Roeg fell in love with Theresa Russell while making this film! I wonder if her performance as Milena in this film affected my eventual choice of life partner, as only really now do I see how much Milena reminds me of my love. When Milena's ex-husband comes in and says "She's alive. She will live" it is like a spell is broken. The tension is broken and he then just turns and looks at the empty room, and only then is he struck by the fact that he has now destroyed that love, and has destroyed it forever. Everyone puts on their jackets and leaves the room forever. He will never find anything this good in his life again, so why did he destroy it. And what was Keitel's police detective just about to say to Alex before Stefan walked in and broke the spell? The final coda in New York is quite devastating. The cold hatred she has for him, and the still despairing obsession he has with her. A great film. I first saw it when I was a teenager I would guess, on BBC2 late one night, and back then I just saw it as a titillating sex film, all breasts and bottoms, and it just turned me on so much. It stuck in my mind forever, and has been with me all these years, till I love it like it is a real person. I feel the same way about *Last Tango in*

Paris, Pierrot le Fou, 8½. All films about a man in love with an unobtainable woman really.

It is a bit of a psychological paradox. If you go out hoping for a good time, some 'high night that persuades us to put off suicide', something or someone that really ignites your senses, and you spend a lot of money in pursuit of this only for nothing to happen, and it be a dud, a dead end, a waste of time, energy and money, you berate yourself and curse yourself for your stupid wasteful dissipation, and despise yourself for your pathetic, tawdry addictions, and think of all the money you could have saved if you had not gone out. And yet if you go out, and your ball lands in your number on the metaphorical roulette wheel, and you have one of those great 'high nights', you congratulate yourself so much for a wise decision in going out, risking that expenditure. It is no different from gambling, going out looking for some sexual excitement. If you lose you despise yourself for your weakness. If you win you respect yourself for your bravery and daring. To dare is to do. You have to speculate to accumulate. And after all what else is the point of having money except to spend it in pursuit of pleasure? What else? Having money to keep you safe and warm and healthy when you get old. If I lived my life not spending money on pleasure I would have so much money to protect me when I am old. Because, however, I spend all my money when young in pursuit of momentary pleasures, I will have nothing to protect me when I am old. It is depressing to know I will have nothing when I am old, but depressing to consider life without pursuing pleasure every day, every minute. One wonders what it must be like to be rich—when you don't have to make that choice, and you can live for pleasure AND still know you will be protected when you get old.

AND YET THESE FINE COLLAPSES ARE NOT LIES. "Through a thousand nights the flesh assaults outright for bolts that linger hidden,—O undirected as the sky that through its black foam has no eyes for this fixed stone of lust. Accumulate such moments to an hour. Account the total of this trembling tabulation." I take these words of Hart Crane to mean you go out night after night, year after year, looking for pleasure, for bolts of pleasure that really linger, really scorch, but if you added up all the fleeting snatched moments of real pleasure that you managed to experience in a year, say, it might only accumulate to one hour's worth, so you put this in your ledger for that year. One year of going out night after night to accumulate a total of one hour of real pleasure. It is like sifting the mud for gold. An accountant's approach to the pursuit of erotic pleasure.

I love having my windows open to the rain. Especially summer rain, in steamy humid July & August, the ferns outside my windows blowing lashing in the approaching storm, black skies turning day into night, and the rain then starts to come down, steadily, relentlessly, until it is lashing down, and I have to turn my classical music up louder to be heard over the roar of the rain and the thunder. And the daddy long legs and butterflies and bumble bees are dashing around madly searching for cover. I wish the world could always be like this. Always raining, always black sky, always this lush green abundant fauna glowing in the rain. Brussels has 200 rainy days a year, and only takes two hours to get to. How can one resist?

*

So for my first day in Brussels let me concentrate on Eros. Tomorrow, disillusioned & depressed & ashamed, I can concentrate on art, and take the long walk to the Fin-de-Siècle and Old Masters museums. Friday I can hunt for shoes. The three great attractions of Brussels apportioned to my three days here. The beautiful Arab girl in the station roll shop surly on my first order of ham & egg roll but smiling sexily on my second. I should have gone back for more (she obviously likes a man who likes a bit of ham & egg). Nothing else of note, after 3½ hours in Brussels.

I love Esmeraldas because I do not want any involvement whatsoever. Involvement is like being stuck in a giant spider web, glued to it, waiting for the giant spider to come back and eat you, like in *Lord of the Rings*. I have to enjoy Belgium & Germany & Austria while I can, before Najat and her ilk take over Europe. In the old days my holidays were a three-way battle between Love, Art & Eros; but I found the one person I can love and so now I never fall in love with anyone on holiday. The trips therefore just become about Art & Eros. And drink and food; more than anything drink and food. My trips are all like *La Grande Bouffe* these days, with the emphasis increasingly on the drink & food. 230PM on my first day back in Brussels, and annoyingly it is hot and sunny. Rain is promised for the next two days. It had better not let me down. Brussels Grill over the road from me here in the Café du Dome, tempting me with its succulent delights. I resist. Let it be the last thing I do before bed.

I have yet to see a really beautiful pair of breasts. Tomorrow I should hang around the Gare du Midi, but oh, there are no longer any bars inside the station. Disgrace. The Pullmans and Murphy's all gone. And Maes Bar, was that a third? That is why Gare du Midi/Ibis is no longer the place I centre myself around, like creatures around a black smoker. I instead stay at the top end of the Boulevard Adolphe Max. Just a shame the ABC and

California have already gone since my first visits back in 2002-2004. I don't ever want to stop enjoying the naughty places, and the big-breasted Esmeraldas, because to me it is the only sign of life in me, it is the only thing that keeps me feeling alive. It is the only thing that gets me out of bed in the morning. In Brussels I want everything at once: I want Brussels Grill steaks, I want Alhambra Cinema, I want Yellow Lily girls. I don't know what to do first because I want all at once.

Belgium—surely there is no more fucked up country in Europe, which is why I like it so much. The racial divides as stark as in Iraq or Africa, yet here they do not blow each other up, they just argue about it. This is the European way. I love and admire Europe so much (at the same time as wanting out of the E.U.). Oh, a new barmaid in the Café du Dome—a blonde North African this time. I might have to stay longer than planned. Oh, these North African girls of Brussels are intoxicating; arousing. As repulsive as the North African boys who try to rob me at night are, the girls during the day are intoxicating & arousing.

I drank too much in the Café du Dome I think, which meant I cannot remember much of the Alhambra Cinema. I didn't stay long, walked past the beautiful street girls of the Rue des Commerçants to Yellow Lily. A beautiful long blonde-haired Swedish-looking girl whose name I cannot remember as she predicted. The beautiful black-haired girl with the big bottom from before. A new black girl in white dress. Again, I did not stay long, feeling so drunk now. Staggered back to Brussels Grill for a steak then back to the hotel to pass out. I will try to drink less today. 1206 Thursday and still no sign of this promised rain. Short walk to the porn cinema or long walk to the museum? Doing cultural things is not easy. But I will feel so much better afterwards, and it will make the sinful things so much more enjoyable because I will feel I have earned them.

The Fin-de-Siècle Museum was a triumph, and a pleasure. Lots of pictures I had not seen before, including some Rops, but the real pleasure was La Figure Tombale. No sign of the Génie du Mal, Alfred Stevens Salome, or Death of Marat, however. Or Temptation of St Anthony by Dali, and the De Chirico picture I have loved for so long (no doubt because they do not fit into the museum's fin-de-siècle time frame). The rain was a merest brief shower; very disappointing. A lovely curvy black girl behind the Dome bar this afternoon. The shoe shops were a disappointment, hardly anything I liked. I was in bed by 8PM last night, passed out. I woke around 330AM and was watching one of those fantastic Euro lesbian vampire movies. The girls spend the whole time naked or in those white see-through nighties. Would love to be able to find out what it was called. It just ended all of a sudden with no credits. I like Brussels. I wouldn't mind staying here forever.

I got to the bar as the barmaid was bending over to put things in the glass washer, and her breasts were hanging so heavy and big in that white blouse. Her black trousers were halfway down her bottom exposing the tiniest purple thong on those massive buttocks. She jumped in shock when she saw me, as the blonde one had done yesterday as I approached behind her. The Dome barmaids have now surpassed the Dorint ones in my imagination. Lotta & Sophia, alas, were a long time ago. The real beauties in Brussels are the North African girls. Walking down to O'Reilly's a young North African man was being put into a police car while other officers stood talking to a tourist couple with two small children. The man had his wallet in his hand and I presume the North African had tried to steal it. In O'Reilly's looking over to the Bourse I was thinking Brussels will be a Muslim capital one day, as will Paris. Capitals of a Muslim caliphate that covers the whole of Europe, and the thought did not particularly bother me. It would be historically interesting. But why when they have disagreements are the Muslim people so violent and so murderous, when we Europeans settle things just by arguing and complaining? God, this barmaid's breasts are impressive. Her behind even more so.

The skies outside are dark, and it makes it look very gloomy here inside the Dome, but still it will not rain. How lovely if there was a proper storm, and I could walk to the Alhambra Cinema in the storm and walk to the Yellow Lily in a storm. There were rumbles of thunder as I climbed the stairs to the Fin-de-Siècle Museum, but nothing came of it. I want to live in a world of tits & arses, pornography & prostitution, sailing forever on a voluptuous sea of scented bosoms. I will work hard in London, so I can spend as much of my time & money on that as possible. This is the pornotopia I want. Blonde in tight pink fluffy sweater and skin-tight almost see-through white trousers. 19, 18? Awesome. I am getting ready for Alhambra Cinema and Yellow Lily. The clouds do not even seem to move. The same grey heavy clouds are just hanging over us, stationary. Oh, now she's bending over to clean the table in front of me, wiggling that massive bottom. There's that purple thong again. That vampire film last night, like *Daughters of Darkness*, ended in what looked like a cold North Sea coast. Finally! A shower! Wow, it is really lashing down now. 5PM. Slowed to a pitter patter by 505 already. Stopped by 508.

For four or five months I really worked hard to bring my credit card debt down each month, but now I no longer bother. It is such a violent world we live in I could meet my end at any moment, so no point living like a monk for month after month to inch my credit card debt down by small

319

amounts. Better to carry on travelling, having pleasure, then die young, owing tens of thousands. My life insurance will be a big help to my loved ones, so they will be happy also. I will come to the Dome early tomorrow on my usual pilgrimage to Gare du Nord, then spend rest of the day snoozing in Alhambra Cinema or Yellow Lily. I wait for the beer goggles to really take over my eyes, then I will move on. I need to start reading Simenon. Maybe after Alhambra Cinema and Yellow Lily I can go back and finish the night in Alhambra Cinema. Nothing better than to be woken up by a porn cinema manager saying "Monsieur, c'est finis" and do myself up and stumble home like that. The barmaid's breasts like two black Zeppelins. Her buttocks, even bigger. This is why I travel.

I travel to places that offer me the pornotopia I crave. Berlin, increasingly, has now become bottom of the list. Stuttgarter Platz has been wiped out and that has really destroyed Berlin for me. Sissi/Angelica is the loveliest Esmeralda I have ever met in my life it is true, but she is now in a laufhaus far in the outskirts and those places are not for me. Brussels always in fourth place out of four, has now risen to become No.1. The Café du Dome has run out of Stella. This is how much I have drunk. Tomorrow it would be lovely to go to Yellow Lily quite sober, and just drink while I am there, instead of arriving drunk, like I do. The umbrellas are up again, 6.29, but I cannot see anything. I am starting to feel hungry—for female flesh, visual and physical.

Unbelievably, it turns out my last day in Brussels, when I planned to do so many things AND BUY MY SHOES, is a holiday day, a religious festival for the Virgin Mary, and everything is closed. Shops, bars, everything. How on Earth can this keep happening to me? How many holidays do they have in Belgium now? Now I am forced to share in the veneration of the Virgin Bloody Mary. A dead, silent city, as the rain gently falls.

Well, the receptionist was right (Spanish again), the closer you get down towards the Grand Place the more places will be open. I even found a shoe shop which I might go back to. So I am forced down to O'Reilly's for a drink, before I head up to Gare du Nord. The Alhambra Cinema films have been a bit rubbish this time but still a lovely luxurious place to crash out in and snooze and relax, away from the world. Leaving there and heading to Yellow Lily I was stopped by a black girl with the most enormous bosoms. I was sorely tempted but pressed on to Yellow. Nothing there took my fancy and I headed back, via Rue des Commerçants street girls, and Brussels Grill. Amazingly, after two solid days of drinking and debauchery I still have the appetite for more. Well, that's my first Irish Breakfast. I know someone who would have loved that. It seems to be the same as an English Breakfast except served by an Irish waitress.

*

So yes I hate plane travel, but flying really is the cheapest, and the least painful way to travel. To Munich in 1 hour 30 minutes, to Vienna in 2 hours. Maximum time then for drinking, eating and fucking. I think I will have to go back to Brussels next, to make sure I am sated with it, THEN I can go on to Munich and Nuremberg, and only after that to Vienna, Café Westend and WSK. But let me do Brussels one more time, to push it to breaking point.

I got SO turned on with Julia in Yellow Lily didn't I! To put alongside the first time with Amanda in Vienna, and busty blonde in Fortuna. Genuine animal top of head blowing off desire which I thought I had left behind years ago. It is back! A new golden age.

Easy to take for granted I was fucking that extraordinary black sexy Sao Paulo girl in every position and was so turned on. And "gangbanged" Amanda in WSK. Incredible things now becoming common. I have to spend everything on travel.

I look for those moments when I can really get turned on, so my head is exploding with lust, like the old days, and I thought they were all gone—but this year in Vienna I met big old blonde in Fortuna and Amanda in WSK, and last week I met Sao Paulo Julia in Brussels Yellow Lily. Add to that Greek Mariana and Bulgarian Zara and Italian Maria in Soho. Extraordinary times once again.

KIMMY AND SPANISH MARY ARE FU MANCHU GIRLS REMEMBER! I AM IN A FU MANCHU FILM. 1905 LONDON. GORGEOUS COCK BETWEEN MY LEGS.

*

460 Snelbus Boom. Busty brown ponytail girl in grey cardigan over big breasts passing the Dome as I arrived. 1345. It starts. Did I come with the black Sao Paulo girl on my last day last time? I can't remember. It doesn't matter. I know it sounds silly, but I don't go to prostitutes in order to come. I go for the visual stimulation, the optical thrill of seeing them undress and then seeing them naked beneath me or above me in a variety of positions. I'd rather not come—as soon as I come the spell is broken and my arousal & excitement is all gone. It is like how horrible the smell of food is after you've eaten a big dinner. I try to put off coming as long as I can, to prolong the

321

excitement, the never-ending anticipation of being about to come. Another discovery from the last day three weeks ago—the Celtica Bar. Happy hour from 1PM to midnight, 1 euro for half pint of beer, and 2 euros for pints! Incredible. Cosy little bar, too, with lots of sports on the TVs. 2PM now. I will hang around until 3 hoping one of the sexy North African girls will take over.

I like to drink until I am numb because then I can go to a porn cinema and blissfully wank and be wanked with no fear of a sudden, ruining explosion, which spoils and ends everything, prematurely. Similarly, I know I can go from the porn cinema to one 'model' after another and f—k three or four girls one after the other without fear of the deadening ruinous ejaculation. No doubt Dr Pamela Stephenson would say I have a problem if sex can only happen for me when it follows drink & pornography, but it makes me so happy, so I don't see it as a problem. Trying to be normal, and suppress these urges, made me unhappy. Indulging and giving free rein to them makes me happy. Oh, yes, at 3PM the beautiful, long blonde hair North African girl has taken over. Like all these Brussels North African girls, with a figure to die for. White blouse pressed tight against her nubile fleshiness. My drinking is speeding up now; I am getting through the small beers more & more rapidly. With my fifth small Stella I can now feel the coldness and the numbness spreading over my entire body and reaching my gonads.

To the Dome by 445, and the gorgeous blonde North African is here again. Lovely. I had two pints in the Celtica (total cost 4 euros, incredible. One pint in O'Reilly's costs more than that) then got the metro up to Gare du Nord. The first videokabin place has three cinema rooms upstairs, two straight and one gay, for 10 euros. The kabin films were mediocre. The kabin place over the road also had very poor kabins as always, and the peep show girls were no better. I was told it is better to go to Gare du Nord windows before 6 because the better girls work then but I would dispute that. Most of the windows were still closed and the few that were open had very average girls. Also, in the bright sunshine it is hard to see in the windows anyway. I will come back at night, 'dangerous' or not.

I really didn't fancy any of the girls in Yellow Lily yesterday, even the black Brazilian from before (who I had slept with). Last time I was out of my head with desire for three or four of them, yet yesterday the same girls did not move me at all. So if Gare du Nord was rubbish, and Yellow Lily not that exciting, what am I to do for the rest of my stay? I was tired yesterday not having slept for more than 24 hours by the time I got to

Yellow Lily or discounting a little nap the previous afternoon more like 32 hours. I was running on empty.

The Dome bar is SO quiet. 5PM, I am the only customer. As I am running a bit later today maybe a chance later to check out Empire and even American Guest Bar. Other than that, there is nothing else I want to do, just Alhambra Cinema, Rue des Commerçants, and Yellow Lily. I look forward to Munich & Nuremberg now. I work to travel. This is how I want it to be for the rest of my life. Oh, the black girl with the massive bosoms and buttocks is here as well. Why on Earth they need two barmaids I do not know. I would like to spend the night with both the Dome girls, more than anything in Yellow Lily. The blonde and the black, they are both so gorgeous and with such fleshy curvy figures. Incredible, but I do not see any barmaids in London as sexy as these two girls. All the pubs I go to in London, I never see anything as sexy as these two girls. The night shift at Gare du Nord will start soon, and darkness starts soon, too.

As soon as I take my place in the Dome, before even sitting down, a beautiful voluptuous brunette, black cardigan over black low-cut vest and most enormous cleavage, skin tight black trousers. Stunning. I really think Brussels has the most beautiful bouncy women in the world. The seats on the Adolphe Max side are so much better for people watching (ogling). I don't know why I ever wasted my time on the other side. Brussels has really boiled down to just three things: Alhambra Cinema, the walk past the street girls of Rue des Commerçants, and Yellow Lily. And I am bored of Yellow Lily now; familiarity has bred if not contempt, at least disinterest. I will try Gare du Nord once more after 6. But I think I am quite sated with Brussels now; good. That leaves me free to enjoy Munich and Nuremberg. I haven't desired anyone enough to do anything this time; when last time I was out of my mind with desire for almost everyone. I wonder if subconsciously I am mindful of saving my money for Munich & Nuremberg. More than anything I think of the Rechthaler Hof steaks.

The Yellow Lily is the only brothel I have ever been to where the girls regularly decline to go to a room with me. They are very choosy. In all other brothels & strip clubs, in Vienna, Berlin, and London, they are so desperate for money, for customers, they fight to take you to the room. Here, the bar is always busy, they can take their pick, they can say no. They can leave as early as they like. They come in for a couple of hours, then leave by 3 or 4, to pick their children up from school, who knows. To get the most out of Yellow Lily, you must arrive early, by 2, 230; if you wait until 7-8 almost all the good ones will have left already. There are lots of girls in Yellow Lily just in the last two days I would have liked to have slept with, but not one of them really blew my mind ENOUGH, to cross that threshold of actually making me ask them. I have restrained myself waiting for the one I cannot resist. Oh my God, brunette in tight green T-shirt and most amazing breasts, and tight leggings over wiggling fat arse. I love Brussels. Now a North African long-black-haired girl so sexy I cannot even describe her.

Yes, Alhambra Cinema has been quite poor again, but oh, it is still a lovely place to doze in when you've had a drink. Yes, Yellow Lily now bores me a little but oh, if you are going to drink where better to drink than in a bar filled with beautiful whores? If this time I have not desired any of them enough to sleep with them then that too is fantastic, as it saves me money for Munich & Nuremberg to come. Wow, 7PM at night, the Dome is really busy. This is how it survives. Most gorgeous gorgeous sexy smile from the black girl as I approached the bar. Probably the sexiest moment of the whole trip. The kind of smile that makes you want to stay in a bar for a long time. "We do not have peanuts" she said in a slow sultry way, which was strange, as she has not given me peanuts the last two days either. Maybe she said "We do not have penis" to let me know that her & her blonde friend were giving me the green light. Typical of my cowardice I did not put it to the test, though God knows I would have loved to. Honestly, she is the most fanciable girl I have met in the three days. I should have said, "I have penis! Lots of it!"

Another little Rubicon crossed yesterday—my first time in one of those one-hour hotels in the Rue des Commerçants—Beatrice, from Bulgaria. A beautiful voluptuous redhead. You pay 20 to the hotel manager, he gives you two towels, two miniature bars of soap and two condoms, and up you go to the bedroom and 50 to the girl (for half an hour). I passed her again later on my way back from Yellow Lily and I was sorely tempted to go with her again but was really too tired & drunk. I was surprised, the Dome closed its doors before 9PM.

I have eaten hardly anything on this trip (apart from Beatrice). On Tuesday I had a McDonald's at midday then a Brussels Grill steak before bed. Wednesday I had nothing all day and just finished the night with a burger & chips. The same yesterday. I have of course been drinking from the moment I woke up to the moment I go back to bed at night. And I am really starting to long for the WSK again. Even Lily in Angelique. I feel naked without a pen & paper in front of me. I am never lonely if I have a pen & paper on the bar table in front of me. I am sure I just saw Beatrice pass by the Dome in black top & blue jeans; I recognised her red ringletted-hair &

voluptuous figure. What a coincidence! How sexy to see her passing a bar I am in, knowing I made love to her the day before!

In the space of about five minutes I have just seen four or five of the most beautiful girls I have ever seen in my life, passing the window of the Dome. This is why I love Brussels. There is literally nowhere in the world I want to go to except Europe. Nothing else fascinates me or enthuses me or interests me except the countries of Europe, the art of Europe, the literature of Europe, the pornography of Europe, the women of Europe, etc etc etc. I am a complete Europhile; I am also completely anti the European Union. I am for the Euro single currency for purely selfish reasons; it makes travelling around Europe so easy. I still remember the nightmare of my first (Interrail) trip to Europe, to Belgium, Germany, Austria, and Sweden, having to take out new currency in every country I came to. The extraordinary beauties of Brussels continue to pass my window. It is now becoming almost unbelievable. I am becoming almost overwhelmed. Almost intoxicated.

*

I love to go to some cheap, low, sleazy night bar or strip bar or tingel tangel, and find the most incredible sexy beauty so much better than her surroundings. What is such a diamond doing amidst such sleaze? That is what I live for, finding these diamonds, like a pig searching for truffles. In Brussels, Berlin, Vienna and Munich. Even in Soho in the last 6 months I have found the most extraordinary beauties: Roxy, Zara, Spanish Maria, Italian Maria, Colombian Lavina, Greek Mariana.

In fact I would say in my experience the more low quality the place the more high quality the girls you will meet, real natural sexy beauties. Not stuck up fake skinny bitches, but real warm curvy sexy girls. That is what makes me think if only I had been able to search those smaller places in Munich I might yet have found some real erotic excitement (at a price). The more 'high quality' the place the more you know you will not find anything genuinely sexy or sexual. They are found in the smaller places, the lower dives.

*

When in Vienna I don't go into the glorious centre much; I tend to stay in the Fünfhaus badlands, and the Gurtel. Surprisingly grey cold misty Vienna when I arrived. A really icy grey mist. Unfortunately, it brightened by the afternoon. 2PM now. I have just settled into the Dorint bar. Cute little

325

(half-Chinese?) barmaid, in the grey waistcoat over white blouse they have to wear now. I cannot imagine Lotta & Sophia in grey waistcoats, hiding those incredible 18-year-old Swedish bosoms. Oh no, they were fully on display back then. The Zipfer beer is MUCH colder than on previous visits. A massive improvement.

Lotta & Sophia really are legends of my life. Yet, just this year I have met a new legend in Vienna, Amanda in WSK. I have barely written a word about her. Often the biggest most important figures of my private life are the ones I say nothing about. I have had two legendary trips to Vienna—the Lotta & Sophia trip in 2002, and the 2005 trip during the thick snow, when I met Maria in Pour Platin, now knocked down and completely gone. Oh, I could add the first visit this year, when I met Amanda in WSK and Nina in Fortuna. But to be really considered legendary, years have to pass to let it richen ever more in my mind, like coal, oil, diamonds. Time gives richness. That is Time's most extraordinary quality. Amazing to think Lotta & Sophia must be 30 years old now, married with children. Would be so so funny to see them again.

I feel like everyone ages except me; I just stay young, like Peter Pan. I attract the flies, I wonder if they have this expression in Vienna? Anyway, this funny little aphid won't leave me alone. I try to squash it and kill it without smashing my beer glass in the process. Beatles All My Loving on the radio. How ubiquitous English culture is. Yet, you can say the same of Viennese culture perhaps. Freud has colonised the world as much as the Beatles. Mozart, Beethoven, Schoenberg, Berg, Webern. Schiele etc etc etc. Cross-fertilisation. This is what I am here for. So here I am in Felberstraße, just down the road from 22 Felberstraße where a young potless Adolf Hitler lived for nine months or so back in 1908-9, sucking Jewish cock and swallowing Jewish cum just to survive. This is what led to gas chambers. Sex—the motor for everything. The greatest catalyst for good & ill. Well, I'm in Vienna—this city makes you think like that.

Café Westend is very quiet on this Monday night. I question why I am here in Vienna now. So I met Amanda in WSK, beautiful girl, beautiful breasts, but felt no desire to do anything with her. Went to Burggasse Peep for the first time and met Athena, beautiful half-Romanian girl, beautiful breasts, but felt no desire to do anything with her. Er, so, what am I to do while here in Vienna?! OK, now let me just enjoy the drinking, and the eating, and the sleeping. Try to see some sights that mean something to me. But that is it. Let me finish THE COLD ICY AIR OF THE MOUNTAINS while I am here. That would be a great monument to this stay—THE COLD ICY AIR OF THE MOUNTAINS was published while I was in Vienna!

The little conversation I had with the Dorint barmaid yesterday was far more sexy than anything I encountered in WSK or Burggasse Peep Show. Today I will try to force myself to do some sightseeing—the Justice Palace, KHM, Elizabethstraße 4 and 20 (two of Karl Kraus's houses), Lothringerstraße 6 (another Kraus house), finally visit the building that was the hotel in *The Night Porter*. The jewel in the crown of this Vienna visit I hope. Then I can try Fortuna Kino. I don't think I will go back to Burggasse Peep again—WSK is a sexier environment for sex. I have yet to see a really sexy girl in Vienna though. In Brussels I see them all the time, an endless stream of mind-blowing girls in the street; even in London I see them all the time. I haven't found a good people-watching place yet here in Vienna—perhaps this is the problem. No doubt they do have sexy girls here in Vienna—just more elusive! So what did I actually do yesterday? Just WSK and Burggasse Peep, after a long Dorint bar session, finishing with a Café Westend steak, which gave me indigestion which woke me up and destroyed my night's sleep, a Vienna tradition. Anyway, it is probably too late for people watching (ogling)—temperatures are as low as 4°C this week and everyone is wrapped up too tightly.

— has politely declined the offer of us sharing a flat together again; therefore, I can continue to devote my life to Tallulah & Esmeralda, with a clear conscience. First of all, let me drink until the point I can get no pleasure out of it. I can't go sightseeing, indeed cannot leave my hotel at all, until I am properly drunk. I don't want to go out until I am in some kind of narcotic trance, alcoholic daze. This is why Amanda is contemptuous of me. Back on my first visit this year she blew my mind, as did the Fortuna blonde: I wonder if I will ever have a mind-blowing experience in Vienna again. I keep looking. At least Vienna has already trumped Munich, as it does have sex, and trumped Munich & Nuremberg as it has sex in a bar environment AND has porn cinemas. No matter I drink too much to enjoy any of it. It makes me happy to know it is there. So readily available. But the drinking and drifting off into my own world is what it is all about and is more important a pleasure than any of the others. If the drink wears off quickly enough to enable me to enjoy some sexual pleasure before I return to the hotel, that is a bonus. Complete numbness of the penis (even when fully erect), and indigestion, are the two prices I pay for my pleasure in this level of drinking. I want the massive beer goggles that it gives me.

Vienna has so many amazing museums, but I have been to them before. Doing something for the first time has so much more of a charge—I have never seen the *Night Porter* hotel building before; I have never seen Kraus's homes before (actually I probably have—I have been along Elizabethstraße and past Lothringerstraße many times, but without knowing he lived there). *Bad Timing* means as much to me as *The Night Porter*, perhaps even more, but there are no actual locations from the film that stick in my mind—most of the meaningful action takes place inside the bedroom, which could be anywhere. The *Last Tango in Paris* flat—now that is something I do want to see; the walk along that bridge leading to it. Visiting film locations means so much more to me, I now realise, than going to art museums. And, indeed, visiting the houses where my favourite writers lived.

I would not list Hitler as one of my favourite writers, yet it is fascinating to stand in front of one of the many Vienna buildings where he lived. True or not, the theory that he survived as a young penniless man in Vienna by sucking Jewish cock, swallowing Jewish cum, and taking Jewish cock up his arse, does offer a fascinating insight into his mindset, and provides a real frisson when one walks in his footsteps—around Westbahnhof in particular, where he volunteered to carry passengers' cases to earn a few pennies. In context of his alleged Jew-cum-swallowing survival method, his writings in *Mein Kampf* do indeed gain extraordinary meaning:-

> "Thus for the first time I recognized the Jews as the cold-hearted, shameless directors of this revolting vice traffic in the scum of the big city.... the more unlimited his fertility, the more the scoundrel ends up splashing his filth in the face of humanity.... But then a flame flared up within me. I no longer avoided the Jewish question, now I sought it... I talked my tongue sore and my throat hoarse... But...Whenever you tried to attack, your hand closed on a jelly-like slime which poured through your fingers."

> Given his obvious attractiveness to Jewish men and reputation as a "sex pervert" might we surmise that perhaps it was Jewish semen that had filled his mouth with distaste, splashed his face or which oozed like "jelly-like slime" through Adolf's effeminate fingers and stroking hand? And what are we to make of Adolf's references to his sore tongue and throat? Perhaps the answers become more obvious when we discover that Adolf Hitler developed a mouth washing compulsion while living in Vienna and that forever after he refused to put meat in his mouth.
> [http://brainmind.com/Hitler2.html]

Coupling the amount of Jewish sperm that he swallowed and the number of Jewish cocks he suffered to be rammed up his arse, with the violent attempted Jewish-led Communist takeover of beautiful Germany after the Great War, and one can start to understand what drove him to the Holocaust. Even in 1918 there were many Jews begging the Jewish Communist revolutionaries to stop what they were doing, because of the retribution it would bring down on all Jews. "A rare case of foresight", Hitler said, years later. Sex is the motor for everything good and bad. And Vienna is the capital of it.

Incredible to think that Hitler, Stalin and Trotsky were all young men in Vienna at the same time—who in Vienna today will we be reading of in 100 years' time? Me, I believe. I write about my love, and sincerely believe that this will make her immortal, too, like Sally Bowles (Jean Ross). This is the Zipfer talking. No, no Dorint barmaids to compare with the legendary Lotta, and Sophia. Drinking gives me the fierce determination that my normal shyness and self-consciousness robs me of. Everyone is wrapped up so tightly outside; it must be freezing. About 14 degrees colder than London perhaps. I drink to the point where I cannot walk straight, and my writing becomes illegible even to myself—only then am I ready to go out. You Were Always on My Mind is on the Dorint bar radio now.

It only takes one girl to bring a whole city to life, it is true—but to be honest there is nowhere else I will be going in Vienna, except back to the WSK and Fortuna, and rest of the time here in the Dorint, so I doubt anyone will bring Vienna to life for me this time. However, I am still very happy to be here, and feel very calm, and very happy. I feel happy to be in a place where pornography & sex are readily available, even if I do not partake of it. In years to come (very soon perhaps) even this will be denied to us. The feminists like Najat and puritanical emasculated prigs like — will see to that. I lead a completely asocial life. I had an asocial baby-hood, an asocial childhood, teenage years, adulthood. So obviously I only seek asocial sex.

Honestly, they have too many staff here in the Dorint. How can they afford so many barstaff? I could quite happily just stay here all day with —. She is very cute. I was, to be honest, thinking about her quite erotically before leaving my hotel room this morning. I was actually thinking there is something so open, and warm, about Hungarians. I have become friendly with so many Hungarians on my travels, yet I have met as many Poles, as many Germans, as many French, who I have never got to know by name. And yet I have become friendly with so many Hungarians. This is quite amazing. And here in my Vienna hotel, the one (of many) barmaid who has actually taken the time to stop and make conversation with me is this Hungarian girl. To be honest, —'s arrival has made me not want to leave and go on to the Justiz Palast, Karl Kraus's houses, *Night Porter* hotel, etc. There is something affecting about her. Well, a few litres

329

of Zipfer later, let's be brutal about it, I would love to f—k her. Oh, the curve of her arse as she bends to her knees to check the wine fridge is most, most affecting. The Dorint uniform trousers are very close-fitting.

Once you get inside the Ring (no sexual pun intended; oh, you dirty perverts) every building is basically a palace. So here I am in the Café Savoy (or Palais Wernburg) facing the *Night Porter* hotel (now Bank of Austria branch). Extraordinarily moving. Surprisingly, judging by the 'Gay Guides' in the pamphlet holders by the door, this might well be a 'gay' café. Very appropriate, for Dirk anyway. I tried to tailgate someone into the Bank of Austria itself, but it seems it is bankcard entry only, so I panicked and turned away. U2 I Still Haven't Found What I'm Looking For on the café radio—not until two hours I think. My God, I am right next to the *Night Porter* hotel of Charlotte Rampling and Dirk Bogarde. So, I have seen the Justice Palace? I couldn't tell which building it is, surely one of them, saw Karl Kraus's houses at Elisabethstraße 4 and 20, been in the café opposite the *Night Porter* hotel, saw the *Night Porter* hotel! A really great thrill. How many years I have loved the film *The Night Porter*; how many times I have watched the film *The Night Porter*; here I am sitting in the café opposite the *Night Porter* hotel. I have to say, it is rather more magnificent now than it is in the film!

Grace Jones La Vie en Rose plays in the Dorint lavatories (& bar) as I return to the hotel from my day of sightseeing. An interesting day, which has restored my faith in Vienna, after I felt rather down this time last night. For the second night in a row the Café Westend waiter tries to sell me a 'pumpkin salad'—no doubt Halloween influenced. I decline. From the Café Savoy I headed to Fortuna Kino. I find it rather more sexy than the WSK; two black-haired Bulgarian girls on hand but I declined on this occasion, though I was in the mood. Instead, I headed back to WSK. As is always the case with Amanda, this time I found her incredibly beautiful again. One time I find her beautiful, next time I don't know why I ever liked her. It alternates almost with mechanical regularity. Anyway, this time her hair was long, and I found her most beautiful, and she was incredibly happy and friendly again. She seems to instantly detect when I am not SO drunk and is pleased as a result. Back to the Dorint, but the menu seemed uninspiring (no rostbraten) so I pushed on to the Café Westend. Indigestion awaits me very soon.

A beautiful rostbraten once again, which I shall pay for very soon, as soon as I fall asleep.

My clothes smell smoky; something I have not known for a long time in London. Indigestion during the night, only minor, thanks God. A better second day in Vienna, which restored so much faith. On my first day, as usual, I was so tired having gone more than 24 hours without sleep and drinking too much, as I was too excited, and so destroyed the charm and thrill of everything. Yesterday I probably drank more than Monday if anything, but after a very good night and morning's sleep I then spent some hours walking around looking at the Justice Palace, Karl Kraus's houses, the *Night Porter* hotel, so by the time I finally got to a naughty place, sensation had returned to my body and I could get full enjoyment, both from the Fortuna and the WSK. Therefore, my time with Amanda was much more pleasurable, and she was much nicer to me, recognising immediately I was not so drunk. We made love again, on the sofa in the tiny cinema upstairs this time. How the incredible becomes commonplace.

I have not even left my room until after 2PM today. This will probably mean I am too late for the Schmetterlinghaus—where I went with Lotta in 2002—so maybe will make do with the KHM (Kunst Historisches Museum) instead. I now realise it is a big mistake to go straight from the bar to the naughty places, as I am so drunk my body is completely desensitised. I must go to some cultural places first, and that gives time for feeling to return to my body. I did not enjoy WSK or Burggasse Peep Show at all on Monday because I was too drunk. In contrast, I felt real pleasure in Fortuna Kino and WSK yesterday, having sobered up in the previous two hours. A coachload of about forty Chinese women & children have just got off outside my bar window and are now filling the reception with a cacophonous racket. Please let them not stay on the 7th floor.

I think I kind of subconsciously/deliberately started later today because I would like to return to the nightbars of the Gurtel tonight, and they don't really open until 9 or 10PM. Pointless as the experience is. Even if you quite fancy a girl, 100 euros for twenty minutes (as they all uniformly seem to charge) is prohibitive, when I can f—k a beautiful girl like Amanda or Athena in WSK or Burggasse Peep Show for half the price. I bemoaned the devastation of the Gurtel since 'Gurtel-King' Steiner's arrest & imprisonment in 2010, but I actually have never had sex in a Gurtel nightbar, since that first time in Pour Platin with Maria. So they are not really that much of a loss. The girls come up to you one after the other, but for 100 euros for twenty minutes she would have to be the most stunning girl ever, and they usually are not. And you will never meet a girl better than Amanda in WSK, so why waste money in the Gurtel night bars? Still, you never know until you look. So let me check again tonight. Walking up to WSK last night most of the places were already lit up in lurid neon, even though probably not yet open—Manhattan, Okay, Bar 6, though worryingly Angelique 1 & 2 were totally dark, and they are the one place I met a really good-looking girl—Lily in Little Angelique. Don't tell me Angelique is the ONE place that has closed down since I was last here?

I didn't go to all the places I had planned yesterday, but I think it is better to not do too much, in one day, otherwise you really tire yourself out and deplete your own energy, depress yourself, give yourself some kind of Stendhal Syndrome—so I left KHM and Karl Kraus's Lothringerstraße 6 home for another day. I was very happy with what I did. If I am too late for the Butterfly House today I can do it Thursday or Friday. I am so glad I chose to stay FIVE days in Vienna this time. It has made everything more relaxed. And if I do nothing else on this trip I am happy because I saw *The Night Porter* hotel and drank in the Café Savoy next to it.

Yes, Lotta & Sophia are legends of my life, but this morning in bed I was thinking so much about the two Café du Dome barmaids—the black one and the North African blonde; both among the sexiest barmaids I have ever met. I would love to "go out" with either of them, preferably both.

Already, just beginning my third day in Vienna, this trip feels much more successful than my stay in Munich & Nuremberg. Everything feels freer here; shocked to turn on my TV at 545 this morning and find the Sport 1 channel was still showing porn clips. Children will be getting up to get ready for school now surely?! This is how Breakfast TV should ALWAYS be! A lovely invigorating start to the day. I will start early tomorrow, as I really want to get to the Butterfly House, and to see Karl Kraus's grave in the Zentralfriedhof. Still I cannot say I have seen a really sexy girl in Vienna. Quite a contrast to Brussels (and even London). No f—kable curvy big sexy arses, or beautiful big bouncy bosoms. 334 already—I doubt I will have time to go anywhere today. Let me just do Fortuna, WSK, Manhattan and the Gurtel nightbars then. Cultural things yesterday and tomorrow, just naughty things today. It is already looking dark.

Amanda was very happy when I finally came ("spritz"); she was cheering & clapping & punching her arms in the air. "Well done, schatzi! Well done!" She is a lovely girl as well as a beautiful girl. Probably the first time in nine or ten visits to WSK I managed to achieve resolution. I tried hard to resist it this time as well; I don't know why but I prefer NOT to finish in these places. Because then my night is over, and I just have to return to my hotel, deflated—literally. This time I was so close to it, I thought, oh, go on then! It made her happy anyway. Yes, cultural things yesterday, just naughty things today. I hate putting pressure on myself; don't want to be rushing anywhere. Get up early tomorrow for KHM and

Butterflies. I am still discovering new things about these four cities I keep visiting, that is the amazing thing. I only discovered the location of the *Night Porter* hotel two weeks ago! The location of Karl Kraus's houses at the same time! I have been googling them for years, with no success at all, but this time, for some reason, the answers just came straight to the top. WSK and Fortuna are discoveries of the last twelve months alone and they are now my top two places in Vienna. The same for Café du Dome, and Yellow Lily, and Alhambra Cinema in Brussels. You have to enjoy them before all these places are gone too. Is that Angelique 1 & 2 gone already? We scorn what is under our noses. Living all my life in London I have still never been to Ernest Dowson's grave in Ladywell, or Mary Kelly's grave in Leytonstone. I need to do these things. Funny thing is Vienna used to be bottom out of my four cities; now I think it has risen to No.1. They do rise and fall like this.

I feel more relaxed in Vienna than I feel in Munich & Nuremberg certainly. In Munich you pay 50 euros just for a contactless private dance; here 50 euros will buy you sex with a girl like Amanda in every position in a porn cinema. And is there any better environment to have sex in than a porn cinema? Of course not. In fact, let me go NOWHERE today that I went yesterday—so no Fortuna or WSK. Let me stay in the hotel bar drinking until late, eating here, then go to ML Revue and the night bars. Today is a rest day. Really twilight outside now. Very gloomy. So I got up in time just to drink and then have my evening meal? Ha. Yes, it seems so! This is what holidays are for! I expect a completely pointless, tiresome night trawling the last few night bars of the Gurtel. Still, they are places that have to be ticked off. So let me tick them off tonight. I think this is what my subconscious was telling me; that is why I did not get out of my room until after 2PM. My subconscious talks to me so much and I have to listen; or I learn to listen. My subconscious is never wrong. For this is truth. If you go your own way you can never go wrong. And this means going the way your subconscious is telling you to go. And only when you are single can you really have the freedom to always follow what your subconscious is telling you. Well, in Vienna you should certainly listen to what your subconscious is telling you!

Nearly 5PM. Yes, let me eat here, and I will go out afterwards, to ML Revue to start with. I hate repeating myself (as I have mentioned before). Yes, yesterday was good, so my temptation today is to do everything the same again; but that actually never works. So I am glad today I am doing THE OPPOSITE. This is the law of the pendulum. You must always do the opposite. You must always swing from one extreme to the other—this is how excitement is generated and maintained. How much nicer and more pleasurable life seems when you feel drunk, when you achieve Debord's perfect point of intoxication. I admire those drinkers like Gary Oldman or

Jimmy Greaves who gave up years ago, but I can't imagine what their lives must be like.

Really, is it just 5:18? It is pitch black outside. The Swedish girls First Aid Kit on the Dorint radio, as if to mock me with the lost Swedish duo of Lotta & Sophia. The Dorint has gone down the road of the 'artistic' meals. One slab of beef sitting on its own on a long plate, five potato wedges artistically spread around it, a couple of pieces of veg artistically around that. A man needs a proper meal, a plate full of food, like the Café Westend serves up. You think anyone will eat an artistic meal again? We order food to admire its artistry? Foolishness. Café Westend it is, from now on then. I want a f—king massive plate of meat & potatoes & veg for f—k's sake! No arty-farty piece of artistic wank. Who inspires these people?

Before I even reach the Dorint bar again I doubt I will get to the Butterfly House today either. I noticed how big my head is compared to the rest of my body when I looked in the mirror in the early hours of this morning, having got back from Tête-à-Tête and Manhattan, which is quite something considering how big my body is. I noticed the same thing today in the lift mirror on the way down to the bar just now. Four solid days of debauchery is making my head bigger, my arse so sore I can hardly sit or shit, and my foreskin stings with soreness. Still I push on! This is my courage. I never moved more than a hundred yards from the hotel yesterday. Drank a lot in the hotel bar, ate a meal which did not fill me at all, so crossed over to Café Westend for a proper filling meal. Back to room to sleep (too long) then started out to Tête-à-Tête and Manhattan. Left Manhattan at 3AM when I was the last man left in the bar (though I think there were a couple in the bedrooms getting their filthy ends away). There were a couple of really sexy girls in Tête-à-Tête (Romanian Flori and Ukrainian Natasha) but I was the only man so that awkwardness made me leave. Manhattan by contrast was loud and busy and full of life. No more than four or five men perhaps, but two of them in particular were very happy and very loud. Again, at least two very sexy girls there, plump Romanian Denitsa and another slimmer black-haired Romanian. The girls here at least make some effort to do a little stage dance (without removing anything) so at least there was something to watch and the other men at least took the girls' attention away from me, so I could have a couple of beers quite undisturbed. The jukebox was the best thing, it showed the videos as well as play the songs. The one disappointment of this trip is no music channel at all on my TV, so it was only by coming here to a brothel that I got to see my first new music of the trip! And some fantastic songs, too. Boris Bukowski Kokain, Arash Salamati, Lasercraft 3D Nein Mann. I sat there at the bar just enjoying the music videos. Until 3AM when the other men one by one drifted away and I returned to my hotel to see how big my head looked in the hotel wardrobe mirror.

I can't get over seeing the *Night Porter* hotel and drinking in the Café Savoy next to it on Tuesday. That is the thrill of this holiday and I can't be bothered to do anything else now. Maybe I will save the Butterfly House and KHM for next time—and I am sure I will want to come straight back at the first opportunity. I am enjoying this visit. Five days was definitely justified. I have discovered on this trip though that doing cultural things is a great aphrodisiac for going on to do naughty things afterwards. To drink and then deny yourself the immediate gratification of the naughty things builds up the volcano inside you and makes it all the more pleasurable when you do get to the naughty places; the longer you can deny it the sexier it is. Obviously, however, this kind of self-control is not my strong point.

Still yet to see a really sexy girl in the street, in the underground, on the trams, in the café, anywhere; the contrast with Brussels (and even London) ever more stark. Oh, for fuck's sake I still haven't been to 22 Felberstraße where Hitler lived in 1908! It is just 100 yards up the road for Christ's sake! Now a coachload of a hundred Turkish-looking men & women. The 2002 Lotta & Sophia Vienna trip is a legend of my life, and the 2005 Maria in Pour Platin trip is a legend of my life, and in time the first journey of this year when I made love with WSK Amanda and finally 'cracked the Vienna nut' will probably come to acquire that status, but I cannot remember a stay I have enjoyed more in a very relaxed and happy way than this five days in Vienna.

A wonderful piano version of No Other Lover playing loudly as I arrive in the Café Westend. My usual waiter greeted me with literally open arms "Hello again, gentleman!", and I wondered for a moment if I should actually embrace him. I think I was right not to. Finally, I saw my first sexy girl of this trip, a blonde sitting at Reumannplatz tram stop, in white coat, black leggings over meaty voluptuous thighs, smoking a cigarette, heavily made-up face; she looked a bit like a whore, and I mean that in a good way. I love heavy make-up. I think there must be a real-live pianist here, as a lot of people just clapped. He seems to have a fixation with Beatles and ex-Beatles music, now it is Yesterday.

I finally made it to the Butterfly House. Very nice to be back there; then on to the KHM. From there to Fortuna, the same two black-haired girls as last time; the one who did not speak to me last time came to me this time; a very sexy black-haired Spanish girl. I resisted the temptation. My visits to kinos are often ruined by being too drunk and insensitive; this time

335

if anything I had sobered up too much and was too sensitised and had to hold myself back. Quite a good film but it went on forever. Monique Covet. I was waiting for the next film to start (*Yacht Party 2*) but had to give up in the end. I didn't want to be too late to get to the Gurtel tonight.

I have no idea what the mad unseen pianist is playing now; I doubt whether even he does. The applause at the end is prolonged and heartfelt, and I sense tinged with relief and/or hysteria. The waiter not only greeted me with open arms but also remembered what I wanted without me saying anything. The more regular you become the quicker the service gets. The meal comes too quick. I never have time to finish even half my beer. I have noticed, however, if you eat in the same steak restaurant every day the steak will get progressively more stringy and fatty on each occasion. Really fatty today. On Monday there was no fat on it at all. The pianist has taken a much-needed pause, which is a cause of relief for many of us. I am just starting to see some not bad-looking girls here in Vienna. Another couple just passed my window of the Westend. Crikey, there was a third one. Then a fourth, and then more once I got to the station to buy my Guardian. There weren't many butterflies in the Butterfly House to be honest; perhaps just three or four I could see. Maybe it is the wrong time of year; perhaps it is more of a Caterpillar House or a Chrysalis House, but I did not see any of those either.

So my final night in Vienna. The stay has flown by; I have not felt bored for a single second. Too busy drinking or eating or sleeping or the other thing. I have done my best to ward off prostate cancer by frequent ejaculation. One must take care of one's health when one gets to my age (and size). Still the eternal mystery—where do all the men go in Berlin and Vienna? The strip pubs & clubs of London are packed with men every night. The strip clubs of Munich are packed with men every night. Yellow Lily in Brussels is packed all day long with men, young & old. So where are these horny young or old men in Vienna or Berlin? I have to say, to answer my own question a little bit, the four porn cinemas of Vienna I have been to are quite well-patronised. The ones that do not have 'hostesses' slightly more well-attended than those two that do—perhaps confirming my observation that most men who go to porn cinemas are in fact gay (even though the films are straight), so the sight of real life women around them might turn them off. One of the Japanese coach party from the other day (I misattributed them as Chinese perhaps) is sitting in the bar now in long red traditional Japanese costume; very beautiful.

So once again I went to all the Gurtel night bars and did nothing in any of them. I get so turned on in WSK and Fortuna but hardly at all in the night bars, so I think why pay if I am not really in the mood? I got perhaps the last U6 up to Josefstadter Straße and walked back from there. The Dream Bar is first; I rang the bell but there was no answer, so I pressed on to Angelique 1 & 2. The two bars are connected so girls you have rejected in the first may well reappear in the second. I was really looking for mega-busen Lily, but her friend said she is home after an operation on her teeth, though if I bought her a drink (27 euros) she would ring Lily and tell her to come in. I declined. On to Bar 6, really beautifully-decorated for Halloween. A magnificent effort. For the first time two other men (local regulars) came in for a while and one was still there when I left. I didn't bother with Okay Bar as I have never met anyone I like there, so finished in Manhattan again. I really intended to do something with Denitsa this time, or black-haired Melissa, but when push came to shove once again I didn't really feel like it, as voluptuous and sexy-looking as she (OK, both) is/are. I did buy Denitsa a drink just to give her something. Oh, and I gave one girl in Angelique a ten euro note, just because she was really sweet and gave me a big cuddle. So, back to my hotel after a relatively cheap night. I am glad I kept my money in my pocket. Earlier in Fortuna I had been so turned on I wanted to do something with the black-haired 'Spanish' girl but thought no, let me save it for the night bars later!

Manhattan is definitely the best of the night bars, though. The girls do make some effort to keep up a constant little stage dance (with nothing coming off but still), their little skirts keep riding up to show off their bottoms which is at least something pleasant to look at. The other bars don't even offer this—why would they? They have NO customers. The Manhattan is the only place where I see two or three or four other men so at least there is some atmosphere in the room, and some attention is distracted from me. I like to be ignored. I don't know if this is perverse or not, but I am quite happy to be ignored, until I am ready to make my choice, and wag my crooked horny little finger. Manhattan is the closest bar to Westbahnhof, which I guess is why it attracts some customers at least. I doubt whether any casual visitor to Vienna will venture any further up the horribly bleak Gurtel as far as Okay, or Bar 6, or Angelique. And Tête-à-Tête is close but hidden in a side street. Manhattan is always the only place I see other customers. Strange to say when there in a brothel I really want to see other men, but it truly makes a world of difference.

I expect nothing from WSK, because I will be going there straight from drinking, so my private parts will all be cold and completely numb, like under local anaesthetic. Fortuna yesterday and Fortuna & WSK on

Tuesday were fantastic as I went there after some hours of walking around sightseeing. So will I come back again in November? It is a long way to come (ahem) just for two good porn kinos; but I feel so happy in a good porn kino; there is nothing better, and with hostesses on hand (ahem) as well. Yesterday in Fortuna Kino was as happy as I've felt in a kino for years; this is why I come to Vienna. The Viennese tourist board should promote these places. And I still want to visit Karl Kraus's grave in Zentralfriedhof, and his house in Lothringerstraße 6. If I go back to Brussels it will be more than anything for the two sexy Café du Dome barmaids, even more than Yellow Lily or Rue des Commerçants or Alhambra Cinema. In Berlin I would like to go to King George and Caligula again, and see if there is any life left at all in the corpse of Stuttgarter Platz, Sissi, Monte Carlo and 77. Still the charm of really low-rent sex persists. Fat, out of shape girls, in really stylish surroundings and cheap prices still retains its carnal thrill.

I have now drunk so much I am pickled. Little point going to the WSK, as I will feel nothing. Prostitutes always react in surprise when I say I DON'T want to be sucked, as I can feel nothing. If I had my eyes shut I would not even know she was doing it. I am going to drink myself to the point of imbecility (a short journey it is true, thank you my love) and then begin my long journey home. Welcome to my life. Eternal Flame on the hotel radio. This is who I am. Culture means high culture. Yes, your Beethoven 5th Symphony, yes your Michelangelo Sistine Chapel ceiling, yes your Mona Lisa, etc etc etc, but the Bangles Eternal Flame is an example of 'low culture' that stands up there with them. And yes, I find myself overwhelmed by the opulent sensuousness of the oil paintings of the KHM, only to then find myself overwhelmed by the porn films on the screen of the Fortuna. One is no different from the other. What really moves us is on the same exalted level (as far as this English gentleman is concerned). And an eye contact and smile with a beautiful girl in the street is above them all.

I want to drink until the point I want to f—k every woman I see. This is when the Beer Goggles have arrived—now I can go to the prostitutes. Now when I am so numb I cannot feel anything when I am with them. I am too drunk to go to WSK now—but I would like to see Amanda before I go home. Amanda has become the face of Vienna for me. A face of derision and annoyance at my drunkenness, but oh, a lovely face. One day I will be famous and the people I have mentioned in my journals will become famous too, and people will want to track down the Amandas, et al, and ask them what was — (me) like? 3.38 still in the Dorint bar. Well, I think my subconscious is telling me I don't WANT to go to WSK even for an hour. I'm at that point where I can't read my own handwriting even immediately after writing it. "I've fallen for you, whatever you do — that I never knew."

338

"Whatever it takes —". I love my ex-wife, as most people do, when they get this drunk. "Whatever you need, you've got it from me." Haha I know she will appreciate this. "Lay your heart on the table —". I can go to Vienna, Berlin, Munich, Brussels, but — never leaves me; she is always with me in every second. I never stop thinking about her; and that is why I will always do anything for her. She is still in my blood, and if you cut me open you will find her. We only get a very short life in this universe, and I am glad I met — and her son in this short life. Amazing good fortune for me.

Wow, my subconscious is dominant. I know my subconscious was always telling me stay in the hotel until 6PM.

It is incredible (I can hardly see my pen but let me try) but the Dorint Hotel is one of my favourite places on Earth. Along with the Berlin Plaza (or Kanthotel) in Berlin. Real deep feelings.

"It's taken me all of my life to find you."

*

The rubbishness of London also prompting me to return to Vienna soon as possible.

When I am at home I just feel I am wasting my time. Better to be at work earning money; and how much more exciting to spend this time in a Vienna hotel room wanking while drinking bottles of beer before heading out to two great porn cinemas, and finishing night in night bar. My life will be very hard when I retire because of this profligacy now but you have to live to the maximum while you are young and healthy. Being at home seems so pointless—EXCEPT FINISH *COLD ICY AIR OF THE MOUNTAINS*.

So was my 3½ year marriage a mistake? Like the academic when asked if the French Revolution was a good thing or a bad thing, "it is too soon to tell". For me it has totally changed my mindset for the better. Before I married I was miserable and depressed, and then I became depressed and miserable. A complete turnaround! Haha! No, since we came back together on Twelfth Night 2010, I have never known a moment of depression. It was cured, and I think has gone forever. The memories of the 3½ years always make me happy, and are like a well I can always draw on. She without a doubt is the best thing that has ever happened to me. It was like a chrysalis stage I had to go through, a metamorphosis. I went in a caterpillar and flew away a butterfly.

*

339

So back in Vienna already. What fresh madness is this? Not feeling anything yet. Totally sober. Not even a minibar in my room this time. 26 hours without sleep and I am sober, and it is a Sunday evening. All conspire to uninspire. Well, my first (free) Zipfer is at least lovely and cold. The intervening nine days since I last was here was in fact a pretty incredible time. Dramatic developments in both work & personal spheres; my broken phone even magically started working last night on my way to work, after months of deadness. On the eve of my flight to Vienna, a miracle. An incredible omen, I thought—and good omens I distrust. A good omen usually leads to a bad trip. Yet the incredible events continued for the rest of the evening. This is November for you. The month of wonders. Well, the month of my birth—need one say more?

What incredibly beautiful girls work in all those little shops in airports. Real black-haired red-lipped Sirens, Circes. They look like slightly better-dressed whores, and I mean that as a compliment. So sexual. So painted. So alluring. The Aspinals girl the absolute pick of them. And your fellow passengers! Travelling is so sexy.

Any plans for this trip to Vienna? Karl Kraus's grave in Zentralfriedhof and the site of Milena's apartment in *Bad Timing*. That is it really. Last night I did nothing but head up to WSK. Just Amanda on 'duty'. I fell asleep, and she had to wake me up to tell me the kino was closing now. Glad I resisted temptation to go into Angelique or Manhattan, instead came straight back on 11PM U6 to Westbahnhof and a McDonald's before bed. A cheap first night in Vienna. And a kind of depressing one as first nights usually are.

Ah, amazing—the No.6 tram from here at Westbahnhof goes all the way to the Zentralfriedhof! The same tram I get to Fortuna. Perfect. Zentralfriedhof it is then. The Zentralfriedhof (Central Cemetery) is so big it seems to have its own tram line (106) to take you around it. It has Jewish sections, Muslim sections; it is the site of the last scene from *The Third Man*. God knows how many famous graves are here that I would love to visit—I will concentrate on Karl Kraus's for now. Hitler's beloved niece Geli Raubal is here somewhere though the location of her grave is lost. The Viennese have a joke about the place apparently. 'The Zentralfriedhof contains two million souls—more than the entire living population of Zurich, and considerably more lively.' Austrian humour. Mind you, it closes at 5, which means leaving my hotel in daylight, something I am always reluctant to do. How I love winter, when the clocks go back, and it is pitch dark by 5PM. I feel so much more comfortable in the dark. Always feel exposed in the daylight.

A good bar is like an auction room, you just have to give the slightest little nod, a rise of an eyebrow, or touch on a cap, to indicate you want another beer. This Chinese-looking barmaid is so cute. A frail-looking thing, but I would enjoy the experience. Even if she wouldn't. How perfect—one tram (the No.6) all the way from Westbahnhof to Zentralfriedhof, and the same tram all the way back (half-way) to Fortuna Kino. Sex and Death, the twin themes of Vienna. Sex & Death in the City of Dreams. I never forget how magical it is to—be in Vienna.

I was only in London for just over a week between the two Vienna visits, but so much seemed to happen in those few days. A lot of developments. All of them may come to nothing once we get to December, but they were dramatic nevertheless. Life is always full of twists & turns. That is why I feel so sorry when you hear about these young people, children at school, who kill themselves in despair—I want to say to them just hang on you fools! Things can change in a moment! Just hang on and around the next corner your life may completely change! Despair is a rich black resource, like a mother chewing on her own placenta. Feed on despair. Let it fill you up with strength & power for when the moment is right, for you to rise again. For you to bloom, and to blossom. For you to rise above your would-be tormentors and let them wither in your shadow. Despair is the greatest resource any human being can ever feed on, and you need to feed on it and gorge yourself on it. It is the fertiliser that will grow your blooms. It gives you all the strength you need, to come again. This perhaps is another theme for my journals—not just impermanence, temporality, good things have to be enjoyed quickly because they will not last long—but the glory of despair. The rich resource that despair is. From despair you can draw all your power, your nutrients, your munitions. Ready to come again. Every time I read some schoolchild has killed himself because he was bullied at school, I think, oh, you didn't realise! How you can use that temporary despair to absolutely fill you with power! The power to totally destroy your pathetic opponents!

I have never met anyone in my life as great as me; except one. That is why I still wear the ring. It is homage to another great person. I do consider myself & my ex-wife as one person. I think I really do. Me and her really are one person. I searched for any woman as great as her—but they all fell short in some way. She is the legend of my life; I revere her; I look up to her. She is an incredible person. She came into the world on Epiphany, January 6, 19—, and she is my Epiphany. And so funny—funny? Destined—she should have come back into my life on Epiphany (just after midnight of Twelfth Night), 2010. The gods do play tricks on us; the gods do pull all our strings; I do believe that. If you keep plugging away; keep trying to achieve what you want, the gods will reward you when they are ready. So many extraordinary twists & turns occur in our lives, it is hard not to believe they are orchestrated by some gods.

So even Milena's apartment can be reached from Westbahnhof—U6 to Niederhofstraße. Tram No.6 to Zentralfriedhof and U6 to Milena. Westbahnhof really is the centre of Vienna, even if the map suggests otherwise. The new 'so-called' Vienna Central Railway Station is a piece of —. It is in the middle of precisely nowhere. Centre of Nowhere Station they should call it—Berlin Hauptbahnhof the same. I have never been to Vienna's CENTRAL railway station and doubt I will ever have cause to. It looks like a petrol garage. Austerity we all have to respect, but for God's sake you could do more with a Central Railway Station than this? Berlin Hauptbahnhof at least has a certain architectural glory, despite being in the middle of nowhere. Vienna's new Hauptbahnhof is in the middle of nowhere but has no architectural merit whatsoever. That is why they call them Central? Because they are in the middle of nowhere. For me, Berlin Zoo is always the centre of Berlin. Westbahnhof is always the centre of Vienna. Lesson to first-time visitors to Europe: Berlin Central Railway Station is in the middle of nowhere. Vienna Central Railway Station is in the middle of nowhere.

And I can say — really is the centre of my life. Even if she seems to be off to the side. When they come to write the biography of my life, and BBC *Arena* come to make the TV documentary, the centre of my life will always have to be —. She is the writing through my Blackpool Rock. I think, genuinely, I am the greatest human being on the planet; except one. I give homage to only one person on this Earth, and that is my ex-wife. She is the only person greater than me. I just hope she doesn't abuse the position; haha and she does! I want that *Arena* documentary. I want my greatness to be recognised. And I want (in my penumbra) my wife's greatness to be recognised. She deserves her own *Arena* documentary in her own right, and in that I necessarily will be in her penumbra (if mentioned at all haha). A real-life Sally Bowles. A modern Jean Ross. Just to mention, for a lot of these three hours I have had tears slowly falling down my face. Yet, I feel quite happy. If I am too late for Zentralfriedhof (5PM) then I can go to Milena instead. I have three days after all.

I got to the Zentralfriedhof too late! 430 already closed (the place looked dead), and then SEVEN No.6 trams went the other way before one came back my way. Seven! Unbelievable. Fortuna film was rubbish. Then got back to my room to find internet still not working since 11 this morning. This is proving to be a disappointing visit so far. Never repeat yourself! No minibar in my room (there is a fridge) but it doesn't matter because there is basically no internet either, except for a random 5 minutes here & there (& no music channel on TV), so I do not stay long in my room except to sleep. I got to the Zentralfriedhof too late yesterday and I cannot be bothered to go again as it is too far. By the time I got to WSK it was almost empty; no girls. Dropped in to Angelique (no Lily), Okay Bar (really beautiful tall African girl with most incredible face; I was sure she must be of some mixed race, but she insists both her parents were African, too), Manhattan. Stayed a long while in Manhattan just enjoying the music videos on the jukebox. I was tempted by Denitsa, Irina and new Bulgarian blonde Nelly, but the more beer I drank the less I felt like it.

 I was so happy in Manhattan last night, sitting at the bar all alone, pretty much undisturbed by the girls as they already know from before I don't do anything, just enjoying the fantastic music videos on the jukebox. The Game Hate It or Love It (how long since I've heard that), T.I. Dead & Gone, Müslüm Süpervitamin. Rainhard Fendrich I Am From Austria (with the whole bar full of Romanian girls singing along at the tops of their voices to the chorus "I am from AUS-TRIA!" A sweet moment). Das Haus von Luci Lied für meine Feinde. Rihanna Man Down. There were four or five other men there the whole time I was there; a couple would leave but another couple would come in at the same time. I actually saw a couple of customers emerging from the rooms in Angelique, and the Okay Bar as well. Ten to 4 already. I didn't wake up until quarter to 2. In Angelique and Okay, as the girls came up one after the other to introduce themselves, I couldn't help noticing their eyes all went straight to my stomach, and they couldn't seem to stop looking at it. It's not that big. I might just go over to the station today, and get some food to bring back, and go straight up to Wahringer Kino and WSK and Burggasse later. Save Milena's apartment for tomorrow. Hungry.

 I drink enough to make me starving hungry, so I can go and stuff my face with food; that out of the way, I can then spend the rest of the night slumped lifelessly in some porn cinema or night bar. Welcome to my life. *La Grande Bouffe* increasingly comes to seem like the key film of my life, even more than *Bad Timing*, or *The Night Porter*, or any of the others. Fellini's *8½* once upon a time seemed like the film of my life. Then it was *Pierrot le Fou*. Then *Last Tango in Paris*, etc, etc. Now, as I get older, and more corpulent, it is *La Grande Bouffe*. Drink yourself stupid, eat until you're stuffed, and then try but fail to make love with a voluptuous big-breasted woman like Andrea Ferréol.

 Irina in Manhattan Bar is a giant St Petersburg blonde, beautiful girl, almost 6ft tall, hourglass figure, but the most massive bottom & thighs you have ever seen in your life. Like something out of a Fellini movie; and crazy; doesn't stop laughing insanely. Melissa is a black-haired Romanian of more dour, watchful countenance, but has very beautiful bosoms, though quite tiny bottom. They are the best two Manhattan girls I think, but it's like when a new film comes out and you watch all the trailers of it and then you feel you've seen the film, so can't be bothered anymore. I've spent so long sitting in this bar, looking at these girls, I feel I have got to know them too well now, and cannot be bothered to do anything with them. I just feel a complete sense of over-familiarity now, without having done anything with any of them.

All these years I have been coming to Vienna and I thought I cannot go to the famous Cafés, the "Coffeehouses", because I do not drink coffee; or tea. So that would rule me out of being able to go to the coffeehouses. Only this year have I discovered that the cafés of Vienna also serve beer and are in fact basically bars. They are the Vienna equivalent of London pubs; in London there is a pub on every corner, in Vienna there is a café on every corner—but you can get drunk in them just the same.

Yes, the coffeehouses are a tradition of Vienna; but another less-publicised Viennese pleasure is the adult cinemas with girls waiting there to service the men in their seats. They have sex kinos in Berlin, but they are such tiny little places, with a little TV-sized screen on the wall. Vienna has proper CINEMAS—like WSK and Fortuna—where you can choose your comfortable seat, but also has the girls. Economising this time, I have stayed away from the Café Westend and its gorgeous Rostbratens (with beer & tip, that is 25 euros a time). Instead making do with a couple of rolls from the station and a foot-long Subway. A much cheaper alternative. The internet in my room actually was working fine yesterday, as well, all day, all night, and all morning until about 11AM when it disappeared again.

Every time I come to Vienna I think yes, I am going to get tanked up on beer, and really turned on, and go to the night bars and f—k all the good-looking girls, one after the other. The reality is my caution, and reticence, and conservatism, and reluctance to spend money, and sheer f—king physical torpor, never leave me, and I drink one beer after another until I am completely sozzled, then waddle off back to my hotel. Apparently, I enjoy drinking more than sex. But once I get back home my pornographic fantasies overwhelm me, and I think oh I wish I had f—ked that massive Russian blonde Irina, and that sexy Romanian black-haired Melissa, and then want to come straight back to f—k them; but then I come back, and still politely say no to them. Too lazy to even f—k, basically; you can put that on my tombstone. Yet you know when you're on a bus, or a train, or in a bar, and you see a sexy girl you so much want to f—k her; but sitting in a brothel languidly looking at all the girls for hour after hour, I can't be bothered.

The Dorint radio has given way to the sound of waves, washing up on a beach. For five minutes now. It sounds like my ejaculate. Wave after wave of English c-m. But, still, quite strange to hear it in a bar. Er, how long are the waves going to last? This is what they call 'ambient'? Yes, so is my ejaculate. The waves are getting harder, and stronger, and more frequent. Yes, this is how my ejaculate comes as well. Plans for my last day/night? Milena's apartment (finally), Fortuna Kino, WSK, Angelique to look for Lily. Back to hotel. Finally, the waves have merged into some kind of Peruvian flute music. And no, that is not a euphemism. Zipfer 1858. In contrast to Fosters, famously, 1888—the year of the events. Oh Christ, I am drinking so much these days and I still don't feel drunk. I think I am becoming immune to its charms. Like I go to the night bars these days and find myself completely immune to the charms of the floozies—however big their bosoms or their buttocks. Anaesthetised to everything. I hate going out of my hotel when it's still daylight outside.

Well, I think now, I have conclusively proved I have no interest in the porn kinos of Vienna, or the porn kino women of Vienna; I much more prefer to drink myself to oblivion and then pass out. The situation in London this time has overshadowed everything. I think, ultimately, I didn't want to sleep with WSK Amanda again; and I didn't want to sleep with any of the Fortuna Kino girls again; my subconscious never lies, and it rules me. Once again I submit. Well, what have you got planned for me, subconscious? What is it later on you are planning for me? You bring me to Vienna and then force me to do nothing in Vienna, until I get back home. I'm quite aware now that I am too drunk to have any sexual experience with anyone (or anything). Why? Why my subconscious has ordained this? Well, perhaps, it has plans for me back at home?

So they really did it. The fools. They knocked down Milena's *Bad Timing* apartment block at Schönbrunner Schloßstraße. You would have thought some Austrian Film Institute or government culture department would have protected it for its place in film history. Why don't you knock down the Sistine Chapel while you're at it? 213AM in the morning; I lie in my hotel room bed with classical music on the radio. I did nothing today except drink a prodigious amount in the hotel bar, find my way to Milena's apartment, come back and stuff my face with food, then sleep for the rest of the evening. No desire to go out again. A low-key trip this time. I never really got the feeling that I actually wanted to be here. Anyway, I was pleased to have stood in the spot where Milena's apartment used to be; and at least turn and look around at all the same buildings she (Theresa Russell) would have seen, at least.

*

Looking back at my first three books I see now I was always depressed, in pain, cut up, feeling completely skinless and naked; things only start to change when I start drinking a lot near the beginning of the third book, and commence a series of three visits to Brussels and three visits to Munich and three visits to Berlin. After that I start to have pleasurable, thrilling, dramatic experiences, I open up like a flower, and start to bloom and blossom and flourish. I have broken hearts and tears and rages, but I am starting to have real experiences; I am really starting to grow, and it was allowing drink into my life that was the catalyst and the fuel for that. It was the combustion engine. If the pressure society put me under was the Bessemer Furnace that produced my writing, then alcohol was the combustion engine that got me moving and going places and doing things, which started to banish depression behind me like shedding a black cloak.

I find it interesting to look back and analyse my own books (of course I do! I love myself. I am completely self obsessed and inward looking), as if reading the books of someone else, and working out what kind of person was he, and how did he change over the years he writes about? The excruciating pain that lacerated my soul screams out of *Autismus, Lotta*, and the start of *The Cold Icy Air of the Mountains*. It is only when I start drinking more, and through that find the courage to start doing more naughty, sexual things on my travels in Europe, that the pain starts to be replaced by pleasure, and the incredible large-bosomed floozies of Berlin and Munich, and I start to come into myself. By the end of the third book and start of the fourth I am actually tired and wearied of all this pleasure and want something more real and substantial! The fifth will see me finally, after a long struggle (a 3-year struggle when I wrote not a word), having this something real, but after a year of marriage to a woman deeply loved, perhaps starting to regret this longing, and thinking perhaps be careful what you wish for! And indeed trying to wriggle my way back to the pleasure without substance of the previous few years. The sixth book I think will see me completely free once more and living a life of mindless pleasure once more, and that is where I am really up to now.

As I always say, it is the strip clubs and the brothels that taught me how to live. First in Soho in London, then Munich Schillerstraße and Berlin Stuttgarter Platz. In Vienna I never actually did very much; from 1999 to 2013 I only ever had sex with one lady of the night; it was only in the first

346

months of this year that Vienna started to come to life for me, with the discoveries of the Fortuna and WSK kinos.

It is so strange when a building is knocked down and completely razed to the ground, and you look at the empty space and think of all the memories that took place in the building that used to stand there, the loves, the sex, the grief, the laughter, the FILMING! Some psychic charge seems left behind, but it is only in your head I suppose. It is very disconcerting. In Vienna I feel it when I look at the empty lot where Milena's *Bad Timing* apartment used to be, when I look at the hole in the Gurtel like a missing tooth where Pour Platin used to be, HQ of the whole red light district where I lost my Vienna virginity to the stunningly beautiful Maria. In London going up Windmill Street past the models' flats opposite the old Red Lion where Marx and Engels attended the first Communist League meeting in London, the flat where I used to see Ana Maria, now a ghastly new hotel and square.

Haha when I suddenly bizarrely feel forces all moving and gathering against me in the shadows is when I come to life and feel most excited. Take me on if you can! I will play you all like a piano. I will defeat you again. Let your moths bash their tiny brains out against my blazing lighthouse. Let us see when they are going to show themselves, and expose themselves. I am actually so excited now. I feel excited for the battle to come. The soldier's minute.

*

All that seemed to be resolving itself is once more occluded in doubt and confusion, and we seem to be back at square one—or worse. This seems to have given me back the nihilism I need to take pleasure in anything.

So here I am sitting in the first floor Max Hotel lounge, drinking cans of Stella. I am so happy to be sitting here in Brussels, drinking my cans of Stella, looking forward to going along the road to drink glasses of Stella in the Dome, then maybe go down to the Alhambra Cinema for a little while, then walk along the Rue des Commerçants and its naughty street-girls to the lovely Yellow Lily and drink some more surrounded by voluptuous floozies. My debts are rising & rising & rising. But like I always say you can't take it with you. You can't use your credit cards when you're dead so might as well enjoy them while you're alive, and young, and still relatively healthy. And single. I feel more at home in Brussels, and Vienna, and Berlin, and Munich, than I have ever felt back in London. This is why I keep travelling, keep coming back, because this is where home is. Stella Artois, from Leuven, anno 1366—bloody hell. 1366! 16.24. Nearly time to—leave the hotel.

So I return to the Dome bar. Without having to say a word the blonde North African (having not seen me for three months) says to me "Stella?" Yes. And instantly readies my nuts for me. My PEAnuts, oh, you disgusting perverts. It is an incredible fact, but I do not know one single barmaid in London as beautiful as her—and I go in a lot of pubs (searching for some girl like this). I have not seen any beauties in the street yet, but—it is winter. Everyone is swaddled in their coats & their scarves. There are other compensations; it gets dark by 4 or 5 o'clock, and this counts for a lot. Just as I was stepping into the bar—the bus turning the corner? 368; to Leuven. Ah, dead on 1700 the black (darker-skinned) girl arrives in her coat to start her shift. A grin & a "bonjour" to me as she comes through the door. These two barmaids, ladies & gentlemen of the jury, are the best thing in Brussels.

I'm trying to think now—any films I love set in Brussels? Hitler spent much time in Brussels? Honestly, these two girls in the Café du Dome are a new Lotta & Sophia. Always the same pattern in Brussels—some cans in the Max lounge, some more (a lot more) glasses in the Café du Dome, down to Alhambra Cinema, along the Rue des Commerçants to Yellow Lily. And it is the rituals that I am addicted to. They are the comfort blanket.

I just had two in the Dome, then walked straight to Yellow Lily as it was already getting quite late. Today I have started earlier, 12.25, so have plenty of time to check out the Alhambra Cinema before Yellow. Woke in the middle of the night with appalling indigestion, got through my last seven or eight Rennies, then lay dozing until about 4 when I had to go to the lavatory to throw up the burger & chips I had before bed. Maybe I drank more than I thought—three cans of Stella in the Hotel Max, two large Stellas in the Dome, then God knows how many small Maes in Yellow, maybe five, maybe more. The one great beauty of Yellow Lily is the busty Romanian who is always there, and normally helps out behind the bar as well, Andrea, and I am glad I finally made her acquaintance (went to the bedroom with her & fucked her like an animal). I did not realise how little English she speaks; she had to ask another girl to ask me if I wanted to go to the room. Yes, yes I did, very much.

A very gloomy, overcast, drizzly day today; though I have probably missed most of the rain. It might have been raining when I got back last night, I cannot remember—I was on a high & in a daze from what I had just done with Andrea, I know that. Just my first day back in Brussels felt so much more enjoyable than the last four I just spent in Vienna. I had other things on my mind then, and that ruined it. I have returned to a more clear, nihilistic frame of mind. Whatever else happens or doesn't happen the fact I finally broke the ice with Andrea in Yellow Lily makes this a great trip to Alhambra. The pendulum has been kept swinging very successfully this time. The amazing thing about that four days in Vienna was I only spent £23 on pornography & prostitution! And that supposedly is the main thing I travel for. My ex-wife being nice to me the night before I travelled completely ruined it. Yesterday's visit to Yellow Lily was so enjoyable I cannot wait to get back again; this time preceded by Alhambra Cinema.

The old California peep show & videokabins still stands miserably closed-up and empty. Better if Brussels council let it stay open; it had at least brought some life and colour and vitality to that end of Boulevard Adolphe Max. The shell of the ABC Cinema next to it similarly depressing. Why I didn't enjoy these places more often when they were still open? I think that is what is propelling me to travel so regularly now; an awareness of how soon all the other great places might be gone, too. The closure of Madame Jojo's in Soho a couple of days ago a shocking confirmation of that.

I took some photos of myself in front of the bathroom mirror this morning. I was shocked how sexy I looked. If only I could lose this blasted belly I would look like some Greek statue. Priapic.

I left Yellow Lily without doing anything; but that place is ridiculous. There were at least seven girls who I would like to have gone with. Instead, I come back to Brussels Grill—not the Rogier Brussels Grill. That is the busiest restaurant I have ever been to; you are not allowed to choose your seat, you basically are slotted in where they tell you. Instead, I walk a bit further and come to the Brouckère Brussels Grill—quieter, and smaller, and always empty. So peaceful. My God, Yellow Lily. So many incredible girls. I miss Mon Cheri and Golden Gate in Berlin, and Pour Platin in Vienna, but Yellow Lily is better than all of them put together to be honest. Alhambra Cinema was busier than I've ever known it. Maybe ten gentlemen in the downstairs kino, another five or so upstairs, three more hanging around the lavatories. Two fantastic films, and a pervert sat next to me and was wanking me; first time for a long, long time that has happened. I left him downstairs, but he followed me upstairs and carried on. What can you do?

A little bit of light rain this Thursday morning it seems, judging by the brollies, but the ground still looks dry. After Brussels Grill I tried to return to Café du Dome but found the doors already locked—at 706PM! The girl could be seen cashing up at the till. I turned and headed straight back to Yellow Lily. I had just come from Alhambra Cinema where I found to my surprise I still had feeling in my nether regions so that encouraged me to return to Yellow. However, about 50 yards before I got there I just turned around and came back to the hotel. My brain and eyes were so flat and tired, and my stomach was already funny. Lucky I did because as I approached my hotel room door, key in hand, I suddenly felt like there was an explosive device in my bottom. I made it just in time. My instincts are never wrong.

The street girls are a disappointment this time; all swaddled in their thick winter coats and fully-covered it is hard to see anything you might fancy anyway. I slept from 730PM until just after midnight, then could not get back to sleep. I just wanted to go out again, back to Alhambra Cinema and Yellow Lily. I forced myself to lie down just after 4 and then slept until after midday—ruining my plans of going down to the *Brussels on German Time* exhibition in the Grand Place and then having an Irish Breakfast in O'Reilly's. There are now black bags under the black bags under my eyes. It is no wonder the Rogier Brussels Grill is always absolutely packed out, surrounded as it is by massive hotels—Sheraton, Thon, Hilton, Crowne Plaza. The De Brouckère Brussels Grill in contrast is always three-quarters empty. A real pleasure. The staff I would say are a little more surly; they probably don't make much in tips. I can't even imagine how much the Rogier waiters & waitresses make in tips—it must be quite astronomical.

I think I will go straight to Yellow Lily today and go to Alhambra Cinema later—there was one girl in particular who caught my eye yesterday, a long dark-blonde-haired slim girl who reminded me of Milena in *Bad Timing*, but she left with an older girl by 445 already! The early bird gets the worm in this place—anyway, Andrea was there, getting up with a big grin as I came in to hug & kiss me, before walking back to her chair, and very warm and friendly, joking to everyone in English "My love! My love!" so it would have been difficult for me to go to the room with anyone else. I would very much like to go with Andrea again as well. It is good that I am still excited and full of anticipation here in Brussels. I have enjoyed this visit to Brussels again, and just cannot wait to get back again. I don't need to look in a mirror—I can FEEL the bags under my eyes.

I have exhausted the shop's supply of Stella and am now on the Jupilers. The *1914-18 Brussels on German Time* exhibition will have to wait for next time (it runs until May), and I will have to go back to the Old Masters Museum too. For some reason I don't feel any desire to return to the Fin-de-Siècle Museum. In retrospect, I liked it less than the old Museum of Modern Art, even though it contains pretty much exactly the same pictures & sculptures. The layout at the old museum seemed far more intense—in one spot I could see Alfred Stevens's Salome, Trésors de Satan, Figure Tombale AND the Génie du Mal (the Génie not even in the new museum?) and there is no spot like that in the new place. I will give it another try to see if my first impressions were wrong. Three days in Brussels is not enough for me now—I could easily stay for five or six days at a time. It is like sinking into a warm bath on a cold day.

I spent my sleepless night in the company of another one of those wonderful (awful) Jean Rollin vampire films, *The Shiver of the Vampires*. In fact, it is one I have seen at least twice before—all see-through nighties and castles and coffins. Followed by another Rollin, *La Morte Vivante*, and on the other side some strange period piece where the girl from the painting on the wall keeps coming down and making love to the young man in the bed. Am I strange in that I never feel 'lonely'? I am just excited to get back to the Alhambra Cinema and Yellow Lily, and the Café du Dome to drink. This is the life I love. I want for nothing else. I used to. I used to crave something real, but I have been through that phase and am once more in clear waters. Complete nihilism. Complete Priapism.

*

I feel like the baby pterodactyl has now broken out of the egg in Brussels; I released the fly from the Brussels amber; the butterfly has emerged from the Brussels chrysalis and flown free in its iridescent glory; all because I broke the ice with Andrea. And when I say "broke the ice", madames et monsieurs, you know very well what I mean. Brussels truly now can bloom and blossom and become a lush green paradise.

I put my books on Amazon like putting them in a bank vault, and sealing them in a time capsule. No one is interested in them now, of course not, but when I am dead, and people start to dig around and wonder who was this strange man, they are all there on Amazon waiting for them, and they will be discovered. Hopefully by then, many many years from now, it will be quite a sizeable and unique body of work. It seems to have little value now, some man going to strip clubs and brothels and night bars, amongst other places, and writing about it, but decades from now, perhaps when prostitution and stripping and pornography and masturbation have long since been banned, my books will be unearthed and dusted off, the cobwebs swept away, and it will be an incredible record of a world long since disappeared, like Charlton Heston discovered the head of the Statue of Liberty sticking out of the beach. Van Gogh only ever sold one painting in his lifetime? Kafka never published a single book in his lifetime? In his last year of life Fitzgerald sold just 7 copies of *The Great Gatsby* and thought himself a failure. I am patient. I can play the long game, long after I am dead if necessary. I want my time on this earth to be recorded in minute detail, every day of it. I want those who betrayed me to be ignored, and those who stood by me to be recorded. Only those who never let my trust down deserve to be remembered. No one remembers the names of the people who spat at Oscar Wilde in the street, but we always remember him, and remember the names of those who helped him.

What a strange life I lead. My jealous hate-filled enemies fill me with power and pleasure, the people who try to love me crush me and suffocate me. Yes, I want to live in this coldness, this bleakness. This fog. This muffled swaddled silence. To go through a whole day without speaking to anyone, and then do it again the next day. Just quietly live my life alone with my books. The cold icy air of the mountains. The cold crashing waves of a bleak North Sea coast. This freshness. This fresh air filling your lungs, those deep gulps of cold icy air filling you with power and excitement.

Only words written in extreme loneliness or when travelling mean anything. Only songs I hear when travelling or see a stripper dancing to mean anything. Travel imprints things on me like a rubber stamp, or a branding iron. A great stripper does the same thing. Intense loneliness does as well because then I am writing in blood. It is pure truth, from the edge of the precipice.

Now I am starting to feel like these really are the Hairy Nights. The old winter solstice German nights, with the night of the Wild Hunt right in the middle of them. I am feeling pagan juices flowing again. Everything I dismissed in London as boring suddenly starts to glow with erotic possibility again.

      Thinking of a Hairy Night trip to Vienna again. A pagan torches flaming wild hunt to Europe once more. The Hairy Nights. When I think about it, that time I went with Andrea was the only time I have been to Brussels without drinking at St Pancras first. And the only time I got to Yellow Lily full of life. Drinking at St Pancras before Eurostar means I am already down by the time I arrive and as I know it is impossible to ever really get up and sparking again after that. I want to fuck all those Yellow Lily girls now, God just to be with them naked! Big girl! Black hair

Romanian. Want to fuck all those Manhattan girls now! Just to lie naked with them, enjoy that naked abandon, soft touches, soft breasts.

COLLECTED WORKS

COLLECTED WORKS

COLLECTED WORKS

A WINTER'S TALE

2015

ERNST GRAF

COLLECTED WORKS

HOW EASY IT IS TO TAKE FOR GRANTED: I AM NO LONGER SAD ANYMORE. All my life I felt so sad until I moved in with my wife.

What did my wife do for me? She banished sadness from my life. Like the cold, permanent sadness gets into your bones, into your marrow, into your soul. A little bit of love will not remove it; it has to be constant, intense love that does not give up and is not deterred and that my wife gave me. I may at times have felt frustrated, shackled, in physical danger, but I never again felt sad. And even now we do not live together anymore I never feel sad; indeed I feel happier now than I did when we were together. Now I love her without resentment. I love her without somehow subconsciously feeling shackled and prevented from "Living! Living the glorious life that is in me!" I love her because she removed the sadness from my life and I shall always worship her for that, whether from near or far.

Sadness was like a permafrost in my life that prevented anything from growing. When she came into my life with her amazing love and amazing beauty, she thawed the permafrost, and enabled shoots to start to grow. Only when we split up though did I feel I was finally able to bloom and blossom. And in that blooming and blossoming I just love her even more, as I know I could not have done it without her loving me, and then without her letting me go. You have to let things go to let them grow.

I had a dream the other night, a very sexy dream; I was in Vienna, and I asked a woman a question and she started singing You Give A Little Love (from *Bugsy Malone*). I asked her "Why Vienna?", and she started singing that.

I absolutely link money with Eros. Money means I can travel to Europe, and sleep with beautiful busty Esmeraldas. Even a single pound coin buys me a naked strip from a girl in London. This is why I follow the financial pages so avidly. This is why I visit the Bourses in every city I visit and worship at them as Temples of Eros.

Of course I will come to a bad end; I expect nothing else. If I am on my own. Being with my wife kept me on the straight and narrow. Very narrow.

If I don't travel anymore I don't know what else is left. I might as well just lay down and ready myself for my coffin. And yet every time I go away my debt just mounts up more and more, but I feel compelled to keep travelling, and keep getting deeper and deeper into debt and this debt really destroys all the excitement of my travel as soon as I set off from my front door, like a heavy sack on my shoulders which gets heavier and heavier as the rain falls on it. This debt is a dead weight robbing all my travels of the excitement and eroticism that I once knew.

The alternative is to stay in London for the rest of my life and never do anything.

When I am with someone I yearn to be free. When free I miss their love so much. When in London I yearn to travel. When I travel I yearn to be back home. As soon as I get home I yearn to rush back to the place I just came from. This is the pendulum of my life. I am a pendulum. I always want the opposite of what I have. Always dissatisfied. Perhaps everyone is like this, dissatisfaction is the only thing that gives any movement to our life.

The only writing I like is really stream of consciousness, sitting in a bar with a beer in one hand, my pen in the other, and it is writing that I do not have to edit, I do not need to change a word. I want to publish it exactly as it came out of my pen. An exact record of how I was feeling at that precise moment. I don't care if I have got my facts wrong, it was what I thought was true at that moment, so it is MY truth.

Travelling is like an illness with me. It is an addiction. But in particular an addiction to Munich, Vienna, Berlin and Brussels. My four 'Cities in the Autumn Stars'. The thought of going anywhere else does not interest me at all. I yearn to be back in my old haunts, my old bars, restaurants, cinemas, Tingel-Tangels, art galleries. It is the familiarity, the home away from home, the memories, the blood on the tracks.

BRUSSELS

To refine things down to their essence, I go on holiday because of my penis. I go in worship of the penis. It is also about oblivion. To be held in suspension, like a piece of silt carried along a river. I never want a train journey to end, a plane journey seems to last forever. This two-hour train journey to Brussels seems to go in the blink of an eye; a two-hour plane journey to Vienna seems to drag on & on forever.

So after checking in my holiday starts by coming down to the lounge from the 8th floor in the lift; the lift closes its door but will not move. I walk down eight flights of stairs to report it and she tells me she knows. OK. Walk back up one flight to lounge, put 20 euros in the change machine to get coins for the vending machine. It swallows my 20 euros and then gives me no option to get anything back. So my holiday begins. Luckily I had a 2 euro coin in my pocket, and got a beer from the machine and—it is ice cold! A great omen!

The Boulevard Adolphe Max seems MUCH calmer than it was last time. A wet and windy day; the flag-poles outside the Hotel Plaza are shaking in the wind. Well, that's my first ice cold can of Stella nearly finished. On my fourth Stella now in the Café du Dome, finally my black barmaid is here. My God, something about her. Rubenesque. So f—g Rubenesque. And that sexy sultry smile. And the way she always says "peanuts" and makes it sound like "Penis?" I feel my first stirring of the holiday so far. Every time I see her she has this effect on me, and there's not that many women you can say that for. I travel around the strip clubs of Europe, and the brothels of Europe, and very very few women stir me like this Dome barmaid does. Time I spend some days in the Dome and just concentrated on her, instead of Yellow Lily and Alhambra Cinema. Time I had a go. Now I'm going to head to Munich tomorrow morning, but I will just be thinking about her. I don't need pornographic cinema to get me ready for Yellow Lily—I just need to come here.

Incredibly, I seem to have only got through 40 euros on my first day in Brussels. I had four Stellas in the Dome, maybe four Maes in Yellow Lily (plus one beer for Ina) then a McDonalds and back home to pass out. A very cheap start to the holiday. Yellow Lily had fewer girls than at any time I have known. Andrea and Ina were the only stars; Andrea disappeared with someone soon after my arrival; I bought Ina a drink and then left when I could drink no more. Now I am on the ICE to Frankfurt, change trains to carry on to Munich.

If you ever hear I have murdered someone, it will not be for any crime of passion, or lust; it will be because they started eating near me, and I could not control my rage and disgust any longer. This c—t across the aisle from me on the train has been eating food on and off, picking it up, typing on his laptop, picking up his bottle of water, gulping it down, typing on his laptop, picking some more food up, for the last hour or more. I hate him, and wish he was dead. Don't eat near me, please don't. It is really the one thing that disgusts me the most. You could shit near me, and that disgust me less.

MUNICH

As usual my Munich Regent Hotel receptionist is Spanish, as is the barman. I think the Regent Hotel has some special deal with some Spanish employment agency, like Eurostar have a deal with Hungary. I notice the sign in the lift has a special Spanish menu on Fridays and Saturdays! I'm not complaining, I just wish they would do a special deal with Italians as well. The first body blow of this trip to Munich—Rechthaler Hof is closed for refurbishment until March 1st! I only booked a second night in Munich so I could have a long drink and meal in Rechthaler Hof on the second day! All I want from Munich is to find just one big bust dancer in one of the numerous strip clubs/cabarets in Schillerstraße. That is all I ask. Will I be lucky? Almost certainly not. Expect I will see nothing but 100 skinny-chested skinny-arsed anorexics, as usual. When I first started to come to Europe, how strange everything seemed, and so how exciting! The girls I met seemed so exciting. Now it is all so familiar, and unexciting, and so therefore are the girls.

Well, escaping from Munich after just one night. I know I always say it, but I mean it now; I will never come to Munich again. I was supposed to stay a second night but couldn't wait to get out. On my way to Vienna now, one day earlier than planned. Christ, all the magical nights I have had in Munich! All the blood I used to leave on the tracks there. I cannot feel anything there now.

    I can't help feeling morose. I hope I can spark some life into myself in Vienna. Anyway, I am certainly pleased I am travelling by train rather than plane.****The train comes to a halt just before we reach Salzburg. Accident ahead of us; police attending; no idea when we can move again. Twelve minutes stationary so far. Look forward to spending three or four days in Vienna and totally relaxing. Occasional visits to Fortuna, WSK and Café Westend but that is it. Twenty minutes stationary. The "prognosis" is we will be 30 minutes late into Salzburg Central Station. This is what I wanted. To be alone. In the snow, and the cold icy air of the mountains. I feel morose and depressed, but I can take pleasure in it, and wallow in it (the sophisticated gentleman can make use of anything, can turn anything to his advantage. Even shit can be used as fertiliser. There is opportunity in everything).

    Spectacular scenery; I almost wish my wife were here with me to see it. Snowing ferociously now.

VIENNA

Vienna is snowing, and very cold. Good. It matches my heart. My blood is ice these days. Thank God for that; after I lost about 8 years of my life to: emotion. Hell is indeed other people, but it is also: emotions. I find it easier to resist the pull of emotions these days. I do not claim this is a good thing, I just state it as an observation. I find I am almost phobic about emotions these days. They taste like poison to me. They used to be mushrooms, now they are toadstools. I really don't think I want them in my life again. So only sin then? I like the idea of sinning more than the reality of actually doing it. So what then? My holidays used to be a battle between Love, Art and Eros. Now it is more like Drinking, Eating and Sleeping.

So I wake up 1AM and sit up in bed with my computer; after about one minute I lose my internet connection and it will not come back. The hotel night manager comes up and confirms he cannot get a signal on his phone, not even in the corridor outside. I stayed too long in the Dorint bar as usual, then headed up to WSK. Nice to see Amanda again (we made love on the sofa at the back of the cinema like two rutting cats) then I came back to the hotel to pass out. This was my Friday night in Vienna. I discovered the pizza slices from the station are lovely, and much quicker and cheaper than a Subway. I discovered it is better to buy single tickets from the machine at the station for just 2,20 rather than buying a three-day Vienna Card for 20 euros or something as I always used to. I usually only take one journey a day, to WSK and back or to Fortuna and back. All the other places I go are pretty much in walking distance, either from the hotel or walking back down from WSK—Angelique, Manhattan, Burggasse Peep. Café Westend. ML Revue. I have been to all the cultural places too recently to go again for a while, Belvedere, KHM, St Stephen's Cathedral, *The Night Porter* hotel and café, the hole in the ground where Milena's *Bad Timing* apartment used to be before being knocked down last year (why why why did I never go to visit in all my years of coming to Vienna before?). Today I will treat myself to bacon & egg breakfast perhaps, move rooms to a room with internet, get housekeeping to fill my minibar up with at least six Gösser beers, start drinking early, head out early, soon after midday, to Fortuna, back to Burggasse and ML Revue maybe. Come back early for a nap and then wake up later to try Manhattan or Angelique. Feel happy to be in Vienna. Just calm and relaxed and at ease. It took me three days to get here, but I will try to get back to Brussels in one day. Early train back to Munich and then straight onto the long train back to Brussels.

    The good thing about me resuming my regular travels is I am starting to get to know the same people and they are getting to know me, the way in the past I became very familiar with the same faces in Munich, Viktoriya, Irina, Susi, and in Berlin, Riccarda, Iga: the bar staff in the Dome know me well now, the bar girl here in the Dorint, Amanda in the WSK, Andrea in Yellow Lily in Brussels. Familiarity has developed with lots of people now; hopefully it will avoid slipping into too much contempt.

Keep deliberating whether to stay in Vienna Monday as well, and take that fourth day, or head back to Brussels on Monday to give me a leisurely two or three days in Brussels. I am thinking it makes more sense to stay longer in Vienna this time, as I need a LONG time off to get to Vienna and back (now I am confining myself to trains). My Vienna trips will therefore necessarily be quite infrequent. So yes, probably I will add a fourth night here in Vienna? We will see; after this Saturday and Sunday I might be completely sated and be happy to get out Monday morning. 4AM now. Starving. Breakfast at 630.

So I am staying in Vienna for a fourth night. Yesterday once again I stayed too long in the hotel bar and by the time I got to Fortuna Kino I was really blotto, I felt on the verge of alcohol poisoning; a real ice in my blood, I was shivering. At some point I discovered I had lost my scarf, which made things much worse. I did not have it leaving Fortuna, but I cannot remember if I had it on the way there or not. I certainly noticed it on the way back, when the shivering set in—an absolutely horrific journey. I grabbed a slice of pizza from the station and after that passed out in bed. Waking at least a couple of times with terrible indigestion, I took some Gaviscon and then slept some more, waking before midnight and deciding I should make the effort to go to Manhattan over the road, as it was a Saturday night. I thought the atmosphere would be better, but I discovered there were only four girls on duty; I have never known so few girls there. Melissa is now blonde, and I found her most attractive (by which I mean we went into one of the bedrooms). I got back to the hotel after 5AM and was planning to stay awake for 630 breakfast but next thing I knew it was after 10, so I did not bother.

I have got these bizarre little cuts on my right hand, just above the little finger. I have no idea how they got there, but every time I look there seem to be more little cuts. The thing is they look more like splits; like my skin is splitting from inside, rather than cut from outside. I often get splitting of the skin on my penis, but never before on my hand. If I met my (ex) wife now, for the first time, I think I would still fall in love with her; I would still think she was the sexiest, most beautiful woman I have ever seen in my life. And I think this is quite a shocking thing to realise. Familiarity makes you take these things for granted, but she is still the most stunningly beautiful girl I have ever seen. If I met her now for the first time, she would still blow my mind. And that is why I still wear the ring. It remains the first and only really good thing that has ever happened in my life. I know sometimes if I put shower gel on my penis, it dries the skin up so much and makes it rough, and then I get the splitting whenever I get an erection, I mean a really powerful erection. My hand too has this rough flaky feel to it all around the little cuts. What is the answer? Wash less? Don't wash my hands? I certainly won't be using the soap on my penis again. I used to write about philosophy and culture, and art; now I write about the skin around my penis splitting. Have I gone backwards, I mean intellectually?

The hotel bar makes me soporific, and apathetic, I realise. I should just fill my minibar with beer and go out straight from my room. I will try that tomorrow. I think I might even go back to my room now, and have that last Gösser in my minibar, while watching some pornography, and get me in the mood to go out. The plan for the afternoon? Train up to WSK, then walk back down the Gurtel to Menzelstraße Peep, Burggasse Peep, Café West End perhaps, then finish with ML Revue before back to hotel. Sleep it off, then back to Manhattan or Angelique tonight. I need to go back to my room and bring myself back to a pornographic high. And then rush to WSK straight from there.

Whether I drank too much or not (I did) the Fortuna Kino film was poor; an old 1990s or early 2000s film. Really rubbish; the two girls weren't much either. I was not in the mood at all. Later, leaving my hotel after 1AM, I felt so much more in the mood.

That h—job from Manuella was the best I ever had. I came a little bit, but then I felt another orgasm surging up behind it, and then came again, this time explosively, a huge cube-shaped glob of white sperm landed on the bridge of her nose, thankfully between her eyes. Never had a double orgasm like that. All those HOURS of masturbating in the room before leaving, then in WSK, then in the Peep videokabins, then watching the peep girls, it had built up so much! It encourages me to really do something with a Yellow Lily girl again. OH AND THAT NEW PLACE BY GARE DU MIDI! YES! SO MUCH looking forward to getting back to Brussels now! That will make the long train journey bearable.

Travelling to Vienna by train has been an unmitigated success. I will always come by train in future. So exciting to leave Vienna now (in the morning) knowing I am heading back to two nights in Brussels. I have written almost nothing on this holiday, final admittance that I have said it all before. Admitting now that it has just become diary, simple list of where I went and what I did. I used to be going through such a metaphysical crisis in my life and my writing reflected that, it was about big themes, Love, Art and Eros. Now I am through those metaphysical crises, there is nothing left to write about. Time I tried to write some fiction at last? Fiction though seems like such a lesser form of art compared to journal writing. I've got to refind a philosophical aspect to my writings. The cold icy of the mountains.

I am living beyond my means, but what fantastic experiences it is bringing me! If I had lived all my life within my means I would have had NONE of the Top 100 greatest memories of my life. That is what I think of when the Governor of the Bank of England says timidity brings stagnation. You have to speculate to accumulate, to dare is to do. You have to swing the pendulum, stand on ledges, roll with the punches. I am very successfully extracting the fly from the amber here in Vienna, releasing the Woolly Mammoth from the ice. I could have lived very frugally here in Vienna and then gone home depressed that I did nothing exciting; instead I have spent handsome amounts of money and go home happy with some great memories.

Well, that was another surprise—snowing as I made my way back to my hotel (via Café West End). I think today I realise I am ready to leave Vienna now. I went to WSK but was not in the mood, went to Burggasse Peep but was not in the mood (and Manuela was not there). Just thinking about the Café West End and my Alt Wiener Zwiebelrostbraten, my first of this trip. I didn't want to do anything in WSK or Burggasse; I think subconsciously I am looking forward to getting back to Brussels and now want to hold myself back for that. Spending this fourth day in Vienna achieved nothing, except allowing me this visit to Café West End—which after all counts for a lot. Consciously, I wanted to stay in Vienna this fourth day; subconsciously, I had, I discovered, already left.

How much happier I am checking out to leave Vienna knowing I am catching a train back to Brussels, rather than having to go to the airport & flying home. I got to the station forty minutes before my 630AM train was due to leave but, as I thought, it was already sitting there waiting for us to board. I treated myself to one last slice of pizza in the station before going to the train. Eleven hours until I reach Brussels. I was always really cold in my room for the whole stay—only in the early hours of this morning did I discover the radiators in the room and bathroom, and it was lovely and warm after that. Another lesson learned. If I had left yesterday morning (Monday morning) I would have been disappointed and feeling that I should have stayed one more day. Instead I travel Tuesday morning feeling I should have gone yesterday. During Monday I became really sated with Vienna, and now I think it may be quite a while before I feel like coming back. If I had left Monday, I would have been dying to rush back at the first opportunity. That is the value of me staying Monday. Memories of this four-day stay? Making love with Amanda in WSK, making love with Melissa in Manhattan, and the hand massage from Manuela in Burggasse Peep. The gorgeous pizza slices from the station Anker. The amazing Alt Wiener Zwiebelrostbraten in Café Westend. The amazing bacon & egg & sausage breakfast I had in the hotel Saturday & Monday; first time I have ever been down for breakfast in the Dorint. The fantastically ice cold Gösser beer and cokes from my minibar; the Dorint have really got their minibar set up properly cold. Disappointments? The continued absence of any music channel on my TV. That was one of the biggest thrills of my holidays in Europe—seeing German, Austrian, French, Belgian pop videos that we would never ever see in England.

The bizarre skin cracking and little cuts on my right hand has got worse and now has spread to my left hand. The two rashes are in the exact place my fingers go when I put soap on my hands and then clasp and rub my hands together, which confirms my suspicion it is the hand gel soap that has caused it. Yesterday the skin along the entire length & breadth of my penis began to sting terribly as well and it came out in that horrible dry flaky skin. It was painful to touch. Don't touch my penis. It seems a little better today, at least. The thought of a two hour flight back to Brussels would fill me with depression; so long a time in a plane; but the prospect of an eleven hour (three-part) train journey back to Brussels (changing at Munich and Frankfurt) leaves me completely sanguine. We will see if I change my mind before the end.

I really look forward to those ice cold cans of Stella from my Max Hotel vending machine now (unless the machine has gone warm again). Yesterday was the first time I tried my new idea of just drinking in my room before going out and missing out the hotel bar. It went very well, and I was fascinated to discover the exact point where I lose my erection. As soon as I started my 6th bottle of Gösser the erection had fallen to half-mast and would not go any more vertical. By the time I finished the 6th it would not come up at all. I had a 7th bottle then headed to WSK where I with difficulty at least managed some kind of erection, and a bit better again in Burggasse Peep, as the drink started to wear off.

Wednesday I get to spend a whole day in Brussels. I will try to start really early, so I can get to the Old Masters and Fin de Siècle museums again, then down to Midi to check out the other "boarding house" (knocking shop) that I read about, before heading back to Alhambra Cinema and Yellow Lily; perhaps even Gare du Nord as well. How relaxed I feel on this train back to Brussels, compared to the tediousness of having to fly straight home. A real pleasure. Fields of snow as far as the eye can see. Having crossed the border at Salzburg, once again a policeman goes along the train and I am the only person he asks to show his passport. Do I look so suspicious? 915AM now. If I had got the plane in Vienna at 630 I would be down on the ground in London by now. Now, instead, I am only just inside Germany around an hour & a quarter away from Munich still. But much happier for it.

I will live with a massive credit card debt all my life; I see that now. It has become too huge to ever make more than a small dent in it; and that only if I stop travelling, and travelling is the best thing in life so that is not an option. The trouble will come if I fall seriously ill and cannot work, or lose my job, then I will not be able to make my repayments each month and will be effectively bankrupt. God knows what will happen when I have to retire and live on a paltry pension.

I have got Vienna out of my system for a while; and dismissed Munich for good (again). And I still don't feel any desire to return to Berlin; so that leaves me free to enjoy Brussels. How much quicker a journey seems if you feel happy and under no pressure. The journey from Vienna back to Munich feels so much quicker than it was when I was going. Truly you carry the weather with you.****I have got a terrible feeling I am going to miss my connection in Munich. A while ago the driver made some announcement but unlike on the way here the announcements going this way are in German only, but the only word I caught was "fünfzig", 50. I hope that doesn't mean arriving 10.50 as that would not give me enough time to catch the 10.54 to Frankfurt. I think I have been so relaxed, and telling myself how fast the journey is going, I didn't realise that at some point we have lost a massive amount of time. I have no idea where. We are still deep in the countryside and we should have arrived ten minutes ago. It means I just have 19 minutes until my connection leaves. If Rechthaler Hof was still open I wouldn't have minded. But this also means I will miss my connection in Frankfurt too! Bloody trains! Bloody German railways! Feeling stressed now.

Well, we did indeed arrive at Munich Hauptbahnhof at 10.50 giving me four minutes to get from platform 13 to 23. Got there by the skin of my teeth, only to be told no, it is not this one, it is the first train, right at the far end of the platform. I ran, with my heavy bag, as best I could. Got on the last carriage just in time, thought I was going to die. Discover I have quite by coincidence booked my favourite seat right behind the driver at the front of the train. Three hours 6 minutes to Frankfurt then three hours 10 minutes to Brussels. I managed to come on holiday with nowhere near enough T-shirts and way too many underpants. I don't know what went wrong with my packing.

Some things I have discovered on this trip? Train travel across Europe really is a joy. I abandoned it some years ago for the speed of planes, but I will not abandon trains again. I have learnt that it can be made more pleasurable if you very carefully choose your seat on the DB's excellent website. Obviously book your tickets in advance and you can travel across Europe and book very cheaply (especially with my Bahn Card 25% discount). I have learned I've been a fool all these years buying the Vienna Card to give me three days of travel around Vienna, when I can just get a couple of single tickets a day for 2,20 each. I learned there is no need for me to be cold in my room as there are radiators in bedroom and bathroom. I have learned I much prefer to drink in my room until the moment I am ready to go out, rather than going down to the bar, where I lose all my priapic momentum and sink into soporific apathy that destroys my aroused mood completely. By all means pop down for one, to see if there is another Lotta & Sophia but then return to my room to continue drinking there.

My Brussels train is running 11 minutes late as it was late getting in from Amsterdam. It is easy to think it is actually very practical to get the train to Vienna; here am I getting back from Vienna to Brussels all in the space of 11 hours. For the joy of avoiding hideous airports and planes that is going to be the option for me now. I always thought no, regrettably train to Vienna is out of the question, it is a stop too far; but in fact it is not. It is easily achievable, and if you choose your seats wisely a really pleasurable relaxing journey. And it allows you to stop off in Munich or anywhere else for a night or two en route as well.

Just never ending snowy white landscape. Snowy trees. I must admit I have never seen so many trees in all my life. On the few occasions I travel anywhere in England I am never conscious of any trees; it's all fields or buildings. Germany and Austria seem like one huge forest, with settlements dotted amongst the trees. Yet another reason to love Germany and Austria. Is there any connection between the rich forest cover of Germany and Austria and the fact that they are two of the most sexually-liberated (i.e. whore-friendly) countries left in Europe? Nature still runs riot in Germany and Austria, thank God. Lushness. Then again, I remember Norway and Sweden being all trees as well, so that theory does not really stand up.

Aix la Chapelle. Leaving Aachen/Aix how do we know when we cross from Germany into Belgium? We don't. The borders are invisible. But suddenly you notice everything is just: smaller. All the houses seem so tiny, the churches, the bridges, the factories. There is I always think something creepy-looking about Belgium; like everyone is engaged in Black Masses.

BRUSSELS

Sitting in the Café du Dome I immediately see a woman driver zoom down the Boulevard Adolphe Max, braking to a halt and turning around when the wall of traffic alerts her. I think women drivers just think I've always gone down this way, so they do, even if they notice the new big red 'NO ENTRY' signs at the entrance they just think "oh, they're not for me I don't think, can't be" and carry on regardless, whereas men are a bit more alert and respond to what they see. I just say this because 99% of the cars I've seen going down the wrong way have been driven by women. Now, whoops, there goes another woman, bless her. She realises after about 10 yards and does a very skilful and quick U-turn. At 8PM I found the doors of the Dome locked, as I expected, even though there were still some customers inside, and my black bargirl and her partner. I carried on along the boulevard but my black barmaid rushed over and was knocking on the window telling me to come back. "I don't know why this was locked," she says, innocently. After I sat down with my drink though she returns and locks the outside door and pulls the chair up against the inner door, in the usual sign they are closed. She gets more adorable every time I see her. Is it my tips or my tits that she loves?

I have discovered Munich really is over for me. Why pay all that money for so little in return, when you can get so much for so comparatively little in Brussels, Vienna and Berlin? The fact my beloved Rechthaler Hof was closed for two months for refurbishment just reinforced that view and made it much much starker. Rechthaler Hof was so much the best thing about Munich for me. This is what it is when a gentleman gets old perhaps: he prefers food over everything else. Sex slips much further down the agenda. Another reason why you are fatter when you are old than when you are young.

Surprised and delighted to discover the Max Hotel has ADDED a music channel to their TVs—MTV Viva! The quality of music was not too great, I have to say! Tove Lo's Habits the one great song I heard but hats off to them for adding a music channel, when all my hotels removed them years ago. Even the Dorint doesn't have any anymore.

*

Suddenly I am starting to think about Berlin, Just to be there. In the Berlin of the 1920s *Blue Angel* Marlene Dietrich cabaret, jazz, cocaine, prostitutes. Einstein, Schopenhauer, Schoenberg, Berg. Birds tweeting when I work up this morning, the clear blue skies have a hint of warmth in them, now I am thinking March in Berlin. My lovely lovely Berlin Plaza bar, those Pilsners, and getting there on a lovely ICE train, and leaving on a lovely ICE train to enjoy a last couple of days in Brussels.

Yes, travelling gives me massive debts, but it also gives me massive rich memories and experiences. How happy I feel in Vienna and Berlin and Brussels. Well, most of the time I feel morose and depressed, but I luxuriate in my moroseness and depression there, and wallow in it till it becomes pleasurable. In London it's just depressing. I resolve to visit one site of literary or historical importance in London every week. Can I then unlock the fly from the amber in London? Release the woolly mammoth from the ice in London? Bring London back to life?

I think I do feel happier in Vienna than in any other city. Just to get on a tram and ride around on the tram makes me happy. Then end the day with a gorgeous rostbraten in the Café West End. I could ride around Munich on a tram but that would not make me happy the way Vienna does. In Berlin there is just the buses (west side anyway). No, right now Vienna really makes me happy and relaxed.

My sex life is: I drink till I am incapable of sex then go to a prostitute.

Sometimes I dread going to Vienna again for all that wasted money, other times I think, yes, Vienna is my favourite city and I feel so happy just drinking there, eating there, riding around on trams.

London so boring. Nowhere to go. Watch girls in Molly Moggs perhaps, that is it. Olivia in Soho Friday night a disaster but maybe a disaster that saves me money. Sports Bar I could return to and start having one private dance a week.

I am an archivist of my own life. I am a researcher and archaeologist into my own life. An Indiana Jones of the mind. I release my records bit by bit on my websites, and lodge my completed books on Amazon; not expecting sales but so there is a permanent record for posterity. One day I want to build a library dedicated to my own life and my writing, like a great Tower of Babel, the rival of the British Library at least. There all my books that I scribbled all my notes in as I go travelling will be kept, and researchers can access them with protective gloves on, like they do old copies of Shakespeare and Goethe and such like.

Marriage was like an illness which I have recovered from, but which can always break out again if you are not careful.

371

Really looking forward to Vienna now, even Berlin Plaza. But Christ my Capital credit card is maxed out, and my Nationwide credit card is maxed out. There is no light at the end of the tunnel, it is just going to get worse. £17,000 will become £18,000 will become £19,000. It is never going to stop. My lifestyle is expensive. Hell yeah but live it. The fucking memories, just last year alone, hottest sex ever with Fortuna Kino blonde, and with WSK Amanda, wild with passion for Brazilian Julia in Yellow Lily then Andrea in Yellow Lily. Amazing hand job from Manuela in Burggasse Peep. Got to go back to Angelique again.

How nice it is to see your cock with even a little bit of swelling. Just a hint of fatness and heaviness. I had massive vertical erection yesterday morning in bed before going to sleep, so there is nothing wrong with the mechanics. If I went to Olivia sober (or just a little drunk) I will be fine, as I was two weeks ago. She was impressed by it, and so was I!

It is already time I reissued my books, but this time annotated. I am completely fascinated by myself; completely in thrall to myself.

I am scathing and bitter about how awful the strip clubs and strip pubs of London now are, but I suppose for someone coming from western Europe it is a real thrill to see so much striptease where the girls take everything off; in the few strip clubs I have found in Brussels, Munich, Vienna and Berlin the knickers never come off, at best will be pulled down just below bottom cheeks for a split second before the music stops and they quickly pull them back and step off stage. It is one of the specialities of London that we still have full nudity striptease. Strange that London and England of all places should be more liberal in this regard!

When I behave shamefully like Thursday night, I wake up feeling ruined, and not wanting to open my eyes, but when I do I want to do great work, intellectual things, I want to go back to classical music & ferns & my books, and I have the most amazing 48 hours or so of inspired creative work, all to run away from the shame of the drunkenness and hedonism of the night before. So doing shameful things has always been good for me; getting that mucky stuff out of your system; and it also gives me deliciously naughty dreams as well.

Just noticed the seven year eras in my life, 1992 first went to Sunset Strip and saw a naked woman for first time and started my lifetime of strip clubs, porn cinemas and whores, 1999 went to Europe for first time and began a lifetime of travelling to Vienna, Berlin, Munich and Brussels, 2006 fell in love with —, 2013 split from — and resumed a new golden age of travelling. Incredible paradigm shifts all seven years apart. Roll on 2020!

*

I look forward to travelling so much, just two nights to get through and then I'm on my way to Vienna! Just one night to get through then I'm on my way to Vienna!, yet here I am on the train to Vienna and I just feel glum, sombre, melancholisch. When I eventually get home, I will look back on the trip fondly; I just don't seem to be able to enjoy it much while I'm actually doing it. I'm only really happy when I'm actually eating, or actually drinking, or actually masturbating. I have to be actively engaged in one of these three activities to really feel "happy" for a little while. It is all the long stretches of time in between that return me to my natural melancholy. The ICEs are really beautiful: the livery, the interiors, the shape. When I think of Europe the ICEs are one of the things I think of first, these white trains with the red stripe. A design classic. I will be happy once I finally get to Vienna, as I can resume eating, drinking and masturbating again. I am a simple creature. I really don't care about politics, or what's going on in the world. Just to hear the train driver mention the word "Berlin" is a thrill. The word Berlin does have a charge to it that no other word has, I think. After leaving Köln it gets suddenly noticeably colder; feels like we have dropped two or three degrees. Spring looks like winter again. The train is really flying now, as we head down to Frankfurt. The sky gets more grey by the minute. Melancholy is the essential me. The story of my marriage was my wife knew I was a pervert but thought I could be reformed, but it turned out I was incurable. She did, however, cure my depression. I may be melancholy, but I don't believe I can ever feel real depression again. For that I will always thank her.

You say how shy people need to develop confidence, but there are some confident people who would do well to develop a bit of shyness.

On the final leg of the journey to Vienna now—the longest leg; four hours until we arrive. Mentally I am loving this long train journey but physically my legs are starting to ache, my knee. And just my luck OBB allotted me a table seat with someone sitting dead opposite me, so leg room: zero. I have sat in an unoccupied seat somewhere else. This train is as musty as the ICE I just left; a real fuggish thick atmosphere. This is going to be a long four hours. Don't even have any music as my phone is dead; I didn't plan that very well.

VIENNA

Arriving in Vienna this Friday night I don't feel in the mood for it at all. My Westbahn Hotel minibar is warm, so I came down to the bar for one bottle then decamped here to the Dorint. Busy. 9PM already. I will try ML Revue then maybe get the U-bahn up to Angelique and stroll back to Manhattan to finish the night. Start early tomorrow and hopefully get myself in the mood for it. Anyway, I am calm—I have three whole days to relax in Vienna. No cultural places I don't think, though the 1814/15 Vienna Peace Talks exhibition at the Belvedere sounds interesting. I might like to go into the centre and find a good drinking (watching) place on the Ring. That would be good.

The food in the Dorint these days is so arty-farty. Serving beautiful artistic food in those ridiculous minuscule portions. No. After a day's sightseeing we want a massive plate FULL of food, you fools. We don't order expensive hotel restaurant food just to look at how artistic it is; we do it to fill our stomach. The Dorint used to serve lovely big meals, back in the days of Lotta & Sophia, and Natalia & Fraulein Wahl; not anymore, I'm afraid. This is why I go to the Café Westend over the road.

The ML Revue films were rather mediocre; the peep show girls were OK, but I didn't stay long; got the U6 two stops up to Thaliastraße and went in Angelique No.1 for one beer and then No.2 where I met Lily again for the first time in more than a year? Two years? She is much smaller than I remember her; she used to have a huge bosom before. She says she has lost 11 kilos; she is quite petite now but amazingly she is much more pretty than I remember her. Back in Hungary she used to be a florist; which perhaps influenced her choice of "stage name". The funny thing is I remember thinking her so beautiful when I first met her, but I took a picture of her (with her permission) and after I got home every time I looked at that picture I was disappointed, because she was not as beautiful as I remembered; beer goggles I thought, disappointed; but now meeting her again she is much more beautiful than her picture, and more beautiful than I remember her. Still I don't think I will go to the room with her. I tipped her twenty euros for her time then came down to Manhattan. Melissa and Denitsa the pick of the bunch, but I only stayed for one beer.

Oh, over the road from Angelique was a place I had never seen before: the Flamingo Bar. There was only one girl on duty, plus barmaid and lady manager I guess, and then a few men emerged but they did not look like customers; maybe bouncers. Amazingly the beer was normal

374

prices, 3,50 for a large bottle of Gösser. Nothing happening here so I pressed on to Manhattan. Stupidly, I only just learned that there are THREE Angelique bars—the Alm Bar, Grosse Angelique and Kleine Angelique, all next to each other. The two Angeliques certainly have a connecting door; probably Alm and Grosse Angelique do as well. They are all managed by a big Austrian man who I think I may have seen at the bar. Perhaps after Richard Steiner's downfall, the bars are all returning to good old Austrian hands. Lily says he is a very good boss, very kind to the girls.

I must have been drunk because I went to bed without flushing the lavatory. Quite a surprise when I walked into the bathroom this morning. The hotel internet works fine, but the minibar is warm, a waste of time. About 200 channels on the TV but still no music channel. That is the biggest change since my first 'Golden Age' of travelling—the strange disappearance of music channels from hotel TVs. But even when they do have a music channel, they no longer show any music. All music channels have reduced their actual music content to about 5%. They might show some videos in the early hours of the morning when they think no one is watching. So many of my strongest memories from my early years of travelling are the great European videos I used to see on my hotel TV—Alcazar Crying at the Discotheque, Alizée, Berenice, Rohff. And those songs forever after remind me of those holidays, like Proustian paving stones. But now I never see any videos on my hotel TV and I have no memories like this to take home. It is a real mystery.

I love drinking. Already down in the Westbahn Hotel bar for a very large bottle of Ottakringer (1837). 5.2% like all the beers seem to be in Europe; I think our lagers in London are more like 4.5% aren't they? I look back on the old Berlin nights from 2004 when I used to get so turned on in the BEC videokabins and would speed up to Stuttgarter Platz with a flagpole erection in my pants not going down a bit. It has been a long time since I felt that kind of lust. Couple of nice girls in Yellow Lily, some attractive busty girls in Carolina, nice girls in Angelique 1 & 2 and Manhattan but I don't feel the lust I would need to be able to go to the room with them. To overcome the drooping effect of the drink I need a very high degree of lust before I can do anything, and I don't seem to feel it these days. I will try Fortuna Kino and WSK and Burggasse Peep today; start out early afternoon hopefully, then I can be back in bed quite early. Back out anywhere tonight? There seems no point: if I don't want to do anything with Lily, or the Manhattan girls, what else is there? Tête-à-Tête is always absolutely empty so I feel uncomfortable going in and having that process of girls coming up to you one after the other. I should be like Smiley in the Hamburg sex club and just tip the barman to tell him I didn't want the girls disturbing me! That would go down like a lead balloon I expect. Really, I just like to have my drink and cast my eye around, ogle them for a while, and only then if I see one I fancy give them the nod. This is how Yellow Lily and Carolina work in Brussels and I think it is a good model. I wish the Vienna clubs would do this; leave the man alone unless he invites you to introduce yourself. So tiresome to have to answer the same questions from ten girls in a row one after the other. I am a curmudgeonly old sod I know.

I will spend my second night in the Westbahn tonight before moving over to the Dorint tomorrow morning. I like the Westbahn; yes, it is old looking, and a bit shabby around the edges (aren't we all), but the internet is fine, and the beer from the bar at least is very cold. As a fallback I wouldn't mind coming here again. And I love the old pictures of the old Westbahnhof station the way it used to look before the war. The 1950s station they have now is so unbelievably bland for such an important station. I think I will write to OBB to complain. If you don't ask you don't get. If Berlin can rebuild their old Schloss then Vienna can rebuild their old Romanesque station.

Tuesday is going to be insane. Leave 6:30 in the morning for the four-hour train to Munich; hope I make my connection for the three-hour train to Frankfurt; hope I make my connection for the three-hour train to Brussels; hope I make my connection for the final Eurostar home to London. If I miss any connection, then I will probably miss the last Eurostar of the night and then I am in deep trouble as there is a national rail strike in Belgium on the Wednesday so I would really be stranded until Thursday. A massively expensive missed train that would be.

2003-2004 was a magical time in my life. The three trips to Munich followed by three trips to Berlin are legends of my life (see THE COLD ICY AIR OF THE MOUNTAINS). I was innocent then, so my sensations were stronger. The magic had seemed to have gone already by 2005 and then at the start of 2006 I fell in love and stopped travelling for four years. In those four years, behind my back, everything happened. Music channels disappeared from all the TVs, Stuttgarter Platz in Berlin was wiped out, including Hanky Panky/Mon Cheri where I lost my Berlin virginity; the Gurtel in Vienna was wiped out, including Pour Platin where I lost my Vienna virginity. Now newly single I resume travelling and find a very different landscape. And yet, on the other side of the coin, I have discovered so many places I never even knew about before: the fantastic porn kinos of Vienna, WSK and Fortuna being the best examples. Yellow Lily and Carolina and Alhambra Cinema in Brussels (ABC Cinema too was a new discovery but that already has gone).

I arrive in the Dorint bar, empty and very quiet music. After attracting some lady manager's attention to get served, the music suddenly is turned up loud and it starts playing Sinead O'Connor, "I love you, my hard Englishman". A funny little moment. Was the manager trying to tell me something? A sudden April Shower breaks out outside. Tiny fine rain. For no apparent reason, Lily started stroking my stomach and saying she likes a man with a big stomach. I woke up OK this morning; I suppose ultimately I did not drink that much last night. One bottle in the Westbahn bar, one small and two large Zipfers in the Dorint, and then four more bottles of beer in the various night bars, so in English terms not much more than five pints in total. I still felt like doing NOTHING with any of the girls I met, in Angelique 1, Angelique 2, Flamingo or Manhattan.

A very fresh 13 or 14 degrees here in Vienna. Banks in Vienna are funny: you have to put your credit card in the slot outside the door to make the door open. The lavatories at Frankfurt Hauptbahnhof are fantastic: you have to pay to go through the barrier, but the machine gives you change! Most lavatory barriers require you to have the right change BEFORE you get there. Fantastic. It then gives you a 0,50 voucher towards, I don't know what, it is all in German. I've got a few of these vouchers now; I don't know what to do with them. I might as well have a few drinks as I won't be drinking anything in Fortuna, WSK or Burggasse. And nowhere I want to go tonight either.

The videokabins at ML Revue are a failure, because it seems there is no menu, so you cannot choose your particular type of film. There is a menu button, but it appears not to be functional. So you have to laboriously scroll through the films one at a time all the time your credit rapidly running down. The other kabin place by Menzelstraße closed a while ago but if memory serves, that was already worse. My third day away from home all of a sudden, and I've still yet to see a really beautiful, sexy girl, in the street or anywhere. I think more than anything I'm looking forward to having a gorgeous Café Westend steak later. This is my life these days.

The single biggest difference in my experience of travelling B.W. Before my Wife and A.W. After my Wife is: music channels. Music videos are such a sheerly pleasurable enjoyable part of life, why on Earth would you delete them all from your hotel TVs? It makes no sense to me. You have 200 boring news and soap channels, yet not a single joyous music video channel? Where is the sense? After the revolution. Just wait and see. After the revolution. Strippers won't have to pay a house fee to work in a pub or club, they will be PAID to work there, like the old days.

No man is an island. Well, I'm as close to it as I've ever met. There may be other people like me but by definition I am not likely to bump into them. I still have the dream, that a hundred years from now sensitive young men will be coming to drink in the Dorint Hotel in Vienna, because it is where their favourite writer Ernst Graf used to drink; and in the Café du Dome in Brussels, and the Berlin Plaza in Berlin. They will be eating Alt Wiener Zwiebel Rostbraten in the Café Westend like their hero did. Will there still BE a Dorint Hotel in 100 years, still a Café Westend, a Berlin Plaza, a Café du Dome? Would be fascinating to know. I want to live forever, I really do. I think *The Makropulos Case* is one of the most affecting operas I have ever seen. I want to be Emilia Marty. I do have a conception of myself as a great person, which, I notice, the rest of the world curiously and bizarrely fails to share.

I reckon in 2014 I had four great days. Four days in 365 I think is not enough. I have not had any such days in 2015. I do have a belief that I am creating a body of work that will one day come to mean something, like the writings of Samuel Pepys. It may not have value now, but like Coal and Diamonds and Oil, it needs Time to bring value to it. This sense of my own specialness was always my best and last defence against depression that dominated most of my life, and eventually the defeater and vanquisher of that depression. My sense of greatness DEFEATED my black depressions; AND my bitter, pathetic little enemies. They had no idea who they had taken on; no idea they had bitten off more than they could chew. I almost felt sorry for them. Their resources were so much less than mine; their "hinterland" was non-existent. The secret source of my Nile was always a bewildering mystery to them. This is how great people always triumph over the small people.

How incredible it seems that Lotta & Sophia ever existed; two stunningly beautiful blonde Swedish 18-year-old girls with the most incredible bosoms. My own history seems like a legend, a myth. I travel more and more, faster and faster, to try to recapture these experiences.

I feel like we are living inside a game, a crystal maze, a treasure island, set up by superior cosmic beings, and they are wagering with each other how long it takes us to discover all the answers to the puzzles. How long until they discover penicillin, how long until they can cure cancer, how long until they fly, how long until they destroy themselves? The answers to everything are all around us, just waiting to be discovered. And the discoveries keep coming and are so amazing, one feels it cannot be coincidence. When dogs crouch to shit they apparently line themselves with the Earth's magnetic field to do so (I'm the same). There is so much gold in the shit we shit it could pay off the national debt. And all the while the gods are looking down on us and enjoying seeing us struggle and enjoying us have our eureka moments when we solve one more little puzzle, one more riddle. We take so long to find the cure for everything, but all the cures are all around us, hidden in plain sight, we just have to find them.

We live in a world of the most unbelievable intelligence: how do the doors work, how does this electric light work, how does this music I am listening to in the bar work? Everything we take for granted we ourselves would not be able to bring about. We know-nothings luxuriate in the world that geniuses have bequeathed us; ungrateful and unaware. This glass I am drinking my beer from, could I make it? No. This beer I am drinking, could I make it? No. Every single simple thing around us is a thing of the most extraordinary wonder, yet we take it for absolute granted. The clothes we wear! Could I make this T-shirt, these jeans, these brown Belgian boots? No!

I stayed too long in the Dorint again, before getting the No.6 tram down to Fortuna Kino. The film was OK, two pretty girls but I did not stay long. I think just two other men there. Back on the No.6 to Westbahnhof then down into the underground for the three stops up to Josefstadter Straße and Weltspiegel Kino. Here there was two much older ladies than I am used to seeing here, and again just a couple of other customers. The films were good enough again and I was in the mood, so headed down to Burggasse Peep (via the Backbone Irish pub). The kabin films here are really not very good, though the Peep Show girls are. But not quite enough to tempt me, and I was by now starving hungry, so I returned to Westbahnhof for two rolls and a slice of pizza then to bed. I woke at 5.30 this morning and was then just on my computer with Anton Webern playing in the background the whole time; I don't listen to enough Viennese music when in Vienna.

Now I am checking out of the Westbahn and walking 20 yards down the road to check in to the Dorint. Though I suddenly wonder why I am bothering? I might as well have stayed here in the Westbahn. The internet here is excellent, much more reliable than the Dorint. No real advantage to be gained from moving to the Dorint; but it is booked now and cannot be undone. Plans for today? I want to eat! I look forward to getting to the Café Westend for a steak at last. All I can think about is food. After that, nice and sleepy, I suppose I will go and doze in the WSK for an hour or so. Nothing else I really want to do. Tonight I will maybe go back to Tête-à-Tête for the ritual embarrassment of being the only customer there and having all the girls come up to me one after the other, and then all of the girls sitting there looking at me for the rest of the time. I may finish the night in Manhattan just for a nightcap. I don't think I will go back to Lily;

she has lost the massive bosoms that really gave her most of her bloom. She is for sure, though, much prettier than I remembered.

No desire to go to any of the museums—Belvedere, Leopold, Albertina or KHM; no desire to return so soon to the Butterfly House, or *The Night Porter* hotel and café. I came here meaning to do naughty things but then never feel tempted enough to do anything. I may try the Wahringer Gurtel kino on Monday, just for a change; perhaps even return to Fortuna. It is a funny thing, but I have so many favourite places in Vienna, in Brussels, in Berlin, even in Munich, but I no longer have ANY favourite places in London. They are all gone or ruined beyond redemption. This is why I travel. In a nutshell I travel to drink, and to eat, and to watch some pornography on a big screen and some scantily-clad floozies in a night bar—but just watch them, mind, rarely anything more than that. The planets and stars have to be in a rare alignment for me to feel any desire to do anything with them; very rare I feel that madness to go to a room with them, that rausch, that intoxication.

Frank Sinatra's My Way on the Dorint bar radio as I arrive, followed by Mack the Knife. Louis Armstrong's version. I think it is time I went to Berlin again. I miss my Berlin Plaza, even if Stuttgarter Platz has been wiped out. Oh, those magical lust-crazed nights in Hanky Panky, Mon Cheri, Golden Gate and Monte Carlo! Legends of my life.

The Palkautaler Weinhaus has confirmed its reputation with me as being rather brutish and aggressive. I write these words later, frightened they would snatch my paper away from me, read my words, and beat me to death for what I have written. I am pampered, for sure; I spend all my time in the international English-speaking hotels, like the Ibis and the Mercure, and then you step outside and go to a proper local beer house and you meet the real Viennese, not too polite, not too much inclined to speak English, and you get rather an aggressive impression. Haha. Obviously I am not offended, but it does make me want to stay in the pampering places; I like to be pampered. Really no desire to do anything today except eat and eat and eat, then sleep.

How unbelievably bland the new (post 1945) Westbahnhof station is; it is basically just a roof. A flat roof. And beneath that are the platforms and the trains. What a comedown from the former glorious massive structure that existed before; where a young Adolf Hitler used to hang around to carry passengers' bags for a few pfennigs. And it was only ruined in the very very very last months of the second world war. And I say this not as a hater of Westbahnhof, but as an absolute lover. Westbahnhof means so much to me. When I die I want part of my body to be buried at Wien

Westbahnhof, part in Berlin Zoo station, and part in Munich Hauptbahnhof. I want nothing of me to remain in London or England. My heart and my mind exist so totally in Mitteleuropa that I want to remain here after my death, in my Union Jack-draped coffin.

Human beings have "evolved" i.e. regressed, to the point of imbecility. When you go into a restaurant and they serve you miniature plates of food arranged with perfect artistry on a plate you realise this. A human being goes to a restaurant because he is HUNGRY, and wants to FILL his stomach with a massive plate-full of food. We do not go to a restaurant to look at the food and admire how artistic it looks. Imbecility. Honestly how do these restaurants get away with it, and how do they thrive? Because human beings have evolved to the point of imbecility. This truly is decadence. When you have become so artificial that you pretend you enjoy eating food like this. All for show.

This Westbahnhof is a massively important station—every train from Western Europe, from England, from France, from Belgium, from Germany, arrives at Westbahnhof. And they arrive in this SHED. When you see pictures of how it used to look before April 1945, it breaks your heart. Yes, the old Romanesque station was perhaps unnecessarily ornate, over the top, impractical—but it was better than this merely functional shed. And yet I love Westbahnhof. I love this bloody shed.

I feared the Café Westend might be packed on a Sunday afternoon but in fact it is as quiet as I've ever known it. I love travel; but I have no interest for "new" places. I have found some places that I love, in Vienna, in Berlin, in Brussels, in Munich, and I just want to keep returning to these places. I have zero interest in Asia, or China, or Australia, or America, or South America, or Scandinavia, or anywhere else. I have found the places I feel at home (not in London anymore, for sure) and I just want to keep coming back to these four places. Frankfurt has a massive red-light district, Hamburg has a massive red-light district, but I have no desire to go to these places; Berlin and Vienna red-light districts are, now, almost non-existent, but I still prefer to keep coming back to these places for my jollies, as "Jack the Ripper" referred to it.

The thing is, we all have dirt in our lives, dirt is an automatic by-product of existence; every human has dirt. And yet papers like the Sun and the Mail take that dirt that we all have and use it to destroy a person; this is the mendacity and the repulsiveness of newspapers like this. The journalists who write these "dirty" stories have exactly the same dirt in their own lives, yet they can keep it in private. We all have dirt; every human has dirt; it is an inescapable by-product of being a normal human being—and to try to smear a human being because of this dirt is the height of repulsiveness.

Wieselburger Bier actually only 5.0% dead. A fraction less than what I am used to in Europe.

Gustav Klimt really was a beautiful painter. He was also a massive shagger I think. He would f—k the women he was painting, go back to his painting, f—k them again, go back to his painting. And I think you can see that in his pictures. His women are so beautiful, so sexual. This painter really f—king loves women, and really loves f—king women. All the painters I love seem to have naked women in nearly all their pictures, like Felicien Rops and Paul Delvaux, who I revere. The only two Magrittes I loved in the old magnificent Museum of Modern Art in Brussels were his Lola de Valence and La Goulue, both paintings of naked women. His other paintings generally bore me. For Brussels to close the Museum of Modern Art and give all that space to a Magritte Museum is a bad joke. Probably they will point to the fact that the visitor numbers have increased; I don't care. Magritte is boring as hell; five or six of his paintings is enough in any museum. A massive disaster.

Bloody hell, there was a gorgeous girl behind the Dorint reception just now as I went to ask for my minibar to be replenished. Dark brown or black hair and wonderfully curvy young body in that grey waistcoat & trousers. I will go back at an opportune moment to book a wake-up call and ask her if she can deliver it in person—preferably in a see-through nightie. Having left my room thinking it would be a long time until I came back to Vienna, I now want to come back quickly to see her. The first sexy-looking girl of this entire trip, amazingly enough. Amazingly there is a Bild in the Dorint paper rack; first time for years. Looks more like a customer has brought it in and left it there as it is very wrinkled like it got rained on (or he ejaculated on it). Perhaps they did it as a protest against the Dorint no longer stocking it themselves?

After several beers and a gorgeous Alt Wiener Zwiebel Rostbraten in Café Westend I came back to the hotel to sleep. I woke later and forced myself to go out to Tête-à-Tête and Manhattan. I really really had no desire for it whatsoever. The Tête girls were nice enough but it never crossed my mind to do anything with them; I was more interested in the lovely little framed pictures on the wall, some miniature Klimts and two rude pictures by an artist I do not know. They look like Thomas Rowlandson but doubt this in Vienna, so guess it may be some Austrian Rowlandson-like painter. It says something about me that I come to a brothel and am more interested in the pictures on the wall. I seem to be becoming increasingly averse to real-life women. In Manhattan, the same. Melissa, who I went with before, the only good one, but I felt no desire even for her. Two beers in Tête and one in Manhattan and I came back to sleep again. Up at 630 for lovely eggs & bacon in the hotel restaurant then back to bed again and then overslept until now, 3PM. No desire at all to go out tonight, my last night, so I might as well just go to WSK and that will be it. The Burggasse Peep kabin films are so rubbish I can't be bothered to go there again; the ML Revue kabin films are rubbish too. I might go back to Fortuna Kino, but it is such a long walk from the tram stop; could try the Wahringer Kino, but probably will just slump in WSK for a while.

All I can think about is the gorgeous curvy receptionist; sexier than anything I have seen in any of the night bars or kinos. I smell so smoky; I had to get out of Manhattan more than anything because the atmosphere was so thick with just about everybody in there smoking. A thing of the past in London—already it feels amazing to think that people were ever allowed to smoke in pubs and restaurants in England. And if I have no interest in the nightbars—not even with Lily back—there seems little point in coming back to Vienna in the near future. The kabins of ML and Burggasse Peep are rubbish, so that just leaves Fortuna and WSK. Not really enough to come all this way for. Tired of Brussels too—Yellow Lily has been rubbish, Alhambra Cinema too full of perverts who won't leave you alone. Next trip has to be Berlin, I think.

Christ, waiting to be served at the bar, I just caught another glimpse of the receptionist girl; she is gorgeous. She is on the Lotta & Sophia level; if only she worked in the bar instead of reception. She looks like a trainee as she is just standing back and not actually doing anything; just watching and listening to the others. Let us hope she stays. A third glimpse, as I go back for another beer. Already these glimpses are the best memory of this holiday.

Once again I managed to get through an entire trip—one night in Brussels and four nights in Vienna—without doing anything with any of the floozies in the night bars or kinos. I went into Yellow Lily, Carolina, Manhattan, Fortuna Kino, Burggasse Peep, WSK x2, Tête-à-Tête, and left with my chastity intact. I didn't fancy anyone, or just was not at all in the mood. The videokabins were rubbish, the kino films were rubbish, so that didn't help. I was just out of sorts the whole time really. I always leave London with lurid pornographic fantasies of what I am going to be getting up to, but then come home having done nothing. I am half pleased and half sad. As soon as I get home I will regret not doing anything. I think this will be my last trip for quite a long time. I have to try to repair my parlous finances now. If I am sated with Vienna and sated with Brussels, and still no real desire for Berlin, then this is a good opportunity to rein myself in. At least I have got a window seat for this four-hour train back to Munich; that makes it slightly less of a pain. Memories of this holiday? Almost nothing whatsoever. I am glad I finally bit the bullet and bought my new boots in Brussels (for 109 euros); I am pleased with them. Other than that, there was just the glimpse of the new trainee receptionist yesterday, who was the one really sexy girl I saw on the entire trip. My financial worries really dogged my entire journey and hung over me like a cloud. As always, I just want to return home and curl up and be very small and stay as much as possible with my mother, away from the world.

It only feels like we left Vienna five minutes ago but here we are arriving at St Polten Hbf 26 minutes away. If all goes well and by some miracle I don't miss any of my connections, I should have two hours 20 minutes between my arrival in Brussels and my Eurostar home. I had planned to leave my bag in a locker and then go to L'Orient Express, the bar that looks like a library, then maybe even down to Carolina for one last look at the floozies, but I feel too dejected now to even do that. I question my whole existence, and way of life. If I no longer have any interest in the naughty things, what is left? I am going through an existential crisis. Next stop Linz. 704AM. I go to the night bars now filled with torpor and lethargy, when back in 2004 I used to hurry from the kabins of BEC or Sarah Young to Stuttgarter Platz almost literally hyperventilating with excitement and anticipation of what voluptuous huge-breasted houris might be waiting for me, in Hanky Panky, or Mon Cheri, or Golden Gate, or Monte Carlo. How long ago those magical nights seem. The drug was new then, and my receptors were very alive to it.

The Alps (?) on the horizon to the south all the way as my train heads back across Austria to Munich. Lucky is he who lives or works in sight of mountains. On my last day in Vienna, I just got the U6 up to WSK but all the young girls who used to work there last year seem to have gone, and there are now just two older ladies, and as I say the films were mediocre as well. I toyed with the idea of going on to Burggasse Peep again, or Fortuna again, but I was feeling hungry again, so delightedly just rushed back to the station for a foot-long Subway AND a slice of pizza; the Subway was delicious, but I struggled to finish the pizza I must say. Then into a deep snooze, waking before midnight and then staying awake the rest of the night. I drink until I am ravenously hungry then stuff myself with food, then go to sleep. These are the only real pleasures of my life these days.

745AM. We arrive in Linz. Another two hours 40 minutes until Munich. Drinking and eating make me happy. Sitting in the nightbars surrounded by floozies no longer makes me happy. They all say to me "You seem upset; what is wrong?" but my addiction makes me keep going, though I get no pleasure out of it. Wasting my time and theirs. These conductors that move down these trains just checking the tickets of the people who got on at the last stop, how on Earth do they remember the people they have already checked? It always puzzles and amazes me. 0811. Rather amazing to think I am not going to get to Brussels until 530PM. 855AM Salzburg.

Well, that is the first hurdle cleared, into Munich dead on time, and now on my train to Frankfurt. Three hours 13 minutes.

Well, it's all gone very smoothly so far. On time in Frankfurt as well, and now on my train to Brussels. Great. Bunch of five or six Finnish young men two rows in front of me, continually talking, and now playing some techno music. This is going to be the longest leg of the journey; it will feel like it anyway. They have to play music, really?

*

People say pornography is bad and strip clubs are bad, because it objectifies women, reduces them to objects; but I would look at it another way: I revere women, I put them on a pedestal and look up to them like goddesses. This is a kind of objectification, but a kind of worshipful objectification, not a bad objectification. I think films were better in the 1970s, I think women looked sexier in the 1970s. If a woman looked at me as a 'sex object' I wouldn't be offended at all; I would love it. If a woman is on a stage, of course, be she musician or actress or singer or dancer, it is even more likely that I will 'objectify' her.

I go to the Wigmore Hall for concerts of chamber music, violin recitals or piano recitals, with the same impulse I go to strip clubs or porn cinemas with. For Priapic arousal. Anything I do in my life is done for Priapic arousal.

One must not comment on the beauty of a violinist or pianist? Her physical attractiveness? Her curvaceousness? So when one checks in one's hat & coat in the cloakroom, one must check in one's natural sexual desires as well? We must go into a concert hall sexless, emasculated, castrated? One must sit there very po-faced, absorbing the experience with one's ears only, no other senses allowed? It is objectifying her to talk of her extreme physical

385

COLLECTED WORKS

desirability? But tell me, before going on stage she puts on her beautiful make up, does her hair beautifully, puts on the most beautiful & alluring dress she can find, all to make herself look as attractive as possible; but then by some bizarre moral omerta we are not then allowed to say "bloody hell, she is attractive!" Is that really being rude to her? Offensive? All human beings size each other up on the tube, the bus, at the airport anyway. Of course it is the same in a concert hall, observing one's fellow audience members, and the people on stage.

On more than one occasion I have had sex with one of my fellow audience members at the Wigmore Hall. It would seem rude and bizarre not to. It is such a heady, arousing environment.

It seems to me most of the greatest art is about sex, most of the greatest philosophy is about sex, most of the greatest classical music is about sex. People think oh, art, philosophy, classical music, is so old, dry and dusty, and boring; but when you realise most of painting, philosophy and classical music is about sex, then it opens up to you like a flower, and you can see how rich and fascinating it is. And then I sit there in a classical music concert lusting after the violinist on stage with a swelling in my trousers, I walk around art museums almost always with an erection. Eros is all around us. Aphrodisiacs are everywhere. I can get turned on by a pot plant, and often have.

I do feel drawn to Brussels, just lazy days drinking and eating, and reading my Guardian, this is the big attraction. Start the day in the Ibis and the Orient Express, then after brief visits to Alhambra Cinema and Yellow Lily END my day in the Dome. Any energy left then pop up to Gare du Nord before back to Midi and chicken & chips then bed. Can I really wait until June?

Vienna was dull, and YET! How fantastic it was (in January) sitting behind that man in WSK who had the girl fucking him on his lap—just no sign of such girls in WSK this time. How fantastic was that incredible TWO ORGASM handjob with Manuela in Burggasse Peep. How sexy it was seeing Melissa walking around Manhattan topless, those lovely big jubblies. Just did not feel ANY of that excitement this time; maybe still too cold. Need to go in hot summer when hormones raging; but the torpor of the Dorint bar is not good, and the complete LACK of people watching. Anyway my finances need to improve A LOT before I can go as far as Vienna again. But when will my finances improve?

BRUSSELS

386

I forced myself to have one beer in the Dome; it was a struggle. Thought I was going to have a heart attack. Then I forced myself on to Yellow Lily, passing Beatrice in the road as I went; I didn't see her as the sun was blazing but she called me back. Yellow Lily was a bit better than recent visits, but I no longer feel comfortable there. I prefer the street environment. Prefer to take Beatrice into Jimmy's Bar for a 'looza peche'. From Yellow back to Alhambra Cinema and at least one really good film; the inevitable Anna Polina in *The Advocate*. I went back to see Beatrice again, and this time we went into the little half-hour hotel together (probably our second such tryst); tried Empire at 9.30 but it was too early apparently; then up to Gare du Nord. The Sexyworld videokabins are actually very very good, and the window girls are fantastic. The street girls were actually fantastic too. Summer is the time to come. It is 22 after midnight. An enjoyable evening in Brussels.

BERLIN

A long journey from Brussels to Berlin (changing at Köln) on crowded ICEs, with someone sitting next to me every step of the way. The transfer from the Central Railway Station to Zoo, however, was as quick and simple as it has ever been. I think I have over-complicated it in the past. Down the escalator from platform 12, up the escalator to platform 16, one-minute wait for the S-Bahn back to Zoo. I didn't bother trying to buy a ticket from the machine because I read an ICE ticket allows you one journey on an S-Bahn train in the central zone when you arrive, so I took advantage of that and hoped it is true. Beautiful big, curvy, brown-bobbed receptionist when I checked in to the Plaza. I tried to keep my eyes from straying to her cleavage at the same time as trying to steal as many looks at her cleavage as I could.

For me Berlin is some kind of Holy City. For some people Jerusalem is a holy city, or Mecca; for me Berlin is a holy city. I feel very emotional just to be here. My last few visits have felt disappointing it is true, but I still come back, because its holiness remains undiminished. All the same, this feels for me a make-or-break visit to Berlin. A last chance for Berlin. Can it still provide any excitement to compare with the old Stuttgarter Platz nights, going to Hanky Panky and Mon Cheri, to Chocolat, to Starlight, to Night Dreams, to Golden Gate, to Blue Bananas, to Sissi Bar, to Monte Carlo—all next to each other? Now? Last time only Sissi & Monte Carlo left, as well as Bon Bon over the road. Tonight we will see.

Found an old map of Berlin three days ago in the suitcase full of stuff I brought back from the house I shared with my wife, and now in Berlin I open it and it smells so musty & dank, and I notice it has mould growing on parts of it, but only on the green parts of the map which denote the Tiergarten, the forest at the heart of Berlin. How strange! Ah, after nine hours of travelling the beer is going down nicely. I will go soon to see if anything at all is left of Stuttgarter Platz. Back in 2003-04 Stuttgarter Platz was a life-changing experience. More than any other street on the planet Stuttgarter Platz released my fly from its amber; brought me to life; released my butterfly from its chrysalis. Now? We will see what is left. An older Swedish/Norwegian couple are sitting at the bar, with their early 20s daughter in between them; with every beer that passes the back (rear) of the daughter becomes more & more compelling to me. What a beautiful, beautiful arse this girl has got.

Surprised how quiet the hotel bar is this Friday night. The Swedish three next to me and another two couples I think on the other side. Berlin is 90% full of ugly, post-war 1950s buildings, then every now & then you will see one of the gorgeous pre-war, 19th century buildings, and they are so beautiful it breaks your heart. How beautiful this city should be today. You see the beauty under your feet still, in the little cobblestones they make the pavements with still. Oh, the old & young Swedish/Norwegian women were not with the man. I got that wrong. Wishful thinking on his part, no doubt. Those Stuttgarter Platz nights were so amazing and as far as I know no books are written about them, no films are made about them. I at least want to preserve their memory here. Thank you to Yulia, and Riccarda, and Iga and all the other girls, who did so much to bring my morbid eroticism flourishing into life.

Insanely, I got lost again on my way to Stuttgarter Platz, and then I got even more lost coming back. I have absolutely no idea how I do it. I have looked at the map and tried to work out which turnings I took, and I still cannot work out how I ended up going in completely the wrong direction every time—I mean like towards Paris when I should have been headed towards Moscow, as bad as that. I had blisters on my feet and I was in a fury. My McDonald's was ice cold by the time I got back as well. Stuttgarter Platz is now a chic upmarket place. Mon Cheri is a cocktail bar called Galander, Starlight and Night-Light are now a cocktail bar called Albert's, Blue Bananas and Golden Gate is a sports bar called Arena. Only Sissi Bar and Monte Carlo kino bar remain. There was just one girl in Sissi, a voluptuous brunette called Lily. In Monte Carlo the usual 6-7 Turks and Bulgarians. I do love the real downmarket sleaziness of these places and I will go back. I tried Club 77, five or six girls but no one to my fancy. I forgot to try Bon Bon. I was shocked how busy the streets were, but I suppose it was Friday night. Tonight will be as bad, I will give it a miss, and head towards

Martin-Luther-Straße instead—King George and Caligula, and later maybe Lustgarten to see if it is still open. I seem to have got through 75 euros on my first day in Berlin, though 20 of it I cannot account for. Oh, to be in a porn cinema with my cock out, and a big breast girl bouncing on the screen. How good it was in Monte Carlo with the blonde giving my naked cock a stroke. The simple pleasures are the best. Hopefully it will start to get dark within an hour then I can go out.

Well, Berlin Erotic Point still has a few kabins left, but if I remember rightly they are in poor repair and the selection of films not great. Sarah Young stopped having kabins years ago but this time I couldn't even see it at all. My years of drunken excess, debauchery, are now catching up with me and giving me serious problems I struggle in vain to combat—while still drinking excessively.

Struggling over these three beers tonight; I will switch to vodka & cokes soon to try to wake me up and spark me to life. I really fancy the curvy receptionist. I was thinking about her earlier in bed. I had a very titillating pleasurable night in Brussels—and looking back I had an OK first night in Berlin. Very sexy-looking brunette and one of the blonde girls in Monte Carlo pulled my jumper back to expose my erect member and gave it a few strokes for free, which was very sexy.

I think I have the stupid delusion that heavy drinking makes me thin—because it makes me feel hungry. So when I feel hungry I feel thin. Then I accidentally spot my face in a mirror. I think we have forgotten how good Lady Gaga was back in 2009—Let's Dance, Poker Face and Bad Romance in particular: three all-time greats, one after the other. Extraordinary. She was the sound of 2009. The hotel bar very busy this Saturday night—inside and out. The service still good. How time flies when I start drinking vodka. It is true, after I give up the beer and switch to vodka, I start to smile again, stupidly. All of a sudden it's dark outside but I no longer want to leave. The barman is amazing—he is giving me "single" vodkas which are getting progressively bigger; this one must be a triple in reality. Oh yes, now, for the first time, I am really tasting the vodka. Every fresh bottom I see now starts to seem like the most f—kable bottom I have ever seen in my life. This is how the vodka brings me back to life.

Is there anything more depressing than checking out of a hotel to start your long journey home? Obviously yes. But it's right up there all the same.

I got the bus easy enough down to Dominicusstraße and the kino. Very pushy girls. Went next door to Lustgarten. Even more pushy girls. On to King George. A very busty black-haired Colombian girl; I bought her a

25-euro drink with three 10 euro notes but I never got the 5 euros change back. In the room she asked for 20 euros but I'd already paid 100 euros to "sleep with as many girls as you want" so said no, so she proceeded to give me a handjob only and would not take her top off, or let me touch her. So much for the flat rate fuck-as-many-as-you-want brothel! I left after that and just made the very long walk back. Anyway, I had to give it a try, so I do not regret the money I spent. The dancing of the two girls who did bother to dance was the sexiest part of the visit, same as last time. They both danced barefeet which I always find sexy.

So at the moment this make-or-break last chance visit to Berlin is leaning towards no, I don't think there is any point coming back to Berlin again. I will try Stuttgarter Platz again as I did quite enjoy my visit there—probably on Monday I will visit the Rosa Luxemburg Straße kino and the Im Ex exhibition at the Alte National Gallery. But at the moment, no, I don't think I will come back to Berlin, unless something spectacular happens today or tomorrow to change my mind.

So two more nights in Berlin to come. I will probably walk back to Stuttgarter Platz tonight; surely the two or three places will still be open on a Sunday. Then Monday should be my early start and doing the cultural things; in the evening nowhere left to try. After my poor experience in King George I am not bothered about Caligula, I don't think.

A beautiful softly raining Berlin evening. 9PM I wake up and make my way down to the bar. Hopefully there will still be some rain around later when I am ready to leave. Earlier I walked to Zoo just to get some rolls and my newspaper; again it was gently raining the whole time. Big slow splatters.

What is this addiction of mine to strip clubs & brothels? I think it's because it is an outsider's world, and it was the first time in my life I ever found a place where I felt comfortable. Even the girls there are kind of outsiders, having some kind of pariah status simply by the job they do. So I always found it easy to get on with girls who were outsiders every bit as much as me. Coupled with that, I am also a scopophiliac—I love LOOKING at women. I generally avoid getting involved with them even if they offer it, as I just want to carry on looking. The relationship is perfect as it is, and I see no need to change it. A girl usually has to hide the fact she is a stripper or a prostitute as much as I hide the fact I spend all my time with these women; therefore we both live the 'double life' every day of our lives, and I find the double life attractive.

Some little 10-year-old boy came up to me while waiting for my bus at Zoo and started talking to me in German; I stopped him and asked "Sprechen sie Englisch, will you, my good man? You are not in Germany now. Oh. Actually, you are, but sprechen sie English anyway will you, there's a good chap." And, of course, he did; he hesitated for a moment then repeated his question to me in Absolutely. Perfect. English. Did I know where Zoo Palast was? I thought it was in that direction but advised him to check with someone else; pleasingly, I was right, as after asking a German he then ran off in the direction I had thought. But seriously how wonderful are Germans, that even their kids can Speak. Perfect. English.

Really struggling with the beer tonight; I think my body is completely saturated with it. Ah, what a pleasure, the curvy receptionist has just come into the bar and is standing there talking with the bar staff. I take the chance to steal long looks at her in profile; she is really, really beautiful. She has been the best memory of this trip to Berlin. She, on her own, might even tip the balance enough to make me want to come all the way back. Fraulein —. Now I am getting an erection just sitting here thinking about her. If only she worked in the bar instead of reception. But I thought that in Vienna too. And in Brussels. Malicia (what a name!) who checked me in. Gorgeous. All the while I have been in Berlin, it is the pretty, pretty receptionist that I think of.

I notice how they keep the vodka in the fridge; they don't do that in London do they? It always hangs upside down over the bar. When the receptionist came in to the bar to talk to the bar staff, she glanced quickly right at me just as I glanced at her and our eyes met—I think she is already aware that I like her, since the first second when I arrived at the desk to check in. I must be that obvious. Feel no desire to walk to Stuttgarter Platz now. I know my signs. I will not even be able to get an erection tonight. The first night, Friday, I was excited and could hardly get it down again. Tonight the opposite. I doubt I will even GET an erection now. Anyway, there is a McDonald's there and that is all I am really looking forward to. It was my custom in the old days to not leave my Berlin bar, or my Brussels bar, until I was almost incapacitated by drink. Only then would I head to the night places and I would still get erections so strong they wouldn't go down. Those days are gone. Alcohol abuse is now starting to show its consequences on my body.

With or Without You on the hotel bar radio. What a timeless classic that is. Some Chinese man just walked in and asked me for "a Berliner beer please". This is how much I appear to belong here. The barman greeted me by name and "You are well known now!" I'll say. With typical stupidity I saved the Alte National Gallery for today (Monday) as I did not want to go on the weekend when it will be too busy; only as I picked my bag up to leave my room just now I suddenly realised it is probably closed on Monday, and sure enough it is! Haha, the one cultural thing I wanted to do on this holiday and it is now impossible. I will head for the Rosa Luxemburg Straße sex kino instead, and maybe look for the site of Hitler's bunker. Raining gently again today, third day in a row. I have been very lucky in that regard. It was raining as I returned from Zoo last night. I walked all the way back from Stuttgarter Platz to Zoo along Kantstraße—passing the famous Theater des Westens where Josephine Baker danced in nothing but a girdle of bananas in 1925—so desperate was I for some food, a 3AM McDonald's (the one by Stuttgarter Platz typically having already closed its doors by the time I got there), then walked back along Ku'Damm in the rain. It was beautiful, raining quite hard, but I was not really getting wet. It was just that big slow splattering rain that barely seems to make my clothes wet at all, just bounces off my head. I stopped in front of all the lingerie shops to take photos of their mannequins; Christ, people must think I am a right old pervert.

So I think the result is no, there is no point returning to Berlin. Sissi Bar, Monte Carlo, Club 77, Bon Bon all still remain at least. In Sissi there seems only ever one girl on duty; Monte Carlo has at least six girls on and last night a very attractive Bulgarian brunette Jessy. I was actually shocked how pretty she was. Club 77 around 6-8 girls, Bon Bon I saw four I think. There was one other man in Monte Carlo when I arrived, which actually made it seem busy, as usually I am on my own. In Bon Bon there was a group of five men at the far end, so glad that took the attention off of me. Twenty euros to get in with one free drink. Bon Bon is unique in that the girl starts dancing on the stage near the door then walks all along the silver bar to the stage at the other end, collecting "dollars" all the while. But there was not enough to detain me in any of them, so I would not come back to Berlin for them. King George was not for me. I think it will be at least a year before I ever consider coming back to Berlin. It is true I have never tried Artemis, La Folie and a few other places; on a future visit I can perhaps be more adventurous, but I did not feel like it this time. Not seen a single sexy girl on this trip to Berlin, though to be fair I have hardly been outside the door except very late. The hotel receptionist was the one great beauty of this stay. I will try to drink a lot now as I will not go out tonight. Oh, was there something about a "happy hour" at Caligula? Before 3 I think. I will check.

Still trying to piece together the events (uneventful) of last night. Let me try again. I must have left the bar around midnight and walked with no enthusiasm towards Stuttgarter Platz. This time I was very careful to record which turnings I was taking to try to work out how I went so spectacularly wrong last time (and the time before that a year ago). I came around Olivaer Platz as usual, crossed Leibnizstraße, rounded the corner of Ku'damm & the magnificent erotically-nippled mannequins of Stottrop fashion store, and then turned up Clausewitzstraße. This brings you to a little tiny star junction and I turned up Griesebrechstraße. After a few steps, I realised this was wrong, so went back and turned up Sybelstraße instead. Sure enough this straightaway brought me to Berlin Erotic Point. This is one thing I have been doing wrong then, though it cannot fully explain the extent of my madness previously. The kabins were not bad certainly, they have a menu button which makes all the difference. I could have stayed longer but the manager was banging on the door saying he wanted to close, so I had to hurriedly "do myself up" and "compose myself". Up to Bon Bon, Monte Carlo and Sissi, so simply so straightforward—how could I ever have got lost? Jessy, as I say, a surprisingly beautiful brunette in Monte Carlo. The girl in the porn film on the screen reminded me so much of the hotel receptionist and that is what detained me for quite a while. Next door to Sissi Bar and Lily there again, who with her huge voluptuousness and brown hair again reminded me of hotel receptionist, so I "stayed" with her for a while, though it was one of those miserable episodes where even as you are taking your clothes off you want to change your mind, but now have to go through with it. Imagining it was the hotel girl made it better. From there the long walk back to Zoo McDonald's and then the walk in the rain back to the hotel. Tawdry, tawdry, wretched sex—is there anything better?

So there is just enough to get me to come back to Berlin one day, but it will be at least a year. Vienna will be on the radar before Berlin will be. No, the Caligula happy hour is still 89 euros (rather than 109); would rather save the money for Brussels. So nothing today except Rosa Luxemburg Straße kino then. I cannot even be bothered to go to the site of Hitler's bunker now. Or Zahringerstraße where Anita Berber lived. I've become so lazy.

As I get older I do not "improve" i.e. become more mature, more of a "family man". On the contrary I become purer me. That means MORE scopophiliac, MORE Priapic, MORE provocative. As I get older all that happens is I become less & less ashamed of my tastes and behaviour and indulge them more purely than ever. I simply cannot understand women who want children, and men who want children. I simply have a completely different mindset to them. Why on Earth would you want to destroy your freedom by having children? I still feel I want to be free to sow my "wild oats". I cannot imagine a time when I DON'T want to sow my "wild oats".

If it starts raining I will go out. I only leave my hotel if it rains. Are there other people who only like to go out when it is raining?

The Rosa Lux kino had less videos than they used to; but the Shione Cooper one was good enough to make it worthwhile. Straight there and straight back. I feel so tired and saturated with drink I had planned to stay in tonight; but I got so turned on in my room I felt suddenly desperate to return to BEC and Monte Carlo! If this is my last night in Berlin for a very long time, as I think it will be, I cannot spend it quietly in bed doing nothing. Still, this late 10PM beer tastes almost poisonous to me now. My body and mind is crying out: "Let me go to bed!" Only my penis is saying "No! Let us go one last time to Stuttgarter Platz!" I may even try just going to BEC, and then see how I feel there. I can always come straight back from there if not in the mood. After all a visit to Monte Carlo will only set me back a further 10 euros, no more.

As always, I feel the complete lack of music videos on this trip keenly.

The number of couples I see here in the hotel bar, and they sit there for an hour or so, and never exchange a single word with each other. Just eventually they quietly get up and leave together in the same silence they had sat. If only me & my wife could have had this kind of relationship. It does seem rather sad, but one presumes they are happy? I remember an American couple I saw in the Porcupine one day. The man was keenly looking through his London maps and his museum guides, planning his next visit, but next to him his wife just sat there with shoulders slumped, staring into space, wondering what happened to her life. Our eyes met a few times; she was pretty and curvy and I felt so hungry for her. I wanted to f—k her so much. She looked like the schoolmaster's wife in *If...* who cures her boredom by walking around the school stark naked; and like the Girl at the Bar of the Folies Bergères.

I have no patience whatsoever to read books again; prefer to read a review paper picking out the best bits for me. No patience for cinema, classical music concerts, relationships; anything except the quick thrills of masturbation or sex. I will just earn money for these two "thrills". For the third night in a row the three Scandinavian ladies are here playing their cards. My gorgeous receptionist was not here today. 00:06. As usual the Priapic excitement of my room has turned to soporific stupor in the bar.

Can you believe after one night in Brussels, and four nights in Berlin, I've not seen one single music video? All that fantastic Belgian, French and German pop music I am completely missing out on. It is a crying shame. And music forms such a strong part of your memories of a holiday (or anything); yet I go home with no musical memories whatsoever. It is really so stupid; I don't know why nobody else feels this loss as I do. You can watch German music on YouTube but IT IS NOT THE SAME! I want to turn on my TV and be surprised by great German music by great German bands I have never heard of! This used to be one of the greatest joys of travelling for me.

I walked all the way to Berlin Erotic Point only to see them pulling the shutters down as I got there. There was no point going on to Monte Carlo without getting turned on first, so I just turned around and headed back. Once again I found my way there so straightforwardly and found my way back so straightforwardly so no idea how I could ever get lost. I walked past my hotel and kept on going for Mazurka (where I had such a legendary time with Olga & Alla in 2006, though no written record seems to exist of it anywhere in my books or notes—although I do still have half a dozen photographs of them that they permitted me to take). I had heard it had closed and indeed I could see no trace of it. I vowed never to set foot in Ciro again but in I went. Twenty euros, two free drinks. A very pretty brunette Romanian, Andrea, came to me and wouldn't take no for an answer, but she was so pretty, and let me touch her all over, and was touching me so I at least bought her a 15-euro cocktail and left her another 15 euros in cash for being sweet. An hour in a room would have cost me 300, half an hour 200, 15 minutes 150 but for that there is just dancing and strip, no sex! I think I was there for an hour and in that time just two girls got up and did a little topless dance on the stage. If they had constant dancing and lowered their prices I think they would do much better.

Another grey rainy Berlin day. 0946 on the train back to Köln and Brussels. An erection all the way, thinking of the nice erotic moments I had in Berlin and those still to come back in Brussels. Christ, I am so turned on, on this train to Brussels. A really grey rainy day. Hard to believe this is summer. On the way to Bielefeld now. 1155 only. Still another 5½ hours until we arrive in Brussels. 1205. We get to Köln 1409. We just passed the big Kaiser Wilhelm statue on the hill by Minden. Now I regret I didn't let Vanessa give me a handjob while I took out her massive breasts, and then finished off by f–king Jessie at the side. Christ, Andrea's body felt good in my hands; her gorgeous arse, her breasts, her thighs, her pussy. I have had so many good erotic moments on this trip; and even when back in my room I was turned on constantly, my cock permanently hard. Just one hour 20 minutes to go until Köln now. Grab a roll then two hours 50 minutes in to Brussels. I am desperate to resume now. I cannot remember the last time I felt as constantly aroused as this.

On the ICE waiting to pull out of Köln. Still grey skies heavy with rainclouds, as it has been all the way since Berlin.

BRUSSELS

The little brunette barmaid with the over-big glasses in the Orient Express, but a gorgeous curvy little arse. I continue to notice delightful little details—like the brass coat-hooks all have little "paintings" on them.

You know I always complain bitterly in London, f—king traffic lights every 50 yards; f—king stupid; but in Brussels you see the reality of what a lack of traffic lights is like, and it is a mind-blowing sight. I am actually in shock that in all these years of coming to Brussels I have NEVER seen a traffic accident—cars, bikes or pedestrians.

I had a large Stella in the Ibis (which made me soporific—same as the Berliner Pilseners and Vienna Zipfers), and a couple of small Jupilers in L'Orient Express followed by two vodkas, then rushed up to Alhambra Cinema. They close at 11, which is good to know. One OK film downstairs, then walked along Rue des Commerçants to Yellow Lily more for somewhere to have another drink than anything else. Had two Maes here but the thrill was sexy Ina in a black backless trouser suit, fitted to her voluptuous arse like a second skin. She has "the fresh bloom of sexuality" on her; like a flower that has just opened. I think she opened a long time ago, but she still maintains the impression of only just opening. It is a quality that can't be faked, manufactured or mistaken. She is the Maria Schneider of Yellow Lily, and only Andrea can compete with her, but she has not been around for a while. From Yellow straight up to Rue d'Aerschot. There was no one in the windows that blew my mind this time, so I spent more time watching the good videos in Sexyworld. I got a metro back after 12. Looking at the signal boards I notice the last train seems to be around 0045.

The conclusion of this trip to Berlin, with a one-night stopover in Brussels on the way there and again on the way back is: I wish I'd spent more time in Brussels. I had a nice time in Berlin but not enough to go back for, any time soon. The best memories of Berlin: the gorgeous brunette receptionist who checked me in, Fraulein —. The free little hand massage the blonde Turkish girl gave me in Monte Carlo when she saw my cock was already up & out. The unexpected prettiness of Jessie in Monte Carlo. The sexiness of Andrea in Ciro. The best memories of this visit to Brussels: the real sexiness of Beatrice on Thursday night. How much I enjoyed the Alhambra Cinema films on both nights. The way Ina stood out in a light of her own at Yellow Lily. The quality of the Sexyworld kabin films, perfect preparation for starting your look at the windows. How much nicer it is to drink in the Orient Express rather than Ibis bar. How Stella just makes me feel soporific but the Jupiler and Maes seems to give me the fire in the blood that I want from beer. It is the same with the Berliner Pilsener I drank in the Berlin hotel, it just makes me soporific. The same with the Zipfers in my Vienna hotel. I don't know why some beers send me into a soporific stupor and others put a fire in my blood. Maybe just the coldness they are served at? I prefer the bars that serve their beer ice cold? Is that all? Another really grey Brussels day. A real grey, rainy depression settled on Europe for the whole six days I was away—strange to have SIX DAYS of grey raininess in July—but of course I was very grateful for it. Just spots of rain on the Eurostar window even now. I always think I do affect the weather and the huge metaphorical cloud and pressure hanging over my head since the morning I left home manifested itself in the bizarre six-day rainy depression over the whole of Europe. I note the forecast for Brussels tomorrow is very hot & sunny again, now that I have gone.

I am actually surprised my fat face and fat stomach did not seem to worsen at all while away, which is amazing after six consecutive days of drinking morning, noon and night. Maybe the stress I have been feeling burnt a lot of calories off all the time; I've always felt that stress has done that to me in the past. Or maybe I just eat less when I am feeling stressed, because my insides feel so knotted up all the time. Amazing I stayed turned on for all six days as well. This has been the sexiest holiday since my glory days of 2003 and 2004—also my most expensive.

Yes, this has been an expensive trip but it is my last long trip for a long while, so I was happy to go a bit mad. "Strange how potent cheap music can be." Strange how potent I find the really cheap sleazy places, like Sissi Bar and Monte Carlo; or the 20-euro hotel rooms of the Rue des Commerçants where the girls take you. "The sight of a whore is profoundly thrilling to a man," said Flaubert. How true. It really is the ideal relationship between a man and a woman.

*

A most bizarre and heavy long dream about 18th century adventurers sailing across southern seas to a land where they believed the second incarnation of Jesus was living, there they meet a man coming out to meet them and they walk across to meet him, a Charles Cogan Lewis. A bearded, brown-suited, top-hatted Victorian gentleman who apparently was Jesus. I cannot remember any more but it was a portentous and ominous dream. I felt the power of their quest, and their belief that this was Jesus, and the momentous moment of their meeting. I wake exhausted, shattered, aching all over.

I am trying to do something quite new in my writing. I record my life almost every minute of the day. They say people think about sex every minute or whatever, I am showing that in my writing. What that actually means. And I am showing someone going from bar, to a strip club, to a porn cinema, to a videokabin, to a night bar, to a prostitute. All the things together, one to the other, with the goal of constant stimulation. I am not sure anyone else writes about this or records it. People write on the sex cinema forums, and other people write on the stripper forums, and other people write on the prostitute forums: I don't know if anybody writes about all these things together. I don't know if other people exist who do this, going from one to the other. Anyway I want to leave behind a record of this way of life. For a time when these places don't exist—already in London NO porn cinemas exist. We have already achieved that state. Effectively in Soho there is now just ONE strip club left. There are only about ten flats where prostitutes work from. In Brussels in the last 5 years they have lost California videokabins and peep show, ABC Cinema, etc. Bete de Nuit, for example, just writes about prostitutes—does he not also enjoy strippers and porn films and kabins? I write about everything in totality, one to the other.

Oh I cannot wait to spend another holiday devoted to the penis. Whether two nights in Brussels or my seven-night trip to Brussels, Munich & Vienna. That is what they are though, devoted to the penis. From the moment I arrive I get my laptop out and start watching porn to get in the mood, before starting to drink and heading out to see naked women, strippers, whores or in a porn film. Cannot wait to be back in Alhambra Cinema again, and Yellow Lily again, and Gare du Nord videokabins again, and Carolina.

More than anything I just like to lie naked with a girl, chatting softly with her, stroking each other's bodies, only at end finishing with sex; I'm not into all this exhausting athletic multi-positional frenzy you others go in for. Sounds like an Army assault course. Just to find a beautiful curvy sympatico girl and lie there naked in each other's arms for a little while till I feel ready for the culmination. Anyone else prefer these gentler pleasures? Am I weird?

I'm like the last of the Medicis. I knew there would be no other after me, so I just gave up; I am just going to stay here and live the life I want to lead.

Live wildly. Live like money is no object. Riches will come later, surely. I don't want to sit at home doing nothing for three days. I will get so depressed. Better to travel! Burn like a firefly. Living wildly is all very well, but I don't know if my body will be up to it.

The melancholy moment. Sex, alcohol and gambling. On my first few visits to Europe, my grand tours, it meant something to get to Venice, or to get to Neuschwanstein, or to go to *The Third Man* sites, pilgrimages, but now I just go for the sex, alcohol and gambling (I don't gamble actually, but I see it as spending a lot of money and seeing if you are going to have a good time tonight or not, that is the gamble). True, last year I found it incredibly moving to visit for the first time the *Night Porter* hotel building and the café opposite, and then to visit the site, knocked down and wiped out, of Milena's apartment in *Bad Timing*. So I do still make some pilgrimages it seems. I wonder what ones are left that would move me like that?

The connection between alcohol & sex. Almost a religious ritual. It's what is most spiritual in my life, going out for sex. And I only really do feel comfortable going out for sex. Same way I only go out for drinking. I never feel so happy drinking at home or having sex at home.

BRUSSELS

Oh, as always, the casually beautiful girls of Brussels! With their casually magnificent bottoms! A dark blonde-haired girl passed me in the Gare du Midi, like a cross between Louane, Peaches from Sunset Strip 1990s and Milena in *Bad Timing*. Mesmerising. The railway workers are protesting from today to Friday, and no trains at all on Friday. Thank God the trains are at least running tomorrow so I can get my early train to Munich. I would find it quite impossible to read a newspaper in Brussels: I can't take my eyes from the window. The black bob African duty manager in black mini-skirt who came to my room to fix my TV; her extraordinary little sticking out arse under that black mini-skirt, black stockings. The silver zip on her skirt such a temptation. Incredibly it's 210PM before I get to the Dome. Wake up, shower, getting my TV fixed, one small beer in the hotel lounge, then here. Lightly raining. Feel very poised, very balanced, knowing I have got Munich to enjoy tomorrow, then three days in Vienna, before final nights in Munich and Brussels on the way back again. I would rather keep my powder dry tonight until Vienna, and the homeward journey. Don't want to spend a fortune on the first night and feel I've shot my bolt before the holiday has even properly begun. Getting a swelling here in the bar just thinking about it.

Oh, effortlessly brilliant; effortlessly beautiful; these Brussels girls.

I always felt I was floating above everyone, on some superior level, like in some balcony looking down on them. And if I ever did step down to speak with them directly, it was just to flirt, then I would step back up to my balcony and continue looking down on them, and the effect I had had.

The driver tells us he has been informed there are pickpockets on this train. Well, we ARE in Brussels; I expect to find pickpockets under my bed or in the shower. ICE to Frankfurt, from whence I head on to Munich. Apparently I spent 65 euros on my first day in Brussels. Alhambra Cinema once again two mediocre films. I complained about the exclusive diet of Marc Dorcel, now they seem to just show awful U.S. porn which is the worst in the world as far as I'm concerned. And the old pervert was back, shuffling to stand next to me at the back, and just staring down at my crotch the whole time hoping for any glimpse of hard English cock. I left about two minutes after I walked in, intending to go back later but suspecting I would be too drunk, as it proved. Got to Yellow Lily about 4PM and it was poor as usual. I was just about to leave when four big Dominican Republic girls came in together, the curvy black Lucy the pick of them. I got turned on just looking at her, but she said she did not speak English and I did not press it. Not sure how many beers I had but eventually I left and had a McDonald's before bed. My TV was not working again, a regular occurrence in the Max. On the way along Rue des Commerçants I am sure I saw the black jacket, blue jeans, black ponytail Moroccan I remember from last time. "Cheri, ça va?" she said. I hope I see her on the way back. Some grizzly kid ruining the peace of this ICE.

MUNICH

3PM. Munich hotel. The newly refurbished Rechthaler Hof was a heart-breaking disappointment. The silver-haired ladies in dirndls are gone, just one man instead. When I asked for a rostbraten he didn't even ask how I wanted it done. Smaller portions than they used to give and no salad with it. Mediocre (and too pink). Spaten beer has been replaced by Ayinger. Bright inside. Too bright. One nice touch is a square of stained glass hanging between seating sections—nod to Munich's monastic origins. Three women receptionists at the Ibis reception, and a gorgeous-bottomed little barmaid. Try to nap as Munich is waste of time during the day. No music on TV of course. Limp Bizkit's classic song Behind Blue Eyes (after The Who) from 2003 on the radio now, before I head out into the Munich night again; a lot less interesting than the night was back then no doubt. Rechthaler Hof used to be an absolute treasure; now I don't think I want to go there again. Their rostbratens used to be a thing of delicious wonder; now quite mediocre. Another treasure ruined.

As always, the eternal mystery and regret that the Ibis ripped out all their beautiful, atmospheric old dark wood bars and replaced them with the cold, hard, modernist mediocrities. The bars are now a place you want to get out of as fast as possible. Their high plastic stools are appalling; so hard to get onto even. Designed for their look and not for comfort, like everything else about the bar. The beer, Maxlrainer, is quite unpleasant, and not even really cold. As I suspected, the sexy little barmaid from earlier has left, replaced by a dour unsmiling black man. The reception staff also gone too. Now the dilemma: do I stay at this hotel on the way back next week, just to see that sexy little barmaid again, or try one of those cheap (relatively) hotels in Schillerstraße? Oh no, a bunch of six or eight Scottish lads have just entered the bar. Oh God, the groom's just arrived, dressed in a Bride to Be sash. My luck, a Scottish stag party arrive in the bar, just at the same time as me. Opposite the hotel I see a Café Central. Oh Jesus, it's just occurred to me, they are going to go on a trawl of all the strip clubs and girlie bars of Schillerstraße aren't they? Actually, that is quite good, as it means I will not be the only man when I walk in as I usually am, and they can take all the girls' attention away from me. I should actually FOLLOW them from club to club! They can be my cover! They are putting a bet on tonight's Scotland v Poland Euro qualifying match: they predict a 6-5 win for Scotland. They are all ordering pizza on the ipad on the bar; this place is going to reek of mouth-watering pizza any minute now; yet another reason to move on, even with just one beer inside me. How atmospheric the old Ibis bars used to be. There was no need to change. It wasn't broken, they should not have fixed it. It is broken now.

Just thinking about taking my love to the Neue Pinakothek and showing her Die Sünde, and incredibly there are tears in my eyes as I think about showing her THAT picture. How can a PAINTING bring tears to your eyes, have this much of an effect on you? I saw it first at a particular time in my life, and it knocked me for six. I just literally wiped a tear off my cheek.

Oh, how exciting, I am on a train to Bologna, Italy. My 0624 to Wien was cancelled, because of the refugee situation, so they have put me on the 0738 to Bologna, changing at 0842 at Wörgl for the train to Vienna. I feel a frisson of excitement at being on a train to Italy, and the temptation is to just stay on it. I get on this train and find 99% of the seats are already reserved "Munich to Wörgl", so it seems everybody else on the Vienna train knew about the cancellation in advance and had already switched their reservations. Why didn't I know? Perhaps because I bought my ticket so far in advance, before the police closed the border on that line.

Munich was crossed off my list a long time ago and this stay has just put a fourth or fifth line through it. I was shocked at the number of girls in Atlantic City, I counted fifteen which was a lot in that small space. There were a lot of good-looking girls, to be honest. Atlantic City has real curves, bosoms & bottoms, but for a ridiculous 50 euros private dances are out of the question. The girls were still very busy giving them. In Munich there is nothing better on offer so men are prepared to pay I suppose. Every club charges the same, so it must be a price set by the authorities one would have thought. Back in 2003/4 they were 25 euros and that was cheap enough to tempt you to have one or two or three, but at 50 euros I won't even have one. Still fifteen euros to get in with two free drinks. The kabins were poor, a very small selection of films. Into Bad Angel, and as expected from my previous visit all the girls are supermodel thin and one or two hideous boob jobs as well. Just two customers (Atlantic City was busy with men), but they looked like rich Americans who were literally showering the girls with banknotes. I left without finishing my free beer, that's how awful it was (twenty euros to get in with one free beer). Up the road into Piano Lounge. Small place, free to get in but seven euros for a beer. The girls come to you and try to sell you the usual 50-euro private dance. It seems crazy they cannot offer you dances for cheaper; are they really not allowed? Again I left without finishing my beer. Into Tiffany. Six girls but no customers at all. I turned around and left. By now I couldn't be bothered with any of the other places, so just went to Sexyland and enjoyed the videokabins, the best I have ever been to. An enormous range of big breast films. Home via the station grabbing a couple of rolls then sleep.

Only leaving my hotel this morning did I realise that Boobs Gentleman's Club is in the same street as my hotel. A more upmarket and expensive place than the Schillerstraße clubs I expect. I did see a few groups of Syrian-looking men at the station, and the area by the side has been fenced off as a kind of reception centre but that is all. Just a longer journey to Vienna than expected though. I have to stay in Munich again Monday night. Better to just save my money for the Sexyland kabins and not waste any anywhere else in Munich.

Bright blue skies as we left Munich; now in the countryside we are encased in a thickening mist.

During my long vigil on platform 11 waiting for the Wörgl train, amazed at the number of nubile young German girls heading to & from the trains. Innumerable. Later a DB employee came and told me my train was in fact leaving from platform 13, otherwise I'd probably have missed it. But apart from that, and the beautiful hotel receptionist and barmaid, I did not see any really beautiful girls in Munich. Nothing to compare with Brussels where they come thick & fast, in a manner of speaking, as would I, given half a chance.

I have about forty minutes to wait on the platform at Wörgl before starting the search for a spare seat for the long four-hour ride to Vienna.

VIENNA

Finally I arrive in Vienna, a febrile Westbahnhof, and already I wish I could stay longer than three days. I read about Austrian taxi drivers making a fortune ferrying refugees from the Hungarian border into Vienna, and sure enough walking to the hotel I saw a big people carrier disgorging what looked like a large Syrian family. Their suitcase had a massive hole in it (my bag has holes too). Amazingly, there is a music channel on my TV! GoTV which was a music channel but then became something else has reverted to music!

I feel tense and stressed because I really haven't done anything naughty three days into my holiday. Just had an argument with the receptionist as she refused to ask housekeeping to put six beers in my minibar instead of just two, as you can only have the "standard". She is young, and she will learn, hopefully. Or I will have to make do with two beers only. One or the other. At St Polten, last stop before Vienna, a most beautiful girl got on, long black hair, eyes heavy with black make up, dark red lipstick, beige trousers so tight they fitted her pussy like a glove. Stunning. Twenty-year-old-ish. Perfect. I do like heavy heavy make-up on a girl, I really do.

Calvin Harris is clever—churn out one piss poor weak track after another but put a stunning, half naked model in the video so perverts like me have to watch it from beginning to end every time it comes on. 4.30 already, and I haven't left the hotel. I never feel ready to leave my hotel until I am almost incapacitated by drink. At this point, my day begins. When I was younger this was no bar whatsoever to achieving and maintaining massive erections; indeed, the problem then was getting them to go down again. Nowadays, I need a little help to counteract the alcohol. Just noticed the Chinese restaurant opposite is now called the Ristorante Mittelmeer and seems to have an Italian flag in the logo. I suspect it may now be an Italian restaurant.

20:00 I arrive in the Café Westend. WSK has a new star, Jackie. She was the only girl on duty, but the WSK was busier than I've known it for a long time, which I don't think was a coincidence. My first day in Vienna flew by like it never happened. Few beers in hotel bar, WSK, Café Westend, then no doubt

I will be sleeping like a log. Ah, I Have A Dream, I recognise that one. This waiter has brought me ketchup and mayonnaise, like he always does, and it will cost me an extra 3 euros each, and I did not request it or want it. I shall try to give it back.

I woke after 10PM and thought about going out but was too drunk still, so went back to sleep until 850 in the morning. The WSK films were fantastic, high quality stuff. There were more men there than I have seen before (still never more than eight) and I think that is all down to Jackie, black hair, young, beautiful, curvy. The Café Westend steak was as fantastic as always. Shame I could not go out for a reconnaissance mission at least to Manhattan but hopefully I can be fresher tonight. Today Fortuna then maybe back to Burggasse Peep, save WSK for later and stay until closing so I can walk back past Angelique back to Manhattan.

10AM I had just started to write a note to leave in the minibar for housekeeping when they knocked at my door. I asked is it possible I can just have eight bottles of beer, and she smiled "Yes! Of course! No problem! Austrian beer is good?" Yes, the best! She was cute. I will tip her tomorrow. So very happy with my stay this time. An absolute thrill to find a great music channel on my TV, and a smiling happy housekeeper (chambermaid, let me call them chambermaids, such a sexier term) supplying me with all the beer I want. A great thrill to discover a new young black-haired beauty in WSK, and a wonderful rostbraten in Westend.

Tinie Tempah Pass Out—not a massive fan, but I must admit it is a little thrill to have proper London music when on holiday in Vienna. There are some beers that make me dull and soporific (my natural state really), but some that put a fire in my blood. Am I imagining it? Is there so much difference between beers that have this different effect? Zipfer makes me soporific.

So, what of Saturday? Got the No.6 tram down to Fortuna. Once again two high quality films. *Drunk Sex Orgy* and the start of a Gabriel Pontello film (*Fatzenschaft?*) but no "hostesses". Back up to Burggasse Peep. The kabin films are better than I gave them credit for (and I already had 36 euros on my card so I did not have to spend anything) but the peep show girls I saw were poor, all skinny. There has been no sign of Manuela since the occasion of my glob of white ejaculate landing squarely between her eyes back in January. I hope that did not discourage her from the job. Left quite quickly as I was hungry. Roll & pizza from station, then, crazily, a 200g steak down in the Dorint restaurant. They have a new steak menu and it is better than before. I had to force myself to finish it, however; I was stuffed. Tried to sleep then but couldn't, so had a couple of beers from minibar then up to WSK. Once again two excellent high-quality films and Jackie there too. I declined her charms this time because I wanted to save it for Angelique and Manhattan bar. Angelique—really three bars in one, Large Angelique, Small Angelique and Alm Bar—Lilly was on holiday, but her friend Sylvia was stunning. I resisted, even at 100 euros for half an hour, and headed on down in the rain to Manhattan. Busy with men, the whole time I was there, a lot of them Syrian-looking (Westbahnhof was packed with them, it is like a refugee camp at night), and SEVERAL beautiful girls, Melissa and Denitsa I know from before, but a new blonde Adelina. The problem is DECIDING which one you want, and I could not, so just drink and drink then stumbled back to my hotel about 2 I think. Melissa for big breasts, Denitsa for big bottom, Adelina neither breasts or arse as big as the others but a little of both—and the most beautiful face you have ever seen in your life.

Manhattan is visible from Westbahnhof, so that is why it always attracts more moths to its light than the other places, lost up the dark and forbidding-looking Gurtel where no one knows they are—I don't know how they survive at all. Wish I could stay in Vienna longer, and now I know I must come back in November. With this amount of alcohol consumption, most of the time I am just thinking about food, and that distracts me from the sex most of the time. Drink, food & sex—these are my holidays. *La Grande Bouffe* in Vienna & Brussels (Berlin & Munich no longer on my list). Plenty of Syrians here in the hotel as well. I dread to think what my 635AM train to Munich is going to be like. I paid for a seat reservation, so they'd better not sit in it. A screaming Syrian child in the Dorint lobby for the past hour. The other good trick Manhattan have got is they have a video jukebox, so even if you say no to the girls there is something for you to sit and pay attention to, and they do make some effort to do a little twirl on the stage (without taking anything off but still). So you can drink your drink and have something to watch, so you don't feel as awkward and pointless and sore thumb-like as you do in all the other Gurtel night bars where you just sit on your own staring into thin air unless you buy the girls hideously expensive drinks. At Manhattan you can sit on your own and still have a pleasant dreamy time. I have to say, the girls in the Gurtel are all unfailingly attractive (to say the least) and pleasant.

Nowadays I tell myself if you go to the naughty places, WSK, Fortuna or wherever, I will reward you and let you have a lovely Westend steak or lovely Westbahnhof pizza (or both). It is food that is what I really yearn for these days. I rush to get the naughty places out of the way, so I can get to the food afterwards.

I have loved this stay in the Dorint hotel Vienna but oh, how magnificent that Lotta & Sophia stay in 2002 feels, more & more & more than ever. Unreal. Like a Swedish fantasy. A Swedish 18-year-old nubile fantasy. Legends of my own life. Last time I felt anything that strong was 2006 when I fell in love with —. After that, emotion was not possible anymore. That is why she is the woman of my life. I was kindling ripe for the great conflagration, that both destroys and brings to flaming life, and she was that great conflagration. Every man only has one great conflagration in his life?

Well, finally, third day in WSK and two rubbish films. I couldn't even get an erection. Jackie climbing on top of me did help, but not enough. I was just thinking about food, so came back here to the Westend. A grey, overcast, quite breezy Sunday afternoon. Jackie was huddling in long cardigan & scarf. Not only were the films bad, not only was I sated after two days of it, not only was I thinking about food and I had eaten nothing all day, I think I was thinking of the three Manhattan girls and wanted to keep myself for them and get back to sleep a bit before then. The subconscious is all powerful. I should have enjoyed Jackie Saturday night when I was so turned on, as I subsequently did nothing in Angelique or Manhattan. Christ, I just want to eat & eat & eat. This is what drinking & drinking & drinking does to me.
    The Westend waiters prowl around, ominously, menacingly. You're never sure if they're going to serve you or beat you up. The Café Westend, and the WSK, and Manhattan, have become part of my life more than anywhere in London. I have nowhere in London that means anything to me (certainly since the final closure of the Flying Scotsman). I could stay in the Café Westend forever.

I felt very tense and stressed getting in the rickety old train to take me out of Vienna. It was packed. After the second stop people were standing all the way along the aisle; but at St Polten it emptied out massively and now is very peaceful and spacious. I head back for a night in Munich, before Brussels the next day.
    On my last day in Vienna I did nothing but go up to WSK and finally my luck ran out: two rubbish films. Jackie was there but I was not in the mood. Once again I was starving, so just rushed back to Café Westend for an unbelievably delicious Alt Wiener Zwiebelrostbraten. Then to bed! I woke in the evening planning to go back to Manhattan, but I just didn't feel like it. Sated. Done enough. I went back to bed and endured a massively sleepless night, hampered by indigestion and restless aching legs. I may

have dropped off about 5 in the morning, about an hour & a half before my alarm went off. So a low-key finish to my stay in Vienna. The money I saved will be needed to pay for my last night in Brussels. 0856 now. One hour into my 4½ hour journey back to Wörgl; before a forty-minute wait, then one-hour journey into Munich. If this rail disruption persists it may decide me against returning to Vienna in November. Bloody refugees!

0914 St Valentin. One hour 18 minutes gone. Three more hours to Wörgl. A clear blue morning, not a cloud in the sky. Nothing to do in Munich except have a few beers in—where? No desire to return to Rechthaler Hof (and how sad it makes me to say that) but where else is there?—then spend an hour or two in the luscious kabins of Sexyland. Then to find an internet café somewhere, if my hotel does not have a computer for guest use (I cannot even remember which hotel I booked. Somewhere in Schillerstraße, but there's quite a lot of hotels in Schillerstraße!). Memories of the holiday: the voluptuous Dominican Republic Lucy in Yellow Lily. Discovering the Dorint DOES have a music channel. Discovering Jackie in WSK. The four sexy girls in Manhattan. 0928 Linz. Three hours to Wörgl. "The feeling of plenitude, of power which seeks to overflow, the happiness of high tension". Nietzsche's *Beyond Good & Evil* is my companion on this long train journey back to Munich. 0942 Wels. 1000 Attnang-Puchheim. 2½ hours to Wörgl. 1006 Vöklabruck. I always feel down when I come to the end of a holiday: tense and scared of the amount of money I have spent. I should be happy, I have a night to spend in Munich and a night to spend in Brussels. Back in Munich there is nothing for me anymore. Atlantic City is poor, but the other places are even worse. At least in Atlantic City there is some dancing to watch by normal curvy women (not the giraffes and stick insects of Bad Angel and Black Boxxx), but even Atlantic City is poor: I do not want to ever again go to a strip club where the girls do not take their knickers off. I do not ever again want to stay in a city where there is not sex for sale. A man needs meat. A man must let off steam. At least Munich has the best videokabin selection I have ever found in Sexyland.

October –. I have the luxury of seven days off in November. I was thinking to return to Vienna, after the delights of new girl Jackie in WSK, great films in Fortuna and WSK, many beautiful girls in Manhattan, AND a music channel on my hotel TV, but this refugee crisis train diversions put me off. It would be nice to spend seven days in Brussels, wouldn't it? Oh, but Alhambra Cinema seems abysmal these days, Yellow Lily is abysmal these days (Dominican Republic girl aside), and that just leaves the good window girls of Gare du Nord and good kabin films in Sexyworld. 1047 Salzburg. Just one hour 45 minutes to go. This seems a much less painful journey than it was coming. The train is half empty and peaceful. It is a

Monday morning not a Friday. There are no football supporters on the train. This train is as docile as the one going was febrile.

This train I have boarded at Wörgl has come from Verona Porta Nuova. How romantic, exotic, thrilling. Leaving from the opposite platform five minutes earlier was the train for Venezia. Any train with an Italian destination name on it sounds thrilling. Stunning scenery around Wörgl and Kufstein, where we cross the border into Germany; gutted that my phone died before we got here, and I cannot film it. Maybe I SHOULD come back this way before the trains go back to normal (will they ever?). Ah, found a seat with a charger but my luck it is on the side of the train with the bland scenery; the spectacular scenery is all on the other side; curses! That's why I didn't notice it on my way here. Just one more stop, Rosenheim, before we get to Munich. 1339 Rosenheim. Just fifty-one minutes into Munich. Oh, the police have got on and turfed off six or seven refugees without papers sitting right opposite me. We are going to be delayed now.

MUNICH

A very low-key disappointing end to the holiday then: Saturday was the high point of the trip; fantastic films in WSK and I really wanted to f—k Jackie, but I said no, because I knew I was heading straight to Angelique and Manhattan so thought keep my powder dry in case I see anyone sexy there, and indeed in Manhattan I wanted to f—k Melissa, Denitsa and Adelina, but in the end did nothing. Thus the potential high night of the trip passed. Sunday was typically miserable and dead, and Munich is always dead.

I really don't want to go back to Atlantic City tonight; but for just fifteen euros which includes two free drinks, it is really not expensive to see some naked bosoms at least, though I find the stage show utterly uninvolving (and I find any strip club where the girls keep their knickers on quite absurd). Hard to believe this place gave me some of the highest nights of my life. It excited me so much back in 2003, 2004. A lot of things excited me back in those days; before I fell in love with my wife. After that nothing really excited me again (except her, of course). Not really enjoying this Spaten beer in the Sports Café (the Café Schiller as was) next to Atlantic City. Nothing wrong with the beer, just the feeling this holiday is already over with two days still to go. It really ended Saturday night, and I won't be home until late Tuesday night. Ah, Blondie Heart of Glass. If I do go to Atlantic City I will just try to lose myself in the music and the beer and try to brush off the endless hustling as best I can. Private dancing—the death of strip clubs.

I think the Syrians are LOVING the pleasure pots of Europe, from the looks on their faces—white European girls having sex with them for such little money. So available, so loose. The "Syrians" I met in Schillerstraße Munich or the Manhattan, Vienna, anyway. This is like their paradise, with forty if not quite virgins waiting for them, forty very nubile young women waiting for them. "I am the dog's bollocks"—a bizarre expression even in English. I wonder if there is any equivalent term in German, or French? I am one of those men who when offered the chance of a decent real relationship with a girl, rather than a life of stripclubs, and whores and porn kinos, prefers the life of strip clubs, and whores and porn kinos. It is at least a life of pure freedom, and lack of shackles, or guilt, or shame.

So Monday night in Munich and I'm in bed by 930PM, ready and eager to sleep. As always at the end I just want to get home. My mojo has gone. The excitement of the outward journey has gone, so I might as well be home as fast as possible. I went in Atlantic City to use up the money I had left on my bonus card but did not spend fifteen euros to go in for the dancers; that says it all. I also used up the money left on an old bonus card in Sexyland so apart from four pints in Café Schiller and the two rolls & two pizzas on my way back that is all I spent in Munich. I hope I make my connection and have time in Brussels to try one more girl—either Dominican Republic or black ponytail, before I finally head for home. Still, cannot believe here I am in Schillerstraße, Munich, and in bed by 930PM.

Fiction to me seems a lesser form of art than journal writing. I can't read it and I can't write it. The only thing which seems of value is to put down one's own thoughts on paper. The real psychological storms people go through in their own heads seem of more value than any invented dramas.

*

My freedom, or the woman I love: that is what my life came down to, and at the end inevitably I will look back and see I threw away the woman I loved because I couldn't give up my freedom. A lonely sad cold old man I will be, missing her for so many years till I eventually die alone and she won't even know I am dead. But I couldn't breathe, from the moment we moved into —, and I cannot live like that again. Not now, perhaps never.

Every time I go to Europe I think THIS TIME I am going to fuck a girl every day, I am going to fuck three girls in a row in Yellow Lily or Manhattan one after the other. But I never do. I hang back and prevaricate, and then they

409

disappear with someone else and I never see them come back, or I get too drunk to move, and stumble home without doing anything. Will I ever do that wild rampant thing of fucking so many? Yes I really want to do this! Oh but then all the girls I fancied in Brussels disappeared!

BRUSSELS

Jesus, I must have drunk a lot last night. My brain cannot put two things together this morning. On the ICE to Frankfurt, then on to Munich then on to Vienna. Couldn't find my scarf this morning so God knows where I left that. Lucy was back at Yellow Lily and I could not tear myself away. Ina too looked amazing. On the walk back, Beatrice looked amazing all in white, like the Ice Queen. I am travelling without a seat reservation for the first time. I got on and every seat in the carriage was reserved. Oh no, I thought. But into the next carriage and every seat was unreserved. This shows to me it is better NOT to reserve a seat. If I had a reservation I would have been sitting in a packed carriage squashed up next to someone all the way for three hours; now I am in an almost empty carriage with two seats to myself. I haven't had a hangover like this for a long time. Last time I went in Diamant Bar and there was a sexy black-haired girl walking around outside. This time I spoke to her. Bruna. Fifty euros for sex and twenty euros for the hotel. The standard. I did not take her up on the offer this time. But there were four 10 out of 10 girls in one evening. Still pitch black this 707AM morning. We pass through Ans. Pouring with rain as we pull into Liege, 714. My erection has been permanent since we left Brussels: thinking about Lucy & Ina & Beatrice & Bruna. Still more than ten hours until I arrive in Vienna.

Well, that was interesting—German customs officers made me leave my seat and bring my bag and they did a complete search of my bag, made me empty my pockets, did a drugs test on my hands, made me show my tickets, hotel reservations, everything. They were quite aggressive, as if they really suspected me in particular, but perhaps this is their manner with everybody. The end of my bag with the broken zip they have now ripped open with a knife so it just hangs open now. So that is a lost scarf and a ripped bag now. This holiday is progressing well. The frisk they gave me was very thorough; I think he even counted my testicles. Well, that certainly woke me up. The Chinese man who had been sitting next to me, and was leaning out of his seat, looking back at me excitedly full of glee the whole time they were searching me, like this was the best thing he had ever seen *in his life*, has now moved to another seat, perhaps fearing I am an unsafe person. Good. Fuck off. My eyes were horridly bloodshot when I left the hotel this morning, and I am a bit befuddled; maybe that is why they picked on me.

So we arrive at Köln and the train driver announces there is an accident on the high speed line to Frankfurt and this train cannot go any further. We all have to get off and get another train in thirty minutes to Frankfurt Airport and then go on from there. Well, there goes my connection to Munich, and therefore there goes my connection from Munich to Vienna. Will I have to buy another ticket? It will cost me an absolute fortune if I do. I try to escape the feeling this trip is becoming a spiralling nightmare. As if this journey to Vienna wasn't going to be long enough. I should not feel too persecuted, after all this line closure has caused travel disruption and chaos to everybody. Everybody is affected equally (although they may not have connections they have to catch, like I do).

This nightmare journey is still ongoing. I had to stand for two hours all the way from Köln to Frankfurt Flughafen. Even the aisles were blocked with people. The seat I thought was free was in fact reserved so I had to give it up. For part of the journey I was just sitting on the floor. Then at Frankfurt Flughafen on to another ICE to Munich. We've been going for 2½ hours so far and we're still forty minutes from Augsburg, last stop before Munich. Quite obviously as it is already 138 I am going to miss my 134 train to Vienna. And once again it looks like I will have to get a train to Wörgl first, then pick up the Railjet for the long four-hour journey into Vienna from there. Hopefully this missed connection will not cost me any money. God knows what time I am going to get to Vienna now. I would guess around 9PM. A shower, something to eat, then straight to Manhattan I guess; presuming it will be too late for WSK.

    While stranded at Köln, and standing for hours on the slow train to Frankfurt Flughafen (it was an ICE but forced to travel on the slow track), I actually toyed with the idea of returning to Brussels and spending the whole week there; my spirits are low, understandably; but I knew this would be a long hard day of travelling and once I do get to Vienna I have three long days of lovely relaxation, just eating & drinking; so I force myself to push on. Once I get there I will be fine; I do wonder what the next blow to fall will be though. Just think about the fantastic films of Fortuna & WSK waiting for me. And the sexy girls of Manhattan at night. The gorgeous Alt Wiener Zwiebelrostbraten in Café West End. Just hold your nerve: once we get to Vienna I'll be fine. I have got the most marvellous job in the world, earning £-,000, working in peace & quiet all on my own. I have complete freedom in my life. Just enjoy the suspension of travel; I thought I said I always did!

411

So remember that, and enjoy the suspension of it now. The nothingness of it.

Turns out there is another stop before Munich Hauptbahnhof—Munich Passing, twenty-one minutes away from there now. If I have to wait a while for my next train from Munich I can at least enjoy the kabins of Sexyland. I'll be glad when I'm on the train to Wörgl and the last lap of my journey will nearly be at hand.

One hour 46 minutes into Salzburg, twenty minute wait, then two hours 22 into Vienna 730, bit earlier than I was fearing; and no extra charge to me, in fact to add to the 25% refund stamp they gave me on the train from Köln, she now has given me a 50% refund sticker, so it is nice to get some money back for my trouble. Well, off to Salzburg. Almost getting there. Typically, before boarding the train I stopped to buy a bottle of water then rushed for my train, only to discover my pile of papers containing my tickets was no longer in my pocket. I rushed back to the counter and sure enough I had left my papers there, and they had put them behind the counter for me. Farcical.

Christ, there were some beautiful nubile young German/Austrian girls on the train to Salzburg; and now on the train to Wien. I need to get my mojo back. I'm now so excited to get to Vienna, I feel like a coke bottle that's been shaken up. I can't keep still. Oh God, the time really can't go quick enough. This is what I travel for: this excitement. How fantastic I can still be excited about arriving in Vienna despite the number of times I have been there! And I certainly had an exciting first night in Brussels.

VIENNA

A low-key first night in Vienna. A few beers in my room, one in the bar then walked down to ML Revue. I won't bother again. The peep show girls were nothing special and the kabins were awful. Videokabins have to have a menu button and an ability to choose categories. A kabin where you can only flick through the videos one at a time forward or back is useless. You use up all your money just flicking through them all. I won't bother again. Up to Manhattan. Same girls as my last visit but this time I just wasn't affected by them. I was so turned on by the girls in Yellow Lily Wednesday night, but here not at all. I will try Fortuna and WSK this afternoon, then try somewhere new later tonight—either Maxim in the centre or Exzess further up the Gurtel. I can't escape the feeling that I wish I had stayed in Brussels; it felt so carnal on Wednesday night.

Pleased I went for the breakfast included option this time; the bacon & scrambled eggs breakfast was lovely. 1237 now. First beer of the day in the bar. I went back to sleep after breakfast. I discovered when I unpacked last night I've also lost my bottle of —; sure those Customs c—ts left it on the floor on the train as they ransacked my belongings. They searched me so aggressively it was like they absolutely knew I was guilty of something. I started to doubt myself. "Empty your pockets. Get EVERYTHING out of your pockets. NOW!" If someone had placed some drugs in my bag and then tipped the customs off, what can you do?

I was supposed to arrive back in Brussels 530 on Monday night, but with all the train trouble it might be closer to 730, which gives me very little time to go to Yellow Lily, Alhambra Cinema or anywhere. Melissa with the heavy big bosoms was at Manhattan last night, and Denitsa with the heavy big bottom; as was big blonde Vienna girl Romy, very nice, but it is the sexy beautiful Adelina who will be the one, if anyone is. Lucky girl! That blue eyes girl with long platinum blonde? almost pink-purplish? hair and beautiful face, with amazing dimples, and nice figure. But let me explore a little first tonight; if I can wake up. Oh my God, about 150 people have just come into reception to check in. I'm not even kidding. They look like Europeans; they literally have filled the reception. Poor Eva & her colleague. It's going to take an hour to check them all in.

Checking in and looking at my reflection in the lift mirror on the way up to my room I was struck by how handsome I still looked, despite my marathon thirteen-hour five-train journey, and I don't know why everyone was looking at me so suspiciously all the way here.

Hitler used to live in this street. The hotel is at 4 Felberstraße and he lived at 22 Felberstraße. Amazing to think he walked up & down this street every day (back in 1908-9); going in & out of Westbahnhof earning some pennies offering to carry passengers' bags for them. Supposedly the rich Jewish bankers & businessmen of Vienna used to use him for sex, and he swallowed so much Jewish cum and took so much Jewish cock up his little effeminate arsehole, that was what inspired his overwhelming revulsion against the Jews. Who knows if this is true or not? If only we could send a miniature little robot camera back in time to see how Hitler really lived in Vienna at that time, who Jack the Ripper really was. I find Bruce Robinson's Michael Maybrick theory compelling, without having yet read the book.

I can't write Vienna off until I have been to the two best porn kinos, because porn kinos are the glory of Vienna for me. Just the memory of those four so sexy girls in Brussels on Wednesday night is overshadowing everything. I will have to work hard and be lucky in Vienna to find anything to compete with them. So, another beer. Strength, adventurer! Courage! Not met a single sexy girl in Vienna. I never do to be honest. The train from

413

Munich to Vienna, yes, always do, but I don't know where they disappear when I get here. In Brussels you see stunning girls every minute. Not here in Vienna. I can't get Lucy off my mind, and Beatrice, and Ina, and Bruna. Oh, but Adelina.

When you think of the amount of shit that people produce, the amount of shit they are flushing down the lavatories every day, it is amazing our cities don't permanently stink of shit. It seems to me shit is the most defining characteristic of human beings, some more than others. Effective shit removal seems to me one of the greatest achievements of human civilisation; what did they do with it back in the 17th century, 16th, 15th, 3rd, 2nd, etc etc? How did they cope without a powerful flush and sewage pipe system? It doesn't bear thinking about.

One more then I go. I will definitely buy some more cans of Gösser at the station on my way back. The Zipfer makes me soporific; or the hotel bar does; or a combination of both. I wonder if I will meet anybody in Vienna to overshadow the four girls I met in Brussels on the first night of this adventure?

A rainy Vienna day, but not heavy. Just drizzle really. Sexy Jackie was in WSK, which made it worthwhile. I confined myself to a 20 euro "hand massage", while she was topless, and me sucking on her breasts, with my hand down her pants on her lovely curvy bottom. Afterwards you think "Was that it? Was that what I came all the way to Vienna for?" Yet still I look forward to seeing Lucy & Ina & the rest back in Brussels again, and maybe other girls tonight in Maxim and Exzess. 437PM. After the meal I will go back and sleep, and head out again after 9 I hope. Two awful films in WSK by the way. If not for Jackie it would have been a disaster. Bloody hell, a giant Budweiser before my meal. I won't be finishing this.

I should perhaps make the effort to do something cultural on this trip, as I am here for three whole days. Belvedere, perhaps, for Richard Gerstl's Laughing Self Portrait and Makart's Five Senses in particular (Klimt's The Kiss interests me little). Or the Leopold for the innumerable Klimts and Schieles but no spectacular stand-out work, I think. Or KHM, for Titian's Mars, Venus & Amor, the best version of the subject I think. Or the Albertina, where I haven't been for so long. Or to *The Night Porter* hotel & café? Milena's *Bad Timing* apartment, or at least the appalling hole where it used to be, tragically.

How at home I feel in the Café West End. I wish I had bought an English newspaper to read. I wonder if I will ever create a great work of art i.e. a great book? Writing still seems to me the supreme art form; as much as I thrill to a great stripper dancing to a great song. But since the death of the Flying Scotsman I wonder if I will ever enjoy that pleasure again. Sunset Strip is the last hope. Europe is a waste of time. They never even take their knickers off. A middle-aged blonde lady sits at the table facing the door. Seeing me unattended by a waiter she gets up and and leaves me a menu. Obviously the manager/owner. Let me try Maxim tonight and then Exzess tomorrow night (Saturday). Will be good to try a couple of new places. I have reached the last page of my Moleskine.

So Saturday I woke planning to go back to Brussels on Sunday rather than Monday; then I came down to check the internet and find the army on the streets of Brussels. All metro lines closed, all shopping centres closed, all football matches cancelled, as a terrorist attack is expected "imminently". This is the city I am travelling back to, Sunday or Monday. Avoid all railway stations they advise, as I prepare to come back into Gare du Nord. My love may be about to claim her life insurance after all. Will Yellow Lily even be open? 1240 I am in the Dorint bar.

The Café West End Alt Wiener Zwiebelrostbraten blew me out as usual, and it was all I could do to stumble back to the hotel to sleep. I woke after 10PM and forced myself out just after midnight to try Maxim at Karlsplatz. It was as bad as I always expected it to be. Lots—lots—of skinny-looking girls, coming up to you one after the other. The dancing was pretty non-stop but as always topless only. You can fuck the girls, so why on Earth can you not see them without knickers? Bizarre. The place had the feel of a Browns or Horns in London, which means pretty awful. So disappointed was I, I just left after one beer and came straight back to the hotel and back to bed. Good thing was the metro runs all night in Vienna on Fridays & Saturdays. Oh, but haha, there was such a long wait for the next metro back to Westbahnhof I ended up walking all the way back to the hotel from Maxim's. A twenty-minute walk perhaps.

So Saturday in Vienna. I will try Fortuna, then try to rebook my Monday train to Brussels for Sunday. That will give me Sunday night and Monday night in Brussels. Though what kind of Brussels will I be returning to? I see pictures of three army trucks outside O'Reilly's! If Sunday is my last night in Vienna, I will try Exzess up the top of the Gurtel, before finishing for a last night cap in Manhattan. If everything in Brussels is going to be closed is there any point going back to Brussels a day early or staying one day more? Their terror alert is raised to 4, the highest, meaning an attack is "imminent". Well, if the metro's not running how will the Yellow Lily girls get to work? As always all I can think about is my own sexual pleasure.

A river cuts its own course. I always follow the path of whatever offers me the best chance of sexual pleasure. So I go today to Fortuna Kino, and let's try Exzess, then finish with Manhattan. And I try to get back to Brussels sooner than planned, despite Brussels being in military lockdown.

820PM. I just want to stay in my big white bed, with my lovely big white pillows. No desire to go back to WSK, or Exzess, or Manhattan.

So with great effort I FORCED myself to go out last night. Forced myself to drink the six bottles of Gösser in my minibar then got the half past midnight metro up to Nußdorfer Straße and I tried the Club Exzess I had heard about. Small, and packed with men, which was good to see. Maybe ten men which was enough to pack the place. Five or six girls, who took it in turns to dance topless on stage. Probably the busiest club I have been to in the Gurtel, and the first I have seen with constant topless dancing. Though why they will fuck you but will not take their knickers off when dancing is something I do not understand. Same for Belgium, Germany, everywhere I've been. Baffling. How lucky we are in London that full strip is the normal. The metro runs all night on Fridays and Saturdays, but only at fifteen-minute intervals and it was my luck every station I entered I had just missed one, so I ended up walking back from Exzess. I stopped off in Bar Josephine for one beer (eight euros), five girls, no dancing, one customer. Picked up a metro at Michelbeuern AKH to Westbahnhof and went for late nightcap in Manhattan. Adelina and black girl were at table with two gentlemen, bottle of champagne, and Adelina was very drunk it seemed. Just watching her walk to & from the jukebox in black bra & knickers was quite intoxicating, so I hung around until she was free, then bought her a drink. If in 2003 I thought Riccarda in Berlin was the most beautiful girl I had ever slept with (in a night club), and then Maria in Pour Platin in Vienna in 2005, then I would say Adelina in Manhattan has just raised the bar. She was very drunk, gabbling at me in Romanian the whole time, and I was too drunk myself to feel anything, but a very good experience. Suddenly I was glad I had forced myself to come out. I had been thinking I will not come back to Vienna again, or not for a very long time, but Adelina has rescued things. I couldn't finish but I told her it was all right, and began to get dressed. She sat on edge of bed and looked like she was going to cry: "Ohhhh! You don't like me!" Oh, I liked her all right.
 Stumbling back into my hotel at 4 in the morning and crossing the Klimtian gold lobby to my lift, I was surprised by the night manager rushing out of his office to hail me: "Mister —! Happy Birthday!" I stopped in my tracks, befuddled, stunned. "Sorry?" "Today is your birthday isn't it?" I

thought about it. I had gone out Saturday night, the day before my birthday, and as it was now 4 the next morning, yes indeed it was now my birthday! "Oh yes! I'd forgotten! You're right!" He grinned triumphantly: "Well—Happy Birthday to you!" How amazing. Not only that he should know—but that he would take the trouble to jump out of his seat in the back office and come running out to give me best wishes. I was touched beyond all words. This truly was the best birthday of my life.

115PM today in the hotel bar. First small beer (after two cans of Gösser in my room). No denying a great deal of trepidation about travelling back to Brussels tomorrow morning (530AM departure to arrive 530PM). The city is still in complete security lockdown; soldiers on the streets. All shopping centres closed, all metro lines closed, all football matches in Belgium cancelled. Avoid crowds, and railway stations they say, and here I am heading into Gare du Nord. Into the vipers' nest. Very good France has forced Europe to reactivate border controls, but it just means the terrorists based in Brussels planning their attacks on France are now forced to attack Brussels instead? All bars were ordered to close by 6PM on Saturday, and I doubt if Yellow Lily will even be open when I get there. I've no luck with that place. No idea what kind of Brussels I will find when I get there.

There are more bars in the Gurtel still open than I thought. Just last night I saw Club Exzess, Bar Josephine, Bar Vienna Night Bar, Queen Night Bar, in addition to the ones I already know, Alm Bar, Angelique 1 & 2, Flamingo, Okay Bar, Bar Haus 6, Manhattan and Tête-à-Tête. I liked the atmosphere in Exzess (probably because all the girls were busy & so not one of them approached me & bothered my peaceful beer!), the number of customers, but its girls were not as sexy as the Manhattan girls. And Adelina, Adelina, is on a level all of her own. Up there with the legends of my travels like Yulia, Riccarda, Iga, Olga & Alla. Maria. I suppose the horrible situation and likely nowhere to go of Brussels when I get back there Monday night kind of forced me into returning to Manhattan and doing something with Adelina, as it may be my last chance of glory on this trip (or ever), and I am glad I did.

Today just WSK I expect, then I will treat myself to a second Café West End Alt Wiener Zwiebelrostbraten. Perhaps pop back to Manhattan later but I don't expect Adelina to be there on a Sunday, so I should get away early tonight to sleep before my 530AM train back to Brussels. Before I even get to WSK all I'm thinking about is food. 153PM. Still plenty of time. 224. Still some time. Well, this is my fourth day in the hotel and I've not seen a single person eating a single mouthful of food in the restaurant. Sad. But I think this is the way for most hotel restaurants? They get so few customers it doesn't pay to even bother? I am as guilty as anyone; I am looking forward to eating in the Café West End a little later. Why not in the hotel? Café West End food is better. This is why hotel restaurants inevitably die. Well, 3PM now. Things are progressing quite fast actually.

0515. On the train out of Vienna. Heading to Salzburg where I have just eight minutes to change platforms to catch the train to Munich, which doesn't seem enough. Then from Munich to Frankfurt (hopefully on the high-speed line this time), and then the final leg of the journey into Brussels—Brussels under army lockdown due to "imminent" attack in "multiple locations simultaneously". I would have loved to have gone back to Manhattan Sunday night, to look for Adelina, but I didn't want to drink before a 5AM check out. In the end Sunday I did nothing but drink in the hotel then go out for a Café West End steak. That was it. Slept all evening and then from midnight to 4AM alarm I was just tossing & turning, too tense to sleep.

The next small blow to fall, arriving at Salzburg a couple of minutes late, and rushing to swap platforms to catch my 0800 Munich train, seeing no sign of it all on the boards. After 0800 passes I go back to Information and they confirm the train was cancelled. Luckily there is another one at 0813—though just one door open on the whole train and security guards checking everybody's bag before letting us on the train by that one door. Even here in Salzburg, so far from France & Belgium, the feeling of fear is palpable. I had a one hour 10 minutes to kill in Munich so I should be all right for my next connection. Perhaps Brussels is a safe place to be right now with the army on the street. It will be less safe once the lockdown ends and "normal" life resumes. The thoughts of enjoying one last bit of carnal pleasure in Brussels may make me go out tonight after all—although I can't believe Yellow Lily will be open, or even Alhambra Cinema; even the street girls? Everyone gets on the trains with their big bag or suitcase; any one of them could have a machine gun or a bomb in their case. Europe suddenly feels a lethally dangerous place.

On the ICE to Frankfurt, waiting its departure. This is the emptiest ICE I have ever been on; one would assume the one from Frankfurt in to Brussels will be even emptier.

Now on the ICE to Brussels. I was thinking this might be the end of my travelling days, but right now I think ironically this might make me go to Vienna MORE, as Vienna feels relatively safe. But still going out for one brief night in Brussels along the way! So what has changed! Might as well go out in Brussels for one brief night tonight then. With all the soldiers on the streets probably the safest time to do it.

BRUSSELS

Well, so here I am in Brussels, 937PM. Brussels under "security lockdown". And yet Alhambra Cinema is open and showing a couple of good films to me and one other discerning customer. The girls are still in the Rue des Commerçants, including my Beatrice. Yellow Lily is still open, including Ina in a stunning floral body suit. Her appeal does not diminish, it just grows. She is like a flower that is just starting to bloom, and she just keeps on blooming. I must admit, when I arrived at Gare du Nord I felt scared. And coming out of the station, passing the soldiers with massive machine guns, I felt scared. And walking down the road from Gare du Nord to my Max Hotel, I felt scared. Every bar and café and restaurant was closed along the whole length of the road, but then, incredibly, Brussels Grill was open, the first place I saw open. And even incredibly the Café du Dome was open! Bravo for them. What if gunmen walk in and start shooting you? Nothing you can do. But you have to go on, don't you. And bravo to them. And then you have a couple of cans of beer and you start to relax. And then you see Alhambra Cinema is open and you relax more. And then you see the street girls in the Rue des Commerçants, and you relax more. And then, amazing, even Yellow Lily is open as normal. Less girls than normal, it is true, but Ina is there, and you relax even more. This is how courage breeds courage. Fear is contagious, but so is courage.

So I wait for my Brussels Grill. No bread or butter this time? Ina looked magnificent but I wasn't turned on this time to even try. I need a Lucy (not there) or Betty or Bulgarian to turn me on enough to even try anything with Ina. Now I am hungry. I will maybe finish with a nightcap in Empire if it is open but that will be it. I have proved a point. I have overcome my very strong fear and hung around in Brussels, out on the streets. I haven't felt this scared since the morning after those two men beheaded the soldier in Woolwich; but then nothing else happened the next day or the day after and slowly courage returns. The terrorists need to do it every day, day after day. I don't want to speak too soon. But Alhambra Cinema, and the street girls, and Yellow Lily being open give me courage and makes me feel better. Brussels Grill playing a slow, jazzy, sexy Pink Panther theme tune now.

The Brussels Grill steak was once more incredibly pleasurable I must say, with a very nice mixed salad which makes a big difference. Once more a real pleasure. From there I was ready for bed. The soldiers outside the Bourse and O'Reilly's in particular seem to have become an extra tourist attraction, everyone taking their pictures with them like with the Horseguards in Whitehall.

*

The fact is I really don't WANT to go back to Vienna again, not right now anyway. It has come down to just WSK and Manhattan. I have given up on Fortuna, and I don't feel at all comfortable in the other Gurtel night bars. Yes Adelina was great but is it worth travelling all those hundreds of miles and all those hours across Europe for? No, it will be a long while before I feel like Vienna again.

People in — are terrified of my sexuality. My sexual power. My sex is out of control. My sex is on fire. They cannot stop thinking about my sex, what I am doing with my sex. How sexy wearing my jeans with no underwear makes me feel.

Though I say my addictive lust for sex and porn has destroyed my relationship, my love, when it is not there, like now, I miss it. I miss that sex drive that gets me out of bed, that sexual hunger that is only motivation for anything. Feel lifeless now, depressed by how suddenly terrifying Brussels has become dampening its carnality. This lust has led me to the greatest nights of my life. Red Riding Hood Night in Soho Cinema, for example, the Sunset Cinema nights. The Godzilla days. STILL though, I would love to go back to Brussels really turned on with lust, my cock bulging against my jeans, no underwear, from Alhambra Cinema along Rue des C, to Yellow Lily and sit in Yellow with massive cock, sizing up which ones. My last two visits to Yellow have led to me getting my big cock out with Betty and then with Lucy, so that place certainly DOES turn me on!

There is a war on carnality, everything must be made increasingly SEXLESS. The cleansing of Soho, Stuttgarter Platz Berlin, the imminent loss of the street girls of Brussels Alhambra. More reason than ever to keep travelling more and more regularly in the short time we have got left till everything is gone and we will truly look back at this as a lost golden age.

BRUSSELS

420

A slightly subdued atmosphere in Brussels, but not as tense as last Monday night when I arrived back from Vienna. Soldiers still on streets on the corner of Rue Neuve and outside the Hotel Plaza. Security guards at the entrance to the City 2 shopping centre. I wouldn't fancy their job. 230PM my first Jupiler of the day. And so the casually beautiful girls of Brussels commence. It is so cheap to drink cans in the hotel lounge—2,80 for two 50cl cans from the shop. This would cost 8 euros in the Dome? Lack of sleep is keeping my mood quite low; I will feel better tomorrow and Friday after a proper sleep. I'll just see how long I can last today. Let me get to Yellow Lily as fast as possible (via Alhambra Cinema and then the Rue des Commerçants) then I can be back in bed as quick as possible! Blue skies when I woke; clouding over a lot now. 350. I've spent an incredible one hour & 20 minutes on these two cans of Jupiler, and still a drop more left.

I went for the smaller cans of Jupiler today, 33cl. Those 50cl cans yesterday were hard work. All I did yesterday was go briefly to Alhambra Cinema and then Yellow Lily, didn't do anything naughty in particular, and yet still seem to have got through 121 euros. The old pervert was back in the Alhambra Cinema. Pathetically hanging around for anyone to fumble with. He was hovering in the reception area when I arrived and as soon as I went in to stand at the back in the dark he followed me in and stood next to me. I went upstairs, he followed me upstairs; I came back down and sat down in the dark. He followed me & found me in the dark & sat next to me. Twice I moved and twice he followed and sat down next to me but then—an unusual event, out of nowhere I noticed there was a young woman in the row a few in front of me, with her top lifted and letting men touch her bosoms, while she played with their members. She came to me but only spoke Italian and French but was trying to get me to give her money to do something with her and her "companion", the man she had come in with. I kept saying no but she just shrugged and carried on handling me regardless. The two of them then sat together on the sofa underneath the screen that I had never noticed before; she came back to me and now pulled her trousers down and wanted me to touch her between the legs. She was offering me various things in a language I did not understand; eventually I declined and disentangled myself from her but gave her 10 euros for the fondle at least. She seemed happy. Italian apparently. Gabriella. I left then and made my way in a state of some arousal to Yellow Lily where I seemed to spend the next several hours, drinking myself into some kind of oblivion. Lucy was there, and so I knew I would be staying. My God, in tiny white & blue sailor-striped top with her cleavage spilling over, small black shorts over black stockings.

421

What a picture. She followed me to my table but after buying her a Red Bull I moved away; she was too desirable and...so why didn't I just do something with her? I always feel I need to be really drunk and wild before I will have sex. In the corridor leading to the smoking room I had another little fondle with the slim black-haired Bulgarian —, she was kissing me with her tongue and pulled my fly down and released my tool from its tense confinement. Another girl walked past laughing, "Oh, a show!" I then sat with the black Brazilian girl, the one I always smile and nod at but had never spoken to before; she has got a beautiful and KIND face, I think it would be lovely to go to a room with her. Her name escapes me, but I remember it was something very beautiful; like Olympia or Ayeesha. I vaguely remember buying her a Red Bull as well, and I think I gave her and Lucy a 10 euro note each, more as an apology for not doing anything with them. I do recall buying a double vodka & coke and being shocked to discover it was 18 euros; I sat for a long time staring at the receipt in my hands, until the manager Victor came over and sat down next to me seeing how upset I looked, and kindly explained I had had a "DOUBLE double vodka, doppel doppel". I must have looked shocked. A McDonald's which I must have paid for with the 100 euro note in my pocket as I see he gave me 94 euros change.

A bright blue-skied Brussels day. 1239. The soldiers still on the street, a reassuring sight; how scary it will suddenly feel when they are withdrawn. Would be nice if they could be there permanently. My first Jupiler of the day. Nothing planned except back to Alhambra Cinema and Yellow Lily. On the way back to the hotel I had a brief chat with a very pretty girl opposite Jimmy's, and then Beatrice who was just a few yards away, grinning at me talking to someone other than her. Spoke briefly with Beatrice then back home. Honestly, why DON'T I — any of the girls? There were three I liked in Yellow Lily, and then two in the street, but I never quite can bring myself to do anything. I was very tired yesterday, after so long without sleep, more than 26 hours. The casually stunning girls continue to pass under my window. It really is a good observation point; even better than the Dome, and cheaper of course. I slept right through to 5AM, then dozed off again until nearly 10AM, so I feel refreshed now.

    No desire to go to any museum. If the old magnificent Museum of Modern Art was reconstituted I would, but no desire to return to the Magritte or Fin-de-Siècle. How I loved the old Museum of Modern Art; in one place Alfred Stevens' Salome, Le Gènie du Mal, La Figure Tombale, Death of Marat, Trésors de Satan, Magritte's La Goulue and Lola de Valence, the room FULL of Paul Delvauxs. It was a special place; destroyed, broken up, most of the pieces I mention now locked away in storage with no place to show them. Fuck the Magritte Museum—a little Magritte goes a long way with me. A museum full of them is way too much. Milking the Magritte cow for all its worth they have killed the goose that lay the golden egg, to mix my metaphors. Ah fantastic (talking of milking cows), I just saw Beatrice and two friends crossing the road under my balcony and walking towards her place!

Here I am, at the Molenbeek Hilton. Having a Molotov Cocktail in the bar. I will miss the street girls if they are indeed banned from the area (Alhambra, I only recently discovered, though it is not marked as such on any map I have seen) as the Mayor intends. A little bit of sex adds such colour & life to a city. Sterilisation, sterilisation, sterilisation. Castration. Emasculation. Whores have been the lifeblood of so much European art & literature & music down the centuries. The sterilisation of Europe is a sign of our cultural decline & enfeeblement. A healthy society can cope with sexuality, eroticism, red in tooth & claw, and should not cower in fear from it. Every time I look up from my notepaper, I see another casually stunning Brussels woman passing beneath my balcony. Better than any pornography. I hope Belgian men realise how lucky they are. When, when, when, am I going to go to Italy? Christ, they go on & on. The women of Brussels really are mindblowing.

I do really like Jupiler beer. Jupiler & Maes. Stella I don't like; it is one of those beers I find soporific. Another reason why I probably won't go back to the Dome. Yesterday's Plaza soldiers wore green berets, passed occasionally by brown beret soldiers on patrol; but today's are black berets. I have also seen purple berets. Another casually sexy 18 or 19-year-old girl goes along the road. My God. The thighs, and bottoms of these Brussels girls! Both white Belgian and darker Moroccans! We hear so much talk about French women and Italian women and South American women and Eastern European women, but no one ever seems to remark on the extraordinary Belgian women. They are just happy to put on a bit of weight it seems, not frightened to appear fleshy, curvy. Just such a natural, curvy beautiful womanliness. It makes them all look so FERTILE. The idea of going to a gym, and working out, and boasting what a flat stomach she has now, would be anathema, bizarre, to a Brussels woman; they are more wise, more relaxed, more spectacular. 117 already. Yellow Lily doesn't really seem to open or at least get going until 230ish, so plenty of time. No Ina yesterday, but I didn't miss her: Lucy, Ayeesha and Emily were so sexy. Emily is a skinny thing so surprising I find her affecting at all, but she is hot, I do have to admit, and naughty.

How happy I am to be STAYING in Brussels this time; and not having to leave at the crack of dawn the next morning for a marathon train journey to Vienna, or Berlin, Though I must admit, after a certain amount of time has passed, I would love to see Adelina again, in Manhattan in Vienna. But my Vienna trips will become fewer & far between from now on. Maybe once a year only. It is too far to travel, unless I return to flying, which I do not intend to do. Though I must admit, on that last leg of the ICE trip back to Brussels from Vienna I felt as suddenly vulnerable and defenceless as I ever do on a plane. Fear was really in the air that week. It was impossible not to become infected by it. The atmosphere was thick with it. It was cloying.

I know I've said it before but it bears repeating: I would love to marry a Belgian girl one day, if she would have me, and didn't mind the huge age difference. Girls like older men, and they like taller men: I read it in the paper this morning. It is scientific fact. And I do agree, I only fancy shorter women. I have never found a tall woman attractive, even if she is still not as tall as me. Something very sexy about short women. Curvy, short women. Another reason why I despise women in high heels. Pointless! Pointless! Where did they get this bizarre idea that it makes them look sexier, more attractive to men? The opposite is true! When strippers take off their high heels, wait for their next turn in their flat little ballet pumps, they look so much more sexy. I know what I am talking about. I am an expert.

The fact is when I got to Yellow Lily yesterday, I felt too sober to have sex. This is how fucked up my attitude to sex and drinking is. I have perfectly conditioned myself to think I can only have sex when absolutely crazy with drink. The thought of having sex sober, or even just slightly drunk, actually scares me; no matter how absolutely sexy the girl; no matter how much my cock is literally poking out of my trousers. Mentally, emotionally, I am not ready, not ready, not ready; always later, later, later. It probably is still shyness, ultimately. Oh God. Two more beautiful teenage sisters just passed by, top two most beautiful women you've ever seen, there they go, just like that. 145. I might give Alhambra Cinema a miss today, head straight to Café Jimmy or Diamant perhaps before Yellow Lily. Can go to Alhambra Cinema later before Empire if I wake up in time.

I always think if I went to Italy (the one night I spent in Venice doesn't count) I will be blown away by the beautiful women in the street; but until that day Brussels will hold the crown; with no other city even coming close. Oh Jesus, and there's another one, as soon as I put my pen down and look up, there's another one. Another casually 10 out of 10 fantastic nubile young Brussels girl. The thighs & bottoms, my God. And in winter, with everyone covered in big winter coats, that is all you can really see. But obviously that would count for nothing without the face, and the faces, my God. Such beauty. 1355. Third can of Jupiler. Gratifyingly ice cold. Bravo. Funny I still feel no desire to go to Paris. I might love Paris as much as Brussels if I gave it a try. Mona Lisa, Musée d'Orsay, Napoleon's tomb, Oscar Wilde's tomb, *Last Tango in Paris* apartment; so much for me to see & do in Paris I would need to stay for a year. Italy & Paris, these are my two big unfulfilled ambitions. But Brussels and Vienna won't let me go. Christ, that Belgian police girl with the huge gun is so pretty.

Police checking the street girls' papers by Café Jimmy; Beatrice just outside joking with some old man sitting in wheelchair. Three euros for a small bottle of Carlsberg is expensive. For the music TV I will stay for at least one.
Checked myself in mirror before I left, and I look drunk. Very attractive. Hiccups again. Always get hiccups in Café Jimmy. Think it's the Carlsberg. Very beautiful black girl with massive bottom & thighs comes in here to the Café Jimmy and sits on her phone (not literally). What a massive loss it will be when the street girls are forced out. How I love being around whores. I always think there is something much sexier seeing these beautiful sexy girls in the street swaddled in their thick winter coats & scarves, than seeing the bikini-clad girls in the Rue d'Aerschot windows. Hiccups didn't last long at least. Beatrice came in begging me for 50 euros; she can't afford a hotel. She had to sleep here last night in the café! Usual sob story but I like her. I only give in to desire, I'm afraid. Watching her arse & thighs as she walked away, then I felt the desire. The music channel of Café Jimmy is SO good, it makes me want to stay.
Three cans of Jupiler in hotel and one Carlsberg here. Every single one of the Balkan music videos is full of girls who look like whores dancing around in lingerie; there is no variety in their videos at all. It is the ONLY concept of Balkan music videos. And a very good concept it is too. Keep on watching. Girls & cars, every video the same. Sometimes big boats. I like this style of music video much better. I must look bad: I nodded hello to one of Beatrice's friends who was coming in to Jimmy's as I was leaving, and she just looked back at me without saying anything, thinking who is this bizarre looking wanker with the pink face? The street girls come in & out of Diamant Bar as casually as they do Café Jimmy. I love this kind of environment. Still, they all giving me very funny looks. Is my face looking that bad? How beautiful whores are. "The sight of a whore is profoundly thrilling to a man" as Flaubert said.

How fast I drink in Yellow Lily. Being in a bar full of whores (who do not approach you but leave you in peace) quickens the blood so much. The metabolism doubles in speed, at least. 305 in Yellow Lily and it is already busy with men & girls. This place thrives. It WAS a beautiful blue-skied day earlier, but now the skies are slate grey, and it is freezing. Here I am in Yellow Lily surrounded by girls (two of whom I really like, Lucy & Ayeesha), but all I can think about is a Brussels Grill steak.

A blazing blue sky Brussels morning. 11AM in the hotel lounge with my first Jupiler of the day. It tastes almost poisonous. I am saturated with beer after two solid days of drinking. Shocked to see there are NO soldiers outside the Plaza anymore. Have the soldiers been withdrawn from the streets? There was I just saying how safe they made me feel. Oh my God some beautiful black-hair girl came walking down the street dressed in nothing but a white bathrobe! What the hell? Just went into the shop next door.

Finally I did something with Lucy, thank God. I remember very little of it as I was so drunk, but I am glad I got it out of the way. Afterwards back in the bar she allowed her friend to take a photo of us together on my phone. I don't remember leaving but there is a McDonald's bag in my bin, so I must have grabbed a McDonald's on the way back; slept through until early hours again. I should make the effort to go up to Rue d'Aerschot today, just to do something different, and I really want to get back to Empire later tonight. Nothing to eat this morning; all I can think about is food.

My God, the street girls of Brussels are lovely. Black-haired Bulgarian Bruna by the Diamant, and Beatrice's friend "Pamela Anderson" on Beatrice's same corner. It will be tragic when the Mayor finally gets his way and bans them from here. But, my mind was on Brussels Grill, so I passed by the two lovely ladies and wait for my "rumsteak". I gave up on Yellow Lily, Lucy still had not appeared, or Ayeesha; and Ina's not been around at all this week; today was all about the steak, and going out later. 4PM now. Yes, it is true, the soldiers have gone from Brussels.

Waking Friday evening I felt NO desire to go out anywhere, so I didn't. Three days of solid drinking left me feeling saturated and fatigued in the brain. Already I look forward to my next visit back to Brussels, but that will probably be the New Year now. Oh, there's a soldier! Just walking slowly down the road checking cars out.

I really am not at ease getting on the Brussels metro at the moment. The trains are so short; at least in London you can get on the last carriage of a very long tube train if you want to avoid crowds, but in Brussels the trains are only like three small carriages long and so you are always pressed quite closely with other people. I feel too defenceless on the underground; I don't even like it in London. I value my life too much. I really have achieved nothing that I want to achieve in life. Some people might say I am leaving it a little bit late, but I still feel so young. I just feel like I am starting in life right now. I feel like I am in my early 20s, just setting out in life. Though if some ugly left a bomb in the back of a taxi or underneath it I would die just as surely; but still, I don't like airplanes and now in Brussels I don't like the metro.

I would definitely like to do something with Lucy again, as I remember next to nothing of the first time. Highlights of this trip? The naughtiness of Yellow Lily, mainly with Lucy, but a little bit with Ayeesha and Emily; the lovely Brussels Grill steak. I said I would not come back again but it has quite quickly returned to my good list, and to have a perfect acceptably big steak for just 15,60 makes it quite affordable actually. When I am drunk these 15,60 steaks are more than enough for me. That's it really. Never got to Rue d'Aerschot, Sexyworld, or Empire. But really Brussels has given me so much pleasure that is just not on offer in London anymore; London has zero of the places that Brussels offers me—Alhambra Cinema, Rue des Commerçants, and Yellow Lily just do not have any equivalent in London. No desire to return to Vienna just yet, but next time I go I will stop off for a night in Nuremberg going and Frankfurt coming back perhaps, so I always have something different to look forward to and break the journey up—though that then makes the trip such a long one. Three days of drinking have wiped me out; seven days hardly bears thinking about. 1142. Still not even 12 yet. My third can of Jupiler commences. I will just go to Jimmy's and Diamant perhaps.

So I decamp to the Diamant, passing the Bulgarian girls opposite the Flamingo Bar. I now realise there are the Pelican girls, on the corner of the Rue du Pelican opposite Jimmy's e.g. Beatrice & her friends, and there are the Flamingo girls, on the corner opposite the Flamingo Bar. You could say there are the Black Beard girls too, on the Black Beard corner; and various other girls in the points in between, but the Pelican girls, Flamingo girls and Black Beard girls are the main hotspots.

I do wonder if the black-haired Bulgarian Diamant bar manager is a former whore; she does have the most massive bosoms (not that massive bosoms makes someone a whore, of course; I'm not saying that; I'm not). I wonder how much longer the street girls will be here. The Mayor was talking about getting rid of them by the end of this year. How massively bland Brussels will seem without them. A whole ecosystem wiped out. And what harm are they causing exactly? 1PM. Another hour. Already I look forward to my return to Brussels. The whores do come into Diamant, but only the older ones it seems, none of the younger ones, like Bruna. No, the

427

bar manager is Alex, not Alice. All I can think about is Brussels Grill. Wow, and then Bruna walks in.

*

When I got this job I thought now I can grow, and bloom & blossom. Now I can start to pick all the fruits that have been ripening. And already I made a good start, with Beatrice, Adelina and Lucy. Now 2016 could be even better. A whole entire year of it. If only I can clear this —, this could be an amazing abundant year. Perhaps the best ever. And really you know you could be struck down by serious illness at any moment, so you have to enjoy the fruits as much as possible now.

Easy to take for granted the naughty things I do on holiday. What I did with Lucy, Betty, Emily in Brussels, with Adelina in Vienna, it is like I am living in my own porn film.

I don't understand these men who don't want their girls to be strippers, or cover themselves up all the time; women are so sexy, and that sexiness should be allowed to bloom & blossom and open up like a flower. Explode into life.

I always feel randy at this time of year, fuck Christmas and its holiness; it is the pagan roots, the heathen roots of our end of year rituals and celebrations and feasts and orgies that enliven my blood, quicken my blood. The hairy nights, the smoky nights of Germanic heathen times, the Wild Hunt, Odin riding out on his wild hunt.

You know how if your headphones leads get tangled up (which they always do) and you angrily furiously try to pull them apart with both hands they just get knotted all the more surely; you must try to patiently choose just one end and slowly unthread that one end and then magically everything comes undone at the same time; isn't this a metaphor for life problems? Just concentrate on one, give that your sole attention, and it's amazing how many other problems are quite unexpectedly unravelled as well.

COLLECTED WORKS

COLLECTED WORKS

ALHAMBRA

2016

ERNST GRAF

COLLECTED WORKS

BEER, PORNOGRAPHY & PROSTITUTION—THE GREATEST THINGS IN LIFE. My three drugs. My three opiums. I travel to indulge these opiums. I do indeed have a mind completely bitten by the serpent of sex, and I cannot understand why everyone is not like me. But, it has to be sex without emotion, sex without "relationship". Pure priapic, erotic rampancy. Sex for the pleasure of sex, sex for the visual pleasure of sex. Sex as just hands on pornography. I am really phobic to emotions. Only one woman has ever got through my defences, and remains "behind my defences" (in a kind of perpetual offside position).

I was born 20 years too late. The 1890s sound fantastic, the 1920s in Berlin sound fantastic, but in the modern era, the 1970s perhaps was the golden age of pornography & prostitution in Europe. I didn't discover these wonderful places until the 1990s, just as they were about to go into decline—due to Internet—easily accessible pornography for everybody—and new bizarre Puritanism. The death of the sex places is understandable even to me. When I was growing up, if I wanted to see a naked woman I had to go to Soho—because it was before internet. Now if I want see a naked woman I just open up my internet. No.1 reason for the death of the sex places right there.

I do not understand people who can live their lives without beer, and pornography and prostitution. I just genuinely cannot. They are so much the crutches of my life, I do not understand anyone who does not need these crutches. Where is their opium? What are their highs? Is this addiction to these opiums sign of my sickness? I honestly feel I am MORE healthy, MORE alive, than those who live their boring mundane lives without these things. We all live life from our own angle, our own perspective, and find it hard to contemplate any other. Certainly, for myself, I can only say I only feel alive when I am doing these "naughty things". It is only the naughty things that make me feel alive. That cost me my marriage, that cost me the love of the one woman who remains "behind my defences", but I have to be true to myself. We only have one life, and it is so short.

I have to get really drunk to find out what my subconscious really wants me to do. It is like the oracle of Delphi. To be able to decipher the message this encourages, I have to be in such a state of perfect inebriation. I am not yet at it. So, a 5th can of Jupiler then. Sober, conscious mind in the saddle, I don't know what to do. Go to the Cine Paris? Or Gare du Nord? Or 5th Avenue? I've no idea. But when I drink, my subconscious takes over and the river starts to cut its own course, and you do what really feels right; and then you can never go wrong. My eyes are over-developed in me to the detriment of all other organs. I do believe that. My scopophiliac love of

433

SEEING dirty things had made my eyes so much bigger than my heart. My heart has atrophied. All I want to do is feed my EYES' love of dirty naughty girls. I only go with whores because I want to see them get undressed and be naked. The actual physical act of penetration is the least exciting part of the encounter. My eyes dominance over me has cost me all hope of a desire for real relationships. Are there really other people like me? Even to me, I feel EXTREME.

But as I get older, I feel my river is more & more cutting its own course, and I am more & more coming closer to my true self, and more & more fulfilling my natural destiny. The prospect of real relationship, marriage, grows ever more & more remote. It can never be for me. I want other things, stronger and stronger. My addictions are not the temptation away from the course of my life; my addictions ARE the main course of my life. My addictions are my Nile, my Mississippi, my Rhine, my Danube. They are the main course of my life which give life to everything else around them. Indulging my addictions brings me to life and invigorates every other area of my life. I can feel happy and relaxed at home and at work as long as I am rampantly indulging my addictions at all other times. A happy life seems to me predicated on the ability to indulge the RAMPANCY of one's true nature.

I am not a bad person, but the only world I feel comfortable in is the world of strip clubs, & brothels, & porn cinemas. The only time I feel at ease, and relaxed, and where I am meant to be; the only time my soul really soars. This precludes me from all normal "healthy" relationships; I feel suffocated, and imprisoned in them. My true nature just becomes ever stronger as I get older; it does not go away; on the contrary, it becomes more insistent; more strident; more unwilling to compromise. There are so many beautiful young women in the world and I want to enjoy as many of them as I can for as long as I can—given I have already lost in London: Carnival Strip, Astral Cinema, Sunset Cinema, Soho Cinema, Boulevard Strip, Peep Show (all of them), Pleasure Lounge; in Berlin: almost ALL of Stuttgarter Platz; in Vienna, Pour Platin and Fortuna Kino; in Brussels California Kabins and Cine ABC; as well as other places I lost before I even knew they existed—the knocking shop right outside the door of Gare du Midi Brussels; the Martin Luther Strasse sex kino in Berlin. Serious ill-health or terrorism or random accident can strike me down at any moment, so I must live every moment as if it is my last. I do not want to die financially healthy with no fantastic memories; I would rather die in extreme debt but with the most fantastic collection of dirty memories, dirty experiences.

*

Some people don't like the fact I am doing very well for myself now! This is understandable. They do not have the intelligence to rise above their baser feelings. That is why they just crawl out from under their stone every now and again. The pondlife.

The death of David Bowie.

Bowie's greatest years were when he was closest to death, on the precipice, 1972 to 1977, with cocaine addiction out of control. After that he wanted to stay safe, and stay alive, and live and love as a normal person. That was when we rather lost interest in him.

When great drinkers stop drinking we lose interest in them; glad they saved themselves but they no longer glow so bright.

People who lead safe lives do not inspire and thrill us and blow our lives apart. We are thrilled by people who put themselves in mortal danger, in some Faustian pact, and such was Bowie from the age of 25 to 30.

Incredible how Bowie's face seemed to age between Starman 1972 and Heroes 1977. By time of Heroes he had got himself back again, from the madness and insanity. But it's those 5 years of madness and insanity that we remember him for, and will always love him for.

Hard to believe just two years separate him from Dick Cavett 1975 to Heroes 1977. Like two different people. One was a monster lost in cocaine addiction, the other had got himself back again.

*

A proper rainy day in Brussels.

A couple of beers in the Max last night then straight to a busy Yellow Lily, playing YMCA as I came through the door. My anthem, I thought. It then changed to another great song, and I was just thinking "I should write these songs down before I forgot them", when the second song (which I've forgotten) switched to Heroes, by David Bowie. Full blast. What a fantastic moment. To be in one of my favourite places in the world, Yellow Lily, surrounded by floozies, and now on comes what has become one of my favourite songs in the world. Ina was there in a short loose red & black dress, but that was it really. I bought her a Jack Daniels (an eye-watering 10 euros) and stumbled back, by now absolutely out of my mind with hunger. Brussels Grill doors were open, but the bar man said "no, we are closed." Domino's Pizza was shuttered up, so I just had a burger & chips in the little

435

burger bar next to the hotel and that was that. Slept well, right through to 10AM this morning.

Stupidly I've been saying they want to get rid of the street girls in Alhambra (the quarter of Brussels still named after the legendary Alhambra Theatre knocked down more than 40 years ago, adorned with Rodin statues and where Josephine Baker once danced) but now I discover it has already in fact happened (in theory). I was reading they have moved to the Chaussée d'Anvers, Boulevard Baudouin, and Albert II Laan. The girls I see in the Rue des Commerçants are just the diehard remnants who have flouted the new instructions? Prostitution is not illegal in Belgium, and street prostitution is not illegal, so I'm not quite sure by what device they can make them move. That would explain why even in summer I was shocked to see so few girls in the Rue des Commerçants. By then they were probably already in the new place (just about 100 yards north). And yet why have I never SEEN any street girls in those places? Last night after leaving Yellow Lily I made a point of walking along the entire length of the Boulevard Baudouin back to Brussels Grill and I never saw a single girl. I will actually go up the Chaussée d'Anvers and Albert II Laan today to look harder. Tuesday morning. Proper raining.

Once again a girl in a floozie bar told me I look "triste" (sad). I have a sad face, I can't help it. Even when happy I look sad. I was born with a sad face. If I'm sad in these places it is because I'm looking for that special someone who will blow my mind and make me feel real desire, and of course it rarely happens. Two brown cap soldiers passing under my balcony. They will finally be withdrawn on March 5th apparently. Between Max and Yellow Lily last night, I finally went in Le Loch Ness for a quick beer. A big L-shaped corner bar, about five other customers in that large space, a large area in the corner which looked like a stage. A soulless cavern. Pretty blonde barmaid though. The Gatsby, as I mentioned, is now a convenience store. The Black Beard is still a bar; I may pop in there tonight. It has some good Black Beard pirate pictures on the walls, but apart from that is also a very soulless large box of a place.

All the way to the end of Rue d'Aerschot and Zinip—big MEGA-bosomed Turkish Zinip. She was simpatico. I like her. Just 30 euros. Back to Brussels Grill. I didn't see her come into Café Jimmy earlier, but when I looked around there was Beatrice—black coat, black trousers; always surprises me how voluptuous she is. She didn't even talk to me this time. In Yellow Lily no one for me, too early even for Ina. Again, I'm not even getting bread & butter. I pinch some from another table. I'd like to go back to Yellow Lily before sleeping, and maybe go back for Beatrice, but after this steak I'll probably just be ready for bed. "Bearnaise or mayonnaise?" said the waitress, mishearing my sauce. Now I understand why I got mayonnaise last time. Hopefully I can get up and out to Empire tonight. Tomorrow? I suppose I could keep Beatrice until tomorrow, last thing I do before I leave. Alhambra Cinema had a half decent film—*Anissa & Lola at the Nurse's School*, and I was undisturbed by the perverts. And the upstairs cinema was closed, for some unknown reason. Maybe all the perverts have been locked inside. Good idea.

716PM. I came back to sleep after my Brussels Grill steak but couldn't sleep, so I'm up again and drinking another Jupiler. I want to see another naked woman tonight. Zinip has given me the taste for it. Beatrice? Bridget? Ina? Or just make do with the topless Empire girls? They should be open in 90 minutes or so.

Well, I managed to do more in one day yesterday than I did in the entire six-days here in January. I went to Churchill's English Pub, Six Nations Pub, Delirium Monasterium, À La Mort Subite, Alhambra Cinema, Café Jimmy, Yellow Lily, made love with mega-bosomed Turkish Zinip in Rue d'Aerschot after a spell in the Sexyworld kabins, had Brussels Grill steak. Then came back to bed, but unable to sleep, I thought "sod it, let's go back out again." Zinip had given me the desire to see MORE naked women. So after a couple more beers I RETURNED to Alhambra Cinema, returned to Yellow Lily—how much sexier and more exciting the same streets feel at night—made love with Beatrice (in the little half-hour hotel), went to Empire and FINALLY took a girl upstairs for 150 euros, Manuela. I got through about 396 euros in the day.

Earlier I had left Yellow Lily thinking there is no point coming here, it is rubbish, dead. Yet returning at night it seemed an incredibly sexy place again—mainly I think because I was now feeling randy. I fancied Emily, Ina and Paloma. I wanted to go with all of them but was just worried I'd drunk too much. Instead I left and went with Beatrice into the Europa 2000 hotel again, but once in the room I found her cold and unfriendly. A massively annoying encounter. On to Empire and there was the sexy little brunette Manuela, half-Spanish half-Romanian. After watching her dance on stage, and enjoying a five-euro lap dance in my chair, I went upstairs with her for thirty minutes for 150 euros—just to see what happens. It turns out to be a non-stop private dance basically but much more close and personal than downstairs. Still she keeps her knickers on, and still my trousers must remain zipped up (!), but you can touch the girl. She sat with me for a while and we discussed why men are so stupid to spend such huge amounts of money for basically nothing. She talked about the window girls of Rue d'Aerschot and the street girls of Rue des Commerçants, and why don't men go there instead where they can get so much more for so much less money, and was "impressed" that I knew so much about them and how much they cost! It was a very pleasant half-hour with a gorgeous sexy girl with a lovely simpatico personality. At 150 euros I don't think I will repeat the experience! But I am very glad I did it this time. She most certainly is girlfriend material.

So I was shocked to find myself really turned on by Bulgarian Emily and Brazilian Paloma as well as Ina, had a poor experience with Beatrice, and lovely experience with Manuela; oh, and let me not forget a good experience with Turkish Zinip earlier. I was rather amazed that after an afternoon of heavy drinking and eating, I was able to go out again in the early evening and just carry straight on heavy drinking again. I think I must be feeling more inspired right now and that means I can absorb alcohol better. If I'm sad or uninspired I get drunk easier and take longer to recover.

*

I honestly didn't think I'd ever go back to Berlin after my last trip. But now having fallen in love with David Bowie (as he was in the 1970s, the Golden Age for almost everything) I need to make pilgrimage to his stay in Berlin, when he was at his most beautiful. Oh Jesus, 1124, we have stopped again. I am so hungry. Same reason again, "person on the track". For f—k's sake. Moving again but that is another five minutes lost. "Fuck all internet fame bitches". Graffiti on the wall. Oh, but we are moving so slowly. A snail's pace. I only have 33 minutes between trains at Köln. The driver advises we are exactly 25 minutes behind schedule. Just leaving Liège (such a beautiful station). The driver is putting his foot down now. Snow on the ground between Liège and Aachen. Leaving Aachen (slowly). 1210. My Berlin train leaves Köln at 1248. Sure enough, the Customs get on at Aachen but thank God they just check my passport and tickets this time and move on. Last time it was so weird because I seemed to be the ONLY person on the carriage they checked, they came straight to me, but today I am reassured to see they are checking EVERYBODY for "papers". They have a very pretty blonde girl with them this time, like she is training.

On a rickety old train to Berlin; a "replacement train" said the announcer. Lots of leg room though as it is an old First Class carriage apparently.

BERLIN

It turns out the "rickety old train" only went as far as Hamm and we then had to switch to the newer modern ICE for the rest of the journey to Berlin. Still arrived on time. In the Plaza Hotel bar now. 20:38. The Berliner Pilsener is no more; replaced by König Pilsener, and I would say it is colder than the old one used to be. Flowing freely, so nice to be back in Berlin which means so much to me. But it means so much to me because of memories from the past, memories of night bars which no longer exist in an extinction event of unprecedented magnitude—is there still life in Berlin for me? We shall see. Anyway I just came for Bowie this time, and the naughty places are just a bonus, hopefully. But the memories are so strong—Berlin is where I bloomed & blossomed, Berlin is where I emerged from the chrysalis a butterfly. My repeated visits to Berlin in 2003 and 2004 were life-changing. As Bowie said of his Berlin albums, "they are my DNA", my Berlin visits from that time are my DNA. They were my womb. 903PM. Sinking prodigious amounts of the König Pilsener, I think I do certainly prefer it to the Berliner Pilsener. No difference in taste, I don't think, but it is colder than I remember. I notice it comes out the tap much faster as well. The Berliner took forever to pour.

Stunning new black ponytail receptionist, unfortunately checking someone else in when I arrived. Low-cut white blouse, falling open very clearly to show the top of her cleavage. Two beautiful girls sitting in the armchairs outside the bar, one black hair, one blonde, are they guests? Or hookers? In Berlin you never, never know. Hell, I need to get up early tomorrow. The Hansa Studio tour starts at 10.30 in Köthener Straße, just south of Potsdamer Platz.

The most extraordinary blazing period of Bowie's genius was 1972 to 1977. He was off his head on cocaine from 1972 to 1977. He had orange hair from 1972 to 1977. After 1977 he decided to clean up, and never did anything interesting again. Do I say this to slight David Bowie? No. What he created, the way he burned himself into the UNIVERSE from 72 to 77 is something so extraordinary, and I honestly think without parallel. In those five years he made himself the greatest ever. Sitting at the bar of the Berlin Plaza, with tears rolling down my cheeks, thinking about David Bowie in Berlin. Strange, isn't it? Strange what emotions really move us. Unpredictable. Going to his studio tomorrow, and feeling already overwhelmed with emotion.

Why do I feel so amazingly happy when I am in the Berlin Plaza bar? Memories? Yes, incredible memories. But a still raging love of being in Berlin. Have I ever felt as comfortable in a bar as I feel in the Berlin Plaza?

First time ever, when I left the hotel just before midnight last night, I could not walk straight; I was literally lurching from one side of the pavement to the other like the proverbial drunken sailor. I was heading towards Stuttgarter Platz but I had to give up and come back to the hotel to sleep. Incredible. Never been so drunk before I couldn't walk straight. Too much vodka on top of all that beer. Now it is 4.15PM before I have my first beer of the day, and it tastes quite poisonous. I am struggling to drink it. Today I got a taxi to Hansa Studio for the tour of the recording studio where Bowie finished *Low* and did the whole of *Heroes*. Incredible to be in the room where Bowie recorded the song 'Heroes', U2 recorded 'One', Iggy Pop recorded 'Passenger', amongst so many others. I then walked all the way to the Rosa Lux sex kino, chafing my thighs so much they are now red raw & unsightly. I was too hungry to go on to the place where Bowie lived; I will try to do that tomorrow.

Back down to the bar at 845PM. I am forcing myself to drink. I cannot spend the whole night in my hotel room. Though that is just what I need to clear my head and recover from the previous night's over-drinking. This holiday is turning into a damp squib. I have felt out of sorts the whole time. So I force myself to do something tonight. You never know, the sexiest girl of all time might be waiting for me in what is left of Stuttgarter Platz. I'll probably shit myself before I get there; it's been that kind of holiday. YMCA on the Berlin Plaza hotel radio now; that song is following me around. 946PM. I just want some sexy experience. Three days into my trip and I've yet to have a genuine unforced erection.

Back in the Plaza bar. Flurries of snow outside, stopped already. I decided I don't want to go to David Bowie's Berlin house and next door café ENOUGH. I can no longer be bothered. It is too damn cold. No, it's snowing again. Wow, hard now. Not sure what to do. I would like to pop back into King George and/or Caligula but the trouble with flat-rate 100 euros entry "f—k all you want" brothels is it deters you from ever going in as you might not fancy anyone. I would love to go in, have a look at the talent on offer, have a couple of drinks and then move on, but at King George and Caligula that would set me back 100 euros even to do that. Better to save that money for Vienna—all those night bars filled with floozies are free to get into, just a beer to pay for. The new black ponytail Yugoslavian receptionist just came through the bar. She is like Princess Mort from *Orpheé*. On check in, she was checking in someone else, her blouse tight over bosoms and low cut and falling open, and you could always see the top of her cleavage. Quite intoxicating.

My train leaves Hauptbahnhof 6.50AM so I don't want to be out too late tonight. So last night—the beer at last started to go down a little easier. Walked straight to Berlin Erotic Point (in Lewishamstraße, always makes me smile; named in honour of the twinning of Charlottenburg with Lewisham, wonderful union of Ernest Dowson and Anita Berber) and it really baffles me how I managed to get lost so badly on recent visits. The kabins were actually very good—if you can find one that is working properly, the selection of films is very very good. It did the job and put me well in the mood for the short walk up to Stuttgarter Platz. Scorning Bon Bon as I usually do (never seen a nice girl there), into Sissi. Big voluptuous brunette Layla I made love with before. Her bottom and bosoms are really a handful; and a long straight black hair slim girl, plus pretty barmaid; all from Bulgaria I am guessing. One other man came in which actually made it seem busy. Into Monte Carlo Kino and two men already there. I'm not used to seeing these places so busy! No particularly beautiful girls this time. On to Club 77; it is a Jacuzzi and sauna club, for around 180 euros I think, or you can just go to a room for 50 euros or so; it has always tempted me to take a girl for Jacuzzi and sauna but there was no one there who I fancied, so I declined again. Long time since the fantastic curvy Angelica was there. And that was it—grabbed a McDonald's and back to hotel. But those kabin films were good enough to make me want to go back and maybe finish with a h—job at least, in Sissi or Monte Carlo. Layla said she could give me a b—job there at the bar, in front of the barmaid, which would be quite titillating. But if I am going to resist the temptation of King George and Caligula, then I must finish in Ciro to at least SEE some other floozies.

Again I managed to get back to the hotel very straightforwardly without getting lost, as I insanely have done a couple of times recently. It is so straightforward & well-trodden a path by me I have no idea how I could possibly have ended up walking the WRONG way along the Ku'damm. Even coming home after another bottle of beer in each of Sissi Bar, Monte Carlo and Club 77, I did not feel drunk. So in the end I think there WAS enough encouragement to come back to Berlin. The kabin films of Berlin Erotic Point were better than I remember; some of the best ever; and the prospect of a naughty h—job at least in the dark of Sissi or Monte Carlo to finish off is tempting enough to come back for. Still, it's a very long way to come if there are no stars—no Yulia, no Riccarda, no Iga, no Olga & Alla. To get me to come back all this way there has to be someone I really really fancy; and it has been a very long time since I've seen someone like that in Berlin. In Vienna I see at least one on every visit; in Brussels there have been several stars recently. I need to find a star in Berlin to get me to come back I think. But even these minor pleasures—a wonderful set of kabin films, followed by a naughty b—job or h—job or full sex in a bar around the corner, are not available in London. I really cannot bear to be in London anymore. It is so so sterile. How on Earth can I stop myself spending all my money on travelling? But when London was more interesting, I used to spend all my money in London, so it doesn't make much difference I suppose.

Quite tempted to try the Bavarium restaurant downstairs in the Europa Centre (that hideous heart-breakingly bland replacement for the legendary Romanisches Café of 1930s glory, where Tucholsky and Anita Berber and so many others used to drink; where have all the flowers gone?) next to the Irish Pub again; that will really make me want to sleep for a couple of hours. It wasn't the best steak dish I've ever had but it is better than what 'Laggis' gave me yesterday. Third beer, starting to think only of food. Good. Unlike Brussels, I don't really have anywhere naughty to go in Berlin during the day. In Brussels, so easy to sit in Alhambra Cinema all afternoon, or sit in Yellow Lily all afternoon. Not got anywhere quite like that in Berlin—though, after all, I could sit in King George all afternoon. If only they didn't charge 100 euros to get in!

I wish I COULD find something/someone to come back to Berlin for, because I do feel so comfortable here—here in the Berlin Plaza bar. In Berlin Erotic Point, and Stuttgarter Platz. But a city always needs a star to get me to come back, and it has been so many years since I found a star in Berlin. Hanky Panky, Mon Cheri, Night Dreams, Chocolat, Starlight, Golden Gate, Blue Angel, all closed down, a cataclysm; also Black & White and Mazurka and more I cannot even remember. Warm blue skies when I woke this morning; that's what made me want to go back to sleep and close the curtains; now lead grey snow heavy skies. Ah, this moment usually comes when I am on holiday—Streets of London on the Plaza hotel radio. Always moving (when I've had a few).

913PM in the hotel bar tonight; I get later every night. My train leaves 0652 in the morning. Well, that was another meal in Berlin I did not enjoy at all; I went for Bavarium's Schwäbischer Zwiebelrostbraten, lured by the promise of fried onion rings. They did not seem fried at all. Cannot remember the last time I had a meal I enjoyed in Berlin; nothing to compare with the Café Westend in Vienna or Brussels Grill. Even my 2AM McDonald's last night I did not enjoy (admittedly it was cold by the time I got it back to my hotel; I walked as fast as my little legs would carry me & was just praying I did not get lost this time). 937PM and just starting my second beer. I need to speed up. It is not going down well at all.

Of course I do regret I did not bother to go see David Bowie's apartment & café next door; next time! If I'm going to make pilgrimage anywhere it should be to the house where they filmed *La Grande Bouffe*, because increasingly that is how I live my life. Dedicated to the pleasures of sex, food & drink, like a connoisseur, with no care for the consequences. I did get a proper erection in Sissi Bar and Monte Carlo last night, so maybe worth a return tonight, and at least suffer a h—job to be performed on me. [Alas, my friend Mr Google tells me the *La Grande Bouffe* mansion was at 68, rue Boileau in the 16th arrondissement of Paris but is now gone, its place taken by the Vietnamese Embassy]. I at least did visit Hansa Studios, where Bowie recorded *Heroes* album and finished *Low*. I stood in the room where Bowie first sang 'Heroes', Iggy Pop first sang 'Passenger', and Bono first sang 'One'. "OK," said Thilo our guide as we entered. "Now get down on your knees; this is the Holy Ground." Not only did I not get to Bowie's house and café, I still haven't been to see Anita Berber's house in Zahringerstraße, OR the site of Hitler's bunker (I thought I'd found it years ago but it turns out I was in the wrong place). So incentives to hang another Berlin visit on. If I could meet a girl (floozie) in Berlin to blow my socks off that would make it easier, but like I say it's been years. It can happen—Adelina and Jackie in Vienna last year, Lucy in Brussels last year. It can still happen, not as completely as back in 2003 or 4 or 5 of course, BEFORE I met and fell in love with my future wife.

I miss my wife, but I still always want to travel. Even if with anybody else, I would want to travel all the time. That is why I can only ever be alone (amongst numerous other reasons). My wanderlust never leaves me, even if it is wanderlust to return to the same places. It cost me just £56 to get to Berlin from Brussels (£56 for a return ticket that is). So hardly a huge expense to come to Berlin, and the hotel is just £35 a night. Those high nights, with Yulia, and Riccarda and Iga, and Olga & Alla, were amazing. A distant memory in Berlin these days. Yes, I get genuine erections in Berlin Erotic Point and Sissi and Monte Carlo, but have I had any really sexy moments in Berlin this time? No. Nothing like an Adelina in Vienna or a Lucy in Brussels. That Brazilian girl passing the bus stop at Alexanderplatz in grey leggings so tight they were see-through over her beautiful big fat arse was the genuinely sexiest moment.

The barmaid in the Plaza bar is very good; we've reached the eyebrow stage. I just need to catch her eye and raise an eyebrow and she nods OK and readies my next beer. And I've reached the stage where I cannot read my own handwriting even after just writing it. Yes, the Plaza bar has gone down the "fancy food" route—individual lumps of food presented artistically all on their own on the vast white expanse of the plate; rather than the fill the plate with gorgeous food so you cannot see the plate-route of places like my beloved Café Westend in Vienna, or the

COLLECTED WORKS

Munich Rechthaler Hof BEFORE new management took over and ruined it, and my old beloved Munich Lamm's (shut down in 2010). I've lost confidence in the Berlin Plaza food I'm afraid; and after the glories of the 'knesepfanne' years (2003-4) it absolutely breaks my heart to say that.

On the train back to Brussels. Another session in the Erotic Point kabins. I still had 9 euros left on my bonuskarte when I was ready to leave, but the button would not work to release it so I had to leave it behind. Lost those 9 euros! I started to walk back to Stuttgarter Platz Sissi and Monte Carlo then changed my mind and went back to Ciro. It was so bitterly cold and already nearly 1AM. A nice curvy black-haired Romanian, Andrea, 200 euros for half an hour of sex, as always prohibitively expensive. After haggling I got it down to a naked private dance for 50 euros. Me lying back on bed, her lying on top of me (me fully clothed of course). Thirty to get in, 25-euro drink for her, then the 50, made it an expensive brief visit but I wanted to finish my Berlin trip with at least SOMETHING. Taxi back to Hauptbahnhof at 615AM. The Berlin Hauptbahnhof really is one of the wonders of the modern world.
　　A very smooth journey until we reach Hagen, just forty minutes from Köln, when we come to a halt and the man on the tannoy makes some very long and important announcement, all in German. I think we are no longer going to Köln but will have to go somewhere else and get another train from there, but I'm just guessing. Not a word in English. So for sure there goes my connection to Brussels. This seems to happen every time I travel on Deutsche Bahn these days; always something. We've been at Hagen for eighteen minutes now. Going on the Bahn.de website and copying to Google Translate, there is some emergency on the line to Wuppertal, our next stop, and we are going to have to go via Düsseldorf, and then I expect change trains. What a nightmare.

So one hour 29 minutes late to Köln; missed my connection to Brussels; now have to wait THREE HOURS until my next one. Arrive 530. So 115 in the Köln station bar, having my first Dom Kölsch beer. F—king DB have done it to me again. Last time I travelled by DB I was TWO HOURS late to Vienna. Now I am going to be FOUR HOURS late to Brussels. Depressing. We are getting there, slowly.

*

Suicide bombings at Brussels Airport and on the Brussels Metro.

A good chance I will be murdered or severely maimed in Europe before 2016 is over. Makes the feral erotic experiences all the more intense. Sex snatched from the jaws of death.

This may be a brief flowering golden age before things turn very very horrible in my life. Whatever happens I will write my masterpiece, *The Willing Cheeks of Fu Manchu. Seeds of the Pope.*

Some big tits in a tight sweater. That is all I need. Don't know why more porn cinemas don't just show porn like this. I wish I owned my own porn cinema. It would be the best porn cinema in the world. There would be ferns everywhere, some places all violin music, some places all old psycho funk 1970s music, old blues 1920s music. In another room a stage with fully nude striptease. My dreams in life are all of a pornographic Priapic nature. That is my pilot light. That is the Nile deep underground inside me. My hinterland is all my erotic memories.

Don't worry about a dirty bomb, all there is is pornography. Go out more rampantly and wildly than ever for all out pornography & prostitution. More likely to die of heart attack or cancer than any random act of terror.

I woke about 4am and then can you believe spent the next seven hours in bed masturbating? An epic masturbation session. This is what I travel for. Great German porn, great German videokabins, those old *Titten Alarm* films and *Katharina & her Wild Horses.* This is what I travel for. Great porn and great big titted whores. Worth all the danger it puts me in. Can just as easily get blown up going through Piccadilly Circus or Charing X Station as I will in Brussels, or Vienna or on ICE from one place to the other.

In Brussels the only really dangerous place I go is Midi Station and in future I will make a point of getting off of Eurostar and leaving the station by the nearest exit as fast as possible. No more queuing up in Panos. Leave via the first side exit and walk around the corner to get to Ibis or taxi. Stay out of the Ibis bar, and after that I am pretty much away from the danger areas, apart from the Brussels Grill window.

I don't think Europe or at least myself have got long before something truly horrific happens, so all the more impetus to travel more faster & faster and seize my erotic pornographic pleasures while I can, in Brussels, Nuremberg and Vienna, and Berlin. Floozies, strippers, they really are my opium. Strippers, pornography & prostitution are my opium. And alcohol.

There are so many pilgrimages I still want to make, to the Brocken Mountain, the Reichenbach Falls, to cross the Rubicon, to visit the Milvian Bridge, but I just keep going back to Vienna, Brussels, Nuremberg, Munich and Berlin. Those other places can wait till I am older perhaps, but I am getting there now. When will Eros ever leave me alone long enough to let me go on the longer journeys to more literary pilgrimages? Always the quick thrill dominates me.

*

A grim, subdued atmosphere in Brussels. Evening rush hour, busy but everyone so quiet. Gare du Midi only has a couple of entrances/exits open and everyone is funnelled in & out of these, with soldiers posted outside. To my surprise, I am really enjoying this Stella in the Ibis bar—cold, and fresh and sharp. Why is the Dome Stella not like this; so creamy and lifeless? This large Stella is going down very nicely. Two soldiers posted outside the hotel door even, which IS reassuring. I am also a little reassured that the Brussels bombers really wanted to attack the Euros in France, and only had to switch to their hometown when they felt the net tightening on them.

A grey, gloomy early evening in Brussels; quite warm but heavy grey skies that look like rain at any moment, further adding to the grim, suppressed atmosphere. This terror threat hanging over Brussels like the heavy clouds could be the final death knell of Yellow Lily—what sexy girls from Spain or Brazil are going to want to come to work in Brussels now? What chance Lucy would ever come back here now?

Drama in the L'Orient Express as some crazy old bag lady is demanding to be served and refusing to leave. Physically fighting with the manager to resist being thrown out. Now she's tripped over the step trying to come back in and the manager rushes to help her up (which is kind of him). Not in the mood for anything at all. A yellow Pompiers van is trying to take the old lady away now, with a white police van standing alongside; the policeman standing outside his van puffing on a fag, Brussels-style. The old lady is a helpless case. Completely pathetic—not in the rude way, but pitiful; you feel pity for her. Drunk, or on drugs, or just lost her mind, or all three. As always, she is probably looking at me thinking the same thing.

The firemen (?) and policemen are having no success in getting her to move from the Orient Express's outside table. They are trying to reason with her, but she is in another world. The Jupiler is at least ice cold, as it always is here. I must admit I was HOPING to find soldiers outside the Ibis; and a large police & army presence around Gare du Midi. 720PM already.

Olympique Marseille v Bordeaux on the Orient Express TV—Christ, French football is so slow & boring. No wonder PSG win the league by 20 points every year. The sun is about one minute away from going down behind the Midi railway tracks, and out of my eyes at least. My train to

446

Nuremberg is not until 10.25 in the morning so at least I should be able to have a long sleep tonight. I need it. I don't know how French football supporters don't slash their wrists; this is dire. Barmaid just brought another beer to my table, I didn't even ask. Well, that decides it; I am having one more then, it seems! It is supposed to rain tonight; that would be lovely; but no sign of it right now. Now the crowd at the football match are rioting. Out of sheer f–king boredom, I expect. As I have been for most of my time here, I am the only customer in L'Orient Express.

So yes, a dire evening in Brussels; but mostly my fault. I was tired, I was late. By the time I got to Yellow Lily almost everyone had gone. Empire was like a tomb. No other customers. On the ICE to Nuremberg now; changing at Frankfurt. Couple of minutes until we leave. We will see if I can salvage any Eros from this holiday at all; even if it is manual only! Let me see what fraught disasters I have on Deutsche Bahn today. Trespassers on the track? Medical emergency on the track? I have just twenty-four minutes to spare to catch my connection at Frankfurt. And I have come to dread the German customs men who get on at Aachen. I am an intensely suspicious-looking character it seems.

 A bit of a hangover in bed this morning but all right now. Three large Jupilers in L'Orient Express, I think perhaps just two small Maes in Yellow Lily and that was it. I will perhaps try to sleep when I get to Nuremberg, as there is nowhere for me to go until after 9PM at least. Blazing blue skies as we speed towards Liège. Three hours to Frankfurt, and then two hours to Nuremberg; not too bad, fingers crossed for a smooth journey this time. Belgium, Germany and Austria feel like home to me now, I have been here so many times, and had just about all of the highest nights of my life here.

 I feel no craving whatsoever for another relationship. It is one of those things you should definitely do once in your life, like climbing Mount Everest or going to the Moon, but you wouldn't want to do it a second time. I never feel lonely anymore. I still feel married to my wife, even though I have not seen her for 300 days. In fact our marriage feels happier than ever. We email each other now & again, keep in touch. It feels a perfect relationship. If only all marriages could be as happy as this. She makes no demands on me and I make no demands on her.

 Remember how excited I was heading to Nuremberg those two or three times looking for Viktoriya; I got off the train almost unable to breathe, hyperventilating, butterflies filling my chest, literally shaking. I wonder if I will ever feel that kind of excitement again. Don't think I am capable anymore. After — everything feels so much less. After conquering

Mount Everest what is left? Just basking in the contentment at having achieved something so great. A lovely smooth journey so far. Into Frankfurt on time, and on our way on time to Nuremberg. I haven't had a genuine unforced erection yet; not seen any pornography yet; not seen a naked woman yet. All these things should change in Nuremberg tonight. Numerous strip clubs (actually topless only apart perhaps for Bella Napoli), videokabins and windows. When you've climbed Mount Everest, you've done it all. The funny thing about my climbing career, though, is Everest was the first mountain I climbed. So I started with the best, and was happy to retire after that.

NUREMBERG

Some girl (Anna in Cabaret Bella Napoli) just guessed my age as 41. I've never had anyone guess my age that old. Most people guess me in the 30s. I nearly slapped her.

So on our way to Wien, four hours 39 minutes away. A grey cloudy morning. My mood slightly improved from 24 hours earlier. I went out after 9PM and found the Hot Legs strip club/videokabins/peepshow was completely closed down! Another one gone. So the ice retreats. I went in Caribic opposite (proper name Stage 2000) and they have very good videokabins. Upstairs in the strip club (now called Crystals Tabledance) there was only one other customer, and five or six skinny-looking girls. I left after one beer and I could not finish it fast enough. If you like Browns or Horns, God help you, you might like Crystals but it is not for me. The Sterntaler Bar (formerly known as the Pils Bar, scene of my legendary encounter with the mega-bosomed Martina years ago) was still there but its door was locked so not sure if that is still in business or not. Then I started my long walk along the windows of Frauentormauer. My God, the quality of the girls is stunning. If I rate Brussels Rue d'Aerschot as a 9, then Frauentormauer must be a 9½. I did not stop as I was really keen to go to Cabaret Bella Napoli which is at the very end of the wall. As always it had some nice-looking girls and they strip NAKED—the only club in Belgium, Germany or Austria I have found where they take their knickers off as well. I queried this with one of the girls and she said "That is because this is a CABARET, not a tabledance club." Oh. Then I wish there were more cabaret clubs. Drink for the girl is 38 euros, a private dance is 50 euros. I did not indulge this time, as I preferred to keep my powder dry for Vienna, but might on the way back; although I just realised I will be back in Nuremberg on Sunday and I do not think they open on Sundays. Back to the station for a roll and a McDonald's, then to bed. Certainly I will enjoy the Caribic videokabins and Frauentormauer windows on my return.

The carpet in my Ibis Altstadt hotel was beautiful—all poppies. Like it was designed by some absolute opium addict. A real German Thomas de Quincey. I was thrilled to discover they had a nice music channel as well! So unusual these days. Rather good one as well, Deluxe. Lots of songs I've never heard before, lots of German music. Excellent. I will certainly always stay at this hotel if I come to Nuremberg again. Next time I travel to Vienna I expect I will give Frankfurt another try. For the first time ever today I will be arriving at the new Wien Hauptbahnhof rather than my beloved Westbahnhof. It means getting a tram to my hotel, if I can work out which one I need to get.

Regensburg, our first stop ticked off. One hour of the journey gone already. 10AM. One & a half hours gone. 1030. Two hours gone. Plattling. A lovely, half-empty peaceful train so far. I've said it before, the ICE is one of the wonders of the modern world (Europe, anyway). On an ICE travelling across Europe, for however many hours, feels a real pleasure. The journey itself is a treat. We are really not picking up hardly any passengers along the way either. At Plattling and Passau the train draws in to an almost totally empty platform. How peaceful Europe feels compared to London!

The only regret I feel from my marriage is that we did not make Phoebe. I feel like she must be angry at us, "Mummy and daddy, why have you still not made me yet! I would love you so much!" And she would be a lovely quiet little girl, like her daddy, not loud & manic like her mother. I have the horrible feeling that if I ever did have a child with another woman, I would never really love her, because I should have made her with —. I love Phoebe like a real child.

Crossing Austria on the ICE listening to Falco's Rock Me Amadeus. Life is sweet. In just over two hours we will be in Vienna. 1125 Wels. Christ, just one hour 40 minutes until we arrive in Vienna. Again no sign of anyone on the Wels platform. This is the quietest train I have ever been on. Normally I go from Munich to Vienna via Salzburg on an Austrian Railways Railjet and that train is always packed, so maybe this route is always the better one to take. Just a nuisance it goes to Wien Hauptbahnhof rather than Westbahnhof. Blazing blue skies now; not a single cloud. Those red Austrian Railjets look so heavy & clunky compared to the smooth sleek airy ICEs. Truly a design classic. Exactly one hour until we arrive at Wien Hauptbahnhof. Well, I take my hat off to Deutsche Bahn this time. Two days of travelling have been smooth & peaceful & dead on time.

VIENNA

How lovely to be back in a Dorint hotel room. Not only was there a Granny Smith apple left in the room for me—the only kind of apple I like—but they had stocked the minibar with just the things I drink, so there were SIX bottles of Gösser beer instead of the normal two, two bottles of sparkling water instead of one sparkling & one flat, and one bottle of coke. It is like they studied my minibar habits and stocked the minibar especially for me! Amazing. That is the personal touch. I just sat down on the edge of the bed, completely gobsmacked. What an amazing thing to do! Really the nicest thing any hotel has ever done for me. After finishing my six bottles of Gösser plus one can I bought from the station, I headed up to WSK. Pleased to see Jackie and a blonde girl just finishing attending to a man in the front row and putting their clothes back on, plus another Bulgarian girl in the lobby, so the floozies are still going strong here. Sadly Jackie left about twenty minutes after I arrived so I left as well then, as the films were rubbish. I have no memory of coming back to the hotel but there is a pizza wrapper in my bin and that makes me remember eating a pizza before falling asleep. I woke 1AM with a raging hangover and knew I felt too bad to go out again. I have three more nights to go out at night.

I forced myself up at 6 this morning to go down for bacon & egg breakfast not because I was hungry but just to feel I was living my life to the full while on holiday. I started this holiday with 350 euros and here on my fourth day I still have 214 left! It has been such a cheap holiday so far.

So my first experience of Wien Hauptbahnhof. Stepping off the train onto the platform with that underwhelming tin roof like a slightly bigger Vauxhall bus station, the comparison with Berlin Hauptbahnhof is unflattering to say the least. Once you descend underground, however, wow. The place is enormous down below (as am I). I had to traipse for MILES to get to the No.18 tram platform (also underground). I kept following the signs, and I thought surely before I get there I will find a machine to buy a ticket, won't I, but then finally I'm on the platform and there is nowhere to buy a ticket at all. The tram was coming so I got on nervously but was scared inspectors were going to catch me and humiliate me in front of everyone—is my ICE ticket good for a short journey on arrival I wondered, as it is in Berlin? Doubtful. At Eisenstraße I saw two menacing-looking men who might have been inspectors so I dashed off and started walking up the Margaretengurtel. The skies were blue, the sun was blazing down, and I was sweating like a pig. Reaching Gumpendorfer Straße U-Bahn station I at last was able to buy a ticket and then got a tram the rest of the way to Westbahnhof. That long walk across the Hauptbahnhof underground was

COLLECTED WORKS

rubbish; I think next time I come to Wien Hauptbahnhof, I will get off the ICE at the stop before, Wien Meidling, which from the map I'm looking at now is just four stops south of Westbahnhof on the U-Bahn. Surely that will be much easier for me. Still, I have to go back to Hauptbahnhof on the No.18 on the way home, unless I get a taxi (which I probably will, as 8AM Sunday morning I will probably have a stinking hangover and will not want to battle my way on the trams).

With no more beer in my minibar, and no sign of the minibar lady (oh voluptuous goddess of beer), I am forced down to the bar at 1120, which I had preferred to avoid on this trip—I don't like the bar's Zipfer as much as I like the minibar Gösser and in my room I can enjoy my music channel (and porn). Plans for today, perhaps the U-Bahn up to Wahringer Gurtel Kino, back down to WSK, maybe Burggasse Peep maybe not, then finish off in Café Westend before crashing out back in the hotel; ready to wake in time to go back out tonight. I will save the Belvedere for tomorrow.

Well, no Lotta & Sophia on this trip again. That was a once in a lifetime event. 1200. On my third beer of the day. Curious to see who is in Manhattan tonight; then Friday & Saturday I can check out Exzess and Angelique. Suppose I might as well check out Tête-à-Tête as it is so close (forty metres?). After three cheap days, Brussels day one, Nuremberg day two, Wien day three, I expect day four will be a little more expensive; though I may save the big splurge for days five or six. But I do feel happier in Vienna than in any other city (including London). Christ, yes, I want to go to the Brocken Mountain, and the Reichenbach Falls, and the Rubicon, and the Milvian Bridge, but the pull of the sleazy nightbars of Vienna and Berlin have a hold on me that will not let go. One day. One day. "The sight of a whore is profoundly thrilling to a man" said Flaubert, and I agree with him so very much. Even if 999 times out of a thousand I won't do anything with them.

To see Beyonce's (minimal) contribution to Coldplay's Hymn for the Weekend followed closely by her own Formation is to throw a stark light on how actually OBJECTIONABLY bland Coldplay's music is, compared to Beyonce's relative fierceness. How I hate newspapers who "expose" someone's private life. Shame, shame, shame on you. We are all entitled to a "private" life. It has no effect on the role we perform when we are in public and at work. I fight against this kind of prurience at every turn (as completely powerless as I am to affect anything; but just to speak against it, if all we can do, is something). I have infinite sympathy and solidarity with any "celebrity" who is exposed in this way. Would they have any sympathy for me? Not at all. This is sign of my greatness. 125. On my sixth beer of the day. Can't wait to get to Café Westend for a rostbraten. Wahringer Gurtel

Kino and WSK are necessary obstacles in between. *La Grande Bouffe*. Is my life. Food, drink (& sex).

I want to be a Shakespeare, a Samuel Pepys. I do not aim low. One hundred years from now, 200, 300, I want people to be reading me to learn what life was like in Western Europe in the early 21st century/late 20th century.

I went out after 1AM Thursday night for the short stroll over the road to Manhattan. A lot of new girls—no Melissa and no Adelina. Denitsa still there and the one shining star. I popped into Tête-à-Tête on my way back, expecting little, but there were actually already a few customers there and it had a good atmosphere. I bought a drink for some busty blonde Hungarian while she massaged my swelling member, and then just about 0250, presumably because some critical mass of men had been reached (there was about ten of us by now), a girl started dancing around the pole by the door, and I was shocked to see she actually stripped completely naked, knickers off as well, something I never expected to see in Vienna. Four girls danced, my busty blonde being the last of them, but by then it seemed some men had left and the critical mass no longer existed so the dancing stopped again. It was really wonderful while it lasted; I spent another 18 euros on beer while enjoying the show, so I think it would make them more money if they made the girls dance in permanent rotation. It makes such a difference if you have something to look at. Turned on by Denitsa and the busty blonde, and the Tête dancing, I felt like it had been a good night.

Friday was a bit of a waste of a day really. Having to change hotels at midday threw me out of sync. I walked down to the Ibis and checked in, ate the two rolls I picked up from the station, then went straight back out to Café Westend for a rostbraten, which to be honest I struggled to finish. I stumbled back to the hotel and slept for the rest of the afternoon. Getting up early enough to prepare for a night out, I really didn't feel in the mood at all. I crossed over to ML Revue just to confirm again that their kabins are rubbish; never wasting my time there again. I have my standards. Train up to Club Exzess. The girls all take turns to dance topless on a small stage but there were none I liked enough to stay for. Back down to Manhattan and Tête-à-Tête but even though I saw all the same girls as last night, this time I just felt no desire or interest at all. Just one beer in each place and I was ready to leave. Thrilled to find the station McDonald's still open, so I brought a hamburger royale & fries back to hotel, but again struggled to finish them, beset by hiccups that would not stop.

So now Saturday morning 10AM, my last day in Vienna. It has gone just like that. If no Adelina no point going back to Manhattan I think, or

Tête, so it's looking like an early night tonight. I will see if I can get to the Belvedere early then back to WSK, finishing with another rostbraten. I leave London thinking I am going to f—k every floozie I see, but then I get to these places and never quite feel like doing anything, and return home having done nothing again.

The Ibis Mariahilfer is a big place; I'm on the 11th floor. Don't think I've ever been in a hotel room this high before.

A beautiful blazing blue-skied Spring day in Vienna. I felt so turned on with Denitsa in Manhattan on Thursday night and so turned on with busty blonde Claudia in Tête-à-Tête on Thursday night, but when I went back to both places Friday night I felt nothing for either of them. I can't help thinking it is being forced to vacate the Dorint and decamp to the Ibis has totally ruined my mojo. The Ibis is a perfectly nice hotel, but it does not feel like home like the Dorint does. So I start my Saturday by walking back to the Dorint bar.

The Dorint have abandoned their practice of serving their peanuts with a spoon, and now serve them in a small jug which is very hard to get the peanuts out of. I don't think that I will go to the Belvedere. I've seen those pictures so many times. I will go next time. Let me just go to the WSK and Café Westend and then have a sleep, then see what I want to do tonight. It will be very boring not going out AT ALL, and yet I feel no desire for Tête-à-Tête or Manhattan again. The discovery of this holiday is that Tête-à-Tête actually seems to get more lively (more customers) than the Manhattan.

No, I will not go to Belvedere this time. My holidays have been reduced to the bestial instincts: drink, sex & food. If I didn't fancy those two girls enough on the second night, then that must mean I didn't fancy them enough to do anything with them at all. It is rare I find a floozie I really want to do something with. My bar is set pretty high, believe it or not. It's got to be someone who blows my mind—an Adelina, a Lucy, a Julia, etc. I've not met anyone who quite reaches that status on this trip. Nuremberg, I think, had a few of them. And that is where I return tomorrow, Sunday. And so if I've not met anyone I really fancy on this trip to Vienna, that puts back any return visit to some indefinite distant point. I've not seen anything to make me rush back for. Saw nothing in Brussels to rush back for. I question my whole way of life, again. I hope I can enjoy Nuremberg on my return. The thing is, if I'd met a really mind-blowing floozie e.g. Adelina from last time, that would have lifted my spirits so much that I WOULD definitely be inspired to go to the Belvedere, and other cultural things; but with my spirits not really being lifted that much by anyone, I have little enthusiasm for the cultural things either. I should perhaps force myself up to Angelique at least tonight. One last try.

So my next holiday? Well, perhaps back to Berlin. Yes. Stuttgarter Platz has been wiped out with just Sissi Bar and Monte Carlo left but there is something so low-down sleazy about those two places that I like (and let's face it, they are cheap, which is the sexiest thing of all). And if King George really is now just 49 euros for entry, then worth trying that again. Oh, it would be lovely if I could just let myself go and f–k someone tonight but I don't think it is going to happen. Apart from Denitsa, the Manhattan's current crop of girls—apparently sans Adelina—depresses me. Tête-à-Tête is at least cheaper, just six euros for a beer. If I go late enough, there may be some dancing. The lesson of my holidays which I always forget is that if I'm going to do anything I need to do it on my first day or second at most. Day after day of seeing the same girls just make me tire of the girls before I have even done anything with them. Jackie at WSK turned me on so much when I first met her, but now even the thought of seeing her later does not excite me.

So I am indeed staying in my Vienna hotel room this Saturday night. I saw the floozies of Tête-à-Tête two nights in a row, the floozies of Manhattan two nights in a row, the floozies of Exzess, the floozies of WSK three days out of four; I am floozied out. Sated with the floozies. Again I've managed to come all the way to Vienna without doing anything naughty; well, it just means I never met anyone I wanted to have sex with enough. No doubt as soon as I get home I will be wishing I had f–ked Jackie in WSK, and wishing I had f–ked Denitsa in Manhattan, but at the time I just didn't feel in the mood enough. So I stay in my big white bed overlooking the Gurtel, listening to classical music on my last night in Vienna. Rachmaninov 2nd Symphony. Check out 12 tomorrow for the 1250 train back to Nuremberg. I think it will be a long while until I come back to Vienna. It remains to be seen whether I can finish my holiday with any erotic flourish and snatched moment of happiness in my last night in Nuremberg and last night in Brussels.

So 930 Sunday morning in Vienna. Still 2½ hours until I have to check out. Don't know what to do with myself. A sad, low-key end to my Vienna trip. I don't want to drink as I have a 4½ hour train journey ahead of me and I don't want to have to keep leaving my seat to pee; I don't want to eat in Café Westend because it always makes me want to s–t.

This Sunday afternoon train back to Nuremberg is absolutely packed. No spare seat; I'm sitting in a seat that is reserved from Passau to Nuremberg, so I will have to be without a seat once we reach Passau. Never travel on a Sunday again. Note to self. I did nothing in Vienna on Saturday; might as well travel Saturday.

So yes, I have lost my faith in Vienna. I will be back but not for eight months at least. Ninety minutes away from Nuremberg now. Sign that this holiday has seemed to have ended badly is on getting on the train I noticed the zip of my bag is broken and it is bulging permanently open. And five minutes ago I noticed my necklace was on the floor almost in the aisle; no idea how long it had been there. Everything is breaking. No real enthusiasm for anything in Nuremberg except to eat. Then 8AM tomorrow train back to Brussels, arrive 130PM for a last night in Brussels. A grey on & off rainy day, since we left hot, blue-skied Vienna. Important thing to remember, even after a disappointing, dispiriting visit, I still always want to keep travelling. I still always remain optimistic and hopeful of a better time next time. If I didn't keep going back to Vienna, I'd never have met Adelina, or WSK Amanda, or WSK Jackie. Or even Lotta & Sophia. Arriving at Regensburg, our last stop before Nuremberg. As soon as I get home, I'll be thinking why didn't I do something with Denitsa, and with Jackie in WSK, and big blonde in Tête-à-Tête? And cursing myself.

Nuremberg restored my faith in Eros at least. Magnificent videokabins in Stage 2000 followed by the stunning window girls/laufhaus girls of the Frauentormauer. Walking along the Frauentormauer on my first stop in Nuremberg on the way to Vienna I remember thinking "A man could make his home in Nuremberg." Daisy, Rubina. So many stunning girls. If I did not do anything it is perhaps because it was already so late, almost midnight, and I had just had a Burger King whopper, large fries AND six onion rings and more than anything needed a s–t. En route to Frankfurt now, twelve minutes delayed at least, but hopefully I'll still make my connection.

On the ICE to Brussels. A much more spacious train than the Nuremberg to Frankfurt one! Sitting in the Caribic videokabins last night I was thinking when I get to Brussels Yellow Lily I'm going to f–k the first half-decent girl there I see, don't care who she is; but of course that feeling has passed, and my old reticence will no doubt still be in force when I get there. And that I realise (again, re-realise) is why Vienna so often does disappoint. To really find a place erotic, to be able to really release the erotic fly from the amber, raise the woolly mammoth from the ice, there needs first of all to be a really good source of pornography. I was happy in Nuremberg because I spent my night in the superb videokabins of Caribic; that made me bursting to f–k anyone, anyone would do, just to stick this throbbing pole into somebody (willing, of course, and cheap). In Vienna I usually am left depressed and dispirited by the poor porn (disregarding what the ancient Chinese always used to say "even bad porn is good porn" or "no porn is bad", depending on your translation). ML Revue kabins awful, Burggasse Peep kabins awful, and the Menzelstraße kabins always were awful and now the place has closed down altogether. That really leaves me WSK, and while it is good to have the floozies there, Jackie in particular, the films shown are often rubbish and so it was on all three visits. That meant I reached Manhattan, Tête-à-Tête and Exzess in already subdued mood. It is often the case in Vienna. Berlin is poor now since Stuttgarter Platz was almost totally wiped out, but at least it has excellent kabins in BEC (Eroticpoint) which make me really desperate to walk on to Sissi or Monte Carlo to do something (I usually don't, but the anticipation is exciting enough). If only I could choose the films at WSK Vienna would be perfect. I have often been tempted to ask a porn cinema manager if I could. Yes, my old reticence will return once I get to Yellow Lily, but if there was a great videokabin place just next door, I would be so much more rampant in Yellow Lily. If I ran a knocking shop I would make sure there were also some high quality videokabins on site. The girls would make so much more money.

BRUSSELS

So no, no miracle on my last day of holiday. I didn't really try very hard. I was in Alhambra Cinema for less than five minutes, two rubbish American films, then to Café Jimmy for one Heineken and watch some Bulgarian music, to Yellow Lily, passing some very poor-looking street girls; no one in Yellow Lily of much interest, except Brazilian Aisha I know from before and Moroccan Leyla. I had a drink with her but then left, for a Brussels Grill. I was now desperate for bed. I awoke in the early hours and watching some mad doctor in white coat French film, and then *The Big Sleep* dubbed into French, before I fell asleep again.

*

Whatever happens at work is totally unimportant, I drop my little grenades then wander off; life is in the lush palms and ferns of Nag's Head with mega-bosomed Sophia, in Berlin and Vienna.

LIVE IN SMUT. SMUT SMUT SMUT. FU MANCHU. I WOULD like to write that Fu Manchu book, *The Willing Cheeks of Fu Manchu*. To capture that smutty, yellow world I live in. Maybe set in Soho of the 1990s, the Fin-de-Siècle naughty nineties, dense fog, thunderstorms, gloom. Rickshaws. Fu Manchu in long yellow silk robe, with bulge of his erection clearly visible. Getting turned on just thinking about it. The yellow mags, the Italian mags. My life is smut. Looking for smut, searching for a great sexual experience.

I like to be controversial. I like to make waves. Then I can return to Soho again.

Yes I want despair, ruin again, that is when EROTICISM comes back to life. When I come back to life. Taste my misery like blood in my mouth. Writing with blue hands in cold stoveless rooms.

A river cuts its own course, and I never go wrong. My instincts are always right. I am bound for better things and this is the route I have to take to get there.

I AM the Protector, the Gran Signore. And I am protecting myself. I am protecting the Garion inside myself. I am protecting the grand genius inside myself, the Neo latent in me who will one day grow and spread his wings, and explode, like a Shakespeare, a Samuel Pepys. You do not yet know my power. I am protecting myself, like they protect Damian in *The Omen*, until he comes into his power.

Pornography raises me to such a heightened state of sublimity, sensitivity, that it raises the pleasure and enjoyment of everything that then follows it. It is also the best temporary cure for fatigue. The best cure for fear. That is why I compare it to opium or some other narcotic drug.

*

1910.

Ten minutes late already after getting stuck at Hamm (as always), we now grind to a halt in the middle of the German countryside—a very waterlogged-looking countryside—halfway to Hannover. As if the journey was not long and arduous enough. Heavy dark grey skies, raining. It will be 930PM before we reach Berlin tonight, and probably 1030PM until I get to the Kanthotel. Quite tempted to get a taxi straight to my hotel, as it is so late. I can treat myself to a bit of luxury, at the end of the journey.

Gliding along at 222 km/h through foul filthy weather. Cold, lashing rain as night begins to fall over the German countryside. Still another twenty minutes to Spandau. 856PM. Ten minutes to Spandau. A silent train. No one talking. So peaceful, civilised. 243 km/h.

BERLIN

So, typical of me, I did nothing in my last two hours in Brussels, just had some drinks in L'Orient Express, something to eat, then on to my train. In Berlin on my first night, I had some drinks in the hotel bar then went out at midnight, started to head towards Club 77 then just thought "I'm not in the mood", so came back for a McDonald's then bed! The Kanthotel no longer has minibars, but you can collect ice cold bottles of beer (or draught beer) from the reception so that's OK. The staff now all wear uniforms; last time I stayed that sexy receptionist was always in tight fluffy sweaters of different colours. Figure-hugging. So yes, lovely to be so close to Monte Carlo and Sissi Bar but how lonely and out of place they now look, surrounded by "respectable" businesses. They LOOK like an anachronism. Twelve midday on my first beer of the day. Cold, but sunny outside. Hopefully it will be raining before I go out. Well, I take it back, a new blonde receptionist in a black lace top.

In David Bowie's Neues Ufer café—scene of his famous 30th birthday pictures. Emotional. Really emotional. Literally tears in my eyes and rolling down my cheeks. Customer in front of me with Ziggy red spiky mullet. Sounds like Amy MacDonald on the jukebox. I went to the carpark that marks the modern site of Hitler's bunker/backgarden of his Chancellery building in Wilhelmstraße. Underwhelming and overwhelming at the same time—that such a bland, genteel, leafy space marks the centre of somewhere once so powerful and "evil". The absolute epicentre of the Nazi madness, now just a leafy genteel carpark and backyard of apartment buildings (can you imagine how it feels to LIVE in these modern apartment buildings knowing what stood on this spot not so long ago?) The dichotomy feels quite overwhelming and disorientating. Well, I've done the two things I came to Berlin for this time, so now let me indulge my Priapism. The pillars & buttresses of the café are fascinating—like dried blood.

I love Berlin. But I honestly don't think I will be coming back. A completely uneventful, unarousing visit. When I think of all the erotic attractions on offer in Nuremberg or Frankfurt, why do I bother with Berlin? 77, Monte Carlo and Sissi were all pretty awful. The ruination of Berlin Zoo station continues—two days in a row I have not even been able to buy a Guardian newspaper here. In the Bavarian restaurant now, waiting for my rumpsteak. Gorgeous salad. So yesterday, what did I do? After several beers in the hotel reception, off to Hitler's bunker and Wilhelmstraße. Then to David Bowie's café and house. King George was rubbish. Six girls, no one took my fancy. Back to hotel, McDonald's, then bed. Woke 1130PM and rushed to BEC (in Lewishamstraße!) but the kabins were rubbish. In a poor state. One kabin the buttons don't work, the next kabin the buttons work but it does not take your coins. Hard work. A lot of money wasted for nothing. 77, Sissi, Monte Carlo all poor. I will try Ciro or Caligula tonight—expensive, but I have to try something. Now all I want is food.

Blazing blue skies as we leave Berlin; not a cloud in the sky after three days of pitiless, remorseless rain. As always when I have a hangover I feel randy yet when I'm actually in the night bars surrounded by floozies I feel NOTHING. All I want to do on this long four-hour trip back to Cologne is masturbate. A low-key trip to Berlin. I did not go out on my last night. Several drinks in the bar, then up to bed. Couldn't be bothered to waste money in Ciro or Caligula, or on the poor kabins of BEC. Save it for Brussels.

I was dizzy with erotic anticipation in the weeks & days leading up to my trip and I wondered whether I would be able to carry it with me and still feel the same when I got there; as I suspected, no. During my stay in Berlin I felt almost completely a-sexual. But as always it just takes one beautiful bottom or one beautiful pair of bosoms to get me in the mood again. I hope it happens in Brussels. My train to Köln is already 21 minutes late, giving me just 13 minutes to spare to catch my connection. I sat drinking my one beer surrounded by floozies in King George, Club 77, Monte Carlo and Sissi Bar and felt completely unmoved and unaroused by all of them. I hope something happens in Brussels to shake me out of my torpor. This is madness.

Blue skies all the way from Berlin to Köln, now as we leave Köln and head towards Belgium the clouds start to thicken. Aachen. I honestly now don't think I will ever return to Berlin. It joins Munich in being crossed off of my list—my famous four "Cities in the Autumn Stars". Just Brussels and Vienna are left, and Vienna was totally underwhelming in April; and Brussels has been totally underwhelming for a long while. Nuremberg maybe my next trip. The last leg of this journey from Köln back to Brussels feels ridiculously, blissfully quick after all these long train journeys across Europe. Just saw more sexy girls on the platform at Liège than I did in my entire stay in Berlin. I love Belgian girls. Three Belgian policemen just checked all our passports between Aachen and Liège.

*

Why am I not rampantly fucking my way around Europe like a wild rutting stag? Tooling like Byron in gondola, in alley, on table, under table, in carriage, etc etc? The infection held me back of course. Hopefully on this next couple of trips I CAN overcome my reticence and be that mad, lust crazed rutting stag. Anyone half fanciable.

The little people, the really really stupid insects, continue to be fascinated by me, obsessed by me. How I torment them. How I run rings around them. How my success tortures them. Oh how I yearn to be back in porn cinema, and videokabin, the smells & the sights & the sounds. It is where I am happiest, where my spirit soars highest. In the dark of a strip club with young girl disrobing to pounding music. In brasseries à femmes or night bar with half-dressed floozies lounging boredly around smoking, not bothering me. Surrounded by butterflies who make no effort to approach me. This is heaven.

Starting to feel a desperation to get to Brussels, and start to stick my iron rod into some soft pussies. But I never do, do I?

That Alphonse Mucha poster actually does remind me why I travel, and the mood I need to keep myself in when I do so. Jeunes filles.

It must be very galling for the small people to know not only did I survive, but how well I am now doing. Married the most beautiful, sexy woman in the world; now got the job of my dreams.

The lesson I learn is make my life in the small places I enjoy: in the Orient Express, in the Café du Dôme. Make my whole life in these places, drinking, watching the world go by. The big themes that play such a huge part in other people's lives, relationships, affairs, marriage, children, house, mortgage, mean absolutely nothing to me. What looms so monumentally large over everything in my life is my little bars, where I can drink, and watch the girls go by. A nice little porn cinema, a nice little bar filled with floozies, some window girls to ogle. A nice strip club to finish the night in.

*

Yellow Lily was poor as always, but oh joy, then Ina arrived! There was an old man sitting just to my left and she came to greet him, squeezing down into the gap between us, her bottom & leg pressed up against mine, neither she nor I making any attempt to move our legs apart, both of us knowingly KEEPING THEM pressed against each other, and I knew I could not resist her any longer. "Can we go upstairs?" "Yes." Finally I did something with Ina, but, sadly, I have absolutely no memory of it, as I was so drunk by this stage. But thank God I have finally scratched that itch, lanced that boil, broken that ice. After three years! I bought a Domino's Pizza and came back to the Max with it then passed out. After 30 hours without sleep it is no surprise I slept right through the night (my usual appalling bout of indigestion apart, the bane of my life) and here I am 11AM in the morning with a couple of hours to kill before my train to Nuremberg. A blazing blue-skied morning. Not a cloud in the sky.

So, yes, the Alhambra Cinema films were rubbish, and the street girls were rubbish, but I knew they would be, and: it doesn't matter! It is still just a joy to be in a place where in walking distance from my hotel is a proper porn cinema, street girls, a daytime floozie bar, window girls, kabins and a strip club. That is why Brussels is still so lovely to come to. We've already lost the ABC Cinema, California Peep Show & kabins, Paradise Peep Show & kabins, so I must treasure what is left while I can.

Little black-haired Japanese or Chinese girl under my window in tight white T-shirt 'La Vie est Belle', over massive bosoms, pulling a suitcase. Let's hope she is staying here. Oh, but thank God I DID something this time! Always I come to these places and I um and ah and think she's nice, but for one reason or another I put off and put off and end up coming home having done nothing. Hope this is a cue for me to do something EVERY DAY on this trip—which is always my intention when I leave boring London.

NUREMBERG

Well, the train to Frankfurt was pretty horrible. Sweating like a pig, there didn't seem to be a breath of cool air on the train. A suffocating hot atmosphere. The train from Frankfurt to Nuremberg was better at least, the cool air hit me as soon as I got on. On the train home now—oops I mean the train back to Brussels. I didn't do much on my one night in Nuremberg in the end. Foolishly I left the hotel too late and the Stage 2000 kabins were already closed! I had a couple of beers in Bella Napoli, then came back. If you like very big-busted black girls (and who on Earth does not?), then the Nuremberg windows are the ones for you. Travelling to Nuremberg with just a small bag was a great success (leaving my big bag in a Max Hotel locker). Not only did it mean I could drop in to Carolina on the way to Midi, but now I can explore Rue d'Aerschot as soon as I get off the train back in Brussels, before I even get down to my hotel. Tomorrow is Belgian National Day, ominously. I don't live for saving, I live for eroticism. Constant priapism. Nothing matters to me except sexual pleasure, pornographic pleasure. I haven't changed at all. All that has happened over the years is I have become more discerning and harder to please. The two-hour train back to Frankfurt so spacious & relaxed, and the journey feels so quick compared to going. And arriving at Frankfurt my Brussels ICE is already sitting quietly waiting for us to get on. The whole train to choose from, so lovely & empty. Happy to be heading back to Brussels.

BRUSSELS

Well, I spoke too soon; after leaving Köln we only went as far as Düren where we had to change trains for the rest of the journey to Brussels. Exchanging quite a cool ICE for another stifling completely airless one. Made it a very gruelling and tiring journey again and arriving at Brussels I wanted to do nothing except come straight to my hotel. Here I am then. Check into my room by 605PM. Tomorrow is Belgian National Day and after Bastille Day in Nice, Brussels I think is braced for the worst. I should try to enjoy tonight as much as I can. Apparently it is 33°C in Brussels right now (doesn't feel that bad) and thunderstorms are expected later. Let us hope I can find a porn cinema or a knocking shop to shelter in. 745PM already. Ridiculous. Going to Nuremberg really has wasted two days for nothing and with tomorrow being Belgian National Day that will be a dead loss as well I expect. Still blue skies outside and no sign of any storms.

    Yes, I finally "broke the ice" with Ina—and yet I have no memory at all of what happened in the room. I have no visual memory; was she on top of me, underneath me, bending over? Me sitting in the Second Empire armchair with her bouncing up & down on my lap? No idea. I have not got a single picture in my mind of what took place. I am sure an encounter took place, but I have no evidence of any kind to prove it. Therefore, I must do it again. Belgium is such a lovable country, and Brussels such a lovable city, it is so perverse it is facing this mortal danger right now; threatened to be blown limb from limb every time we go shopping. This perversity must surely end soon; every band of losers has their shelf life; let us hope this one is nearer its end than its beginning. In the million ways I am likely to die, crossing a road without looking is No.1 top of the list, being killed in a "terrorist" loser outrage is at around No.1 million. It remains the most unlikely way to die. So, keep things in proportion (I tell myself). The population of France is 66.03 million, and only ONE person chose to murder anyone on Bastille Day.

Four days into my five-day holiday and I've only heard one good song, Black Strobe's 'Girl from the Bayou' while in Nuremberg. It is nice to have two music channels on my TV here in Brussels but MTV Viva only plays pretty mainstream stuff from the charts (and only has music in the mornings anyway), and D17 by contrast plays a lot of French music which is great, if only it wasn't all so weak and rubbish. Where are the Alizées these days!? The Berenices? Something with a bit of punch. Yes, French music but with a bit of oomph behind it. Massive tunes. Sexy Lolitas. The best music channel I find these days is Go TV in my Vienna hotel. Really interesting great songs old & new which I have never heard before.

So Wednesday night after my return from Nuremberg, it was so late by the time I left the hotel I headed straight to Yellow Lily. Ina behind the bar pulling beers. Then later in the corridor leading to the smoking room. She was sweet, and simpatico, tactile, so I think she must have a good feeling towards me since our encounter; I myself, as I said, have no memory of it. Later, as she returned behind the bar, she touched my arm with her hand; another good sign. She is the ONLY girl there now of any interest. It is sad. Yellow Lily now IS Ina. Back in my first discovery of the place there would always be four or five alternatives. Now just her. Really sad. I think the terrorism has scared off so many quality girls. Ina went to the room quite soon with another man, so I left at that point and headed down to Alhambra Cinema. The doors were open, but the lady was hoovering and the cinema lights were on, and the show had already finished. It was only just after 10PM. Down to Empire but no girls of any interest—no Manuela, no Jennifer that means—so I left after one beer. So another cheap day in Brussels. In Nuremberg the kabins were closed so I just had three beers in Bella Napoli and that was it. In Brussels just the beers in Yellow Lily, but Alhambra Cinema was closed, so two very cheap nights. Still 225 euros in my pocket for Thursday and Friday.

I feel so at home in the Max Hotel. I really could live here forever. If I was able to do that, I would be a happy man. And yes, the Alhambra Cinema films have been crap again, the street girls have been crap again, the Yellow Lily girls are really crap, the Empire dancers are really crap—but it doesn't matter; it is enough that these places exist. Finding the occasional diamond in these places is worth the wait. There was AMAZING quality in the Nuremberg windows and laufhauses and I did nothing with any of them. It is about finding places I feel comfortable, and I have that in Brussels. I will wait for the odd diamond to come to the surface; hopefully one day soon these jihadist losers will fade away and Brussels can really start to bloom & blossom again (erotically speaking). Berlin for me is dead, erotically speaking. When Stuttgarter Platz was wiped out, then for me Berlin was wiped out. The memories from those nights in Hanky Panky, Mon Cheri and Golden Gate in particular are so strong, so glorious. Munich for me is dead, erotically speaking, nothing on offer except 50-euro private dances! Waste of time and money. And Nuremberg I don't think I will return to. So that leaves Brussels and Vienna. And from this week's experience NOTE TO SELF—no more long train journeys in summer. So Brussels only for summer. Vienna can wait for winter.

One day, one day, I still want to go to the Reichenbach Falls, and the Brocken Mountain, and to Italy, all of Italy; and to Sils Maria. But for now my narrow erotic interests in quick thrills lead me always back to Brussels, and Vienna, and the dwindling last few red lights. I have lost so much in London (Carnival Strip, Astral Cinema, Sunset Cinema, Soho Cinema, Boulevard Strip, Flying Scotsman, Robert Peel, Queen Anne, White Horse Charlton, Horse & Groom, so many models' flats), lost so much in Berlin, Stuttgarter Platz almost entirely, lost so much in Brussels, ABC Cinema, California, Paradise, I must treasure the last few resources that are left before they too are gone. In Vienna already I have lost Fortuna Kino and Pour Platin.

How to tell toadstools from mushrooms? Does anyone know? When we buy mushrooms from our local supermarket we just have to trust they are mushrooms and not toadstools, don't we. So yes, an early visit to rubbish Alhambra Cinema, and early visit to rubbish Yellow Lily today; and after Rue d'Aerschot back down for a steak or a pizza then bed. This my life in Brussels. And it makes me happy. Try Empire again tonight. After finally crossing Ina off my list, Jennifer at Empire is the next sacred cow in my sights, and those wonderful sacred udders, heavy with wonderful sacred milk.

When they built the Hotel le Dôme around 1904 they must have thought wow, this is a massive building. "Look wife! Look children! Look how high it is!" Now it is dwarfed by the Sheratons, and the Thons, and the Crowne Plazas all around it. 230 already. Maybe time to go. So let me salute Belgium on its National Day—a country I love, and Brussels a city I love. Let us hope the perverse clouds of pathetic "Islamist" murders will be behind it soon. Losers always lose in the end. There are many more of us than there are of them. Those may well be famous last words. So be it. Let it be: "I love my wife! I love —! I love my mother!"

So I finally burnt a big hole in my money. Alhambra Cinema, Café Jimmy, Yellow Lily (twice), Sexyworld kabins, Rue d'Aerschot, Fiesta Café, Domino's Pizza (large!), and Empire to finish. I take back a lot of what I said yesterday. The Alhambra Cinema films must have changed Tuesday or Wednesday, and these ones were much better. I in fact went in FOUR times yesterday. The street girls had some promise—two petite curvy black-haired Bulgarians outside Jimmy, who could be sisters, are quite cute. There was a Colombian outside Europe 2000 hotel who really tempted me. And Yellow Lily has a blonde girl who looks the spitting image of Perrie from Little Mix, and a black-bobbed girl who is all right. Ina was not there yesterday. And in Rue d'Aerschot I found Mariana, like Nicole Sherzinger but with huge bosoms—I indulged, her on top of me smashing me in the face with those wonderful knockers. The kabin films, however, were poor. The machines are in good working order, but the selection of films gets worse every time I go. In Empire to finish the night, Jennifer was there but as usual eluded me—stepping off stage and going straight into private dance with someone. Though at 60 euros for a private dance (maybe she charges more) and 10 euros for each 25cl beer, maybe it is better if she does elude me. Don't think I will go back.

A new development yesterday—there was a floozie in Alhambra Cinema going around the men in the dark (and it is absolutely pitch black in there) offering her services—50 euros for suck & f–k. I had passed her in the lobby earlier and presumed her to be the cleaning lady. During the night, a new custom of my nights in Brussels now, *The Big Sleep* dubbed into French on TV. Has there ever been anything finer on a cinema screen than Humphrey Bogart and Lauren Bacall together? Even if I cannot understand what they are saying. Things I've learned from this week: 1. Never go on a long train journey across Europe in summer. The heat and often lack of effective AC on the trains make it too horrible. Stick to Brussels in summer. 2. I won't bother with Nuremberg again. There were AMAZING girls in Frauentormauer, but if I did nothing this time then I never will so no point. 3. I finally "broke the ice" with Ina, and that is such a relief. Like an Albanian Maria Schneider; an Albanian Selena Gomez. Having done the Alhambra Cinema to death (four times there yesterday alone), done the Yellow Lily to death, not really sure what to do today—to get myself in the mood for anything I mean.

So, yes, I went to Alhambra Cinema, and felt nothing. Went to Café Jimmy, and Yellow Lily, and felt nothing. So, rather than flog this dead horse even further, I came straight to Brussels Grill. Maybe I will go on to Rue d'Aerschot afterwards; I doubt it. The horse has bolted. No point locking the stable doors now, my cow. My Eros has gone, sodden, like a drowned rat. Nothing left. Still early, 430PM, though, Friday night. If even Alhambra Cinema and Yellow Lily do not arouse me, then what chance do I have? I am mentally dead, subdued; as I say, sodden. Nothing can spark when it is so flooded, flooded with five solid days of booze. Even before the steak arrives, I am thinking about another Domino's Pizza. Or a burger in the bar next to my hotel. 1659. This has been an UNUSUALLY long wait for my steak. Because I tried to order before I even sat down? "No," she said, "you must sit down first." Did she deliberately delay my food because of that?

Gorgeous steak completely knocked me out. Five days of drinking had caught up with me and the steak just put the top hat on it. Numb, like a zombie, I slowly plodded up to Rue d'Aerschot just to see Mariana one last time, as the last thing I did on this holiday. Just to SEE her; no way I could do anything with her. But getting there at 530 I found every single window empty. I know it is near change of shift time, but I didn't expect the windows to be left empty. So a complete waste of time. I had one beer in Fiesta Café and walked back; they were still empty.

    A misty Saturday morning, after last night's rain. Feeling quite maudlin, not sure why. Just my natural state when sober I suppose. Five days of drinking has left me dull, numb, flat. How excited I always feel on my first day away. If I had not done something with Ina on the first night, I would not have done anything with her all week again. I managed to find some more life on Thursday because of a whole new set of films at Alhambra Cinema, good ones too.

*

There is a kind of dangerous desire for defeat, for only in complete abject defeat and despair, can one experience that release of pure nihilism, that eroticism of despair that enables real sexual ecstacy to flower, to bloom and blossom from the absolute fertiliser of shit in which one is now wallowing. For instance one can yearn for a wonderful blessed marriage to a beautiful woman to be lost because it restricts one's true desire too much so one can be free to wallow in shame and degradation again, one can yearn for wonderful job and career to be ruined because it forces one not to refrain from certain practices, so one can be free to wallow in shame and degradation again. This yearning for disaster, defeat, shame, humiliation, as only then can you achieve real sexual highs. Only in the most abject lows can you experience the most sublime sexual and spiritual highs. A real Sadeian Nihilism. A French cyclist who wants never to win stages of the

Tour de France or to ever again win the race itself so the despair and the bitterness can become richer and richer, like a child biting down on a loose tooth to release that amazing sweet taste of blood and feel that amazing pain. This whole attitude is prevalent through the life of the Marquis de Sade, and I recognise it so strongly in myself. It is both terrifying, and disgusting, and makes me want to cry, at the same time as filling me with a dangerous excitement, a devilish desire, a feeling that is my true desire. So sitting with my beautiful never to be unloved wife in a pub together looking at some lonely old man sitting alone all afternoon with his pint, quietly and with dignity speaking to no one, but just periodically returning to the bar to politely take another drink, I finding myself yearning to be that lonely old man myself as I get older. There is a dignity to them, a beauty. Like sad abused old dogs recovering from their terrible wounds in some dog sanctuary seem so much more lovable than happy dogs.

"They thought to wear me down with constant attacks; they just filled me up with power and gave me the air I needed to fill my balloon and rise up above them. They gave me the fertiliser I needed to bloom and blossom to rise and flower above them, and leave them withering in my shade. They did not realise I was Fantomas looming over Paris pulling all their strings. I provoked them into everything so they would give me what I needed. Their smiles of gloating triumph sadly misplaced started to fade, to looks of worry and bewilderment. This was not going as they had planned. They had never had a supposed victim play them like a piano before. I took over their small minds, I wormed my way into their consciousness, so they took me home with them and infected their entire home lives with me. They are obsessed with me, and they will never be free of me now."

(*To Confound* has got to be written in voice of strident hubris, madman genius shaking his fist at the world cackling. Yes he is mad, but mad like Fantomas. Fu Manchu. Surely *Confound* CAN be the very tiny germ from which my great book can arise. But MIXED with all the Berlin stuff, "I suffer gravity only to defeat it again!" Return to it but with mad surrealism, don't stick to narrow chronology of diary.)

More than ever I can become pure Priapism. I have not even started. Now I must reboot and start again. I have the pills now, and I am free of the infection, and I have more money than ever before. And I am free. This can become the start of the most rampant time in my life. I started using the pills last summer but at one and the same time, chance or not, was crippled by this infection. At same time I got new job with more money. Only now I have beaten the infection can I start my rampant life for real. Inna and Mariana were just the start of it.

467

Now I WANT to go to Munich! I want to stand in the portico of the Justizpalast again. Don't care how rubbish Atlantic City is or how expensive the private dances or pushy the girls. Don't care. It is the memories. It is the wellstone, the lodestone. Bella Rosa Jay Z Build the Sands on You. Patricia handjob coming over her tits. Emily running cotton wool bud dipped in champagne around head of my penis. Extraordinary nights in Munich. Irina! "I want to come back to your hotel!" Suzy. Viktoria. Surely I could find SOME new excitement in Munich??? Since I split up with — in August 2013 have I felt drawn to ANY woman, in terms of a relationship? No. Not one. Quite the opposite. I have veered happily away from every one of them who showed any interest in me.

It is amazing what a sexual pornotopia is out there, and which I am enjoying. To think I was there in the WSK cinema lobby while a completely naked Jackie stood there getting dressed. What pleasures I enjoy. Haha and to think the little people laugh at me and try to make me feel ASHAMED of these delicious pleasures I enjoy. Hahahaha.

Christ what a magnificent life I have had. All the magnificent floozies I have fucked, groped, ogled. The Irinas, Patricias, Bella Rosa, Viktoriyas, Emilys, Riccardas in those magnificent Berlin rooms, Iga, Diana, the Monte Carlo kino girls, the Vienna WSK and Fortuna girls, and Pour Platin and Manhattan, the Brussels girls, Lucy, Inna, Julia, Andrea. The magnificent hours, days in the great porn cinemas, the magnificent slow stroking back and forth.

How great to think Summer Solstice was June 22, already more than a MONTH past! The nights are drawing in already!

I wonder if I will ever meet someone I will fall for again? I mean EVER again? Will I ever fall for a girl again? There is Ina at Yellow Lily I am attracted to. Adelina at Manhattan I was attracted to. Christ she WAS beautiful wasn't she! Maybe she was just on holiday last time. HAHAHA how my exploits drive my enemies mad, even just wondering wondering wondering WHAT is he getting up to? Hahahahahahaha.

*

Feeling quite depressed, but trying to force myself to spark to life, I came back to Alhambra Cinema. Films were OK actually, but downstairs I was treated to a live show! Some curvy blonde woman was fucking some young Moroccan boy on the sofa under the screen itself, while the tubby husband (?) watched with pleasure. One or two other men were standing close by with their members out, and I moved in to stroke her beautiful naked voluptuous arse under her raised black negligee top—but her husband shooed me away. I think they are obviously swingers—the woman was really enjoying it, she seemed absolutely lost in the delirious abandon of her fucking—but I think there might be money involved too. People who wanted to partake had to pay for the privilege, I suspect. She then leant over the Moroccan boy (wearing a T-shirt only, his trousers & underwear nowhere to be seen) and proceeded to suck him off (uncovered). Amazing scenes! Of depravity! Filth! And quite a good film on screen as well—was that Anna Polina?—but you know what, I still couldn't feel sexy. Yes, I had a full erection, but an erection in name only if you know what I mean. That is to say yes, I had a full erection, of iron hard magnificence, but I didn't feel any sexiness in my head. Still had no desire to put my erection INTO anything. It was a real lifeless erection.

After she had finished off the very happy looking Moroccan boy (Belgian boy of Moroccan descent no doubt, I mean; not wanting to be rude), she, hubby, manager, and another gentleman who had been standing with his member out were in very animated discussion for a long time at the back of the cinema. Eventually the gentleman with his member out took the blonde back down to the sofa under the screen and she got it on again, hubby sitting next to them with kitchen roll in hand. Then, blow me, the manager got his little man out and she was sucking him off as well! I made my excuses and left.

It was dark then, after 9PM, and I headed up to Gare du Nord, with no enthusiasm. Still feeling completely sexless. Spent about ten minutes in the Sexyworld kabins, again a full erection but again no sexual arousal in my brain. Normally the kabins will turn me on so much I want to rush out and do something with one of the window girls, but now I felt no desire for it. I walked up as far as Fiesta Café only (about one quarter of the Rue d'Aerschot only? Perhaps less); surprised how few windows were open actually. Turned back and had two small beers in La Dernière Minute café, mainly because the barmaid looked cute and she had the most amazing hair, braids, and devil's horn buns and all sorts, really lovely—must have taken HOURS to get her hair like that! Watched a bit of Liverpool's pre-season destruction of Barcelona at Wembley on the TV screen then came back; all I could think of was a burger in the burger bar beside my house, so rushed back for that and then bed. A cheap first evening in Brussels, but rather sad that I felt so completely unaroused the whole time. Hope I can feel SOME sexiness on this trip.

Belgian girls have such beautiful, curvy figures. I would love to do something with a Brussels girl. But all I ever meet of course are the floozies of Romania, Albania, Brazil, Bulgaria etc. Belgian girls have become something of a fantasy figure to me.

I have had an amazing life—for the first 30 years it is true I did live like a rabbit in a hutch, and only after that did I start to bloom & blossom and live like a normal human being; and I felt the need to make up for lost time. After all those years of sexual repression, the dam burst and après that, le deluge indeed. So many beautiful girls in Brussels. Really casually stunning. Not "beach body ready" in that rather stupid phrase, but just curvy, cuddly, totally sexy. But my life HAS, belatedly, been amazing. When I think of the stunning girls (floozies, 90% of them) I have slept with, it is absolutely mind-blowing. One hundred or more of the most beautiful women you have ever seen in your life, and I have — them, for very little money. What a life, of sexual adventure (and misadventure).

*

I AM enthused by *To Confound*! I think I can make something wonderful and florid and lurid out of it; and if I do that then I can do something with *Nellie's Band* as well, even smaller of course. Those two summers. Of rain and thunder. Christ now I realise there is SO much great stuff in *Fin-de-Siècle*. Perhaps I can do two versions, brief miniature *To Confound*, and long detailed *Fin-de-Siècle*. One the abbreviated speed read of the second. A man on the edge of madness, depression, completely bitten by the serpent of sex in Fin-de-Siècle Munich 1996-1999. Addicted to sex, revelling in it more and more, and the growing hatred and jealousy this attracts, till it is all out war.

Fascinating to put my four books into chronological order in one document, I had forgotten so much stuff that was put into my reissued books. Long lost material that I only recently uncovered and put back in. Fascinating too to read through my Munich *To Confound* stuff as well. This claustrophobic, Wilhelmine world. Stuffy, sickly, suffocating, but struggling to break through and fly, emerge from my chrysalis. The electricity provided by the outside world's attacks was what I needed to finish my metamorphosis and emerge as the glorious iridescent butterfly, flapping above their heads, terrifying them, like the pterodactyl at the Geographical Society at the end of *The Lost World*. What have they unleashed on the world! What have they done! Why couldn't they just have ignored me and let me be! They cannot put me back in my box, back in my egg, back in my chrysalis now. They have sowed the wind, now let them reap the whirlwind. NOW the books at last started to emerge, *Autismus, Lotta & Sophia, The Cold Icy Air of the Mountains, Casanova*. The butterfly's journeys around Europe.

How lovely it is NOT to want to be in a relationship with anyone. Not to crave sex with anyone. To be completely free like that. Free to save my money, and travel more selectively. Thank God Berlin is over now. I can concentrate totally on the Brussels and Vienna route. Haha let my legend spread, and let them spread it for me. They think they are smearing me, they are just spreading my seed even further and doing it for me, like bees carrying pollen to germinate the whole world. They spread my legend for me and make it sure I will flourish and bloom and blossom even more. A bad reputation is a good reputation.

Ah the more they laugh and think to crush me, the more I rise above them, and their smiles turn to worried looks. This is not going the way they planned. Haha they act all cocky, as stupid people do that to try and hide their fear of someone above their level, but really they are frustrated and fearful and feel small.

Now they are more than ever tormented by their obsession with me. Their desire for vengeance may have made — and — do worse to me since Thursday, so they have smeared me more than before, but all they have done is tormented and fixated themselves even more in their jealous obsession with me and seething obsession with defeating me. Hahahah now I am on their minds all the time.

I have forced them to do WORSE to try to beat me, and still they do not succeed. I have forced them to shame themselves MORE. Everything — tried to do to hurt me just backfired on her and made things worse for her; now — and — are discovering the same thing. I force my enemies to damn and shame THEMSELVES in desperate vain attempts to land one single blow on me.

I almost crave the old despair, so I can return to the mountains and cold stoveless rooms. In this time of plenty & warmth, I must fill my boots & save as much money as I can. When disaster comes as it must, I will be ready with stockpile to head back to the cold icy air with. Sils Maria too. I am one of life's outsiders; you can try to bring me in but I will never feel comfortable or happy; and will have to fly away again. Like Wendy tried to lure Peter in, but he had to go.

"Take some down time, enjoy where you are, reflect on what it took to get here...would you do it again, was the investment worth the cost."

471

"All your hard work is paying off, you've invested yourself well, and you are putting your unique mark on it all."

"What you're doing is leaving a lasting impression, you're in home stretch, & will soon be going even further; even a new direction perhaps."

In January to September alone I have spent £2,242 on strippers, and that does not include all the beer I consume while doing it, all the drinks I bought for them & bar staff. STOPPING going to strip pubs for rest of the year will make a massive difference. That is the turning point. THAT is only thing that will bring my credit card debt down, bring my credit card minimum payments down. Just think that £2,242 I had not spent on strippers I could have spent in Vienna and Brussels! Much better use of the money. That £234 I spent in — last week alone could have gone on paying off my cards, and been used as spending money in Brussels and Vienna. That is the incentive. I am doing well, in August I reduced my credit card debt by £74 and in September by a further £240. Without — I can be reducing it by almost £500 a MONTH. That is reducing my credit card debt by a thousand pounds every two months, potentially. The prize is there, and it is attainable. The low lying fruit is there.

My personal debt as percentage of GDP i.e. salary is 68.9%. I will track this figure every month now. Compared to 60.8% a year ago. Difference of 8.1%. Interesting to note my debt ratio in last month in Wandsworth Road back in 2007 was just 27% rising to 71% in 2012 just before E– money, then rising again to 69.9% two months ago.

Just in next two weeks, Monday & Tuesday this week and Monday to Wednesday next week, I have chance to save up to £348 by NOT going to —. That shows what can be done! Suddenly that is £348 I could spend in Brussels at end of October or Vienna in December! And many weeks till we get to Vienna.

The thing is working at — I SHOULD be rich, I should be PERFECTLY capable of renting a little studio flat of my own based on my £– monthly paycheque; it is only the £1,000 a month minimum credit card repayments that makes that impossible. If I COULD reduce this credit card debt significantly now, suddenly everything in my life becomes possible. From being on the brink of ruin and disaster, I can pull back to a very comfortable place, where I should be while working at —.

But of course as always I cannot be down on myself too much, all that debt was incurred on pleasure, and in particular travel, so was any of that money wasted? No, it was all spent on travel. And if I had all that money back again, I would just straightaway spend it all on travel again. So it is not like I wasted all the money on some terrible investment, or on something that then got stolen and lost. I spend it doing exactly the most important thing I want to spend money on. That money brought me the most fantastic sexual experiences with Adelina in Manhattan, Fortuna blonde, Manuela in Burggasse Peep, Amanda and Jackie in WSK, Andrea and Julia, and Ina and Lucy in Yellow Lily, Maria in Pour Platin, Riccarda, Diana, Olga & Alla in Berlin etc etc etc. The only thing is for my safety and later harder life, I have to try to rein this in now. Rein it in for a while, just so I can go again. There is no point living like a monk and owing zero pounds and just carry on living like a monk till the day you die. I have to try to indulge as much of my pleasure as I can, while still young and fit and healthy (and single). I have to put all that pleasure in my bank, so when I am old and infirm at least I can look back and think well at least I did something, at least I travelled to some amazing places, and slept with some incredible women. That is why every penny of that debt is worth it. Not a single penny is wasted or do I regret. Yes, there have been some bad trips, but you never know until you get there. You have to keep spinning the roulette wheel to enjoy those occasional massive successes that live with you forever. The successes are of so much greater value than whatever they cost me in pure monetary terms. Adelina, Lucy, Andrea, Amanda, etc etc etc absolutely mind blowing experiences. The highs that you remember for all your life. Important to reach a philosophical position on debt, as much as a practical management position on it.

Living with — the worst thing was all my debt was because of giving all my money to our private landlord. At least now I can look at my debt and know this time it was all incurred on pleasure, and pretty much erotic pleasure at that. If you are going to go into debt, nothing better to go into debt over than erotic pleasure. But now I have to give consideration to the roof over my head, and my quality of life when I have to live alone again. I can have a wonderful quality of life, based purely on my excellent salary, if only it was not for the debt repayments taking it all away. So a period of sensibleness must ensue, while still allowing myself my occasional pleasures like Brussels this month and Vienna at Xmas.

On Brussels Klara classical radio you hear music from composers I have NEVER HEARD OF. Johann Joachim Quantz. But it all sounds totally normal music from the romantic canon, it could be Bach or Mozart or Beethoven. Why do we never hear these composers in England? Niels Wilhelm Gade. Fascinating. I actually think they are just playing Bach or Mozart, they just add made up names to it to make it sound more exotic, it sounds just like I would hear on Radio 3 but with totally unknown names added.

What an incredible sexual life I have had, belatedly, catching up for lost time, when I had such an incredible long life of repression when I was young; to think I did not lose my virginity till I was 27. I have been making up for lost time ever since. But still those missed chances will never leave me. If there was one person in this life I would dearly love to meet again it is —.

        I have managed to make a wonderful life out of all the muck of my life.

        But us writers do, don't we? Throw us sunshine we will bask in the sunshine, throw us rain and we will bathe in the rain. Throw us flowers and we will write about flowers, throw us shit and we will write about shit. Throw us your all-consuming jealousy and savage envy and we will write with great amusement about your all-consuming jealousy and savage envy; "Oh! How sad! Look at their poor twisted seething ugly little faces! As I go on enjoying all my voluptuous pleasures! How difficult for them! How I must torment them!"

*

The 1970s are raw, sensual, decaying—that is when sensuality is at its height; when it is starting to decay and turn rotten, then it glows brightest and burns fiercest. I no longer hope to meet a great beauty when I travel, or to fall in love; I hope to drink & drink & eat & eat, and anything else pulchritude-wise is a bonus.

        So, 11:53 Sunday morning (or possibly 10:53 Sunday morning—the clocks went back last night and I'm not sure if my phone automatically updated or not). I missed out on Saturday night unfortunately; I was looking forward to a Saturday night Empire or Gascogne: hoping at least there would be a nice crowd & good atmosphere; but after leaving Yellow Lily I just grabbed a lovely Domino's Pizza and back to hotel then sleep; right the way through to 6AM. A wee then slept some more through to 9. Now on my second Jupiler of the day. Lovely to see Ina at Yellow on my arrival yesterday evening. I took her up to a bedroom again. We had a nice chat about many things while laying naked in each other's arms, none of which I will repeat, as I cannot remember any of it. At least this time I do remember being in the room with her, and have some visual memories stuck in my head; some pictures in my head at least. The piano is gone and as I stood at the back where it used to be, she was sitting in the chair in front of me, her back to me, in that long black satin halter-neck catsuit she wears. Her jet-black hair falling around her alabaster white skin reminding me of those old little black inkpots you used to get at school, to fill the inkwells with! Yes, I am old enough to remember inkwells at school! Like an explosion of black ink against her white skin. I became aroused just looking at her back so knew I would have to do something with her again.

So Yellow Lily had Ina, the star as always, Brazilian Aisha I always like to look at, the black bob Eastern European who is a bit too thin for my taste, and another long dark-haired girl was OK, but that was it. No competition for Ina for sure, though she claimed I was her first customer of the day. She says she lives in a flat by the ——. A bright blue-skied Sunday midday in Brussels. Wish it was dark & stormy & rainy as always. My soul soars and spirit flies when it is dark & stormy & rainy. Feel meek and self conscious when it is fine & blue-skied & sunny. The weather affects me greatly. Are other people like this? I mean, I know normal people feel really happy when it is bright & sunny, but I am the opposite. I am happy when it is dark & raining. Thunder? Oh! My dream.

RFM TV. I cannot walk out of a bar that's playing Lady Gaga Paparazzi; I cannot. So I booked TWO more nights in my Brussels hotel, coming home on Thursday afternoon COACH for £16. I realised, if I'm going to stay in Brussels for two more days let me NOT try and save money for two days because that is pointless. To come on holiday and save money makes the holiday a complete WASTE of money. I have done almost nothing of any note in my three days here already, so let me finally DO something on these extra two days. So I go on a bar crawl of the Rue d'Aerschot. Really I should spend more time in the Rue d'Aerschot instead of Yellow Lily. The quality of window girls in Rue d'Aerschot is ridiculously high. A lot of 10 out of 10 girls, the only problem is deciding WHO to go with. Really I was planning to come back from Rue d'Aerschot to Yellow Lily, but after the quality of the Rue d'Aerschot girls it would be so depressing to go back to Yellow Lily, same old mediocre girls (Ina excepted). I should have a drink in a Rue d'Aerschot bar, fuck a girl, have another drink, fuck another one, etc and repeat.

The usual ridiculously sexy girls in the Rue d'Aerschot windows; I walked all the way to the end and had a couple of beers in the Retro Bar then a few more in the Red Devil bar then came back down the road thinking to do something with at least one of the beauties I'd seen on the way up, and couldn't see any of them haha. So I just came back to Yellow Lily, and my God, there were so many beautiful girls here too! A new Moroccan girl Leyla who I don't think I'd seen before, and spoke no English, so her "sister" translated for us. I took her up to a bedroom. One of the most beautiful, adorable girls I'd ever met in a place like this. Fall in love-able. When I finally tore myself away it was nearly 8PM and I had a five-euro pizza from a packed solid Domino's Pizza (Tuesdays must be the cheap day) then bed. A most enjoyable day; vindication for staying in Brussels and not going on somewhere else—a better day than the three that preceded it. Now the only problem is I am broke, don't know what card I'll be able to get any more money from—and I think I've fallen in love with Leyla. Apart from that everything is fine.

Absolute vindication for taking the time to have a McDonald's at 11AM; because of that I was able to keep drinking right the way through the day without thinking obsessively about food. Finally yesterday I broke through to the other side, instead of the boring abstention of the first three days. And today, it is always a mistake, but I will try to repeat yesterday. Spend a good deal of time in Rue d'Aerschot, going up the full length and having a drink or two in each bar; only when it gets to mid-afternoon returning to Yellow Lily. That big Moroccan with black bob I quite liked Monday in jumper & jeans and who I thought might be spectacular in a sexy black dress, was indeed spectacular in a black dress yesterday—it was like she had read my mind—her huge bosoms spilling over the top of it. Very appealing. Yellow Lily last night was the best I have known it for a very long time. This is why I keep trying. If you don't keep trying you will never have these good nights. I felt Brussels spectacularly came back to life for me yesterday, and I wouldn't have known that if I'd gone away somewhere on Tuesday as planned.

So Day of the Dead was a spectacularly good one for me; as always death represents transformation & rebirth. An unforgettable Day of the Dead in Brussels. If nothing else happens on the remaining day & a half of this holiday it will have been a success—a last minute victory snatched from the jaws of defeat. Suddenly all those boring songs on my TV now seem exciting, after yesterday. It only takes one girl to bring a club to life, and a city to life. All the year I've been saying this year hasn't caught fire yet, and it finally happens on Day of the Dead. Everything that kills me makes me feel alive. Everything that financially ruins me makes me feel alive. Oh God, just walking round my room with a beer, a full erection just thinking about Leyla. It was about this time last year I met Lucy in Yellow Lily and Adelina in Vienna, who both had a similar effect on me, but I never saw either of them again. You keep looking, these diamonds keep turning up.

I'm interested to see Leyla again, to see if I find her as affecting as I did last night. I was massively drunk last night; maybe that was why I liked her so much. But I am interested to see. I did drink a massive amount yesterday but feel absolutely fine, took my pizza at 815PM, went to bed no problem, with no hangover whatsoever. When I am excited, enervated, turned on, I do not feel drunk, and I do not suffer hangovers. There was something so sweet and vulnerable about Leyla, as if she is new to the game and had no confidence in herself; she just wears jeans, T-shirt and shirt; if she wore a sexy evening dress like the others she would blow everybody else out of the water. No other girl would stand a chance.

So yesterday was a disaster in the end. In my entire life, whenever I have had one of the great, high, magical nights like Wednesday, the next day I try to repeat it and it turns out to be a disaster. I always tell myself "don't repeat yourself!" But what can you do, when going up & down Rue d'Aerschot was so exciting, and then arriving late at Yellow Lily to see Leyla was so sexy, how could I not retrace my steps the next day? But as always, repeating myself I do everything too soon, I am too excited, so I got to Rue d'Aerschot too early and got back to Yellow Lily too early and Leyla had not arrived yet. She would not be arriving until 5, an hour or so ahead. I carried on drinking but when she arrived I did not even recognise her to be honest. Some girl came in and touched my arm as she passed, and it was the glimpse of white & black check shirt that made me realise it was her. She sat at the back and I made eye contact with her a couple of times as I came out of the lavatories and we smiled at each other, but I still carried on sitting at the front of the bar and never said a word to her. After forty minutes I just saw her leaving with her coat on and though I waited an hour or so hoping she would return, she never did. I left in somewhat of a daze, my mind scrambled. I had been waiting ALL DAY, with increasing excitement to see her again, and then never said a word to her. I stumbled back to Domino's Pizza in a daze of grief & despair; so frazzled was I after finishing my pizza I went out for a Royal Cheese McDonald's & large fries, which I could not even half-finish. Suddenly there was no question of going out later to Empire or Gascogne. All my sexual desire had just died. What a fool I was. But I honestly did not recognise this girl I saw in Yellow Lily yesterday; was it really the girl who blew my mind the night before? When things happen naturally & unexpectedly they are magical; as soon as you try to repeat yourself it becomes precise & all the magic dies.

A nice lunchtime session in the Alhambra Cinema to get me started, then straight up to Rue d'Aerschot. Usual stunning girls, but the two I liked most went with customers just before I got there. He who hesitates is lost. I had four beers before I left the hotel, two more in the Alhambra Cinema, now on my seventh here in the Red Devil bar. They have the best music channel & best lavatories. I could go up & down the road looking in the windows all day & night. It is better than any porn film. It is already 2:50; I have passed the time well today, thanks to that long Alhambra Cinema session. Let me have a long Retro Bar and Red Devil bar session at least, before chancing Yellow. Hope tonight I can finally get awake in time to try Empire.

Better to stay in the erotic paradise of Brussels for as long as possible. Porn cinema, window girls of fabulous sexiness, and maybe even a beauty or two in Yellow Lily. None of this is possible in London. The short stretch between Red Devil and Retro Bar actually seems the poorest stretch of the road; no one of any great interest. Just relax; stroll up & down the Rue d'Aerschot for as many hours as you like. Stay in the Retro or the Red Devil as long as you like. Back in the Red Devil. I don't think I'm going to do anything in the windows, to be honest. My money is too tight, stretched to the absolute maximum, and I still subconsciously know I have TWO more remote possibilities of seeing Leyla again. To see Leyla again would be amazing. I cannot deny it. Hahaha. You saw her yesterday and you ignored her for forty-five minutes? An hour? Until she walked out. Yes. Subconsciously I must have done this for a reason. I always seem to need this element of masochism in my relationships. Now—now—I want to see her, talk to her, be with her. I do not think I will ever see her again. Same as with Lucy, Adelina, et al. These girls are like clouds in the sky.

Starboy has quietly turned into the song of this holiday. The Weeknd sounds like Jason Derulo and looks like Derulo, but his songs and his videos are so much more interesting than Derulo's. A real edge, and fire to them.

So a rapprochement with Leyla. I came back down the whole length of the Rue d'Aerschot without doing anything with anyone, as I knew I would; a last small beer in La Dernière Minute then back to Yellow Lily. After my second visit to the lavatory, I saw there she was sitting in the armchair at the back as usual. She was talking with two Moroccan men but when I got the chance I sat down next to her—and things took their natural course from there i.e. I took her up to a bedroom again. Now, ironically, having extended my holiday to Saturday night, I feel ready to return Friday night after all. But presuming I can find enough credit on one of my cards, I will indulge in Brussels for one more day (with no money). This means I will have spent SEVEN consecutive days in Brussels; I've never done that before. I knew my jollies would take in Halloween, but I didn't think I'd still be here by Guy Fawkes Day.

I tell myself today I am NOT going to drink, so I can go to a floozie and actually be able to FEEL something. But I know I cannot do it. I wouldn't know how else to fill my time except drinking. And anyway I cannot afford any more floozies, so let this be a day of drinking & eating & sleeping only. Maybe finally that nightcap in Empire. I should perhaps pop into Yellow early, hoping to see one of Leyla's Moroccan friends who can tell her I WON'T be coming tonight anymore after all, though I told her I would. Just in case she thought she would have at least one definite customer in me, come all the way from Antwerp and then sit there waiting for me to come in when I won't. I feel sated with the naughty places, and rather horrified by how much money I have spent on these seven days. Let me enjoy the pleasure of drink & food & sleep today, before my return home Saturday. Oh, the Brussels Grill steak last night was gorgeous. Following the ruinous new management in the Berlin Plaza bar & the loss of the old gorgeous knesepfanne, and the ruinous new management in Munich's Rechthaler Hof (and much earlier closure of Lamm's), it only has Vienna's Café Westend for competition in the steak stakes, as it were.

Why is it that McDonald's in Europe are SO much more tasty than ours in London? Royal Cheese is SO tasty. And restaurants in Europe are SO cheap compared to London. Brussels Grill steak, fries & little bit of salad (enough) plus two sauces last night (mayonnaise AND garlic, complimentary as my choice of Bearnaise wasn't available) all for 15,90?! Even with disastrous exchange rates post-Brexit that is still no more than £13! In London that would cost you £30 at least. This, too, is why I come to Brussels.

Christ, Ina came into Yellow Lily last night like a ball of lightning; like the ball of fire in *Tintin & the Seven Crystal Balls*. Looking hot in that shock of black hair, black tight top exposing her midriff, black miniskirt & black stockings, a little pocket rocket; and from the moment she surged in & hung her coat up, stopping for a brief kiss on the cheek with me which was sweet, she was taken up to a room and I think one or more gentlemen kept her there for all the time I was there. At one point she came back down to get some drinks then was gone again.

I really do miss my old days of travelling, when I used to do something cultural every day; it was the centrepiece around which the naughty things radiated. Nowadays I just relentlessly focus on the drinking & the porn & the whoring & whatever. My trips have lost something because of this. I have no desire to go back to Alhambra Cinema today and see the same films again; no desire to go back up & along Rue d'Aerschot again, as stunningly beautiful & sexy as the girls are. No desire to go back to Yellow Lily (no money either). So perfect opportunity to do something cultural—except my old beloved Museum of Modern Art (modern in the sense of 1789-1939 sort of range) was broken up, scandalously, years ago and replaced by a Magritte Museum instead—wall to wall nothing but

Magritte for room after room is too much. The 6 or 8 or 10 Magrittes on show in the old Modern Art Museum was perfect. No doubt putting a Magritte Museum in the halls that used to house the Modern Art collection has been a massive cash cow for them, with the token 1890s Fin-de-Siècle Museum tagged on underneath it like an afterthought, with its ridiculously low ceilings & APPALLING lighting, but it has deprived us of so many of the great treasures of the Modern Art that I loved so much, the Paul Delvauxs uppermost amongst them. He does not fit into the Fin-de-Siècle timeframe so that is it, hidden away in storage! It crosses my mind to finally go to Saint-Idesbald and visit the Delvaux Museum, or Namur and finally visit the Rops Museum, but I cannot be bothered and I can scarcely afford the train fare or museum admission charges. I could go back to the Wiertz Museum after many many years. We will see.

So finally my holiday is almost at its end. Friday night in Brussels and I stay in my room, in my huge white bed listening to classical music on the radio, Klara. So no, I did not get to the Wiertz Museum, sadly; instead I spent about 4½ hours in Alhambra Cinema—the longest session in a porn kino I've had for years & years & years. I think the fact I knew this was my last chance to enjoy it before the end of my holiday, and that I had no money to do anything more than that, gave a keenness to my arousal. Films that would have had me walking out within ten seconds normally kept me highly aroused this time. And if you invest a bit of time & effort into a porn film you can usually get into it—*Auto École* which yesterday I walked out on as it was absolutely rubbish now really turned me on. The actresses I thought unattractive yesterday now turned me on immensely (Tiffany Doll a new discovery). It is all in your mind. You carry the weather with you. You carry the eroticism with you, depending on what mood you are in.

    Auto-École was on upstairs with *Première Orgie pour ma Femme*—I just caught the first & last scenes of this one and both were very good indeed. Downstairs had a rather poor film that had been running for a couple of days, and *Anissa & Lola à l'école d'infirmières*, which also had a couple of absolutely fantastic scenes. Towards the end the film jammed, as luck would have it, as when this happens the manager puts in a completely new film—this one the very good Marc Dorcel airline film. By the time I left my cock was red raw and pretty numb. I didn't get to the end of the airline film, and I would have liked to have watched *Première Orgie* again to see all the scenes I missed last time—in fact it is only 8:20; I do still have two hours to go back before they close! But no, I cannot be bothered now. I am in that down, depressed, end of holiday mood; depressed and subdued by the massive expenditure, so much more than I expected. But out of all that expenditure is there anything I can really look back on and think I shouldn't have spent that? The three great extravagances were the 3 x 75 euros to take Ina and Leyla (twice) to the Yellow Lily bedrooms, and I absolutely NEEDED to do that. If I hadn't, on all three occurrences, I would have been cursing my missed opportunity and would have spent more money coming BACK to put it right. This time I did everything I wanted and needed to do, so no need to come back for a long while. Apart from that I just paid fourteen euros almost every day for Alhambra Cinema, lots of beer but only in cheap places, no more than 1,60-1,80 for small beers every bar—and avoided all the rip-off places like Empire and their ten euros small beers. I managed to avoid Empire all week, and am quite pleased about that. I DIDN'T go with any Rue d'Aerschot window girls which is absolutely remarkable given their astonishing beauty & sexiness. It was only my fidelity to Leyla, and wanting to save money for her, that kept me from doing anything in Rue d'Aerschot, so I would have spent the same money in Rue d'Aerschot if I hadn't spent it in Yellow Lily. No, I cannot regret anything—this is one of those holidays where I really did EVERYTHING I wanted to do, and do not go home regretting any foolish abstentions.

I really indulged in Rue d'Aerschot and Alhambra Cinema more than before and got a LOT more erotic succour in return as a result. Some wonderful memories stored away from those two places, as well as Leyla, of course, one of the loveliest women I've met anywhere, let alone in a place like that.

My room stinks; because of my trousers, sitting for 4½ hours on all those stinking disgusting Alhambra Cinema seats (although the Alhambra Cinema is the cleanest porn kino I've ever been to, but still some filthy things go on there). My trousers need fumigating, or burning.

Guy Fawkes Day. I cannot be too down on myself for the money I have spent on this elongated Brussels adventure—it has been a wonderfully pornographic, erotic week, and that is precisely what I try to save my money for. Tuesday's long stay in Rue d'Aerschot was deliciously exciting; Friday's long stay in Alhambra Cinema was deliciously exciting. My Tuesday night tryst with Leyla was deliciously exciting; if it went wrong after that it was only because I felt too emotional about her and that is not what I go to places like Yellow Lily for. I go for a purely erotic sexual experience; when I start having feelings for them it all becomes confused.

I think about cancelling the trip to Vienna, but it would make such little difference—the hotel & travel money is already spent & is not refundable (a little bit of refund on the train tickets only)—so the only expense would be a little bit of spending money when there, and I can live very cheaply in Europe if I have to. Better to go and hope to have as delicious an experience as I did here in Brussels.

So my hoped-for cheap, short little trip to Brussels at the end of October, just to tide me over till the long trip to Vienna, turned into an expensive 7-nighter, my longest ever stay in Brussels. My financial recovery will be delayed somewhat. I learned some new things—I MUST eat something for breakfast when on holiday; it transforms the whole day to come. I must force myself to spend a long time in Alhambra Cinema. I must spend more time in Rue d'Aerschot, having now discovered the Retro Bar right at the end, and Red Devil just before that. I did feel I went further than before in Brussels this time—with Leyla, in Alhambra Cinema and in Rue d'Aerschot. I hope I can break through to a deeper level in Vienna as well. Don't hold back. Spend the money, break through to the other side.

*

Whenever I am tense, stressed, nervous, I wake up with hard erections, and desire for nothing but to masturbate and fuck. Just eyes closed shut out the world, just masturbate and fuck like an animal. That is why periods of greatest despair in my life are the times of greatest, most wild and rampant sexuality. When calm and happy, my sex drive disappears.

My Eros so infused by von Stuck, Menzel, Makart, a 19th Century erotic aesthetic.

It is amazing when you turn the corner, how quickly things can start to improve and pace of improvement quickens, it is turning the corner that is the hard bit. After that it gets easier.

*

On our way to Frankfurt. Half-full train, maybe a bit more. My eyes very very tired. Three hours to Frankfurt. Change. Then three hours plus to Munich. A lot more people getting on here at Gare du Nord. I just dread crossing the German border at Aachen and having the German customs guards pulling me out of my seat again. Making me turn out my bag in front of everyone, turn out my pockets in front of everyone, swabbing my hands in front of everyone; so embarrassing. And of course I am the most suspicious-looking person on the whole train.

Oh, I wish I could fall asleep on trains & planes the way other people do, but I can't. I struggle to even fall asleep for more than 3-4 hours in my own bed. In all seriousness I wonder how I am still alive considering the lack of sleep I suffer from day after day.

On the train to Munich. Three hours 13 minutes. 625PM Aschaffenburg. ETA Munich 907PM. Just two hours 42 to go! 735PM. So the man who cannot sleep in planes & trains now cannot stay awake. Feel like just going straight to bed when I get to Munich, and stay there until the morning. 818. Nuremberg town of Kaspar Hauser behind us. Ingolstadt, town of Frankenstein ahead of us; then just—Munich. 234 km per hour. 249. 254. 258. I think we are going to take off soon. "Frohe Weihnachten!" Just one more hour to go. I am almost delirious with tiredness. It will only take a couple of beers until I am exposing myself in public I expect.

MUNICH

Well, the first blow has fallen. The Regent Hotel bar does not open on Mondays. Last time I come here on a Monday. No music channel on my TV, and the radio beside the bed does not work; so no music at all. Just one beer (warm) in the minibar. Think this is going to be a very long night in Munich.

I wandered along Arnulfstraße looking for some other bar to have a drink in, tried a couple of hotel bars but they were small & bland, then settled down in the lovely old Hotel Wolff. Charming bar, real log fire. Atlantic City, no one took my fancy but for 15 euros and two free drinks it is not expensive to have a look. The kabins were unusable. Stuck my head in most of the "cabaret" bars in Schillerstraße—Piano Bar, Imperial, Femina, Tiffany, Dolly Bar, Broadway, Candy Bar. As always Tiffany was the only one with more than one customer or two, and as it usually is it was packed. Attractive busty blonde barmaid Nena from Serbia; big Romanian girl Gabriella. 50 euros for a private dance declined. I tried to tempt the barmaid, but she laughed and said "200". Some nice girls in Dolly Bar and Candy actually; one day I will have to say yes to their 50-euro private dance and see how enjoyable (naughty) it is. If I hadn't been on my way to Vienna I might have had a go last night. Walking back to my hotel, two girls standing outside the Amba Hotel, I think, next to the one red light bar in the road; they called out to me "Hallo!" and were both holding a bottle of beer. At first I thought they were hookers, pretty blonde Fanny and beautiful busty brunette Jenny. Wedding dress designers from northern Germany. I wanted them so much, especially Jenny, but after a little chat I bid them goodnight (sensing their initial friendliness was becoming more guarded & reluctant). It was them I was thinking about before I went to sleep, if you know what I mean. On the 725AM train now to Vienna. It goes to the new Hauptbahnhof, not

Westbahnhof. No hangover to speak of. A lovely Yorma's roll for breakfast and I am ready for my four-hour journey. On our way.

I never even remembered to go to the Sexyland kabins. Means I got through just 65 euros on my one night in Munich; to go with the twelve before I left Brussels. My Regent Hotel bedroom was like a monk's room; in tribute to Munich's historic past I presume. Like the room you'd put a penitent sinner in. The bed inside a wooden box. I nearly smashed my head open when my room phone rang with my wake up call at 6 this morning and I had to jump from my bed to the desk, only noticing the wooden post at the end of my bed with a SPLIT second to spare. The conductor has just pointed out to me my ticket is actually for a FIRST class seat. I remember now booking the ticket weeks in advance it was only a few euros more expensive for a first class seat so I thought yes, why not, let me treat myself! First time I've ever booked a first class seat and then I forget to use it. Anyway, I don't want to move now and probably find the first class carriages are nearly full when I get there. I stay. Idiot. I booked the ticket such a long time ago I'd forgotten all about it. I blame myself.

Curiosity about how much more comfortable my bottom might feel in first class is starting to irritate me. Suddenly I feel stuck in a carriage full of 'plebs', when I could be breathing more rarefied air. Rosenheim. On our way to Salzburg. Suddenly my lack of a footrest here in second class grows in my mind; I imagine what luxurious foot rests they might have in first class; lovely pouffés to put one's feet on. Waited on by busty Bavarian maidens. Oh Christ! This is haunting me. Their huge bosoms accidentally on purpose falling out of their low-cut dirndls as they bend to serve me. I have an erection now. Austria is picture-book beautiful (we might even still be in Bavaria). Like something out of the Brothers Grimm fairy tales you read as a child. How lovely to finally get some sleep last night (or early hours of the morning anyway)! All I could think about yesterday was my fatigue; thirty-three hours without sleep I went.

I must admit I am curious now about what a 50-euro private dance in a place like Dolly Bar or Candy Bar would be like; I think those girls would be quite naughty; more so than in the bigger Atlantic City or Tiffany. I will give it a go next time I stop over in Munich. Perhaps there IS some bang for your buck. Anyway, I'm stopping off in Frankfurt on my way back (presuming I don't change it at the last minute and carry on all the way to Brussels). Not particularly cold; for December ridiculously mild. Boringly so. Maybe not particularly exciting in Munich last night, but it was titillating enough to get me in the mood for it now. A rising sense of excitement as we head towards Vienna. 0848. Still two hours 40 minutes to go. But a lovely quiet train (first class would have been even better of course). My erections coming & going in a pleasantly heady, lubricious mood.

VIENNA

Back in my old seat in the Dorint bar; first song Pet Shop Boys "It's taken me all of my life to find you"; that song I first heard here two years ago and hadn't heard since. I hope I'm not going to get emotional about my wife again. 220 already. Need to get a move on to get to WSK. Last time I saw Jackie there, she got changed and left by 5 (maybe because she saw me). A bunch of very loud Americans all around the lobby & bar since I checked in and still, making very angry phone calls to various people. GoTV has disappeared from the hotel TV? Hard to be sure, as they now have more than 90 channels it seems, but I could not find it on a couple of sweeps through. Deluxe Music is there. Just ONE bottle of beer in my minibar; I rang reception for more; she couldn't help laughing when I said eight. "Eight?!" she queried. Yes, that's right. "OK, no problem sir" she was laughing a little bit more. Last time I came here, they put SIX in my minibar ready for my arrival. That was truly amazing.

I start with 305 euros. The test of this holiday is if that lasts me all the way until I get the train out of Vienna Friday morning—if so then it's been a pretty poor holiday. If I've already got through that and have had to draw out more, then it's probably been a good one! Poor show in Westbahnhof books & magazine shop—no English newspapers at all. Always this nervousness at the start of a stay, that it's going to turn out to be rubbish, a complete anti-climax. Or I won't have the nerve to go out of the hotel and do anything. But then again, I've really done everything I wanted to do in Vienna—I went to *The Night Porter* hotel and café next door, I went to the hole in the ground where Milena's *Bad Timing* apartment used to be, I went to all the main art museums a dozen times, been on *The Third Man* tour (sewers included). Been to Judenplatz and the Whiteread memorial. So all of that taken care of, I just concentrate on the naughty places; but I lose something because of this focus on the naughty places alone.

The usual gorgeous slice of pizza from the station on my arrival, and a roll to have later. Very pretty new blonde barmaid but desperately thin. If she gained another 5-stone in weight she'd be sensational, and if I lost 5 we'd be almost compatible. Still, still, still, I have the feeling I could even now bring Munich to some kind of life—if I tried to do something with one of the Schillerstraße girls. In my first Munich Golden Age I had great experiences because I was prepared to splash the cash—and, therefore, got to splash something else as well. I never do in Munich anymore; I still wonder if—expensive as it might be, as much money as it might require—if there is SOME fly I could awake from the amber. It would be one of the small places. Not Atlantic City or Tiffany. They are too regulated and boring. The small places up the road are a little bit more "wild west" as it were. I'm talking myself into returning to Munich but I've ruled out any more long train journeys for a long while; just make do with Brussels only in 2017 for a long time, to save money. 2017 is going to be a year for finally TACKLING my debts. Not just keep hoping by some miracle they will come down by themselves, but actually doing something and making sacrifices to make sure it happens. I've already started, but it will be a while before the improvements really show through in the figures. "Stop drinking! Stop looking at pussy!" I can almost hear my beloved ex-wife saying, bless her. What a truly wonderful person she quite often can be. I don't know if it is my imagination but the Dorint Zipfer seems a fraction colder than usual. 328. Just started another large beer. Let me get a move on now. 3PM the male barman has started and the girls disappeared. I will get here earlier tomorrow. I think I am thinking much more about Manhattan and Tête tonight, and am not really thinking much about WSK. By the time I wake up tomorrow I will know which is better—WSK during the day or Manhattan/Tête at night. Place your bets now, ladies & gentlemen. Release my balls!

After leaving the Dorint bar, an eventful trip to WSK. The floozies still there. Three of them, all very nice, in their blowsy floozie way. None of them would make it into a Rue d'Aerschot window, but for a dark porn kino all three of them were just right. Just what the doctor ordered. Christina the busty older Austrian blonde. A Turkish-looking brunette with a ponytail—the most reticent. And Mongolian Anita. Anita one of these girls you meet in these places periodically—a star. Charismatic. Because of her I stayed rather too long. Now, here I am, back in the Café Westend.

After three bottles of Gösser in the room, back in the Dorint bar for my first Zipfer. The little Vietnamese barmaid greeted me "Grüß Gott! Grosses bier?" and the other barmaid burst out laughing. They remember me well! Always the eternal question: why? Why serve peanuts with a spoon? If I actually USED the spoon and ate my peanuts with the spoon people would look at me like I was a f—king retard, and I am not. I am not. Lots of people eating in the other end of the restaurant; maybe part of a conference event. Gorgeous Mongolian-looking barmaid/waitress serving them, wish she would stay behind the bar! I will speak more about Mongolians presently.

So OK, let me try to recap events of yesterday. Well, quite simply, WSK, Café Westend, bed. Slept right through until 4.50 in the morning! So, so much for my plan of going back out at night for the night bars. WSK. Three eminently naughty-looking women in the bar; just ONE customer in the cinema, and he left soon after as well. I allowed Mongolian Anita and big blonde Austrian Christina to perform "hand massage" on me in the cinema (pointless of course, without resolution, "spritz", as I was so benumbed by drink) but the films were pretty rubbish. After that I sat at the bar drinking Gösser, bought Anita the Mongolian a beer too, pulled down my fly and got out my erect cock, and she sat with me at the bar openly wanking me in front of everyone. I bought Christina a drink too and she came up and joined in the wanking. A very pleasant time. I encouraged Anita to spit on my cock to lubricate it and she happily did so. Like I say, when I travel it is like I am starring in my own porn film. This is why I travel. Back to the Café Westend after 7PM, and surprised to find it so empty. A customarily gorgeous Alt Wiener Zwiebelrostbraten (with no drink) then back to bed.

Today I want to concentrate on the night bars, which means not drinking too much during the day and being in bed early this afternoon, so I am up early tonight to go out again. Therefore I might just get the train up to Burggasse Peep (or walk) then back for a pizza slice and Subway from the station then back here again! Let me concentrate on the night bars tonight. I can even get up to WSK for the last hour before walking back down. I don't know, this new bargirl might be more Vietnamese than Mongolian, but she is gorgeous. The typical beautiful Asian features but a real curvaceousness to her body as well. Ah, if only she could be behind the bar more often. At least I got her to serve me this second beer. A great addition to the Dorint team.

This Asian barmaid is the best thing to have happened at the Dorint in a very long time. I am attracted to her. I might even just stay here drinking as long as she is around, then go to the station, stuff myself with food—pizza & roll & Subway then come back and sleep until tonight. Leave Belvedere and Burggasse Peep until my last day tomorrow. I have been to the art museums of Vienna so many times, but Belvedere has so many treasures it is always a pleasure to go back—Richard Gerstl's Laughing Self Portrait among the most important pictures of my whole life, Makart's Five Senses. How fantastic it is to go to a porn cinema in Europe, and sit there at the bar, and calmly unzip my trousers and get my cock out, and have one of the girls calmly wanking me in front of everyone. This is the glory of Europe. E.U., no. Europe yes. And what harm does it do to ANYONE if some floozie in a Vienna porn kino manually pleasures me? Of course none.

Yet still, it is forbidden in so many places. Can you imagine what that c—t — would do about this? Priggish c—t. Please, please, do not let the prigs win.

I would like to go back to the *Bad Timing* apartment of Milena (now just a massive hole—thanks to a monstrous act of sacrilege. Would you just toss the Mona Lisa into a skip? Knock down the Sistine Chapel? *Bad Timing* is a work of art of similar magnitude), as it is the black heart of Vienna for me. Why not today? No, let me concentrate on the night bars for today. And I would like to go back to *The Night Porter* hotel and café, the other black heart of Vienna for me. Not even thinking about *The Third Man* sites. Vienna means so much to me. It colonised my mind and soul at such a young age and will never lose its grip. Cinema mainly the cause of that, it would appear. If I concentrate on the night bars today, then let me do the cultural things tomorrow. For today, nothing but drink, eat, sleep. PERHAPS Burggasse Peep. Oh, I'm supposed to be looking at the Christmas lights in the Ring aren't I! If there are any. Tomorrow for that. I could happily live in Vienna.

Ah, this new Asian barmaid is gorgeous. She shyly berated me, "I can also bring the drink to you", because I always wait at the end of the bar for my drink instead of letting her bring it to my table, but sweetly. So I have broken my imposition, to always make sure I eat breakfast when on holiday. But Vienna is a different dynamic to Brussels—the real places to go are at night, even after midnight. Daytime is not important. There is just WSK really. Just got a map from reception—just marking the *Bad Timing* and *Night Porter* sites on the map makes me want to visit them—now. U6 down to Längenfeldgasse (two stops) for *Bad Timing*. Then from Meidling (closest to *Bad Timing*), U4 to Kettenbrückengasse (four stops) for *The Night Porter* hotel and café. Then back to Westbahnhof for food, then sleep. Tempted. This Asian barmaid has inspired me, put fire in my blood. Barmaids until 3 then the night barman starts. Not long to enjoy my Asian love. Or alternatively let me just eat today then sleep, and tomorrow do the *Bad Timing* and *Night Porter* things? Yes, better. Because today really is about the night bars. I'd rather leave now, before the night man starts, so I can give my tip to the gorgeous Asian. My MONETARY tip. Oh, you filthy perverts.

So here I am in the Café Savoy, next to the *Night Porter* hotel. The hotel last time I came was a Bank Austria branch, now a dm pharmacy. Finally this time I went inside. Amazing. Amazing. Powerful. It is thanks to BBC2 foreign film nights that I discovered so many places like this. Jean-Luc Godard, Jean Cocteau, *The Night Porter, Bad Timing*. All thanks to BBC2. During the formative years of my life 16-22 all of them. God bless BBC2.

Here I am in the extraordinarily beautiful Café Savoy. They sell an Alt Wiener Zwiebelrostbraten for 11,90 but the kitchen does not open until 4PM, so I will have to pass. But what a pleasure to be here. Let me get back to Westbahnhof now, and grab some food and sleep.

When & why did Kings of Leon become so DREARY? All their songs are so DREARY now, aren't they? Wow, they were the great hope of rock & roll when they burst on the scene. London was mad for them. My last afternoon in Vienna and here I am in my big white bed, listening to classical music on the radio. I drank too much yesterday and last night. Terrible headache all morning, and sick feeling. Just want to stay in now, drinking nothing but water. Later I may or may not go out for a last Café Westend and a last Manhattan. Three solid days of drinking have, as always, left me tired and down. And such a horrible long journey to get back home from here. I don't want to drink any more beer tonight, don't want to go to any more naughty places, don't want to spend any more money. I just have a craving for lots of water. And classical music. I will go out at 7 to see if I can grab any food from the station; if not I will go to Café Westend. But mainly I'm thinking I need to drink more sparkling water. I feel an unquenchable thirst. Friday afternoon I arrive in Frankfurt. The train ticket is paid for and the hotel is paid for. Maybe I will take a stroll to the Städel art museum when I arrive. I have overdone drink, and overdone the floozies. I feel suddenly allergic to both. But then again I think it is "anti-life" not to go out on my last night in Vienna, when it will be such a long time until I come all this way again, if ever. Better, my devil argues, to squeeze as much as I can out of this last night. We will see. I need to see if I can get some food from the station first of all. A foot-long Subway would go down nicely. Well, I have to say that 0,5l can of Gösser went down very nicely and very quickly. I think I'm recovering.

So 0645 I wait for my ICE to leave Vienna for Frankfurt, six hours 40 minutes hence. The end of my last long visit. I love Vienna but it will be a long time until I come back again. On our way. Still pitch black. On my way to Frankfurt with no enthusiasm except that it at least brings me halfway home. I did very little in Vienna this time. Tuesday an amazingly dirty visit to WSK, followed by a lovely Westend steak. Wednesday a nice return visit to the two black hearts of Vienna—the *Bad Timing* apartment of Milena, and *The Night Porter* hotel and café, and later a brief visit to Manhattan and Tête-à-Tête ruined by a splitting headache. The headache and sick feeling persisted into Thursday which wiped out Thursday as well. I did very little except lay in bed listening to classical music on Radio Stephansdom;

just popped out twice to the station for food. And that was what I went all the way to Vienna for!? But I feel it needed to be done, and now I have got it out of my system; I can safely cross it off my list. That just leaves Brussels—until one day, one day, one day I finally make the effort and can afford to go to all those long wished-for places—the Brocken mountain, Reichenbach Falls, the Rubicon river, the Milvian Bridge, house where Mona Lisa lived, etc, etc, etc. Paris locations of *La Grande Bouffe* and *Last Tango in Paris*.

I did do something new on this trip. Last time I just went to the door of the *Night Porter* hotel but this time I calmly went in and walked around. Last time it was still a branch of Bank Austria but now it is a dm pharmacy. It was very moving to finally be inside that building that has meant so much to me over the years. I had another beer in the Café Savoy next to it (which also features in the film) and was delighted to see they have Alt Wiener Zwiebelrostbraten on the menu! For just 11,90! Unfortunately I was too early for the kitchen to be open. Another time. In WSK the films were poor so I just sat at the bar and asked the Mongolian girl if she would masturbate me there, so then I sat with my erect cock out and she happily stroking me in front of everyone. Big older blonde Christina came up and joined in as well. Incredible scenes but it felt totally relaxed. The manager kept his face in his computer screen the whole time, desperately pretending not to notice, and let us get on with it; other customers came in and out and quite calmly let us get on with it. You cannot do that in London. There isn't even a single porn cinema left. Disgusting. There were three really attractive girls in Manhattan—Denitsa my long time "friend" who I am always tempted to do something with but then never do, plus new blonde frizzy asymmetric bob Croatian-Romanian, and big voluptuous beautiful Ghanaian girl. If it had not been for my splitting headache I might well have done something with all three of them. So on to a last night in Frankfurt which I don't really want. The hotel is already paid for so I can just stay in all night and stop myself spending any more money I can ill afford; as I try to go out with a bang, literally & metaphorically. If this is my very last holiday, I should have plenty of time to repair my finances once I get back home.

St Polten. 720. Almost everyone gets off here; now the train is really quiet. This is the shakiest, rattliest ICE I've ever been on. Bit of a bone-shaker. 751. One hour gone already. 812 Linz. 852 Wels.

Now at this very late stage I'm starting to think it would be so nice to book ANOTHER train ticket, and go straight on to Brussels this afternoon, no matter the extra cost. That would also get Brussels out of my sights for a long while. Kill all the birds with one stone. Is it possible?

Means on arrival at Frankfurt going straight to the information desk and check to find out cost of ticket for immediate travel. If the cost of the DB ticket is not too prohibitive, then I think I would prefer to do that. I have 290 euros cash; a small amount of credit on my Nationwide, Capital and Egg cards. If the train costs me no more than 100 euros, that will still leave me 190 to spend in Brussels tonight. And it is just three hours from Frankfurt, I can surely be there by 6PM, 7PM at latest. I really feel no desire to be in Frankfurt tonight. I will make the enquiries on arrival at Frankfurt Hauptbahnhof. 905. Let my saving and financial rebirth start from January. Let me allow myself this last blow-out. It doesn't help that I am now one by one deleting all the Vienna songs from my phone as they are playing, which pretty much just leaves the Brussels songs, making me think of it even more. Probably the breaking point is 100 euros—if another DB ticket to Brussels costs more than that, I will bail out & stay in Frankfurt tonight.

1020. That is 3½ hours gone already. This agony whether to press on to Brussels or not (at great expense) has certainly made the time fly. 1026 Regensburg. It is so annoying, I'm pretty sure I could get a free train ride to Brussels, I have amassed so many points on my Bahncard. Stupidly, I should have pursued this possibility Thursday when stuck all day in my Vienna hotel. It never even crossed my mind. I was all set to just stay in Frankfurt as planned. Which I may well still do. Realistically I just need to go straight to the DB Reisezentrum in Frankfurt Hauptbahnhof and ask them for the best price they can give me with my Bahncard, which looks like the 86 euros.

If I do go all the way to Brussels tonight, then I could have a last Brussels Grill steak AND Domino's Pizza tonight! I could go to Alhambra Cinema tonight until closing time then for that nightcap in Empire. 1122 Nuremberg. Let's face it, whatever it costs to get back to Brussels tonight I'm going to pay it. 1142. Christ, just an hour & a half to go until we are in Frankfurt. More than anything I want to be on that train to Brussels at 229. 1222 Wurzburg. Just one hour to go.

OK so the train to Brussels has cost me 94,55. I console myself with a few things. That 94 euros ticket is offset by the 11-euro refund on the other one I cancelled, so that is really 83 euros, and in pounds that is around £69 only. And I always said my saving and financial fightback begins in January. NO MORE TRAVELLING AFTER THIS!

BRUSSELS

So in the Max by 545PM, and in the lounge with my Jupiler beer by 640PM. I'd better get a move on or it'll be too late to go to Yellow Lily. It has been a long, and unnecessarily expensive journey to get here, but at last I feel where I belong. As always at the end of a long journey across Europe and back, I can't help feeling I wish I'd stayed in Brussels the whole time. Really pretty Christmas lights—multicoloured cubes of light. Very nice.

So you tell yourself with all honesty your travelling is over, and you are going to stop. Then after a brief stay in a rather poor Alhambra Cinema you walk into a Yellow Lily BETTER THAN IT HAS EVER BEEN. Perhaps *ten* completely fuckable girls and now the problem is you don't know which one to choose, but in the end the choice is clear—Brazilian blonde Diane (pronounced the Brazilian way—Dian*y*).

A night in Brussels so good I can barely bring myself to think about it. I am in shock and rather frightened how good it was. A couple of fairly rubbish films in Alhambra Cinema. A stunning bottle blonde with heavy make-up in the Rue des C, Amanda I think. So tempted. Then the best collection of girls I have ever seen in Yellow Lily. Ina grinning when she saw me, spectacularly sexy. 'Perrie Edwards' blonde all in white now looked so appealing. The black bob East European in red glitter dress. And so many others. And Brazilian Diane—like a voluptuous Demi Lovato. Demi Lovato face with purple lipstick, tight red top over voluptuous bosoms, skin-tight jeans over wonderfully voluptuous arse & thighs. Standing a few feet in front of me, dancing along with her Brazilian friend to Maître Gims Bella. I could not resist, I felt drawn towards her like the moth to the flame. I took her up to a bedroom. Then I went to Brussels Grill for what seemed like the most delicious steak I have ever had there. To Empire for one beer and I could barely finish it. Pretty girl on stage but I thought I'll just wait to see the next girl and if it is NOT my Indian-Hungarian Jennifer then I'm going. Of course, up stepped Indian-Hungarian Jennifer. As always, quite possibly the most beautiful body I have ever seen on a strip stage. After she finished as usual she went around asking men if they wanted brief five-euro lap dances in their seats and I prayed, prayed this time she would turn and come to me instead of deliberately ignoring me as she always does. She turned and with a big smile came to me. Finally my chance to ask for a private dance, 60 euros for six minutes. Yes. Topless only but touching allowed, I had her breasts in my hands, in my mouth. Of course 60 euros is ridiculous for a private dance but I do not regret it, on the contrary, thank God I finally did it. If anyone is worth it, she is. After that, I still was unable to finish my beer so stumbled back to the hotel in a complete daze. What happened tonight? And oh God, how on Earth can I save money and rebuild my finances now, when I want to come back to Brussels at the earliest opportunity and repeatedly again?

492

My eleventh-hour decision to switch from Frankfurt to Brussels on Friday night was vindicated a thousand-fold. My best ever night in Brussels. And God help me, now I cannot wait to come back. My pen has run out, and now I am out of paper too. Thank God, you might be saying. I spent more last night than in the previous four days put together. But the frightening thing is I wanted to have Diane again, straightaway, and it was only the fact she went upstairs with another man that stopped me. I wanted to take Jennifer for an hour (200 euros). I wanted the street girl Amanda as well.

A very quiet 9AM Saturday morning in Brussels. The streets nearly empty. The Christmas lights turned off. I buy an energy drink & can of Jupiler and bring it back to the hotel. I must control myself. Allow myself one trip to Brussels a month and always after pay day. Which means it must be at least twenty-four days until I come back. I could have stayed in bed until just before time to leave but that is boring. Let me have a last little session in Alhambra Cinema. I managed to spend 380 in total yesterday, might as well finish off this last 65 in my pocket. Amazing to think of all that money I spent going all the way to Munich and all the way to Vienna, then all the way back to Frankfurt, then all the way back to Brussels—I could have kept all that just to spend in Brussels; with the amazing girls of Yellow Lily, Rue des C and Rue d'Aerschot. I am never travelling anywhere again. Finally this year has caught fire—I've been coming to Brussels all year, why did I never feel excited like this before? Just wasn't in the right mood, it wasn't the right time perhaps. Now I am ready, 2017 could be extraordinary. After finally breaking the ice with Ina, thank God, this year, now I have finally broken the ice with Jennifer in Empire. I didn't hang about with Brazilian Diane at all; I struck while my iron was hot for once. And when I say "iron" I think you know very well to what I allude.

1105 the Alhambra Cinema shutters were still closed so I came back for a McDonald's instead, and sat in the McDonald's eating it. Absolutely gorgeous brunette ponytail girl serving me, her heavy bosoms (Moroccan perhaps) straining so hard against the tight green McDonald's top, and beautiful curvy bottom straining against her black jeans. Better than anything I would see in the porn cinema. Oh Brussels. I am under your spell, and defenceless. Hardly worth going to Alhambra Cinema now even if it's open; so back to the lounge for one last Jupiler. More than ever, I love this city. Even after all these years I realise now I have only just scratched the surface of the pleasures it could offer me. And there was I just twenty-four hours ago with all sincerity saying NO MORE BRUSSELS. Well,

I'm fucked now. Brussels has me in its thrall more than ever before. My whole life now revolves around getting back to Brussels as often as I can.

Venice was already symbol to me in 1998—I am sinking, and stinking, but how beautiful and elegant and steamy with lubriciousness, and illicit sexual energy, decadent, compulsive, self destructive, liquid pleasure. Can I be saved? Yes save me from complete inundation, but do not lose the thing that gives me my dangerous charm and power. Same as the Leaning Tower, yes save me from collapse, but don't put my tower straight because that would defeat the object of the exercise! I would lose all interest! Yes, I am sinking but I want to remain sodden and moist with lubriciousness, not lifted clear of the water completely!

I realise all my favourite films are about uncontrollable passion, uncontrollable obsession. Love and lust that is too strong and becomes pathology. *Bad Timing, The Night Porter, Last Tango in Paris. Pierrot le Fou.*

COLLECTED WORKS

COLLECTED WORKS

BRUSSELS

IN THE YEARS
OF
RECAPITALISATION

2017-2019

ERNST GRAF

CHAPTER 1
THIS IS
A MASSIVE YEAR
FOR ME

THIS IS A MASSIVE YEAR FOR ME. The year I finally control my spending and focus everything on reducing my credit card debt massively. That will set me up for the rest of my life. Oh my God, can you believe tonight is the TWENTY-SECOND anniversary of first seeing a naked woman at Sunset Strip? Dancing to 'Tallulah'. 'I live till I die. I'll take what you give me. And I won't ask why.' She set me on my path. My career in infamy.

I love Brussels as I see more beautiful women here than I have ever seen anywhere else in the world. Big, curvy, voluptuous, womanly women. "Monstrous bosoms typically developing quite precociously, swelling like swamps owing to the humidity of the climate and the gluttony of the women," as Baudelaire put it when he lived here hating Belgium and the Belgians with a passion. "What to say on hearing a Belgian has died?" he pondered. "At last!" "Baudelaire was planning a book on Belgium where he lived from 1864 to 67. He had a muse here (whore) Appollonie Sabatier. Here he began to drink to excess. It was here he suffered massive stroke and paralysis which he had for the last two years of his life." "There is an invincible taste for prostitution in the heart of man, from which comes his horror of solitude."

Christ, amazing reading about all the literary figures who spent time and wrote great things in Brussels. Baudelaire, the Brontë sisters, Hugo, Marx, etc etc. I have so MANY pilgrimages to do. Baudelaire's hotel Le Grand Miroir in rue de Montagne 28 just behind Grand Place, the hospital he was taken to (same one Rimbaud went to after Verlaine shot him) which is now the Passage 44 car park. The Swan restaurant in Grand Place where Marx used to go and probably completed the Communist Manifesto. Charlotte Brontë wrote two novels inspired by her professor in Brussels who she fell in love with. So many places for me to make pilgrimage to. So many Brussels poems to read too. And Venice Italy tar—

"No matter what you come up against today, be a presence so stirring, so self confident and focused. Use your willpower and discipline to your advantage. You will be triumphant (even if it catches you by surprise)." "If you are flexible, balanced and self assured, what drives you internally will absolutely show up in the tangible. You may pursue something with single-minded intent, and it leads you to a fathomless well of abundance. What it's about in the beginning is never what it's about in the end. There is a feeling of strength in knowing your own worth, a deep sense of well being on every front." "You will find the answers, if you stand back, and view everything from a larger perspective." How apposite. What can I say I really long for in my life? To get back to Yellow Lily, to get back to Vienna. To find another girl like Adelaide, –, Cassia. To greatly reduce my credit card debt. "People are admiring you." "You have presence." "Get out of your own way." Who knows these negotiations may even work out BETTER for me? Don't need to be caught up in all this whirlstorm of fear, anxiety and angst. "You stand on the threshold of abundance. Align yourself with like-minded people, with people who see your value. People trying to pull you down are pulling you down out of fear." Fear you are having more sex than them, fear you are having more sexual pleasure than them, fear you are more intelligent than them, more gifted than them, more beautiful than them. "Tap into your gifts".

Beautiful girls have always tapped into their 'gifts' but for not much longer. Darts 'walk on' girls and Formula 1 'grid girls' both banned! Soon we won't even be allowed to use these girls in our Black Masses! What on Earth is the world coming to? One day there may be a #timesup against feminazis & the beta men who weakly, meekly comply with their own castration. A #metoo movement of all those beautiful women who lost their jobs because they were more annoyingly beautiful than the feminazis could bear. As I always say, you never see beautiful women protesting outside strip clubs. You very rarely hear a beautiful woman shouting 'pervert!' at you. As a Freudian of course I believe everything is about sex. People tried to destroy Bill Clinton, & tried to destroy Oscar Wilde, & tried to destroy Byron, etc, etc, etc, as they SEEMED TO BE enjoying so much more deliciously dirty sex, & getting away with it. We all have to tap into whatever gifts we have to make our way in this world. Beautiful women can tap into their beauty, but from now on the feminazis are going to close down every possible career for these women that they can. You must NOT be able to make money out of your beauty! You must NOT be able to make money out of your sexual desirability! But sexual desire is so much a central part of life. None of us would be here if not for uncontrollable sexual desire between our makers. These feminazis and their weak, cowering beta men enablers are terrified of beauty, terrified of sexual desire, anti-life. As Henry Miller said, we need men and women with dynamos between their legs! As Oscar Wilde said, a new hedonism, that is what our century needs! Fight back! Rise up!

I CANNOT BE HORRIFIED AT THAT HUGE DEBT OF MINE, BECAUSE IT WAS SPENT ON TRAVELLING AND HAVING SEX WITH FANTASTIC WHORES IN EUROPE. EVERYTHING AND THE ONLY THING I WANT TO DO. It was all money well spent. Starting to wonder if my austerity is going too far now. I JUST COUNT DOWN THE DAYS TILL I CAN GET BACK TO WSK IN VIENNA AND YELLOW LILY IN BRUSSELS. TILL I CAN BE NAKED IN A DARK ROOM WITH A NAKED FLOOZIE AGAIN IN BRUSSELS OR VIENNA.

"Some of the greatest writers throughout history have called Brussels home, and many of their works were influenced by their time spent in the Belgian capital. Though you can't travel back in time, you can still visit the roads where several of these great writers roamed, many of which have remained essentially unchanged. Discover these spots that showcase Brussels' rich literary history." "In fact, after the revolution (1830), Belgium established a very liberal constitution, and many persecuted writers chose Brussels as their place of solace. In an attempt to flee their home countries, where their social ideas displeased the government, eminent authors and thinkers sought refuge in Brussels."

Fascinating reading about Baudelaire and Verlaine's haunts in Brussels, their favourite inns, and thinking one day people will write books about my footsteps. The Café du Dome where he was in love with a big black Moroccan girl, the Victoria Regina Hotel in the Boulevard du Jardin Botanique where he stayed on the top floor amidst his ferns, and lamps, and rugs, and gramophone horn, the Brussels Grill, the Alhambra Cinema, an establishment that showed pornographic films (imagine!), Yellow Lily.

*

I loved the old Brussels Museum of Modern Art (modern in this sense roughly 1789-1939) which had 6-8 wonderful Magrittes on its walls; but then they decided they would take over all the space of the Museum of Modern Art and turn it into a Magritte Museum only; wall to wall Magrittes, complete Magritte overkill. Milking the Magritte cow for all it's worth. Killing the golden Magritte goose that laid the golden egg. Devastating. The Belgian Government it seems has forced Brussels city to put back all the other pieces in the original building—criminally all the wonderful treasures have been IN STORAGE, hidden from view, all these years. They did open a Fin de Siècle Museum down in the basement levels, appallingly lit, appallingly laid out, like a Token Afterthought Museum—it pains me to go there despite the wonderful works of art it contains. The old Museum of Modern Art was one of my favourite places in all the world, its continued closure is an open wound, and I look forward impatiently to its resurrection—but things move slowly in Brussels.

And it doesn't matter how poor or unarousing my stay in Brussels is, I still want to be here. There is always the thought that there MIGHT be a great film in Alhambra Cinema today, or there MIGHT be a great girl in Yellow Lily today—one of those girls that blows your mind. It only takes one girl to bring a whole city to life, as I always say. That is the incredible power of woman.

There are a few cultural things I would like to do in Brussels—visit Rue de la Montagne, the site of the famous Hôtel du Grand Miroir where Baudelaire stayed during his unhappy sojourn in Brussels which he hated, and where he kept a bat in a cage as his pet that he captured in a nearby cemetery. Place Rouppe where Verlaine tried to shoot poor Rimbaud for a SECOND time; only after this was he arrested and charged and began his two years in prison. He had been escorting Rimbaud to the Gare du Midi to see him off to Paris when his jealousy overcame him again. The Rue Ducale 51 where Byron stayed for two nights after fleeing England once & for all. And most of all the corner of Rue des Cendres and Rue de la Blanchisserie (after all, just a hundred yards away from where I am sitting now!)—where the Duchess of Richmond gave "the most famous ball in history", attended by Wellington and his generals on the eve of the Battle of Quatre Bras (four bras? Phwoar!), which preceded the Battle of Waterloo by two days. It goes without saying I have been to almost all these places already without realising the historical importance of the place I was. That is why it really does pay to do some research before visiting a city, even one I have visited a million times—it adds so much value to a visit to know the history under your feet every street you walk down. On Rue des Cendres of course is also the site of the Hospital St Jean that Baudelaire was taken to after his massive stroke, and where Rimbaud was taken after Verlaine shot him. The hospital in fact took up the whole block; the side entrance was in the little Rue des Cendres (Ashes) but the main part of the hospital faced the Botanical Gardens (much grander then than they are now alas), as I myself did now.

I am pretty sure I have walked through Place Rouppe, on my way to Carolina, but had no idea of its historical significance (where Verlaine tried to shoot Rimbaud a second time); and I've been to Rue des Cendres once or twice visiting that awful little hostess bar which has gone by various names; have probably even been along Rue de la Montagne; but I never realised the historical significance of these streets I am walking. It adds so much excitement to just walking down a street to know the artistic heroes who have walked the same street before. This is how INTELLIGENCE and KNOWLEDGE make life more pleasurable. How thin life must seem for dumb, ignorant, mentally lazy people. I cannot imagine it.

Ah, my crazy man! My first sight since I arrived. Over outside the Botanical Gardens with a crutch. He is rubbing his chin, looking up in this direction, probably seeing me and thinking the same thing, "Ah, that crazy Englishman in the hotel! My first sight of him in a long time!" We never see ourselves as others see us. As always, I wonder what is his story? He does not look like an unintelligent man, why does he live this empty life? As always, he could say exactly the same thing about me, with great justification. But what gives a life "point"? To settle down, get married, have a mortgage, 2.4 children, once a year holiday in Spain? Or live alone, travelling several times a year to Brussels, Vienna, Berlin, Munich, always alone? Does one have more "point" than the other? Discuss. A river cuts its own course. I do what gives me pleasure. Or try to. When at home in London, on the treadmill, I crave the erotic pleasures of Brussels, and think when I get back there I am going to f–k every half-decent floozie I see! But then I get here, and feel nothing but reluctance, and reticence, to get involved, and do anything, even though it is all there on offer. This reluctance, and reticence, only grows & grows the older I get; but still I carry on. Like Phèdre "continuing to seduce long after seduction has ceased to be a pleasure". Like *Smiles of a Summer Night*, "flirting with rescue when one has no intention of being saved". Increasingly locked up within myself, I discover I have become LESS rampant the older I get, not more. More confident, more freedom, more money, yet I do less than I ever did before, when I was so much crippled by shame, poverty, etc.

*

"When walking along a street I just think I am SCANDAL, I am blood red scandal, I am suffused with scandal, and feel the glory and the sexiness and the power of that; how that attracts and fascinates people. FILLED WITH SCANDAL remember that. Always unpredictable. People never know what I am going to do next. POWERFUL, WITH SCANDAL. THE POWER THAT GIVES ME. ALL THE DIRTY SEX I HAVE HAD WITH THE MOST BEAUTIFUL FLOOZIES IMAGINABLE. Wanked in the foyer of the WSK. Fucking girls in the back of the dark cinema in the WSK. Coming over Patricia's tits in Atlantic City Munich. Emily on the Night of the Snow. POWERFUL WITH SMUT."

"Society is warped by my presence in their midst. They attack me but this betrays how they are fascinated by me, which means they are attracted to me. They cannot stop thinking about WHAT I am getting up to. I find it delicious the effect I have on them, and I am not going to back down now. I am not going to let them off the hook. My behaviour just becomes more rampant, more flagrant, more provocative. Every time they attack me they betray how I have got under their skin, how they are obsessed with me. And they have done another thing they can never ever take back, and stored up even more bad karma for themselves, waiting for them just around the corner."

"I may be sick, but it is a delirious, delicious sickness. It is a fever that arouses and allows one to see the truth with penetrating clarity. A fever that excites and intoxicates."

"Oh God how floozies make my life worth living, and porn. It is my opium, it is my richness."

"Think of all the beautiful women I have slept with, for real. Then the incredible floozies! What a life I have had. And so much more to look forward to. A late start but I have made up for it, exploded all the more riotously into my sexual life because of it. When the dam finally burst, the flood was tremendous. And still is. Like after the Big Bang the universe has kept on expanding and maybe even is speeding up, so has my erotic flood continued since the moment the dam finally burst (first naked woman I saw

1992 and first sex 1997) and maybe even now is speeding up. I am grateful now to my late start. I am ripening late, blooming and blossoming late; that is why I still look so ridiculously young. People still call me 'son' and I think I must be 10 or so years older than them! An impatience now, to do more, to go further and deeper. Sense even now I have only just dipped my toes into what is possible erotically. I feel like I am 25 years old, as I count my age as having started the moment I first saw a naked woman, at Sunset Strip in Dean Street, London, dancing to Tallulah. That is when MY life began. Before that there was nothing."

Got erection now in my seat, just writing these words. My credit card debt coming down by £500 every month; that is every month my return to travelling and floozies and the pornotopian life comes closer. Yes, that is £3,000 every six months. £6,000 a year. So £17,900 by end of this year and potentially £11,900 by end of next year. Oh but that all depends on the unlikely event of this – paradise continuing as it is, and mother carrying on as she is, and me carrying on as I am. THIS IS MY ONCE IN A LIFETIME CHANCE TO BRING DOWN MY CREDIT CARD DEBT. And I don't know how long this window of opportunity will last, so I must go for it all out.

*

YOU DID A GOOD THING. YOU PUT THE CAT AMONG THE PIGEONS. START AGAIN. RISE LIKE A PHOENIX FROM THE FLAMES AGAIN. IT IS WHAT I ALWAYS DO. ALL THAT MATTERS IS PORN. RETREATING VERY SMALL & HUMBLE AGAIN. FERNS AND CLASSICAL MUSIC. WAITING FOR WORLD TO COLLAPSE AROUND ME. WAITING FOR NEXT BLOW TO FALL, AN EVEN BIGGER ONE THIS TIME. But don't I kind of like it when the world collapses around me! And I have to start again! Turns me on. I find it exciting. A rebirth, a sloughing of old skin. When in despair, as always, retreat into the dreamy sleazy pleasures, of WSK, Alhambra Cinema, etc. Porn and whores. Vienna, Munich, sink myself into these places. Debt is there to be enjoyed. I can live in any tiny room, with no possessions except my ferns and my classical music. I will be happy. As long as I can work for some money and then TRAVEL, TRAVEL, TRAVEL. "Thinking about me all night were you, little people? Boring people? Thinking about my scandalous sex-filled life? Carry on!" How those who miss out despise those who indulge. How DESPERATELY they try to get my attention. PUSH THEM MORE! SCANDALISE THEM MORE! PROVOKE THEM MORE! PLAY THEM LIKE A PIANO.

I AM HEADING INTO THE MOST DRAMATIC STORMY SEAS OF MY LIFE NOW. I CAN ONLY LOSE ULTIMATELY BUT I WILL ENJOY IT. YES HEADING INTO MOST STORMY SEAS OF MY LIFE, AND DON'T I LOVE THAT! I AM A SINGLE MAN NOW AND THAT MAKES ME INVINCIBLE. BRING IT ON. BYRON WENT THROUGH THIS. DON'T THINK ABOUT WORK. THINK ABOUT ADELINA IN MANHATTAN, DIANE IN YELLOW LILY. WSK WANKS. THAT IS ALL THAT MATTERS. PRIAPISM. BEAUTIFUL NUBILE YOUNG PAINTED FLOOZIES. HA! I AM STILL WINDING THEM UP. I AM STILL GETTING UNDER THEIR SKIN. I AM STILL PLAYING THEM LIKE A PIANO. STILL INFURIATING THEM AND TORMENTING THEM. STILL POISONING THEM. REALISE AGAIN MY SUPREME POWER AND DOMINANCE OVER THEM. THE GIANT BLACK BUTTERFLY LOOMING ABOVE THEM.

CHAPTER 2
DON'T BURN
YOUR BRIDGES

Absolutely great video from Venice Italy Tarot. "Don't burn your bridges, because the person who seemed to have let you down will in the next moment offer you everything you wanted. So don't throw yourself into a shooting match, stay humble, and what you want is coming to you, very soon. Person you thought was your enemy, is not, a lot of the time it was just timing." If I just wait, then I will get what I wanted. Do not go getting angry now, when the other side is just about to give you all you wanted. Don't go putting in claims now, then they will take their – offer away. Be good boy, humble, respect their decision, and you may yet get what you dreamed of. There are always twists & turns to come. Avoid enmity at all costs.

"What it's about in the beginning is never what it's about in the end. There is a feeling of strength in knowing your own worth, a deep sense of well being on every front." What a great quote. Yes. "What it's about in the beginning is never what it's about in the end." "A new sense of optimism fills the air around you. Things are getting better and better financially, whether you realise it or not. It's invisible for the moment, but only because there are some cups that must be sacrificed first. Not love or ambition, but personal regrets and grudges. How is that different from any other month? Once you can put your belief in an energy that believes in you, the collective push towards success is inevitable. The world can and will be yours if you can trust the love being presented to you. Channel it into material success." Stop waiting for money to come out of the sky to save me, I hold the key myself to feel rich. Now I am slowly getting it and being able to do it. When you let go you feel empowered. I let go of the – fight, and I feel empowered, stronger. To hold it in reserve. For when I need it. It is INCREDIBLE how quickly I can EARN money by not going to the pub on my days off! And that is how it feels, it is more than just saving, not spending, it feels like EARNING new money, suddenly I can send so much money to my credit cards. It feels like NEW money. It is incredible. When you give up something, that is when the greatest flowers bloom & blossom. Give up coke, give up strippers, give up Brussels pubs. Give up the – fight.

I AM TURNING LEAD INTO GOLD RIGHT NOW. I AM BECOMING AN ALCHEMIST OF MY LIFE. What was burdening me and making me heavy, I am now going to earn from. NEVER FORGET WHO YOUR TRUE ENEMY IS. THERE ARE INFINITE POSSIBILITIES, AND THINGS YOU CAN MANIFEST, FROM THIS POINT ON. I am manifesting, there is a magic about me which is quick and instant. "The universe will always bring you what you need". Trust in the universe, do not obsess or fret over when something is going to happen. Go with the flow, and you will get it, keep doing your inner work, and it will come to you. Stay grounded in your power. Remember who you are.

THIS WILL WORK OUT BETTER FOR ME. THIS IS THE BEST THING THAT COULD EVER HAVE HAPPENED. I NEED TO DO SOMETHING ELSE. THIS IS THE START OF A BRAND NEW CHAPTER IN MY LIFE. THIS IS WHERE I RISE TO MY GLORY. THIS IS WHERE MY PHOENIX RISES FROM THE FLAMES. THE NEXT JOB IS GOING TO BE THE BEST JOB OF MY LIFE. EVERY MOVE I HAVE EVER MADE HAS BEEN FOR THE BETTER. I LIKE TO MAKE THINGS HARD FOR MYSELF. I AM A REBEL & A REVOLUTIONARY. I AM NAUGHTY. I HAVE TO PUSH PEOPLE. HAHAHA! WOUNDED INNOCENCE. GOOD! I LIKE THIS FEELING. THIS IS HOW I WANT TO FEEL. A SCORPIO ALWAYS CRAVES DESTRUCTION JUST SO HE CAN RISE LIKE A PHOENIX FROM THE FLAMES ALL OVER AGAIN. I WILL RISE FROM THIS MORE GLORIOUS THAN EVER BEFORE.

"I am the English opium addict, travelling around Europe in search of his sleazy fixes, his dreams, his reveries, and these are my confessions."

"They are thinking about me all the time. They are infecting themselves. They do my job for me. I am taking over their minds, their lives. I've got my enemies where I want them: trapped on the horns of their own obsession. Trapped on the horns of their own obsession. I can imagine how agonising it is for them. They cannot stop, as that would be to let me get away with it, and admit that I had won. So they must carry on, and so will be trapped forever in their obsession with me."

"High honour coming to you." I AM A WRITER. I AM THE WRITER OF
THE ERNST GRAF JOURNALS. I BLOOM AND BLOSSOM OVER ALL OF
THEM. I HAVE BALLS AND COURAGE TO SPEAK MY MIND. I AM
BYRON. I AM MAD, BAD AND DANGEROUS TO KNOW. BE
SCANDALOUS. BE NOTORIOUS. SMILE, AND BE HAPPY. I HAVE THE
BOOKS. FERNS. CLASSICAL MUSIC. I DELIBERATELY did this, to
provoke them. TO test them. TO ride the waves again; to create the stormy
seas I need again. SLICK BLACK-HAIRED F.G.LORCA, STARING
SILENTLY AT CAMERA, WITH TWINKLY EYES (OR COLD HATRED).
Rain against my balcony windows at night. A NEW BEGINNING.
ZARATHUSTRA. Ah, I am going through one of my regenerations again; I
realise it is just like Dr Who. This incarnation has reached its end, painful
death and rebirth before I am born into new glorious, next incarnation. The
snake is shedding its skin again. I think my soul is crying out for something
new. WRITING gives me my power. I DO NOT REGRET WHAT I DID and
SAID. I NEEDED TO BREAK INTO THE NEXT LEVEL. My world is inside
the porn cinemas and brothels. That is my paradise. That is why I can be
cocky here now: BYRON. SCANDAL. NOTORIOUS. SHAMELESS.
UNREPENTANT. People look at me with a sense of wonder. Dangerous. DO
NOT BACK OFF. DO NOT RETREAT. DO NOT RUN AWAY. STAND YOUR
GROUND. Coming back to life tonight, after the long dark night of the soul
of the previous 24 hours. Regaining my defiance, my mojo. Take me on if
you wish. I AM BYRON. DARK SCANDALOUS UNREPENTANT. A WILD
CARD. A DISTURBER OF THE PEACE. A WAVE-MAKER. NOT BACKING
DOWN ONE INCH OR BEING ASHAMED ONE JOT. WITH THIS
"DESPAIR" HOW MY EROTIC LIFE CAN FLARE BACK TO
MAGNIFICENCE. I'M LAUGHING NOW. RELIEVED. LAUGHING THAT
— THINK THEY HAVE POWER OVER ME, THAT I AM THE MOUSE
UNDER THEIR PAW, AND THAT I AM SCARED OF THEM. THEY HAVE
NO IDEA OF MY POWER. I feel a need for destruction and rebirth again.
Revolt. Revolt of my senses, of my Flesh. A carnal revolt. How wonderful
now: the thought of being removed from — leaves me completely unmoved!
In fact twitching, quivering with excitement. What power this gives me!
Likewise, how wonderful now I no longer crave female company
whatsoever! What power this gives me! When you don't need anything
anymore, you have power over it. Mastery is to free yourself of need.
Pornography is so lovely, so perfect. Older I get, the more I love it.

In 1888 Jack the Ripper (Michael Maybrick, if you believe Bruce Robinson;
I do) was terrorising Whitechapel, and becoming the most infamous
uncaptured murderer of all time; in 1888 Nietzsche was in the last sane year

of his life, and completing FOUR books in the one year; in 1886 a young physician called Sigmund Freud established a small medical practice in Vienna. What a time to be alive! Who will we remember from 2018? I, Ernst Graf, was living and writing in Brussels, in the top floor room of the Hotel Victoria Regina looking down into the Botanical Gardens, surrounded by ferns, and lamps, and an old gramophone player with a huge horn.

"Ladies compete for his strawberries."

"My husband mistrusted water closets." A man after my own heart.

"There's always naked tits in the finest establishments."

Laughed six times in the first scene.

I am very partial to Natalie Dormer. *Picnic at Hanging Rock*, the 1976 film, is one of my ur films from my ur year 1989. I was compelled, therefore, to give the new BBC adaptation a try. "You are a ruinously spoiled child. You're not unattractive. But you lack refinement."

"Bad timing will define your life, Edith."

Fascinating research in early hours of this morning about the Solvay Conference of 1927 in Leopold Park when Lemaître met Einstein; about the old location of the Gare du Midi just kind of level with Carolina; the hotel where Van Gogh stayed at Boulevard du Midi 71, which now is right under the huge railway bridge between Rue Terre Neuve and Boulevard Stalingrad (which just used to be meadows bordering the River Senne in those days). And incredible to discover that the studio of Van Rappard that Van Gogh used to work in while in Brussels was at Rue Traveriere 8, the exact site of the Van Gogh Youth Hostel where I stayed in 2003! Also Gestapo HQ was at Avenue Louise 1000, and of course Byron stayed in Rue Ducale 51 while writing the third canto of *Childe Harolde's Pilgrimage* dealing with the Battle of Waterloo. Enjoyed the Vienna programmes as well. Especially the bits about the extraordinary Congress of Vienna in 1815. Held in Metternich's palace which is now the Austrian Chancellery in Ballhausplatz, and those two megavamps who lived in the same building on the same floor on opposite sides of the landing in Palais Palm in Schenkenstraße. Got my first pilgrimages lined up for when I return.

NO LONGER ANY REASON TO SAVE MONEY FOR NEST MONEY. AS IT WILL BE IMPOSSIBLE. JUST A CRUMMY SINGLE ROOM FOR ME WILL BE MY LIFE FROM NOW ON. FUCK THE PAIN AWAY THAT IS WHAT I WANT. THAT TOTAL DESPAIR & NIHILISTIC SELF-DESTRUCTION AGAIN WHEN EROTICISM CAN GLOW AGAIN.

"I am a thorn in their flesh. To see me doing so well drives them around the bend. To see me blooming and blossoming, rising above them more and more, flourishing in my lush steamy pornotopia. I am a Prince among peasants. They resent me for still living amongst them. My richness, beauty, intelligence, is a constant daily reminder of their lack of it. My unspoken yet unshakeable air of superiority. My ex-wife says I am in denial about my drinking. No I am not. I'm not. Oh no I'm not. I am in acceptance. Acceptance that alcohol plays a necessarily stimulating effect on my entire life force and in moderation is a force for good in my life. Just two cans enough to remind me 'Oh Christ I am so much better than these pitiful retards who attack me!' Can you imagine the smallness of their wretched lives? I am a giant and I am tormenting them. I am torturing them. Carry on."

"This is what power looks like."

"People are obsessed with me. All the snatches of shocking gossip they have heard about me. They cannot get enough. I lure them into exposing their stupidity. They expose themselves. They give themselves away how much they are thinking about me all the time. The fact they try so hard to get at me, to hurt me, mock me, bring me down in any way, exposes how much I am hurting THEM."

"I honestly don't feel I have come into my power yet. That is almost frightening to realise. In terms of my physical beauty, sexual indulgence, sexual success, financial power, literary success. The Berlin golden age 2003-5 and Vienna *12th Night* golden age 2014-16 were nothing compared to what is about to unfold from next year. My blooming and blossoming, my flourishing has not even started. And that requires the destruction, not just reduction, the destruction of my debt. That has held me back for so long. A ferocious reconcentration on saving money now."

"My books are all about women. The beautiful women who have crossed my path, like so many black cats. Only thing that gets me out of bed is thought of the beautiful women I might meet today. Just to see some beautiful boobies bouncing past my window."

*

I will try to head to Rue Ducale 51 where Byron stayed for a while after fleeing England in 1816. In this house he wrote the third canto of *Childe*

Harold's Pilgrimage, on the Battle of Waterloo (maybe one day people will be coming to the Hotel Victoria Regina overlooking the Botanical Gardens as it is where Ernst Graf wrote *Brussels in the Years of Recapitalisation*, and so much of *Twelfth Night, A Winter's Tale* and *Alhambra*?). Then make my way down to Carolina via a couple of the beautiful churches of Brussels perhaps. I should make the effort to go to see the 'Space Egg' of the despised European Union—more despised by me now than ever after their Brexit machinations with the help of their even more despised British MPs and the wretched Prime Minister May. I would like to be back in bed for a drunken sleep early today, so I have the time to wake up & rouse a bit and head out to Empire tonight—Friday night being the best chance for a bit of atmosphere, a few other customers, and the best selection of girls (I hope).

Stunningly beautiful black ponytail girl in long purple coat over black floral jumper over huge bosoms—passing under my balcony. I've said it before and I will say it again, I see more beautiful girls in Brussels than I see anywhere else in the world. Yellow Lily rather poor, but always I feel like I wish I could stay in Brussels forever. Feel so, so at ease here. Just an escape from reality; live in the opium dream forever. Not seen a single soldier on the streets so that has relaxed too. Let us hope Brussels never suffers any more attacks. A grey dark on the verge of raining day, the Orangery flags blowing hard in the wind.

In the Brussels Grill at De Brouckère—gorgeous blonde waitress, but she appears to be the ONLY one. Five minutes after sitting down still waiting for my order to be taken. She is in animated discussion beside the till with a colleague who looks like a chef. They seem to be trying to divide up tips. A tense matter. This is ridiculous, must be ten minutes now. OK. She really is lovely. Braces on teeth which is always sexy (when I'm not the one paying for them). Prettiest waitress I've ever seen in Brussels Grill, so I excuse her the wait. But this is ridiculous—only ONE waitress? Now she seems to be talking to the manager, deep discussion. Not got any bread & butter. They always play old black & white silent films—this time Chaplin's *The Great Dictator*. Wonderful.

Well, the bread & butter came as soon as I wrote those words and before I finished the second piece the meal came so bravo madame! She was on top of the whole situation; one waitress for the entire restaurant. So how to piece together the events of the day? I headed out towards Rue Ducale 51, where Lord Byron stayed after fleeing England in 1816, and where he wrote the third canto of *Childe Harold's Pilgrimage* on the Battle of Waterloo, after I first passed down Rue des Cendres (site of the hospital where Baudelaire was taken after suffering his life-ending collapse, and also where Rimbaud was taken after being shot by Verlaine), around the corner of Cendres and Blanchisserie which was the site of the Duchess of Richmond's mansion, where was staged "the most famous ball in history" which Wellington and his generals attended on the eve of the Battle of Waterloo. Indeed, it was while here that they received the shock news that Napoleon's army was on the march and would be in Paris in three days. I found Rue Ducale 51 easy enough—facing the Royal Park and in a street full of embassies it seems, US, GB, Swiss, and more, and just around the corner from the Royal Palace. I now attempted to head across town to Carolina. However, I was stopped in my tracks by sight of a *Berlin 1912-32* exhibition at the museum and felt compelled to visit. When I came out it was 235PM and now pouring with rain. I had of course left my umbrella at the hotel. I stopped off in the beautiful Sablon church then pressed on in the rain, but soon became enveloped in the maze of little streets and no longer knew where I was, completely lost my bearings and rapidly my mind. I was by now like a drowned rat. Eventually I had to ask a policeman and he directed me back in the direction I had just come from! Found my way to Carolina quite quickly then but oh dear, the worst and oldest collection of girls I'd ever seen there. Last year I had seen the best collection I'd ever seen there; now it was the worst. I was in no mood for it anyway, after my hell trek across Brussels, so I left as fast as I could finish my beer. Passing back up through Place Rouppe where Verlaine tried to shoot Rimbaud for a second time, while escorting him to Gare du Midi for Rimbaud to catch his train to Paris, leaving Verlaine behind (Midi station was just south of Place Rouppe in those days), finally taking shelter from the rain in Brussels Grill and the absolutely gorgeous Vjolca.

I read so many comments online saying "Brussels is a shithole"—often it seems from people who have never actually set foot here; but I beg to differ. It has problems of course, some very dangerous problems, but which major city does not? However, it is a most beautiful, most charming, and most walkable city. Being so small (compared to London) every street has some amazing historical heritage in it. Verlaine and Rimbaud stayed here, around the corner Baudelaire stayed, around the corner Victor Hugo stayed, around the corner Karl Marx and Friedrich Engels wrote the Communist Manifesto, around that corner Charlotte Brontë fell in love with her schoolteacher & wrote two books about him, around this corner Byron wrote the third canto of *Childe Harold*, in this cinema Ernst Graf ejaculated or fucked some girl from behind as she bent over the seats in front. I do love this place..

CHAPTER 3
ALL WORKS OF ART ARE MONUMENTS TO A CRISIS

"All works of art are monuments to a crisis. My books are all monuments to a period of anxiety in my life. They are each an erupting volcano, when the underlying pressure couldn't be restrained anymore, and the words explode out. That is so true for *Therapy* (1996-98), *Soho* (1998-99), *Autismus* (1999-2001), *Lotta* (2002) and *The Cold Icy Air of the Mountains* (2003-4). Then I started to be able to cope with life better and didn't feel such pressure and anxiety so then found it harder to write any more books! I was still putting my thoughts down on paper but they had nothing to coalesce around anymore, no particular pinch points. That is why from 2005 onwards I have preferred to publish my diaries only."

The Dorcel chambermaid film in the Alhambra reminded me of the wonderful Oscar Wilde films with Rupert Everett—*An Ideal Husband* and *The Importance of Being Earnest*; the wonderful Victorian-looking rooms filled with ferns and chaise-longues and I thought I'd love them to make those films again but with pornographic scenes as well; keep the wonderful dialogue just add in the pornography as well. I'm sure Oscar of all people would not mind. These are the kind of films I want to see—marry high culture with "low". Like I always dreamed of them making pornographic versions of the Fu Manchu books. Same plot, same dialogue, just add in the pornographic scenes (like the *Oriental Cumpots* porno I saw in Soho

Cinema in 2002). My life constantly aspires to the condition of a porn film. I go from porn cinema to hooker bar to strip club, nowhere else. If I am alcohol-dependent (NOT alcoholic—an important distinction which my ex-wife resolutely claimed not to understand) I am also pornography-dependent. It is not out of control, it is perfectly in control—I just need a certain constant amount of alcohol and a certain constant amount of pornography at all times. They are my two crutches which carry me through life. Life would feel totally empty and terrifyingly empty without both of them. They make life more pleasurable. I derive ALL my pleasure from alcohol and pornography.

Look at how beautiful, intelligent, dark I am. How that torments them. The books I have sucked out of their abuse and hatred and jealousy, *Soho* (1998-99), *Autismus* (1999-2001), *Lotta* (2002), *The Cold Icy Air of the Mountains* (2003-4). Delicious delicious to be stirring people up again. Look at the quality of those who attack you and try not to kill yourself laughing. Love of mother and love for mother all that matters. Sure there is a desperate new campaign starting. How, how delicious. I am going to drive the pond life into a frenzy and feed on the rich blood, the rich electricity. A society is warped by a strange person in its midst. They become obsessed with him. Seethingly jealous that he keeps on 'getting away with it'. Become more provocative. Become more annoying. They are the ones who are being annoyed and stirred up by your continuing presence. And still I progress. Still I bloom. Still more books coming out. Love love love the electricity, feed on the seething jealousy against me like a mother eating her own placenta.

You are the one in the strong position, they in the weak position.

How they hate you for your continued blooming and blossoming. And now the heat of spring is coming, I am just going to blossom more than ever. Piling up the money now, debt down to £6,300 soon, and once I hit zero I will be invincible. Continually in the Alhambra Cinema or WSK Vienna. How strong I am now. Stronger than March last year. And then I was stronger than March the year before. How invincible I will be when I hit zero. Exult in this summer now. The power it is going to fill me with. And my books carry on being published. People's obsession with me CONTINUES! Can you believe? My power over them remains total. My grip over them just tightens. I grip them in my black fist. They are still absolutely eaten away by thinking about me and my undimmed power. How delicious this summer is going to be now. How funny reading the Vienna section of

Autismus (1999) and to think the same blight is with me twenty years later but haha better to say the same blight is on THEM twenty years later. They still cannot escape from my greater beauty, greater intelligence, greater genius, my blooming and blossoming over them which absolutely torments and ruins their entire lives, while I go on publishing book after book, go on getting richer & richer, go on fucking one sexy curvy beautiful floozie after another.

Christ, how WONDERFUL I still have everyone in the palm of my hand, in my back pocket. How they hate my cockiness, my flaunting of my pleasures. Any coincidence this new campaign seemed to begin the day after I went to Alhambra?! "Casanova was recognised by his contemporaries as an extraordinary person, a man of far-ranging intellect and curiosity. Casanova has been recognised by posterity as one of the foremost chroniclers of his age. He was a true adventurer." How my CONTINUED presence must disturb the stupid people of –! I foment them into a constant frenzy of agitation, annoyance I am STILL here, and still so fucking cocky and unperturbed. A prince in their midst. How sexy was that moment Sunday when I pulled my trousers down with Lala before a half hour handjob. Go on, go on disturbing the stupid people of –, more and more and more. I am the thorn in their flesh. The bacteria inside their tiny brains.

I disturb people, I shake them up, I make them obsessed with me. Sometimes with my silence, my apparent complete lack of personality, sometimes with my wild shocking debauchery. It is a strange mixture, and it makes me impossible to get out of their minds. And I am still getting away with it. I think that should be the title of my autobiography. STILL GETTING AWAY WITH IT. Or, possibly, WELCOME TO THE PONDLIFE. No—THE UPPER HAND.

*

I've said it a hundred times before, and I will say it again now—the most beautiful women I ever see in my life are here in Brussels. I don't think the men of Brussels know how lucky they are. Within five minutes of sitting out on my balcony, I've just seen three or four of the most sensationally beautiful women you will ever see in your life. Quite, quite extraordinary. Better than any porn cinema—so I reconsider my plan of heading to Alhambra Cinema. Nothing the Alhambra Cinema can be showing will compare with the two or three girls I just ogled as they passed under my balcony. Oh, there goes another one. I really don't want to shut myself away in a dark porn cinema, and shut myself away in a dark knocking shop bar in Yellow Lily—when there are these stunning, stunning young nubile women on the streets of Brussels right outside my window. I NEVER feel this, experience this, see this, say this, in Berlin, Vienna, Munich or anywhere else I ever travel to. It is Brussels—it is only Brussels—that produces this incredible, incredible pulchritude. And it is so funny but Brussels women are still so similar to Baudelaire's description of Brussels' "monstrous bosoms!" and "fat, moist Flemish women"! They have not changed in 160 years—there goes another one.

Just as I was coming back from the shop, black hair, black cardigan, long black skirt tight over most beautiful bouncing little buttocks, heading along the road. The beautiful women of Brussels. Thursday I did nothing but go straight to Yellow and there I stayed—until I finally took new Romanian Sophia up to a bedroom for a tryst of appalling tawdriness and lack of pleasure. My fault—I was beyond drunk. If she had been warm, kind, sympatico, it would not have been so bad, but she was surly, uncommunicative, unhelpful. I don't blame her. No point going to a bedroom when I am that drunk.

Alhambra Cinema two poor films but with my large can of Jupiler I enjoyed my twenty minutes well enough; to Rue d'Aerschot for usual ridiculously pretty girls, but I really felt like doing nothing. After one beer in the Red Devils bar, back to Yellow—by 2PM! Too early again but still already quite busy with girls and men. When Sophia came in I immediately straightaway got an erection! Now I realised why I had gone to the bedroom with her—it was with very good reason. She is really pretty, and has that shyness about her of someone new to the job which is always very appealing. However, after buying her a couple of drinks I departed, and was in Brussels Grill before 4PM for a gorgeous rumpsteak then Victoria to sleep.

*

I want my books to be like *The Pyat Quartet*, rich dense prose, a character locked in his own private sensual world, we follow a young man through the snow of Berlin, pissing against a tree with a full erection, before tramping on to Stuttgarter Platz and the loss of my Berlin virginity, and anal sex (?) with black hair Pole Yulia. I wanted my book to be a manifesto, a grenade, a pistol shot--a pistol shot that would start a war. Except the war had already started. They attacked me and tried to shame me because of my sexual exploits, but I was PROUD of my sexual exploits! How infuriating for them!

517

How enraging! And then I actually started going out with one of these naughty Soho strippers, and was fucking her every day AND every night, in my own bed! How that shot them up the arse once & for all! They never had much to say after that, funnily enough! Meanwhile my stripper lover took to the stage with my white sperm occasionally leaking out and running down her thighs as she was dancing. This was the extent of their humiliating defeat, and my sublime victory.

Funny how my hero now is Byron when before it was Dowson. Yes, I feel so strong when I identify with Byron. I woke and found myself famous overnight HAHA. How my continued presence excites the pondlife into a frenzy. It stirs them up to a point they cannot control or bear. I'm the constant thorn in their flesh. I shall carry on. I am playing my own game and holding to my own line. How small they feel next to me. Whenever you are abused just think of Byron. The vile abuse even such a great man as he endured, and now look what an all time hero. And how thrilling to know, even if I am forced into exile, the exile will be the most exciting chapter of my life yet. I yearn for exile, but delay only so I can go with as much savings as possible! All the dunces do just plays into my hands more. It was after exile Byron settled at Diodati and the most famous sojourn in literary history. So it will be for me. That is why I yearn for exile, and yearn for it to be forced on me, as if left to me I will delay indefinitely. I need need to be forced into it. Come cretins, come envious dunces, come pond life. Please help ME do it. Sweetest most polite person I know yet most abused, on level of Byron, Wilde, Van Gogh. Oh my, these cretins are so far below me, and with every year that passes they are just further below me.

I am every day doing what I love most—writing and publishing my own books! What is there to be unhappy about! I am ejaculating whenever I want. I am going to Alhambra whenever I want. I am going to Vienna whenever I want. Life is good. Enjoy it to the full in the next 15 years. I AM CONVINCED I WILL DIE OF A HEART ATTACK ANY DAY NOW SO NO POINT WORRYING ABOUT RETIREMENT. LIVE LIFE TO THE FULL NOW. It's easy to say "oh if only I had started saving sooner!" But then I would have missed out on those mind-blowing fucks with Andrea, Lucy, Vienna Adelina, WSK Amanda and Jackie, Diane, Leyla. The best memories of my life were brought with that £22,000 debt. Beatrice, private dance with Empire Indian! So what, so fucking what if I don't have money to live on when I'm 65??? Just live in massive pleasure and massive joy for the next 10 years, fucking fuck myself to death! Go out with a fucking bang. The last great memory was 2016—three long years ago. Go back to Yellow Lily

518

repeatedly and repeatedly fuck this Sophia. Live live live. Live the fucking life that is in you while you are still pretty, can still get it up, and these places still survive.

*

On the street corner I passed a gorgeous little black-haired Bulgarian, Susanna. On the walk to Yellow I was surprised to see so many girls back on the streets. I presume the 350 euro fines are still in place? I passed Nora by Café Jimmy, the huge-bosomed girl I took back to my hotel a few years ago. She remembered me, and my hotel! "If you need me, you know where I am!" she said. Hopefully the police have got more important things to worry about than lurking around corners fining customers 350 euros, surely?

No titillation so far at all. No erection—well, except for briefly in Alhambra Cinema. No visit to the Alhambra is complete until I have seen Anna Polina being fucked up the bottom. So it was I hung around in the downstairs screen long enough to see Anna being fucked up the bottom in *The Godfather's Daughter*, then before leaving I just popped up to the upstairs screen where there was Anna Polina being fucked up the bottom in some other film. Lovely. Pleased now, I headed to Yellow. Few girls in the street, but not of the quality of that delectable dark little Susanna on Sunday night. Yellow busy with men again, around 3PM now I think, but the girls were all very average indeed. No stars like Ina or Sophia. Hung around until after 5 then could wait no more. Back for Domino's Pizza then bed again. Woke after 9 with indigestion and headache and no desire to go out again so that was my day in Brussels.

Surprised how few sexy girls I've seen in the street in Brussels—I mean just passing under my hotel window or the Café du Dome where I am now. In fact, none. The beer is really tiring me out quickly and hard; I think because I'm not excited, not turned on. When turned on, excited, I can drink prodigious amounts with no ill effects. Feeling so flat, becalmed, I feel drunk almost straight away. And not in a good way. Not high, intoxicated drunk. Just heavy, sodden drunk with headache immediate. Well, good, that means it will be a very cheap couple of days. Still with one more visit to Yellow to come, I wonder if I will see a star there at last, or will these be a completely uninspiring set of visits to Yellow? There's usually one, at least, isn't there? But so far this time, nothing. August of course. Holiday season. Graveyard month. One large can, one small can, now halfway through my first large Stella in the Dome, and already my headache is gathering. So, I finally asked, "is it possible to sit upstairs?", and was met by a very polite but shocked refusal. "*No*, sir! Upstairs is *closed*, sir!" It is my dream for some porn cinema to allow me to choose their programming—if only for the days I am there. I would have a Titten Alarm season, a French season, a Titten Alarm season, an Italian season, a Titten Alarm season, and so on (Roy Alexandre is the greatest pornographer ever). As I've said before, if I ran a porn cinema, it would be the best porn cinema in the world. Ferns, & violin music, and only the most exquisitely curated films. Really disappointed with the quality/paucity of the young ladies passing by my window. It is counter-intuitive. You think in hot summer there will be more, but I find I see less sexy girls in summer than I do in winter.

I finally achieved my holy grail—of going out drinking early then coming back for a nap and going out AGAIN in the evening. A midday session in Alhambra Cinema—sadly the two good films of Monday had now been changed to two pretty rubbish ones. However, I got turned on, and went to the Dome for one beer, then up to Rue d'Aerschot. A brief visit to Sexyworld videokabins—they are really rubbish. Just SIX films in the BIG TITS category, and 153 in the ANAL! That says it all. The world we live in. Do men really enjoy seeing girls being fucked in the bottom more than they enjoy seeing a girl with lovely big bouncing boobies? I don't. So I settled on the FRENCH category (six films) and, blow me, found myself watching the same Anna Polina film I had just seen in Alhambra Cinema upstairs on Monday—now I discover it is SECRETAIRE PARTICULAIRE. Once more I got to see Anna being "pleasured" up the bottom. A rather sad and melancholy end, but I am not depressed, because I know November, December and January are when I have my greatest adventures so I will look forward to them. On the way back to Domino's after leaving Yellow I bumped into Nora again (in the main road this time, last place I'd expect to see her). She told me this was her last night in Brussels, tomorrow she was going back to Spain, forever. "Tout. Finis." She had finished with this life. Had enough of it. We hugged and kissed on the cheeks and she said "I am so glad I met you before I left!" A sweet moment. A lovely girl.

*

Standing on the train to — , shaking, nervous, heart racing, it was already starting to get dark and lash with rain, and the windows of the train were all getting steamed up so it looked like thick mist outside, and with Pluto now gone direct it really did feel like our train was entering the Underworld, and made me think it WAS a right thing I was doing, and it was in this rather magical frame of mind I entered the dark — and first girl this voluptuous Amazonian — , massive voluptuous bottom, instant erection. And — 's dark naughty face almost as arousing. It was quite a powerful moment, that first 15 minutes in the — . Worth it. Vindication.

I am turning lead into gold. This is alchemy. Under the influence of Pluto direct. I was going to hibernate but this is the most magical time to go out, October November mists and fogs. A state of mind.

*

If I was to choose the nationality of my next wife, I would choose Belgian. These Belgian girls are absolutely gob-smacking. On the way to the shop for Red Bull this morning, black hair, black coat, black jeans over curvy gorgeous bottom. Just back in shop now for two beers, two girls came in both 10 out of 10. Leaving shop and coming back to the Victoria two more coming towards me both 10 out of 10. It absolutely takes your breath away. Grey clouds here in Brussels but no chance of rain. Yesterday a couple of beers in the Victoria, and to Alhambra Cinema. I walked into the cinema to see some woman on screen being fucked up the bottom and sure enough it was my old friend, Anna Polina. As I said last time, no trip to the Alhambra is complete without seeing Anna Polina being fucked up the bottom, and here she was, as soon as I walk in. So happy (her & me). Stayed long enough to finish my can of beer then to Yellow Lily by 4. Busy with girls and men but no one for me, though I hung around for a couple of hours. A giant Domino's Pizza then bed (not before the arm fell off my spectacles and I smashed them to pieces against the bathroom floor in a rage; I now need new spectacles unfortunately).

I find to my surprise I actually wrote a note on my phone while I was in Yellow Lily: "This is a bar of monstrosities. If I ever ever ever find a diamond here again, I will be staggered. Surely this is over for Yellow. Everything gets worse and then terminates. Yellow at that point. It has become a cabinet of horrors. My censor is off. I speak nakedly. Ever ever again will there be a diamond?" I put this down to being in a bad mood as I was so tired.

Black hair, grey dress over massive tits. 19? 20? The girls of Brussels are absolutely mind-blowing. I was thinking when I think of all the great sexual adventures of my life, the Adelinas in Vienna, the Amandas in Vienna, the Andreas in Brussels, Lucys in Brussels, Riccardas in Berlin, etc etc, I

NEVER recall any of my nine, ten, twelve? who knows how many fucks with the Rue d'Aerschot girls. Though the girls of the Rue d'Aerschot windows are probably the most beautiful floozies I ever see, from sheer beauty point of view, I never recall the trysts themselves. Environment makes such a difference. If I fuck in an environment not pleasant to me, I do not remember them afterwards. Better a less beautiful girl in a more salubrious environment! It seems crazy but it is absolutely true.

So two good films in Alhambra Cinema, a Penthouse Black and a Dorcel upstairs. With fine erection I left and headed down to the Notre Dame de la Chapelle to see the Madonna that was apparently a favourite of Baudelaire. I am not a religious person at all—on the contrary—but to step into one of these great churches is always such a powerful feeling. Leaving the church I tried to walk down to Carolina but evidently turned in the wrong direction from the word go and became hopelessly furiously lost again. In the end I had to get on the metro at Munthof for the two stops to Gare du Midi. The metro stuffy and absolutely pungent with the odour of sweat. Leaving Midi I thought as I am here I might as well go for a drink in my old favourite bar, L'Orient Express, only to be shocked to find it totally gone. The entire building replaced by a hideous modern B&B hotel, hideous in its blandness. Appalling. Another appalling loss. Then got a little bit more lost finding Carolina but eventually got in around 510PM. It was evidently on its last knockings, five girls and six men, and by 6 everyone had gone. I was the last to leave. But! They had two stunning girls, a voluptuous blonde bob Brazilian-looking girl, and a slimmer but still curvy long blonde hair girl. These were the best two girls I saw, better than anything in Yellow Lily on my two visits, though after arriving in Yellow after the long walk up from Carolina there were three girls who looked like sisters who were evidently Brazilian but looked like South Sea Islanders, something strongly Fijian or Tongan in their features, and it was one of them that I was most attracted to. However, I was by now very over drunk so gave up and came back for a gorgeous Brussels Grill steak. As usual I struggled to finish it, then staggered back to the Victoria to pass out, not before an enormous shit which blocked my lavatory and would not flush. That was my day in Brussels.

*

Oh, casually, staggeringly beautiful, these Brussels girls. 1150 Friday—I crack open my first beer of the day. Bitterly cold. This discourages me from going on my planned long walk to the 'Space Egg' E.U. building, and Solvay

Park where in 1927 Belgian priest/physicist Lemaître went for a stroll with Einstein and told him of his theory of a 'Big Bang' at the start of the universe—the 'Primeval Atom'—to Einstein's scoffing & ridicule, and to my old special place—the Wiertz Museum. Instead I shall probably concentrate on Alhambra Cinema, long walk down to Carolina, then finish back in Yellow. After midnight I will see if I can go out again for a nightcap in Empire—surely on a Friday night it will have SOME customers?

Thursday I went to Alhambra Cinema for a nice little session, one OK film upstairs while I had my large can of Jupiler, then to Yellow by about 3PM. Ina already there and the only attractive one. Busy with old men. Then three black-haired girls came in; they must be quite new because they didn't stop to greet the other girls or customers before going to the back to get changed. And oh Christ, they looked good once they got changed. Two of them were immediately taken up to the rooms as soon as they sat down in the bar, so I think the men had been waiting for them. No one else of note, so easy to leave for a Domino's Pizza then out like a light. Woke in the night with indigestion, unable to take an inward breath, bane of my life, massive shit which blocked the lavatory again, then back to sleep until 6AM.

Oh, Ina. As I said Ina was the only attractive girl when I got to Yellow yesterday, and then after a little while she got up and changed into—oh my—a skin-tight, skin-COLOURED, shoulderless catsuit that fitted her like a glove, that massively curvy arse and thighs and pussy. I was so tempted, after a long while having lost a little interest, but only my extreme tiredness (more than 24 hours without sleep) made me pass. I wonder if I WILL go with her again (for a third time)? Christ, it's bitterly cold out there now; the real grey gloom that presages snow. I so rarely have sex these days. The visit before last when I went upstairs with Yellow Lily Sophia was the first time I'd had sex in Brussels for two & a half years (!) which rather belies my sordid reputation. She was absolutely stunning, but the sex was so clumsy & rubbish, I felt that I'd almost forgotten how to do it. Would love to see her again though, but sadly she seems long gone. Sex, actually doing it, is an almost non-existent part of my life right now. Watching, and pornography, and trying to unblock my lavatory of shit has become pretty predominant.

When Brussels first turned the centre of their city into a car-free zone, it looked like a zombie apocalypse. Absolutely horrific, terrifying, chilling. Just this massive long north-south central boulevard absolutely devoid of cars and people. Now, people have started to feel comfortable, it seems, to fill the void left by the cars. I was thinking these words as I walked down the middle of the road, and at that moment I saw someone coming towards me who looked familiar. I looked again and sure enough—it was Ina, Yellow Lily Ina. We avoided eye contact, of course. A gentleman never acknowledges a floozie outside of their place of acquaintance, unless SHE initiates it. Always a thrill to walk through Place Rouppe, the square where Verlaine tried to shoot Rimbaud for a second time, and it was this second occasion that Verlaine was jailed for. How much more rich and interesting a city is when you research its streets before you go there. I don't do enough of it. The two stars I saw last time at Carolina are still here. They now look like twin sisters; the one with long blonde hair now has it cut into a long bob like the other one. And it is this one I feel most attracted to, though I feel attracted to them both. 234. Not a bad time to head back to Yellow before long. I think no long sight-seeing walk for me today.

*

So I finally, finally, crossed the Rubicon at Carolina. Christy, one of the two sisters from last time. Albanian. Beautiful, beautiful, beautiful. I of course had managed to completely anaesthetise myself with beer before then, so could get no real pleasure from it except the visual, and the tactile. She was adorable. Before returning to Yellow, I stop off in the De Brouckère Brussels Grill for a steak. No bread & butter it seems. I will be back to Carolina many times now. The first time is always the hardest. The De Brouckère Brussels Grill have lost their chandelier. Chandeliers are dying everywhere. The E.N.O. lost their one years ago, now the De Brouckère Brussels Grill. Sad. Finally get one piece of bread & butter. Gorgeous. No breakfast before I left home today so I am understandably starving. Christ, Christy was gorgeous.

Friday then, little session in Alhambra Cinema, again the films upstairs were the better ones, but soon on my way for the long walk down to Carolina. Direct this time, with no diversions, and therefore no getting furiously disastrously lost. The same two stars—they look like sisters I now realise. One slightly slimmer, and slightly shorter blonde hair. After SEVERAL 25cl bottles of Jupiler, I finally give the nod to the slimmer one and finally the Rubicon was crossed. My first time in a Carolina bedroom. Christy from Albania, absolutely beautiful, absolutely lovely. Completely naked, never said no to anything, a proper "girlfriend experience" as they say in the trade. Of course I was so benumbed by beer I got no real pleasure out of it whatsoever bar the visual. 23 to the house, 50 to the girl, and I added 20 for her sweetness and being so sympatico. Then the long walk back up to Yellow, but by now I was feeling "metallic". This is how I feel when my veins are so filled with cold beer. Therefore I stopped off in De Brouckère Brussels Grill for a customarily gorgeous steak, then waddled off once more in the direction of Yellow. Packed with men and girls, and several several gorgeous sexy girls. Yellow Lily lives. Unfortunately, however, I was so blown out by the steak (and several hours of beer that preceded it) my chest felt like it was going to explode, my heart felt like it was about to explode. I could not seriously consider doing anything. I had to leave. Straight back to the Victoria and out like a light. I woke just after midnight, in good time for my Friday night planned visit to Empire, but no, I just wanted to stay in my huge white bed, so I did. 1124AM Saturday morning now. I wait for Alhambra Cinema to open (if it has not already).

Christ, I love Brussels. I never want to leave. So yes, Carolina had two stars, two sisters I am sure, but that was all. Bear this in mind. And she said she'd only been there two months so be cautious about putting too much importance on Carolina rather than Yellow. Without those two it would have been a really long and wasted walk. And that is Brussels for me, isn't it? Alhambra Cinema, Yellow Lily and Carolina. Occasional nightcaps in the topless-only strip club Empire, and the sightseeing pilgrimages to various places. But it is enough. Because London does not have an Alhambra Cinema (anymore), a Yellow Lily or a Carolina. And without these two sisters, even Carolina would be pointless. Funny, when there yesterday, the only customers other than me were old Moroccan goats. Moroccan men 40-90 years old. They seem to be 90% of the clientele. A young English boy like myself is quite a rarity. Yellow for sure has lots of Moroccan men, but younger, and so many more white Belgians, "European" Belgians as it were. I am not criticising one way or the other, just simply stating my observation.

Brussels has become my home from home in the most wonderful way. So let me be the English chronicler of Brussels. The chronicler of certain parts of Brussels anyway.

*

Forced to decamp for one night to the Hotel Manhattan as my hotel has suffered a sewage overflow caused by a blocked drain. It took me about an hour to flush all the shit and lavatory paper down my bowl last night so I hope it was not me that has caused it. It was one of the most disastrously huge shits of my life and my poor little lavatory could not cope with it.

The Hotel Manhattan is the oldest, shabbiest hotel I have stayed in for many, many years; perhaps ever. I was frightened to open a wardrobe in case there was a dead body in it. Around 640AM this morning it sounded like a gunshot from further along the corridor. They still use metal keys for the doors! I had a vast cavernous room (more like a hall) with four single beds, and after entering by one door I was surprised to observe another door at the distant far end of the room which opened into another corridor on the other side which led you into a completely different part of the hotel. The architecture of the place is actually really interesting, so many strange little corridors and nooks and crannies and spiral staircases, like something out of a horror film. If some company closed it for a year and spent 20 million renovating it into a modern hotel it would be quite an amazing place to stay.

Leaving the hotel after just one can of beer around 6PM I cut along Rue des Malines on my way to Yellow Lily. The old DM café was shut down but next to it L'Entracht has been reopened in garish phosphorescently bright blandness, behind the bar there was a beautiful young blonde girl in tight yellow sweater over huge bosoms—like Christina Hendricks out of *Mad Men*. I actually stopped, doubled back and crossed over to go in, but realising I was already quite late for Yellow, I pressed on, meaning to try again later. Later, however, I passed it two or three times more but never saw her behind the bar so did not go in. I shall try again later. Yellow busy with men and girls—the pick of them the three Bulgarian Kylie Jenners I saw last time, and the three "South Sea Island" Brazilians. The middle Jenner i.e the younger of the two who really looked like Kylie Jenner (the third one did not really) was the pick of them and we exchanged many looks & grins. Not only a Kylie Jenner, she had the look of a young Anna Polina. She was chewing gum like a teenager and she looked the type who will be mean and unsympatico once in the room. Not taking her bra off, not allowing kissing, that kind of thing, which deters me (a bit). The pick of the three South Sea Islanders would be warmer, more generous, sympatico I am sure. I will return later afternoon today to think about it again. I am not sure if I can face that long long walk down to Carolina again today. Maybe I will try the Rue d'Aerschot again (with little enthusiasm). Still I put off the long walk to Space Egg/Solvay Park/Wiertz Museum.

Grey and cold in Brussels but no rain, and none predicted. Leaving Yellow last night, I stopped off in Domino's Pizza to order my small pizza and popped next door to Carrefour to buy a bar of chocolate and behind the counter was the most stunningly beautiful black-haired Moroccan girl. I will go back later to look for her as well. It was her and the yellow-top L'Entracht girl I was thinking about in bed this morning, if you know what I mean, as well as the South Sea Island girl and the middle Kylie Jenner. How wonderful just to meet four women that rouse me this much. That in itself makes the night worthwhile.

The fabulous curvy Brussels girls already passing under my window; even swaddled in their winter clothes, their voluptuous buttocks pressing magnificently against their tight trousers.

It will be nice to see Carolina Christy again, and her "sister", I cannot deny. Depends how I feel when I leave Alhambra Cinema in a little while. Oh my, just saw one of the Yellow Lily girls passing under my window. One wonders if she spent the night at someone's hotel and is now heading back home, on the "walk of shame". She has a big grin on her face so doesn't look very ashamed, I must say. Did not see her at Yellow last night, however, nor on my last trip last week. The other girl of interest at Yellow right now is a black girl with very large bosoms, on prominent display. Another possible.

Happy birthday to myself. An hour or so in Alhambra Cinema, good Marc Dorcel upstairs—schoolgirls *Orgy for Lucy* with Tiffany Doll, then to Yellow. Sophia was there, looking sexy as —, but two men took her up to the room one after the other, and I could not wait any longer. Domino's Pizza then bed. As always, the overwhelming thought—I should have spent more time in Alhambra Cinema.

*

My first beer of the day. Just starting to rain as I write these words. Should be quite an afternoon of showers. Having vowed to finally spend more time in Alhambra Cinema the films yesterday were, of course, rubbish. Upstairs now just seems to be permanent rolling Marc Dorcel TV and downstairs rolling American porn channel, either Brazzers TV or Hustlers TV. As I have said before, American porn is the worst in the world (excepting British only). If there was a Top 20 for porn film-producing countries, American would be No.19 and GB No.20. No, actually they wouldn't even make the Top 20. So so unsexy, unarousing. In American porn the men fuck the girls like they don't even like women, viciously, like they want to hurt them, whereas in European porn you feel the women are worshipped. In British porn the men just look pathetically grateful to be getting any at all; like they can't believe their luck. Not the weather for people watching, really, so I shall return to my room shortly, to prepare to go out—to Alhambra Cinema and Carolina or Alhambra Cinema and the long sightseeing walk to Space Egg and Solvay Park that I have been threatening to do all year. Yellow Lily was also poor—not one single viable option for me. I will try again later.

After an enjoyable two-beer session in Alhambra Cinema watching the Marc Dorcel TV upstairs, I decide to head down to Carolina on a pub crawl. So after a small beer in a packed Celtica (all teenagers, about sixty of them or more) here I am in the Café Bebo in Place Rouppe, one of my Holy of Holies sites in Brussels, where Verlaine tried to shoot Rimbaud for a second time, and it was this that led to Verlaine's imprisonment. A nice cold Cavée des Trolls. How learning about the history of a city increases your pleasure, and Brussels is so absolutely packed with it. To think I, little me, am in the same square where Verlaine and Rimbaud were 136 years ago. How exhilarating. One day people will come here and say "Here am I, where the great Ernst Graf was drinking a glass of Cavée des Trolls! On his way to get his rocks off in the Carolina knocking shop just down the road!" Heading to Carolina, yes, but I will be so totally anaesthetised and cold with drink it will be pointless; even more when I get back up to Yellow Lily later. Never mind. I like looking at the floozies more than doing anything. Ah, the barmaid just came by me to close the door that was stuck ajar—sexy beauty in blue jeans—her perfume now completely enveloping me even though she has returned behind the bar. This is the worth of coming on this pub crawl. Just to be enveloped in a barmaid's perfume is so, so sexy.

Oh, and then right next to it, an even lovelier bar, Santana, with a curvy Moroccan barmaid and innumerable paintings on the walls. Jupiler 2,20. And just beginning on the jukebox as I walk in—the modern classic Billie Eilish Bad Guy. Every so often a song like this comes along—instant classic. Honestly lost all interest in reaching Carolina now; this bar and this barmaid are very lovely. Beautiful wall lamps, beautiful paintings, beautiful barmaid, 2,20 Jupilers—what a lovely bar. I will be here again. The value, as always, of trying new places. Invigorating. Thrilling. Dua Lipa 'New Rules'. The beautiful barmaid has turned the lights down now. Even lovelier. Ah, now she's bending over lighting all the candles on the tables. I want to see D— again. What a beautiful fucking arse. I would fuck that and never stop fucking it.

I did not do anything in Carolina but I had a fun ten minutes with Christy sitting beside me and letting me hold her hand on top of my bulging cock, much to the amusement of her friend (another Albanian? Bulgarian?)

sitting opposite us. They were particularly amused when I suddenly changed the subject and pointed up at the big brown painting of the river inquiring where it was set—with Christy's hand still on my cock. I honestly am obsessed by that painting. Who painted it? Where? But she told me she finished at 5 and it was now 20 to 5 and I was of course cold with drink so I released her, but a lovely ten minutes or so. Only after she moved back to her seat by the window, and was talking to the man who came in selling clothes, did I realise who it was she so strongly reminded me of—of course it was Tana from Greece, at the —! Just a more voluptuous version of Tana from Greece, but the same face, and, I now realised, exactly the same voice. They could have been sisters. I am very fond of Christy—I was thinking I will have to try and stay in the Ibis Midi one night so I then am just a short walk away from Carolina and I can get there not so drunk. Perhaps, after all, one more jolly before Christmas! Christy informed me that her beautiful black & gold blouse was from Albania, her pussy was from Albania, her left breast was from Albania but her right breast was from Brussels, "ici!". A lovely girl.

From Carolina I stumbled back to Yellow (giving Christy 10 euros on my way out of Carolina for being so sweet) but again there was no one I fancied. A giant Domino's Pizza then out like a light. I really wanted to go back to Alhambra Cinema as the films I had left had been so good and I lay there thinking about it, but next thing I knew it was 2 in the morning and I was lying there with my contact lenses still in, stuck to my eyeballs of course. Lenses out, and back to sleep. So a low-key week (i.e. no sex) and I was happy to leave it for the rest of the year, but now I wonder if I can find the money in December for a last hurrah. Finally do that long walk to Solvay Park where Lemaître told a mocking Einstein of his theory of a 'Big Bang'. I wonder if I can end my year with one.

CHAPTER 4
THEY'RE DOING
MY JOB FOR ME!

"They're doing my job for me! I infect their minds, then they take me home with them and they infect their whole family, their little children become infected with me. Every generation of their family becomes infected with me. So their entire family is thinking about me, every single day. This is how I take over an entire family, an entire town, an entire city, an entire continent. The full realisation of what it is to be me. This is the richest time for my writing. Fine, let them do what they want, meanwhile I am building my own empire. They are shooting themselves in the foot. I am languid, in my voluptuousness. Every attack gives me electricity. Gives me power. They cannot understand why my power is increasing! Ha so stupid they are! So dumb they are! One day they will realise it was they themselves who were giving me my power."

I woke 5AM with balcony windows open to sound of rain or snow falling outside, traffic hissing sibilantly along the Boulevard du Jardin Botanique, ice cold, but naked & mostly uncovered, & loving the coldness. Desperate for a piss, but then started to think of Tongan and then got erection that just would not go away. My battle with the thugs yesterday had left me high on adrenalin and that was now converted into sexual desire. WHAT IT SHOWS IS I AM WINNING. I AM UNNERVING THEM SO MUCH. I HAVE TAKEN OVER THEIR MINDS. What is my plan now? I intend to KEEP THE PRESSURE ON! I intend to NOT LET THEM OFF THE HOOK!

"Whenever someone who does not deserve an apology from you demands one, never hesitate. Apologise in such a way they regret demanding one. Apology should belittle them. Humiliate them. The ability to shower apologies on the little people is sign of your greatness. 'Oh I am so *terribly* sorry!' Confuse them."

*

Back in my lovely Ibis Gare du Midi and my lovely old arched bedroom again! Such strong visceral memories being back here, where I stayed in all of my first twenty or more stays in Brussels. Quick shower then down to the bar by 120PM. Bad start—Stella beer tap empty and chap covering the bar doesn't normally work in bar and is not sure what to do. But they have a lovely corner table for me to sit at again. The Ibis lobby and bar has undergone a major renovation—more comfortable now. Soft browns & blues. Oh Christ, the proper barmaid has arrived, frizzy blonde bob and absolutely massive knockers in tight white T-shirt! I will be here a long, long time now. Remember her from my last stay a couple of years ago I'm sure, but don't remember them being THAT huge. Beer warm—as it's a new barrel I guess.

Christ, here I am again—in my corner seat of the Ibis, watching the trams & buses rolling in & out of Gare du Midi station. The memories. Back then I did not know of Carolina, or Yellow Lily, or even Alhambra Cinema. Incredible to think all that time I used to spend in Brussels, the only jollies I ever got here were in the Rue d'Aerschot. What I was missing out on!

At home I have erotic pornographic fantasies of what I am going to get up to as soon as I get to Alhambra, or Vienna, or wherever, but when I get here my usual reticence and reluctance takes over. Brasserie de la Senne says the beermat (the Senne being the river that used to run through the centre of Brussels, now covered over by roads, and commemorated by so many of the roads bearing names like Pont or Quai to remind you what is invisibly under your feet)—is that the name of the bar now? It was the Café Belge when I first used to come here. 202PM—literally waiting fifteen minutes for my second beer. This is not impressive—but I persevere: because I need to drink to get me started, and I don't know where she's gone, but I need to see that bargirl again (or to be more specific I need to see her knockers again). Oh God, still waiting but now Gaga's Bad Romance comes on the bar radio. Ah, after 17 minutes I get my second beer, big knockers girl delivered it, then vanished again. So 215 already—on my second large Stella. Will of course be pickled by the time I get to Carolina—by 3? By time I get up to Yellow Lily (via Alhambra Cinema) it should be 430-5ish. Perfect time. Let me use today as recon, to see if the two "sisters" are still at Carolina, then decide tomorrow if I shall indulge again. Just a real pleasure to be back in the Ibis again.

So, Friday in Brussels. Left the Ibis and got to Carolina about 3. Sat with the one who I thought was Christy's big sister, but now I realise is not. Christina, from Bulgaria (Christy being from Albania), like a voluptuous Florence Pugh. Again, these were the only two girls of any attraction for me. Three or four bottles of Jupiler, a coffee for Christina, then I was on my way straight up to Yellow Lily. No one of any special note—sad to not see Sophia. The middle Kylie Jenner sister still looks so cute, and then, curses, just before I left around 7, one of the South Sea Islander Brazilians arrived, looking fantastic in HEAVY make-up and sparkling silver short dress. I fancied her so much but I was really blotto so had to leave. My timing is nearly always wrong in this place.

I did not even go to Alhambra Cinema yesterday; I will put that right today. Loving sitting here in the corner seat of the Ibis bar, looking across the bar into the reception area, as I used to do back in Stephanie's day. I have returned to the stool at the bar. From this higher elevation I can properly see the buses & trams coming in & out of the station. Much better. When I started travelling, I used to write down all my philosophical thoughts on life and the universe; now I write about which chair I'm sitting in. But, like I said, I want to record my life in minute detail. I will leave here soon and start my trek across Brussels in Carolina but I doubt whether I will do anything with Christy again. Really, however amazingly sexy & gorgeous a girl is, I only ever want to sleep with her once. After that, I'm just thinking "who next?"

So many black people use this Ibis bar. Eight other people in the bar with me now and all black; and being in Brussels this probably means from Congo (or of Congolese descent, at least). Inevitably reminded then, of course, of the epic moment when that Congolese gentleman in white suit in the Ibis lavatories showed me his absolutely prodigious cock—still the largest cock I have ever set eyes on in the flesh. Yes, I doubt I will do anything with Christy, I prefer to drink & drink & drink and ogle the floozies while I'm doing it. Very rare I am sufficiently moved to do anything. Oh, but I would so much like to see that South Sea Island girl this afternoon. Having started drinking earlier today, I expect I will be blotto even sooner so little chance. 81 Montgomery. I've said it before, I love the place names in Brussels, and the street names. 82 Droglos Chateau. Drogenloos.

I think my sightseeing in Brussels should confine itself to places inside the 'Pentagon'. As much as I'd like to go to Solvay Park, and the Space Egg and the Wiertz Museum, they are awfully far to walk to (now I abstain from the metro). Let me concentrate on the Holy Trinity—Carolina, Alhambra Cinema and Yellow Lily. 'Chelsea Dagger' playing here in the Ibis bar—lovely. Just walking from the top of the Pentagon to the bottom (from Yellow Lily back to the Ibis) was long enough! I really do not want to submit myself to anything longer; maybe in summer. My chief explorations must be the same as always—sexual, and philosophical.

Just asked the bar lady for a third large Stella. She said nothing at all, just raised her eyebrows for a few seconds, then wordlessly went to pour it. Three large Stellas is not so excessive, surely? This is only the START of my day. I'll be going to at least two other bars after this, plus a can or two in the porn cinema. Halfway through my third large Stella and only 2PM. Will I or will I not have sexual relations on this, my final day out in Brussels of the year, and indeed of the whole 17-19 period? I have, after all, made one pilgrimage this week to the site of the hotel Van Gogh stayed in while living in Brussels, 72 Boulevard du Midi (only as it was about 50 yards from Carolina, ha ha). Let my book *Brussels in the Years of Recapitalisation* be the standard work on whoring in Brussels in the years 2017-19. With almost no mention of the voluminous window girls of the Rue d'Aerschot. Sitting in Yellow Lily last night, however poor it was, I did think to myself "I've NO desire for Rue d'Aerschot. However poor it is here in Yellow Lily, I'd still rather stay here in Yellow Lily."

81 Marius Renard. No interest to do anything in Carolina today. Couple of Jupilers, ogle lovely Christy, then after a Brussels Grill Brouckère for steak, Alhambra Cinema, then to Yellow Lily. The fact is I just love DRINKING in a bar full of floozies. No real need to do anything with them, except in exceptional circumstances. You never know who is going to walk in the door.

Well, Carolina was a bit of a disaster, but subconsciously I knew I didn't really want to go there. I think I can't get the visual memory of the South Sea Island Yellow girl from my mind. She is the one I want next. In the lovely Santana Bar now, on the corner of Place Rouppe, one of my holy places in Brussels (where Verlaine tried to shoot Rimbaud for a second time; and it was for this outrage he was imprisoned—did I mention that?) Ah, Carolina—what I was going to say—got my Jupiler and seeing Christy greeted her with a smile and "hi!", but within 60 seconds some man quickly took her upstairs—as if sensing that I might be about to steal her from him & not fancying "sloppy seconds" after I had had my way with her (you should be honoured to have sloppy seconds after ME, sir!), so that resolved that particular tension/opportunity. Then this Algerian in a bobble hat next to me started to explain to me in an almost inaudible mumble his theory about, well, I'm not exactly clear about what. His obsession seemed to revolve around the number "79", and the concept of passing time, and 8 is nothing but 7 is very significant, and he wanted to be remembered as a "good" person, not a "bad" person. Half-suspecting these were his last words before he killed me with a knife and cut my head off, I left after downing my one beer as fast as I could, and so, here I am, in the Santana. If I sleep with Christy again, it will be in some far future time. I realise now: I have scratched that itch. I have lanced that boil. And that is how my sexuality is. 315PM. The Santana very nicely decorated for Christmas.

The Moroccan barmaid here in Santana, very nice bottom, not fat but nice. Black really tight trousers, black vest over the lacy bra, black cardigan. Dark blonde hair. Ah I like it here, but I like everywhere that has beer don't I. But better to drink beer surrounded by floozies so I push on to Yellow. Too early as always. I'd hoped for a big finish to my year but I don't think it is going to happen. Oh, I could stay in Brussels forever. I could live here forever quite happily. Very strange North African music now playing here in the Santana bar, and I love it.

After Brussels Grill, a brief stop in Alhambra Cinema, and the Marc Dorcel channel is now playing downstairs rather than upstairs. A very beautiful brunette bob girl in the one scene I saw; but, curses, with no credits at the end I could not see her name. Next scene was rubbish, so I pushed on to Yellow. There were NO girls on show when I walked in! At least a dozen men but no girls whatsoever. Saturday nights at Yellow are the worst nights to come. Soon enough three or four of Ina's crew turned up, then the three Kylie Jenners, but the middle one (the best one) was taken to a room as soon as she got there and never reappeared. She must have been getting a right good seeing-to. If only I was. And that was it. I hung on until after 7 hoping the South Sea Islanders would turn up but then had to give up. Not being able to face the hideous long walk back again, I broke my prohibition and got the metro down to Midi. A packed metro carriage of course, but as I stood by the door there in the seats right in front of me and under me, as it were, was the most beautiful girl I had seen for a very long time. Some office girl perhaps, dressed smart, brown hair flat on top but all frizzy and curly down the sides like something out of a Klimt painting. Light green coat, black leggings, breathtakingly beautiful. Out of the corner of her eyes I think she knew I was looking as her chest started rising & falling faster and her face slightly flushed. When I got off at Midi she stayed on, but seeing her was the best moment of the whole year. The kind of woman you remember for your whole life.

So, great lover, another day out where you did nothing, never even saw a naked woman. Now with my improved finances I should be able to allow myself an Alhambra visit every couple of months; but oh, when am I going to try Amsterdam? Hamburg? And February is set for Vienna. Sexy AF black-haired girl at the shop in front of me in the queue. 19 perhaps, pink sweater with cartoon figure on front, blue cut-off denim shorts, over black leggings. Sexy AF. Curvy AF. Even from quite a distance apart our eyes met. Is eye contact across a crowded room ever really accidental?

Printed in Great Britain
by Amazon

36192152R00304